THE COUNT OF MONTE-CRISTO

ALEXANDRE DUMAS

TRUE FRIENDS

THE COUNT

of

MONTE-CRISTO

VOL. I

By

ALEXANDRE
DUMAS

ODHAMS PRESS LIMITED
LONG ACRE, LONDON, W.C.2

Printed and Bound in Great Britain by
Greycaine Limited, Watford. Herts.

INTRODUCTION

In spite of the grimly practical lives that most of us lead
to-day, romance in one form or another still glimmers like a
will o' the wisp to lead us down the by-paths of adventure.
And of all forms of romance surely the search for treasure is
the most alluring. That is why Cocos Island and the Tober-
mory Galleon—to mention only two from an almost endless
list—remain perpetual sources of news and legend, and why
whenever men shall talk of buried riches, the name of Monte-
Cristo is inevitably mentioned. For it is the prototype of all
such stories; not "The Gold Bug" nor "Treasure Island"
itself have had so powerful an effect upon the imaginations of
writers and readers.

Like all great books its strength lies in its reality. A great
deal of the action passes in real places. The Château d'If—
castle of the Yew Tree—for example, still stands on the little
island off Marseilles, though the gloomy trees which gave their
name to it have long since disappeared. Dumas, too, is half
identified with his hero, and the combination is again transformed into a likeness of himself by the reader. For Edmond
Dantès represents romance for us all—romance and accomplished revenge. More than half the book is devoted to the
adventures of Dantès during the pursuit of his enemies; and
his ultimate triumph over the misfortunes that ruined his
early life. But it is the treasure that overshadows the
book—the treasure that makes possible all the half-fantastic,
exciting events that crowd its pages. And it is the glittering
lure of those heaps of gold and precious stones that enchant
us. Few indeed of us are lucky enough to discover stores
of fabulous wealth; but we can dream, and "Monte-Cristo"
is the stuff of which our dreams are made.

Here is a novel long even by modern standards, yet
packed with incident and adventure enough for a whole

library. Here are storms at sea, delicate negotiations over secret documents of vital importance, escape from imprisonment worse than Cayenne, pirates, treasure, love—and a happy ending to crown the whole. What prodigality of invention! There is material here for a dozen books, but Dumas has boiled down the bones of his plot, as it were, throwing in lavish handfuls of incident and description, until the resultant stock is the richest and most nourishing fare for the epicure of romantic fiction.

An astonishing fact about "The Count of Monte-Cristo" is that it is only one of a vast series of over one hundred novels which include "The Three Musketeers" and its sequels, though for any one man to produce two such widely diverse masterpieces as those mentioned is in itself a literary miracle.

Dumas' own life runs parallel to his hero's, Dantès, in that he amassed a tremendous fortune and spent it lavishly. The legends of his castle at St. Germain, his private theatre and his extravagance are more fantastic than the incidents he describes; but his life had an unhappy ending. His rise had been too meteoric and his old age was clouded by the inevitable debts that followed him. With a weakened mind, with friends, health, self-respect all gone, Alexandre Dumas the elder, ended his life at 67, as poor as he began it.

But he left behind a priceless gift to the young in heart, and here is part of it—"The Count of Monte-Cristo."

CONTENTS

OF

THE FIRST VOLUME

CONTENTS OF THE FIRST VOLUME

CONTENTS OF THE FIRST VOLUME

THE COUNT OF MONTE-CRISTO

CHAPTER 1

MARSEILLES—THE ARRIVAL

On the 28th of February, 1815, the watch-tower of Notre-Dame de la Garde signalled the three-master, the Pharaon, from Smyrna, Trieste, and Naples.

As usual, a pilot put off immediately, and, rounding the Château d'If, got on board the vessel between Cape Morgion and the Isle of Rion.

Immediately, and according to custom, the platform of Fort Saint-Jean was covered with lookers-on; it is always an event at Marseilles for a ship to come into port, especially when this ship, like the Pharaon, had been built, rigged, and laden on the stocks of the old Phocée, and belonged to an owner of the city.

The ship drew on: it had safely passed the strait, which some volcanic shock had made between the Isle of Calasareigne and the Isle of Jaros: had doubled Pomégue, and approached the harbour under topsails, jib, and foresail, but so slowly and sedately that the idlers, with that instinct which misfortune sends before it, asked one another what misfortune could have happened on board. However, those experienced in navigation saw plainly that if any accident had occurred, it was not to the vessel herself, for she bore down with all the evidence of being skilfully handled, the anchor ready to be dropped, the bowsprit-shrouds loose, and beside the pilot, who was steering the Pharaon by the narrow entrance of the port of Marseilles, was a young man, who, with activity and vigilant eye, watched every motion of the ship, and repeated each direction of the pilot.

The vague disquietude which prevailed amongst the spectators had so much affected one of the crowd that he did not await the arrival of the vessel in harbour, but jumping into a small skiff, desired to be pulled alongside the Pharaon, which he reached as she rounded the creek of La Réserve.

When the young man on board saw this individual approach

15

he left his station by the pilot, and came, hat in hand, to the side of the ship's bulwarks.

He was a fine tall, slim, young fellow, with black eyes, and hair as dark as the raven's wing; and his whole appearance bespoke that calmness and resolution peculiar to men accustomed from their cradle to contend with danger.

"Ah! is it you, Dantès?" cried the man in the skiff. "What's the matter? and why have you such an air of sadness aboard?"

"A great misfortune, M. Morrel!" replied the young man,— "a great misfortune, for me especially! Off Civita Vecchia we lost our brave Captain Leclere."

"And the cargo?" inquired the owner eagerly.

"Is all safe, M. Morrel; and I think you will be satisfied on that head. But poor Captain Leclere——"

"What happened to him?" asked the owner, with an air of considerable resignation. "What happened to the worthy captain?"

"He died."

"Fell into the sea?"

"No, sir, he died of the brain-fever in dreadful agony." Then turning to the crew, he said,—

"Look out there! all ready to drop anchor!"

All hands obeyed. At the same moment the eight or ten seamen, who composed the crew, sprung some to the main sheets, others to the braces, others to the halliards, others to the jib-ropes, and others to the topsail brails.

The young sailor gave a look to see his orders were promptly and accurately obeyed, and then turned again to the owner.

"And how did this misfortune occur?" inquired he, resuming the inquiry suspended for a moment.

"Alas! sir, in the most unexpected manner. After a long conversation with the harbour-master, Captain Leclere left Naples greatly disturbed in his mind. At the end of twenty-four hours he was attacked by a fever, and died three days afterwards. We performed the usual burial-service, and he is at his rest sewn up in his hammock, with two bullets of thirty-six pounds each at his head and heels, off the Island of El Giglio. We bring to his widow his sword and cross of honour. It was worth while, truly," added the young man, with a melancholy smile, "to make war against the English for ten years and to die in his bed at last like every body else."

"Why, you see, Edmond," replied the owner, who appeared more comforted at every moment, "we are all mortal, and the old must make way for the young. If not, why, there would be no promotion; and as you have assured me that the cargo——"

"Is all safe and sound, M. Morrel, take my word for it; and I advise you not to take 1000l. for the profits of the voyage."

Then, as they were just passing the Round Tower the young man shouted out, "Ready, there, to lower topsails, foresail, and jib!"

The order was executed as promptly as if on board a man-of-war.

"Let go! and brail all!"

At this last word all the sails were lowered, and the bark moved almost imperceptibly onwards.

"Now, if you will come on board, M. Morrel," said Dantès, observing the owner's impatience, "here is your supercargo, M. Danglars, coming out of his cabin, who will furnish you with every particular. As for me, I must look after the anchoring, and dress the ship in mourning."

The owner did not wait to be twice invited. He seized a rope which Dantès flung to him, and, with an activity that would have done credit to a sailor, climbed up the side of the ship, whilst the young man, going to his task, left the conversation to the individual whom he had announced under the name of Danglars, who now came towards the owner. He was a man of twenty-five or twenty-six years of age, of unprepossessing countenance, obsequious to his superiors, insolent to his inferiors; and then, besides his position as responsible agent on board, which is always obnoxious to the sailors, he was as much disliked by the crew as Edmond Dantès was beloved by them.

"Well, M. Morrel," said Danglars, "you have heard of the misfortune that has befallen us?"

"Yes—yes! poor Captain Leclere! He was a brave and an honest man!"

"And a first-rate seaman, grown old between sky and ocean, as should a man charged with the interests of a house so important as that of Morrel and Son," replied Danglars.

"But," replied the owner, following with his look Dantès, who was watching the anchoring of his vessel, "it seems to me that a sailor needs not to be so old as you say, Danglars, to understand his business; for our friend Edmond seems to understand it thoroughly, and not to require instruction from any one."

"Yes," said Danglars, casting towards Edmond a look in which a feeling of envy was strongly visible. "Yes, he is young, and youth is invariably self-confident. Scarcely was the captain's breath out of his body than he assumed the command without consulting any one, and he caused us to lose a day and a half at the Isle of Elba, instead of making for Marseilles direct."

"As to taking the command of the vessel," replied Morrel, "that was his duty as captain's mate; as to losing a day and a half off the Isle of Elba he was wrong, unless the ship wanted some repair."

"The ship was as well as I am, and as, I hope, you are, M. Morrel, and this day and a half was lost from pure whim, for the pleasure of going ashore, and nothing else."

"Dantès!" said the shipowner, turning towards the young man, "come this way!"

"In a moment, sir," answered Dantès, "and I'm with you!" Then, calling to the crew, he said,—

"Let go!"

The anchor was instantly dropped, and the chain ran rattling through the port-hole. Dantès continued at his post, in spite of the presence of the pilot, until this manœuvre was completed, and then he added, "Lower the pennant half-mast high—put the ensign in a weft, and slope the yards!"

"You see," said Danglars, "he fancies himself captain already, upon my word."

"And so, in fact, he is," said the owner.

"Except your signature and your partner's, M. Morrel."

"And why should he not have this?" asked the owner; "he is young, it is true, but he seems to me a thorough seaman, and of full experience."

A cloud passed over Danglar's brow.

"Your pardon, M. Morrel," said Dantès, approaching, "the ship now rides at anchor, and I am at your service. You hailed me, I think?"

Danglars retreated a step or two.

"I wished to inquire why you stopped at the Isle of Elba?"

"I do not know, sir; it was to fulfil a last instruction of Captain Leclere, who, when dying, gave me a packet for the Maréchal Bertrand."

"Then did you see him, Edmond?"

"Who?"

"The maréchal?"

"Yes."

Morrel looked around him, and then, drawing Dantès on one side, he said, suddenly,—

"And how is the emperor?"

"Very well, as far as I could judge from my eyes."

"You saw the emperor, then?"

"He entered the maréchal's apartment whilst I was there."

"And you spoke to him?"

"Why, it was he who spoke to me, sir," said Dantès. with a smile.

"And what did he say to you?"

"Asked me questions about the ship, the time it left Marseilles, the course she had taken, and what was her cargo. I believe, if she had not been laden, and I had been master, he would have bought her. But I told him I was only mate, and that she belonged to the firm of Morrel and Son. 'Ah! ah!'

he said, 'I know them! The Morrels have been shipowners from father to son; and there was a Morrel who served in the same regiment with me when I was in garrison at Valence.'"

"*Pardieu!* and that is true!" cried the owner, greatly delighted. "And that was Policar Morrel, my uncle, who was afterwards a captain. Dantès, you must tell my uncle that the emperor remembered him, and you will see it will bring tears into the old soldier's eyes. Come, come!" continued he, patting Edmond's shoulder kindly. "You did very right, Dantès, to follow Captain Leclere's instruction, and touch at the Isle of Elba, although, if it were known that you had conveyed a packet to the maréchal and had conversed with the emperor, it might bring you into trouble."

"How could that bring me into trouble, sir?" asked Dantès; "for I did not even know of what I was the bearer; and the emperor merely made such inquiries as he would of the first comer. But your pardon; here are the officers of health and the customs, coming alongside!" and the young man went to the gangway. As he departed Danglars approached and said,—

"Well, it appears that he has given you satisfactory reasons for his landing at Porto-Ferrajo?"

"Yes, most satisfactory, my dear Danglars."

"Well, so much the better," said the supercargo; "for it is always painful to see a comrade who does not do his duty."

"Dantès has done his," replied the owner, "and that is not saying much. It was Captain Leclere who gave orders for this delay."

"Talking of Captain Leclere, has not Dantès given you a letter from him?"

"To me?—no—was there one?"

"I believe, that, besides the packet, Captain Leclere had confided a letter to his care."

"Of what packet are you speaking, Danglars?"

"Why, that which Dantès left at Porto-Ferrajo."

"How do you know he had a packet to leave at Porto-Ferrajo?"

Danglars turned very red.

"I was passing close to the door of the captain's cabin, which was half open, and I saw him give the packet and letter to Dantès."

"He did not speak to me of it," replied the shipowner; "but if there be any letter he will give it to me."

Danglars reflected for a moment.

"Then, M. Morrel, I beg of you," said he, "not to say a word to Dantès on the subject, I may have been mistaken."

At this moment the young man returned, and Danglars retreated as before.

"Well, my dear Dantès, are you now free?" inquired the owner.

"Yes, sir."

"You have not been long detained?"

"No. I gave the customhouse officers a copy of our bill of lading; and as to the other papers, they sent a man off with the pilot, to whom I gave them."

"Then you have nothing more to do here?"

"No; all is arranged now."

"Then, you can come and dine with me?"

"Excuse me, M. Morrel, excuse me, if you please: but my first visit is due to my father, though I am not the less grateful for the honour you have done me."

"Right, Dantès, quite right. I always knew you were a good son."

"And," inquired Dantès, with some hesitation, "do you know how my father is?"

"Well, I believe, my dear Edmond, although I have not seen him lately."

"Yes, he likes to keep himself shut up in his little room."

"That proves, at least, that he has wanted for nothing during your absence."

Dantès smiled.

"My father is proud, sir; and if he had not a meal left I doubt if he would have asked any thing from any one, except God."

"Well, then, after this first visit has been made we rely on you."

"I must again excuse myself M. Morrel; for after this first visit has been paid I have another, which I am most anxious to pay."

"True, Dantès, I forgot that there was at the Catalans some one who expects you no less impatiently than your father—the lovely Mercédès."

Dantès blushed.

"Ah! ah!" said the shipowner, "that does not astonish me, for she has been to me three times, inquiring if there were any news of the Pharaon. *Peste!* Edmond, you have a very handsome mistress!"

"She is not my mistress," replied the young sailor, gravely; "she is my betrothed."

"Sometimes one and the same thing," said Morrel, with a smile.

"Not with us, sir," replied Dantès.

"Well, well, my dear Edmond," continued the owner, "do not let me detain you. You have managed my affairs so well, that I ought to allow you all the time you require for your own. Do you want any money?"

"No, sir; I have all my pay to take,—nearly three months' wages."

"You are a careful fellow, Edmond."

"Say I have a poor father, sir."

"Yes, yes, I know how good a son you are, so now haste away to see your father. I have a son too, and I should be very wroth with those who detained him from me after a three months' voyage."

"Then I have your leave, sir?"

"Yes, if you have nothing more to say to me."

"Nothing."

"Captain Leclere did not, before he died, give you a letter for me?"

"He was unable to write, sir. But that reminds me that I must ask your leave of absence for some days."

"To get married?"

"Yes, first, and then to go to Paris."

"Very good; have what time you require, Dantès. It will take quite six weeks to unload the cargo, and we cannot get you ready for sea until three months after that; only be back again in three months, for the Pharaon," added the owner, patting the young sailor on the back, "cannot sail without her captain."

"Without her captain!" cried Dantès, his eyes sparkling with animation; "pray mind what you say, for you are touching on the most secret wishes of my heart. Is it really your intention to nominate me captain of the Pharaon?"

"If I were sole owner I would nominate you this moment, my dear Dantès, and say it is settled; but I have a partner, and you know the Italian proverb—*Che a compagno a padrone*—'He who has a partner has a master.' But the thing is at least half done, as you have one out of two voices. Rely on me to procure you the other; I will do my best."

"Ah! M. Morrel," exclaimed the young seaman, with tears in his eyes, and grasping the owner's hand, "M. Morrel, I thank you in the name of my father and of Mercédès."

"Good, good! Edmond. There's a sweet little cherub that sits up aloft that keeps a good watch for good fellows! Go to your father; go and see Mercédès, and come to me afterwards."

"Shall I row you on shore?"

"No, I thank you, I shall remain and look over the accounts with Danglars. Have you been satisfied with him this voyage?"

"That is according to the sense you attach to the question, sir. Do you mean, is he a good comrade? No, for I think he never liked me since the day when I was silly enough, after a little quarrel we had, to propose to him to stop for ten minutes at the Isle of Monte-Cristo to settle the dispute, a proposition which I was wrong to suggest, and he quite right to refuse. If you mean as responsible agent that you ask me the question, I believe there is nothing to say against him, and that you will be content with the way in which he has performed his duty."

"But tell me, Dantès, if you had the command of the Pharaon, should you have pleasure in retaining Danglars?"

"Captain or mate, M. Morrel," replied Dantès, "I shall always have the greatest respect for those who possess our owners' confidence."

"Good! good! Dantès. I see you are a thorough good fellow, and will detain you no longer. Go, for I see how impatient you are."

"Then I have leave?"

"Go, I tell you."

"May I have the use of your skiff?"

"Certainly."

"Then for the present, M. Morrel, farewell, and a thousand thanks!"

"I hope soon to see you again, my dear Edmond. Good luck to you!"

The young sailor jumped into the skiff, and sat down in the stern, desiring to be put ashore at the Canebière. The two rowers bent to their work, and the little boat glided away as rapidly as possible in the midst of the thousand vessels which choke up the narrow way which leads between the two rows of ships from the mouth of the harbour to the Quai d'Orleans.

The shipowner, smiling, followed him with his eyes, until he saw him spring out on the quay, and disappear in the midst of the throng which, from five o'clock in the morning until nine o'clock at night, choke up this famous street of La Canebière, of which the modern Phocéens are so proud, and say with all the gravity in the world, and with that accent which gives so much character to what is said, " If Paris had La Canebière, Paris would be a second Marseilles." On turning round, the owner saw Danglars behind him, who apparently attended his orders; but in reality followed, as he did, the young sailor with his eyes, only there was a great difference in the expression of the looks of the two men who thus watched the movements of Edmond Dantès.

CHAPTER II

FATHER AND SON

WE will leave Danglars struggling with the feelings of hatred, and endeavouring to insinuate in the ear of the shipowner, Morrel, some evil suspicions against his comrade, and follow Dantès; who, after having traversed the Canebière, took the Rue de Noailles, and entering into a small house, situated on the left side of the Allées de Meillan, rapidly ascended four stories of a dark staircase, holding the baluster in his hand, whilst with the other he repressed the beatings of his heart, and paused before a half-opened door, which revealed all the interior of a small apartment.

This apartment was occupied by Dantès' father.

The news of the arrival of the Pharaon had not yet reached the old man, who, mounted on a chair, was amusing himself with staking some nasturtiums with tremulous hand, which, mingled with clematis, formed a kind of trellis at his window.

Suddenly he felt an arm thrown round his body, and a well-known voice behind him exclaimed, "Father! dear father!"

The old man uttered a cry, and turned round; then, seeing his son, he fell into his arms, pale and trembling.

"What ails you, my dearest father? Are you ill?" inquired the young man, much alarmed.

"No, no, my dear Edmond—my boy—my son!—no; but I did not expect you; and joy, the surprise of seeing you so suddenly—Ah! I really seem as if I were going to die!"

"Come, come, cheer up, my dear father! 'Tis I—really I! They say joy never hurts, and so I come to you without any warning. Come now look cheerfully at me, instead of gazing as you do with your eyes so wild. Here I am back again, and we will now be happy."

"Yes, yes, my boy, so we will—so we will," replied the old man; "but how shall we be happy?—Will you never leave me again?—Come, tell me all the good fortune that has befallen you."

"God forgive me," said the young man, "for rejoicing at happiness derived from the misery of others; but Heaven knows I did not seek this good fortune; it has happened, and I really cannot affect to lament. The good captain Leclere is dead, father, and it is probable that, with the aid of M.

23

Morrel, I shall have his place. Do you understand, father? Only imagine me a captain at twenty, with a hundred louis pay, and a share in the profits! Is not this more than a poor sailor, like me, could have hoped for?"

"Yes, my dear boy," replied the old man, "and much more than you could have expected."

"Well, then, with the first money I touch, I mean you to have a small house, with a garden to plant your clematis, your nasturtiums, and your honeysuckles. But what ails you, father? Are not you well?"

"'Tis nothing, nothing; it will soon pass away;" and as he said so the old man's strength failed him, and he fell back-wards.

"Come, come," said the young man, "a glass of wine, father, will revive you. Where do you keep your wine?"

"No, no; thank ye. You need not look for it; I do not want it," said the old man.

"Yes, yes, father, tell me where it is;" and he opened two or three cupboards.

"It is no use," said the old man; "there is no wine."

"What! no wine?" said Dantès, turning pale, and looking alternately at the hollow cheeks of the old man and the empty cupboards. "What! no wine? Have you wanted money, father?"

"I wanted nothing since I see you," said the old man.

"Yet," stammered Dantès, wiping the perspiration from his brow,—"yet I gave you two hundred francs when I left three months ago."

"Yes, yes, Edmond, that is true; but you forgot at that time a little debt to our neighbour Caderousse. He reminded me of it, telling me if I did not pay for you, he would be paid by M. Morrel; and so, you see, lest he might do you an injury——"

"Well?"

"Why I paid him."

"But," cried Dantès, "it was a hundred and forty francs I owed Caderousse."

"Yes," stammered the old man.

"And you paid him out of the two hundred francs I left you?"

The old man made a sign in the affirmative.

"So that you have lived for three months on sixty francs?" muttered the young man.

"You know how little I require," said the old man.

"Heaven pardon me," cried Edmond, going on his knees before the old man.

"What are you doing?"

"You have wounded my very heart."

"Never mind it, for I see you once more," said the old man; "and now all is forgotten—all is well again."

"Yes, here I am," said the young man, "with a happy prospect and a little money. Here, father! here!" he said, "take this—take it, and send for something immediately."

And he emptied his pockets on the table, whose contents consisted of a dozen pieces of gold, five or six crowns, and some smaller coin.

The countenance of old Dantès brightened.

"Whom does this belong to?" he inquired.

"To me! to you! to us! Take it; buy some provisions; be happy, and to-morrow we shall have more."

"Gently, gently," said the old man, with a smile; "and by your leave I will use your purse moderately, for they would say, if they saw me buy too many things at a time, that I had been obliged to await your return, in order to be able to purchase them."

"Do as you please; but, first of all, pray have a servant, father. I will not have you left alone so long. I have some smuggled coffee, and most capital tobacco, in a small chest in the hold, which you shall have to-morrow. But, hush! here comes somebody."

"'Tis Caderousse, who has heard of your arrival, and, no doubt, comes to congratulate you on your fortunate return."

"Ah! lips that say one thing, whilst the heart thinks another," murmured Edmond. "But, never mind, he is a neighbour who has done us a service on a time, so he's welcome."

As Edmond finished his sentence in a low voice, there appeared at the door the black and shock head of Caderousse. He was a man of twenty-five or twenty-six years of age, and held in his hand a morsel of cloth, which, in his capacity as a tailor, he was about to turn into the lining of a coat.

"What! it is you, Edmond, returned?" said he, with a broad Marseillaise accent, and a grin that displayed his teeth as white as ivory.

"Yes, as you see, neighbour Caderousse; and ready to be agreeable to you in any and every way," replied Dantès, but ill concealing his feeling under this appearance of civility.

"Thanks—thanks; but, fortunately, I do not want for any thing; and it chances that at times there are others who have need of me." Dantès made a gesture. "I do not allude to you, my boy. No!—no! I lent you money, and you returned it: that's like good neighbours, and we are quits."

"We are never quits with those who oblige us," was Dantès' reply: "for when we do not owe them money, we owe them gratitude."

"What's the use of mentioning that? What is done is done. Let us talk of your happy return, my boy. I had gone on the quay to match a piece of mulberry cloth, when I met friend Danglars.

"'What! you at Marseilles?'

"'Yes,' says he.

"'I thought you were at Smyrna.'

"'I was; but am now back again.'

"'And where is the dear boy, our little Edmond?'

"'Why, with his father, no doubt,' replied Danglars. And so I came," added Caderousse, "as fast as I could to have the pleasure of shaking hands with a friend."

"Worthy Caderousse!" said the old man, "he is so much attached to us!"

"Yes, to be sure I am. I love and esteem you, because honest folks are so rare! But it seems you have come back rich, my boy," continued the tailor, looking askance at the handful of gold and silver which Dantès had thrown on the table.

The young man remarked the greedy glance which shone in the dark eyes of his neighbour.

"Eh!" he said, negligently, "this money is not mine: I was expressing to my father my fears that he had wanted many things in my absence, and to convince me, he emptied his purse on the table. Come, father," added Dantès, "put this money back in your box—unless neighbour Caderousse wants any thing, and in that case it is at his service."

"No, my boy, no," said Caderousse. "I am not in any want, thank God! the State nourishes me. Keep your money—keep it, I say;—one never has too much;—but at the same time, my boy, I am as much obliged by your offer as if I took advantage of it."

"It was offered with good-will," said Dantès.

"No doubt, my boy; no doubt. Well, you stand well with M. Morrel, I hear,—you insinuating dog, you!"

"M. Morrel has always been exceedingly kind to me," replied Dantès.

"Then you were wrong to refuse to dine with him."

"What! did you refuse to dine with him?" said old Dantès; " and did he invite you to dine?"

"Yes, my dear father," replied Edmond, smiling at his father's astonishment at the excessive honour paid to his son.

"And why did you refuse, my son?" inquired the old man.

"That I might the sooner see you again, my dear father," replied the young man. "I was most anxious to see you."

"But it must have vexed M. Morrel, good, worthy man," said Caderousse. "And when you are looking forward to be captain, it was wrong to annoy the owner."

"But I explained to him the cause of my refusal," replied Dantès; "and I hope he fully understood it."

"Yes, but to be captain one must give way a little to one's patrons."

"I hope to be captain without that," said Dantès.

"So much the better—so much the better! Nothing will give greater pleasure to all your old friends; and I know one down there behind the citadel of Saint Nicolas, who will not be sorry to hear it."

"Mercédès?" said the old man.

"Yes, my dear father, and with your permission, now I have seen you, and know you are well, and have all you require, I will ask your consent to go and pay a visit to the Catalans."

"Go, my dear boy," said old Dantès; "and Heaven bless you in your wife, as it has blessed me in my son!"

"His wife!" said Caderousse; "why, how fast you can go, father Dantès; she is not his wife yet, it appears."

"No, but according to all probability she soon will be," replied Edmond.

"Yes—yes," said Caderousse; "but you were right to return as soon as possible, my boy."

"And why?"

"Because Mercédès is a very fine girl, and fine girls never lack lovers; she, particularly, has them by dozens."

"Really?" answered Edmond, with a smile which had in it traces of slight uneasiness.

"Ah, yes," continued Caderousse, "and capital offers too; but you know you will be captain, and who could refuse you then?"

"Meaning to say," replied Dantès, with a smile which but ill concealed his trouble, "that if I were not a captain——"

"Eh—eh!" said Caderousse, shaking his head.

"Come, come," said the sailor, "I have a better opinion than you of women in general, and of Mercédès in particular; and I am certain that, captain or not, she will remain ever faithful to me."

"So much the better—so much the better," said Caderousse. "When one is going to be married, there is nothing like implicit confidence; but never mind that, my boy, —but go and announce your arrival, and let her know all your hopes and prospects."

"I will go directly," was Edmond's reply; and, embracing his father, and saluting Caderousse, he left the apartment.

Caderousse lingered for a moment, then taking leave of old Dantès, he went downstairs to rejoin Danglars, who awaited him at the corner of the Rue Senac.

"Well," said Danglars, "did you see him?"

"I have just left him," answered Caderousse.

"Did he allude to his hope of being captain?"

"He spoke of it as a thing already decided."

"Patience!" said Danglars, "he is in too much hurry, it appears to me."

"Why, it seems M. Morrel has promised him the thing."

"So that he is quite elate about it."

"That is to say, he is actually insolent on the matter—has already offered me his patronage, as if he were a grand personage, and proffered me a loan of money, as though he were a banker."

"Which you refused."

"Most assuredly; although I might easily have accepted, for it was I who put into his hands the first silver he ever earned; but now, M. Dantès has no longer any occasion for assistance —he is about to become a captain."

"Pooh!" said Danglars, "he is not one yet."

"*Ma foi!*—and it will be as well he never should be," answered Caderousse; "for if he should be, there will be really no speaking to him."

"If we choose," replied Danglars, "he will remain what he is, and, perhaps, become even less than he is."

"What do you mean?"

"Nothing—I was speaking to myself. And is he still in love with the Catalane?"

"Over head and ears: but unless I am much mistaken, there will be a storm in that quarter."

"Explain yourself."

"Why should I?"

"It is more important than you think, perhaps. You do not love Dantès?"

"I never like upstarts."

"Then tell me all you know relative to the Catalane."

"I know nothing for certain; only I have seen things which induce me to believe, as I told you, that the future captain will find some annoyance in the environs of the Vieilles Infirmeries."

"What do you know?—come, tell me!"

"Well, every time I have seen Mercédès come into the city, she has been accompanied by a tall, strapping, black-eyed Catalan, with a red complexion, brown skin, and fierce air, whom she calls cousin."

"Really; and you think this cousin pays her attentions?"

"I only suppose so. What else can a strapping chap of twenty-one mean with a fine wench of seventeen?"

"And you say Dantès has gone to the Catalans?"

"He went before I came down."

"Let us go the same way; we will stop at La Réserve, and we can drink a glass of La Malgue. whilst we wait for news."

"Come along," said Caderousse; "but mind you pay the shot."

"Certainly," replied Danglars; and going quickly to the spot alluded to, they called for a bottle of wine and two glasses.

Père Pamphile had seen Dantès pass not ten minutes before; and, assured that he was at the Catalans, they sat down under the budding foliage of the planes and sycamores, in the branches of which the birds were joyously singing on a lovely day in early spring.

CHAPTER III

THE CATALANS

ABOUT a hundred paces from the spot where the two friends were, with their looks fixed on the distance, and their ears attentive, whilst they imbibed the sparkling wine of La Malgue, behind a bare, and torn, and weather-worn wall. was the small village of the Catalans.

One day a mysterious colony quitted Spain and settled on the tongue of land on which it is to this day. It arrived from no one knew where, and spoke an unknown tongue. One of its chiefs, who understood Provençal, begged the commune of Marseilles to give them this bare and barren promontory, on which, like the sailors of the ancient times, they had run their boats ashore. The request was granted, and three months afterwards, around the twelve or fifteen small vessels which had brought these gipsies of the sea, a small village sprung up.

This village, constructed in a singular and picturesque manner, half Moorish, half Spanish, is that we behold at the present day inhabited by the descendants of those men who speak the language of their fathers. For three or four centuries they remained faithful to this small promontory, on which they had settled like a flight of seabirds, without mixing with the Marseillaise population, intermarrying, and preserving their original customs and the costume of their mother country, as they have preserved its language.

Our readers will follow us along the only street of this little village, and enter with us into one of the houses, on the outside of which the sun had stamped that beautiful colour of the dead leaf peculiar to the buildings of the country, and within a coat of limewash, of that white tint which forms the only ornament of Spanish posadas.

A young and beautiful girl, with hair as black as jet, her eyes as velvety as the gazelle's, was leaning with her back against the wainscot, rubbing in her slender fingers, moulded after the antique, a bunch of heath-blossoms, the flowers of which she was picking off and strewing on the floor; her arms, bare to the elbow, embrowned, and resembling those of the Venus at Arles, moved with a kind of restless impatience, and she tapped the earth with her pliant and well-formed foot so as to display the pure and full shape of her well-turned leg, in its red cotton stocking with grey and blue clocks.

At three paces from her, seated in a chair which he balanced on two legs, leaning his elbow on an old worm-eaten table, was a tall young man of twenty or two-and-twenty, who was looking at her with an air in which vexation and uneasiness were mingled. He questioned her with his eyes, but the firm and steady gaze of the young girl controlled his look.

"You see, Mercédès," said the young man, "here is Easter come round again, tell me, is this the moment for a wedding?"

"I have answered you a hundred times, Fernand, and really you must be your own enemy to ask me again."

"Well, repeat it,—repeat it, I beg of you, that I may at last believe it! Tell me for the hundredth time that you refuse my love, which had your mother's sanction. Make me fully comprehend that you are trifling with my happiness, that my life or death are immaterial to you. Ah! to have dreamed for ten years of being your husband, Mercédès, and to lose that hope, which was the only stay of my existence!"

"At least it was not I who ever encouraged you in that shape, Fernand," replied Mercédès; "you cannot reproach me with the slightest coquetry. I have always said to you, I love you as a brother, but do not ask from me more than sisterly affection, for my heart is another's. Is not this true, Fernand?"

"Yes, I know it well, Mercédès," replied the young man. "Yes, you have been cruelly frank with me; but do not forget that it is among the Catalans a sacred law to intermarry?"

"You mistake, Fernand, it is not a law, but merely a custom; and, I pray of you, do not cite this custom in your favour. You are included in the conscription, Fernand, and are only at liberty on sufferance, liable at any moment to be called upon to take up arms. Once a soldier, what would you do with me, a poor orphan, forlorn, without fortune, with nothing but a hut, half in ruins, containing some ragged nets, a miserable inheritance left by my father to my mother, and by my mother to me? She has been dead a year, and, you know, Fernand, I have subsisted almost entirely on public charity. Sometimes you pretend I am useful to you, and that is an excuse to share with me the produce of your fishing, and I accept it, Fernand, because you are the son of my father's brother, because we were brought up together, and still more because it would give you so much pain if I refuse. But I feel deeply that this fish which I go and sell, and with the produce of which I buy the flax I spin,—I feel very keenly, Fernand, that this is charity!"

"And if it were, Mercédès, poor and lone as you are, you suit me as well as the daughter of the first shipowner or the richest banker of Marseilles! What do such as we desire but a good wife and careful housekeeper, and where can I look for these better than in you?"

"Fernand," answered Mercédès, shaking her head, "a woman becomes a bad manager, and who shall say she will remain an honest woman, when she loves another man better than her husband? Rest content with my friendship, for I repeat to you that is all I can promise, and I will promise no more than I can bestow."

"I understand," replied Fernand, "you can endure your own wretchedness patiently, but you are afraid of mine. Well, Mercédès, beloved by you I would tempt fortune; you would bring me good luck, and I should become rich. I could extend my occupation as a fisherman, might get a place as clerk in a warehouse, and become myself a dealer in time."

"You could do no such thing, Fernand; you are a soldier, and if you remain at the Catalans it is because there is not a war; so remain a fisherman, and contented with my friendship, as I cannot give you more."

"Well, you are right, Mercédès. I will be a sailor; instead of the costume of our fathers, which you despise, I will wear a varnished hat, a striped shirt, and a blue jacket with an anchor on the buttons. Would not that dress please you?"

"What do you mean?" asked Mercédès, darting at him an angry glance,—"what do you mean? I do not understand you."

"I mean, Mercédès, that you are thus harsh and cruel with me, because you are expecting some one who is thus attired; but, perhaps, he you await is inconstant, or, if he is not, the sea is so to him."

"Fernand!" cried Mercédès, "I believed you were good-hearted, and I was mistaken! Fernand, you are wicked to call to your aid jealousy and the anger of God! Yes, I will not deny it, I do await, and I do love him to whom you allude; and, if he does not return, instead of accusing him of the inconstancy which you insinuate, I will tell you that he died loving me and me only."

The young Catalan made a gesture of rage.

"I understand you, Fernand; you would be revenged on him because I do not love you; you would cross your Catalan knife with his dirk. What end would that answer? To lose you my friendship if he were conquered, and see that friendship changed into hate if you were conqueror. Believe me, to seek a quarrel with a man is a bad method of pleasing the woman who loves that man. No, Fernand, you will not thus give way to evil thoughts. Unable to have me for your wife, you will content yourself with having me for your friend and sister; and besides," she added, her eyes troubled and moistened with tears, "wait, wait, Fernand, you said just now that the sea was treacherous, and he has been gone four months, and during these four months we have had some terrible storms."

Fernand made no reply, nor did he attempt to check the tears which flowed down the cheeks of Mercédès, although for each of these tears he would have shed his heart's blood; but these tears flowed for another. He rose, paced awhile up and down the hut, and then, suddenly stopping before Mercédès, with his eyes glowing and his hands clenched,—

"Say, Mercédès," he said, "once for all, is this your final determination?"

"I love Edmond Dantès," the young girl calmly replied, "and none but Edmond shall ever be my husband."

"And you will always love him?"

"As long as I live."

Fernand let fall his head like a defeated man, heaved a sigh which resembled a groan, and then, suddenly looking her full in the face, with clenched teeth and expanded nostrils, said,—

"But if he is dead——"

"If he is dead, I shall die too."

"If he has forgotten you——"

"Mercédès!" cried a voice, joyously, outside the house,— "Mercédès!"

"Ah!" exclaimed the young girl, blushing with delight, and springing up with love, "you see he has not forgotten me, for here he is!" And, rushing towards the door, she opened it, saying, "Here, Edmond, here I am!"

Fernand, pale and trembling, receded like a traveller at the sight of a serpent, and fell into a chair beside him.

Edmond and Mercédès were clasped in each other's arms. The burning sun of Marseilles, which penetrated the room by the open door, covered them with a flood of light. At first they saw nothing around them. Their intense happiness isolated them from all the rest of the world, and they only spoke in broken words, which are the tokens of a joy so extreme that they seem rather the expression of sorrow.

Suddenly Edmond saw the gloomy countenance of Fernand, as it was defined in the shadow, pale and threatening, and by a movement, for which he could scarcely account to himself, the young Catalan placed his hands on the knife at his belt.

"Ah! your pardon," said Dantès, frowning in his turn. "I did not perceive that there were three of us." Then, turning to Mercédès, he inquired, "Who is this gentleman?"

"One who will be your best friend, Dantès, for he is my friend, my cousin, my brother,—it is Fernand—the man whom, after you, Edmond, I love the most in the world. Do you not remember him?"

C.M.—B

"Yes!" said Edmond, and without relinquishing Mercédès' hand clasped in one of his own, he extended the other to the Catalan with a cordial air.

But Fernand, instead of responding to this amicable gesture, remained mute and trembling.

Edmond then cast his eyes scrutinisingly at Mercédès, agitated and embarrassed, and then again on Fernand gloomy and menacing.

This look told him all, and his brow became suffused and angry.

"I did not know, when I came with such haste to you, that I was to meet an enemy here."

"An enemy!" cried Mercédès, with an angry look at her cousin. "An enemy in my house, do you say, Edmond! If I believed that I would place my arm under yours and go with you to Marseilles, leaving the house to return to it no more."

Fernand's eye darted lightning.

"And, should any misfortune occur to you, dear Edmond," she continued, with the same calmness, which proved to Fernand that the young girl had read the very innermost depths of his sinister thought, "if misfortune should occur to you I would ascend the highest point of the Cape de Morgion, and cast myself headlong from it."

Fernand became deadly pale.

"But you are deceived, Edmond," she continued. "You have no enemy here—there is no one but Fernand, my brother, who will grasp your hand as a devoted friend."

And at these words the young girl fixed her imperious look on the Catalan, who, as if fascinated by it, came slowly towards Edmond, and offered him his hand.

His hatred, like a powerless though furious wave, was broken against the strong ascendancy which Mercédès exercised over him.

Scarcely, however, had he touched Edmond's hand than he felt he had done all he could do, and rushed hastily out of the house.

"Oh!" he exclaimed, running furiously, and tearing his hair,—"Oh! who will deliver me from this man? Wretched—wretched that I am!"

"Hallo! Catalan! Hallo, Fernand! where are you running to?" exclaimed a voice.

The young man stopped suddenly, looked around him, and perceived Caderousse sitting at table with Danglars under an arbour.

"Well," said Caderousse, "why don't you come? Are you really in such a hurry that you have not time to say 'how do' to your friends?"

"Particularly when they have still a full bottle before them," added Danglars.   Fernand looked at them both with a stupefied air, but did not say a word.

"He seems besotted," said Danglars, pushing Caderousse with his knee.   "Are we mistaken, and is Dantès triumphant in spite of all we have believed?"

"Why, we must inquire into that," was Caderousse's reply; and turning towards the young man, said, "Well, Catalan, can't you make up your mind?"

Fernand wiped away the perspiration steaming from his brow, and slowly entered the arbour, whose shade seemed to restore somewhat of calmness to his senses, and whose coolness, somewhat of refreshment to his exhausted body.

"Good day," said he.   "You called me, didn't you?" And he fell rather than sat down on one of the seats which surrounded the table.

"I called you because you were running like a madman; and I was afraid you would throw yourself into the sea," said Caderousse, laughing.   "Why! when a man has friends, they are not only to offer him a glass of wine, but, moreover, to prevent his swallowing three or four pints of water unnecessarily!"

Fernand gave a groan, which resembled a sob, and dropped his head into his hands, his elbows leaning on the table.

"Well, Fernand, I must say," said Caderousse, beginning the conversation, with that brutality of the common people, in which curiosity destroys all diplomacy, "you look uncommonly like a rejected lover;" and he burst into a hoarse laugh.

"Bah!" said Danglars, "a lad of his make was not born to be unhappy in love.   You are laughing at him, Caderousse!"

"No," he replied, "only hark how he sighs! Come, come, Fernand!" said Caderousse, "hold up your head and answer us.   It's not polite not to reply to friends who ask news of your health."

"My health is well enough," said Fernand, clenching his hands without raising his head.

"Ah! you see, Danglars," said Caderousse, winking at his friend, "this it is, Fernand whom you see here is a good and brave Catalan, one of the best fishermen in Marseilles, and he is in love with a very fine girl named Mercédès; but it appears, unfortunately, that the fine girl is in love with the second in command on board the Pharaon; and, as the Pharaon arrived to-day—why, you understand!"

"No, I do not understand," said Danglars.

"Poor Fernand has been dismissed," continued Caderousse.

"Well, and what then?" said Fernand, lifting up his head, and looking at Caderousse like a man who looks for some one on whom to vent his anger; "Mercédès is not accountable to any person, is she? Is she not free to love whomsoever she will?"

"Oh! if you take it in that sense," said Caderousse, "it is another thing! But I thought you were a Catalan, and they told me the Catalans were not men to allow themselves to be supplanted by a rival. It was even told me that Fernand, especially, was terrible in his vengeance."

Fernand smiled piteously. "A lover is never terrible," he said.

"Poor fellow!" remarked Danglars, affecting to pity the young man from the bottom of his heart. "Why, you see, he did not expect to see Dantès return so suddenly! he thought he was dead, perhaps; or, perchance, faithless! These things always come on us more severely when they come suddenly."

"Ah, *ma foi*, under any circumstances!" said Caderousse, who drank as he spoke, and on whom the fumes of the wine of La Malgue began to take effect,—"under any circumstances Fernand is not the only person put out by the fortunate arrival of Dantès; is he, Danglars?"

"No, you are right—and I should say that would bring him ill luck."

"Well, never mind," answered Caderousse, pouring out a glass of wine for Fernand, and filling his own for the eighth or ninth time, whilst Danglars had merely sipped his. "Never mind—in the meantime he marries Mercédès—the lovely Mercédès—at least, he returns to do that."

During this time Danglars fixed his piercing glance on the young man, on whose heart Caderousse's words fell like molten lead.

"And when is the wedding to be?" he asked.

"Oh, it is not yet fixed!" murmured Fernand.

"No, but it will be," said Caderousse, "as surely as Dantès will be captain of the Pharaon—eh, Danglars?"

Danglars shuddered at this unexpected attack, and turned to Caderousse, whose countenance he scrutinised to try and detect whether the blow was premeditated; but he read nothing but envy in a countenance already rendered brutal and stupid by drunkenness.

"Well," said he, filling the glasses, "let us drink to Captain Edmond Dantès, husband of the beautiful Catalane!"

Caderousse raised his glass to his mouth with unsteady hand, and swallowed the contents at a gulp. Fernand dashed his on the ground.

"Eh! eh! eh!" stammered Caderousse. "What do I see down there by the wall in the direction of the Catalans? Look, Fernand! your eyes are better than mine. I believe I see double. You know wine is a deceiver: but I should say it was two lovers walking side by side, and hand in hand. Heaven forgive me! they do not know that we can see them, and they are actually embracing!"

Danglars did not lose one pang that Fernand endured.

"Do you know them, M. Fernand?" he said.

"Yes," was the reply, in a low voice. "It is M. Edmond and Mademoiselle Mercédès!"

"Ah! see there, now!" said Caderousse; "and I did not recognise them! Holla, Dantès! holla, lovely damsel! Come this way, and let us know when the wedding is to be, for M. Fernand here is so obstinate he will not tell us!"

"Hold your tongue! will you?" said Danglars, pretending to restrain Caderousse, who, with the tenacity of drunkards, leaned out of the arbour. "Try to stand upright, and let the lovers make love without interruption. See, look at M. Fernand, and follow his example—he is well behaved!"

Fernand, probably excited beyond bearing, pricked by Danglars, as the bull is by the bandilleros, was about to rush out; for he had risen from his seat, and seemed to be collecting himself to dash headlong upon his rival, when Mercédès, smiling and graceful, lifted up her lovely head, and shewed her clear and bright eye. At this Fernand recollected her threat of dying if Edmond died, and dropped again heavily on his seat.

Danglars looked at the two men, one after the other, the one brutalised by liquor, the other overwhelmed with love.

"I shall extract nothing from these fools," he muttered; "and I am very much afraid of being here between a drunkard and a coward. Yet this Catalan has eyes that glisten like the Spaniards, Sicilians, and Calabrians, who practise revenge so well. Unquestionably, Edmond's star is in the ascendant, and he will marry the splendid girl—he will be captain, too, and laugh at us all, unless——" a sinister smile passed over Danglar's lips—"unless I mingle in the affair," he added.

"Hallo!" continued Caderousse, half rising, and with his fist on the table, "hallo, Edmond! do you not see your friends, or are you too proud to speak to them?"

"No! my dear fellow," replied Dantès, "I am not proud, but I am happy; and happiness blinds, I think, more than pride."

"Ah! very well, that's an explanation!" said Caderousse. "Well, good day, Madame Dantès!"

Mercédès curtseyed gravely, and said,—

"That is not my name, and in my country it bodes ill fortune, they say, to call young girls by the name of their betrothed before he becomes their husband. Call me, then, Mercédès, if you please."

"We must excuse our worthy neighbour, Caderousse," said Dantès, "he is so easily mistaken."

"So, then, the wedding is to take place immediately, M. Dantès," said Danglars, bowing to the young couple.

"As soon as possible, M. Danglars; to-day all preliminaries will be arranged at my father's, and to-morrow, or next day at latest, the wedding festival here at La Réserve. My friends will be there, I hope; that is to say, you are invited, M. Danglars, and you, Caderousse."

"And Fernand," said Caderousse, with a chuckle, "Fernand, too, is invited?"

"My wife's brother is my brother," said Edmond; "and we, Mercédès and I, should be very sorry if he were absent at such a time."

Fernand opened his mouth to reply, but his voice died on his lips, and he could not utter a word.

"To-day the preliminaries, to-morrow or next day the ceremony! you are in a hurry, captain!"

"Danglars," said Edmond, smiling, "I will say to you as Mercédès said just now to Caderousse, 'Do not give me a title which does not belong to me;' that may bring me bad luck."

"Your pardon," replied Danglars, "I merely said you seemed in a hurry, and we have lots of time, the Pharaon cannot be under weigh again in less than three months."

"We are always in a hurry to be happy, M. Danglars; for when we have suffered a long time, we have great difficulty in believing in good fortune. But it is not selfishness alone that makes me thus in haste; I must go to Paris."

"To Paris! really! and will it be the first time you have ever been there, Dantès?"

"Yes."

"Have you business there?"

"Not of my own; the last commission of poor Captain Leclere; you know to what I allude, Danglars,—it is sacred. Besides, I shall only take the time to go and return."

"Yes, yes, I understand," said Danglars, and then, in a low tone he added,—

"To Paris, no doubt to deliver the letter which the Grand Marshal gave him. Ah! this letter gives me an idea,—a capital idea! Ah! Dantès, my friend, you are not yet registered number One on board the good ship Pharaon," then turning towards Edmond, who was walking away, "Good journey," he cried.

"Thank ye," said Edmond, with a friendly nod, and the two lovers continued their route, calm and joyous.

CHAPTER IV

CONSPIRACY

DANGLARS followed Edmond and Mercédès with his eyes until the two lovers disappeared behind one of the angles of Fort Saint-Nicolas, then turning round, he perceived Fernand, who had fallen pale and trembling into his chair, whilst Caderousse stammered out the words of a drinking song.

"Well, my dear sir," said Danglars to Fernand, "here is a marriage which does not appear to make every body happy."

"It drives me to despair," said Fernand.

"Do you, then, love Mercédès?"

"I adore her!"

"Have you loved her long?"

"Ever since I have known her."

"And you sit there, tearing your hair instead of seeking to remedy your condition! I did not think it was thus your nation acted."

"What would you have me do?" said Fernand.

"How do I know? Is it my affair? I am not in love with Mademoiselle Mercédès, but for you—seek, and you shall find."

"I have found already."

"What?"

"I would stab the man, but the woman told me that if any misfortune happened to her betrothed she would kill herself."

"Pooh! women say those things, but never do them."

"You do not know Mercédès; what she threatens she will do."

"Idiot!" muttered Danglars, "whether she kill herself or not, what matter provided Dantès is not captain?"

"Before Mercédès should die," replied Fernand, with the accents of unshaken resolution, "I would die myself!"

"That's what I call love!" said Caderousse, with a voice more tipsy than ever. "That's love, or I don't know what love is."

"Come," said Danglars, "you appear to me a good sort of fellow, and, hang me! but I should like to help you, but——"

"Yes," said Caderousse, "but how?"

"My dear fellow," replied Danglars, "you are three parts drunk; finish the bottle, and you will be completely so.

39

Drink, then, and do not meddle with what we are discussing, for that requires all one's wit and cool judgment."

"I—drunk?" said Caderousse, "well, that's a good one! I could drink four more such bottles; they are no bigger than Eau-de-Cologne flasks. Père Pamphile, more wine!" and Caderousse rattled his glass upon the table.

"You were saying, sir——" said Fernand, awaiting with great anxiety the end of this interrupted remark.

"What was I saying? I forget. This drunken Caderousse has made me lose the thread of my sentence."

"Drunk, if you like; so much the worse for those who fear wine, for it is because they have some bad thoughts which they are afraid the liquor will extract from their hearts;" and Caderousse began to sing the two last lines of a song very popular at the time,——

> " 'Tous les méchants sont buveurs d'eau;
> C'est bien prouvé par le déluge.' "

"You said, sir, you would like to help me, but——"

"Yes; but, I added, to help you it would be sufficient that Dantès did not marry her you love; and the marriage may easily be thwarted, methinks, and yet Dantès need not die."

"Death alone can separate them," remarked Fernand.

"You talk like a noodle, my friend," said Caderousse, "and here is Danglars, who is a wide-awake, clever, deep fellow, who will prove to you that you are wrong. Prove it, Danglars. I have answered for you. Say there is no need why Dantès should die: it would, indeed, be a pity he should. Dantès is a good fellow; I like Dantès; Dantès, your health!"

Fernand rose impatiently.

"Let him run on," said Danglars, restraining the young man; "drunk as he is, he is not much out in what he says. Absence severs as well as death, and if the walls of a prison were between Edmond and Mercédès they would be as effectually separated as if they lay under a tombstone."

"Yes; only people get out of prison," said Caderousse, who, with what sense was left him, listened eagerly to the conversation, "and when they get out, and their names are Edmond Dantès, they revenge——"

"What matters that?" muttered Fernand.

"And why, I should like to know," persisted Caderousse, "should they put Dantès in prison; he has neither robbed, nor killed, nor murdered."

"Hold your tongue!" said Danglars.

"I won't hold my tongue!" replied Caderousse, "I say I want to know why they should put Dantès in prison; I like Dantès; Dantès, your health!" And he swallowed another glass of wine.

Danglars saw in the muddled look of the tailor the progress of his intoxication, and turning towards Fernand, said,——

"Well, you understand there is no need to kill him."

"Certainly not, if, as you said just now, you have the means of having Dantès arrested. Have you that means?"

"It is to be found for the searching. But, why should I meddle in the matter? it is no affair of mine."

"I know not why you meddle," said Fernand, seizing his arm, "but this I know, you have some motive of personal hatred against Dantès, for he who himself hates is never mistaken in the sentiments of others."

"I! motives of hatred against Dantès? None, on my word! I saw you were unhappy, and your unhappiness interested me; that's all; but the moment you believe I act for my own account, adieu, my dear friend, get out of the affair as best you may;" and Danglars rose as if he meant to depart.

"No, no," said Fernand, restraining him, "stay! It is of very little consequence to me at the end of the matter whether you have any angry feeling or not against Dantès. I hate him! I confess it openly. Do you find the means, I will execute it, provided it is not to kill the man, for Mercédès has declared she will kill herself if Dantès is killed."

Caderousse, who had let his head drop on the table, now raised it, and looking at Fernand with his dulled and fishy eyes, he said,——

"Kill Dantès! who talks of killing Dantès? I won't have him killed—I won't! He's my friend, and this morning offered to share his money with me, as I shared mine with him. I won't have Dantès killed—I won't!"

"And who has said a word about killing him, muddlehead!" replied Danglars. "We were merely joking: drink to his health," he added, filling Caderousse's glass, "and do not interfere with us."

"Yes, yes, Dantès, good health!" said Caderousse, emptying his glass, "here's to his health! his health—hurrah!"

"But the means—the means?" said Fernand.

"Have you not hit upon any?"

"No!—you undertook to do so."

"True," replied Danglars; "the French have the superiority over the Spaniards, that the Spaniards ruminate whilst the French invent."

"Do you invent then!" said Fernand, impatiently.

"Waiter," said Danglars, "pen, ink, and paper!"

"Pen, ink, and paper," muttered Fernand.

"Yes; I am a supercargo; pen, ink, and paper, are my tools and without my tools I am fit for nothing."

"Pen, ink, and paper!" then called Fernand, loudly.

C.M.—B*

"All you require is a table," said the waiter, pointing to the writing materials.

"Bring them here."

The waiter did as he was desired.

"When one thinks," said Caderousse, letting his hand drop on the paper, "there is here wherewithal to kill a man more sure than if we waited at the corner of a wood to assassinate him. I have always had more dread of a pen, a bottle of ink, and a sheet of paper, than of a sword or pistol."

"The fellow is not so drunk as he appears to be," said Danglars. "Give him some more wine, Fernand." Fernand filled Caderousse's glass, who, toper as he was, lifted his hand from the paper and seized the glass.

The Catalan watched him until Caderousse, almost overcome by this fresh assault on his senses, rested, or rather allowed his glass to fall, upon the table.

"Well?" resumed the Catalan, as he saw the final glimmer of Caderousse's reason vanishing before the last glass of wine.

"Well, then; I should say, for instance," resumed Danglars, "that after a voyage such as Dantès has just made, and in which he touched the Isle of Elba, some one were to denounce him to the king's procureur as a Bonapartist agent——"

"I will denounce him!" exclaimed the young man hastily.

"Yes, but they will make you then sign your declaration, and confront you with him you have denounced. I will supply you with the means of supporting your accusation, for I know the fact well. But Dantès cannot remain for ever in prison, and one day or other he will leave it, and the day when he comes out, woe betide him who was the cause of his incarceration!"

"Oh, I should wish nothing better than that he would come and seek a quarrel with me."

"Yes, and Mercédès! Mercédès, who will detest you if you have only the misfortune to scratch the skin of her dearly beloved Edmond!"

"True!" said Fernand.

"No! no!" continued Danglars, "if we resolve on such a step, it would be much better to take, as I now do, this pen, dip it into this ink, and write with the left hand (that the writing may not be recognised) the denunciation we propose." And Danglars, uniting practice with theory, wrote with his left hand, and in a writing reversed from his usual style, and totally unlike it, the following lines which he handed to Fernand, and which Fernand read in an under tone:—

"Monsieur,—The procureur du roi is informed by a friend of the throne and religion, that one Edmond Dantès, mate of the ship Pharaon, arrived this morning from Smyrna, after having touched at Naples and Porto-Ferrajo, has been intrusted by Murat with a letter for the usurper, and by the usurper with a letter for the Bonapartist committee in Paris.

"Proof of this crime will be found on arresting him, for the letter will be found upon him, or at his father's, or in his cabin on board the Pharaon."

"Very good," resumed Danglars: "now your revenge looks like common sense, for in no way can it revert to yourself, and the matter will thus work its own way; there is nothing to do now but fold the letter as I am doing, and write upon it, 'To M. le Procureur Royal,' and that's all settled."

And Danglars wrote the address as he spoke.

"Yes, and that's all settled," exclaimed Caderousse, who, by a last effort of intellect, had followed the reading of the letter, and instinctively comprehended all the misery which such a denunciation must entail. "Yes, and that's all settled: only it will be an infamous shame;" and he stretched out his hand to reach the letter.

"Yes," said Danglars, taking it from his reach; "and as what I say and do is merely in jest, and I amongst the first and foremost should be sorry if any thing happened to Dantès—the worthy Dantès—Look here!"

And taking the letter he squeezed it up in his hands, and threw it into a corner of the arbour.

"All right!" said Caderousse. "Dantès is my friend, and I won't have him ill-used."

"And who thinks of using him ill? Certainly neither I nor Fernand!" said Danglars, rising, and looking at the young man who still remained seated, but whose eye was fixed on the denunciatory sheet of paper flung into the corner.

"In this case," replied Caderousse, "let's have some more wine. I wish to drink to the health of Edmond and the lovely Mercédès."

"You have had too much already, drunkard," said Danglars; "and if you continue you will be compelled to sleep here, because unable to stand on your legs."

"I?" said Caderousse, rising with all the offended dignity of a drunken man, "I can't keep on my legs! Why, I'll bet a wager I go up into the belfry of the Accoules, and without staggering, too!"

"Well done!" said Danglars, "I'll take your bet; but to-morrow—to-day it is time to return. Give me your arm, and let us go."

"Very well, let us go," said Caderousse; "but I don't want your arm at all. Come, Fernand, won't you return to Marseilles with us?"

"No," said Fernand; "I shall return to the Catalans."

"You're wrong. Come with us to Marseilles—come along."

" I will not."

"What do you mean? you will not? Well, just as you like, my prince; there's liberty for all the world. Come along, Danglars, and let the young gentleman return to the Catalans if he chooses."

Danglars took advantage of Caderousse's temper at the moment, to take him off towards Marseilles by the Porte-Saint-Victor, staggering as he went.

When they had advanced about twenty yards, Danglars looked back and saw Fernand stoop, pick up the crumpled paper, and, putting it into his pocket, then rush out of the arbour towards Pillon.

"Well," said Caderousse, "why, what a lie he told! He said he was going to the Catalans, and he is going to the city. Halloa, Fernand!"

"Oh, you see wrong," said Danglars, "he's gone right enough."

"Well," said Caderousse, "I should have said not—how treacherous wine is!"

"Come, come," said Danglars to himself, "now the thing is at work, and it will effect its purpose unassisted."

CHAPTER V

THE MARRIAGE-FEAST

THE morning's sun rose clear and resplendent, gilding the heavens, and even the foamy waves with its bright refulgent beams.

The plenteous feast had been prepared at La Réserve, with whose arbour the reader is already familiar. The apartment destined for the purpose was spacious, and lighted by a number of windows, over each of which was written in golden letters the name of one of the principal cities of France; beneath these windows a wooden balcony extended the entire length of the house. And although the entertainment was fixed for twelve o'clock at noon, an hour previous to that time the balcony was filled with impatient and expectant guests, consisting of the favoured part of the crew of the Pharaon, and other personal friends of the bridegroom, the whole of whom had arrayed themselves in their choicest costumes, in order to do greater honour to the day.

Various rumours were afloat, to the effect that the owners of the Pharaon had promised to attend the nuptial feast; but all seemed unanimous in doubting that an act of such rare and exceeding condescension could possibly be intended.

Danglars, however, who now made his appearance, accompanied by Caderousse, effectually confirmed the report, stating that he had recently conversed with M. Morrel, who had himself assured him he intended joining the festive party upon the occasion of their second officer's marriage.

Even while relating this aloud an enthusiastic burst of applause from the crew of the Pharaon announced the presence of M. Morrel, who hailed the visit of the shipowner as a sure indication that the man whose wedding-feast he thus delighted to honour would ere long be first in command of the Pharaon; and as Dantès was universally beloved on board his vessel, the sailors put no restraint on their tumultuous joy at finding the opinion and choice of their superiors so exactly coincide with their own.

This noisy though hearty welcome over, Danglars and Caderousse were despatched to the residence of the bridegroom to convey to him the intelligence of the arrival of the important personage who had recently joined them, and to desire he would hasten to receive his honourable guest.

The above-mentioned individuals started off upon their errand at full speed; but ere they had gone many steps they perceived a group advancing towards them, composed of the betrothed pair, a party of young girls in attendance on the bride, by whose side walked Dantès' father; the whole brought up by Fernand, whose lips wore their usual sinister smile.

Neither Mercédès nor Edmond observed the strange expression of his countenance; basking in the sunshine of each other's love they heeded not the dark louring look that scowled on their innocent felicity.

Having acquitted themselves of their errand, and exchanged a hearty shake of the hand with Edmond, Danglars and Caderousse took their places beside Fernand and old Dantès,—the latter of whom attracted universal notice. The old man was attired in a suit of black, trimmed with steel buttons, beautifully cut and polished. His thin but still powerful legs were arrayed in a pair of richly embroidered clocked stockings, evidently of English manufacture; while from his three-cornered hat depended a long streaming knot of white and blue ribands. Thus he came along supporting himself on a curiously carved stick, his aged countenance lit up with happiness, while beside him crept Caderousse, whose desire to partake of the good things provided for the wedding party had induced him to become reconciled to the Dantès' father and son, although there still lingered in his mind a faint and imperfect recollection of the events of the preceding night; just as the brain retains on waking the dim and misty outline of the dream that has "murdered sleep."

As Danglars approached the disappointed lover, he cast on him a look of deep meaning, while Fernand, as he slowly paced behind the happy pair, who seemed, in their own unmixed content, to have entirely forgotten that such a being as himself existed, was pale and abstracted: occasionally, however, a deep flush would overspread his countenance, and a nervous contraction distort his features, while, with an agitated and restless gaze, he would glance in the direction of Marseilles, like one who either anticipated or foresaw some great and important event.

Dantès himself was simply, though becomingly, clad in the dress peculiar to the merchant-service,—a costume somewhat between a military and a civil garb; and with his fine countenance radiant with joy and happiness, a more perfect specimen of manly beauty could scarcely be imagined.

Lovely as the Greeks of Cyprus or Chios, Mercédès boasted the same bright flashing eyes of jet, and ripe, round, coral lips.

One more practised in the arts of great cities would have hid her blushes beneath a veil, or, at least, have cast down her thickly fringed lashes, so as to have concealed the liquid lustre of her animated eyes; but, on the contrary, the delighted girl looked round her with a smile that seemed to invite all who saw her to behold, and beholding, to rejoice with her in her exceeding happiness.

Immediately the bridal *cortège* came in sight of La Réserve, M. Morrel came forth to meet it, followed by the soldiers and sailors there assembled, to whom he had repeated the promise already given, that Dantès should be the successor to the late Captain Leclere. Edmond, at the approach of his patron, respectfully placed the arm of his affianced bride within that of M. Morrel, who forthwith conducting her up the flight of wooden steps leading to the chamber in which the feast was prepared, was gaily followed by the guests, beneath whose thronging numbers the slight structure creaked and groaned as though alarmed at the unusual pressure.

"Father," said Mercédès, stopping when she had reached the centre of the table, "sit, I pray you, on my right hand; on my left I will place him who has ever been as a brother to me," pointing with a soft and gentle smile to Fernand; but her words and look seemed to inflict the direst torture on him, for his lips became ghastly pale, and even beneath the dark hue of his complexion the blood might be seen retreating as though some sudden pang drove it back to the heart.

During this time, Dantès, at the opposite side of the table, had been occupied in similarly placing his most honoured guests. M. Morrel was seated at his right hand, Danglars at his left, while at a sign from Edmond, the rest of the company arranged themselves as they found it most agreeable.

And now commenced the work of devastation upon the many good things with which the table was loaded. Sausages of Arles, with their delicate seasoning and piquant flavour, lobsters in their dazzling red cuirasses, prawns of large size and brilliant colour, the echinus, with its prickly outside and dainty morsel within; the clovis, esteemed by the epicures of the south as more than rivalling the exquisite flavour of the oyster. All these in conjunction with the numerous delicacies cast up by the wash of waters on the sandy beach, and styled by the grateful fishermen "sea-fruits," served to furnish forth this marriage-table.

"A pretty silence, truly!" said the old father of the bride-groom, as he carried to his lips a glass of wine of the hue and brightness of the topaz, and which had just been placed before Mercédès herself. "Now, would any body think that this room contained a happy, merry party, who desire nothing better than to laugh and dance the hours away?"

"Ah!" sighed Caderousse, "a man cannot always feel happy because he is about to be married!"

"The truth is," replied Dantès, "that I am too happy for noisy mirth; if that is what you meant by your observation, my worthy friend, you were right; joy takes a strange effect at times, it seems to oppress us almost the same as sorrow."

Danglars looked towards Fernand, whose excitable nature received and betrayed each fresh impression.

"Why, what ails you?" asked he of Edmond. "Do you fear any approaching evil? I should say that you were the happiest man alive at this instant."

"And that is the very thing that alarms me," returned Dantès. "Man does not appear to me to be intended to enjoy felicity so unmixed; happiness is like the enchanted palaces we read of in our childhood, where fierce, fiery dragons defend the entrance and approach; and monsters of all shapes and kinds, requiring to be overcome ere victory is ours. I own that I am lost in wonder to find myself promoted to an honour of which I feel myself unworthy,—that of being the husband of Mercédès."

"Nay, nay!" cried Caderousse, smiling, "you have not attained that honour yet. Mercédès is not yet your wife. Just assume the tone and manner of a husband, and see how she will remind you that your hour has not yet come!"

The bride blushed, and seemed half inclined to be angry, while Fernand, restless and uneasy, seemed to start at every fresh sound, occasionally applying his handkerchief to his brow to wipe away the large drops of perspiration that gathered again, almost as soon as they were removed.

"Well, never mind that, neighbour Caderousse, it is not worth while to contradict me for such a trifle as that. 'Tis true that Mercédès is not actually my wife; but," added he, drawing out his watch, "in an hour and a half from this she will be as fast and firm as holy church can make her."

A general exclamation of surprise ran round the table, with the exception of the elder Dantès, whose laugh displayed the still perfect beauty of his large white teeth. Mercédès looked pleased and gratified, while Fernand grasped the handle of his knife with a convulsive clutch.

"In an hour?" inquired Danglars, turning pale. "How is that, my friend?"

"Why, thus it is," replied Dantès. "Thanks to the influence of M. Morrel, to whom, next to my father, I owe every blessing I enjoy, every difficulty has been removed. We have purchased permission to waive the usual delay; and at half-past two o'clock the mayor of Marseilles will be waiting for us at the Hôtel-de-Ville. Now, as a quarter past one has already struck, I do not consider I have asserted too much in saying, that in another hour and thirty minutes Mercédès will have become Madame Dantès."

Fernand closed his eyes, a burning sensation passed across his brow, and he was compelled to support himself by the table to prevent his falling from his chair; but in spite of all his efforts, he could not refrain from uttering a deep groan, which, however, was lost amid the noisy felicitations of the company.

"Upon my word," cried the old man, "you make short work of these kinds of affairs. Arrived here only yesterday morning, and married to-day at three o'clock! Commend me to a sailor for going the quick way to work!"

"But," asked Danglars, in a timid tone, "how did you manage about the other formalities—the contract—the settlement?"

"Oh, bless you!" answered Dantès, laughingly, "our papers were soon drawn up. Mercédès has no fortune; I have none to settle on her. So, you see, our papers were quickly written out, and certainly do not come very expensive."

This joke elicited a fresh burst of applause.

"So that what we presumed to be merely the betrothed feast turns out to be the actual wedding-dinner?" said Danglars.

"No, no!" answered Dantès; "don't imagine I am going to put you off in that shabby manner. To-morrow morning I start for Paris: five days to go, and the same to return, with one day to discharge the commission intrusted to me, is all the time I shall be absent. I shall be back here by the twelfth of March, and the next day I give my real marriage-feast."

This prospect of fresh festivity redoubled the hilarity of the guests to such a degree, that the elder Dantès, who at the commencement of the repast had commented upon the silence that prevailed, now found it difficult, amid the general din of voices, to obtain a moment's tranquillity in which to drink to the health and prosperity of the bride and bridegroom.

Dantès, perceiving the affectionate eagerness of his father, responded by a look of grateful pleasure, while Mercédès, whose eyes had been constantly consulting the pendule which decked the chamber, made an expressive gesture to Edmond.

Around the festive board reigned that mirthful freedom from all restraint which is usually found at the termination of social meetings, among those at least whose inferior station in the world gives them a happy dispensation from the frigid rules of etiquette; and so it was with the party now assembled. Such as at the commencement of the repast had not been able to seat themselves according to their inclination, rose unceremoniously, and exchanged their place for the more immediate proximity of some preferred individual, male or female, as the case might be. All spoke at the same time, and yet none heeded a reply, but appeared as though merely addressing their own thoughts.

The paleness of Fernand appeared to have communicated itself to Danglars. As for Fernand himself, he seemed as though undergoing the tortures of the damned; unable to rest, he was among the first to quit the table, and as though seeking to avoid the hilarious mirth that rose in such deafening sounds, he continued, in utter silence, to pace the farther end of the salon.

Caderousse approached him just as Danglars, whom Fernand seemed most anxious to avoid, had joined him in a corner of the room.

"Upon my word," said Caderousse, from whose mind the friendly treatment of Dantès, united with the effect of the excellent wine he had partaken of, had effaced every feeling of envy or jealousy at Dantès' good fortune,—"upon my word, Dantès is a downright good fellow, and when I see him sitting there beside his pretty wife that is so soon to be, I cannot help thinking it would have been a great pity to have served him that trick you were planning yesterday."

"Oh, there was no harm meant!" answered Danglars; "at first I certainly did feel somewhat uneasy as regarded what Fernand might be tempted to do, but when I saw how completely he had mastered his feelings, even so far as to become one of his rival's bride's-men, I knew there was no further cause for apprehension."

Caderousse looked full at Fernand—he was ghastly pale.

"Certainly," continued Danglars, "the sacrifice was no trifling one when the beauty of the bride is considered. Upon my soul that future captain of mine is a lucky dog! Gad! I only wish he would let me take his place!"

"Shall we not set forth?" asked the sweet, silvery voice of Mercédès; "two o'clock has just struck, and you know we are expected at the Hôtel-de-Ville in a quarter of an hour."

"To be sure!—to be sure!" cried Dantès, eagerly quitting the table; "let us go directly!"

His words were re-echoed by the whole party, who rose with a simultaneous cheer, and commenced forming themselves into procession.

At this moment Danglars, who had been incessantly observing every change in Fernand's look and manner, perceived him stagger and fall back, with an almost convulsive spasm, against a seat placed near one of the open windows. At the same instant the ear caught a sort of indistinct sound on the stairs, followed by the measured tread of soldiery, with the clanking of swords and military accoutrements; then came a hum and buzz as of many voices, so as to deaden even the noisy mirth of the bridal party, among whom a vague feeling of curiosity and apprehension quelled every disposition to talk, and almost instantaneously the most deathlike stillness prevailed.

Nearer and nearer came those sounds of terror. Three distinct knocks, as though from the hilt of a sword, against the door, increased the fears of the before gay party. Each looked inquiringly in the countenance of his neighbour, while all wished themselves quietly and safely at home.

"I demand admittance," said a loud voice outside the room, "in the name of the law!"

As no attempt was made to prevent it, the door was opened, and a magistrate, wearing his official scarf, presented himself, followed by four soldiers and a corporal. Uneasiness now yielded to the most extreme dread on the part of those present.

"May I venture to inquire the reason of this unexpected visit?" said M. Morrel, addressing the magistrate, whom he evidently knew; "there is doubtless some mistake easily explained."

"If it be so," replied the magistrate, "rely upon every reparation being made; meanwhile, I am the bearer of an order of arrest, and although I most reluctantly perform the task assigned me, it must, nevertheless, be fulfilled. Who among the persons here assembled answers to the name of Edmond Dantès?"

Every eye was turned towards the individual so described, who, spite of the agitation he could not but feel, advanced with dignity, and said in a firm voice, "I am he! what is your pleasure with me?"

"Edmond Dantès," replied the magistrate, "I arrest you in the name of the law!"

"Me!" repeated Edmond, slightly changing colour, "and wherefore, I pray?"

"I cannot inform you, but you will be duly acquainted with the reasons that have rendered such a step necessary at your first examination."

M. Morrel felt that further resistance or remonstrance was useless. He saw before him an officer delegated to enforce the law, and perfectly well knew that it would be as unavailing to seek pity from a magistrate decked with his official scarf as to address a petition to some cold, marble effigy. Old Dantès, however, saw not all this. His paternal heart could not contemplate the idea of such an outrage as consigning his beloved child to prison amid the joys of his wedding-feast. Rushing forwards, therefore, he threw himself at the magistrate's feet, and prayed and supplicated in terms so moving, that even the officer was touched; and although firm to his duty, he kindly said, "My worthy friend, let me beg of you to calm your apprehensions. Your son has probably neglected some proscribed form or attention in registering his cargo, and it is more than probable he will be set at liberty directly he has given the information required, whether touching the health of his crew or the value of his freight."

"What is the meaning of all this?" inquired Caderousse, frowningly, of Danglars, who had assumed an air of utter surprise.

"How can I tell you?" replied he; "I am, like yourself, utterly bewildered at all that is going on, not a word of which do I understand."

Caderousse then looked around for Fernand, but he had disappeared.

The scene of the previous night now came back to his mind with startling accuracy. The painful catastrophe he had just witnessed appeared effectually to have rent away the veil which the intoxication of the evening before had raised between himself and his memory.

"So! so!" said he, in a hoarse and choking voice, to Danglars, "this, then, I suppose, is a part of the trick you were concerting yesterday? All I can say is, that if it be so, 'tis an ill turn, and well deserves to bring double evil on those who have projected it."

"Nonsense!" returned Danglars, "I tell you again I have nothing whatever to do with it; besides, you know very well that I tore the paper to pieces."

"No, you did not!" answered Caderousse, "you merely threw it by—I saw it lying in a corner."

"Hold your tongue, you fool!—what should you know about it?—why, you were drunk!"

"Where is Fernand?" inquired Caderousse.

"How do I know?" replied Danglars; "gone, as every prudent man ought to do, to look after his own affairs, most likely. Never mind where he is, let you and I go and see what is to be done for our poor friends in this their affliction."

During this conversation Dantès, after having exchanged a cheerful shake of the hand with all his sympathising friends, had surrendered himself to the officer sent to arrest him, merely saying, "Make yourselves quite easy, my good fellows, there is some little mistake to clear up, that's all, depend upon it! and very likely I may not have to go so far as the prison to effect that."

"Oh, to be sure!" responded Danglars, who had now approached the group, "nothing more than a mistake I feel quite certain."

Dantès descended the staircase, preceded by the magistrate and followed by the soldiers. A carriage awaited him at the door; he got in, followed by two soldiers and the magistrate, and the vehicle drove off towards Marseilles.

"Adieu! adieu! dearest Edmond!" cried Mercédès, stretching out her arms to him from the balcony.

The prisoner, whose ready ear caught the despairing accents of his betrothed, felt as though the chill hand of death pressed on his heart, as leaning from the coach he tried to reply in cheerful tones.

"Good-bye, my sweet Mercédès!—we shall soon meet again!"

The rapid progress of the vehicle, which disappeared round one of the turnings of Fort Saint-Nicolas, prevented his adding more.

"Wait for me here, all of you!" cried M. Morrel; "I will take the first conveyance I find, and hurry to Marseilles, whence I will bring you word how all is going on."

"That's right!" exclaimed a multitude of voices, "go, and return as quickly as you can!"

This second departure was followed by a long and fearful state of terrified silence on the part of those who were left behind. The old father and Mercédès remained for some time apart, each absorbed in their separate griefs; but at length the two poor victims of the same blow raised their eyes, and with a simultaneous burst of feeling rushed into each other's arms.

Meanwhile Fernand made his reappearance, poured out for himself a glass of water with a trembling hand; then hastily swallowing it, went to sit down on the first vacant chair he perceived, and this was, by mere chance, placed next to the seat on which poor Mercédès had fallen, half fainting, when released from the warm and affectionate embrace of old Dantès. Instinctively Fernand drew back his chair.

"He is the cause of all this misery—I am quite sure of it," whispered Caderousse, who had never taken his eyes off Fernand, to Danglars.

"I really do not think so," answered the other; "he is too stupid to imagine such a scheme. I only hope the mischief will fall upon the head of whoever wrought it."

"You don't mention those who aided and abetted the cruel deed, any more than of those who advised it," said Caderousse.

"Surely," answered Danglars, "one cannot be expected to become responsible for all the idle words one may have been obliged to listen to in the course of our lives."

Meantime the subject of the arrest was being canvassed in every different form.

"What think you, Danglars," said one of the party, turning towards him, "of the late unfortunate event?"

"Why, upon my word, I know not what to say," replied he. "I think, however, that it is just possible Dantès may have been detected with some trifling article on board his ship considered here as contraband."

"But how could he have done so without your knowledge, Danglars, who was the ship's supercargo?"

"Why, as for that, I could only know what I was told respecting the merchandise with which the vessel was laden. I know she was loaded with cotton, and that she took in her freight at Alexandria from the magazine of M. Pastret, and at Smyrna from M. Pascal's; that is all I was obliged to know, and I beg I may not be asked for any further particulars."

"Now, I recollect!" cried the afflicted old father; "my poor boy told me yesterday he had got a small case of coffee and another of tobacco for me!"

"There, you see!" exclaimed Danglars. "Now the mischief is out; depend upon it the custom-house people went rummaging about the ship in our absence, and discovered poor Dantès' hidden treasures."

Mercédès, however, paid no heed to this explanation of her lover's arrest. Her grief, which she had hitherto tried to restrain, now burst out in a violent fit of hysterical sobbing.

"Come, come!" said the old man, "be comforted, my poor child; there is still hope!"

"Hope!" repeated Danglars.

"Hope!" faintly murmured Fernand; but the word seemed to die away on his pale agitated lips, and a convulsive spasm passed over his countenance.

"Good news! good news!" shouted forth one of the party stationed in the balcony on the look-out. "Here comes M. Morrel back. No doubt, now, we shall hear that our friend is released!"

Mercédès and the old man rushed to meet the person from whom they hoped so much; but the first glance of the pale, desponding countenance of M. Morrel prepared them for evil tidings.

"What news?" exclaimed a general burst of voices.

"Alas! my friends," replied M. Morrel, with a mournful shake of his head, "the thing has assumed a more serious aspect than I expected."

"Oh! indeed—indeed, sir, he is innocent!" sobbed forth Mercédès.

"That I believe!" answered M. Morrel; "but still he is charged——"

"With what?" inquired the elder Dantès.

"With being an agent of the Bonapartist faction!"

Many of my readers may be able to recollect how formidable such an accusation became in the period at which our story is dated.

A despairing cry escaped the pale lips of Mercédès, while the heart-stricken father fell listlessly into a chair, kindly placed for him by one of the pitying guests.

"Ah, Danglars!" whispered Caderousse, "you have deceived me—the trick you spoke of last night has been played off, I see; but I cannot suffer a poor old man or an innocent girl to die of grief through your fault. I am determined to tell them all about it."

"Be silent, you simpleton!" cried Danglars, grasping him by the arm, "or I will not answer even for your own safety. Who can tell whether Dantès be innocent or guilty? The vessel did touch at Elba, where he quitted it, and passed a whole day in the island. Now, should any letters or other documents of a compromising character be found upon him, will it not be taken for granted that all who uphold him are his accomplices?"

With the rapid instinct of selfishness Caderousse readily perceived the solidity of this mode of reasoning; he gazed doubtfully, wistfully on Danglars, and then insensibly continued to retreat from the dangerous proximity in which he found himself.

"Suppose we wait a while, and see what comes of it!" said he, casting a bewildered look on his companion.

"To be sure!" answered Danglars. "Let us wait, by all means! If he be innocent, of course he will be set at liberty; if guilty, why, it is no use involving ourselves in his conspiracy."

"Then let us go hence. I cannot stay to endure the sight of that old man's distress."

"With all my heart!" replied Danglars, but too pleased to find a partner in his retreat. "Let us take ourselves out of the way, and leave every one else to do the same thing, if they please."

After their departure, Fernand, who had now again become the only friend and protector poor Mercédès could find in this trying hour, led the weeping girl back to her home, which she had quitted with such different hopes and feelings in the morning, while some friends of Dantès' conducted the poor heart-broken parent to his childless and dreary abode.

The rumour of Edmond's arrest as a Bonapartist agent was not slow in circulating throughout the city.

"Could you ever have credited such a thing, my dear Danglars?" asked M. Morrel, as on his return to the port for the purpose of gleaning fresh tidings of Dantès he overtook his supercargo and Caderousse. "Could you have believed such a thing possible?"

"Why, you know I told you," replied Danglars, "that I considered the circumstance of his having anchored in the Isle of Elba as a very suspicious circumstance."

"And did you mention these suspicions to any person besides myself?"

"Certainly not!" returned Danglars. Then added in a low whisper, "You understand that, on account of your uncle, M. Policar Morrel, who served under the other government, and who does not altogether conceal what he thinks on the subject, you are strongly suspected of regretting the abdication of Napoleon. I should have feared to injure both Edmond and yourself, had I divulged my own apprehensions to a soul. I am too well aware that though a subordinate, like myself, is bound to acquaint the shipowner with every thing that occurs, there are many things he ought most carefully to conceal from all else."

"'Tis well, Danglars—'tis well!" replied M. Morrel. "You are a worthy fellow; and I had already thought of your interests in the event of poor Edmond having become captain of the Pharaon."

"Is it possible you were so kind?"

"Yes, indeed; I had previously inquired of Dantès what was his opinion of you, and if he should have any reluctance to continue you in your post, for somehow I have perceived a sort of coolness between you two that led me to believe that he would rather have another in your place as supercargo."

"And what was his reply?"

"That he certainly did think he had given you offence in an affair which he merely referred to without entering into particulars, but that whoever possessed the good opinion and confidence of the ship's owners would have his preference also."

"The hypocrite!" murmured Danglars between his teeth.

"Poor Dantès!" said Caderousse. "No one can deny his being a noble-hearted young fellow!"

"But in the midst of all our trouble," continued M. Morrel, "we must not forget that the Pharaon has at present no captain."

"Oh!" replied Danglars, "since we cannot leave this port for the next three months, let us hope that ere the expiration of that period Dantès will be set at liberty."

"Of that I entertain no doubt; but in the meantime what are we to do?"

"I am entirely at your service, M. Morrel," answered Danglars. "You know that I am as capable of managing a ship as the most experienced captain in the service; and it will be so far advantageous to you to accept my services, that upon Edmond's release from prison no further change will be requisite on board the Pharaon than for Dantès and myself each to resume our respective posts."

"Thanks! thanks! my good friend, for your excellent idea and acceptable proposition—that will smooth all difficulties. I fully authorise you at once to assume the command of the Pharaon, and look carefully to the unloading of her freight.

Private misfortunes must never induce us to neglect public affairs."

"Depend upon my zeal and attention, M. Morrel; but when do you think it likely we may be permitted to visit our poor friend in his prison?"

"I will let you know that directly. I have seen M. de Villefort, whom I shall endeavour to interest in Edmond's favour. I am aware he is a furious royalist; but, spite of that, and of his being the 'king's procureur,' he is a man like ourselves, and I fancy not a bad sort of one!"

"Perhaps not," replied Danglars; "but he is universally spoken of as extremely ambitious, and ambition is a sore hardener of the heart!"

"Well, well!" returned M. Morrel, "we shall see! But now hasten on board, I will join you there ere long." So saying, the worthy shipowner quitted the two allies, and proceeded in the direction of the Palais de Justice.

"You see," said Danglars, addressing Caderousse, "the turn things have taken. Do you still feel any desire to stand up in his defence?"

"Not the slightest! but yet it seems to me a shocking thing a mere joke should lead to such frightful consequences."

"But who perpetrated that joke? let me ask; neither you nor myself, but Fernand; you know very well that I threw the paper into a corner of the room,—indeed, I fancied I had destroyed it."

"Oh, no!" replied Caderousse; "that I can answer for, you did not. I only wish I could see it now as plainly as I saw it lying all crushed and crumpled in a corner of the arbour."

"Well, then, if you did, depend upon it, Fernand picked it up, and either copied it or caused it to be copied; perhaps, even, he did not take the trouble of recopying it. And now I think of it, by heavens! he has sent the letter itself! Fortunately, for me, the handwriting was disguised."

"Then you were aware of Dantès being engaged in a conspiracy?"

"Not I. As I before said, I thought the whole thing was a joke, nothing more. It seems, however, that I have unconsciously stumbled upon the truth."

"Still," argued Caderousse, "I would give a great deal nothing of the kind had happened; or, at least, that I had had no hand in it. You will see, Danglars, that it will turn out an unlucky job for both of us."

"Nonsense! If any harm comes of it, it should fall on the guilty person; and that, you know, is Fernand. How can we be implicated in any way? All we have got to do is, to keep our own counsel and remain perfectly quiet, not breathing a word to any living soul; and you will see that the storm will pass away without in the least affecting us."

"Amen!" responded Caderousse, waving his hand in token of adieu to Danglars, and bending his steps towards the Allées de Meillan, moving his head to and fro, and muttering as he went, after the manner of one whose mind was overcharged with one absorbing idea.

"So far, then," said Danglars, mentally, "all has gone as I would have it! I am temporarily commander of the Pharaon, with the certainty of being permanently so, if that fool of a Caderousse can be persuaded to hold his tongue. My only fear is the chance of Dantès being released. But bah! he is in the hands of justice; and," added he, with a smile, "she will take her own."

So saying, he leaped into a boat, desiring to be rowed on board the Pharaon, where M. Morrel had appointed to meet him.

CHAPTER VI

THE DEPUTY PROCUREUR DU ROI

In one of the large aristocratical mansions situated in the Rue du Grand Cours, opposite the fountain of Medusa, a second marriage-feast was being celebrated almost at the same hour with the ill-fated nuptial repast given by Dantès.

In this case, however, although the occasion of the entertainment was similar, the company assembled formed a striking difference. Instead of a rude mixture of sailors, soldiers, and those belonging to the humblest grade of life, the present *réunion* was composed of the very flower and *élite* of Marseillese society. Magistrates who had resigned their office during the usurper's reign; officers who, scorning to fight under his banners, had offered their services to foreign powers, with younger members of the family, brought up to hate and execrate the man whom five years of exile would have converted into a martyr, and fifteen of restoration elevated to the rank of a demigod.

The guests were still at table, and the heated and energetic conversation that prevailed betrayed the violent and vindictive passions that then agitated each dweller of the south, where, unhappily, religious strife had long given increased bitterness to the violence of party feeling.

The emperor,—now king of the petty Isle of Elba, after having held sovereign sway over one half of the world, counting us, his subjects, a small population of twenty millions, after having been accustomed to hear the "*Vive Napoleons*" of, at least, six times that number of human beings uttered in nearly every language of the globe,—was looked upon among the *haute société* of Marseilles as a ruined man, separated for ever from any fresh connexion with France or claim to her throne.

The magistrates freely discussed their political views; the military part of the company talked unreservedly of Moscow and Leipsic, while the females indulged in open comments upon the divorce of the Empress Josephine.

All seemed to evince that in this focus of royalism it was not over the downfall of one man they rejoiced, but in the bright and cheering prospect of a revivified political existence for themselves.

An old man, decorated with the cross of Saint Louis, now rose and proposed the health of King Louis XVIII. This aged individual was the Marquis de Saint-Méran.

This toast, recalling at once the patient exile of Hartwell, and the peace-loving king of France, excited universal enthusiasm; glasses were elevated in the air *à l'Anglais ;* and the ladies, snatching their bouquets from their fair bosoms, strewed the table with their floral treasures. In a word, an almost poetical fervour prevailed.

"Ah!" said the Marquise de Saint-Méran, a woman with a stern, forbidding eye, though still noble and elegant-looking, despite her having reached her fiftieth year—"Ah! these revolutionists who have driven us from those very possessions they afterwards purchased for a mere trifle during the Reign of Terror, would be compelled to own, were they here, that all true devotion was on our side, since we were content to follow the fortunes of a falling monarch, while they, on the contrary, made their fortune by worshipping the rising sun;—yes—yes, they could not help admitting that the king, for whom we sacrificed rank, wealth, and station, was truly our 'Louis the Well-beloved!' while their wretched usurper has been, and ever will be, to them their evil genius, their 'Napoleon the Accursed!' Am I not right, Villefort?"

"I beg your pardon, madame! I really must pray you to excuse me—but—in truth—I was not attending to the conversation."

"Marquise!—marquise!" interposed the same elderly personage who had proposed the toast, "let the young people alone; let me tell you, on one's wedding-day there are more agreeable subjects of conversation than dry politics!"

"Never mind, dearest mother," said a young and lovely girl, with a profusion of light brown hair, and eyes that seemed to float in liquid crystal; "'tis all my fault for seizing upon M. de Villefort, so as to prevent his listening to what you said. But there—now take him—he is all your own, for as long as you like. M. Villefort, I beg to remind you, my mother speaks to you."

"If Madame la Marquise will deign to repeat the words I but imperfectly caught, I shall be delighted to answer," said M. de Villefort.

"Never mind, Renée," replied the marquise, with such a look of tenderness, as all were astonished to see her harsh, dry features capable of expressing; for however all other feelings may be withered in a woman's nature, there is always one bright, smiling spot in the maternal breast, and that is where a dearly-beloved child is concerned, "I forgive you. What I was saying, Villefort, was, that the Bonapartists had neither our sincerity, enthusiasm, nor devotion."

"They had, however, what supplied the place of those fine qualities," replied the young man, "and that was fanaticism. Napoleon is the Mahomet of the West, and is worshipped by his commonplace but ambitious followers, not only as a leader and law-giver, but also as the personification of equality."

"He!" cried the marquise,—"Napoleon the type of equality!—for mercy's sake, then, what would you call Robespierre?—Come, come, do not strip the latter of his just rights to bestow them on one who has usurped enough, methinks."

"Nay, madame! I would place each of these heroes on his right pedestal—that of Robespierre to be built where his scaffold was erected; that of Napoleon on the column of the Place Vendôme. The only difference consists in the opposite character of the equality supported by these two men; the one advocates the equality that elevates, the other professes the equality that depresses;—the one brings a king within reach of the guillotine, the other elevates the people to a level with the throne. Observe," said Villefort, smiling, "I do not mean to deny, that both the individuals we have been referring to were revolutionary scoundrels, and that the 9th Thermidor and 4th of April were lucky days for France, worthy of being grate-fully remembered by every friend to monarchy and civil order; and that explains how it comes to pass, that, fallen as I trust he is for ever, Napoleon has still preserved a train of parasitical satellites. Still, marquise, it has been so with other usurpers; Cromwell, for instance, who was not half so bad as Napoleon, had his partisans and advocates."

"Do you know, Villefort, that you are talking in a most dreadfully revolutionary strain?—but I excuse it—it is impossible to expect the son of a Girondin to be free from a small spice of the old leaven."

A deep crimson suffused the countenance of Villefort.

"'Tis true, madame," answered he, "that my father was a Girondin, but he was not among the number of those who voted for the king's death; he was an equal sufferer with yourself during the Reign of Terror, and had well-nigh lost his head on the same scaffold as your own father."

"True!" replied the marquise, without wincing in the slightest degree at the tragical remembrance thus called up; "but bear in mind, if you please, that our respective parents underwent persecution and proscription from diametrically opposite principles; in proof of which I may remark, that while my family remained among the stanchest adherents of the exiled princes, your father lost no time in joining the new government; and that after the Citizen Noirtier had become a Girondin, the Count Noirtier appeared as a senator and statesman."

"Dear mother!" interposed Renée, "you know very well it was agreed that all these disagreeable reminiscences should for ever be laid aside."

"Suffer me also, madame, to add my earnest request that you will kindly allow the veil of oblivion to cover and conceal the past. What avails retrospection and recrimination touching circumstances wholly past recall? for my own part, I have laid aside even the name of my father, and altogether disown his political principles. He was—nay, probably may still be—a Bonapartist, and is called Noirtier; I, on the contrary, am a stanch royalist, and style myself De Villefort. Let what may remain of revolutionary sap exhaust itself and die away with the old trunk, and condescend only to regard the young shoot which has started up at a distance from the parent tree, without having the power, any more than the wish, to separate entirely from the stock from which it sprung."

"Bravo, Villefort!" cried the marquis; "excellently well said! Come, now, I have hopes of obtaining what I have been for years endeavouring to persuade the marquise to promise—namely, a perfect amnesty and forgetfulness of the past."

"With all my heart!" replied the marquise; "let the past be for ever forgotten! I promise you, it affords *me* as little pleasure to revive it as it does you. All I ask, is, that Villefort will be firm and inflexible for the future in marking his political principles. Remember also, Villefort, that we have pledged ourselves to his majesty for your fealty and strict loyalty, and that at our recommendation, the king consented to forget the past, as I do" (and here she extended to him her hand), "as I now do at your entreaty. But bear in mind, that should there fall in your way any one guilty of conspiring against the government, you will be so much the more bound to visit the offence with rigorous punishment, as it is known you belong to a suspected family."

"Alas! madame," returned Villefort, "my profession, as well as the times in which we live, compel me to be severe. I have already successfully conducted several public prosecutions, and brought the offenders to merited punishment. But we have not done with the thing yet."

"Do you, indeed, think so?" inquired the marquise.

"I am, at least, fearful of it. Napoleon, in the island of Elba, is too near France, and his proximity keeps up the hopes of his partisans. Marseilles is filled with half-pay officers, who are daily, under one frivolous pretext or other, getting up quarrels with the royalists; from hence arise continual and fatal duels among the higher classes of persons, and assassinations in the lower."

"You have heard, perhaps," said the Count de Salvieux, one of M. de Saint-Méran's oldest friends, and chamberlain to the Count d'Artois, "that the Holy Alliance purpose removing him from thence?"

"Ah! they were talking about it when we left Paris," said M. de Saint-Méran; "and where is it decided to transfer him?"

"To Saint Helena!"

"For heaven's sake, where is that?" asked the marquise.

"An island situated on the other side of the equator, at least two thousand leagues from hence," replied the count.

"So much the better! As Villefort observes, it is a great act of folly to have left such a man between Corsica, where he was born, Naples, of which his brother-in-law is king, and Italy, the sovereignty of which he coveted for his son."

"Well," said the marquise, "it seems probable, that by the aid of the Holy Alliance, we shall be rid of Napoleon; and we must trust to the vigilance of M. de Villefort to purify Marseilles of his partisans. The king is either a king or no king; if he be acknowledged as sovereign of France, he should be upheld in peace and tranquillity, and this can best be effected by employing the most inflexible agents to put down every attempt at conspiracy—'tis the best and surest means of preventing mischief."

"Unfortunately, madam," answered Villefort, "the strong arm of the law is not called upon to interfere until the evil has taken place."

"Then all he has got to do is to endeavour to repair it."

"Nay, madame, the law is frequently powerless to effect this; all it can do is to avenge the wrong done."

"Oh! M. de Villefort," cried a beautiful young creature, daughter to Count Salvieux, and the cherished friend of Mademoiselle de Saint-Méran,—"do try and get up some famous trial while we are at Marseilles. I never was in a law court; I am told it is so very amusing!"

"Amusing, certainly!" replied the young man, "inasmuch as, instead of shedding tears as at the fictitious tale of woe produced at a theatre, you behold in a law-court a case of real and genuine distress—a drama of life. The prisoner whom you there see pale, agitated, and alarmed, instead of—as is the case when the curtain falls on a tragedy—going home to sup peacefully with his family, and then retiring to rest, that he may recommence his mimic woes on the morrow, is removed from your sight merely to be reconducted to his prison and delivered up to the executioner. I leave you to judge how far your nerves are calculated to bear you through such a scene. Of this, however, be assured, that should any favourable opportunity present itself, I will not fail to offer you the choice of being present at it."

"For shame, M. de Villefort!" said Renée, becoming quite

pale; "don't you see how you are frightening us?—and yet you laugh."

"Why, I stand almost in the light of one engaged in a duel. I have already recorded sentence of death, five or six times, against the movers of political conspiracies, and who can say how many daggers may be ready sharpened and only waiting a favourable opportunity to be buried in my heart?"

"Gracious heavens! M. de Villefort," said Renée, becoming more and more terrified; "you surely are not in earnest."

"Indeed, I am," replied the young magistrate, with a smile; "and in the interesting trial that young lady is anxious to witness, the case would only be still more aggravated. Suppose, for instance, the prisoner, as is more than probable, to have served under Napoleon—well, can you expect for an instant, that one accustomed, at the word of his commander, to rush fearlessly on the very bayonets of his foe, will scruple more to drive a stiletto into the heart of one he knows to be his personal enemy, than to slaughter his fellow-creatures, merely because bidden to do so by one he is bound to obey? Besides, one requires the excitement of being hateful in the eyes of the accused, in order to lash one's self into a state of sufficient vehemence and power. I would not choose to see the man against whom I pleaded smile as though in mockery of my words. No! my pride is to see the accused pale, agitated, and as though beaten out of all composure by the fire of my eloquence."

"Bravo!" cried one of the guests, "that is what I call talking to some purpose."

"Just the person we require at a time like the present," said a second.

"What a splendid business that last cause of yours was, my dear Villefort!" remarked a third. "I mean the trial of the man for murdering his father. Upon my word you killed him ere the executioner had laid his hand upon him."

"Oh! as for parricides and such dreadful people as that," interposed Renée, "it matters very little what is done to them; but as regards poor unfortunate creatures whose only crime consists in having mixed themselves up in political intrigues——"

"Why, that is the very worst offence they could possibly commit; for, don't you see, Renée, the king is the father of his people, and he who shall plot or contrive aught against the life and safety of the parent of thirty-two millions of souls, is a parricide upon a fearfully great scale?"

"I don't know any thing about that," replied Renée; "but, M. de Villefort, you have promised me—have you not?—always to shew mercy to those I plead for."

"Make yourself quite easy on that point," answered Villefort, with one of his sweetest smiles, "you and I will always consult upon our verdicts."

"My love," said the marquise, "attend to your doves, your lap-dogs, and embroidery, but do not meddle with what you understand not. Nowadays the military profession has rest, and its brave sons repose under their well-earned laurels. Now is the time for those of the long robe, like M. de Villefort, to achieve a splendid notoriety; seek not, therefore, to cross the brilliant career your betrothed husband may otherwise pursue."

"Well," said Renée, "I cannot help regretting you had not chosen some other profession than your own—a physician, for instance. Do you know I always felt a shudder at the idea of even a *destroying* angel?"

"Dear good Renée!" whispered Villefort, as he gazed with unutterable tenderness on the lovely speaker.

"Let us hope, my child," cried the marquis, "that M. de Villefort may prove the moral and political physician of this province; if so, he will have achieved a noble work."

"And one which will go far to efface the recollection of his father's conduct," added the incorrigible marquise.

"Madame," replied Villefort, with a mournful smile, "I have already had the honour to observe, that my father has (at least I hope so) abjured his past errors, and that he is, at the present moment, a firm and zealous friend to religion and order, a better royalist possibly than his son, for he has to atone for past dereliction, while I have no other impulse than warm, decided preference and conviction."

Having made this well-turned speech, Villefort looked carefully round to mark the effect of his oratory, such as he would have done had he been addressing the bench in open court.

"Do you know, my dear Villefort," cried the Count de Salvieux, "that is as nearly as possible what I myself said the other day at the Tuileries when questioned by his majesty's principal chamberlain, touching the singularity of an alliance between the son of a Girondin and the daughter of an officer of the Duke de Condé; and I assure you he seemed fully to comprehend that this mode of reconciling political differences was based upon sound and excellent principles. Then the king, who, without our suspecting it, had overheard our conversation, interrupted us by saying, 'Villefort,'—observe that the king did not pronounce the word Noirtier, but on the contrary placed considerable emphasis on that of Villefort,— 'Villefort,' said his majesty, 'is a young man of great judgment and discretion, who will be sure to make a figure in his profession. I like him much, and it gave me great pleasure to hear that he was about to become the son-in-law of M. le Marquis and Madame la Marquise de Saint-Méran. I should myself have recommended the match, had not the noble marquis anticipated my wishes by requesting my consent to it.'"

"Is it possible the king could have condescended so far as to express himself so favourably of me?" asked the enraptured Villefort.

"I give you his very words; and if the marquis chooses to be candid, he will confess that they perfectly agree with what his majesty said to him when he went six months ago to consult him upon the subject of your espousing his daughter."

"Certainly," answered the marquis; "you state but the truth."

"How much do I owe this gracious prince! What is there I would not do to evince my earnest gratitude?"

"That is right," cried the marquise. "I love to see you thus. Now, then, were a conspirator to fall into your hands he would be most welcome."

"For my part, dear mother," interposed Renée, "I trust your wishes will not prosper, and that Providence will only permit petty offenders, poor debtors, and miserable cheats, to fall into M. de Villefort's hands, then I shall be contented."

"Just the same as though you prayed that a physician might only be called upon to prescribe for headaches, measles, and the stings of wasps, or any other slight affection of the epidermis. If you wish to see me the king's procureur, you must desire for me some of those violent and dangerous diseases, from the cure of which so much honour redounds to the physician."

At this moment, and as though the utterance of Villefort's wish had sufficed to effect its accomplishment, a servant entered the room and whispered a few words in his ear. Villefort immediately rose from table and quitted the room upon the plea of urgent business; he soon, however, returned, his whole face beaming with delight.

Renée regarded him with fond affection; and certainly his handsome features, lit up as they then were with more than usual fire and animation, seemed formed to excite the innocent admiration with which she gazed on her graceful and intelligent lover.

"You were wishing just now," said Villefort, addressing her, "that I were a doctor instead of a lawyer. Well, I at least resemble the disciples of Esculapius in one thing, that of not being able to call a day my own, not even that of my betrothal."

"And wherefore were you called away just now?" asked Mademoiselle de Saint-Méran, with an air of deep interest.

"For a very serious affair, which bids well to afford our executioner here some work."

"How dreadful!" exclaimed Renée. Her cheeks that were before glowing with emotion becoming pale as marble.

"Is it possible?" burst simultaneously from all who were near enough to the magistrate to hear his words.

"Why, if my information prove correct, a sort of Bonaparte conspiracy has just been discovered."

"Can I believe my ears?" cried the marquise.

"I will read you the letter containing the accusation at least," said Villefort:—

"'The procureur du roi is informed by a friend to the throne and the religious institutions of his country, that an individual, named Edmond Dantès, second in command on board the Pharaon, this day arrived from Smyrna, after having touched at Naples and Porto-Ferrajo, has been the bearer of a letter from Murat to the usurper, and again taken charge of another letter from the usurper to the Bonapartist club in Paris. Ample corroboration of this statement may be obtained by arresting the above-mentioned Edmond Dantès, who either carries the letter for Paris about with him, or has it at his father's abode. Should it not be found in the possession of father or son, then it will assuredly be discovered in the cabin belonging to the said Dantès on board the Pharaon.'"

"But," said Renée, "this letter, which, after all, is but an anonymous scrawl, is not even addressed to you but to the procureur du roi."

"True; but that gentleman being absent, his secretary, by his orders, opened his letters; thinking this one of importance, he sent for me, but not finding me, took upon himself to give the necessary orders for arresting the accused party."

"Then the guilty person is absolutely in custody?" said the marquise.

"Nay, dear mother, say the accused person. You know we cannot yet pronounce him guilty."

"He is in safe custody," answered Villefort; "and rely upon it, if the letter alluded to is found, he will not be likely to be trusted abroad again, unless he goes forth under the especial protection of the headsman."

"And where is the unfortunate being?" asked Renée.

"He is at my house!"

"Come, come, my friend," interrupted the marquis, "do not neglect your duty to linger with us. You are the king's servant, and must go whithersoever that service calls you."

"Oh, Villefort!" cried Renée, clasping her hands, and looking towards her lover with piteous earnestness, "be merciful on this the day of our betrothal."

The young man passed round to the side of the table where the fair pleader sat, and leaning over her chair said tenderly,—

"To give you pleasure, my sweet Renée, I promise to shew

all the lenity in my power; but if the charges brought against this Bonapartean hero prove correct, why, then, you really must give me leave to order his head to be cut off."

Renée, with an almost convulsive shudder, turned away her head, as though the very mention of killing a fellow-creature in cold blood was more than her tender nature could endure.

"Never mind that foolish girl, Villefort," said the marquise, "she will soon get over these things."

So saying, Madame de Saint-Méran extended her dry, bony hand to Villefort, who, while imprinting a son-in-law's respectful salute on it, looked at Renée, as much as to say, "I must try and fancy 'tis your dear hand I kiss, as it should have been."

"These are mournful auspices to accompany a betrothal!" sighed poor Renée.

"Upon my word, child!" exclaimed the angry marquise, "your folly exceeds all bounds. I should be glad to know what connexion there can possibly be between your sickly sentimentality and the affairs of state!"

"Oh, mother!" murmured Renée.

"Nay, madame, I pray you pardon this little traitor; I promise you, that to make up for her want of loyalty I will be most inflexibly severe;" then casting an expressive glance at his betrothed, which seemed to say, "Fear not, for your dear sake my justice shall be tempered with mercy," and receiving a sweet and approving smile in return, Villefort quitted the room.

CHAPTER VII

THE EXAMINATION

No sooner had Villefort left the saloon, than he assumed the grave air of a man who holds the balance of life and death in his hands. Except the recollection of the line of politics his father had adopted, and which might interfere, unless he acted with the greatest prudence, with his own career, Villefort was as happy as a man could be. Already rich, he held a high official situation, though only twenty-seven. He was about to marry a young and charming woman, and besides her personal attractions, which were very great, Mademoiselle de Saint-Méran's family possessed considerable political influence, which they would of course exert in his favour. The dowry of his wife amounted to six thousand pounds, besides the prospect of inheriting twenty thousand more at her father's death.

At the door he met the commissary of police, who was waiting for him. The sight of this officer recalled Villefort from the third heaven to earth; he composed his face as we have before described, and said, " I have read the letter, monsieur, and you have acted rightly in arresting this man; now inform me what you have discovered concerning him and the conspiracy."

"We know nothing as yet of the conspiracy, monsieur; all the papers found have been sealed up and placed on your bureau. The prisoner himself is named Edmond Dantès, mate on board the three-master, the Pharaon, trading in cotton with Alexandria and Smyrna, and belonging to Morrel and Son, of Marseilles."

"Before he entered the navy had he ever served in the marines?"

"Oh, no, monsieur, he is very young."

"How old?"

"Nineteen or twenty at the most."

At this moment, and as Villefort had arrived at the corner of the Rue des Conseils, a man, who seemed to have been waiting for him, approached: it was M. Morrel.

"Ah, M. de Villefort," cried he, " I am delighted to see you. Some of your people have committed the strangest mistake— they have just arrested Edmond Dantès, the mate of my ship."

"I know it, monsieur," replied Villefort, "and I am now going to examine him."

"Oh," said Morrel, carried away by his friendship, "you do not know him, and I do. He is the most estimable, the most trustworthy creature in the world, and I will venture to say, there is not a better seaman in all the merchant-service. Oh, M. de Villefort, I beseech your indulgence for him."

Villefort, as we have seen, belonged to the aristocratic party at Marseilles, Morrel to the plebeian; the first was a royalist, the other suspected of Bonapartism. Villefort looked disdainfully at Morrel, and replied,—

"You are aware, monsieur, that a man may be estimable and trustworthy in private life, and the best seaman in the merchant-service, and yet be, politically speaking, a great criminal. Is it not true?"

The magistrate laid emphasis on these words, as if he wished to apply them to the owner himself, whilst his eyes seemed to plunge into the heart of him who, whilst he interceded for another, had himself need of indulgence. Morrel reddened, for his own conscience was not quite clear on politics; besides, what Dantès had told him of his interview with the grand-marshal, and what the emperor had said to him, embarrassed him. He replied, however,—

"I entreat you, M. de Villefort, be, as you always are, kind and equitable, and give him back to us soon."

This *give us* sounded revolutionary in the sub-prefect's ears.

"Ah! ah!" murmured he, "is Dantès then a member of some Carbonari society, that his protector thus employs the collective form? He was, if I recollect, arrested in a cabaret in company with a great many others." Then he added, "Monsieur, you may rest assured I shall perform my duty impartially, and that if he be innocent you shall not have appealed to me in vain; should he, however, be guilty, in this present epoch impunity would furnish a dangerous example, and I must do my duty."

As he had now arrived at the door of his own house, which adjoined the Palais de Justice, he entered, after having saluted the shipowner, who stood, as if petrified, on the spot where Villefort had left him.

The antechamber was full of agents of police and gendarmes, in the midst of whom, carefully watched, but calm and smiling, stood the prisoner. Villefort traversed the antechamber, cast a side glance at Dantès, and taking a packet which a gendarme offered him, disappeared, saying, "Bring in the prisoner."

Rapid as had been Villefort's glance, it had served to give him an idea of the man he was about to interrogate. He had recognised intelligence in the high forehead, courage in the dark eye and bent brow, and frankness in the thick lips that shewed a set of pearly teeth.

Villefort's first impression was favourable, but he had been so often warned to mistrust first impulses that he applied the maxim to the impression, forgetting the difference between the two words. He stifled, therefore, the feelings of compassion that were rising, composed his features, and sat down at his bureau. An instant after Dantès entered.

He was pale, but calm and collected, and saluting his judge with easy politeness, looked round for a seat, as if he had been in the saloon of M. Morrel.

It was then that he encountered, for the first time, Ville-fort's look, that look peculiar to justice; which, whilst it seems to read the culprit's thoughts, betrays nought of its own.

"Who and what are you?" demanded Villefort, turning over a pile of papers, containing information relative to the prisoner that an agent of police had given to him on his entry.

"My name is Edmond Dantès," replied the young man calmly. "I am mate of the Pharaon, belonging to Messrs. Morrel and Son."

"Your age?" continued Villefort.

"Nineteen," returned Dantès.

"What were you doing at the moment you were arrested?"

"I was at the festival of my marriage, monsieur," said the young man, his voice slightly tremulous, so great was the contrast between that happy moment and the painful ceremony he was now undergoing; so great was the contrast between the sombre aspect of M. de Villefort and the radiant face of Mercédès.

"You were at the festival of your marriage?" said the deputy, shuddering in spite of himself.

"Yes, monsieur, I am on the point of marrying a young girl I have been attached to for three years."

Villefort, impassive as he was, was struck with this co-incidence; and the tremulous voice of Dantès, surprised in the midst of his happiness, struck a sympathetic chord in his own bosom; he also was on the point of being married, and he was summoned from his own happiness to destroy that of another.

This philosophic reflection, thought he, will make a great sensation at M. de Saint-Méran's, and he arranged mentally, whilst Dantès awaited further questions, the antitheses by which orators often create a reputation for eloquence.

When this speech was arranged, Villefort turned to Dantès.

"Continue, sir," said he.

"What would you have me continue?"

"To give all the information in your power."

"Tell me on which point you desire information, and I will tell all I know; only," added he, with a smile, " I warn you I know very little."

"Have you served under the usurper?"

"I was about to be incorporated in the royal marines when he fell."

"It is reported your political opinions are extreme," said Villefort, who had never heard anything of the kind, but was not sorry to take this inquiry as if it were an accusation.

"My political opinions!" replied Dantès. "Alas! sir, I never had any opinions. I am hardly nineteen; I know nothing; I have no part to play. If I obtain the situation I desire, I shall owe it to M. Morrel. Thus all my opinions,—I will not say public, but private, are confined to these three sentiments—I love my father, I respect M. Morrel, and I adore Mercédès. This, sir, is all I can tell you, and you see how uninteresting it is."

As Dantès spoke, Villefort gazed at his ingenuous and open countenance, and recollected the words of Renée, who, without knowing who the culprit was, had besought his indulgence for him. With the deputy's knowledge of crime and criminals, every word the young man uttered convinced him more and more of his innocence.

This lad, for he was scarcely a man, simple, natural, eloquent with that eloquence of the heart, never found when sought for, full of affection for everybody, because he was happy, and because happiness renders even the wicked good, extended his affection even to his judge, spite of Villefort's severe look and stern accent. Dantès seemed full of kindness.

"*Pardieu!*" said Villefort, "he is a noble fellow! I hope I shall gain Renée's favour easily by obeying the first command she ever imposed on me. I shall have at least a pressure of the hand in public and a sweet kiss in private."

Full of this idea, Villefort's face became so joyous, that when he turned to Dantès, the latter, who had watched the change on his physiognomy, was smiling also.

"Sir," said Villefort, "have you any enemies, at least that you know?"

"I have enemies?" replied Dantès; "my position is not sufficiently elevated for that. As for my character, that is, perhaps, somewhat too hasty, but I have striven to repress it. I have had ten or twelve sailors under me; and if you question them, they will tell you that they love and respect me, not as a father, for I am too young, but as an elder brother."

"But instead of enemies you may have excited jealousy. You are about to become captain at nineteen, an elevated post; you are about to marry a pretty girl, who loves you, and these two pieces of good fortune may have excited the envy of some one."

"You are right; you know men better than I do, and what you say may possibly be the case, I confess; I prefer not knowing them, because then I should be forced to hate them."

"You are wrong; you should always strive to see clearly

around you. You seem a worthy young man; I will depart from the strict line of my duty to aid you in discovering the author of this accusation. Here is the paper; do you know the writing?"

As he spoke, Villefort drew the letter from his pocket, and presented it to Dantès. Dantès read it. A cloud passed over his brow as he said:—

"No, monsieur, I do not know the writing, and yet it is tolerably plain. Whoever did it writes well. I am very fortunate," added he, looking gratefully at Villefort, "to be examined by such a man as you, for this envious person is a real enemy."

And by the rapid glance that the young man's eyes shot forth, Villefort saw how much energy lay hid beneath this mildness.

"Now," said the deputy, "answer me frankly, not as a prisoner to a judge, but as one man to another who takes an interest in him, what truth is there in the accusation contained in this anonymous letter?"

And Villefort threw disdainfully on his bureau the letter Dantès had just given back to him.

"None at all. I will tell you the real facts. I swear by my honour as a sailor, by my love for Mercédès, by the life of my father——"

"Speak, monsieur," said Villefort. Then, internally, "If Renée could see me, I hope she would be satisfied, and would no longer call me a decapitator."

"Well, when we quitted Naples, Captain Leclere was attacked with a brain-fever. As we had no doctor on board, and he was so anxious to arrive at Elba, that he would not touch at any other port, his disorder rose to such a height, that at the end of the third day, feeling he was dying, he called me to him. 'My dear Dantès,' said he, 'swear to perform what I am going to tell you, for it is a matter of the deepest importance.'

"'I swear, captain,' replied I.

"'Well, as after my death the command devolves on you as mate, assume the command, and bear up for the Isle of Elba, disembark at Porto-Ferrajo, ask for the grand-marshal, give him this letter, perhaps they will give you another letter, and charge you with a commission. You will accomplish what I was to have done, and derive all the honour and profit from it.'

"'I will do it, captain; but, perhaps, I shall not be admitted to the grand-marshal's presence as easily as you expect?'

"'Here is a ring that will obtain audience of him, and remove every difficulty,' said the captain.

"At these words he gave me a ring.

"It was time: two hours after he was delirious; the next day he died."

"And what did you do then?"

"What I ought to have done, and what every one would have done in my place. Every where the last requests of a dying man are sacred; but amongst sailors the last requests of his superior are commands. I sailed for the Isle of Elba, where I arrived the next day; I ordered every body to remain on board, and went on shore alone. As I had expected, I found some difficulty in obtaining access to the grand-marshal; but I sent the ring I had received from the captain to him, and was instantly admitted. He questioned me concerning Captain Leclere's death; and, as the latter had told me, gave me a letter to carry on to a person in Paris. I undertook it because it was what my captain had bade me do. I landed here, regulated the affairs of the vessel, and hastened to visit my affianced bride, whom I found more lovely than ever. Thanks to M. Morrel, all the forms were got over; in a word, I was, as I told you, at my marriage-feast, and I should have been married in an hour, and to-morrow I intended to start for Paris."

"Ah!" said Villefort, "this seems to me the truth. If you have been culpable, it was imprudence, and this imprudence was legitimised by the orders of your captain. Give up this letter you have brought from Elba, and pass your word you will appear should you be required, and go and rejoin your friends."

"I am free, then, sir?" cried Dantès joyfully.

"Yes; but first give me this letter."

"You have it already; for it was taken from me with some others which I see in that packet."

"Stop a moment," said the deputy, as Dantès took his hat and gloves. "To whom is it addressed?"

"To Monsieur Noirtier, Rue Coq-Héron, Paris."

Had a thunderbolt fallen into the room, Villefort could not have been more stupefied. He sank into his seat, and hastily turning over the packet, drew forth the fatal letter, at which he glanced with an expression of terror.

"M. Noirtier, Rue Coq-Héron, No. 13," murmured he, growing still paler.

"Yes," said Dantès; "do you then know him?"

"No," replied Villefort; "a faithful servant of the king does not know conspirators."

"It is a conspiracy, then?" asked Dantès, who, after believing himself free, now began to feel a tenfold alarm. "I have already told you, however, sir, I was ignorant of the contents of the letter."

"Yes, but you knew the name of the person to whom it was addressed?" said Villefort.

"I was forced to read the address to know to whom to give it."

"Have you shewn this letter to any one?" asked Villefort, becoming still more pale.

"To no one, on my honour."

"Every body is ignorant that you are the bearer of a letter from the Isle of Elba, and addressed to M. Noirtier?"

"Every body, except the person who gave it to me."

"This is too much," murmured Villefort.

Villefort's brow darkened more and more, his white lips and clenched teeth filled Dantès with apprehension.

After reading the letter, Villefort covered his face with his hands.

"Oh!" said Dantès, timidly, "what is the matter?"

Villefort made no answer but raised his head at the expiration of a few seconds, and again perused the letter.

"You give me your honour that you are ignorant of the contents of this letter?"

"I give you my honour, sir," said Dantès; "but what is the matter? You are ill;—shall I ring for assistance?—shall I call?"

"No," said Villefort, rising hastily; "stay where you are. It is for me to give orders here, and not you."

"Monsieur," replied Dantès, proudly, "it was only to summon assistance for you."

"I want none; it was a temporary indisposition. Attend to yourself; answer me."

Dantès waited, expecting a question, but in vain. Villefort fell back on his chair, passed his hand over his brow, moist with perspiration, and, for the third time, read the letter.

"Oh! if he knows the contents of this!" murmured he, "and that Noirtier is the father of Villefort, I am lost!" And he fixed his eyes upon Edmond as if he would have penetrated his thoughts.

"Oh! it is impossible to doubt it," cried he suddenly.

"In Heaven's name!" cried the unhappy young man, "if you doubt me, question me; I will answer you."

Villefort made a violent effort, and in a tone he strove to render firm,—

"Sir," said he, "I am no longer able, as I had hoped, to restore you immediately to liberty; before doing so, I must consult the judge of instruction; but you see how I behave towards you."

"Oh! monsieur," cried Dantès, "you have been rather a friend than a judge."

"Well, I must detain you some time longer, but I will strive to make it as short as possible. The principal charge against you is this letter, and you see——"

Villefort approached the fire, cast it in, and waited until it was entirely consumed.

"You see I destroy it?"

"Oh!" exclaimed Dantès, "you are goodness itself."

"Listen," continued Villefort, "you can now have confidence in me after what I have done."

"Oh! order me, and I will obey."

"Listen! this is not an order, but a counsel I give you."

"Speak, and I will follow your advice."

"I shall detain you until this evening in the Palais de Justice. Should any one else interrogate you, do not breathe a word of this letter."

"I promise."

It was Villefort who seemed to entreat, and the prisoner who reassured him.

"You see," continued he, "the letter is destroyed, you and I alone knew of its existence; should you, therefore, be questioned, deny all knowledge of it."

"Fear nothing, I will deny it."

"It was the only letter you had?"

"It was."

"Swear it."

"I swear it."

Villefort rang. An agent of police entered. Villefort whispered some words in his ear, to which the officer replied by a motion of his head.

"Follow him," said Villefort to Dantès.

Dantès saluted Villefort and retired.

Hardly had the door closed, than Villefort threw himself into a chair.

"Alas! alas!" murmured he, "if the procureur du roi had been at Marseilles, I should have been ruined. This accursed letter would have destroyed all my hopes. Oh! my father, must your past career always interfere with my successes?"

Suddenly a light passed over his face, a smile played round his mouth, and his lips became unclenched.

"This will do," said he, "and from this letter, which might have ruined me, I will make my fortune."

And after having assured himself the prisoner was gone, the deputy procureur hastened to the house of his bride.

CHAPTER VIII

THE CHÂTEAU D'IF

The commissary of police, as he traversed the antechamber, made a sign to two gendarmes, who placed themselves one on Dantès' right and the other on his left. A door that communicated with the Palais de Justice was opened, and they traversed a long range of gloomy corridors, whose appearance might have made even the boldest shudder.

The Palais de Justice communicated with the prison—a sombre edifice, that from its grated windows looks on the clock-tower of the Accoules.

After numberless windings Dantès saw an iron door. The commissary knocked thrice, every blow seeming to Dantès as if struck on his heart. The door opened, the two gendarmes gently pushed him forward, and the door closed with a loud sound behind him. The air he inhaled was no longer pure, but thick and mephitic,—he was in prison.

He was conducted to a tolerably neat chamber, but grated and barred, and its appearance, therefore, did not greatly alarm him; besides the words of Villefort, who seemed to interest himself so much, resounded still in his ears like a promise of freedom.

It was four o'clock when Dantès was placed in this chamber. It was, as we have said, the 1st of March, and the prisoner was soon buried in darkness.

The obscurity augmented the acuteness of his hearing: at the slightest sound he rose and hastened to the door, convinced they were about to liberate him, but the sound died away, and Dantès sank again into his seat.

At last, about ten o'clock, and just as Dantès began to despair, steps were heard in the corridor, a key turned in the lock, the bolts creaked, the massy oaken door flew open, and a flood of light from two torches pervaded the apartment.

By the torchlight Dantès saw the glittering sabres and carbines of four gendarmes. He had advanced at first, but stopped at the sight of this fresh accession of force.

"Are you come to fetch me?" asked he.

"Yes," replied a gendarme.

"By the orders of the deputy of the king's procureur?"

"I believe so."

77

The conviction that they came from M. de Villefort relieved all Dantès' apprehension, he advanced calmly and placed himself in the centre of the escort.

A carriage waited at the door, the coachman was on the box, and an exempt seated beside him.

"Is this carriage for me?" said Dantès.

"It is for you," replied the gendarme.

Dantès was about to speak, but feeling himself urged forward, and having neither the power nor the intention to resist, he mounted the steps, and was in an instant seated inside between two gendarmes, the two others took their places opposite, and the carriage rolled heavily over the stones.

The prisoner glanced at the windows, they were grated; he had changed his prison for another that was conveying him he knew not whither. Through the grating, however, Dantès saw they were passing through the Rue Caisserie, and by the quay Saint-Laurent and the Rue Taramis, to the port.

The carriage stopped, the exempt descended, approached the guard-house, a dozen soldiers came out and formed themselves in order, Dantès saw the reflection of their muskets by the light of the lamps on the quay.

"Can all this force be summoned on my account?" thought he.

The exempt opened the door, which was locked, and without speaking a word answered Dantès' question, for he saw between the ranks of the soldiers a passage formed from the carriage to the port.

The two gendarmes who were opposite to him descended first, then he was ordered to alight, and the gendarmes on each side of him followed his example. They advanced towards a boat, which a custom house officer held by a chain, near the quay.

The soldiers looked at Dantès with an air of stupid curiosity. In an instant he was placed in the stern-sheets of the boat between the gendarmes, whilst the exempt stationed himself at the bow; a shove sent the boat adrift, and four sturdy oarsmen impelled it rapidly towards the Pilon. At a shout from the boat the chain that closes the mouth of the port was lowered, and in a second they were outside the harbour.

The prisoner's first feeling was joy at again breathing the pure air, for air is freedom; but he soon sighed, for he passed before La Réserve, where he had that morning been so happy, and now through the open windows came the laughter and revelry of a ball.

Dantès folded his hands, raised his eyes to heaven, and prayed fervently.

The boat continued her voyage. They had passed the

Tête de More, were now in front of the lighthouse, and about to double the battery; this manœuvre was incomprehensible to Dantès.

"Whither are you taking me?" asked he.

"You will soon know."

"But still——"

"We are forbidden to give you any explanation."

Dantès knew that nothing would be more absurd than to question subordinates, who were forbidden to reply, and remained silent.

The most vague and wild thoughts passed through his mind. The boat they were in could not make a long voyage, there was no vessel at anchor outside the harbour; he thought, perhaps, they were going to leave him on some distant point. He was not bound, nor had they made any attempt to hand-cuff him; this seemed a good augury. Besides had not the deputy who had been so kind to him told him that provided he did not pronounce the dreaded name of Noirtier, he had nothing to apprehend? Had not Villefort in his presence destroyed the fatal letter, the only proof against him? He waited silently, striving to pierce through the darkness.

They had left the Ile Ratonneau, where the lighthouse stood, on the right, and were now opposite the Point des Catalans. It seemed to the prisoner that he could distinguish a female form on the beach, for it was there Mercédès dwelt.

How was it that a presentiment did not warn Mercédès her lover was near her?

One light alone was visible, and Dantès recognised it as coming from the chamber of Mercédès. A loud cry could be heard by her. He did not utter it. What would his guards think if they heard him shout like a madman?

He remained silent, his eyes fixed upon the light: the boat went on, but the prisoner only thought of Mercédès. A rising ground hid the light, Dantès turned and perceived they had got out to sea. Whilst he had been absorbed in thought they had hoisted the sail.

In spite of his repugnance to address his guards, Dantès turned to the nearest gendarme, and taking his hand,—

"Comrade," said he, "I adjure you as a Christian and a soldier to tell me where we are going. I am Captain Dantès, a loyal Frenchman, though accused of treason, tell me where you are conducting me, and I promise you on my honour I will submit to my fate."

The gendarme looked irresolutely at his companion, who returned for answer a sign that said, "I see no great harm in telling him now," and the gendarme replied,—

"You are a native of Marseilles and a sailor, and yet you do not know where you are going?"

"On my honour I have no idea."

"That is impossible."

"I swear to you it is true. Tell me, I entreat."

"But my orders?"

"Your orders do not forbid your telling me what I must know in ten minutes, in half an hour, or an hour. You see I cannot escape even if I intended."

"Unless you are blind, or have never been outside the harbour, you must know."

"I do not."

"Look round you then."

Dantès rose and looked forward, when he saw rise within a hundred yards of him the black and frowning rock on which stands the Château d'If. This gloomy fortress, which has for more than three hundred years furnished food for so many wild legends, seemed to Dantès like a scaffold to a malefactor.

"The Château d'If!" cried he, "what are we going there for?"

The gendarme smiled.

"I am not going there to be imprisoned," said Dantès; "it is only used for political prisoners, I have committed no crime. Are there any magistrates or judges at the Château d'If?"

"There are only," said the gendarme, "a governor, a garrison, turnkeys, and good thick walls. Come, come, do not look so astonished, or you will make me think you are laughing at me in return for my good nature."

Dantès pressed the gendarme's hand as though he would crush it.

"You think, then," said he, "that I am conducted to the Château to be imprisoned there?"

"It is probable; but there is no occasion to squeeze so hard."

"Without any formality?"

"All the formalities have been gone through."

"In spite of M. de Villefort's promises?"

"I do not know what M. de Villefort promised you," said the gendarme, "but I know we are taking you to the Château d'If. But what are you doing? Help! comrades, help!"

By a rapid movement, which the gendarme's practised eye had perceived, Dantès sprang forward to precipitate himself into the sea, but four vigorous arms seized him as his feet quitted the flooring of the boat. He fell back foaming with rage.

"Good!" said the gendarme, placing his knee on his chest; "believe soft-spoken gentlemen again! Harkye, my friend, I have disobeyed my first order, but I will not disobey the second, and if you move I lodge a bullet in your brain."

And he levelled his carbine at Dantès, who felt the muzzle touch his head.

For a moment the idea of struggling crossed his mind, and so end the unexpected evil that had overtaken him. But he bethought him of M. de Villefort's promise; and, besides, death in a boat from the hand of a gendarme seemed too terrible. He remained motionless, but gnashing his teeth with fury.

At this moment a violent shock made the bark tremble. One of the sailors leaped on shore, a cord creaked as it ran through a pulley, and Dantès guessed they were at the end of the voyage.

His guardians, taking hold of his arms, forced him to rise, and dragged him towards the steps that lead to the gate of the fortress, whilst the exempt followed, armed with a carbine and bayonet.

Dantès made no resistance, he was like a man in a dream, he saw soldiers who stationed themselves on the sides, he felt himself forced up fresh stairs, he perceived he passed through a door, and the door closed behind him; but all this as mechanically as through a mist, nothing distinctly.

They halted for a minute, during which he strove to collect his thoughts; he looked around; he was in a court surrounded by high walls; he heard the measured tread of sentinels, and as they passed before the light he saw the barrels of their muskets shine.

They waited upwards of ten minutes. Certain Dantès could not escape, the gendarmes released him; they seemed awaiting orders. The orders arrived.

"Where is the prisoner?" said a voice.

"Here," replied the gendarmes.

"Let him follow me; I am going to conduct him to his room."

"Go!" said the gendarmes, pushing Dantès.

The prisoner followed his conductor, who led him into a room almost under ground, whose bare and reeking walls seemed as though impregnated with tears; a lamp placed on a stool illumined the apartment faintly, and shewed Dantès the features of his conductor, an under-gaoler, ill clothed, and of sullen appearance.

"Here is your chamber for to-night," said he. "It is late, and Monsieur le Gouverneur is asleep; to-morrow, perhaps, he may change you. In the meantime there is bread, water, and fresh straw, and that is all a prisoner can wish for. Good night!"

And before Dantès could open his mouth,—before he had noticed where the gaoler placed his bread or the water,—before he had glanced towards the corner where the straw was, the gaoler disappeared, taking with him the lamp.

Dantès was alone in darkness and in silence: cold as the shadows that he felt breathe on his burning forehead.

With the first dawn of day the gaoler returned, with orders to leave Dantès where he was. He found the prisoner in the same position as if fixed there,—his eyes swollen with weeping.

He had passed the night standing and without sleep.

The gaoler advanced: Dantès appeared not to perceive him. He touched him on the shoulder: Edmond started.

"Have you not slept?" said the gaoler.

"I do not know," replied Dantès.

The gaoler stared.

"Are you hungry?" continued he.

"I do not know."

"Do you wish for anything?"

"I wish to see the governor."

The gaoler shrugged his shoulders and left the chamber.

Dantès followed him with his eyes, and stretched forth his hands towards the open door; but the door closed.

All his emotion then burst forth; he cast himself on the ground weeping bitterly, and asking himself what crime he had committed that he was thus punished.

The day passed thus; he scarcely tasted food, but walked round and round the cell like a wild beast in its cage.

One thought in particular tormented him, namely, that during his journey hither he had sat so still, whereas he might, a dozen times, have plunged into the sea, and, thanks to his powers of swimming, for which he was famous, have gained the shore, concealed himself until the arrival of a Genoese or Spanish vessel; escaped to Spain or Italy, where Mercédès and his father could have joined him. He had no fears as to how he should live; good seamen are welcome everywhere; he spoke Italian like a Tuscan, and Spanish like a Castilian; he would have then been happy, whereas he was now confined in the Château d'If, ignorant of the future destiny of his father and Mercédès; and all this because he had trusted to Villefort's promise. The thought was maddening, and Dantès threw himself furiously down on his straw.

The next morning the gaoler made his appearance.

"Well," said the gaoler, "are you more reasonable to-day?"

Dantès made no reply.

"Come, take courage, do you want any thing in my power to do for you?"

"I wish to see the governor."

"I have already told you it was impossible."

"Why so?"

"Because it is not allowed by the rules."

"What is allowed then?"

"Better fare, if you pay for it, books, and leave to walk about."

"I do not want books, I am satisfied with my food, and I do not care to walk about; but I wish to see the governor."

"If you worry me by repeating the same thing I will not bring you any more to eat."

"Well, then," said Edmond, "if you do not I shall die of famine, that is all."

The gaoler saw by his tone he would be happy to die; and, as every prisoner is worth sixpence a day to his gaoler, he replied in a more subdued tone,—

"What you ask is impossible; but if you are very well behaved you will be allowed to walk about, and some day you will meet the governor; and if he chooses to reply, that is his affair."

"But," asked Dantès, "how long shall I have to wait?"

"Ah! a month—six months—a year."

"It is too long a time. I wish to see him at once."

"Ah!" said the gaoler, "do not always brood over what is impossible, or you will be mad in a fortnight."

"You think so?"

"Yes, we have an instance here; it was by always offering a million of francs to the governor for his liberty that an abbé became mad, who was in this chamber before you."

"How long has he left it?"

"Two years."

"Was he liberated then?"

"No; he was put in a dungeon."

"Listen!" said Dantès; "I am not an abbé, I am not mad; perhaps I shall be; but at present, unfortunately, I am not. I will make you another offer."

"What is that?"

"I do not offer you a million, because I have it not; but I will give you a hundred crowns if the first time you go to Marseilles you will seek out a young girl, named Mercédès, at the Catalans, and give her two lines from me."

"If I took them, and were detected, I should lose my place, which is worth two thousand francs a-year; so that I should be a great fool to run such a risk for three hundred."

"Well," said Dantès, "mark this, if you refuse, at least, to tell Mercédès I am here, I will some day hide myself behind the door, and when you enter I will dash out your brains with this stool."

"Threats!" cried the gaoler, retreating, and putting himself on the defensive, "you are certainly going mad. The abbé began like you; and in three days you will want a strait-waistcoat; but, fortunately, there are dungeons here."

Dantès whirled the stool round his head.

"Oh!" said the gaoler, "you shall see the governor at once."

"That is right!" returned Dantès, dropping the stool, and sitting on it as if he were in reality mad.

The gaoler went out, and returned in an instant with a corporal and four soldiers.

"By the governor's orders," said he, "conduct the prisoner to the story beneath."

"To the dungeon, then," said the corporal.

"Yes, we must put the madmen with the madmen."

The soldiers seized Dantès, who followed passively.

He descended fifteen steps, and the door of a dungeon was opened, and he was thrust in.

The door closed, and Dantès advanced with outstretched hands until he touched the wall; he then sat down in the corner until his eyes became accustomed to the darkness.

The gaoler was right, Dantès wanted but little of being utterly mad.

CHAPTER IX

THE EVENING OF THE BETROTHAL

VILLEFORT had, as we have said, hastened back to the Place du Grand Cours, and on entering the house found all the guests in the salon at coffee. Renée was, with all the rest of the company, anxiously awaiting him, and his entrance was followed by a general exclamation.

"Well, Decapitator, Guardian of the State, Brutus, what is the matter?" said one.

"Are we threatened with a fresh Reign of Terror?" asked another.

"Has the Corsican ogre broken loose?" cried a third.

"Madame la Marquise," said Villefort, approaching his future mother-in-law, "I request your pardon for thus leaving you. M. le Marquis, honour me by a few moments' private conversation!"

"Ah! this affair is really serious, then?" asked the marquis, remarking the cloud on Villefort's brow.

"So serious, that I must take leave of you for a few days; so," added he, turning to Renée, "judge for yourself if it be not important?"

"You are going to leave us?" cried Renée, unable to hide her emotion.

"Alas!" returned Villefort, "I must!"

"Where, then, are you going?" asked the marquise.

"That, madame, is the secret of justice, but if you have any commissions for Paris, a friend of mine is going there to-night."

The guests looked at each other.

"You wish to speak to me alone?" said the marquis.

"Yes, let us go into your cabinet."

The marquis took his arm, and left the salon.

"Well!" asked he, as soon as they were in his closet, "tell me, what is it?"

"An affair of the greatest importance, that demands my immediate presence in Paris. Now, excuse the indiscretion, marquis, but have you any funded property?"

"All my fortune is in the funds; seven or eight hundred thousand francs."

"Then sell out,—sell out, marquis, as soon as you can."

85

"Eh! how can I sell out here?"

"You have a broker; have you not?"

"Yes."

"Then give me a letter to him, and tell him to sell out without an instant's delay, perhaps even now I shall arrive too late."

"What say you?" said the marquis, "let us lose no time, then!"

And, sitting down, he wrote a letter to his broker, ordering him to sell out at any loss.

"Now, then," said Villefort, placing the letter in his pocket-book, "write another!"

"To whom?"

"To the king."

"I dare not write to his majesty."

"I do not ask you to write to his majesty, but ask M. de Salvieux to do so. I want a letter that will enable me to reach the king's presence without all the formalities of demanding an audience, that would occasion a loss of time."

"But address yourself to the keeper of the seals, he has the right of entry, and can procure you audience."

"Doubtless; but there is no occasion to divide the merit of my discovery with him. The keeper would leave me in the background, and take all the honour to himself. I tell you, marquis, my fortune is made if I only reach the Tuileries the first, for the king will not forget the service I do him."

"In that case make your preparations, and I will write the letter."

"Be as quick as possible, I must be *en route* in a quarter of an hour."

"Make your carriage stop at the door."

"You will present my excuses to the marquise and Mademoiselle Renée, whom I leave on such a day with great regret."

"They are both in my room, you can say all this for yourself."

"A thousand thanks, busy yourself with the letter."

The marquis rang: a servant entered.

"Inform the Count de Salvieux I am waiting for him."

"Now, then, go!" said the marquis.

"I only go for a few moments."

Villefort hastily quitted the apartment, but reflecting that the sight of the deputy-procureur running through the streets would be enough to throw the whole city into confusion, he resumed his ordinary pace. At his door he perceived a figure in the shadow that seemed to wait for him. It was Mercédès who, hearing no news of her lover, had come herself to inquire after him.

As Villefort drew near, she advanced and stood before him.

Dantès had spoken of his bride, and Villefort instantly recognised her. Her beauty and high-bearing surprised him, and when she inquired what had become of her lover, it seemed to him that she was the judge, and he the accused.

"The young man you speak of," said Villefort, abruptly, "is a great criminal, and I can do nothing for him, mademoiselle."

Mercédès burst into tears, and, as Villefort strove to pass her, again addressed him.

"But, at least, tell me where he is, that I may learn if he is alive or dead," said she.

"I do not know, he is no longer in my hands," replied Villefort.

And desirous of putting an end to the interview, he pushed by her, and closed the door, as if to exclude the pain he felt. But remorse is not thus banished; like the wounded hero of Virgil, the arrow remained in the wound, and, arrived at the salon, Villefort, in his turn, burst into tears, and sank into a chair.

The man he sacrificed to his ambition, that innocent victim he made pay the penalty of his father's faults, appeared to him pale and threatening, leading his affianced bride by the hand, and bringing with him remorse, not such as the ancients figured, furious and terrible, but that slow and consuming agony, whose pangs cease only with life. Then he had a moment's hesitation. He had frequently called for capital punishment on criminals, and owing to his irresistible eloquence they had been condemned, and yet the slightest shadow of remorse had never clouded Villefort's brow, because they were guilty; at least, he believed so; but here was an innocent man whose happiness he had destroyed: in this case he was not the judge, but the executioner.

As he thus reflected, he felt the sensation we have described, and which had hitherto been unknown to him, arise in his bosom, and fill him with vague apprehensions. It is thus that a wounded man trembles instinctively at the approach of the finger to his wound until it be healed, but Villefort's was one of those that never close, or if they do, only close to reopen more agonising than ever. If, at this moment, the sweet voice of Renée had sounded in his ears pleading for mercy, or the fair Mercédès had entered, and said, "In the name of God, I conjure you to restore me my affianced husband," his cold and trembling hands would have signed his release; but no voice broke the stillness of the chamber, and the door was opened only by Villefort's valet, who came to tell him the travelling-carriage was in readiness.

Villefort rose, or rather sprang, from his chair, hastily opened one of the drawers of his *sécrétaire*, emptied all the gold it contained into his pocket, stood motionless an instant, his hand pressed to his head, muttered a few inarticulate sounds, and then perceiving his servant had placed his cloak on his shoulders, he sprang into the carriage, ordering the postilions to go, Rue du Grand Cours, to the house of M. de Saint-Méran.

As the marquis had promised, Villefort found the letter. He started when he saw Renée, for he fancied she was again about to plead for Dantès. Alas! she was thinking only of Villefort's departure.

She loved Villefort, and he left her at the moment he was about to become her husband. Villefort knew not when he should return, and Renée, far from pleading for Dantès, hated the man whose crime separated her from her lover. What had Mercédès to say?

Mercédès had met Fernand at the corner of the Rue de la Loge, she had returned to the Catalans, and had despairingly cast herself on her couch. Fernand, kneeling by her side, took her hand, and covered it with kisses that Mercédès did not even feel.

She passed the night thus, and the day returned without her noticing it. Grief had made her blind to all but one object, that was Edmond.

" Ah! you are there," said she, at length.

" I have not quitted you since yesterday," returned Fernand, sorrowfully.

M. Morrel had learned that Dantès had been conducted to prison, and he had gone to all his friends, and the influential persons of the city, but the report was already in circulation that Dantès was arrested as a Bonapartist agent; and as the most sanguine looked upon any attempt of Napoleon to remount the throne as impossible, he met with nothing but refusal, and had returned home in despair.

Caderousse was equally restless and uneasy, but instead of seeking to aid Dantès, he had shut himself up with two bottles of wine, in the hope of drowning reflection. But he did not succeed, and became too intoxicated to fetch any more wine, and yet not so intoxicated as to forget what had happened.

Danglars alone was content and joyous, he had got rid of an enemy, and preserved his situation on board the Pharaon; Danglars was one of those men born with a pen behind the ear, and an inkstand in place of a heart. Every thing with him was multiplication or subtraction, and he estimated the life of a man as less precious than a figure when that figure could increase, and that life would diminish, the total of the amount.

Villefort, after having received M. de Salvieux' letter, embraced Renée, kissed the marquise's hand, and shaken hands with the marquis, started for Paris.

Old Dantès was dying with anxiety to know what had become of Edmond.

CHAPTER X

THE SMALL CABINET OF THE TUILERIES

WE will leave Villefort on the road to Paris, travelling with all speed, and penetrating the two or three apartments which precede it, enter the small cabinet of the Tuileries with the arched window, so well known as having been the favourite cabinet of Napoleon and Louis XVIII, as now that of Louis Philippe.

There in this closet, seated before a walnut-tree table he had brought with him from Hartwell, and to which, from one of those fancies not uncommon to great people, he was particularly attached, the King Louis XVIII was carelessly listening to a man of fifty or fifty-two years of age, with grey hairs, aristocratic bearing, and exceedingly gentlemanly attire, whilst he was making a note in a volume of Horace, Gryphius's edition, which was much indebted to the sagacious observations of the philosophical monarch.

"You say, sir——" said the king.

"That I am exceedingly disquieted, sire."

"Really, have you had a visit of the seven fat kine and seven lean kine?"

"No, sire, for that would only betoken for us seven years of plenty and seven years of scarcity, and with a king as full of foresight as your majesty scarcity is not a thing to be feared."

"Then of what other scourge are you afraid, my dear Blacas?"

"Sire, I have every reason to believe that a storm is brewing in the south."

"Well, my dear duke," replied Louis XVIII, "I think you are wrongly informed, and know positively that, on the contrary, it is very fine weather in that direction."

Man of ability as he was, Louis XVIII liked a pleasant jest.

"Sire," continued M. de Blacas, "if it only be to reassure a faithful servant, will your majesty send into Languedoc, Provence, and Dauphiné, trusty men who will bring you back a faithful report as to the feeling in these three provinces?"

"*Canimus surdis!*" replied the king, continuing the annotations in his Horace.

"Sire," replied the courtier, laughing, in order that he might seem to comprehend the quotation, "your majesty may

89

be perfectly right in relying on the good feeling of France, but I fear I am not altogether wrong in dreading some desperate attempt."

"By whom?"

"By Bonaparte, or, at least, his party."

"My dear Blacas," said the king, "you with your alarms prevent me from working."

"And you, sire, prevent me from sleeping with your security."

"Wait, my dear sir, wait a moment, for I have such a delightful note on the *Pastor quùm traheret*,—wait, and I will listen to you afterwards."

There was a brief pause, during which Louis XVIII wrote, in a hand as small as possible, another note on the margin of his Horace, and then looking at the duke with the air of a man who thinks he has an idea of his own, whilst he is but commenting upon the idea of another, he said,—

"Go on, my dear duke, go on—I listen."

"Sire," said Blacas, who had for a moment the hope of sacrificing Villefort to his own profit, "I am compelled to tell you that these are not mere rumours destitute of foundation which thus disquiet me; but a reflective man, deserving all my confidence, and charged by me to watch over the south (the duke hesitated as he pronounced these words), has arrived post to tell me a great peril threatens the king, and then I hastened to you, sire."

"*Mala ducis avi domum*," continued Louis XVIII, still annotating.

"Does your majesty wish me to cease as to this subject?"

"By no means, dear duke; but just stretch out your hand."

"Which?"

"Whichever you please—there to the left."

"Here, sire."

"I tell you to the left, and you seek the right,—I mean on my right!—yes, there! You will find the report of the minister of police of yesterday. But here is M. Dandré himself;" and M. Dandré, announced by the chamberlain in waiting, entered.

"Come in," said Louis XVIII, with an imperceptible smile, "come in, baron, and tell the duke all you know—the latest news of M. de Bonaparte; do not conceal any thing, however serious—let us see the island of Elba as a volcano, and we may expect to have issuing thence flaming and bristling war,—*bella, horrida bella!*"

M. Dandré leaned very respectfully on the back of a chair with his two hands, and said,—

"Has your majesty perused yesterday's report?"

"Yes, yes! but tell the count himself, who cannot find any

thing, what the report contains; give him the particulars of what the usurper is doing in his islet."

"Monsieur," said the baron to the count, "all the servants of his majesty must approve of the latest intelligence which we have from the island of Elba. Bonaparte," M. Dandré looked at Louis XVIII, who, employed in writing a note, did not even raise his head,—"Bonaparte," continued the baron, "is mortally wearied, and passes whole days in watching his miners at work at Porto-Longone."

"And scratches himself for amusement," added the king.

"Scratches himself?" inquired the count, "what does your majesty mean?"

"Yes, indeed, my dear count; did you forget that this great man, this hero, this demigod, is attacked with a malady of the skin which worries him to death, *prurigo?*"

"And, moreover, M. le Comte," continued the minister of police, "we are almost assured that, in a very short time, the usurper will be insane."

"Insane?"

"Insane to a degree; his head becomes weaker. Sometimes he weeps bitterly, sometimes laughs boisterously; at other times he passes hours on the sea-shore, flinging stones in the water, and when the flint makes 'duck-and-drake' five or six times he appears as delighted as if he had gained another Marengo or Austerlitz. Now you must agree these are indubitable symptoms of weakness?"

"Or of wisdom, M. le Baron—or of wisdom," said Louis XVIII, laughing; "the greatest captains of antiquity recreated themselves with casting pebbles into the ocean: see Plutarch's Life of Scipio Africanus."

M. de Blacas pondered deeply on this blind repose of monarch and minister. Villefort, who did not choose to reveal the whole secret, lest another should reap all the benefit of the disclosure, had yet communicated enough to cause him the greatest uneasiness.

"Well, well, Dandré," said Louis XVIII, "Blacas is not yet convinced, let us proceed therefore to the usurper's conversion."

The minister of police bowed.

"The usurper's conversion!" murmured the count, looking at the king and Dandré, who spoke alternately, like Virgil's shepherds,—"the usurper converted!"

"Decidedly, my dear count."

"In what way converted?"

"To good principles; explain all about it, baron."

"Why this it is, M. le Comte," said the minister, with the gravest air in the world: "Napoleon lately had a review, and as two or three of his old veterans testified a desire to return to France, he gave them their dismissal, and exported them to 'serve the good king;' these were his own words, M. le Comte, I am certain of that."

"Well, Blacas, what think you of this?" inquired the king, triumphantly, and pausing for a moment from the voluminous scholiast before him.

"I say, sire, that M. the minister of police, or I am greatly deceived, and as it is impossible it can be the minister of police, as he has the guardianship of the safety and honour of your majesty, it is probable I am in error. However, sire, if I might advise, your majesty will interrogate the person of whom I spoke to you, and I will urge your majesty to do him this honour."

"Most willingly, count; under your auspices I will receive any person you please, but with arms in hand. M. le Ministre, have you any report more recent than this, dated the 20th February, and this is the 4th of March?"

"No, sire, but I am hourly expecting one; it may have arrived since I left my office."

"Go thither, and if there be none—well, well," continued Louis XVIII, "make one, that is the usual way, is it not?" and the king laughed facetiously.

"Oh, sire," replied the minister, "we have no occasion to invent any; every day our desks are loaded with most circumstantial denunciations, coming from crowds of individuals who hope for some return for services which they seek to render, but cannot; they trust to fortune, and rely that some unexpected event will give a kind of reality to their predictions."

"Well, sir, go," said Louis XVIII, "and remember I am waiting for you."

"I will but go and return, sire; I shall be back in ten minutes."

"And I, sire," said M. de Blacas, "will go and find my messenger."

"Wait, sir, wait," said Louis XVIII; "really, M. de Blacas, I must change your armorial bearings; I will give you an eagle with outstretched wings, holding in its claws a prey which tries in vain to escape, and bearing this device, *Tenax*."

"Sire, I listen," said De Blacas, biting his nails with impatience.

"I wish to consult you on this passage, '*Molli fugies anhelitu;*' you know it refers to a stag flying from a wolf. Are you not a sportsman and a great wolf-hunter? Well, then, what do you think of the *molli anhelitu?*"

"Admirable, sire; but my messenger is like the stag you refer to, for he has posted two hundred and twenty leagues in little more than three days."

"Which is undergoing great fatigue and anxiety, my dear count, when we have a telegraph which corresponds in three or four hours, and that without putting it the least in the world out of breath."

"Ah, sire, you recompense but badly this poor young man, who has come so far and with so much ardour to give your majesty useful information. If only for the sake of M. de Salvieux, who recommends him to me, I entreat your majesty to receive him graciously."

"M. de Salvieux, my brother's chamberlain?"

"Yes, sire."

"He is at Marseilles."

"And writes me thence."

"Does he speak to you of this conspiracy?"

"No, but strongly recommends M. de Villefort, and begs me to present him to your majesty."

"M. de Villefort!" cried the king, "is the messenger's name M. de Villefort?"

"Yes, sire."

"And he comes from Marseilles?"

"In person."

"Why did you not mention his name at once?" replied the king, betraying some uneasiness.

"Sire, I thought his name was unknown to your majesty."

"No, no, Blacas; he is a man of strong and elevated understanding, ambitious too, and, *pardieu!* you know his father's name!"

"His father?"

"Yes, Noirtier."

"Noirtier the Girondin?—Noirtier the senator?"

"He himself."

"And your majesty has employed the son of such a man?"

"Blacas, my friend, you have but limited comprehension. I told you Villefort was ambitious, and to attain his ambition Villefort would sacrifice every thing, even his father."

"Then, sire, may I present him?"

"This instant, count! Where is he?"

"Waiting below in my carriage."

"Seek him at once."

"I hasten to do so."

The count left the royal presence with the speed of a young man; his really sincere royalism made him youthful again. Louis XVIII remained alone, and turning his eyes on his half-opened Horace, muttered, "*Justum et tenacem propositi virum.*"

M. de Blacas returned with the same rapidity he had descended, but in the antechamber he was forced to appeal to the king's authority. Villefort's dusty garb, his costume, which was not of courtly cut, excited the susceptibility of M. de Brezé, who was all astonishment at finding that this young man had the pretension to enter before the king in such attire. The count, however, superseded all difficulties with a word— his majesty's order, and, in spite of the observations which the master of the ceremonies made for the honour of his office and principles, Villefort was introduced.

The king was seated in the same place where the count had left him. On opening the door, Villefort found himself facing him, and the young magistrate's first impulse was to pause.

"Come in, M. de Villefort," said the king, "come in."

Villefort bowed, and, advancing a few steps, waited until the king should interrogate him.

"M. de Villefort," said Louis XVIII, "the Count de Blacas assures me you have some interesting information to communicate."

"Sire, the count is right, and I believe your majesty will think it equally important."

"In the first place, and before every thing else sir, is the bad news as great in your opinion as it is wished to make me believe?"

"Sire, I believe it to be most urgent, but I hope, by the speed I have used, that it is not irreparable."

"Speak as fully as you please, sir," said the king, who began to give way to the emotion which had shewed itself in Blacas' face and affected Villefort's voice,—"speak, sir, and pray begin at the beginning; I like order in every thing."

"Sire," said Villefort, "I will render a faithful report to your majesty, but I must entreat your forgiveness if my anxiety creates some obscurity in my language."

A glance at the king after this discreet and subtle exordium assured Villefort of the benignity of his august auditor, and he continued:—

"Sire, I have come as rapidly to Paris as possible, to inform your majesty that I have discovered, in the exercise of my duties, not a commonplace and insignificant plot, such as is every day got up in the lower ranks of the people, and in the army, but an actual conspiracy, a storm which menaces no less than the throne of your majesty. Sire, the usurper is arming three ships, he meditates some project, which, however mad, is yet, perhaps, terrible. At this moment he will have left Elba, to go whither I know not, but assuredly to attempt a landing either at Naples, or on the coast of Tuscany, or, perhaps, on the shore of France. Your majesty is well aware that the sovereign of the Isle of Elba has maintained his relations with Italy and France?"

"I am, sir," said the king, much agitated; "and recently we have had information that the Bonapartist clubs have had meetings in the Rue Saint-Jacques.   But proceed, I beg of you; how did you obtain these details?"

"Sire, they are the results of an examination which I have made of a man of Marseilles, whom I have watched for some time, and arrested on the day of my departure.   This person, a sailor, of turbulent character, and whom I suspected of Bonapartism, has been secretly to the Isle of Elba.   There he saw the grand marshal, who charged him with a verbal mission to a Bonapartist in Paris, whose name I could not extract from him; but this mission was to prepare men's minds for a return (it is the man who says this, sire)—a return which will soon occur."

"And where is this man?"

"In prison, sire?"

"And the matter seems serious to you?"

"So serious, sire, that when the circumstance surprised me in the midst of a family festival, on the very day of my betrothal, I left my bride and friends, postponing every thing, that I might hasten to lay at your majesty's feet the fears which impressed me, and the assurance of my devotion."

"True," said Louis XVIII, "was there not a marriage engagement between you and Mademoiselle de Saint-Méran?"

"Daughter of one of your majesty's most faithful servants."

"Yes, yes; but let us talk of this plot, M. de Villefort."

"Sire, I fear it is more than a plot; I fear it is a conspiracy."

"A conspiracy in these times," said Louis XVIII, smiling, "is a thing very easy to meditate, but more difficult to conduct to an end; inasmuch as re-established so recently on the throne of our ancestors, we have our eyes open at once upon the past, the present, and the future.   For the last ten months my ministers have redoubled their vigilance, in order to watch the shore of the Mediterranean.   If Bonaparte landed at Naples, the whole coalition would be on foot before he could even reach Piombino; if he land in Tuscany, he will be in an unfriendly territory; if he land in France, it must be with a handful of men, and the result of that is easily foretold, execrated as he is by the population.   Take courage, sir; but at the same time rely on our royal gratitude."

"Ah, here is M. Dandré!" cried De Blacas.

At this instant the minister of police appeared at the door, pale, trembling, and as if ready to faint.

Villefort was about to retire, but M. de Blacas, taking his hand, restrained him.

CHAPTER XI

THE OGRE OF CORSICA

AT the sight of this agitation Louis XVIII pushed from him violently the table at which he was writing.

"What ails you, M. le Baron?" he exclaimed. "You appear quite aghast. This trouble—this hesitation—have they any thing to do with what M. de Blacas has told me, and M. de Villefort has just confirmed?"

M. de Blacas moved suddenly towards the baron, but the fright of the courtier precluded the triumph of the statesman; and besides, as matters were, it was much more to his advantage that the prefect of police should triumph over him than that he should humiliate the prefect.

"Sire——" stammered the baron.

"Well, what is it?" asked Louis XVIII.

The minister of police, giving way to an impulse of despair, was about to throw himself at the feet of Louis XVIII, who retreated a step and frowned.

"Will you speak?" he said.

"Oh! sire, what a dreadful misfortune! I am, indeed, to be pitied. I can never forgive myself."

"Monsieur," said Louis XVIII, "I command you to speak."

"Well, sire, the usurper left Elba on the 26th February, and landed on the 1st of March."

"And where? In Italy?" asked the king eagerly.

"In France, sire, at a small port near Antibes, in the Gulf of Juan."

"The usurper landed in France, near Antibes, in the Gulf of Juan, 250 leagues from Paris, on the 1st of March, and you only acquired this information to-day, the 4th of March! Well, sir, what you tell me is impossible. You must have received a false report, or you have gone mad."

"Alas! sire, it is but too true!"

Louis made a gesture of indescribable anger and alarm, and then drew himself up as if this sudden blow had struck him at the same moment in heart and countenance.

"In France!" he cried, "the usurper in France! Then they did not watch over this man. Who knows? they were, perhaps, in league with him."

"Oh, sire!" exclaimed the Comte de Blacas, "M. Dandré is

96

not a man to be accused of treason! Sire, we have all been blind, and the minister of police has shared the general blindness, that is all."

"But——" said Villefort, and then suddenly checking himself, he was silent; then he continued, " Your pardon, sire," he said bowing, "my zeal carried me away. Will your majesty deign to excuse me?"

"Speak, sir, speak boldly," replied Louis. "You alone forewarned us of the evil; now try and aid us with the remedy!"

"Sire," said Villefort, "the usurper is detested in the south; and it seems to me that if he ventured into the south, it would be easy to raise Languedoc and Provence against him."

"Yes, assuredly," replied the minister; "but he is advancing by Gap and Sisteron."

"Advancing! he is advancing!" said Louis XVIII. "Is he then advancing on Paris?"

The minister of police kept a silence which was equivalent to a complete avowal.

"And Dauphiné, sir?" inquired the king of Villefort. "Do you think it possible to rouse that as well as Provence?"

"Sire, I am sorry to tell your majesty a cruel fact; but the feeling in Dauphiné is far from resembling that of Provence or Languedoc. The mountaineers are Bonapartists, sire."

"Then," murmured Louis, "he was well informed. And how many men had he with him?"

"I do not know, sire," answered the minister of police.

"What! you do not know? Have you neglected to obtain information of this circumstance? It is true this is of small importance," he added, with a withering smile.

"Sire, it was impossible to learn; the despatch simply stated the fact of the landing and the route taken by the usurper."

"And how did this despatch reach you?" inquired the king.

The minister bowed his head, and whilst a deep colour overspread his cheeks, he stammered out,—

"By the telegraph, sire."

Louis XVIII advanced a step, and folded his arms over his chest as Napoleon would have done.

"So then!" he exclaimed, turning pale with anger, "seven conjoined and allied armies overthrew that man. A miracle of Heaven replaced me on the throne of my fathers after five-and-twenty years of exile. I have, during those five-and-twenty years, studied, sounded, analysed the men and things of that France which was promised to me; and when I have attained the end of all my wishes the power I hold in my hands bursts and shatters me to atoms!"

"Sire, it is fatality!" murmured the minister, feeling that such a pressure, however, light for destiny, was sufficient to overwhelm a man.

C.M.——D

"What our enemies say of us is then true. We have learnt nothing, forgotten nothing! If I were betrayed as he was, I would console myself; but to be in the midst of persons elevated by myself to dignities, who ought to watch over me more preciously than over themselves; for my fortune is theirs!—before me they were nothing—after me they will be nothing, and perish miserably from incapacity—ineptitude! Oh, yes, sir! you are right—it is fatality!"

The minister was bowed beneath this crushing sarcasm. M. de Blacas wiped the moisture from his brow. Villefort smiled within himself, for he felt his increased importance.

"To fall!" continued King Louis, who at the first glance had sounded the abyss on which the monarchy hung suspended,—"to fall, and learn that fall by the telegraph! Oh! I would rather mount the scaffold of my brother, Louis XVI, than thus descend the staircase of the Tuileries driven away by ridicule. Ridicule, sir—why, you know not its power in France, and yet you ought to know it!"

"Sire, sire," murmured the minister, "for pity's——"

"Approach, M. de Villefort," resumed the king, addressing the young man, who, motionless and breathless, was listening to a conversation on which depended the destiny of a kingdom. "Approach, and tell monsieur that it is possible to know beforehand all that he has not known."

"Sire, it was really impossible to learn secrets which that man concealed from all the world."

"Really impossible! Yes—that is a great word, sir. Unfortunately, there are great words as there are great men; I have measured them. Really impossible for a minister who has an office, agents, spies, and fifteen hundred thousand francs for secret service money, to know what is going on at sixty leagues from the coast of France! Well, then, see, here is a gentleman who had none of these resources at his disposal—a gentleman, only a simple magistrate, who learned more than you with all your police, and who would have saved my crown, if, like you, he had the power of directing a telegraph."

The look of the minister of police was turned with concentrated spite on Villefort, who bent his head with the modesty of triumph.

"I do not mean that for you, Blacas," continued Louis XVIII; "for if you have discovered nothing, at least you have had the good sense to persevere in your suspicions. Any other than yourself would have considered the disclosure of M. de Villefort as insignificant, or else, dictated by a venal ambition."

These words were meant to allude to those which the minister of police had uttered with so much confidence an hour before.

Villefort understood the drift of the king. Any other person would, perhaps, have been too much overcome by the intoxication of praise; but he feared to make for himself a mortal enemy of the police minister, although he perceived Dandré was irrevocably lost. In fact, the minister who, in the plenitude of his power, had been unable to penetrate Napoleon's secret, might in the convulsions of his dying throes penetrate his (Villefort's) secret, for which end he had but to interrogate Dantès. He, therefore, came to the rescue of the crestfallen minister, instead of aiding to crush him.

"Sire," said Villefort, "the rapidity of the event must prove to your majesty that God alone can prevent it, by raising a tempest; what your majesty is pleased to attribute to me as profound perspicacity is simply owing to chance; and I have profited by that chance, like a good and devoted servant, that's all. Do not attribute to me more than I deserve, sire, that your majesty may never have occasion to recall the first opinion you have been pleased to form of me."

The minister of police thanked the young man by an eloquent look, and Villefort understood that he had succeeded in his design; that is to say, that without forfeiting the gratitude of the king, he had made a friend of one on whom, in case of necessity, he might rely.

"'T is well!" resumed the king. "And now, gentlemen," he continued, turning towards M. de Blacas and the minister of police, "I have no further occasion for you, and you may retire; what now remains to do is in the department of the minister of war."

"Fortunately, sire," said M. de Blacas, "we can rely on the army; your majesty knows how every report confirms their loyalty and attachment."

"Do not mention reports, sir, to me! for I know now what confidence to place in them. Yet, *àpropos* of reports, M. le Baron, what intelligence have you as to our affair in the Rue Saint-Jacques?"

"The affair in the Rue Saint-Jacques!" exclaimed Villefort, unable to repress an exclamation. Then suddenly pausing, he added, "Your pardon, sire, but my devotion to your majesty has made me forget, not the respect I have, for that is too deeply engraven in my heart, but the rules of etiquette."

"Say and act, sir!" replied the king; "you have acquired the right to inquire."

"Sire," replied the minister of police, "I came this moment to give your majesty fresh information which I had obtained on this head, when your majesty's attention was attracted by this terrible affair of the gulf, and now these facts will cease to interest your majesty."

"On the contrary, sir,—on the contrary," said Louis XVIII, "this affair seems to me to have a decided connexion with that which occupies our attention; and the death of General Quesnel will, perhaps, put us on the direct track of a great internal conspiracy."

At the name of General Quesnel Villefort trembled.

"All combines, sire," said the minister of police, "to ensure the probability that this death is not the result of a suicide, as we at first believed, but of an assassination. General Quesnel had quitted, as it appears, a Bonapartist club when he disappeared. An unknown person had been with him that morning, and made an appointment with him in the Rue Saint-Jacques; unfortunately, the general's valet-de-chambre, who was dressing his hair at the moment when the stranger entered, heard the street mentioned, but did not catch the number."

As the police minister related this to the king, Villefort, who seemed as if his very existence hung on his lips, turned alternately red and pale. The king looked towards him.

"Do you not think with me, M. de Villefort, that General Quesnel, whom they believed attached to the usurper, but who was really entirely devoted to me, has perished the victim of a Bonapartist ambush?"

"It is probable, sire," replied Villefort. "But is this all that is known?"

"They are on the traces of the man who appointed the meeting with him?"

"On his traces?" said Villefort.

"Yes, the servant has given his description. He is a man of from fifty to fifty-two years of age, brown, with black eyes, covered with shaggy eyebrows, and a thick moustache. He was dressed in a blue frock-coat, buttoned up to the chin, and wore at his button-hole the rosette of an officer of the Legion of Honour. Yesterday an individual was followed exactly corresponding with this description, but he was lost sight of at the corner of the Rue de la Jussienne and the Rue Coq-Héron."

Villefort leaned on the back of an arm-chair, for in proportion as the minister of police spoke, he felt his legs bend under him; but when he learnt that the unknown had escaped the vigilance of the agent who followed him, he breathed again.

"Continue to seek for this man, sir," said the king to the minister of police; "for if, as all conspires to convince me, General Quesnel, who would have been so useful to us at this moment, has been murdered, his assassins, Bonapartists or not, shall be cruelly punished."

It required all Villefort's *sang-froid* not to betray the terror with which this declaration of the king inspired him.

"How strange!" continued the king, with some asperity, "the police thinks all is said when it says, 'A murder has been committed,' and particularly when it adds, 'And we are on the trace of the guilty persons.'"

"Sire, your majesty will, I trust, be amply satisfied on this point, at least."

"We shall see; I will no longer detain you, baron. M. de Villefort, you must be fatigued after so long a journey, go and repose yourself. Of course you stopped at your father's?"

A faintness came over Villefort.

"No, sire," he replied, "I alighted at the Hôtel de Madrid, in the Rue de Tournon."

"But you have seen him?"

"Sire, I went straight to M. the Comte de Blacas."

"But you will see him, then?"

"I think not, sire."

"Ah, I forgot," said Louis, smiling in a manner which proved that all these questions were not made without a motive,— "I forgot you and M. Noirtier are not on the best terms possible, and that this is another sacrifice made to the royal cause, and for which you should be recompensed."

"Sire, the kindness your majesty deigns to evince towards me is a recompense which so far surpasses my utmost ambition that I have nothing more to request."

"Never mind, sir, we will not forget you, make your mind easy, in the meanwhile" (the king here detached the cross of the Legion of Honour he usually wore over his blue coat, near the cross of Saint-Louis, above the order of Notre-Dame-du-Mont-Carmel and Saint-Lazare, and gave it to Villefort)— "in the meanwhile take this cross."

"Sire," said Villefort, "your majesty mistakes, this cross is that of an officer."

"*Ma foi!*" said Louis XVIII, "take it, such as it is, for I have not the time to procure you another. Blacas, let it be your care to see that the brevet is made out and sent to M. de Villefort."

Villefort's eyes were filled with tears of joy and pride, he took the cross and kissed it.

"And now," he said, "may I inquire what are the orders with which your majesty deigns to honour me?"

"Take what rest you require, and remember that, unable to serve me here in Paris, you may be of the greatest service to me at Marseilles."

"Sire," replied Villefort, bowing, "in an hour I shall have quitted Paris."

"Go, sir," said the king; "and should I forget you (king's memories are short) do not be afraid to bring yourself to my recollection. M. le Baron, send for the minister of war. Blacas, remain."

"Ah, sir," said the minister of police to Villefort, as they left the Tuileries, "you enter by the right door, your fortune is made."

"Will it be long first?" muttered Villefort, saluting the minister, whose career was ended, and looking about him for a hackney-coach. One passed at the moment, which he hailed: he gave his address to the driver, and springing in, threw himself on the seat, and gave loose to dreams of ambition.

Ten minutes afterwards Villefort reached his hotel, ordered his horses in two hours, and desired to have his breakfast brought to him. He was about to commence his repast when the sound of the bell, rung by a free and firm hand, was heard. The valet opened the door, and Villefort heard his name pronounced.

"Who could know that I was here already?" said the young man.

The valet entered.

"Well," said Villefort, "what is it?—Who rang?—Who asked for me?"

"A stranger, who will not send in his name."

"A stranger who will not send in his name! What can he want with me?"

"He wishes to speak to you."

"To me?"

"Yes."

"Did he mention my name?"

"Yes."

"What sort of person is he?"

"Why, sir, a man of about fifty."

"Short or tall?"

"About your own height, sir."

"Dark or fair?"

"Dark—very dark: with black eyes, black hair, black eyebrows."

"And how dressed?" asked Villefort, quickly.

"In a blue frock-coat, buttoned up close, decorated with the Legion of Honour."

"It is he!" said Villefort, turning pale.

"Eh, *pardieu!*" said the individual whose description we have twice given, entering the door, "what a great deal of ceremony! Is it the custom of Marseilles for sons to keep their fathers waiting in their anterooms?"

"Father!" cried Villefort, "then I was not deceived; I felt sure it must be you."

"Well, then, if you felt so sure," replied the new comer, putting his cane in a corner and his hat on a chair, "allow me to say, my dear Gérard, that it was not very filial of you to keep me waiting at the door."

"Leave us, Germain," said Villefort.

The servant quitted the apartment with evident signs of astonishment.

CHAPTER XII

FATHER AND SON

M. NOIRTIER—for it was, indeed, he who entered—followed with his eyes the servant until he had closed the door, and then, fearing, no doubt, that he might be overheard in the antechamber, he opened the door again, nor was the precaution useless, as appeared from the rapid retreat of Germain, who proved that he was not exempt from the sin which ruined our first parents.

M. Noirtier then took the trouble to close carefully the door of the antechamber, then that of the bedchamber, and then extended his hand to Villefort, who had followed all his motions with surprise, which he could not conceal.

"Well, now, my dear Gérard," said he to the young man, with a very significant look, "do you know you seem as if you were not very glad to see me?"

"My dear father," said Villefort, "I am, on the contrary, delighted, but I so little expected your visit that it has somewhat overcome me."

"But, my dear fellow," replied M. Noirtier, seating himself, "I might say the same thing to you when you announce to me your wedding for the 28th of February and on the 4th of March here you are in Paris."

"And if I have come, my dear father," said Gérard, drawing closer to M. Noirtier, "do not complain, for it is for you that I came, and my journey will save you."

"Ah, indeed!" said M. Noirtier, stretching himself out at his ease in the chair. "Really, pray tell me all about it, M. le Magistrat, for it must be interesting."

"Father, you have heard speak of a certain club of Bonapartists held in the Rue Saint-Jacques?"

"No. 53: yes, I am vice-president."

"Father, your coolness makes me shudder."

"Why, my dear boy, when a man has been proscribed by the mountaineers, has escaped from Paris in a hay-cart, been hunted in the *landes* of Bordeaux by M. Robespierre's bloodhounds, he becomes accustomed to most things. But go on, what about the club in the Rue Saint-Jacques?"

"Why they induced General Quesnel to go there, and General Quesnel, who quitted his own house at nine o'clock in the evening, was found the next day in the Seine."

"And who told you this fine story?"

"The king himself."

"Well, then, in return for your story," continued Noirtier, " I will tell you one."

"My dear father, I think I already know what you are about to tell me."

"Ah, you have heard of the landing of the emperor?"

"Not so loud, father, I entreat of you—for your own sake as well as mine. Yes, I heard this news, and knew it even before you could; for three days ago I posted from Marseilles to Paris with all possible speed, and half desperate because I could not send with a wish two hundred leagues a-head of me the thought which was agitating my brain."

"Three days ago? you are crazy. Why three days ago the emperor had not landed."

"No matter, I was aware of his project."

"How did you learn it?"

"By a letter addressed to you from the Isle of Elba."

"To me?"

"To you, and which I discovered in the pocket-book of the messenger; had that letter fallen into the hands of another, you, my dear father, would, probably, ere this have been shot."

Villefort's father laughed.

"Come, come," said he, "it appears that the Restoration has learned from the Empire the mode of settling affairs speedily. Shot, my dear boy! you go ahead with a vengeance. Where is this letter you talk about? I know you too well to suppose you would allow such a thing to pass you."

"I burnt it, for fear that even a fragment should remain; for that letter must have effected your condemnation."

"And the destruction of your future prospects," replied Noirtier; "yes, I can easily comprehend that. But I have nothing to fear whilst I have you to protect me."

"I do better than that, sir—I save you."

"You do? why really, the thing becomes more and more dramatic—explain yourself."

"I must refer again to the club in the Rue Saint-Jacques."

"It appears that this club is rather a bore to the police. Why didn't they search more vigilantly? they would have found——"

"They have not found, but they are on the track."

"Yes, that's the usual phrase, I know it well. When the police is at fault it declares that it is on the track, and the government patiently awaits the day when it comes to say, with a sneaking air, that the track is lost."

"Yes, but they have found a corpse; the general has been killed, and in all countries they call that a murder."

C.M.—D*

"A murder do you call it? why there is nothing to prove that the general was murdered. People are found every day in the Seine, having thrown themselves in, or have been drowned from not knowing how to swim."

"Father, you know very well that the general was not a man to drown himself in despair, and people do not bathe in the Seine in the month of January. No, no, do not mistake, this death was a murder in every sense of the word."

"And who thus designated it?"

"The king himself."

"The king! I thought he was philosopher enough to allow that there was no murder in politics. In politics, my dear fellow, you know, as well as I do, there are no men, but ideas—no feelings, but interests; in politics we do not kill a man, we only remove an obstacle, that is all. Would you like to know how matters have progressed? Well, I will tell you. It was thought reliance might be placed in General Quesnel, he was recommended to us from the Isle of Elba; one of us went to him and invited him to the Rue Saint-Jacques, where he would find some friends. He came there, and the plan was unfolded to him of the leaving Elba, the projected landing, &c. When he had heard and comprehended all to the fullest extent, he replied that he was a royalist. Then all looked at each other,—he was made to take an oath, and did so, but with such an ill grace that it was really tempting Providence to swear thus, and yet, in spite of that, the general was allowed to depart free—perfectly free. Yet he did not return home. What could that mean? why, my dear fellow, that on leaving us he lost his way, that's all. A murder! really, Villefort, you surprise me. You, a deputy procureur, to found an accusation on such bad premises! Did I ever say to you, when you were fulfilling your character as a royalist, and cut off the head of one of my party, 'My son, you have committed a murder?' No, I said, 'Very well, sir, you have gained the victory, to-morrow, perchance, it will be our turn.'"

"But, father, take care when our turn comes, our revenge will be sweeping."

"I do not understand you."

"You rely on the usurper's return?"

"We do."

"You are mistaken, he will not advance two leagues into the interior of France without being followed, tracked, and caught like a wild beast."

"My dear fellow, the emperor is at this moment on the way to Grenoble, on the 10th or 12th he will be at Lyons, and on the 20th or 25th at Paris."

"The population will rise."

"Yes, to go and meet him."

"He has but a handful of men with him, and armies will be despatched against him."

"Yes, to escort him into the capital. Really, my dear Gérard, you are but a child; you think yourself well informed because a telegraph has told you three days after the landing, 'The usurper has landed at Cannes with several men. He is pursued.' But where is he? what is he doing? You do not know well, and in this way they will pursue him to Paris without drawing a trigger."

"Grenoble and Lyons are faithful cities, and will oppose to him an impassable barrier."

"Grenoble will open her gates to him with enthusiasm—all Lyons will hasten to welcome him. Believe me, we are as well informed as you, and our police is as good as your own. Would you like a proof of it? well, you wished to conceal your journey from me, and yet I knew of your arrival half an hour after you had passed the barrier. You gave your direction to no one but your postilion, yet I have your address, and in proof I am here the very instant you are going to sit at table. Ring, then, if you please, for a second knife, fork, and plate, and we will dine together."

"Indeed!" replied Villefort, looking at his father with astonishment, "you really do seem very well informed."

"Eh? the thing is simple enough. You who are in power have only the means that money produces—we who are in expectation have those which devotion prompts."

"Devotion!" said Villefort, with a sneer.

"Yes, devotion, for that is, I believe, the phrase for hopeful ambition."

And Villefort's father extended his hand to the bell-rope, to summon the servant whom his son had not called. Villefort arrested his arm.

"Wait, my dear father," said the young man, "one other word."

"Say it."

"However ill-conducted is the royalist police, they yet know one terrible thing."

"What is that?"

"The description of the man who, on the morning of the day when General Quesnel disappeared, presented himself at his house."

"Oh, the admirable police have found out that, have they? And what may be that description?"

"Brown complexion; hair, eyebrows, and whiskers, black; blue frock coat, buttoned up to the chin; rosette of an officer of the Legion of Honour in his button-hole, a hat with wide brim, and a cane."

"Ah! ah! that is it, is it?" said Noirtier, "and why, then have they not laid hands on the individual?"

"Because yesterday, or the day before, they lost sight of him at the corner of the Rue Coq-Héron."

"Didn't I say your police was good for nothing?"

"Yes, but still it may lay hands on him."

"True," said Noirtier, looking carelessly around him, "true, if this individual were not warned as he is;" and he added with a smile, "he will consequently change looks and costume."

At these words he rose, and put off his frock-coat and cravat, went towards a table on which lay all the requisites of the toilette for his son, lathered his face, took a razor, and, with a firm hand, cut off the whiskers that might have compromised him and gave the police so decided a trace. Villefort watched him with alarm, not divested of admiration.

His whiskers cut off, Noirtier gave another turn to his hair, took, instead of his black cravat, a coloured neckerchief, which lay at the top of an open portmanteau, put on in lieu of his blue and high-buttoned frock-coat a coat of Villefort's, of dark brown, and sloped away in front, tried on before the glass a narrow-brimmed hat of his son's, which appeared to fit him perfectly, and leaving his cane in the corner where he had deposited it, he made to whistle in his powerful hand a small bamboo switch, which the dandy deputy used when he walked, and which aided in giving him that easy swagger, which was one of his principal characteristics.

"Well," he said, turning towards his wondering son, when this disguise was completed,—"well, do you think your police will recognise me now?"

"No, father," stammered Villefort, "at least, I hope not."

"And now, my dear boy," continued Noirtier, "I rely on your prudence to remove all the things which I leave in your care."

"Oh, rely on me," said Villefort.

"Yes, yes! and now I believe you are right, and that you have really saved my life, but be assured I will return the obligation to you hereafter."

Villefort shook his head.

"You are not convinced yet?"

"I hope, at least, that you may be mistaken."

"Shall you see the king again?"

"Perhaps."

"Would you pass in his eyes for a prophet?"

"Prophets of evil are not in favour at the court, father."

"True, but some day they do them justice; and supposing a second restoration, you would then pass for a great man."

"Well, what should I say to the king?"

"Say this to him:—'Sire, you are deceived as to the feeling in France, as to the opinions of the towns, and the prejudices of the army; he whom in Paris you call the ogre of Corsica, who at Nevers is styled the usurper, is already saluted as Bonaparte at Lyons, and emperor at Grenoble. You think he is tracked, pursued, captured: he is advancing as rapidly as his own eagles. The soldiers you believe dying with hunger, worn out with fatigue, ready to desert, increase like atoms of snow about the rolling ball which hastens onward. Sire, go, leave France to its real master, to him who did not buy, but acquired it—go, sire, not that you incur any risk, for your adversary is powerful enough to shew you mercy, but because it would be humiliating for a grandson of Saint-Louis to owe his life to the man of Arcola, Marengo, Austerlitz. Tell him this, Gérard, or, rather, tell him nothing. Keep your journey a secret, do not boast of what you have come to Paris to do, or have done; return with all speed, enter Marseilles at night, and your house by the back-door, and there remain quiet, submissive, secret, and, above all, inoffensive, for this time I swear to you we shall act like powerful men who know their enemies. Go, my son—go, my dear Gérard, and by your obedience to my paternal orders, or, if you prefer it, friendly counsels, we will keep you in your place. This will be," added Noirtier, with a smile, "one means by which you may a second time save me, if the political balance should one day place you high and me low. Adieu, my dear Gérard, and at your next journey alight at my door."

Noirtier left the room when he had finished, with the same calmness that had characterised him during the whole of this remarkable and trying conversation.

Villefort, pale and agitated, ran to the window, put aside the curtain, and saw him pass, cool and collected, by two or three ill-looking men at the corner of the street, and were there, perhaps, to arrest a man with black whiskers, and a blue frock-coat, and hat with broad brim.

Villefort stood watching, breathless, until his father had disappeared at the Rue Bussy. Then he turned to the various articles he had left behind him, put at the bottom of his portmanteau his black cravat and blue frock-coat, threw the hat into a dark closet, broke the cane into small bits, and flung it in the fire, put on his travelling-cap, and calling his valet, checked with a look the thousand questions he was ready to ask, paid his bill, sprung into his carriage, which was ready, learned at Lyons that Bonaparte had entered Grenoble, and in the midst of the tumult which prevailed along the road, at length reached Marseilles, a prey to all the hopes and fears which enter into the heart of man with ambition and its first successes.

CHAPTER XIII

THE HUNDRED DAYS

M. NOIRTIER was a true prophet, and things progressed rapidly as he had predicted. Every one knows the history of the famous return from Elba, a return which, without example in the past, will probably remain without imitation in the future.

Louis XVIII made but a faint attempt to parry this unexpected blow; the monarchy he had scarcely reconstructed tottered on its precarious foundation, and it needed but a sign of the emperor to hurl to the ground all this edifice composed of ancient prejudices and new ideas. Villefort therefore gained nothing save the king's gratitude (which was rather likely to injure him at the present time), and the cross of the Legion of Honour, which he had the prudence not to wear, although M. de Blacas had duly forwarded the brevet.

Napoleon would, doubtless, have deprived Villefort of his office had it not been for Noirtier, who was all-powerful at the court; and thus the Girondin of '93 and the Senator of 1806 protected him who so lately had been his protector.

All Villefort's influence barely enabled him to stifle the secret Dantès had so nearly divulged.

The king's procureur alone was deprived of his office, being suspected of royalism.

However, scarcely was the imperial power established, that is, scarcely had the emperor re-entered the Tuileries and issued his numerous orders from that little cabinet into which we have introduced our readers, and on the table of which he found Louis XVIII's snuff-box, half full, than Marseilles began to rekindle the flames of civil war, and it required but little to excite the populace to acts of far greater violence than the shouts and insults with which they assailed the royalists whenever they ventured abroad.

Owing to this change, the worthy shipowner became at that moment, we will not say all-powerful—because Morrel was a prudent and rather a timid man, so much so, that many of the most zealous partisans of Bonaparte accused him of "*moderation*,"—but sufficiently influential to make a demand in favour of Dantès.

Villefort retained his place, but his marriage was put off until a more favourable opportunity. If the emperor remained on the throne, Gérard required a different alliance to aid his career; if Louis XVIII returned, the influence of M. Saint-Méran and himself became double, and the marriage must be still more suitable.

The deputy-procureur was, therefore, the first magistrate of Marseilles, when one morning his door opened, and M. Morrel was announced.

Any one else would have hastened to receive him, but Villefort was a man of ability, and he knew this would be a sign of weakness. He made Morrel wait in the antechamber, although he had no one with him, for the simple reason that the king's procureur always makes every one wait; and after quarter of an hour passed in reading the papers, he ordered M. Morrel to be admitted.

Morrel expected Villefort would be dejected; he found him, as he had found him six weeks before, calm, firm, and full of that glacial politeness, that most insurmountable barrier which separates the well-bred and the vulgar man.

He had penetrated into Villefort's cabinet, convinced the magistrate would tremble at the sight of him; on the contrary, he felt a cold shudder all over him when he beheld Villefort seated, his elbow on his desk, and his head leaning on his hand. He stopped at the door; Villefort gazed at him as if he had some difficulty in recognising him; then, after a brief interval, during which the honest shipowner turned his hat in his hands,—

"M. Morrel, I believe?" said Villefort.

"Yes, sir."

"Come nearer," said the magistrate, with a patronising wave of the hand; "and tell me to what circumstance I owe the honour of this visit?"

"Do you not guess, monsieur?" asked Morrel.

"Not in the least; but if I can serve you in any way I shall be delighted."

"Every thing depends on you."

"Explain yourself, pray."

"Monsieur," said Morrel, recovering his assurance as he proceeded, "do you recollect that a few days before the landing of his majesty the emperor, I came to intercede for a young man, the mate of my ship, who was accused of being concerned in a correspondence with the Isle of Elba, and what was the other day a crime is to-day a title to favour; you then served Louis XVIII, and you did not shew any favour —it was your duty; to-day you serve Napoleon, and you ought to protect him—it is equally your duty; I come, therefore, to ask what has become of him?"

Villefort made a violent effort. "What is his name?" said he; "tell me his name."

"Edmond Dantès."

Villefort would evidently rather have stood opposite the muzzle of a pistol, at five-and-twenty paces, than have heard this name pronounced; but he betrayed no emotion.

"Dantès!" repeated he; "Edmond Dantès?"

"Yes, monsieur."

Villefort opened a large register, then went to a table, from the table turned to his registers, and then turning to Morrel:

"Are you quite sure you are not mistaken, monsieur?" said he, in the most natural tone in the world.

Had Morrel been a more quick-sighted man, or better versed in these matters, he would have been surprised at the king's procureur answering him on such a subject, instead of referring him to the governors of the prison or the prefect of the department. But Morrel, disappointed in his expectations of exciting fear, saw only in its place condescension. Villefort had calculated rightly.

"No," said Morrel, "I am not mistaken. I have known him ten years, and the last four he has been in my service. Do not you recollect, I came about six weeks ago to beseech your clemency, as I come to-day to beseech your justice; you received me very coldly? Oh! the royalists were very severe with the Bonapartists in those days."

"Monsieur," returned Villefort, "I was then a royalist, because I believe the Bourbons not only the heirs to the throne but the chosen of the nation. The miraculous return of Napoleon has conquered me; the legitimate monarch is he who is loved by his people."

"That's right!" cried Morrel. "I like to hear you speak thus; and I augur well for Edmond from it."

"Wait a moment," said Villefort, turning over the leaves of a register.

"I have it!—a sailor, who was about to marry a young Catalan girl. I recollect now, it was a very serious charge."

"How so?"

"You know that when he left here he was taken to the Palais de Justice."

"Well?"

"I made my report to the authorities at Paris, and a week after he was carried off."

"Carried off!" said Morrel. "What can they have done with him?"

"Oh! he has been taken to Fenestrelles, to Pignerol, or to the Iles Sainte-Marguerite. Some fine morning he will return to assume the command of your vessel."

"Come when he will, it shall be kept for him. But how is it he is not already returned? It seems to me the first care of government should be to set at liberty those who have suffered for their adherence to it."

"Do not be too hasty, M. Morrel," replied Villefort. "The order of imprisonment came from high authority, and the order for his liberation must proceed from the same source: and, as Napoleon has scarcely been reinstated a fortnight, the letters have not yet been forwarded."

"But," said Morrel, "is there no way of expediting all these formalities of releasing him from his arrest?"

"There has been no arrest."

"How?"

"It is sometimes essential to government to cause a man's disappearance without leaving any traces, so that no written forms or documents may defeat their wishes."

"It might be so under the Bourbons; but at present——"

"It is always the same, my dear Morrel, since the reign of Louis XIV. The emperor is more strict in prison discipline than even Louis himself, and the number of prisoners whose names are not on the register is incalculable."

Had Morrel even any suspicions, so much kindness would have dispelled them.

"Well, M. de Villefort, how would you advise me to act?" asked he.

"Petition the minister."

"Oh, I know what that is; the minister receives two hundred every day, and does not read three."

"That is true; but he will read a petition countersigned and presented by me."

"And will you undertake to deliver it?"

"With the greatest pleasure. Dantès was then guilty, and now he is innocent; and it is as much my duty to free him as it was to condemn him."

"But how shall I address the minister?"

"Sit down there," said Villefort, giving up his place to Morrel, "and write what I dictate."

"Will you be so good?"

"Certainly. But lose no time; we have lost too much already."

"That is true. Only think that perhaps this poor young man is pining in captivity."

Villefort shuddered at this picture; but he was too far gone to recede: Dantès must be crushed beneath the weight of Villefort's ambition.

Villefort dictated a petition, in which, from an excellent intention no doubt, Dantès' services were exaggerated, and he was made out one of the most active agents of Napoleon's return. It was evident that at the sight of this document the minister would instantly release him.

The petition finished, Villefort read it aloud.

"That will do," said he; "leave the rest to me."

"Will the petition go soon?"

"To-day."

"Countersigned by you?"

"The best thing I can do will be to certify the truth of the contents of your petition."'

And, sitting down, Villefort wrote the certificate at the bottom.

"What more is to be done?"

"I will answer for every thing."

This assurance charmed Morrel, who took leave of Villefort, and hastened to announce to old Dantès that he would soon see his son.

As for Villefort, instead of sending it to Paris, he carefully preserved the petition that so fearfully compromised Dantès, in the hopes of an event that seemed not unlikely, that is, a second restoration.

Dantès remained a prisoner, and heard not the noise of the fall of Louis XVIII's throne.

Twice during the Hundred Days had Morrel renewed his demand, and twice had Villefort soothed him with promises. At last there was Waterloo, and Morrel came no more: he had done all that was in his power, and any fresh attempt would only compromise himself uselessly.

Louis XVIII remounted the throne, Villefort demanded and obtained the situation of king's procureur at Toulouse, and a fortnight afterwards married Renée.

Danglars comprehended the full extent of the wretched fate that overwhelmed Dantès, and, like all men of small abilities, he termed this a *decree of Providence*. But when Napoleon returned to Paris Danglars' heart failed him, and he feared at every instant to behold Dantès eager for vengeance: he therefore informed M. Morrel of his wish to quit the sea, and obtained a recommendation from him to a Spanish merchant, into whose service he entered at the end of March, that is, ten or twelve days after Napoleon's return. He then left for Madrid, and was no more heard of.

Fernand understood nothing except that Dantès was absent. What had become of him? He cared not to inquire. Only during the respite the absence of his rival afforded him, he reflected partly on the means of deceiving Mercédès as to the cause of his absence, partly on plans of emigration and abduction, as from time to time he sat sad and motionless on the summit of Cape Pharo, at the spot from whence Marseilles and the village des Catalans are visible, watching for the apparition of a young and handsome man, who was for him also the messenger of vengeance. Fernand's mind was made up: he would shoot Dantès, and then kill himself. But

Fernand was mistaken; a man of his disposition never kills himself, for he constantly hopes.

During this time the empire made a last appeal, and every man in France capable of bearing arms rushed to obey the summons of their emperor.

Fernand departed with the rest, bearing with him the terrible thought, that perhaps his rival was behind him, and would marry Mercédès.

Had Fernand really meant to kill himself, he would have done so when he parted from Mercédès. His devotion, and the compassion he showed for her misfortunes, produced the effect they always produce on noble minds; Mercédès had always had a sincere regard for Fernand, and this was now strengthened by gratitude.

"My brother," said she, as she placed his knapsack on his shoulders, "be careful of yourself; for if you are killed I shall be alone in the world."

These words infused a ray of hope into Fernand's heart. Should Dantès not return Mercédès might one day be his. Mercédès was left alone to gaze on this vast plain that had never seemed so barren, and the sea that had never seemed so vast.

Sometimes she stood mute and motionless as a statue, gazing towards Marseilles; at other times gazing on the sea, and debating as to whether it were not better to cast herself into the abysses of the ocean, and thus end her woes.

It was not want of courage that prevented her putting this resolution into execution; but her religious feelings came to her aid and saved her.

Caderousse was, like Fernand, enrolled in the army; but, being married, and eight years older, he was merely sent to the frontier.

Old Dantès, who was only sustained by hope, lost all hope at Napoleon's downfall. Five months after he had been separated from his son, and almost at the very hour at which he was arrested, he breathed his last in Mercédès' arms.

M. Morrel paid the expenses of his funeral and the few small debts the poor old man had contracted.

There was more than benevolence in this action; there was courage; for to assist, even on his death-bed, the father of so dangerous a Bonapartist as Dantès was stigmatised as a crime.

CHAPTER XIV

THE TWO PRISONERS

A YEAR after Louis XVIII's restoration a visit was made by the inspector-general of prisons.

Dantès heard from the recesses of his cell the noises made by the preparations for receiving him,—sounds that at the depth where he lay would have been inaudible to any but the ear of a prisoner, who could distinguish the plash of the drop of water that every hour fell from the roof of his dungeon. He guessed something uncommon was passing among the living; but he had so long ceased to have any intercourse with the world that he looked upon himself as dead.

The inspector visited the cells and dungeons, one after another, of several of the prisoners, whose good behaviour or stupidity recommended them to the clemency of the government, the inspector inquired how they were fed, and if they had any thing to demand. The universal response was, that the fare was detestable, and that they required their freedom.

The inspector asked if they had anything else to demand. They shook their heads! What could they desire beyond their liberty?

The inspector turned smilingly to the governor.

"I do not know what reason government can assign for these useless visits: when you see one prisoner you see all,—always the same thing,—ill-fed and innocent. Are there any others?"

"Yes, the dangerous and mad prisoners are in the dungeons."

"Let us visit them," said the inspector, with an air of fatigue. "I must fulfil my mission. Let us descend."

"Let us first send for two soldiers," said the governor. "The prisoners sometimes, through mere uneasiness of life, and in order to be sentenced to death, commit acts of useless violence, and you might fall a victim."

"Take all needful precautions," replied the inspector.

Two soldiers were accordingly sent for, and the inspector descended a stair so foul, so humid, so dark, that the very sight affected the eye, the smell, and the respiration.

"Oh," cried the inspector, "who can live here?"

"A most dangerous conspirator, a man we are ordered to keep the most strict watch over, as he is daring and resolute."

"He is alone?"

"Certainly."

"How long has he been there?"

"Nearly a year."

"Was he placed here when he first arrived?"

"No, not until he attempted to kill the turnkey."

"To kill the turnkey!"

"Yes, the very one who is lighting us. Is it not true, Antoine?" asked the governor.

"True enough; he wanted to kill me!" replied the turnkey.

"He must be mad," said the inspector.

"He is worse than that; he is a devil!" returned the turnkey.

"Shall I complain of him?" demanded the inspector.

"Oh, no; it is useless. Besides, he is almost mad now, and in another year he will be quite so."

"So much the better for him; he will suffer less," said the inspector.

He was, as this remark shews, a man full of philanthropy, and in every way fit for his office.

"You are right, sir," replied the governor; "and this remark proves that you have deeply considered the subject. Now we have in a dungeon about twenty feet distant, and to which you descend by another stair, an abbé, ancient leader of a party in Italy, who has been here since 1811, and in 1813 he went mad, and the change is astonishing. He used to weep, he now laughs; he grew thin, he now grows fat. You had better see him, for his madness is amusing."

"I will see them both," returned the inspector; "I must conscientiously perform my duty."

This was the inspector's first visit: he wished to display his authority.

"Let us visit this one first," added he.

"Willingly," replied the governor, and he signed to the turnkey to open the door. At the sound of the key turning in the lock, and the creaking of the hinges, Dantès, who was crouched in a corner of the dungeon, raised his head.

At the sight of a stranger, lighted by two turnkeys, accompanied by two soldiers, and to whom the governor spoke bareheaded, Dantès, who guessed the truth, and that the moment to address himself to the superior authorities was come, sprang forward with clasped hands.

The soldiers presented their bayonets, for they thought he was about to attack the inspector, and the latter recoiled two or three steps. Dantès saw he was represented as a dangerous prisoner. Then infusing all the humility he possessed into his eyes and voice, he addressed the inspector, and sought to inspire him with pity.

The inspector listened attentively, then turning to the governor observed, "He will become religious—he is already more gentle; he is afraid and retreated before the bayonets—madmen are not afraid of any thing; I made some curious observations on this at Clarenton." Then turning to the prisoner, "What do you demand?" said he.

"What crime I have committed—to be tried; and if I am guilty, I may be shot; if innocent, I may be set at liberty."

"Are you well fed?" asked the inspector.

"I believe so—I know not, but that matters little; what matters really, not only to me, but to every one, is that an innocent man should languish in prison, the victim of an infamous denunciation."

"You are very humble to-day," remarked the governor, "you are not so always; the other day, for instance, when you tried to kill the turnkey."

"It is true, sir, and I beg his pardon, for he has always been very good to me: but I was mad."

"And you are not so any longer?"

"No! captivity has subdued me—I have been here so long."

"So long?—when were you arrested, then?" asked the inspector.

"The 28th of February, 1815, at half-past two in the afternoon."

"To-day is the 30th of June, 1816; why, it is but seventeen months."

"Only seventeen months!" replied Dantès; "oh, you do not know what is seventeen months in prison!—seventeen ages rather, especially to a man who, like me, had arrived at the summit of his ambition—to a man who, like me, was on the point of marrying a woman he adored, who saw an honourable career open before him, and who loses all in an instant, who sees his prospects destroyed, and is ignorant of the fate of his affianced wife, and whether his aged father be still living! Seventeen months' captivity to a sailor accustomed to the boundless ocean is a worse punishment than human crime ever merited. Have pity on me, then, and ask for me, not indulgence, but a trial—let me know my crime and my sentence, for incertitude is worse than all."

"We shall see," said the inspector; then turning to the governor, "On my word, the poor devil touches me; you must shew me the proofs against him."

"Certainly, but you will find terrible notes against him."

"Monsieur," continued Dantès, "I know it is not in your

power to release me, but you can plead for me, you can have me tried, and that is all I ask."

"Light me," said the inspector.

"Monsieur," cried Dantès, "I can tell by your voice you are touched with pity; tell me at least to hope."

"I cannot tell you that," replied the inspector; "I can only promise to examine into your case."

"Oh, I am free!—then I am saved!"

"Who arrested you?"

"M. Villefort; see him, and hear what he says."

"M. Villefort is no longer at Marseilles, he is now at Toulouse."

"I am no longer surprised at my detention," murmured Dantès, "since my only protector is removed."

"Had M. de Villefort any cause of personal dislike to you?"

"None, on the contrary, he was very kind to me."

"I can then rely on the notes he has left concerning you?"

"Entirely."

"That is well; wait patiently, then."

Dantès fell on his knees, and prayed earnestly. The door closed, but this time a fresh inmate was left with Dantès, Hope.

"Will you see the register at once," asked the governor, "or proceed to the other cell?"

"Let us visit them all," said the inspector; "if I once mounted the stairs I should never have the courage to descend."

"Ah, this one is not like the other, and his madness is less affecting than the reason of his neighbour."

"What is his folly?"

"He fancies he possesses an immense treasure: the first year he offered government a million francs (40,000*l*.) for his release, the second two, the third three, and so on progressively, he is now in his fifth year of captivity, he will ask to speak to you in private, and offer you five millions."

"How curious! what is his name?"

"L'Abbé Faria."

"No. 27," said the inspector.

"It is here; unlock the door, Antoine."

The turnkey obeyed, and the inspector gazed curiously into the chamber of the *mad abbé*.

In the centre of the cell, in a circle traced with a fragment of plaster detached from the wall, sat a man whose tattered garments scarcely covered him. He was drawing in this circle geometrical lines, and seemed as much absorbed in his problem as Archimedes when the soldier of Marcellus slew him.

He did not move at the sound of the door, and continued

his problem until the flash of the torches lighted up with an unwonted glare the sombre walls of his cell, then raising his head he perceived with astonishment the number of persons in his cell.

"What do you demand?" said the inspector.

"I, monsieur!" replied the abbé, with an air of surprise, "I demand nothing."

"You do not understand," continued the inspector; "I am sent here by government to visit the prisoners, and hear the requests of the prisoners."

"Oh, that is different," cried the abbé; "and we shall understand each other, I hope."

"There now," whispered the governor, "it is just as I told you."

"Monsieur," continued the prisoner, "I am the Abbé Faria, born at Rome. I was for twenty years Cardinal Spada's secretary; I was arrested, why I know not, in 1811, since then I have demanded my liberty from the Italian and French government."

"Why from the French government?"

"Because I was arrested at Piombino, and I presume that, like Milan and Florence, Piombino has become the capital of some French department."

"Ah!" said the inspector, "you have not the latest intelligence from Italy."

"They date from the day on which I was arrested," returned the Abbé Faria; "and as the Emperor had created the kingdom of Rome for his infant son, I presume that he has realised the dream of Machiavel and Cæsar Borgia, which was to make Italy one vast kingdom."

"Monsieur," returned the inspector, "Providence has changed this gigantic plan you advocate so warmly."

"It is the only means of rendering Italy happy and independent."

"Very possibly, only I am not come to discuss politics, but to inquire if you have any thing to ask or complain of."

"The food is the same as in other prisons,—that is very bad, the lodging is very unwholesome, but on the whole passable for a dungeon, but it is not that which I speak of, but a secret I have to reveal of the greatest importance."

"We are coming to the point," whispered the governor.

"It is for that reason I am delighted to see you," continued the abbé, "although you have disturbed me in a most important calculation, which if it succeeded would possibly change Newton's system. Could you allow me a few words in private?"

"What did I tell you?" said the governor.

"You knew him," returned the inspector.

"What you ask is impossible, monsieur," continued he, addressing Faria.

"But," said the abbé, "I would speak to you of a large sum amounting to five millions."

"The very sum you named," whispered in his turn the Inspector.

"However," continued Faria, perceiving the inspector was about to depart, "it is not absolutely necessary we should be alone; Monsieur the Governor can be present."

"Unfortunately," said the governor, "I know beforehand what you are about to say; it concerns your treasures, does it not?"

Faria fixed his eyes on him with an expression that would have convinced any one else of his sanity.

"Doubtless," said he; "of what else should I speak?"

"Monsieur l'Inspecteur," continued the governor, "I can tell you the story as well, for it has been dinned in my ears for the last four or five years."

"That proves," returned the abbé, "that you are like the idols of Holy Writ, who have ears and hear not."

"The government does not want your treasures," replied the inspector; "keep them until you are liberated."

The abbé's eyes glistened; he seized the inspector's hand.

"But what if I am not liberated," cried he, "and am detained here until my death? Had not government better profit by it? I will offer six millions, and I will content myself with the rest."

"On my word," said the inspector, in a low tone, "had I not been told beforehand this man was mad I should believe what he says."

"I am not mad!" replied Faria, with that acuteness of hearing peculiar to prisoners. "The treasure I speak of really exists, and I offer to sign a treaty with you, in which I promise to lead you to the spot you shall dig, and, if I deceive you, bring me here again,—I ask no more."

The governor laughed. "Is the spot far from here?"

"A hundred leagues."

"It is not a bad idea," said the governor.

"If every prisoner took it into his head to travel a hundred leagues, and their guardians consented to accompany them, they would have a capital chance of escaping."

"The scheme is well known," said the governor; "and M. l'Abbé has not even the merit of its invention."

Then turning to Faria,—

"I inquired if you are well fed?" said he.

"Swear to me," replied Faria, "to free me if what I tell you prove true, and I will stay here whilst you go to the spot."

"Are you well fed?" repeated the inspector.

"Monsieur, you run no risk, for, as I told you, I will stay here, so there is no chance of my escaping."

"You do not reply to my question," replied the inspector, impatiently.

"Nor you to mine," cried the abbé. "You will not accept my gold; I will keep it for myself. You refuse me my liberty; God will give it me."

And the abbé, casting away his coverlid, resumed his place, and continued his calculations.

"What is he doing there?" said the inspector.

"Counting his treasures," replied the governor.

Faria replied to this sarcasm by a glance of profound contempt.

"He has been wealthy once, perhaps?" said the inspector.

"Or dreamed he was and awoke mad."

"After all," said the inspector, "if he had been rich he would not have been here."

Thus finished the adventure of the Abbé Faria. He remained in his cell, and this visit only increased the belief of his insanity.

Caligula or Nero, those treasure-seekers, those desirers of the impossible, would have accorded to the poor wretch, in exchange for his wealth, the liberty and the air he so earnestly prayed for.

But the kings of modern ages, retained within the limits of probability, have neither the courage nor the desire. They fear the ear that hears their orders, and the eye that scrutinises their actions. Formerly they believed themselves sprung from Jupiter, and shielded by their birth; but, nowadays, they are not inviolable.

It has always been against the policy of despotic governments to suffer the victims of their policy to reappear. As the Inquisition rarely suffered their victims to be seen with their limbs distorted, and their flesh lacerated by torture, so madness is always concealed in its cell, from whence, should it depart, it is conveyed to some gloomy hospital, where the doctor recognises neither man nor mind in the mutilated being the gaolor delivers to him.

The very madness of the Abbé Faria, gone mad in prison, condemned him to perpetual captivity.

The inspector kept his word with Dantès: he examined the register, and found the following note concerning him,—

EDMOND DANTÈS. { Violent Bonapartist; took an active part in the return from Elba.

The greatest watchfulness and care to be exercised.

This note was in a different hand from the rest, which proved it had been added since his confinement.

The inspector could not contend against this accusation; he simply wrote,—

"Nothing to be done."

This visit had infused new vigour into Dantès; he had, till then, forgotten the date; but now, with a fragment of plaster, he wrote the date, 30th July, 1816; and made a mark every day, in order not to lose his reckoning again.   Days and weeks passed away, then months, Dantès still waited; he at first expected to be freed in a fortnight.   This fortnight expired; he reflected the inspector would do nothing until his return to Paris; and that he would not reach there until his circuit was finished; he, therefore, fixed three months: three months passed away, then six more.   During these ten months no favourable change had taken place; and Dantès began to fancy the inspector's visit was but a dream, an illusion of the brain.

At the expiration of a year the governor was changed; he had obtained the government of Ham.   He took with him several of his subordinates, and amongst them Dantès' gaoler. A fresh governor arrived; it would have been too tedious to acquire the names of the prisoners, he learned their numbers instead.

This horrible place consisted of fifty chambers; their inhabitants were designated by the number of their chamber; and the unhappy young man was no longer called Edmond Dantès, he was now number 34.

CHAPTER XV

DANTÈS passed through all the degrees of misfortune that
prisoners, forgotten in their dungeon, suffer. He commenced
with pride, a natural consequence of hope, and a consciousness
of innocence; then he began to doubt his own innocence,
which justified in some measure the governor's belief in his
mental alienation; and then falling into the opposite extreme,
he supplicated, not heaven, but his gaoler.

Dantès entreated to be removed from his present dungeon
into another; for a change, however disadvantageous, was
still a change, and would afford him some amusement. He
entreated to be allowed to walk about, to have books and
instruments. Nothing was granted; no matter, he asked all
the same. He accustomed himself to speak to his fresh gaoler,
although he was, if possible, more taciturn than the former;
but still, to speak to a man, even though mute, was something.
Dantès spoke for the sake of hearing his own voice; he had
tried to speak when alone, but the sound of his voice terrified
him. Often before his captivity Dantès' mind had revolted
at the idea of those assemblages of prisoners, composed of
thieves, vagabonds, and murderers. He now wished to be
amongst them, in order to see some other face besides that of
his gaoler; he sighed for the galleys, with their infamous
costume, their chain, and the brand on the shoulder. The
galley-slaves breathed the fresh air of heaven, and saw each
other. They were very happy.

He besought the gaoler one day to let him have a companion, were it even the mad abbé.

The gaoler, though rude and hardened by the constant
sight of so much suffering, was yet a man. At the bottom
of his heart he had often compassionated the unhappy young
man who suffered thus; and he laid the request of number 34
before the governor; but the latter sapiently imagined that
Dantès wished to conspire, or attempt an escape, and refused
his request.

Dantès had exhausted all human resources; and he then
turned to God.

All the pious ideas that had been so long forgotten returned; he recollected the prayers his mother had taught him,

and discovered a new meaning in every word. For in prosperity prayers seem but a mere assemblage of words until the day when misfortune comes to explain to the unhappy sufferer the sublime language by which he invokes the pity of heaven! He prayed, and prayed aloud, no longer terrified at the sound of his voice; for he fell into a species of ecstasy. He laid every action of his life before the Almighty, proposed tasks to accomplish, and at the end of every prayer introduced the entreaty oftener addressed to man than to God, "Forgive us our trespasses as we forgive them that trespass against us."

Spite of his earnest prayers Dantès remained a prisoner. Then a gloomy feeling took possession of him. He was simple and without education; he could not, therefore, in the solitude of his dungeon, and of his own thoughts, reconstruct the ages that had passed, reanimate the nations that had perished, and rebuild the ancient cities that imagination renders so vast and so stupendous, and that pass before our eyes, illumined by the fires of heaven, as in Martin's pictures. He could not do this, he whose past life was so short, whose present so melancholy, and his future so doubtful. Nineteen years of light to reflect upon in eternal darkness. No distraction could come to his aid; his energetic spirit that would have exulted in thus revisiting the past was imprisoned like an eagle in a cage. He clung to one idea, that of his happiness, destroyed without apparent cause by an unheard-of fatality; he considered and reconsidered this idea, devoured it (thus to speak) as Ugolino devours the skull of the Archbishop Roger in the Inferno of Dante.

Rage succeeded to this. Dantès uttered blasphemies that made his gaoler recoil with horror, dashed himself furiously against the walls of his prison, attacked every thing, and chiefly himself, and the least thing, a grain of sand, a straw, or a breath of air that annoyed him. Then, the letter he had seen that Villefort had shewed to him recurred to his mind, and every line seemed visible in fiery letters on the wall, like the *Mene, Tekel, Upharsin* of Belshazzar. He said that it was the vengeance of man, and not of heaven, that had thus plunged him into the deepest misery. He devoted these unknown persecutors to the most horrible tortures he could imagine, and found them all insufficient, because, after torture came death, and after death, if not repose, at least that insensibility that resembles it.

By dint of constantly dwelling on the idea that repose was death, and in order to punish, other tortures than death must be invented, he began to reflect on suicide. Unhappy he, who, on the brink of misfortune, broods over these ideas!

It is one of those dead seas that seem clear and smooth to

the eye: but he who unwearily ventures within its embrace finds himself entangled in a quagmire that attracts and swallows him. Once thus ensnared, unless the protecting hand of God snatch him thence, all is over, and his struggles but tend to hasten his destruction. This state of mental anguish is, however, less terrible than the sufferings that precede, and the punishment that awaits it. A sort of consolation that points to the yawning abyss, at the bottom of which is darkness and obscurity.

Edmond found some solace in these ideas. All his sorrows, all his sufferings, with their train of gloomy spectres, fled from his cell, where the angel of death seemed about to enter. Dantès reviewed with composure his past life, and looking forward with terror to his future existence chose that middle line that seemed to afford him a refuge.

"Sometimes," said he, "in my voyages, when I was a man and commanded other men, I have seen the heavens become overcast, the sea rage and foam, the storm arise, and, like a monstrous bird, cover the sky with its wings. Then I felt that my vessel was a vain refuge that trembled and shook before the tempest. Soon the fury of the waves and the sight of the sharp rocks announced the approach of death, and death then terrified me, and I used all my skill and intelligence as a man and a sailor to escape. But I did so because I was happy, because I had not courted death, because this repose on a bed of rocks and sea-weed seemed terrible, because I was unwilling that I, a creature made for the service of God, should serve for food to the gulls and ravens. But now it is different, I have lost all that bound me to life; death smiles and invites me to repose, I die after my own manner, I die exhausted and broken-spirited, as I fall asleep when I have paced three thousand times round my cell."

No sooner had this idea taken possession of him than he became more composed, arranged his couch to the best of his power, ate little, and slept less, and found this existence almost supportable, because he felt he could throw it off at pleasure, like a worn-out garment. He had two means of dying; the one was to hang himself with his handkerchief to the staunchions of the window; the other, to refuse food and starve himself. But the former means were repugnant to him. Dantès had always entertained the greatest horror of pirates, who are hung up to the yard-arm, he would not die by what seemed an infamous death; he resolved to adopt the second, and began that day to execute his resolve. Nearly four years had passed away; at the end of the second he had ceased to mark the lapse of time.

Dantès said, "I wish to die," and had chosen the manner of his death; and fearful of changing his mind, he had taken an oath to die. "When my morning and evening meals are brought," thought he, "I will cast them out of the window, and I shall be believed to have eaten them."

He kept his word; twice a-day he cast out, by the barred aperture, the provisions his gaoler brought him, at first gaily, then with deliberation, and at last with regret; nothing but the recollection of his oath gave him strength to proceed. Hunger rendered these viands, once so repugnant, acceptable to him; he held the plate in his hand for an hour at a time, and gazed on the morsel of bad meat, of tainted fish, of black and mouldy bread. It was the last struggle of life, which occasionally vanquished his resolve; then his dungeon seemed less sombre, his prospects less desperate. He was still young, he was only four or five-and-twenty, he had nearly fifty years to live. What unforeseen events might not open his prison-door and restore him to liberty? Then he raised to his lips the repast that, like a voluntary Tantalus, he refused himself; but he thought of his oath, and he would not break it. He persisted until, at last, he had not sufficient force to cast his supper out of the loophole.

The next morning he could not see or hear; the gaoler feared he was dangerously ill. Edmond hoped he was dying.

The day passed away thus: Edmond felt a species of stupor creeping over him, the gnawing pain at his stomach had ceased, his thirst had abated, when he closed his eyes he saw myriads of lights dancing before them, like the meteors that play about the marshes. It was the twilight of that mysterious country called Death!

Suddenly, about nine o'clock in the evening, Edmond heard a hollow sound in the wall against which he was lying.

So many loathsome animals inhabited the prison, that their noise did not, in general, awake him; but whether abstinence had quickened his faculties, or whether the noise was really louder than usual, Edmond raised his head and listened.

It was a continual scratching, as if made by a huge claw, a powerful tooth, or some iron instrument, attacking the stones.

Although weakened, the young man's brain instantly recurred to the idea that haunts all prisoners—liberty! It seemed to him that Heaven had at length taken pity on him, and had sent this noise to warn him on the very brink of the abyss. Perhaps one of those beloved ones he had so often thought of was thinking of him, and striving to diminish the distance that separated them.

No! no! doubtless he was deceived, and it was but one of those dreams that forerun death!

Edmond still heard the sound. It lasted nearly three

hours; he then heard a noise of something falling, and all was silent.

Some hours afterwards, it began nearer and more distinct; Edmond became already interested in that labour, when the gaoler entered.

For a week that he had resolved to die, and for four days that he put this resolution into execution, Edmond had not spoken to this man, had not answered him when he inquired what was the matter with him, and turned his face to the wall when he looked too curiously at him; but now the gaoler might hear this noise and put an end to it, thus destroying a ray of something like hope that soothed his last moments.

The gaoler brought him his breakfast. Dantès raised himself up, and began to speak on everything; on the bad quality of his food, on the coldness of his dungeon, grumbling and complaining, in order to have an excuse for speaking louder, and wearying the patience of his gaoler, who had solicited some broth and white bread for his prisoner, and who had brought it.

Fortunately he fancied Dantès was delirious; and placing his food on the rickety table, he withdrew.

Edmond listened and the sound became more and more distinct.

There can be no doubt, thought he, it is some prisoner who is striving to obtain his freedom.

Suddenly another idea took possession of his mind, so used to misfortune, that it could scarcely understand hope; yet this idea possessed him, that the noise arose from the workmen the governor had ordered to repair the neighbouring dungeon.

It was easy to ascertain this; but how could he risk the question? It was easy to call his gaoler's attention to the noise, and watch his countenance as he listened, but might he not by this means betray interests far more precious than this short-lived satisfaction? Unfortunately Edmond's brain was still so feeble that he could not bend his thoughts to anything in particular.

He saw but one means of restoring lucidity and clearness to his judgment. He turned his eyes towards the soup his gaoler had brought him, rose, staggered towards it, raised the vessel to his lips, and drank off the contents with a feeling of indescribable pleasure. He had often heard that shipwrecked persons had died through having eagerly devoured too much food, Edmond replaced on the table the bread he was about to devour, and returned to his couch: he did not wish to die. He soon felt that his ideas became again collected, he could think and strengthen his thoughts by reasoning. Then he said to himself, " I must put this to the test but without compromising anybody. If it is a workman I need but knock against the wall, and he will cease to work in order to find out who is knocking, and why he does so, but as his occupation is sanctioned by the governor he will soon resume it; if, on the contrary, it is a prisoner the noise I make will alarm him, he will cease and not recommence until he thinks every one is asleep."

Edmond rose again but this time his legs did not tremble, and his eyes were free from mists: he advanced to a corner of his dungeon, detached a stone, and with it knocked against the wall where the sound came. He struck thrice.

At the first blow the sound ceased, as if by magic.

Edmond listened intently, an hour passed, two hours passed, and no sound was heard from the wall, all was silent there.

Full of hope, Edmond swallowed a few mouthfuls of bread and water, and, thanks to the excellence of his constitution, found himself well-nigh recovered.

The day passed away in utter silence—night came without the noise having recommenced.

"It is a prisoner," said Edmond, joyfully.

The night passed in perfect silence. Edmond did not close his eyes.

In the morning the gaoler brought him fresh provisions, he had already devoured those of the previous day, he ate these, listening anxiously for the sound, walking round and round his cell, shaking the iron bars of the loophole, restoring by exercise vigour and agility to his limbs, and preparing himself thus for his future destiny. At intervals he listened if the noise had not began again, and grew impatient at the prudence of the prisoner who did not guess he had been disturbed by a captive as anxious for liberty as himself.

Three days passed—seventy-two long tedious hours!

At length one evening as the gaoler was visiting him for the last time that night, Dantès fancied he heard an almost imperceptible movement among the stones.

Edmond recoiled from the wall, walked up and down his cell to collect his thoughts, and replaced his ear against the wall.

There could be no doubt something was passing on the other side, the prisoner had discovered the danger, and had substituted the lever for the chisel.

Encouraged by this discovery, Edmond determined to assist the indefatigable labourer, he began by moving his bed, and sought with his eyes for anything with which he could pierce the wall, penetrate the cement, and displace a stone.

He saw nothing, he had no knife or sharp instrument, the grating of his window alone was of iron, and he had too often assured himself of its solidity. All his furniture consisted of

C.M.—E

a bed, a chair, a table, a pail, and a jug. The bed had iron clamps but they were screwed to the wood, and it would have required a screw-driver to take them off. The table and chair had nothing, the pail had had a handle, but that had been removed.

Dantès had but one resource, which was to break the jug, and with one of the sharp fragments attack the wall. He let the jug fall on the floor, and it broke in pieces.

Dantès concealed two or three of the sharpest fragments in his bed, leaving the rest on the floor. The breaking of his jug was too natural an accident to excite suspicion, Edmond had all the night to work in, but in the darkness he could not do much; and he soon felt his instrument was blunted against something hard; he pushed back his bed and awaited the day.

All night he heard the subterranean workman, who continued to mine his way. The day came, the gaoler entered. Dantès told him the jug had fallen from his hands in drinking, and the gaoler went grumblingly to fetch another, without giving himself the trouble to remove the fragments of the broken one.

He returned speedily, recommended the prisoner to be more careful, and departed.

Dantès heard joyfully the key grate in the lock, he listened until the sound of steps died away and then hastily displacing his bed, saw by the faint light that penetrated into his cell, that he had laboured uselessly the previous evening, in attacking the stone instead of removing the plaster that surrounded it.

The damp had rendered it friable and Dantès saw joyfully the plaster detach itself, in small morsels, it is true, but at the end of half an hour he had scraped off a handful: a mathematician might have calculated that in two years, supposing that the rock was not encountered, a passage, twenty feet long, and two feet broad, might be formed.

The prisoner reproached himself with not having thus employed the hours he had passed in prayers and despair.

In six years (the space he had been confined) what might he not have accomplished?

In three days he had succeeded, with the utmost precaution, in removing the cement, and exposing the stone; the wall was formed of rough stones, to give solidity to which were embedded at intervals, blocks of hewn stone. It was one of these he had uncovered, and which he must remove from its socket.

Dantès strove to do so with his nails, but they were too weak. The fragments of the jug broke, and after an hour of useless toil Dantès paused.

Was he to be thus stopped at the beginning, and was he to wait inactive until his fellow-workman had completed his toils?

Suddenly an idea occurred to him, he smiled and the perspiration dried on his forehead.

The gaoler always brought Dantès' soup in an iron saucepan, this saucepan contained the soup of a second prisoner, for Dantès had remarked that it was either quite full, or half empty, according as the turnkey gave it to himself or his companion first.

The handle of this saucepan was of iron. Dantès would have given ten years of his life in exchange for it.

The gaoler poured the contents of this saucepan into Dantès' plate, who, after eating his soup with a wooden spoon, washed the plate, which thus served for every day. In the evening Dantès placed his plate on the ground near the door, the gaoler as he entered stepped on it and broke it.

This time he could not blame Dantès. He was wrong to leave it there, but the gaoler was wrong not to have looked before him.

The gaoler, therefore, contented himself with grumbling. Then he looked about him for something to pour the soup into; Dantès's whole furniture consisted of one plate, there was no alternative.

"Leave the saucepan," said Dantès, "you can take it away when you bring me my breakfast."

This advice was to the gaoler's taste, as it spared him the necessity of ascending, descending, and ascending again.

He left the saucepan.

Dantès was beside himself with joy. He rapidly devoured his food, and after waiting an hour lest the gaoler should change his mind and return, he removed his bed, took the handle of the saucepan, inserted the point between the hewn stone and rough stones of the wall, and employed it as a lever. A slight oscillation shewed Dantès all went well.

At the end of an hour the stone was extricated from the wall, leaving a cavity of a foot and a half in diameter.

Dantès carefully collected the plaster, carried it into the corners of his cell, and covered it with earth. Then wishing to make the best use of this night, in which chance, or rather, his own stratagem, had placed so precious an instrument in his hands, he continued to work without ceasing.

At the dawn of day he replaced the stone, pushed his bed against the wall, and lay down.

The breakfast consisted of a piece of bread, the gaoler entered and placed the bread on the table.

"Well, you do not bring me another plate?" said Dantès.

"No," replied the turnkey, "you destroy every thing; first you break your jug, then you make me break your plate; if all the prisoners followed your example, the government would be ruined; I shall leave you the saucepan, and pour your soup into that, so for the future I hope you will not be so destructive to your furniture."

Dantès raised his eyes to heaven, clasped his hands beneath the coverlid, and prayed.

He felt more gratitude for the possession of this piece of iron than he had ever felt for anything; he had however remarked that the prisoner on the other side had ceased to labour.

No matter, this was a greater reason for proceeding; if his neighbour would not come to him, he would go to him.

All day he toiled on untiringly, and by the evening he had succeeded in extracting ten handfuls of plaster and fragments of stone.

When the hour for his gaoler's visit arrived, Dantès straightened the handle of the saucepan as well as he could and placed it in its accustomed place.   The turnkey poured his ration of soup into it, together with the fish, for thrice a-week the prisoners were made to abstain from meat: this would have been a method of reckoning time had not Dantès long ceased to do so.

Having poured out the soup, the turnkey retired.

Dantès wished to ascertain whether his neighbour had really ceased to work.

He listened.

All was silent as it had been for the last three days.

Dantès sighed; it was evident that his neighbour distrusted him.

However, he toiled on all the night, without being discouraged; but after two or three hours he encountered an obstacle.

The iron made no impression, but met with a smooth surface; Dantès touched it, and found it was a beam.

This beam crossed, or rather blocked up, the hole Dantès had made.

It was necessary therefore to dig above or under it.

The unhappy young man had not thought of this.

"Oh, my God! my God!" murmured he, "I have so earnestly prayed to you, that I hoped my prayers have been heard.   After having deprived me of my liberty, after having deprived me of death, after having re-called me to existence, my God! have pity on me, and do not let me die in despair."

"Who talks of God and despair at the same time?" said a voice that seemed to come from beneath the earth, and, deadened by the distance, sounded hollow and sepulchral in the young man's ears.

Edmond's hair stood on end, and he rose on his knees.

"Ah!" said he, "I hear a human voice."   Edmond had not heard any one speak save his gaoler for four or five years, and a gaoler is not a man to a prisoner, he is a living door added to his door of oak, a barrier of flesh and blood added to his barriers of iron.

"In the name of Heaven," cried Dantès, "speak again though the sound of your voice terrifies me."

"Who are you?" said the voice.

"An unhappy prisoner," replied Dantès, who made no hesitation in answering.

"Of what country?"

"A Frenchman."

"Your name?"

"Edmond Dantès."

"Your profession?"

"A sailor."

"How long have you been here?"

"Since the 28th of February, 1815."

"Your crime?"

"I am innocent."

"But of what are you accused?"

"Of having conspired to aid the emperor's return."

"How for the emperor's return? the emperor is no longer on the throne then?"

"He abdicated at Fontainebleau in 1814, and was sent to the island of Elba: but how long have you been here that you are ignorant of all this?"

"Since 1811."

Dantès shuddered, this man had been four years longer than himself in prison.

"Do not dig any more," said the voice; "only tell me how high up is your excavation?"

"On a level with the floor."

"How is it concealed?"

"Behind my bed."

"Has your bed been moved since you have been a prisoner?"

"No."

"What does your chamber open on?"

"A corridor."

"And the corridor?"

"On a court."

"Alas!" murmured the voice.

"Oh, what is the matter?" cried Dantès.

"I am deceived, and the imperfection of my plans has ruined all. An error of a line in the plan has been equivalent to fifteen feet in reality, and I took the wall you are mining for the wall of the fortress."

"But then you were close to the sea?"

"That is what I hoped."

"And supposing you succeeded?"

"I should have thrown myself into the sea, gained one of the islands near here,—the Isle de Daume or the Isle de Tiboulen, and then I was safe."

"Could you have swam so far?"

"Heaven would have given me strength, but now all is lost."

"All?"

"Yes; stop up your excavation carefully: do not work any more, and wait until you hear from me."

"Tell me, at least, who you are?"

"I am—I am Number 27."

"You mistrust me, then?" said Dantès.

Edmond fancied he heard a bitter laugh proceed from the unknown.

"Oh! I am a Christian," cried Dantès, guessing instinctively that this man meant to abandon him. "I swear to you by Him who died for us that nought shall induce me to breathe one syllable to my gaolers, but I conjure you do not abandon me. If you do, I swear to you that I will dash my brains out against the wall, and you will have my death to reproach yourself with."

"How old are you? Your voice is that of a young man."

"I do not know my age, for I have not counted the years I have been here. All I do know is, that I was just nineteen when I was arrested the 28th of February, 1815."

"Not quite twenty-six!" murmured the voice; "at that age he cannot be a traitor."

"Oh! no, no!" cried Dantès. "I swear to you again, rather than betray you they shall hew me to pieces!"

"You have done well to speak to me, and entreat me, for I was about to form another plan, and leave you; but your age reassures me. I will not forget you; expect me."

"When?"

"I must calculate our chances; I will give you the signal."

"But you will not leave me; you will come to me, or you will let me come to you. We will escape, and if we cannot escape, we will talk, you of those whom you love, and I of those whom I love. You must love somebody?"

"No, I am alone in the world."

"Then you will love me. If you are young, I will be your comrade; if you are old, I will be your son. I have a father, who is seventy, if he yet lives; I only love him and a young girl called Mercédès. My father has not yet forgotten me, I am sure; but God alone knows if she loves me still: I shall love you as I loved my father."

"It is well," returned the voice; "to-morrow."

These few words were uttered with an accent that left no

doubt of his sincerity; Dantès rose, dispersed the fragments with the same precaution as before, and pushed back his bed against the wall. He then gave himself up to his happiness: he would no longer be alone. He was, perhaps, about to regain his liberty; at the worst, he would have a companion, and captivity that is shared is but half captivity.

All day Dantès walked up and down his cell. He sat down occasionally on his bed, pressing his hand on his heart. At the slightest noise he bounded towards the door. Once or twice the thought crossed his mind that he might be separated from this unknown, whom he loved already, and then his mind was made up,—when the gaoler moved his bed and stooped to examine the opening, he would kill him with his water-jug.

He would be condemned to die, but he was about to die of grief and despair when this miraculous noise recalled him to life.

The gaoler came in the evening: Dantès was on his bed. It seemed to him that thus he better guarded the unfinished opening. Doubtless there was a strange expression in his eyes, for the gaoler said, "Come, are you going mad again?"

Dantès did not answer: he feared that the emotion of his voice would betray him.

The gaoler retired, shaking his head.

The night came; Dantès hoped that his neighbour would profit by the silence to address him, but he was mistaken. The next morning, however, just as he removed his bed from the wall, he heard three knocks; he threw himself on his knees.

"Is it you?" said he, "I am here."

"Is your gaoler gone?"

"Yes," said Dantès, "he will not return until the evening, so that we have twelve hours before us."

"I can work then," said the voice.

"Oh! yes, yes, this instant, I entreat you."

In an instant the portion of the floor on which Dantès (half buried in the opening) was leaning his two hands, gave way; he cast himself back, whilst a mass of stones and earth disappeared in a hole that opened beneath the aperture he himself had formed. Then from the bottom of this passage, the depth of which it was impossible to measure, he saw appear, first the head, then the shoulders, and lastly the body of a man, who sprang lightly into his cell.

CHAPTER XVI

A LEARNED ITALIAN

RUSHING towards the friend so long and ardently desired, Dantès almost carried him towards the window, in order to obtain a better view of his features by the aid of the imperfect light that struggled through the grating of the prison.

He was a man of small stature, with hair blanched rather by suffering and sorrow than years. A deep-set, penetrating eye, almost buried beneath the thick grey eyebrow, and a long (and still black) beard reaching down to his breast.

The meagreness of his features, deeply furrowed by care, joined to the bold outline of his strongly marked features, announced a man more accustomed to exercise his moral faculties than his physical strength. Large drops of perspiration were now standing on his brow, while his garments hung about him in such rags as to render it useless to form a guess as to their primitive description.

The stranger might have numbered sixty, or sixty-five years, but a certain briskness and appearance of vigour in his movements made it probable that he was aged more from captivity than the course of time. He received the enthusiastic greeting of his young acquaintance with evident pleasure, as though his chilled affections seemed re-kindled and invigorated by his contact with one so warm and ardent. He thanked him with grateful cordiality for his kindly welcome, although he must at that moment have been suffering bitterly to find another dungeon where he had fondly reckoned on discovering a means of regaining his liberty.

"Let us first see," said he, "whether it is possible to remove the traces of my entrance here—our future comforts depend upon our gaolers being entirely ignorant of it." Advancing to the opening, he stooped and raised the stone as easily as though it had not weighed an ounce; then fitting it into its place, he said,—

"You removed this stone very carelessly; but I suppose you had no tools to aid you."

"Why!" exclaimed Dantès, with astonishment, "do you possess any?"

"I made myself some; and with the exception of a file, I have all that are necessary—a chisel, pincers, and lever."

"Oh! how I should like to see these products of your industry and patience!"

"Well! in the first place, here is my chisel!"

So saying, he displayed a sharp strong blade, with a handle made of beech-wood.

"And with what did you contrive to make that?" inquired Dantès.

"With one of the clamps of my bedstead; and this very tool has sufficed me to hollow out the road by which I came hither, a distance of at least fifty feet."

"Fifty feet!" re-echoed Dantès, with a species of terror.

"Do not speak so loud, young man!—don't speak so loud! It frequently occurs in a state prison like this, that persons are stationed outside the doors of the cells purposely to overhear the conversation of the prisoners."

"But they believe I am shut up alone here!"

"That makes no difference."

"And you say that you penetrated a length of fifty feet to arrive here?"

"I do; that is about the distance that separates your chamber from mine—only unfortunately I did not curve aright: for want of the necessary geometrical instruments to calculate my scale of proportion; instead of taking an ellipsis of forty feet, I have made fifty.   I expected, as I told you, to reach the outer wall, pierce through it, and throw myself into the sea; I have, however, kept along the corridor on which your chamber opens, instead of going beneath it.   My labour is all in vain, for I find that the corridor looks into a courtyard filled with soldiers."

"That's true," said Dantès; "but the corridor you speak of only bounds *one* side of my cell; there are three others,—do you know any thing of their situation?"

"This one is built against the solid rock, and it would take ten experienced miners, duly furnished with the requisite tools, as many years to perforate it;—this adjoins the lower part of the governor's apartments, and were we to work our way through, we should only get into some lock-up cellars, where we must necessarily be recaptured:—the fourth and last side of your cell looks out—looks out—stop a minute, now where does it open to?"

The side which thus excited curiosity was the one in which was fixed the loophole by which light was admitted into the chamber.   This loophole, which gradually diminished as it approached the outside, until only an opening through which a child could not have passed, was, for better security, furnished with three iron bars, so as to quiet all apprehensions even in the mind of the most suspicious gaoler as to the possibility of a prisoner's escape.

C.M.—E*

As the stranger finished his self-put question, he dragged the table beneath the window.

"Climb up," said he to Dantès.—The young man obeyed, mounted on the table, and, divining the intentions of his companion, placed his back securely against the wall, and held out both hands.   The stranger, whom as yet Dantès knew only by his assumed title of the number of his cell, sprang up with an agility by no means to be expected in a person of his years, and, light and steady as the bound of a cat or a lizard, climbed from the table to the outstretched hands of Dantès, and from them to his shoulders; then, almost doubling himself in two, for the ceiling of the dungeon prevented his holding himself erect, he managed to slip his head through the top bar of the window, so as to be able to command a perfect view from top to bottom.

An instant afterwards he hastily drew back his head, saying, "I thought so!" and sliding from the shoulders of Dantès, as dexterously as he had ascended, he nimbly leapt from the table to the ground.

"What made you say those words?" asked the young man, in an anxious tone, in his turn descending from the table.

The elder prisoner appeared to meditate; "Yes," said he at length, "it is so.   This side of your chamber looks out upon a kind of open gallery, where patrols are continually passing, and sentries keep watch day and night."

"Are you quite sure of that?"

"Certain.   I saw the soldier's shako and the top of his musquet: that made me draw my head in so quickly, for I was fearful he might also see me."

"Well?" inquired Dantès.

"You perceive, then, the utter impossibility of escaping through your dungeon?"

"Then," pursued the young man eagerly——

"Then," answered the elder prisoner, "the will of God be done!" and as the old man slowly pronounced those words, an air of profound resignation spread itself over his care-worn countenance.

Dantès gazed on the individual who could thus philosophically resign hopes so long and ardently nourished with an astonishment mingled with admiration.

"Tell me, I entreat of you, who and what you are?" said he at length; "never have I met with so remarkable a person as yourself."

"Willingly," answered the stranger; "if, indeed, you feel any curiosity respecting one, now, alas! powerless to aid you in any way!"

"Say not so; you can console and support me by the

strength of your own powerful mind. Pray let me know who you really are?"

The stranger smiled a melancholy smile. "Then listen," said he; "I am the Abbé Faria, and have been imprisoned in this Château d'If since the year 1811: previously to which I had been confined for three years in the fortress of Fenestrelle. In the year 1811 I was transferred to Piedmont in France; it was at this period I learned that the destiny which seemed subservient to every wish formed by Napoleon had bestowed on him a son, named King of Rome even in his cradle. I was very far then from expecting the change you have just informed me of, namely, that four years afterwards this colossus of power would be overthrown. Then who reigns in France at this moment? Napoleon II?"

"No, Louis XVIII!"

"The brother of Louis XVI!—How inscrutable are the ways of Providence!—for what great and mysterious purpose has it pleased Heaven to abase the man once so elevated, and raise up the individual so beaten down and depressed?"

Dantès' whole attention was riveted on a man who could thus forget his own misfortunes while occupying himself with the destinies of others.

"But so it was," continued he, "in England. After Charles I came Cromwell; to Cromwell succeeded Charles II, and then James II, who was succeeded by some son-in-law or relation. Ah! my friend!" said the abbé, turning towards Dantès, and surveying him with the kindling gaze of a prophet; "these are the changes and vicissitudes that give liberty to a nation. Mark what I say!—you are young, and may see my words come to pass that such will be the case with France— you will see it, I say."

"Probably, if ever I get out of prison!"

"True," replied Faria, "we are prisoners; but I forget this sometimes, and there are even moments when my mental vision transports me beyond these walls, and I fancy myself at liberty."

"But wherefore are you here?"

"Because in 1807 I meditated the very scheme Napoleon wished to realise in 1811; because, like Machiavel, I desired to alter the political face of Italy, and instead of allowing it to be split up into a quantity of petty principalities, each held by some weak or tyrannical ruler, I sought to form one large, compact, and powerful empire; and, lastly, because I fancied I had found my Cæsar Borgia in a crowned simpleton, who feigned to enter into my views only to betray me. It was projected equally by Alexander VI and Clement VII, but it will never succeed now, for they attempted it fruitlessly, and Napoleon was unable to complete his work. Italy seems fated to be unlucky." The old man uttered these last words in a tone of deep dejection, and his head fell listlessly on his breast.

To Dantès all this was perfectly incomprehensible. In the first place, he could not understand a man risking his life and liberty for such unimportant matters as the division of a kingdom; then, again, the persons referred to were wholly unknown to him. Napoleon certainly he knew something of, inasmuch as he had seen and spoken with him; but the other individuals alluded to were strangers to him even by name.

"Pray excuse my question," said Dantès, beginning to partake of the gaoler's opinion touching the state of the abbé's brain; "but are you not the priest who is considered throughout the Château d'If — to — be — ill?"

"Mad, you mean, don't you?"

"I did not like to say so," answered Dantès, smiling.

"Well, then," resumed Faria, with a bitter smile, "let me answer your question in full, by acknowledging that I am the poor mad prisoner of the Château d'If; for many years permitted to amuse the different visitants to the prison with what is said to be my insanity; and, in all probability, I should be promoted to the honour of making sport for the children, if such innocent things could be found in an abode devoted like this to suffering and despair."

Dantès remained for a short time mute and motionless; at length he said, "Then you abandon all hope of flight?"

"I perceive its utter impossibility; and I consider it impious to attempt that which the Almighty evidently does not approve."

"Nay, be not discouraged. Would it not be expecting too much to hope to succeed at your first attempt? Why not try to find an opening in another direction to that which had so unfortunately failed?"

"Alas! it shews how little notion you can have of all it has cost me to effect a purpose so unexpectedly frustrated that you talk of beginning over again. In the first place, I was four years making the tools I possess; and have been two years scraping and digging out earth, hard as granite itself; then what toil and fatigue has it not been to remove huge stones I should once have deemed impossible to loosen! Whole days have I passed in these Titanic efforts, considering my labour well repaid if by night-time I had contrived to carry away a square inch of this hard-bound cement, changed by ages into a substance unyielding as the stones themselves; then, to conceal the mass of earth and rubbish I dug up, I was compelled to break through a staircase, and throw the fruits of my labour into the hollow part of it; but the well is now so completely choked up, that I scarcely think it would be possible to add another handful of dust without leading to a discovery. Consider, also, that I fully believed I had accomplished the end and aim of my undertaking, for which I had so exactly husbanded my strength as to make it just hold out to the termination of my enterprise; and just at the moment when I reckoned upon success, my hopes are for ever dashed from me. No, I repeat, again, that nothing shall induce me to renew attempts evidently at variance with the Almighty's pleasure."

Dantès held down his head, that his companion might not perceive how little of real regret at the failure of the scheme was expressed on his countenance; but, in truth, the young man could entertain no other feeling than delight at finding his prison would be no longer solitary or uncheered by human participation.

The abbé sunk upon Edmond's bed, while Edmond himself remained standing, lost in a train of deep meditation. Flight had never once occurred to him—There are, indeed, some things which appear so morally impossible that the mind does not dwell on them for an instant. To undermine the ground for fifty feet—to devote three years to a labour which, if successful, would conduct you to a precipice overhanging the sea—to plunge into the waves at a height of fifty or sixty feet, at the risk of being dashed to pieces against the rocks, should you have been fortunate enough to have escaped the balls from the sentinel's musquet; and even, supposing all these perils past, then to have to swim for your life a distance of at least three miles ere you could reach the shore—were difficulties so startling and formidable that Dantès had never even dreamed of such a scheme, but resigned himself to his fate. But the sight of an old man clinging to life with so desperate a courage gave a fresh turn to his ideas, and inspired him with new courage and energy. An instance was before him of one less adroit, as well as weaker and older, having devised a plan which nothing but an unfortunate mistake in geometrical calculation could have rendered abortive. This same individual, with almost incredible patience and perseverance, had contrived to provide himself with tools requisite for so unparalleled an attempt. If, then, one man had already conquered the seeming impossibility, why should not he, Dantès, also try to regain his liberty? Faria had made his way through fifty feet of the prison, Dantès resolved to penetrate through double that distance. Faria, at the age of fifty, had devoted three years to the task; he, who was but half as old, would sacrifice six. Faria, a churchman and philosopher, had not shrunk from risking his life by trying to swim a distance of three miles to reach the isles of Daume, Rattonneau, or Lemaire, should a hardy sailor, an experienced diver, like himself, shrink from a similar task? Should he, who had so often for mere amusement's sake plunged to the bottom of the sea to fetch up the bright coral-branch, hesitate to swim a distance of three miles? He could do it in an hour, and how many times had he for pure pastime continued in the water for more than twice as long! At once Dantès resolved to follow the brave example of his energetic companion, and to remember that what has once been done may be done again.

After continuing some time in profound meditation, the young man suddenly exclaimed, " I have found what you were in search of."

Faria started: "Have you, indeed?" cried he, raising his head with quick anxiety; "pray let me know what it is you have discovered?"

"The corridor through which you have bored your way from the cell you occupy here extends in the same direction as the outer gallery, does it not?"

"It does!"

"And is not above fifteen steps from it?"

"About that!"

"Well, then, I will tell you what we must do. We must pierce through the corridor by forming a side opening about the middle, as it were the top part of a cross. This time you will lay your plans more accurately; we shall get out into the gallery you have described; kill the sentinel who guards it, and make our escape. All we require to ensure success is courage, and that you possess, and strength, which I am not deficient in; as for patience, you have abundantly proved yours—you shall now see me prove mine."

"One instant, my dear friend," replied the abbé; "it is clear you do not understand the nature of the courage with which I am endowed, and what use I intend making of my strength. As for patience, I consider I have abundantly exercised that on recommencing every morning the task of the over night, and every night beginning again the task of the day. But then, young man (and I pray of you to give me your full attention), then I thought I could not be doing any thing displeasing to the Almighty in trying to set an innocent being at liberty,—one who had committed no offence, and merited not condemnation."

"And have your notions changed?" asked Dantès, with much surprise; "do you think yourself more guilty in making the attempt since you have encountered me?"

"No; neither do I wish to incur guilt. Hitherto I have fancied myself merely waging war against circumstances, not men. I have thought it no sin to bore through a wall, or destroy a staircase, but I cannot so easily persuade myself to pierce a heart or take away a life."

A slight movement of surprise escaped Dantès. "Is it

possible," said he, "that where your liberty is at stake you can allow any such scruple to deter you from obtaining it?"

"Tell me," replied Faria, "what has hindered you from knocking down your gaoler with a piece of wood torn from your bedstead, dressing yourself in his clothes, and endeavouring to escape?"

"Simply that I never thought of such a scheme," answered Dantès.

"Because," said the old man, "the natural repugnance to the commission of such a crime prevented its bare idea from occurring to you; and so it ever is with all simple and allowable things. Our natural instincts keep us from deviating from the strict line of duty. The tiger, whose nature teaches him to delight in shedding blood, needs but the organ of smelling to know when his prey is within his reach; and by following this instinct he is enabled to measure the leap necessary to enable him to spring on his victim; but man, on the contrary, loathes the idea of blood;—it is not alone that the laws of social life inspire him with a shrinking dread of taking life; his natural construction and physiological formation——"

Dantès remained confused and silenced by this explanation of the thoughts which had unconsciously been working in his mind, or rather soul; for there are two distinct sorts of ideas, those that proceed from the head and those that emanate from the heart.

"Since my imprisonment," said Faria, "I have thought over all the most celebrated cases of escape recorded. Among the many that have failed in obtaining the ultimate release of the prisoner, I consider there has been a precipitation—a haste, wholly incompatible with such undertakings. Those escapes that have been crowned with full success have been long meditated upon and carefully arranged—such, for instance, as the escape of the Duke de Beaufort from the Château de Vincennes, that of the Abbé Dubuquoi from For l'Evêque; Latude's from the Bastille, with similar cases of successful evasion; and I have come to the conclusion, that chance frequently affords opportunities we should never ourselves have thought of. Let us, therefore, wait patiently for some favourable moment; rely upon it, you will not find me more backward than yourself in seizing it."

"Ah!" said Dantès, "you might well endure the tedious delay; you were constantly occupied in the task you set yourself, and when weary with toil, you had your hopes to refresh and encourage you."

"I assure you," replied the old man, "I did not turn to that source for recreation or support."

"What did you do then?"

"I wrote or studied?"

"Were you then permitted the use of pens, ink, and paper?"

"Oh, no!" answered the abbé; "I had none but what I made for myself."

"Do you mean to tell me," exclaimed Dantès, "that you could invent all those things—for real ones you could not procure unaided?"

"I do, indeed, truly say so."

Dantès gazed with kindling eyes and rapidly increasing admiration on the wonderful being whose hand seemed gifted with the power of a magician's wand; some doubt, however, still lingered in his mind, which was quickly perceived by the penetrating eye of the abbé.

"When you pay me a visit in my cell, my young friend," said he, "I will shew you an entire work, the fruits of the thoughts and reflections of my whole life; many of them meditated over in the ruins of the Coliseum of Rome, at the foot of St. Mark's Column at Venice, and on the borders of the Arno at Florence, little imagining at the time that they would be arranged in order within the walls of the Château d'If. The work I speak of is called '*A Treatise on the Practicability of forming Italy into one General Monarchy*,' and will make one large quarto volume."

"And on what have you written all this?"

"On two of my shirts. I invented a preparation that makes linen as smooth and as easy to write on as parchment."

"You are, then, a chemist?"

"Somewhat:—I know Lavoisier, and was the intimate friend of Cabanis."

"But for such a work you must have needed books;—had you any?"

"I possessed nearly 5,000 volumes in my library at Rome, but after reading them over many times, I found out that with 150 well-chosen books a man possesses a complete analysis of all human knowledge, or at least all that is either useful or desirable to be acquainted with. I devoted three years of my life to reading and studying these 150 volumes, till I knew them nearly by heart. So that since I have been in prison, a very slight effort of memory has enabled me to recall their contents as readily as though the pages were open before me. I could recite you the whole of Thucydides, Xenophon, Plutarch, Titus Livius, Tacitus, Strada, Jornandès, Dante, Montaigne, Shakespeare, Spinosa, Machiavel, and Bossuet. Observe, I merely quote the most important names and writers."

"You are, doubtless, acquainted with a variety of languages, so as to have been able to read all these?"

"Yes; I speak five of the modern tongues; that is to say, German, French, Italian, English, and Spanish; by the aid of ancient Greek I learned modern Greek—I don't speak it so well as I could wish, but I am still trying to improve myself."

"Improve yourself!" repeated Dantès; "why, how can you manage to do so?"

"Why, I made a vocabulary of the words I knew; turned, re-turned, and arranged them, so as to enable me to express my thoughts through their medium. I know nearly one thousand words, which is all that is absolutely necessary, although I believe there are nearly one hundred thousand in the dictionaries. I cannot hope to be very fluent, but I certainly should have no difficulty in explaining my wants and wishes; and that would be quite as much as I should ever require."

Stronger grew the wonder of Dantès, who almost fancied he had to do with one gifted with supernatural powers—still hoping to find some imperfection which might bring him down to a level with human beings, he added, "Then if you were not furnished with pens, how did you manage to write the work you speak of?"

"I made myself some excellent ones, which would be universally preferred to all others, if once known?"

"You are aware what huge whitings are served to us on *maigre* days. Well, I selected the cartilages of the heads of these fishes, and you can scarcely imagine the delight with which I welcomed the arrival of each Wednesday, Friday, and Saturday, as affording me the means of increasing my stock of pens; for I will freely confess that my historical labours have been my greatest solace and relief. While retracing the past, I forget the present; and while following the free and independent course of historical record, I cease to remember that I am myself immured within the gloomy walls of a dungeon."

"But the ink requisite for copying down your ideas," said Dantès; "how have you procured that?"

"I will tell you," replied Faria; "there was formerly a fireplace in my dungeon, but closed up long ere I became an occupant of this prison. Still it must have been many years in use, for it was thickly covered with a coating of soot; this soot I dissolved in a portion of the wine brought to me every Sunday; and I assure you a better ink cannot be desired; for very important notes, for which closer attention is required, I have pricked one of my fingers, and written the facts claiming notice in blood."

"And when," asked Dantès, "will you shew me all this?"

"Whenever you please," replied the abbé.

"Oh, then! let it be directly," exclaimed the young man.

"Follow me, then," said the abbé, as he re-entered the subterraneous passage, in which he soon disappeared, followed by Dantès.

CHAPTER XVII

THE ABBÉ'S CHAMBER

AFTER having passed with tolerable ease through the subterranean passage, which, however, did not permit of their holding themselves erect, the two friends reached the further end of the corridor, into which the cell of the abbé opened; from that point, the opening became much narrower, barely permitting an individual to creep through on his hands and knees. The floor of the abbé's cell was paved, and it had been by raising one of the stones in the most obscure corner that Faria had been able to commence the laborious task of which Dantès had witnessed the completion.

As he entered the chamber of his friend, Dantès cast around one eager and searching glance in quest of the expected marvels; but nothing more than common met his view.

"It is well," said the abbé, "we have some hours before us; it is now just a quarter past twelve o'clock."

Instinctively Dantès turned round to observe by what watch or clock the abbé had been able so accurately to specify the hour.

"Look at this ray of light, which enters by my window," said the abbé, "and then observe the lines traced on the wall. Well: by means of these lines, which are in accordance with the double motion of the earth, as well as the ellipses it describes round the sun, I am enabled to ascertain the precise hour with more minuteness than if I possessed a watch, for that might be broken or deranged in its movements, while the sun and earth never vary in their appointed paths."

This last explanation was wholly lost upon Dantès, who had always imagined, from seeing the sun rise from behind the mountains and set in the Mediterranean, that it moved, and not the earth. A double movement in the globe he inhabited, and of which he could feel nothing, appeared to him perfectly impossible; still, though unable to comprehend the full meaning of his companion's allusions, each word that fell from his lips seemed fraught with the wonders of science, as admirably deserving of being brought fully to light as were the glittering treasures he could just recollect having visited during his earliest youth in a voyage he made to Guzerat and Golconda.

"Come!" said he to the abbé, "shew me the wonderful

inventions you told me of—I am all impatience to behold them."

The abbé smiled, and proceeding to the disused fireplace, raised, by the help of his chisel, a long stone which had doubtless been the hearth, beneath which was a cavity of considerable depth, serving as a safe depository of the articles mentioned to Dantès.

"What do you wish to see first?" asked the abbé.

"Oh! your great work on the monarchy of Italy!"

Faria then drew forth from its hiding-place three or four rolls of linen, laid one over the other, like the folds of papyrus found in mummy-cases; these rolls consisted of slips of cloth about four inches wide and eighteen long; they were all carefully numbered and closely covered with writing, so legible that Dantès could easily read it, as well as make out the sense —it being in Italian, a language he, as a Provençal, perfectly understood.

"There!" said he, "there is the work complete—I wrote the word *finis* at the end of the last page about a week ago. I have torn up two of my shirts, and as many handkerchiefs as I was master of, to complete the precious pages. Should I ever get out of prison, and find a printer courageous enough to publish what I have composed, my literary reputation is for ever secured."

"I see," answered Dantès. "Now let me behold the curious pens with which you have written your work."

"Look!" said Faria, shewing to the young man a slender stick about six inches long, and much resembling the size of the handle of a fine painting-brush, to the end of which was tied by a piece of thread one of those cartilages of which the abbé had before spoken to Dantès—it was pointed, and divided at the nib like an ordinary pen.

Dantès examined it with intense admiration then looked around to see the instrument with which it had been shaped so correctly into form.

"Ah, I see!" said Faria, "you are wondering where I found my penknife, are you not? Well, I must confess that I look upon that article of my ingenuity as the very perfection of all my handiworks. I made it, as well as this knife, out of an old iron candlestick." The penknife was sharp and keen as a razor;—as for the other knife, it possessed the double advantage of being capable of serving either as a dagger or a knife.

Dantès examined the various articles shewn to him with the same attention he had bestowed on the curiosities and strange tools exhibited in the shops at Marseilles as the works of the savages in the South Seas, from whence they had been brought by the different trading vessels.

"As for the ink," said Faria, "I told you how I managed to obtain that—and I only just make it from time to time, as I require it."

"There is one thing puzzles me still," observed Dantès, "and that is how you managed to do all this by daylight?"

"I worked at night also," replied Faria.

"Night!—why, for Heaven's sake, are your eyes like cats' that you can see to work in the dark?"

"Indeed they are not; but a beneficent Creator has supplied man with intelligence and ability to supply the want of the power you allude to. I furnished myself with a light quite as good as that possessed by the cat."

"You did?—Pray tell me how."

"I separated the fat from the meat served to me, melted it, and made a most capital oil; here is my lamp." So saying, the abbé exhibited a sort of vessel very similar to those employed upon the occasion of public illuminations.

"But how do you procure a light?"

"Oh, here are two flints, and a morsel of burnt linen."

"And your matches?"

"Were easily prepared—I feigned a disorder of the skin, and asked for a little sulphur, which was readily supplied."

Dantès laid the different things he had been looking at gently on the table, and stood with his head drooping on his breast, as though overwhelmed by the persevering spirit and strength of character developed in each fresh trait of his new-found friend's conduct.

"You have not seen all yet," continued Faria, "for I did not think it wise to trust all my treasures in the same hiding-place; let us shut this one up, and then you shall see what else I have to display."

Dantès helped him to replace the stone as they first found it; the abbé sprinkled a little dust over it to conceal the traces of its having been removed, rubbed his foot well on it to make it assume the same appearance as the other, and then, going towards his bed, he removed it from the spot it stood in. Behind the head of the bed, and concealed by a stone fitting in so closely as to defy all suspicion, was a hollow space, and in this space a ladder of cords between twenty-five and thirty feet in length.

Dantès closely and eagerly examined it—he found it firm, solid, and compact enough to bear any weight.

"Who supplied you with the materials for making this wonderful work?" asked Dantès.

"No one but myself. I tore up several of my shirts, and unravelled the sheets of my bed, during my three years' imprisonment at Fenestrelle; and when I was removed to the

Château d'If, I managed to bring the ravellings with me, so that I have been able to finish my work here."

"And was it not discovered that your sheets were un-hemmed?"

"Oh, no! for when I had taken out the thread I required, I hemmed the edges over again."

"With what?"

"With this needle!" said the abbé, as, opening his ragged vestments, he shewed Dantès a long, sharp fish-bone, with a small perforated eye for the thread, a small portion of which still remained in it. "I once thought," continued Faria, "of removing these iron bars, and letting myself down from the window, which, as you see, is somewhat wider than yours—although I should have enlarged it still more preparatory to my flight;—however, I discovered that I should merely have dropped into a sort of inner court, and I therefore renounced the project altogether as too full of risk and danger. Nevertheless, I carefully preserved my ladder against one of those unforeseen opportunities of which I spoke just now, and which sudden chance frequently brings about."

While affecting to be deeply engaged in examining the ladder, the mind of Dantès was, in fact, busily occupied by the idea that a person so intelligent, ingenious, and clear-sighted as the abbé, might probably be enabled to dive into the dark recesses of his own misfortunes, and cause that light to shine upon the mystery connected with them he had in vain sought to elicit.

"What are you thinking of?" asked the abbé, smilingly, imputing the deep abstraction in which his visitor was plunged to the excess of his awe and wonder.

"I was reflecting, in the first place," replied Dantès, "upon the enormous degree of intelligence and ability you must have employed to reach the high perfection to which you have attained;—if you thus surpass all mankind while but a prisoner, what would you not have accomplished free?"

"Possibly nothing at all;—the overflow of my brain would probably, in a state of freedom, have evaporated in a thousand follies; it needs trouble and difficulty and danger to hollow out various mysterious and hidden mines of human intelligence. Pressure is required, you know, to ignite powder; captivity has collected into one single focus all the floating faculties of my mind; they have come into close contact in the narrow space in which they have been wedged, and you are well aware that from the collision of clouds electricity is produced—from electricity comes the lightning, from whose flash we have light amid our greatest darkness."

"Alas, no!" replied Dantès; "I know not that these things follow in such natural order. Oh, I am very ignorant; and you must be blessed, indeed, to possess the knowledge you have."

The abbé smiled. "Well," said he, "but you had another subject for your thoughts besides admiration for me; did you not say so just now?"

"I did!"

"You have told me as yet but one of them,—let me hear the other."

"It was this:—that while you had related to me all the particulars of your past life, you were perfectly unacquainted with mine."

"Your life, my young friend, has not been of sufficient length to admit of your having passed through any very important events."

"It has been long enough to inflict on me a misfortune so great, so crushingly overwhelming, that unconscious as I am of having in any way deserved it, I would fain know who, of all mankind, has been the accursed author of it, that I may no longer accuse Heaven, as I have done in my fury and despair, of wilful injustice towards an innocent and injured man."

"Then you profess ignorance of the crime with which you are charged?"

"I do, indeed; and this I swear by the two beings most dear to me upon earth—my father and Mercédès."

"Come," said the abbé, closing his hiding-place, and pushing the bed back to its original situation, "let me hear your story."

Dantès obeyed, and commenced what he called his history, but which consisted only of the account of a voyage to India and two or three in the Levant, until he arrived at the recital of his last cruise, with the death of Captain Leclere, and the receipt of a packet to be delivered by himself to the grand maréchal; his interview with that personage, and his receiving in place of the packet brought a letter addressed to M. Noirtier —his arrival at Marseilles and interview with his father—his affection for Mercédès and their nuptial fête—his arrest and subsequent examination in the temporary prison of the Palais de Justice, ending in his final imprisonment in the Château d'If. From the period of his arrival all was a blank to Dantès—he knew nothing, not even the length of time he had been imprisoned. His recital finished, the abbé reflected long and earnestly.

"There is," said he, at the end of his meditations, "a clever maxim which bears upon what I was saying to you some little while ago, and that is, that unless wicked ideas take root in a naturally depraved mind, human nature, in a right and wholesome state, revolts at crime. Still, from an artificial civilisation have originated wants, vices, and false tastes, which occasionally become so powerful as to stifle within us all good feelings, and ultimately to lead us into guilt and wickedness—from this view of things then comes the axiom I alluded to—that if you wish to discover the author of any bad action, seek first to discover the person to whom the perpetration of that bad action could be in any way advantageous. Now to apply it in your case:—to whom could your disappearance have been serviceable?"

"To no breathing soul. Why, who could have cared about the removal of so insignificant a person as myself?"

"Do not speak thus, for your reply evinces neither logic nor philosophy; every thing is relative, my dear young friend, from the king who obstructs his successor's immediate possession of the throne, to the occupant of a place for which the supernumerary to whom it has been promised ardently longs. Now, in the event of the king's death, his successor inherits a crown; when the placeman dies, the supernumerary steps into his shoes, and receives his salary of twelve thousand livres. Well, these twelve thousand livres are his civil list, and are as essential to him as the twelve millions of a king. Every individual, from the highest to the lowest degree, has his place in the ladder of social life, and around him are grouped a little world of interests, composed of stormy passions and conflicting atoms; but let us return to your world. You say you were on the point of being appointed captain of the Pharaon?"

"I was."

"And about to become the husband of a young and lovely girl?"

"True."

"Now could any one have had an interest in preventing the accomplishment of these two circumstances? But let us first settle the question as to its being the interest of any one to hinder you from being captain of the Pharaon. What say you?"

"I cannot believe such was the case. I was generally liked on board; and had the sailors possessed the right of selecting a captain themselves, I feel convinced their choice would have fallen on me. There was only one person among the crew who had any feeling of ill-will towards me. I had quarrelled with him some time previously, and had even challenged him to fight me; but he refused."

"Now we are getting on. And what was this man's name?"

"Danglars."

"What rank did he hold on board?"

"He was supercargo."

"And had you been captain, should you have retained him in his employment?"

"Not if the choice had remained with me; for I had frequently observed inaccuracies in his accounts."

"Good again! Now then tell me was any person present during your last conversation with Captain Leclere?"

"No; we were quite alone."

"Could your conversation be overheard by any one?"

"It might, for the cabin-door was open;—and—stay; now I recollect,—Danglars himself passed by just as Captain Leclere was giving me the packet for the grand maréchal."

"That will do," cried the abbé; "now we are on the right scent. Did you take any body with you when you put into the port of Elba?"

"Nobody."

"Somebody there received your packet, and gave you a letter in place of it, I think?"

"Yes, the grand maréchal did."

"And what did you do with that letter?"

"Put it into my pocket-book."

"Ah! indeed! You had your pocket-book with you, then? Now, how could a pocket-book, large enough to contain an official letter, find sufficient room in the pockets of a sailor?"

"You are right: I had it not with me,—it was left on board."

"Then it was not till your return to the ship that you placed the letter in the pocket-book?"

"No."

"And what did you do with this same letter while returning from Porto-Ferrajo to your vessel?"

"I carried it in my hand."

"So that when you went on board the Pharaon, every body could perceive you held a letter in your hand?"

"To be sure they could."

"Danglars as well as the rest?"

"Yes; he as well as others."

"Now, listen to me, and try to recall every circumstance attending your arrest. Do you recollect the words in which the information against you was couched?"

"Oh, yes! I read it over three times, and the words sunk deeply into my memory."

"Repeat it to me."

Dantès paused for a few instants as though collecting his ideas, then said, "This is it word for word:—'M. le Procureur du Roi is informed by a friend to the throne and religion, that an individual, named Edmond Dantès, second in command on board the Pharaon, this day arrived from Smyrna, after having touched at Naples and Porto-Ferrajo, has been charged by Murat with a packet for the usurper; again, by the usurper, with a letter for the Bonapartist Club in Paris.

This proof of his guilt may be procured by his immediate arrest, as the letter will be found either about his person, at his father's residence, or in his cabin on board the Pharaon.'"

The abbé shrugged up his shoulders. "The thing is clear as day," said he; "and you must have had a very unsuspecting nature, as well as a good heart, not to have suspected the origin of the whole affair."

"Do you really think so? Ah, that would, indeed, be the treachery of a villain!"

"How did Danglars usually write?"

"Oh! extremely well."

"And how was the anonymous letter written?"

"All the wrong way—backwards, you know."

Again the abbé smiled. "In fact it was a disguised hand?"

"I don't know; it was very boldly written, if disguised."

"Stop a bit," said the abbé, taking up what he called his pen, and, after dipping it into the ink, he wrote on a morsel of prepared linen with his left hand the first two or three words of the accusation. Dantès drew back, and gazed on the abbé with a sensation almost amounting to terror.

"How very astonishing!" cried he, at length. "Why your writing exactly resembles that of the accusation!"

"Simply because that accusation had been written with the left hand; and I have always remarked one thing——"

"What is that?"

"That whereas all writing done with the right hand varies, that performed with the left hand is invariably similar."

"You have evidently seen and observed every thing."

"Let us proceed."

"Oh! yes, yes! Let us go on."

"Now as regards the second question. Was there any person whose interest it was to prevent your marriage with Mercédès?"

"Yes, a young man who loved her."

"And his name was——"

"Fernand."

"That is a Spanish name, I think?"

"He was a Catalan."

"You imagine him capable of writing the letter?"

"Oh, no! he would more likely have got rid of me by sticking a knife into me."

"That is in strict accordance with the Spanish character; an assassination they will unhesitatingly commit, but an act of cowardice never."

"Besides," said Dantès, "the various circumstances mentioned in the letter were wholly unknown to him."

"You had never spoken of them yourself to any one?"

"To no person whatever."

"Not even to your mistress?"

"No, not even to my betrothed bride."

"Then it is Danglars beyond a doubt."

"I feel quite sure of it now."

"Wait a little. Pray was Danglars acquainted with Fernand?"

"No——yes, he was. Now I recollect——"

"What?"

"To have seen them both sitting at table together beneath an arbour at Père Pamphile the evening before the day fixed for my wedding. They were in earnest conversation. Danglars was joking in a friendly way, but Fernand looked pale and agitated."

"Were they alone?"

"There was a third person with them whom I knew perfectly well, and who had, in all probability, made their acquaintance; he was a tailor named Caderousse, but he was quite intoxicated. Stay!—stay!— How strange that it should not have occurred to me before! Now I remember quite well that on the table round which they were sitting were pens, ink, and paper. Oh! the heartless, treacherous scoundrels!" exclaimed Dantès, pressing his hand to his throbbing brows.

"Is there any thing else I can assist you in discovering besides the villainy of your friends?" inquired the abbé.

"Yes, yes," replied Dantès, eagerly; "I would beg of you, who see so completely to the depths of things, and to whom the greatest mystery seems but an easy riddle, to explain to me, how it was that I underwent no second examination, was never brought to trial, and, above all, my being condemned without ever having had sentence passed on me?"

"That is altogether a different and more serious matter," responded the abbé. "The ways of justice are frequently too dark and mysterious to be easily penetrated. All we have hitherto done in the matter has been child's play. If you wish me to enter upon the more difficult part of the business, you must assist me by the most minute information on every point."

"That I will gladly. So pray begin, my dear abbé, and ask me whatever questions you please; for, in good truth, you seem to turn over the pages of my past life far better than I could do myself."

"In the first place, then, who examined you,—the procureur du roi, his deputy, or a magistrate?"

"The deputy."

"Was he young or old?"

"About six or seven-and-twenty years of age, I should say."

"To be sure," answered the abbé. "Old enough to be ambitious, but not sufficiently so to have hardened his heart. And how did he treat you?"

"With more of mildness than severity."

"Did you tell him your whole story?"

"I did."

"And did his conduct change at all in the course of your examination?"

"Yes; certainly he did appear much disturbed when he read the letter that had brought me into this scrape. He seemed quite overcome at the thoughts of the danger I was in."

"*You* were in?"

"Yes; for whom else could he have felt any apprehensions?"

"Then you feel quite convinced he sincerely pitied your misfortune?"

"Why he gave me one great proof of his sympathy, at least."

"And what was that?"

"He burnt the sole proof that could at all have criminated me."

"Do you mean the letter of accusation?"

"Oh, no! the letter I was intrusted to convey to Paris."

"Are you sure he burnt it?"

"He did so before my eyes."

"Ay, indeed! that alters the case, and leads to the conclusion, that this man might, after all, be a greater scoundrel than I at first believed."

"Upon my word," said Dantès, "you make me shudder. If I listen much longer to you, I shall believe the world is filled with tigers and crocodiles."

"Only remember that two-legged tigers and crocodiles are more dangerous than those that walk on four."

"Never mind, let us go on."

"With all my heart! You tell me he burnt the letter in your presence?"

"He did; saying at the same time, 'You see I thus destroy the only proof existing against you.'"

"This action is somewhat too sublime to be natural."

"You think so?"

"I am sure of it. To whom was this letter addressed?"

"To M. Noirtier, No. 13 Rue Coq-Héron, Paris."

"Now can you conceive any interest your heroic deputy procureur could by possibility have had in the destruction of that letter?"

"Why, it is not altogether impossible he might have had, for he made me promise several times never to speak of that letter to any one, assuring me he so advised me for my own interest; and, more than this, he insisted on my taking a solemn oath never to utter the name mentioned in the address."

"Noirtier!" repeated the abbé; "Noirtier!—I knew a person of that name at the court of the Queen of Etruria,—a Noirtier, who had been a Girondin during the revolution! What was your deputy called?"

"De Villefort!"

The abbé burst into a fit of laughter; while Dantès gazed on him in utter astonishment.

"What ails you?" said he at length.

"Do you see this ray of light?"

"I do."

"Well! I see my way into the full meaning of all the proceedings against you more clearly than you even discern that sunbeam. Poor fellow! poor young man! And you tell me this magistrate expressed great sympathy and commiseration for you?"

"He did!"

"And the worthy man destroyed your compromising letter?"

"He burnt it before me!"

"And then made you swear never to utter the name of Noirtier?"

"Certainly!"

"Why, you poor short-sighted simpleton, can you not guess who this Noirtier was, whose very name he was so careful to keep concealed?"

"Indeed I cannot!"

"No other than the father of your sympathetic deputy procureur."

Had a thunderbolt fallen at the feet of Dantès, or hell opened its yawning gulf before him, he could not have been more completely transfixed with horror than at the sound of words so wholly unexpected, revealing as they did the fiendish perfidy which had consigned him to wear out his days in the dark cell of a prison, that was to him as a living grave. Starting up, he clasped his hands around his head as though to prevent his very brain from bursting, as in a choked and almost inarticulate voice he exclaimed, "His father! oh, no! not his father surely!"

"His own father, I assure you," replied the abbé; "his right name was Noirtier de Villefort!"

At this instant a bright light shot through the mind of Dantès, and cleared up all that had been dark and obscure before. The change that had come over Villefort during the examination; the destruction of the letter, the exacted promise, the almost supplicating tones of the magistrate, who seemed rather to implore mercy than denounce punishment,—all returned with a stunning force to his memory. A cry of mental agony escaped his lips, and he staggered against the wall almost like a drunken man; then, as the paroxysm passed away, he hurried to the opening conducting from the abbé's cell to his own, and said,—

"I must be alone to think over all this."

When he regained his dungeon he threw himself on his bed, where the turnkey found him at his evening visit sitting, with fixed gaze and contracted features, still and motionless as a statue; but, during hours of deep meditation, which to him had seemed but as minutes, he had formed a fearful resolution, and bound himself to its fulfilment by a solemn oath.

Dantès was at length roused from his reverie by the voice of Faria, who, having also been visited by his gaoler, had come to invite his fellow-sufferer to share his supper.

The reputation of being out of his mind, though harmlessly, and even amusingly so, had procured for the abbé greater privileges than were allowed to prisoners in general. He was supplied with bread of a finer, whiter description than the usual prison fare, and even regaled each Sunday with a small quantity of wine: the present day chanced to be Sunday, and the abbé came delighted at having such luxuries to offer his new friend.

Dantès followed him with a firm and assured step; his features had lost their almost spasmodic contraction, and now wore their usual expression; but there was that in his whole appearance that bespoke one who had come to a fixed and desperate resolve.

Faria bent on him his penetrating eye: "I regret now," said he, "having helped you in your late inquiries, or having given you the information I did."

"Why so?" inquired Dantès.

"Because it has instilled a new passion in your heart—that of vengeance."

A bitter smile played over the features of the young man, "Let us talk of something else," said he.

Again the abbé looked at him, then mournfully shook his head; but, in accordance with Dantès' request, he began to speak of other matters.

The elder prisoner was one of those persons whose conversation, like that of all who have experienced many trials, contained many useful and important hints as well as sound information; but it was never egotistical, for the unfortunate man never alluded to his own sorrows.

Dantès listened with admiring attention to all he said: some of his remarks corresponded with what he already knew, or applied to the sort of knowledge his nautical life had enabled him to acquire. A part of the good abbé's words, however,

were wholly incomprehensible to him; but, like those auroræ
boreales which serve to light the navigators in southern
latitudes, they sufficed to open fresh views to the inquiring
mind of the listener, and to give a glimpse of new horizons,
illumined by the wild meteoric flash, enabling him justly to
estimate the delight an intellectual mind would have in
following the high and towering spirit of one so richly gifted
as Faria in all the giddiest heights or lowest depths of science.

"You must teach me a small part of what you know," said
Dantès, "if only to prevent your growing weary of me.   I can
well believe that so learned a person as yourself would prefer
absolute solitude to being tormented with the company of one
as ignorant and uninformed as myself.   If you will only agree
to my request, I promise you never to mention another word
about escaping."

The abbé smiled.   "Alas! my child," said he, "human
knowledge is confined within very narrow limits; and when I
have taught you mathematics, physics, history, and the three
or four modern languages with which I am acquainted, you
will know as much as I do myself.   Now it will scarcely require
two years for me to communicate to you the stock of learning
I possess."

"Two years!" exclaimed Dantès; "do you really believe I
can acquire all these things in so short a time?"

"Not their application certainly, but their principles you
may; to learn is not to know, there are the learners and the
learned.   Memory makes the one, philosophy the other."

"But can I not learn philosophy as well as other things?"

"My son, philosophy, as I understand it, is reducible to no
rules by which it can be learned; it is the amalgamation
of all the sciences, the golden cloud which bears the soul to
heaven."

"Well, then," said Dantès, "leaving philosophy out of the
question, tell me what you shall teach me first?   I feel my
great need of scientific knowledge, and long to begin the work
of improvement, say when shall we commence?"

"Directly, if you will," said the abbé.

And that very evening the prisoners sketched a plan of
education to be entered upon the following day.

Dantès possessed a prodigious memory, combined with an
astonishing quickness and readiness of conception; the mathe-
matical turn of his mind rendered him apt at all kinds of
calculation, while his naturally poetical feelings threw a light
and pleasing veil over the dry reality of arithmetical compu-
tation or the rigid severity of lines.   He already knew Italian,
and had also picked up a little of the Romaic dialect during
his different voyages to the East, and by the aid of these two
languages he easily comprehended the construction of all the

others, so that at the end of six months he began to speak Spanish, English, and German.

In strict accordance with the promise made to the abbé, Dantès never even alluded to flight; it might have been that the delight his studies afforded him supplied the place of liberty; or, probably, the recollection of his pledged word (a point, as we have already seen, to which he paid a rigid attention) kept him from reverting to any plan for escape: but absorbed in the acquisition of knowledge, days, even months, passed by unheeded in one rapid and instructive course; time flew on, and at the end of a year Dantès was a new man. With Faria, on the contrary, Dantès remarked, that, spite of the relief his society afforded, he daily grew sadder: one thought seemed incessantly to harass and distract his mind. Sometimes he would fall into long reveries, sigh heavily and involuntarily, then suddenly rise, and, with folded arms, begin pacing the confined space of his dungeon.

One day he stopped all at once in the midst of these so-often-repeated promenades, and exclaimed, "Ah! if there were no sentinel!"

"There shall not be one a minute longer than you please," said Dantès, who had followed the working of his thoughts as accurately as though his brain were enclosed in crystal, so clear as to display its minutest operations.

"I have already told you," answered the abbé, "that I loathe the idea of shedding blood."

"Still in our case the death we should bestow would not be dictated by any wild or savage propensity, but as a necessary step to secure our own personal safety and preservation."

"No matter! I could never agree to it?"

"Still you have thought of it?"

"Incessantly, alas!" cried the abbé.

"And you have discovered a means of regaining our freedom; have you not?" asked Dantès, eagerly.

"I have; if it were only possible to place a deaf and blind sentinel in the gallery beyond us."

"I will undertake to render him both," replied the young man, with an air of determined resolution that made his companion shudder.

"No, no!" cried the abbé; "I tell you the thing is impossible: name it no more!"

In vain did Dantès endeavour to renew the subject; the abbé shook his head in token of disapproval, but refused any further conversation respecting it.

Three months passed away.

"Do you feel yourself strong?" inquired the abbé of Dantès.

The young man, in reply, took up the chisel, bent it into the form of a horse-shoe, and then as readily straightened it

"And will you engage not to do any harm to the sentry, except as a last extremity?"

"I promise on my honour not to hurt a hair of his head, unless positively obliged for our mutual preservation."

"Then," said the abbé, "we may hope to put our design into execution."

"And how long shall we be in accomplishing the necessary work?"

"At least a year."

"And shall we begin at once?"

"Directly!"

"We have lost a year to no purpose," cried Dantès.

"Do you consider the last twelve months as wasted?" asked the abbé, in a tone of mild reproach.

"Forgive me!" cried Edmond, blushing deeply; "I am indeed ungrateful to have hinted such a thing."

"Tut! tut!" answered the abbé: "man is but man at last, and you are about the best specimen of the genus I have ever known. Come, let me shew you my plan."

The abbé then shewed Dantès the sketch he had made for their escape: it consisted of a plan of his own cell and that of Dantès, with the corridor which united them. In this passage he proposed to form a tunnel, such as is employed in mines; this tunnel would conduct the two prisoners immediately beneath the gallery where the sentry kept watch; once there, a large excavation would be made, and one of the flag-stones with which the gallery was paved be so completely loosened, that at the desired moment it would give way beneath the soldier's feet, who falling into the excavation below, would be immediately bound and gagged, ere, stunned by the effects of his fall, he had power to offer any resistance. The prisoners were then to make their way through one of the gallery windows, and to let themselves down from the outer walls by means of the abbé's ladder of cords. The eyes of Dantès sparkled with joy, and he rubbed his hands with delight at the idea of a plan so simple, yet apparently so certain to succeed.

That very day the miners commenced their labours; and that with so much more vigour and alacrity as it succeeded to a long rest from fatigue, and was destined, in all probability, to carry out the dearest wish of the heart of each.

Nothing interrupted the progress of their work except the necessity of returning to their respective cells against the hour in which their gaoler was in the habit of visiting them; they had learned to distinguish the almost imperceptible sound of his footsteps, as he descended towards their dungeons, and happily never failed being prepared for his coming.

The fresh earth excavated during their present work, and which would have entirely blocked up the old passage, was thrown, by degrees and with the utmost precaution, out of the window in either Faria's or Dantès' cell; the rubbish being first pulverised so finely that the night-wind carried it far away without permitting the smallest trace to remain.

More than a year had been consumed in this undertaking; the only tools for which had been a chisel, a knife, and a wooden lever. Faria, still continuing to instruct Dantès by conversing with him, sometimes in one language, sometimes in another; at others relating to him the history of nations and great men who from time to time have left behind them one of those bright tracks called glory.

The abbé was a man of the world, and had moreover mixed in the first society of the day; his appearance was impressed with that air of melancholy dignity, which Dantès, thanks to the imitative powers bestowed on him by nature, easily acquired, as well that outward polish and politeness he had before been wanting in, and which is seldom possessed except by those who have been placed in constant intercourse with persons of high birth and breeding.

At the end of fifteen months the tunnel was made, and the excavation completed beneath the gallery, and the two workmen could distinctly hear the measured tread of the sentinel as he paced to and fro over their heads.

Compelled, as they were, to await a night sufficiently dark to favour their flight, they were obliged to defer their final attempt till that auspicious moment should arrive; their greatest dread now was lest the stone through which the sentry was doomed to fall should give way before its right time, and this they had in some measure provided against by placing under it as a kind of prop a sort of bearer they had discovered among the foundations through which they had worked their way. Dantès was occupied in arranging this piece of wood when he heard Faria, who had remained in Edmond's cell for the purpose of cutting a peg to secure their rope-ladder, call to him in accents of pain and suffering. Dantès hastened to his dungeon, where he found him standing in the middle of the room, pale as death, his forehead streaming with perspiration, and his hands clenched tightly together.

"Gracious heavens!" exclaimed Dantès; "what is the matter? what has happened?"

"Quick! quick!" returned the abbé; "listen to what I have to say."

Dantès looked in fear and wonder at the livid countenance of Faria, whose eyes, already dull and sunken, were circled by a halo of a bluish cast, his lips were white as those of a corpse, and his very hair seemed to stand on end.

C.M.—F

"For God's sake!" cried Dantès, "what is the meaning of this? Tell me, I beseech you, what ails you?"

"Alas!" faltered out the abbé, "all is over with me. I am seized with a terrible, perhaps mortal illness; I can feel that the paroxysm is fast approaching: I had a similar attack the year previous to my imprisonment. This malady admits but of one remedy; I will tell you what that is; go into my cell as quickly as you can—draw out one of the feet that support the bed, you will find it has been hollowed out for the purpose of containing a small phial you will see there half-filled with a red-looking fluid, bring it to me—or rather—no, no!—I may be found here, therefore help me back to my room while I have any strength to drag myself along; who knows what may happen? or how long the fit may last?"

In spite of the magnitude of the misfortune which thus suddenly frustrated his hopes, Dantès did not lose his presence of mind, but descended into the corridor dragging his unfortunate companion with him; then, half carrying, half supporting him, he managed to reach the abbé's chamber, when he immediately laid the sufferer on his bed.

"Thanks!" said the poor abbé, shivering as though his veins were filled with ice. "Now that I am safely here, let me explain to you the nature or my attack, and the appearance it will present. I am seized with a fit of catalepsy; when it comes to its height, I may probably lie still and motionless as though dead, uttering neither sigh nor groan. On the other hand, the symptoms may be much more violent and cause me to fall into fearful convulsions, cover my lips with foaming, and force from me the most piercing shrieks;—this last evil you must carefully guard against, for, were my cries to be heard, it is more than probable I should be removed to another part of the prison, and we be separated for ever. When I become quite motionless, cold, and rigid as a corpse, then, and not before—you understand—force open my teeth with a chisel, pour from eight to ten drops of the liquor contained in the phial down my throat, and I may perhaps revive."

"Perhaps!" exclaimed Dantès, in grief-stricken tones.

"Help! help!" cried the abbé; "I—I—die—I——"

So sudden and violent was the fit, that the unfortunate prisoner was unable to complete the sentence began: a violent convulsion shook his whole frame, his eyes started from their sockets, his mouth was drawn on one side, his cheeks became purple, he struggled, foamed, dashed himself about, and uttered the most dreadful cries, which, however, Dantès prevented from being heard by covering his head with the blanket; the fit lasted two hours, then, more helpless than an infant, and colder and paler than marble, more crushed and broken than a reed trampled under foot, he stretched himself out as though in the agonies of death, and became of the ghastly hue of the tomb.

Edmond waited till life seemed extinct in the body of his friend; then taking up the chisel, he with difficulty forced open the closely fixed jaws, carefully poured the appointed number of drops down the rigid throat, and anxiously awaited the result.

An hour passed away without the old man's giving the least sign of returning animation; Dantès began to fear he had delayed too long ere he administered the remedy, and, thrusting his hands into his hair, continued gazing on the lifeless features of his friend in an agony of despair. At length a slight colour tinged the livid cheeks, consciousness returned to the dull open eyeballs; a faint sigh issued from the lips, and the sufferer made a feeble effort to move.

"He is saved!—he is saved!" cried Dantès, in a paroxysm of delight.

The sick man was not yet able to speak, but he pointed with evident anxiety towards the door. Dantès listened, and plainly distinguished the approaching steps of the gaoler; it was therefore near seven o'clock; but Edmond's anxiety had put all thoughts of time out of his head.

The young man sprang to the entrance, darted through it, carefully drawing the stone over the opening, and hurried to his cell. He had scarcely done so before the door opened and disclosed to the gaoler's inquisitorial gaze the prisoner seated as usual on the side of his bed.

Almost before the key had turned in the lock, and before the departing steps of the gaoler had died away in the long corridor he had to traverse, Dantès, whose restless anxiety concerning his friend left him no desire to touch the food brought him, hurried back to the abbé's chamber and, raising the stone by pressing his head against it, was soon beside the sick man's couch.

Faria had now fully regained his consciousness, but he still lay helpless and exhausted on his miserable bed.

"I did not expect to see you again," said he feebly to Dantès.

"And why not?" asked the young man; "did you fancy yourself dying?"

"No, I had no such idea; but, knowing that all was ready for your flight, I considered you had availed yourself of it and were gone."

The deep glow of indignation suffused the cheeks of Dantès.

"And did you really think so meanly of me," cried he, "as to believe I would depart without you?"

"At least," said the abbé, "I now see how wrong such an

opinion would have been. Alas! alas! I am fearfully exhausted and debilitated by this attack."

"Be of good cheer!" replied Dantès. "Your strength will return;" and as he spoke he seated himself on the bed beside Faria and tenderly chafed his chilled hands. The abbé shook his head.

"The former of these fits," said he, "lasted but half-an-hour. At the termination of which I experienced no other feeling than a great sensation of hunger; and I rose from my bed without requiring the least help. Now I can neither move my right arm nor leg, and my head seems uncomfortable, proving a rush of blood to the brain. The next of these fits will either carry me off or leave me paralysed for life."

"No, no!" cried Dantès. "You are mistaken—you will not die! And your third attack (if, indeed, you should have another) will find you at liberty. We shall save you another time, as we have done this, only with a better chance, because we shall be able to command every requisite assistance."

"My good Edmond," answered the abbé "be not deceived. The attack which has just passed away condemns me for ever to the walls of a prison. None can fly from their dungeon but those who can walk."

"Well, well, perhaps just now you are not in a condition to effect your escape; but there is no hurry; we have waited so long we can very easily defer our purpose a little longer; say a week, a month,—two, if necessary; by that time you will be quite well and strong; and as it only remains with us to fix the hour and minute, we will choose the first instant that you feel able to swim, to execute our project."

"I shall never swim again," replied Faria. "This arm is paralysed; not for a time, but for ever. Lift it, and judge by its weight if I am mistaken."

The young man raised the arm, which fell back by its own weight perfectly inanimate and helpless. A sigh escaped him.

"You are convinced now, Edmond, are you not?" asked the abbé. "Depend upon it, I know what I say. Since the first attack I experienced of this malady I have continually reflected on it. Indeed, I expected it, for it is a family inheritance; both my father and grandfather having been taken off by it. The physician who prepared for me the remedy I have twice successfully taken was no other than the celebrated Cabanis; and he predicted a similar end for me."

"The physician may be mistaken!" exclaimed Dantès. "And as for your poor arm, what difference will that make in our escape? Never mind, if you cannot swim I can take you on my shoulders and swim for both of us."

"My son," said the abbé, "you who are a sailor and a swimmer must know as well as I do, that a man so loaded would sink ere he had advanced fifty yards in the sea. Cease, then, to allow yourself to be duped by vain hopes, that even your own excellent heart refuses to believe in. Here I shall remain till the hour of my deliverance arrives; and that, in all human probability, will be the hour of my death. As for you, who are young and active, delay not on my account, but fly—go—I give you back your promise."

"It is well," said Dantès. "And now hear my determination also." Then rising and extending his hand with an air of solemnity over the old man's head, he slowly added, "Here I swear to remain with you so long as life is spared to you, and that death only shall divide us."

Faria gazed fondly on his noble-minded but single-hearted young friend, and read in his honest, open countenance ample confirmation of truthfulness, as well as sincere, affectionate, and faithful devotion.

"Thanks, my child," murmured the invalid, extending the one hand of which he still retained the use. "Thanks for your generous offer, which I accept as frankly as it was made." Then, after a short pause, he added, "You may one of these days reap the reward of your disinterested devotion; but as I cannot, and you will not, quit this place, it becomes necessary to fill up the excavation beneath the soldier's gallery; he might, by chance, find out the hollow sound produced by his footsteps over the excavated ground, and call the attention of his officer to the circumstance; that would bring about a discovery which would inevitably lead to our being separated. Go, then, and set about this work, in which, unhappily, I can offer you no assistance; keep at it all night, if necessary, and do not return here to-morrow till after the gaoler has visited me. I shall have something of the greatest importance to communicate to you."

Dantès took the hand of the abbé in his, and affectionately pressed it. Faria smiled encouragingly on him, and the young man retired to his task filled with a religious determination faithfully and unflinchingly to discharge the vow which bound him to his afflicted friend.

CHAPTER XVIII

THE TREASURE

When Dantès returned next morning to the chamber of his companion in captivity, he found Faria seated and looking composed. In the ray of light which entered by the narrow window of his cell, he held open in his left hand, of which alone, it will be recollected, he retained the use, a morsel of paper, which, from being constantly rolled into a small compass, had the form of a cylinder, and was not easily kept open. He did not speak, but shewed the paper to Dantès.

"What is that?" he inquired.

"Look at it," said the abbé, with a smile.

"I have looked at it with all possible attention," said Dantès, "and I only see a half-burnt paper on which are traces of Gothic characters traced with peculiar kind of ink."

"This paper, my friend," said Faria, "I may now avow to you, since I have proved you,—this paper is my treasure, of which, from this day forth, one half belongs to you."

A cold damp started to Dantès brow. Until this day,—and what a space of time!—he had avoided talking to the abbé of this treasure, the source whence accusation of madness against the poor abbé was derived. With his instinctive delicacy Edmond had preferred avoiding any touch of this painful chord, and Faria had been equally silent. He had taken the silence of the old man for a return to reason, and now these few words uttered by Faria, after so painful a crisis, seemed to announce a serious relapse of mental alienation.

"Your treasure?" stammered Dantès. Faria smiled.

"Yes," said he. "You are, indeed, a noble heart, Edmond; and I see by your paleness and your shudder what is passing in your heart at this moment. No, be assured, I am not mad. This treasure exists, Dantès; and if I have not been allowed to possess it, you will. Yes—you! No one would listen to me or believe me because they thought me mad; but you, who must know that I am not, listen to me, and believe me afterwards if you will."

"Alas!" murmured Edmond to himself, "this is a terrible relapse! There was only this blow wanting." Then he said aloud, "My dear friend, your attack has, perhaps fatigued you, had you not better repose a while? To-morrow, if you will, I will hear your narrative; but to-day I wish to nurse you carefully. Beside," he said, "a treasure is not a thing we need hurry."

"On the contrary, it must be hurried, Edmond!" replied the old man. "Who knows if to-morrow, or the next day after, the third attack may not come on? and then must not all be finished? Yes, indeed, I have often thought with a bitter joy that these riches, which would make the wealth of a dozen families, will be for ever lost to those men who persecute me. This idea was one of vengeance to me, and I tasted it slowly in the night of my dungeon and the despair of my captivity. But now I have forgiven the world for the love of you; now I see you young and full of hope and prospect,—now that I think of all that may result to you in the good fortune of such a disclosure, I shudder at any delay, and tremble lest I should not assure to one so worthy as yourself the possession of so vast an amount of hidden treasure."

Edmond turned away his head with a sigh.

"You persist in your incredulity, Edmond," continued Faria. "My words have not convinced you. I see you require proofs. Well, then, read this paper which I have never shewn to any one."

"To-morrow, my dear friend," said Edmond, desirous of not yielding to the old man's madness. "I thought it was understood that we should not talk of that until to-morrow."

"Then we will not talk of it until to-morrow; but read this paper to-day."

"I will not irritate him," thought Edmond, and taking the paper, of which half was wanting, having been burnt, no doubt, by some accident, he read,—

"'This treasure, which may amount to two
of Roman crowns in the most distant a
of the second opening wh
declare to belong to him alo
heir.
"'25th April, 149

"Well!" said Faria, when the young man had finished reading it.

"Why," replied Dantès, "I see nothing but broken lines and unconnected words, which are rendered illegible by fire."

"Yes, to you, my friend, who read them for the first time, but not for me, who have grown pale over them by many nights' study, and have re-constructed every phrase, completed every thought."

"And do you believe you have discovered the concealed sense?"

"I am sure I have, and you shall judge for yourself; but first listen to the history of this paper."

"Silence!" exclaimed Dantès. "Steps approach, I go, adieu."

And Dantès, happy to escape the history and explanation which could not fail to confirm to him his friend's malady, glided like a snake along the narrow passage, whilst Faria, restored by his alarm to a kind of activity, pushed with his foot the stone into its place, and covered it with a mat in order the more effectually to avoid discovery.

It was the governor, who, hearing of Faria's accident from the gaoler, had come in person to see him.

Faria sat up to receive him, and continued to conceal from the governor the paralysis that had already half stricken him with death. His fear was, lest the governor, touched with pity might order him to be removed to a prison more wholesome, and thus separate him from his young companion; but fortunately this was not the case, and the governor left him convinced that the poor madman, for whom in his heart he felt a kind of affection, was only affected with a slight indisposition.

During this time, Edmond, seated on his bed with his head in his hands, tried to collect his scattered thoughts. All was so rational, so grand, so logical with Faria, since he had known him that he could not understand how so much wisdom on all points could be allied to madness in any one;—was Faria deceived as to his treasure, or was all the world deceived as to Faria?

Dantès remained in his cell all day, not daring to return to his friend, thinking thus to defer the moment when he should acquire the certainty that the abbé was mad—such a conviction would be so terrible!

But towards the evening, after the usual visitation, Faria, not seeing the young man appear, tried to move, and get over the distance which separated them. Edmond shuddered when he heard the painful efforts which the old man made to drag himself along; his leg was inert, and he could no longer make use of one arm. Edmond was compelled to draw him towards himself, for otherwise he could not enter by the small aperture which led to Dantès's chamber.

"Here I am, pursuing you remorselessly," he said, with a benignant smile. "You thought to escape my munificence, but it is in vain. Listen to me."

Edmond saw there was no escape, and placing the old man on his bed, he seated himself on the stool beside him.

"You know," said the abbé, "that I was the secretary and intimate friend of the Cardinal Spada, the last of the princes of that name. I owe to this worthy lord all the happiness I ever knew. He was not rich, although the wealth of his family had passed into a proverb, and I heard the phrase very often, 'As rich as a Spada.' But he, like public rumour, lived on this reputation for wealth; his palace was my paradise. I instructed his nephews, who are dead, and when he was alone in the world I returned to him, by an absolute devotion to his will, all he had done for me during ten years.

"The house of the cardinal had no secrets for me. I had often seen my noble patron annotating ancient volumes, and eagerly searching amongst dusty family manuscripts. One day when I was reproaching him for his unavailing searches, and the kind of prostration of mind that followed them, he looked at me, and, smiling bitterly, opened a volume relating to the History of the City of Rome. There in the twenty-ninth chapter of the Life of Pope Alexander VI, were the following lines, which I can never forget:—

"'The great wars of Romagne had ended; Cæsar Borgia, who had completed his conquest, had need of money to purchase all Italy. The pope had also need of money to conclude with Louis, the twelfth king of France, formidable still in spite of his recent reverses; and it was necessary, therefore, to have recourse to some profitable speculation, which was a matter of great difficulty in the impoverished condition of exhausted Italy. His holiness had an idea. He determined to make two cardinals.'

"By choosing two of the greatest personages of Rome, especially rich men,—*this* was the return the holy father looked for from his speculation. In the first place, he had to sell the great appointments and splendid offices which the cardinals already held, and then he had the two hats to sell besides.

"There was a third view in the speculation, which will appear hereafter.

"The pope and Cæsar Borgia first found the two future cardinals; they were Jean Rospigliosi, who held four of the highest dignities of the holy seat; and Cæsar Spada, one of the noblest and richest of the Roman nobility: both felt the high honour of such a favour from the pope. They were ambitious: and these found, Cæsar Borgia soon found purchasers for their appointments.

"The result was that Rospigliosi and Spada paid for being cardinals, and eight other persons paid for the offices the cardinals held before their elevation, and thus eight hundred thousand crowns entered into the coffers of the speculators.

"It is time now to proceed to the last part of the speculation. The pope having almost smothered Rospigliosi and Spada with caresses, having bestowed upon them the insignia of cardinal, and induced them to realise their fortunes, and

fix themselves at Rome, the pope and Cæsar Borgia invited
the two cardinals to dinner.

"This was a matter of contest between the holy father and
his son. Cæsar thought they could make use of one of the
means which he always had ready for his friends; that is to say,
in the first place the famous key with which they requested
certain persons to go and open a particular cupboard. This
key was furnished with a small iron point,—a negligence on
the part of the locksmith. When this was pressed to effect
the opening of the cupboard, of which the lock was difficult,
the person was pricked by this small point, and died the next
day. Then there was the ring with the lion's head, which
Cæsar wore when he meant to give certain squeezes of the
hand. The lion bit the hand thus favoured, and at the end
of twenty-four hours, the bite was mortal.

"Cæsar then proposed to his father, either to ask the
cardinals to open the cupboard or give each a cordial squeeze
of the hand, but Alexander VI replied to him:—

"'Whilst we are thinking of those worthy cardinals, Spada
and Rospigliosi, let us ask both of them to a dinner. Something
tells me that we shall regain this money. Besides, you forget,
Cæsar, an indigestion declares itself immediately, whilst a
prick or a bite occasions a day or two's delay."

"Cæsar gave way before such cogent reasoning, and the
cardinals were consequently invited to dinner.

"The table was laid in a vineyard belonging to the pope,
near Saint-Pierre-ès-Liens, a charming retreat which the
cardinals knew very well by report.

"Rospigliosi, quite giddy with his dignity, prepared his
stomach, and assumed his best looks. Spada, a prudent man,
and greatly attached to his only nephew, a young captain of
highest promise, took paper and pen and made his will.

"He then sent to his nephew to await him in the vicinity of
the vineyard, but it appeared the servant did not find him.

"Spada knew the nature of these invitations; since Christianity, so eminently civilising, had made progress in Rome, it
was no longer a centurion who came from the tyrant with a
message, 'Cæsar wills that you die,' but it was legate à latere,
who came with a smile on his lips to say from the pope, 'His
holiness requests you will dine with him.'

"Spada set out about two o'clock to Saint-Pierre-ès-Liens.
The pope awaited him. The first figure that struck the eyes of
Spada was that of his nephew, in full costume, and Cæsar
Borgia paying him most marked attentions. Spada turned
pale, as Cæsar looked at him with an ironical air, which proved
that he had anticipated all, and that the snare was well spread.

"They began dinner, and Spada was only able to inquire
of his nephew if he had received his message. The nephew

replied no, perfectly comprehending the meaning of the question. It was too late, for he had already drank a glass of excellent wine, placed for him expressly by the pope's butler. Spada at the same moment saw another bottle approach him, which he was pressed to taste. An hour afterwards a physician declared they were both poisoned through eating mushrooms. Spada died on the threshold of the vineyard; the nephew expired at his own door, making signs which his wife could not comprehend.

"Then Cæsar and the pope hastened to lay hands on the heritage, under pretence of seeking for the papers of the dead man. But the inheritance consisted in this only, a scrap of paper on which Spada had written:—

"'I bequeath to my beloved nephew my coffers, my books, and, amongst other, my breviary with the golden corners, which I beg he will preserve in remembrance of his affectionate uncle.'

"The heirs sought every where, admired the breviary, laid hands on the furniture, and were greatly astonished that Spada, the rich man, was really the most miserable of uncles— no treasures—unless they were those of science composed in the library and laboratories. This was all, Cæsar and his father searched, examined, scrutinised, but found nothing, or at least very little; not exceeding a few thousand crowns in plate, and about the same in ready money; but the nephew had time to say to his wife before he expired,—

"'Look well among my uncle's papers; there is a will.'"

"They sought even more thoroughly than the august heirs had done, but it was fruitless. There were two palaces and a vineyard behind the Palatine Hill, but in these days landed property had not much value, and the two palaces and the vineyard remained to the family as beneath the rapacity of the pope and his son.

"Months and years rolled on. Alexander VI died poisoned, —you know by what mistake. Cæsar, poisoned at the same time, escaped with colouring his skin like a snake, and assumed a new cuticle, on which the poison left spots like those we see on the skin of a tiger; then, compelled to quit Rome, he went and killed himself in obscurity in a night skirmish, scarcely noticed in history.

"After the pope's death and his son's exile, it was supposed the Spada family would again make the splendid figure they had before the cardinal's time; but this was not the case. The Spadas remained in doubtful ease, a mystery hung over this dark affair, and the public rumour was, that Cæsar, a better politician than his father, had carried off from the pope the fortune of the two cardinals. I say the two, because

Cardinal Rospigliosi, who had not taken any precaution, was completely despoiled.

"Up to this time," said Faria, interrupting the thread of his narrative, "this seems to you very ridiculous, no doubt, eh?"

"Oh! my friend," said Dantès, "on the contrary, it seems as if I were reading a most interesting narrative; go on, I pray of you."

"I will.

"The family began to feel accustomed to this obscurity. Years rolled on, and amongst the descendants some were soldiers, others diplomatists, some churchmen, some bankers, some grew rich, and some were ruined. I come now to the last of the family, whose secretary I was,—the Comte de Spada.

"I had often heard him complain of the disproportion of his rank with his fortune; and I advised him to sink all he had in an annuity. He did so, and thus doubled his income.

"The celebrated breviary remained in the family, and was in the comte's possession. It had been handed down from father to son, for the singular clause of the only will that had been found, had rendered it a real relique, preserved in the family with superstitious veneration. It was an illuminated book with beautiful Gothic characters, and so weighty with gold, that a servant always carried it before the cardinal on days of great solemnity.

"At the sight of papers of all sorts, titles, contracts, parchments, which were kept in the archives of the family, all descending from the poisoned cardinal, I, like twenty servitors, stewards, secretaries before me, in my turn examined the immense bundles of documents; but in spite of the most accurate researches, I found—nothing. Yet I had read, I had even written a precise history of the Borgia family, for the sole purpose of assuring myself whether any increase of fortune had occurred to them on the death of the Cardinal Cæsar Spada; but could only trace the acquisition of the property of the Cardinal Rospigliosi, his companion in misfortune.

"I was then almost assured that the inheritance had neither profited the Borgias nor the family, but had remained unpossessed like the treasures of the Arabian Nights, which slept in the bosom of the earth under the eyes of a genii. I searched, ransacked, counted, calculated a thousand and a thousand times the income and expenditure of the family for three hundred years. It was useless. I remained in my ignorance, and the Comte de Spada in his poverty.

"My patron died. He had reserved from his annuity his family papers, his library composed of 5,000 volumes, and his famous breviary. All these he bequeathed to me, with a thousand Roman crowns, which he had in ready money, on condition, that I would have said anniversary masses for the repose of his soul, and that I would draw up a genealogical tree and history of his house; all this I did scrupulously.

"Be easy, my dear Edmond, we are near the conclusion.

"In 1807, a month before I was arrested, and fifteen days after the death of Comte de Spada, on the 25th of December (you will see presently how the date became fixed in my memory), I was reading, for the thousandth time, the papers I was arranging, for the palace was sold to a stranger; and I was going to leave Rome and settle at Florence, intending to take with me twelve thousand francs I possessed, my library, and famous breviary; when, tired with my constant labour at the same thing, and overcome by a heavy dinner I had eaten, my head dropped on my hands, and I fell asleep about three o'clock in the afternoon.

"I awoke as the clock was striking six.

"I raised my head, all was in darkness. I rang for a light, but as no one came, I determined to find one for myself. It was indeed the habit of a philosopher which I should soon be under the necessity of adopting. I took a wax-candle in one hand, and with the other groped about for a piece of paper (my match-box being empty), with which I hoped to produce a light from the small flame still playing on the embers. Fearing, however, to make use of any valuable piece of paper, I hesitated for a moment, then recollected that I had seen in the famous breviary which was on the table beside me, an old paper quite yellow with age, and which had served as a marker for centuries, kept there by the request of the heirs. I felt for it, found it, twisted it up together, and putting it to the expiring flame, set light to it.

"But beneath my fingers as if by magic, in proportion as the fire ascended, I saw yellowish characters appear on the paper, I grasped it in my hand, put out the flame as quickly as I could, lighted my taper in the fire itself, and opened the crumpled paper with inexpressible emotion, recognising, when I had done so, that these characters had been traced in mysterious and sympathetic ink, only appearing when exposed to the fire: nearly one-third of the paper had been consumed by the flame. It was that paper you read this morning; read it again, Dantès, and then I will complete for you the incomplete words and unconnected sense."

Faria, with an air of triumph, offered the paper to Dantès, who this time read the following words traced with an ink of a colour which most nearly resembled rust:—

"This 25th day of April, 1498, be...
Alexander VI and fearing that not...
he may desire to become my heir, and re...
and Bentivoglio, who were poisoned...

my sole heir, that I have bu...
and has visited with me, that is in...
island of Monte-Cristo all I poss...
jewels, diamonds, gems, that I alone...
may amount to nearly two mil...
will find on raising the twentieth ro...
creek to the east in a right line. Two open...
in these caves: the treasure is in the furthest a...
which treasure I bequeath and leave en...
as my sole heir.
      "25th April, 1498.

                                        "Cæs. .

"And now," said the abbé, "read this other paper;" and
he presented to Dantès a second leaf with fragments of lines
written on it which Edmond read as follows:—

...ing invited to dine by his Holiness
...content with making me pay for my hat
...serves for me the fate of Cardinals Caprara
...I declare to my nephew Guido Spada,
...ried in a place he knows
...the caves of the small
...essed of ingots, gold, money,
...know of the existence of this treasure, which
...lions of Roman crowns, and which he
...ck from the small
...ings have been made
...ngle in the second;
...tire to him

                              AR † Spada."

Faria followed him with excited look.
"And now," he said, when he saw Dantès had read the last
line, "put the two fragments together and judge for yourself."
Dantès obeyed, and the conjoined pieces gave the following:—

"This 25th day of April, 1498, be..ing invited to dine with
his holiness Alexander VI, and fearing that not..content with
making me pay for my hat, he may desire to become my heir
and re..serves for me the fate of Cardinals Caprara and Bentivoglio, who were poisoned,..I declare to my nephew Guido
Spada, my sole heir, that I have bu..ried in a place he knows
and has visited with me,..that is, in..the caves of the small
island of Monte-Cristo, all I poss..essed of ingots, gold, money,
jewels, diamonds, gems: that I alone..know of the existence
of this treasure, which may amount to nearly two mil..lions
of Roman crowns, and which he will find on raising the twentieth ro..ck from the small creek to the east in a right line.

Two open..ings have been made in these caves; the treasure
is in the furthest a..ngle in the second: which treasure I
bequeath and leave en..tire to him as my sole heir.

"25th April, 1498.

"CÆS..AR † SPADA."

"Well, do you comprehend now?" inquired Faria.

"It is the declaration of Cardinal Spada, and the will so
long sought for," replied Edmond, still incredulous.

"Of course; what else could it be?"

"And who completed it as it now is?"

"I did. Aided by the remaining fragment I guessed the
rest; measuring the length of the lines by those of the paper,
and divining the hidden meaning, by means of what was in
part revealed, as we are guided in a cavern by the small ray of
light above us."

"And what did you do when you arrived at this conclusion?"

"I resolved to set out, and did set out that very instant,
carrying with me the beginning of my great work on forming
Italy into one kingdom; but for some time the infernal police
(who at this period, quite contrary to what Napoleon desired
so soon as he had a son born to him, wished for a partition of
provinces,) had their eyes on me and my hasty departure, the
cause of which they were unable to guess. Having aroused
their suspicions, I was arrested at the very moment I was
leaving Piombino.

"Now," continued Faria, addressing Dantès with an almost
paternal expression,—"now, my dear fellow, you know as
much as I do myself. If we ever escape together, half this
treasure is yours; if I die here and you escape alone, the whole
belongs to you."

"But," inquired Dantès, hesitating, "has this treasure no
more legitimate possessor in this world than ourselves?"

"No, no, be easy on that score; the family is extinct. The
last Comte de Spada, moreover, made me his heir; bequeathing
to me this symbolic breviary, he bequeathed to me all it
contained: no, no, make your mind satisfied on that point.
If we lay hands on this fortune, we may enjoy it without
remorse."

"And you say this treasure amounts to——"

"Two millions of Roman crowns; nearly thirteen millions
of our money."

"Impossible!" said Dantès, staggered at the enormous
amount.

"Impossible! and why?" asked the old man. "The Spada
family was one of the oldest and most powerful families of the
fifteenth century; and in these times, when all speculation

and occupation were wanting, those accumulations of gold and jewels were by no means rare; there are at this day Roman families perishing of hunger, though possessed of nearly a million in diamonds and jewels, handed down as heir-looms, and which they cannot touch."

Edmond thought he was in a dream—he wavered between incredulity and joy.

"I have only kept this secret so long from you," continued Faria, "that I might prove you, and then surprise you. Had we escaped before my attack of catalepsy, I should have conducted you to Monte-Cristo; now," he added, with a sigh, "it is you who will conduct me thither. Well! Dantès, you do not thank me?"

"This treasure belongs to you, my dear friend," replied Dantès, "and to you only. I have no right to it. I am no relation of yours."

"You are my son, Dantès," exclaimed the old man. "You are the child of my captivity. My profession condemns me to celibacy. God has sent you to me to console, at one and the same time, the man who could not be a father, and the prisoner who could not get free."

And Faria extended the arm of which alone the use remained to him to the young man, who threw himself around his neck and wept bitterly.

CHAPTER XIX

THE THIRD ATTACK

Now that this treasure which had so long been the object of the abbé's meditations could ensure the future happiness of him whom Faria really loved as a son, it had doubled its value in his eyes, and every day he expatiated on the amount, explaining to Dantès all the good which with thirteen or fourteen millions of francs a man could do in these days to his friends; and then Dantès' countenance became gloomy, for the oath of vengeance he had taken recurred to his memory, and he reflected how much ill in these times a man with thirteen or fourteen millions could do to his enemies.

The abbé did not know the Isle of Monte-Cristo, but Dantès knew it, and had often passed it, situated twenty-five miles from Pianosa, between Corsica and the isle of Elba, and had once touched at it. This island was, always had been, and still is, completely deserted. It is a rock of almost conical form, which seems as though produced by some volcanic effort from the depth to the surface of the ocean.

Dantès traced a plan of the island to Faria, and Faria gave Dantès advice as to the means he should employ to recover the treasure.

But Dantès was far from being as enthusiastic and confident as the old man. It was past a question now that Faria was not a lunatic, and the way in which he had achieved the discovery, which had given rise to the suspicion of his madness, increased his admiration of him; but at the same time he could not believe that that deposit, supposing it had ever existed, still existed, and though he considered the treasure as by no means chimerical, he yet believed it was no longer there.

However, as if fate resolved on depriving the prisoners of their last chance, and making them understand that they were condemned to perpetual imprisonment, a new misfortune befell them; the gallery on the sea-side, which had long been in ruins, was rebuilt. They had repaired it completely, and stopped up, with vast masses of stone, the hole Dantès had partly filled in. But for this precaution, which it will be remembered, the abbé had made to Edmond, the misfortune would have been still greater, for their attempt to escape would have been detected, and they would unfortunately have been separated. Thus, a fresh and even stronger door was closed upon them.

"You see," said the young man, with an air of sorrowful resignation to Faria, "that God deems it right to take from me even what you call my devotion to you. I have promised you to remain for ever with you, and now I could not break my promise if I would. I shall no more have the treasure than you, and neither of us will quit this prison. But my real treasure is not that, my dear friend, which awaits me beneath the sombre rocks of Monte-Cristo, but it is your presence, our living together five or six hours a-day in spite of our gaolers; it is those rays of intelligence you have elicited from my brain, the languages you have implanted in my memory, and which spring there with all their philological ramifications. These different sciences that you have made so easy to me by the depth of the knowledge you possess of them, and the clearness of the principles to which you have reduced them,—this is my treasure, my beloved friend, and with this you have made me rich and happy. Believe me, and take comfort, this is better for me than tons of gold and cases of diamonds, even were they not as problematical as the clouds we see in the morning floating over the sea which we take for *terra firma*, and which evaporate and vanish as we draw near to them. To have you as long as possible near me, to hear your eloquent voice which I trust embellishes my mind, strengthens my soul, and makes my whole frame capable of great and terrible things, if I should ever be free, so fills my whole existence, that the despair to which I was just on the point of yielding when I knew you, has no longer any hold over me; and this—this is my fortune—not chimerical but actual. I owe you my real good, my present happiness; and all the sovereigns of the earth, were they Cæsar Borgias, could not deprive me of this."

Thus, if not actually happy, yet the days these two unfortunates passed together went quickly. Faria, who, for so long a time had kept silence as to the treasure, now perpetually talked of it. As he had said, he remained paralysed in the right arm and the left leg, and had given up all hope of ever enjoying it himself. But he was continually thinking over some means of escape for his young companion, and he enjoyed it for him. For fear the letter might be some day lost or abstracted, he compelled Dantès to learn it by heart, and he thus knew it from one end to the other.

Then he destroyed the second portion, assured that if the first were seized no one would be able to penetrate its real meaning. Whole hours sometimes passed whilst Faria was giving instructions to Dantès,—instructions which were to serve him when he was at liberty. Then once free, from the day and hour and moment when he was so, he could have but one only thought, which was to gain Monte-Cristo by some means, and remain there alone under some pretext, which would give no suspicions, and once there to endeavour to find the wonderful caverns, and search in the appointed spot. The appointed spot, be it remembered, being the farthest angle in the second opening.

In the meanwhile the hours passed, if not rapidly, at least tolerably. Faria, as we have said, without having recovered the use of his hand and foot, had resumed all the clearness of his understanding; and had gradually, besides the moral instructions we have detailed, taught his youthful companion the patient and sublime duty of a prisoner, who learns to make something from nothing. They were thus perpetually employed. Faria, that he might not see himself grow old; Dantès, for fear of recalling the almost extinct past which now only floated in his memory like a distant light wandering in the night. All went on as if in existences in which misfortune has deranged nothing, and which glide on mechanically and tranquilly beneath the eye of Providence.

But beneath this superficial calm there were in the heart of the young man, and, perhaps, in that of the old man, many repressed desires, many stifled sighs, which found vent when Faria was left alone, and when Edmond returned to his cell.

One night Edmond awoke suddenly, believing he heard some one calling him.

He opened his eyes, and tried to pierce through the gloom.

His name, or rather a plaintive voice, which essayed to pronounce his name, reached him.

"Alas!" murmured Edmond, "can it be?"

He moved his bed, drew up the stone, rushed into the passage, and reached the opposite extremity; the secret entrance was open.

By the light of the wretched and wavering lamp, of which we have spoken, Dantès saw the old man, pale, but yet erect, clinging to the bedstead. His features were writhing with those horrible symptoms which he already knew, and which had so seriously alarmed him when he saw them for the first time.

"Alas! my dear friend," said Faria, in a resigned tone, "you understand, do you not, and I need not attempt to explain to you?"

Edmond uttered a cry of agony, and, quite out of his senses, rushed towards the door exclaiming,——

"Help! help!"

Faria had just sufficient strength to retain him.

"Silence!" he said, "or you are lost. Think now of yourself; only, my dear friend, act so as to render your captivity supportable or your flight possible. It would require years to renew only what I have done here, and which would be instantly destroyed if our gaolers knew we had communicated with each other. Besides, be assured, my dear Edmond, the dungeon I am about to leave will not long remain empty; some other unfortunate being will soon take my place, and to him you will appear like an angel of salvation. Perhaps, he will be young, strong, and enduring, like yourself, and will aid you in your escape, whilst I have been but a hindrance. You will no longer have half a dead body tied to you to paralyse all your movements. At length Providence has done something for you; he restores to you more than he takes away, and it was time I should die."

Edmond could only clasp his hands, and exclaim,—

"Oh, my friend! my friend! speak not thus!" and then resuming all his presence of mind, which had for a moment staggered under this blow, and his strength, which had failed at the words of the old man, he said,—

"Oh! I have saved you once, and I will save you a second time!"

And raising the foot of the bed he drew out the phial, still a third filled with the red liquor.

"See!" he exclaimed, "there remains still some of this saving draught. Quick! quick! tell me what I must do this time,—are there any fresh instructions? Speak, my friend, I listen."

"There is not a hope," replied Faria, shaking his head; "but no matter, God wills it that man whom He has created, and in whose heart He has so profoundly rooted the love of life, should do all in his power to preserve that existence which, however painful it may be, is yet always so dear."

"Oh! yes, yes!" exclaimed Dantès, "and I tell you you shall be saved!"

"Well, then, try! the cold gains upon me. I feel the blood flowing towards my brain. This horrible trembling, which makes my teeth chatter and seems to dislocate my bones, begins to pervade my whole frame; in five minutes the malady will reach its height, and in a quarter of an hour there will be nothing left of me but a dead corpse."

"Oh!" exclaimed Dantès, his heart wrung with anguish.

"Do as you did before, only do not wait so long. All the springs of life are now exhausted in me, and death," he continued, looking at his paralysed arm and leg, "has but half its work to do. If, after having made me swallow twelve drops instead of ten, you see that I do not recover, then pour the rest down my throat. Now lift me on my bed, for I can no longer support myself."

Edmond took the old man in his arms and laid him on the bed.

"And now, my dear friend," said Faria, "sole consolation of my wretched existence,—you whom Heaven gave me somewhat late, but still gave me, a priceless gift, and for which I am most grateful,—at the moment of separating from you for ever, I wish you all the happiness and all the prosperity you so well deserve. My son, I bless thee!"

The young man cast himself on his knees, leaning his head against the old man's bed.

"Listen, now, to what I say in this my dying moment. The treasure of the Spadas exists. God grants me that there no longer exists for me distance or obstacle. I see it in the depths of the inner cavern. My eyes pierce the inmost recesses of the earth, and are dazzled at the sight of so much riches. If you do escape, remember that the poor abbé, whom all the world called mad, was not so. Hasten to Monte-Cristo—avail yourself of the fortune—for you have indeed suffered long enough."

A violent shock interrupted the old man. Dantès raised his head, and saw Faria's eyes injected with blood. It seemed as if a flow of blood had ascended from the chest to the head.

"Adieu! adieu!" murmured the old man, clasping Edmond's hand convulsively—"adieu!"

"Oh, no—no, not yet," he cried, "do not forsake me! Oh! succour him! Help!—help!—help!"

"Hush! hush!" murmured the dying man, "that they may not separate us if you save me!"

"You are right. Oh, yes, yes! be assured, I shall save you! Besides, although you suffer much, you do not seem in such agony as before."

"Do not mistake! I suffer less because there is in me less strength to endure it. At your age we have faith in life; it is the privilege of youth to believe and hope, but old men see death more clearly. Oh! 'tis here—'tis here—'tis over—my sight is gone—my reason escapes! Your hand, Dantès! Adieu!—adieu!"

And raising himself by a final effort, in which he summoned all his faculties, he said,——

"Monte-Cristo! forget not Monte-Cristo!"

And he fell back in his bed.

The crisis was terrible, his twisted limbs, his swollen eyelids, a foam of blood and froth in his lips, a frame quite rigid, was soon extended on this bed of agony in place of the intellectual being who was there but so lately.

Dantès took the lamp, placed it on a projecting stone above the bed, whence its tremulous light fell with strange and fantastic ray on this discomposed countenance and this motionless and stiffened body.

With fixed eyes he awaited boldly the moment for administering the hoped-for restorative.

When he believed the instant had arrived, he took the knife, unclosed the teeth, which offered less resistance than before, counted one after the other twelve drops, and watched; the phial contained, perhaps, twice as much more.

He waited ten minutes, a quarter of an hour, half an hour, nothing moved. Trembling, his hair erect, his brow bathed with perspiration, he counted the seconds by the beatings of his heart.

Then he thought it was time to make the last trial, and he put the phial to the violet lips of Faria, and without having occasion to force open his jaws which had remained extended, he poured the whole of the liquid down his throat.

The draught produced a galvanic effect, a violent trembling pervaded the old man's limbs, his eyes opened until it was fearful to gaze upon them, he heaved a sigh which resembled a shriek, and then all this vibrating frame returned gradually to its state of immobility, only the eyes remained open.

Half an hour, an hour, an hour and a half elapsed, and during this time of anguish Edmond leaned over his friend, his hand applied to his heart, and felt the body gradually grow cold, and the heart's pulsation become more and more deep and dull, until at length all stopped: the last movement of the heart ceased, the face became livid, the eyes remained open, but the look was glazed.

It was six o'clock in the morning, the dawn was just breaking, and its weak ray came into the dungeon and paled the ineffectual light of the lamp. Singular shadows passed over the countenance of the dead man, which at times gave it the appearance of life. Whilst this struggle between day and night lasted, Dantès still doubted; but as soon as the daylight gained the pre-eminence, he saw that he was alone with a corpse.

Then an invincible and extreme terror seized upon him, and he dared not again press the hand that hung out of bed, he dared no longer to gaze on those fixed and vacant eyes which he tried many times to close, but in vain—they opened again as soon as shut. He extinguished the lamp, carefully concealed it, and then went away, closing as well as he could the entrance to the secret passage by the large stone as he descended.

It was time, for the gaoler was coming. On this occasion he began his rounds at Dantès' cell, and on leaving him he went on to Faria's dungeon, where he was taking breakfast and some linen.

Nothing betokened that the man knew anything of what had occurred. He went on his way.

Dantès was then seized with an indescribable desire to know what was going on in the dungeon of his unfortunate friend. He therefore returned by the subterranean gallery, and arrived in time to hear the exclamations of the turnkey who called out for help.

Other turnkeys came, and then was heard the regular tramp of soldiers even when not on duty—behind them came the governor.

Edmond heard the noise of the bed in which they were moving the corpse, heard the voice of the governor, who desired them to throw water on the face, and seeing that in spite of this application the prisoner did not recover, sent for the doctor.

The governor then went out, and some words of pity fell on Dantès' listening ears, mingled with brutal laughter.

"Well! well!" said one, "the madman has gone to look after his treasure. Good journey to him!"

"With all his millions he will not have enough to pay for his shroud!" said another.

"Oh!" added a third voice, "the shrouds of the Château d'If are not dear!"

"Perhaps," said one of the previous speakers, "as he was a churchman, they may go to some expense in his behalf."

"They may give him the honours of the sack."

Edmond did not lose a word, but comprehended very little of what was said. The voices soon ceased, and it seemed to him as if the persons had all left the cell. Still he dared not to enter as they might have left some turnkey to watch the dead.

He remained, therefore, mute and motionless, restraining even his respiration.

At the end of an hour he heard a faint noise which increased. It was the governor who returned, followed by the doctor and other attendants.

There was a moment's silence, it was evident that the doctor was examining the dead body.

The inquiries soon commenced.

The doctor analysed the symptoms of the malady under which the prisoner had sunk, and declared he was dead.

Questions and answers followed in a manner that made Dantès indignant, for he felt that all the world should experience for the poor abbé the love he bore him.

"I am very sorry for what you tell me," said the governor, replying to the assurance of the doctor, "that the old man is really dead, for he was a quiet, inoffensive prisoner, happy in his folly, and required no watching."

"Ah!" added the turnkey, "there was no occasion for watching him; he would have stayed here fifty years, I'll answer for it, without any attempt to escape."

"Still," said the governor, "I believe it will be requisite, notwithstanding your certainty, and not that I doubt your science, but for my own responsibility's sake, that we should be perfectly assured that the prisoner is dead."

There was a moment of complete silence, during which Dantès, still listening, felt assured that the doctor was examining and touching the corpse a second time.

"You may make your mind easy," said the doctor; "he is dead. I will answer for that."

"You know, sir," said the governor, persisting, "that we are not content in such cases as this with such a simple examination.   In spite of all appearances, be so kind, therefore, as finish your duty by fulfilling the formalities prescribed by law."

"Let the irons be heated," said the doctor; "but really it is an useless precaution."

This order to heat the irons made Dantès shudder.   He heard hasty steps, the creaking of a door, people going and coming, and some minutes afterwards a turnkey entered saying,——

"Here is the brazier lighted."

There was a moment's silence, and then was heard the noise made by burning flesh, of which the peculiar and nauseous smell penetrated even behind the wall where Dantès was listening horrified.

At this smell of human flesh carbonised, the damp came over the young man's brow, and he felt as if he should faint.

"You see, sir, he is really dead," said the doctor; "this burn in the heel is decisive; the poor fool is cured of his folly, and delivered from his captivity."

"Wasn't his name Faria?" inquired one of the officers who accompanied the governor.

"Yes, sir; and as he said, it was an ancient name; he was, too, very learned, and rational enough on all points which did not relate to his treasure; but on that, indeed, he was obstinate."

"It is the sort of malady which we call monomania," said the doctor.

"You never had any thing to complain of?" said the governor to the gaoler who had charge of the abbé.

"Never, sir," replied the gaoler, "never—on the contrary, he sometimes amused me very much by telling me stories. One day, too, when my wife was ill, he gave me a prescription which cured her."

"Ah, ah!" said the doctor, "I was ignorant that I had a competitor; but I hope, M. le Gouverneur, that you will shew him all proper respect in consequence."

"Yes, yes; make your mind easy; he shall be decently interred in the newest sack we can find.   Will that satisfy you?"

"Must we do this last formality in your presence, sir?" inquired a turnkey.

"Certainly. But make haste. I cannot stay here all day."

Fresh footsteps, going and coming, were now heard, and a moment afterwards the noise of cloth being rubbed reached Dantès ears, the bed creaked on its hinges, and the heavy foot of a man, who lifts a weight, resounded on the floor; then the bed again creaked under the weight deposited upon it.

"In the evening!" said the governor.

"Will there be any mass?" asked one of the attendants.

"That is impossible," replied the governor. "The chaplain of the Château came to me yesterday to beg for leave of absence in order to take a trip to Hyères for a week. I told him I would attend to the prisoners in his absence. If the poor abbé had not been in such a hurry he might have had his requiem."

"Pooh! pooh!" said the doctor, with the accustomed impiety of persons of his profession, "he is a churchman. God will respect his profession, and not give the devil the wicked delight of sending him a priest."

A shout of laughter followed this brutal jest.

During this time the operation of putting the body in the sack was going on.

"This evening," said the governor, when the task was ended.

"At what o'clock?" inquired a turnkey.

"Why, about ten or eleven o'clock."

"Shall we watch by the corpse?"

"Of what use would it be? Shut the dungeon as if he were alive—that is all."

Then the steps retreated, and the voices died away in the distance; the noise of the door with its creaking hinges and bolts ceased, and a silence duller than any solitude ensued, the silence of death, which pervaded all, and struck its icy chill through the young man's whole frame. Then he raised the flag-stone cautiously with his head, and looked carefully round the chamber.

It was empty, and Dantès, quitting the passage, entered it.

CHAPTER XX

THE CEMETERY OF THE CHÂTEAU D'IF

ON the bed, at full length, and faintly lighted by the pale ray that penetrated the window, was visible a sack of coarse cloth, under the large folds of which was stretched a long and stiffened form; it was Faria's last winding-sheet,—a winding-sheet which, as the turnkey said, cost so little. All then was completed. A material separation had taken place between Dantès and his old friend,—he could no longer see those eyes which had remained open as if to look even beyond death,—he could no longer clasp that hand of industry which had lifted for him the veil that had concealed hidden and obscure things. Faria, the usual and the good companion, with whom he was accustomed to live so intimately, no longer breathed. He seated himself on the edge of that terrible bed, and fell into a melancholy and gloomy reverie.

Alone! he was alone again! again relapsed into silence! he found himself once again in the presence of nothingness!

Alone! no longer to see,—no longer to hear the voice of the only human being who attached him to life! Was it not better, like Faria, to seek the presence of his Maker and learn the enigma of life at the risk of passing through the mournful gate of intense suffering?

The idea of suicide, driven away by his friend, and forgotten in his presence whilst living, arose like a phantom before him in presence of his dead body.

"If I could die," he said, "I should go where he goes, and should assuredly find him again. But how to die? It is very easy," he continued, with a smile of bitterness, "I will remain here, rush on the first person that opens the door, will strangle him, and then they will guillotine me."

But as it happens that in excessive griefs, as in great tempests, the abyss is found between the tops of the loftiest waves, Dantès recoiled from the idea of this infamous death, and passed suddenly from despair to an ardent desire for life and liberty.

"Die! oh, no," he exclaimed, "not die now, after having lived and suffered so long, and so much! Die! yes, had I died years since, but now it would be indeed to give way to my bitter destiny. No, I desire to live, I desire to struggle to the

186

very last, I wish to re-conquer the happiness of which I have been deprived. Before I die, I must not forget that I have my executioners to punish, and, perhaps, too, who knows, some friends to reward. Yet they will forget me here, and I shall die in my dungeon like Faria."

As he said this, he remained motionless, his eyes fixed like a man struck with a sudden idea, but whom this idea fills with amazement. Suddenly he rose, lifted his hand to his brow as if his brain were giddy, paced twice or thrice round his chamber, and then paused abruptly at the bed.

"Ah! ah!" he muttered, "who inspires me with this thought? Is that thou, gracious God? Since none but the dead pass freely from this dungeon, let me assume the place of the dead!"

Without giving himself time to re-consider his decision, and indeed that he might not allow his thoughts to be distracted from his desperate resolution, he bent over the appalling sack, opened it with the knife which Faria had made, drew the corpse from the sack, and transported it along the gallery to his own chamber, laid it on his couch, passed round its head the rag he wore at night round his own, covered it with his counterpane, once again kissed the ice-cold brow, and tried vainly to close the resisting eyes which glared horribly, turned the head towards the wall, so that the gaoler might, when he brought his evening meal, believe that he was asleep, as was his frequent custom; returned along the gallery, threw the bed against the wall, returned to the other cell, took from the hiding-place the needle and thread, flung off his rags that they might feel naked flesh only beneath the coarse sackcloth, and getting inside the sack, placed himself in the posture in which the dead body had been laid, and sewed up the mouth of the sack withinside.

The beating of his heart might have been heard, if by any mischance the gaolers had entered at that moment.

Dantès might have waited until the evening visit was over, but he was afraid the governor might change his resolution, and order the dead body to be removed earlier.

In that case his last hope would have been destroyed.

Now his project was settled under any circumstances, and he hoped thus to carry it into effect.

If during the time he was being conveyed the grave-diggers should discover that they were conveying a live instead of a dead body, Dantès did not intend to give them time to recognize him, but with a sudden cut of the knife, he meant to open the sack from top to bottom, and, profiting by their alarm, escape; if they tried to catch him he would use his knife.

If they conducted him to the cemetery and laid him in the grave, he would allow himself to be covered with earth, and then as it was night, the grave-diggers could scarcely have turned their backs, ere he would have worked his way through the soft soil and escape, hoping that the weight would not be too heavy for him to support.

If he was deceived in this and the earth proved too heavy, he would be stifled, and then, so much the better, all would be over.

Dantès had not eaten since the previous evening, but he had not thought of hunger or thirst, nor did he now think of it. His position was too precarious to allow even time to reflect on any thought but one.

The first risk that Dantès run was, that the gaoler when he brought him his supper at seven o'clock, might perceive the substitution he had effected; fortunately, twenty times at least from misanthropy or fatigue, Dantès had received his gaoler in bed, and then the man placed his bread and soup on the table and went away without saying a word.

This time the gaoler might not be silent as usual, but speak to Dantès, and seeing that he received no reply go to the bed, and thus discover all.

When seven o'clock came Dantès' agony really commenced. His hand placed on his heart was unable to repress its throbbings, whilst, with the other, he wiped the perspiration from his temples. From time to time shudderings ran through his whole frame, and collapsed his heart as if it were frozen. Then he thought he was going to die. Yet the hours passed on without any stir in the Château, and Dantès felt he had escaped this first danger: it was a good augury. At length about the hour the governor had appointed, footsteps were heard on the stairs. Edmond felt that the moment had arrived, and summoning up all his courage, held his breath, happy if at the same time he could have repressed in like manner the hasty pulsation of his arteries.

They stopped at the door—there were two steps, and Dantès guessed it was the two grave-diggers who came to seek him—this idea was soon converted into certainty, when he heard the noise they made in putting down the hand-bier.

The door opened, and a dim light reached Dantès' eyes through the coarse sack that covered him, he saw two shadows approach his bed, a third remaining at the door with a torch in his hand. Each of these two men, approaching the ends of the bed, took the sack by its extremities.

"He's heavy though for an old and thin man," said one, as he raised the head.

"They say every year adds half a pound to the weight of the bones," said another, lifting the feet.

"Have you tied the knot?" inquired the first speaker.

"What would be the use of carrying so much more

weight?" was the reply; "I can do that when we get there."

"Yes, you're right," replied the companion.

"What's the knot for?" thought Dantès.

They deposited the supposed corpse on the bier. Edmond stiffened himself in order to play his part of a dead man, and then the party lighted by the man with the torch who went first, ascended the stairs.

Suddenly he felt the fresh and sharp night air, and Dantès recognised the *Mistral*. It was a sudden sensation, at the same time replete with delight and agony.

The bearers advanced twenty paces, then stopped, putting their bier down on the ground.

One of them went away, and Dantès heard his shoes on the pavement.

"Where am I then?" he asked himself.

"Really, he is by no means a light load!" said the other bearer, sitting on the edge of the hand-barrow.

Dantès' first impulse was to escape, but fortunately he did not attempt it.

"Light me, you sir," said the other bearer, "or I shall not find what I am looking for."

The man with the torch complied, although not asked in the most polite terms.

"What can he be looking for?" thought Edmond. "The spade, perhaps."

An exclamation of satisfaction indicated that the grave-digger had found the object of his search.

"Here it is at last," he said, "not without some trouble though."

"Yes," was the answer, "but it has lost nothing by waiting."

As he said this the man came towards Edmond, who heard a heavy and sounding substance laid down beside him, and at the same moment a cord was fastened round his feet with sudden and painful violence.

"Well, have you tied the knot?" inquired the grave-digger, who was looking on.

"Yes, and pretty tight, too, I can tell you," was the answer.

"Move on, then."

And the bier was lifted once more, and they proceeded.

They advanced fifty paces farther, and then stopped to open a door, then went forward again. The noise of the waves dashing against the rocks, on which the Château is built, reached Dantès' ear distinctly as they progressed.

"Bad weather!" observed one of the bearers; "not a pleasant night for a dip in the sea."

"Why, yes, the abbé runs a chance of being wet," said the other; and then there was a burst of brutal laughter.

Dantès did not comprehend the jest, but his hair stood erect on his head.

"Well, here we are at last," said one of them; "a little farther—a little farther," said the other. "You know very well that the last was stopped on his way, dashed on the rocks, and the governor told us next day that we were careless fellows."

They ascended five or six more steps, and then Dantès felt that they took him one by the head and the other by the heels, and swung him to and fro.

"One!" said the grave-diggers. "Two!   Three, and away!"

And at the same instant Dantès felt himself flung into the air like a wounded bird falling, falling with a rapidity that made his blood curdle.   Although drawn downwards by the same heavy weight which hastened his rapid descent, it seemed to him as if the time were a century.   At last, with a terrific dash, he entered the ice-cold water, and as he did so he uttered a shrill cry, stifled in a moment by his immersion beneath the waves.

Dantès had been flung into the sea, into whose depths he was dragged by a thirty-six pound shot tied to his feet.

The sea is the Cemetery of Château d'If.

CHAPTER XXI

THE ISLE OF TIBOULEN

DANTÈS, although giddy, and almost suffocated, had yet sufficient presence of mind to hold his breath; and as his right hand (prepared as he was for every chance) held his knife open, he rapidly ripped up the sack, extricated his arm, and then his body; but in spite of all his efforts to free himself from the bullet he felt it dragging him down still lower; he then bent his body, and by a desperate effort severed the cord that bound his legs at the moment he was suffocating. With a vigorous spring he rose to the surface of the sea, whilst the bullet bore to its depths the sack that had so nearly become his shroud.

Dantès merely paused to breathe, and then dived again in order to avoid being seen.

When he rose a second time he was fifty paces from where he had first sunk. He saw overhead a black and tempestuous sky, over which the wind was driving the fleeting vapours that occasionally suffered a twinkling star to appear: before him was the vast expanse of waters, sombre and terrible, whose waves foamed and roared as if before the approach of a storm. Behind him, blacker than the sea, blacker than the sky, rose like a phantom the giant of granite, whose projecting crags seemed like arms extended to seize their prey; and on the highest rock was a torch that lighted two figures. He fancied these two forms were looking at the sea; doubtless these strange grave-diggers had heard his cry. Dantès dived again, and remained a long time beneath the water. This manœuvre was already familiar to him, and usually attracted a crowd of spectators in the bay before the lighthouse at Marseilles when he swam there, and who, with one accord, pronounced him the best swimmer in the port.

When he reappeared the light had disappeared.

It was necessary to strike out to sea; Ratonneau and Pomègue are the nearest isles of all those that surround the Château d'If. But Ratonneau and Pomègue are inhabited together with the islet of Daume; Tiboulen or Lemaire were the most secure. The isles of Tiboulen and Lemaire are a league from the Château d'If. Dantès, nevertheless, determined to make for them; but how could he find his way in the darkness of the night!

At this moment he saw before him, like a brilliant star, the lighthouse of Planier.

By leaving this light on the right he kept the isle of Tiboulen a little on the left; by turning to the left, therefore, he would find it. But as we have said, it was at least a league from the Château d'If to the island.

Often in prison Faria had said to him when he saw him idle and inactive,—

"Dantès, you must not give way to this listlessness, you will be drowned, if you seek to escape; and your strength has not been properly exercised and prepared for exertion."

These words rang in Dantès' ears even beneath the waves; he hastened to cleave his way through them to see if he had not lost his strength; he found with pleasure that his captivity had taken away nothing of his power, and that he was still master of that element on whose bosom he had so often sported as a boy.

Fear, that relentless pursuer, clogged Dantès' efforts; he listened if any noise was audible; each time that he rose over the waves his looks scanned the horizon, and strove to penetrate the darkness; every wave seemed a boat in his pursuit, and he redoubled exertions that increased his distance from the Château, but the repetition of which weakened his strength. He swam on still, and already the terrible Château had disappeared in the darkness. He could not see it, but he *felt* its presence. An hour passed, during which Dantès, excited by the feeling of freedom, continued to cleave the waves.

"Let us see," said he, "I have swam above an hour; but as the wind is against me, that has retarded my speed: however, if I am not mistaken, I must be close to the isle of Tiboulen. But what if I were mistaken?"

A shudder passed over him. He sought to tread water in order to rest himself, but the sea was too violent, and he felt that he could not make use of this means of repose.

"Well," said he, "I will swim on until I am worn out, or the cramp seizes me, and then I shall sink;" and he struck out with the energy of despair.

Suddenly the sky seemed to him to become still darker and more dense, and compact clouds lowered towards him; at the same time he felt a violent pain in his knee, his imagination told him a ball had struck him, and that in a moment he would hear the report; but he heard nothing. Dantès put out his hand, and felt resistance; he then extended his leg and felt the land, and in an instant guessed the nature of the object he had taken for a cloud.

Before him rose a mass of strangely formed rocks that resembled nothing so much as a vast fire petrified at the moment of its most fervent combustion.   It was the isle of Tiboulen.

Dantès rose, advanced a few steps, and with a fervent prayer of gratitude stretched himself on the granite, which seemed to him softer than down.   Then, in spite of the wind and rain, he fell into the deep sweet sleep of those worn out by fatigue.

At the expiration of an hour Edmond was awakened by the roar of the thunder.   The tempest was unchained and let loose in all its fury; from time to time a flash of lightning stretched across the heavens like a fiery serpent lighting up the clouds that rolled on like the waves of an immense chaos.

Dantès had not been deceived, he had reached the first of the two isles, which was in reality Tiboulen.   He knew that it was barren and without shelter; but when the sea became more calm, he resolved to plunge into its waves again, and swim to Lemaire, equally arid, but larger, and consequently better adapted for concealment.

An overhanging rock offered him a temporary shelter; and scarcely had he availed himself of it when the tempest burst forth in all its fury.   Edmond felt the rock beneath which he lay tremble; the waves dashing themselves against the granite rock wetted him with their spray.   In safety as he was, he felt himself become giddy in the midst of this war of the elements, and the dazzling brightness of the lightning.   It seemed to him that the island trembled to its base, and that it would, like a vessel at anchor, break her moorings, and bear him off into the centre of the storm.

He then recollected that he had not eaten or drunk for four-and-twenty hours.   He extended his hands and drank greedily of the rain-water that had lodged in a hollow of the rock.

As he rose, a flash of lightning, that seemed as if the whole of the heavens were opened, illumined the darkness.   By its light, between the isle of Lemaire and Cape Croiselle, a quarter of a league distant, Dantès saw, like a spectre, a fishing-boat driven rapidly on by the force of the winds and waves.   A second after he saw it again approaching nearer.   Dantès cried at the top of his voice to warn them of their danger, but they saw it themselves.   Another flash shewed him four men clinging to the shattered mast and the rigging, while a fifth clung to the broken rudder.

The men he beheld saw him doubtless, for their cries were carried to his ears by the wind.   Above the splintered mast a sail rent to tatters was waving, suddenly the ropes that still held it gave way, and it disappeared in the darkness of the night like a vast sea-bird.   At the same moment a violent crash was heard, and cries of distress.   Perched on the

C.M.—G

summit of the rock, Dantès saw by the lightning the vessel in pieces; and amongst the fragments were visible the agonised features of the unhappy sailors. Then all became dark again.

Dantès ran down the rocks at the risk of being himself dashed to pieces; he listened, he strove to examine, but he heard and saw nothing,—all human cries had ceased; and the tempest alone continued to rage.

By degrees the wind abated; vast grey clouds rolled towards the west; and the blue firmament appeared studded with bright stars. Soon a red streak became visible in the horizon; the waves whitened, a light played over them, and gilded their foaming crests with gold. It was day.

Dantès stood silent and motionless before this vast spectacle; for since his captivity he had forgotten it. He turned towards the fortress, and looked both at the sea and the land.

The gloomy building rose from the bosom of the ocean with that imposing majesty of inanimate objects that seems at once to watch and to command.

It was about five o'clock; the sea continued to grow calmer.

"In two or three hours," thought Dantès, "the turnkey will enter my chamber, find the body of my poor friend, recognise it, seek for me in vain; and give the alarm. Then the passage will be discovered, the men who cast me into the sea, and who must have heard the cry I uttered, will be questioned. Then boats filled with armed soldiers will pursue the wretched fugitive. The cannon will warn every one to refuse shelter to a man wandering about naked and famished. The police of Marseilles will be on the alert by land, whilst the governor pursues me by sea. I am cold, I am hungry. I have lost even the knife that saved me. Oh, my God! I have suffered enough, surely. Have pity on me, and do for me what I am unable to do for myself."

As Dantès (his eyes turned in the direction of the Château d'If) uttered this prayer, he saw appear at the extremity of the isle of Pomègue, like a bird skimming over the sea, a small bark, that the eye of a sailor alone could recognise as a Genoese tartane. She was coming out of Marseilles harbour, and was standing out to sea rapidly, her sharp prow cleaving through the waves.

"Oh!" cried Edmond, "to think that in half an hour I could join her, did I not fear being questioned, detected, and conveyed back to Marseilles. What can I do? What story can I invent? Under pretext of trading along the coast, these men, who are in reality smugglers, will prefer selling me to doing a good action. I must wait. But I cannot, I am starving. In a few hours my strength will be utterly exhausted; besides, perhaps, I have not been missed at the

fortress. I can pass as one of the sailors wrecked last night.
This story will pass current, for there is no one left to contradict
me."

As he spoke, Dantès looked towards the spot where the
fishing vessel had been wrecked, and started.   The red cap of
one of the sailors hung to a point of the rock; and some beams
that had formed a part of the vessel's keel, floated at the foot
of the crags.

In an instant Dantès' plan was formed. He swam to the
cap, placed it on his head, seized one of the beams, and
struck out so as to cross the line the vessel was taking.

"I am saved," murmured he.

And this conviction restored his strength.

He soon perceived the vessel, which, having the wind right
a-head, was tacking between the Château d'If and the tower
of Planier. For an instant he feared lest the bark, instead of
keeping in shore, should stand out to sea; but he soon saw
by her manœuvres that she wished to pass, like most vessels
bound for Italy, between the islands of Jaros and Calaseraigne.
However, the vessel and the swimmer insensibly neared one
another; and in one of its tacks the bark approached within
a quarter of a mile of him. He rose on the waves, making
signs of distress, but no one on board perceived him; and the
vessel stood on another tack. Dantès would have cried out
but he reflected that the wind would drown his voice.

It was then he rejoiced at his precaution in taking the
beam, for without it he would have been unable, perhaps, to
reach the vessel,—certainly to return to shore, should he be
unsuccessful in attracting attention.

Dantès, although almost sure as to what course the bark
would take, had yet watched it anxiously until it tacked and
stood towards him.   Then he advanced; but, before they had
met, the vessel again changed her direction. By a violent
effort, he rose half out of the water, waving his cap, and
uttering a loud shout peculiar to sailors.

This time he was both seen and heard, and the tartane
instantly steered towards him.   At the same time, he saw
they were about to lower the boat.

An instant after, the boat, rowed by two men, advanced
rapidly towards him. Dantès abandoned the beam, which
he thought now useless, and swam vigorously to meet them.
But he had reckoned too much upon his strength, and then he
felt how serviceable the beam had been to him. His arms
grew stiff, his legs had lost their flexibility, and he was almost
breathless.

He uttered a second cry. The two sailors redoubled their
efforts, and one of them cried in Italian, "Courage!"

The word reached his ear as a wave, which he no longer

had the strength to surmount, passed over his head. He rose again to the surface, supporting himself by one of those desperate efforts a drowning man makes, uttered a third cry, and felt himself sink again, as if the fatal bullet were again tied to his feet.

The water passed over his head and the sky seemed livid. A violent effort again brought him to the surface. He felt as if something seized him by the hair; but he saw and heard nothing. He had fainted.

When he opened his eyes Dantès found himself on the deck of the tartane. His first care was to see what direction they were pursuing. They were rapidly leaving the Château d'If behind. Dantès was so exhausted that the exclamation of joy he uttered was mistaken for a sigh.

As we have said, he was lying on the deck, a sailor was rubbing his limbs with a woollen cloth; another, whom he recognised as the one who had cried out "Courage!" held a gourd full of rum to his mouth; whilst the third, an old sailor, at once the pilot and captain, looked on with that egotistical pity men feel for a misfortune that they have escaped yesterday and which may overtake them to-morrow.

A few drops of the rum restored suspended animation, whilst the friction of his limbs restored their elasticity.

"Who are you?" said the pilot, in bad French.

"I am," replied Dantès, in bad Italian, "a Maltese sailor. We were coming from Syracuse laden with grain. The storm of last night overtook us at Cape Morgion, and we were wrecked on these rocks."

"Where do you come from?"

"From these rocks, that I had the good luck to cling to whilst our captain and the rest of the crew were all lost. I saw your ship, and fearful of being left to perish on the desolate island, I swam off on a fragment of the vessel in order to try and gain your bark. You have saved my life, and I thank you," continued Dantès. "I was lost when one of your sailors caught hold of my hair."

"It was I," said a sailor, of a frank and manly appearance; "and it was time, for you were sinking."

"Yes," returned Dantès, holding out his hand, "I thank you again."

"I almost hesitated though," replied the sailor, "you looked more like a brigand than an honest man, with your beard six inches and your hair a foot long."

Dantès recollected that his hair and beard had not been cut all the time he was at the Château d'If.

"Yes," said he, "I made a vow to our Lady of the Grotto not to cut my hair or beard for ten years if I were saved in a moment of danger; but to-day the vow expires."

"Now what are we to do with you?" said the captain.

"Alas! any thing you please. My captain is dead; I have barely escaped; but I am a good sailor. Leave me at the first port you make; I shall be sure to find employment."

"Do you know the Mediterranean?"

"I have sailed over it since my childhood."

"You know the best harbours?"

"There are few ports that I could not enter or leave with my eyes blinded."

"I say, captain," said the sailor, who had cried "Courage!" to Dantès, "if what he says is true, what hinders his staying with us?"

"If he says true," said the captain, doubtingly. "But in his present condition he will promise any thing, and take his chance of keeping it afterwards."

"I will do more than I promise," said Dantès.

"We shall see," returned the other, smiling.

"Where are you going to?" asked Dantès.

"To Leghorn."

"Then why, instead of tacking so frequently, do you not sail nearer the wind?"

"Because we should run straight on to the island of Rion."

"You shall pass it by twenty fathoms."

"Take the helm, and let us see what you know."

The young man took the helm, ascertaining by a slight pressure if the vessel answered the rudder, and seeing that, without being a first-rate sailer, she yet was tolerably obedient,—

"To the braces," said he.

The four seamen, who composed the crew, obeyed, whilst the pilot looked on.

"Haul taut."

They obeyed.

"Belay."

This order was also executed, and the vessel passed, as Dantès had predicted, twenty fathoms to the right.

"Bravo!" said the captain.

"Bravo!" repeated the sailors.

And they all regarded with astonishment this man whose eye had recovered an intelligence and his body a vigour they were far from suspecting.

"You see," said Dantès, quitting the helm, "I shall be of some use to you, at least, during the voyage. If you do not want me at Leghorn, you can leave me there, and I will pay you out of the first wages I get for my food and the clothes you lend me."

"Ah," said the captain, "we can agree very well if you are reasonable."

"Give me what you give the others, and all will be arranged," returned Dantès.

"That's not fair," said the seaman who had saved Dantès. "For you know more than we do."

"What is that to you, Jacopo?" returned the captain. "Every one is free to ask what he pleases."

"That's true," replied Jacopo. "I only made a remark."

"Well, you would do much better to lend him a jacket and a pair of trousers if you have them."

"No," said Jacopo; "but I have a shirt and a pair of trousers."

"That is all I want," interrupted Dantès.

Jacopo dived into the hold, and soon returned with what Edmond wanted.

"Now, then, do you wish for any thing else?" said the patron.

"A piece of bread and another glass of the capital rum I tasted, for I have not eaten or drunk for a long time."

He had not tasted food for forty hours.

A piece of bread was brought, and Jacopo offered him the gourd.

"Larboard your helm," cried the captain to the steersman.

Dantès glanced to the same side as he lifted the gourd to his mouth; but his hand stopped.

"Halloa! what's the matter at the Château d'If?" said the captain.

A small white cloud, which had attracted Dantès' attention, crowned the summit of the bastion of the Château d'If.

At the same moment the faint report of a gun was heard. The sailors looked at one another.

"What is this?" asked the captain.

"A prisoner has escaped from the Château d'If, and they are firing the alarm gun," replied Dantès.

The captain glanced at him, but he had lifted the rum to his lips, and was drinking it with so much composure, that his suspicions, if he had any, died away.

"At any rate," murmured he, "if it be, so much the better, for I have made a rare acquisition."

Under pretence of being fatigued, Dantès asked to take the helm, the steersman, enchanted to be relieved, looked at the captain, and the latter by a sign indicated that he might abandon it to his new comrade. Dantès could thus keep his eyes on Marseilles.

"What is the day of the month?" asked he of Jacopo, who sat down beside him.

"The 28th of February!"

"In what year?"

"In what year—you ask me in what year?"

"Yes," replied the young man, "I ask you in what year!"

"You have forgotten then?"

"I have been so frightened last night," replied Dantès, smiling, "that I have almost lost my memory. I ask you what year is it?"

"The year 1829," returned Jacopo.

It was fourteen years day for day since Dantès' arrest.

He was nineteen when he entered the Château d'If; he was thirty-three when he escaped.

A sorrowful smile passed over his face, he asked himself what had become of Mercédès, who must have believed him dead.

Then his eyes lighted up with hatred as he thought of the three men who had caused him so long and wretched a captivity.

He renewed against Danglars, Fernand, and Villefort, the oath of implacable vengeance he had made in his dungeon.

This oath was no longer a vain menace, for the fastest sailer in the Mediterranean would have been unable to overtake the little tartane, that with every stitch of canvas set was flying before the wind to Leghorn.

CHAPTER XXII

THE SMUGGLERS

DANTÈS had not been a day on board before he had an insight into the persons with whom he sailed. Without having been in the school of the Abbé Faria, the worthy master of La Jeune Amélie (the name of the Genoese tartane) knew a smattering of all the tongues spoken on the shores of that large lake called the Mediterranean, from the Arabic to the Provincial; and this, whilst it spared him interpreters, persons always troublesome and frequently indiscreet, gave him great facilities of communication, either with the vessels he met at sea, with the small barks sailing along the coast, or with those persons without name, country, or apparent calling, who are always seen on the quays of seaports, and who live by those hidden and mysterious means, which we must suppose come in a right line from Providence, as they have no visible means of existence. We may thus suppose that Dantès was on board a smuggling lugger.

In the first instance the master had received Dantès on board with a certain degree of mistrust. He was very well known to the custom-house officers of the coast, and as there was between these worthies and himself an exchange of the most cunning stratagems, he had at first thought that Dantès might be an emissary of these illustrious executors of rights and duties, who employed this ingenious means of penetrating some of the secrets of his trade. But the skilful manner in which Dantès had manœuvred the little bark had entirely reassured him, and then when he saw the light smoke floating like a plume above the bastion of the Château d'If, and heard the distant explosion, he was instantly struck with the idea that he had on board his vessel one for whom, like the goings in and comings out of kings, they accord salutes of cannons. This made him less uneasy, it must be owned, than if the new comer had proved a custom-house officer, but this latter supposition also disappeared like the first, when he beheld the perfect tranquillity of his recruit.

Edmond thus had the advantage of knowing what the owner was, without the owner knowing who he was; and, however the old sailor and his crew tried to "pump" him, they extracted nothing more from him; giving accurate descriptions of Naples and Malta, which he knew as well as Marseilles, and persisting stoutly in his first statement. Thus the Genoese, subtle as he was, was duped by Edmond, in whose favour his mild demeanour, his nautical skill, and his admirable dissimulation, pleaded. Moreover, it is possible that the Genoese was one of those shrewd persons who know nothing but what they should know, and believe nothing but what they should believe.

It was thus, in this reciprocal position, that they reached Leghorn.

Here Edmond was to undergo another trial; it was to see if he should recognise himself, never having beheld his features for fourteen years. He had preserved a tolerably good remembrance of what the youth had been, and was now to find what the man had become. His comrades believed that his vow was fulfilled, as he had twenty times touched at Leghorn before he remembered a barber in the Rue Saint-Ferdinand: he went there to have his beard and hair cut.

The barber gazed in amaze at this man with the long hair and beard, thick and black as it was, and resembling one of Titian's glorious heads. At this period it was not the fashion to wear so large a beard and hair so long; now a barber would only be surprised if a man gifted with such advantages should consent voluntarily to deprive himself of them. The Leghorn barber went to work without a single observation.

When the operation was concluded, when Edmond felt his chin was completely smooth, and his hair reduced to its usual length, he requested a looking-glass in which he might see himself. He was now, as we have said, three-and-thirty years of age, and his fourteen years' imprisonment had produced a great moral change in his appearance.

Dantès had entered the Château d'If with the round, open, smiling face of a young and happy man, with whom the early paths of life have been smooth, and who rely on the future as a natural deduction of the past. This was now all changed.

His oval face was lengthened, his smiling mouth had assumed the firm and marked lines which betoken resolution; his eyebrows were arched beneath a large and thoughtful wrinkle; his eyes were full of melancholy, and from their depths occasionally sparkled gloomy fires of misanthropy and hatred; his complexion, so long kept from the sun, had now that pale colour which produces, when the features are encircled with black hair, the aristocratic beauty of the men of the north; the deep learning he had acquired had besides diffused over his features the rays of extreme intellect; and he had also acquired, although previously a tall man, that vigour which a frame possesses which has so long concentrated all its force within itself.

C.M.—G*

To the elegance of a nervous and slight form had succeeded the solidity of a rounded and muscular figure. As to his voice, prayers, sobs, and imprecations, had changed it now into a soft and singularly touching tone, and now into a sound rude and almost hoarse. Moreover, being perpetually in twilight or darkness, his eyes had acquired that singular faculty of distinguishing objects in the night common to the hyena and the wolf.

Edmond smiled when he beheld himself: it was impossible that his best friend—if, indeed, he had any friend left—could recognise himself.

The master of La Jeune Amélie, who was very desirous of retaining amongst his crew a man of Edmond's value, had offered to him some advances out of his future profits, which Edmond had accepted. His next care on leaving the barber's, who had achieved his first metamorphosis, was to enter a shop and buy a complete sailor's suit, a garb, as we all know, very simple, and consisting of white trousers, a striped shirt, and a cap.

It was in this costume, and bringing back to Jacopo the shirt and trousers he had lent him, that Edmond reappeared before the patron of La Jeune Amélie, who made him tell his story over and over again before he could believe him, or recognise in the neat and trim sailor the man with thick and matted beard, his hair tangled with seaweed, and his body soaking in sea-brine, whom he had picked up naked and nearly drowned.

Attracted by his prepossessing appearance, he renewed his offers of an engagement to Dantès; but Dantès, who had his own projects, would not agree for a longer time than three months.

La Jeune Amélie had a very active crew, very obedient to their captain, who lost as little time as possible. He had scarcely been a week at Leghorn before the hold of his vessel was filled with painted muslins, prohibited cottons, English powder, and tobacco on which the crown had forgotten to put its mark. The master was to get all this out of Leghorn free of duties and land it on the shores of Corsica, where certain speculators undertook to forward the cargo to France.

They sailed; Edmond was again cleaving the azure sea which had been the first horizon of his youth, and which he had so often dreamed of in prison. He left Gorgone on his right and La Pianosa on his left, and went towards the country of Paoli and Napoleon.

The next morning going on deck, which he always did at an early hour, the patron found Dantès leaning against the bulwarks gazing with intense earnestness at a pile of granite rocks, which the rising sun tinged with rosy light. It was the Isle of Monte-Cristo.

La Jeune Amélie left it three quarters of a league to the larboard, and kept on for Corsica.

Dantès thought, as they passed thus closely the island whose name was so interesting to him, that he had only to leap into the sea and in half an hour he would be on the promised land. But then what could he do without instruments to discover his treasure, without arms to defend himself? Besides, what would the sailors say? What would the patron think? He must wait.

Fortunately, Dantès had learned how to wait; he had waited fourteen years for his liberty, and now he was free he could wait at least six months or a year for wealth.

Would he not have accepted liberty without riches, if it had been offered to him?

Besides, were not these riches chimerical?—offspring of the brain of the poor Abbé Faria, had they not died with him?

It is true, this letter of the Cardinal Spada was singularly circumstantial, and Dantès repeated to himself, from one end to the other, the letter of which he had not forgotten a word.

The evening came on, and Edmond saw the island covered with every tint that twilight brings with it, and disappear in the darkness from all eyes; but he with his gaze accustomed to the gloom of a prison continued to see it after all the others, for he remained last upon deck.

The next morning broke off the coast of Aleria; all day they coasted, and in the evening saw the fires lighted on land; when they were extinguished, they no doubt recognised the signals for landing, for a ship's lantern was hung up at the mast-head instead of the streamer, and they neared the shore within gunshot.

Dantès remarked that at this time, too, the patron of La Jeune Amélie had, as he neared the land, mounted two small culverines, which, without making much noise, can throw a ball of four to the pound a thousand paces or so.

But on this occasion the precaution was superfluous, and every thing proceeded with the utmost smoothness and politeness. Four shallops came off with very little noise along-side the bark, which, no doubt in acknowledgment of the compliment, lowered her own shallop into the sea, and the five boats worked so well that by two o'clock in the morning all the cargo was out of La Jeune Amélie and on *terra firma*.

The same night, such a man of regularity was the patron of La Jeune Amélie, that the profits were shared out, and each man had a hundred Tuscan livres, or about three guineas English.

But the voyage was not ended. They turned the bowsprit towards Sardinia, where they intended to take in a cargo, which was to replace what had been discharged.

The second operation was as successful as the first, La Jeune Amélie was in luck.

This new cargo was destined for the coast of the Duchy of Lucca, and consisted almost entirely of Havannah cigars, sherry, and Malaga wines.

There they had a bit of a skirmish in getting rid of the duties, the *gabelle* was in truth the everlasting enemy of the patron of La Jeune Amélie. A custom-house officer was laid low, and two sailors were wounded; Dantès was one of the latter, a ball having touched him in the left shoulder.

Dantès was almost glad of this affray, and almost pleased at being wounded; for they were rude lessons which taught him with what eye he could view danger, and with what endurance he could bear suffering. He had contemplated danger with a smile, and when wounded had exclaimed with the great philosopher, "Pain, thou art not an evil."

He had, moreover, looked upon the custom-house officer wounded to death; and, whether from heat of blood produced by the rencontre, or the chill of human sentiment, this sight had made but slight impression upon him; Dantès was on the way he desired to follow, and was moving towards the end he wished to achieve: his heart was in a fair way of petrifying in his bosom. Jacopo, seeing him fall, had believed him killed, and rushing towards him raised him up, and then attended to him with all the kindness of an attached comrade.

This world was not then so good as Voltaire's Doctor Pangloss believed it, neither was it so wicked as Dantès thought it, since this man who had nothing to expect from his comrade, but the inheritance of his share of the prize-money, testified so much sorrow when he saw him fall.

Fortunately, as we have said, Edmond was only wounded, and with certain herbs gathered at certain seasons and sold to the smugglers by the old Sardinian women, the wound soon closed. Edmond then resolved to try Jacopo, and offered him in return for his attention a share of his prize-money, but Jacopo refused it indignantly.

It resulted, therefore, from this kind of sympathetic devotion which Jacopo had bestowed on Edmond from the first time he saw him, that Edmond felt for Jacopo a certain degree of affection. But this sufficed for Jacopo, who already instinctively felt that Edmond had a right to superiority of position—a superiority which Edmond had concealed from all others. And from this time the kindness which Edmond shewed him was enough for the brave seaman.

Then in the long days on board ship when the vessel gliding on with security over the azure sea required nothing, thanks to the favourable wind that swelled her sails, but the hand of the helmsman, Edmond, with a chart in his hand, became the instructor of Jacopo, as the poor Abbé Faria had been his tutor. He pointed out to him the bearings of the coast, explained to him the variations of the compass, and taught him to read in that vast book opened over our heads which they call heaven, and where God writes in azure with letters of diamonds. And when Jacopo inquired of him, "What is the use of teaching all these things to a poor sailor like me?" Edmond replied,—

"Who knows? you may one day be the captain of a vessel; your fellow-countryman, Bonaparte, became Emperor."

We had forgotten to say that Jacopo was a Corsican.

Two months and a half elapsed in these trips, and Edmond had become as skilful a coaster as he had been a hardy seaman; he had formed an acquaintance with all the smugglers on the coast, and learned all the masonic signs by which these half pirates recognise each other. He had passed and re-passed his isle of Monte-Cristo twenty times, but not once had he found an opportunity of landing there.

He then formed a resolution. This was, as soon as his engagement with the patron of La Jeune Amélie ended, he would hire a small bark on his own account (for in his several voyages he had amassed a hundred piastres), and under some pretext land at the isle of Monte-Cristo.

Then he would be free to make his researches, not perhaps entirely at liberty, for he would be doubtless watched by those who accompanied him. But in this world we must risk something.

Prison had made Edmond prudent, and he was desirous of running no risk whatever.

But in vain did he rack his imagination; fertile as it was, he could not devise any plan for reaching the wished-for isle without being accompanied thither.

Dantès was tossed about on these doubts and wishes, when the patron who had great confidence in him, and was very desirous of retaining him in his service, took him by the arm one evening and led him to a tavern on the Via del'Oglio, where the leading smugglers of Leghorn used to congregate.

It was here they discussed the affairs of the coast. Already Dantès had visited this maritime Bourse two or three times, and seeing all these hardy free-traders, who supplied the whole coast for nearly two hundred leagues in extent, he had asked himself what power might not that man attain who should give the impulse of his will to all these contrary and diverging links.

This time it was a great matter that was under discussion, connected with a vessel laden with Turkey carpets, stuffs of the Levant, and cachmeres. It was requisite to find some neutral ground on which an exchange could be made, and then to try and land these goods on the coast of France.

If successful the profit would be enormous, there would be a gain of fifty or sixty piastres each for the crew.

The patron of La Jeune Amélie proposed as a place of landing the isle of Monte-Cristo, which being completely deserted, and having neither soldiers nor revenue officers, seemed to have been placed in the midst of the ocean since the time of the heathen Olympus by Mercury, the god of merchants and robbers, classes which we in modern times have separated if not made distinct, but which antiquity appears to have included in the same category.

At the mention of Monte-Cristo Dantès started with joy, he rose to conceal his emotion, and took a turn round the smoky tavern, where all the languages of the known world were jumbled in a *lingua franca*. When he again joined the two persons who had been discussing, it had been decided that they should touch at Monte-Cristo, and set out on the following night.

Edmond, being consulted, was of opinion that the island offered every possible security, and that great enterprises to be well done, should be done quickly. Nothing then was altered in the plan arranged, and orders were given to get under weigh next night, and, wind and weather permitting, to gain the day after the waters of the neutral isle.

CHAPTER XXIII

THE ISLE OF MONTE-CRISTO

THUS at length, by one of those pieces of unlooked-for good fortune which sometimes occur to those on whom misfortune has for a long time spent itself, Dantès was about to arrive at his wished-for opportunity by simple and natural means, and land in the island without incurring any suspicion. One night only separated him from his departure so ardently wished for.

This night was one of the most feverish that Dantès had ever passed, and during its progress all the charms good and evil passed through his brain. If he closed his eyes, he saw the letters of Cardinal Spada written on the wall in characters of flame; if he slept for a moment the wildest dreams haunted his brain. He descended into grottoes paved with emeralds, with panels of rubies, and the roof glowing with diamond stalactites. Pearls fell drop by drop as subterranean waters filter in their caves. Edmond, amazed—wonderstruck, filled his pockets with the radiant gems and then returned to daylight, when he discovered that his prizes were all converted into common pebbles. He then endeavoured to re-enter these marvellous grottoes, but then beheld them only in the distance; and now the way serpentined into countless paths, and then the entrance became invisible, and in vain did he tax his memory for the magic and mysterious word which opened the splendid caverns of Ali Baba to the Arabian fisherman. All was useless, the treasure disappeared, and had again reverted to the genii from whom for a moment he had hoped to carry it off.

The day came at length, and was almost as feverish as the night had been, but it brought reason to aid his imagination, and Dantès was thus enabled to arrange a plan which had hitherto been vague and unsettled in his brain.

Night came, and with it the preparation for departure, and these preparations served to conceal Dantès' agitation. He had by degrees assumed such authority over his companions that he was almost like a commander on board; and as his orders were always clear, distinct, and easy of execution, his comrades obeyed him with celerity and pleasure.

207

The old patron did not interfere, for he, too, had recognised the superiority of Dantès over the crew and himself.   He saw in the young man his natural successor, and regretted that he had not a daughter that he might have bound Edmond to him by a distinguished alliance.

At seven o'clock in the evening all was ready, and at ten minutes past seven they doubled the light-house just as the beacon was kindled.

The sea was calm, and with a fresh breeze from the south-east they sailed beneath a bright blue sky, in which God also lighted up in turn his beacon lights, each of which is a world. Dantès told them that all hands might turn in and he would take the helm.

When the Maltese (for so they called Dantès) had said this it was sufficient, and all went to their cots contentedly.   This frequently happened.   Dantès, rejected by all the world, frequently experienced a desire for solitude, and what solitude is at the same time more complete, more poetical, than that of a bark floating isolated on the sea during the obscurity of the night, in the silence of immensity and under the eye of heaven?

Now this solitude was peopled with his thoughts, the night lighted up by his illusions, and the silence animated by his anticipations.   When the patron awoke the vessel was hurrying on with every sail set, and every sail full with the breeze. They were making nearly ten knots an hour.

The isle of Monte-Cristo loomed large in the horizon.

Edmond resigned the bark to the master's care and went and lay down in his hammock, but in spite of a sleepless night he could not close his eyes for a moment.

Two hours afterwards he came on deck as the boat was about to double the isle of Elba.   They were just abreast of Mareciana, and beyond the flat but verdant island of La Pianosa.   The peak of Monte-Cristo, reddened by the burning sun, was seen against the azure sky.

Dantès desired the helmsman to put down his helm in order to leave La Pianosa on the right hand, as he knew that he should thus decrease the distance by two or three knots.

About five o'clock in the evening the island was quite distinct, and every thing on it was plainly perceptible, owing to that clearness of the atmosphere which is peculiar to the light which the rays of the sun cast at its setting.

Edmond gazed most earnestly at the mass of rocks which gave out all the variety of twilight colours from the brightest pink to the deepest blue, and from time to time his cheeks flushed, his brow became purple, and a mist passed over his eyes.

Never did gamester whose whole fortune is staked on one cast of the die, experience the anguish which Edmond felt in his paroxysms of hope. Night came, and at ten o'clock p.m. they anchored. La Jeune Amélie was the first at the rendezvous.

In spite of his usual command over himself, Dantès could not restrain his impetuosity. He was the first who jumped on shore, and had he dared he would, like Lucius Brutus, have "kissed his mother Earth." It was dark, but at eleven o'clock the moon rose in the midst of the ocean whose every wave she silvered, and then, "ascending high," played in floods of pale light on the rocky hills of this second Pelion.

The island was familiar to the crew of La Jeune Amélie: it was one of her halting places. As to Dantès, he had passed it on each of his voyages to and from the Levant, but never touched at it.

He questioned Jacopo. "Where shall we pass the night?" he inquired.

"Why on board the tartane," replied the sailor.

"Should we not be better in the grottoes?"

"What grottoes?"

"Why the grottoes—caves of the island."

"I do not know of any grottoes," replied Jacopo.

A cold damp sprang to Dantès' brow.

"What! are there no grottoes at Monte-Cristo?" he asked. "None."

For a moment Dantès was speechless, then he remembered that these caves might have been filled up by some accident, or even stopped up for the sake of greater security by Cardinal Spada.

The point was then to discover the last opening. It was useless to search at night, and Dantès therefore delayed all investigation until the morning. Besides, a signal made half a league out at sea, and to which La Jeune Amélie also replied by a similar signal, indicated that the moment was arrived for business.

The boat that now arrived, assured by the answering signal that all was right, soon came in sight, white and silent as a phantom, and cast anchor within a cable's length of shore.

Then the landing began. Dantès reflected, as he worked, on the shout of joy which with a single word he could produce from amongst all these men if he gave utterance to the one unchanging thought that pervaded his heart. But, far from disclosing this precious secret, he almost feared that he had already said too much, and by his restlessness and continual questions, his minute observations and evident preoccupation, had aroused suspicions. Fortunately, as regarded this circumstance, at least, with him the painful past reflected on his countenance an indelible sadness, and the glimmerings of gaiety seen beneath this cloud were indeed but transitory.

No one had the slightest suspicion; and when next day, taking a fowling-piece, powder, and shot, Dantès testified a desire to go and kill some of the wild goats that were seen springing from rock to rock, his wish was construed into a love of sport or a desire for solitude. However, Jacopo insisted on following him, and Dantès did not oppose this, fearing if he did so that he might incur distrust. Scarcely, however, had he gone a quarter of a league than, having killed a kid, he begged Jacopo to take it to his comrades and request them to cook it, and when ready to let him know by firing a gun. This, and some dried fruits, and a flask of the wine of Monte Pulciano, was the bill of fare.

Dantès went forwards, looking behind and round about him from time to time. Having reached the summit of a rock, he saw, a thousand feet beneath him, his companions, whom Jacopo had rejoined, and who were all busy preparing the repast which Edmond's skill as a marksman had augmented with a capital dish.

Edmond looked at them for a moment with the sad and soft smile of a man superior to his fellows.

"In two hours' time," said he, "these persons will depart richer by fifty piastres each to go and risk their lives again by endeavouring to gain fifty more such pieces. Then they will return with a fortune of six hundred francs and waste this treasure in some city with the pride of sultans and the insolence of nabobs. At this moment Hope makes me despise their riches, which seem to me contemptible. Yet, perchance, to-morrow deception will so act on me that I shall, on compulsion, consider such a contemptible possession as the utmost happiness. Oh, no!" exclaimed Edmond, "that will not be. The wise, unerring Faria could not be mistaken in this one thing. Besides, it were better to die than continue to lead this low and wretched life."

Thus Dantès, who but three months before had no desire but liberty, had now not liberty enough, and panted for wealth. The cause was not in Dantès, but in Providence, who, whilst limiting the power of man, has filled him with boundless desires.

Meanwhile, by a way between two walls of rock, following a path worn by a torrent, and which, in all human probability, human foot had never before trod, Dantès approached the spot where he supposed the grottoes must have existed. Keeping along the coast, and examining the smallest object with serious attention, he thought he could trace on certain rocks marks made by the hand of man.

Time, which encrusts all physical substances with its mossy mantle, as it invests all things moral with its mantle of forgetfulness, seemed to have respected these signs, traced

with a certain regularity, and probably with the design of
leaving traces. Occasionally these marks disappeared beneath
tufts of myrtle, which spread into large bushes laden with
blossoms, or beneath parasitical lichen. It was thus requisite
that Edmond should move branches on one side or remove the
mosses in order to retrace the indicating marks which were to
be his guides in this labyrinth. These signs had renewed the
best hopes in Edmond's mind. Why should it not have been
the cardinal who had first traced them, in order that they
might, in the event of a catastrophe, which he could not
foresee would have been so complete, serve as a guide for his
nephew? This solitary place was precisely suited for a man
desirous of burying a treasure. Only, might not these betraying marks have attracted other eyes than those for whom they
were made? and had the dark and wondrous isle indeed faithfully guarded its precious secret?

It seemed, however, to Edmond, who was hidden from his
comrades by the inequalities of the ground, that at sixty
paces from the harbour the marks ceased; nor did they
terminate at any grotto. A large round rock, placed solidly
on its base, was the only spot to which they seemed to lead.
Edmond reflected that perhaps instead of having reached the
end he might have only touched on the beginning, and he
therefore turned round and retraced his steps.

During this time his comrades had prepared the repast,
had got some water from a spring, spread out the fruit and
bread, and cooked the kid. Just at the moment when they
were taking the dainty animal from the spit, they saw Edmond,
who, light and daring as a chamois, was springing from rock
to rock, and they fired the signal agreed upon. The sportsman
instantly changed his direction, and ran quickly towards them.
But at the moment when they were all following with their
eyes his agile bounds with a rashness which gave them alarm,
Edmond's foot slipped, and they saw him stagger on the edge
of a rock and disappear. They all rushed towards him, for all
loved Edmond in spite of his superiority; yet Jacopo reached
him first.

He found Edmond stretched bleeding and almost senseless.
He had rolled down a height of twelve or fifteen feet. They
poured some drops of rum down his throat, and this remedy,
which had before been so beneficial to him, produced the same
effect as formerly. Edmond opened his eyes, complained of
great pain in his knee, a feeling of heaviness in his head, and
severe pains in his loins. They wished to carry him to the
shore, but when they touched him, although under Jacopo's
directions, he declared, with heavy groans, that he could not
bear to be moved.

It may be supposed that Dantès did not now think of his

dinner; but he insisted that his comrades, who had not his reasons for fasting, should have their meal. As for himself, he declared that he had only need of a little rest, and that when they returned he should be easier. The sailors did not require much urging. They were hungry, and the smell of the roasted kid was very savoury, and your tars are not very ceremonious. An hour afterwards they returned. All that Edmond had been able to do was to drag himself about a dozen paces forward to lean against a moss-grown rock.

But, far from being easier, Dantès' pains had appeared to increase in violence. The old patron, who was obliged to sail in the morning in order to land his cargo on the frontiers of Piedmont and France between Nice and Frejus, urged Dantès to try and rise. Edmond made great exertions in order to comply; but at each effort he fell back, moaning and turning pale.

"He has broken his ribs," said the commander, in a low voice. "No matter; he is an excellent fellow, and we must not leave him. We will try and carry him on board the tartane."

Dantès declared, however, that he would rather die where he was than undergo the agony caused by the slightest movement he made.

"Well," said the patron, "let what may happen, it shall never be said that we deserted a good comrade like you. We will not go till evening."

This very much astonished the sailors, although not one opposed it. The patron was so strict that this was the first time they had ever seen him give up an enterprise, or even delay an arrangement.

Dantès would not allow that any such infraction of regular and proper rules should be made in his favour.

"No, no," he said to the patron, " I was awkward, and it is just that I pay the penalty of my clumsiness. Leave me a small supply of biscuit, a gun, powder, and balls, to kill the kids or defend myself at need, and a pickaxe, to build me something like a shed if you delay in coming back for me."

"But you'll die of hunger," said the patron.

"I would rather do so," was Edmond's reply, "than suffer the inexpressible agonies which the slightest motion brings on."

The patron turned towards his vessel, which was undulating in the small harbour, and, with her sails partly set, was ready for sea when all her toilette should be completed.

"What are we to do, Maltese?" asked the captain. "We cannot leave you here so, and yet we cannot stay."

"Go, go!" exclaimed Dantès.

"We shall be absent at least a week," said the patron, "and

then we must run out of our course to come here and take you up again."

"Why," said Dantès, "if in two or three days you hail any fishing-boat, desire them to come here to me. I will pay twenty-five piastres for my passage back to Leghorn. If you do not come across one, return for me."

The patron shook his head.

"Listen, Captain Baldi; there's one way of settling this," said Jacopo. "Do you go, and I will stay and take care of the wounded man."

"And give up your share of the venture," said Edmond, "to remain with me?"

"Yes," said Jacopo, "and without any hesitation."

"You are a good fellow and a kind-hearted messmate," replied Edmond, "and Heaven will recompense you for your generous intentions; but I do not wish any one to stay with me. A day or two's rest will set me up, and I hope I shall find amongst the rocks certain herbs most excellent for contusions."

A singular smile passed over Dantès' lips; he squeezed Jacopo's hand warmly; but nothing could shake his determination to remain—and remain alone.

The smugglers left with Edmond what he had requested, and set sail; but not without turning about several times, and each time making signs of a cordial leave-taking, to which Edmond replied with his hand only, as if he could not move the rest of his body.

Then, when they had disappeared, he said with a smile,—

"'Tis strange that it should be amongst such men that we find proofs of friendship and devotion."

Then he dragged himself cautiously to the top of a rock, from which he had a full view of the sea, and thence he saw the tartane complete her preparations for sailing, weigh anchor, and, balancing herself as gracefully as a water-fowl ere it takes to the wing, set sail. At the end of an hour she was completely out of sight; at least, it was impossible for the wounded man to see her any longer from the spot where he was.

Then Dantès rose more agile and light than the kid amongst the myrtles and shrubs of these wild rocks, took his gun in one hand, his pickaxe in the other, and hastened towards the rock on which the marks he had noted terminated.

"And now," he exclaimed, remembering the tale of the Arabian fisherman, which Faria had related to him —"now open sesame!"

CHAPTER XXIV

THE SECRET CAVE

THE sun had nearly reached the meridian, and his scorching rays fell full on the rocks, which seemed themselves sensible of the heat. Thousands of grasshoppers, hidden in the bushes, chirped with a monotonous and dull note; the leaves of the myrtle and olive-trees waved and rustled in the wind. At every step that Edmond took he disturbed the lizards glittering with the hues of the emerald: afar off he saw the wild goats bounding from crag to crag. In a word, the isle was inhabited, yet Edmond felt himself alone, guided by the hand of God. He felt an indescribable sensation somewhat akin to dread,— that dread of the daylight which even in the desert makes us fear we are watched and observed.

This feeling was so strong, that at the moment when Edmond was about to commence his labour, he stopped, laid down his pickaxe, seized his gun, mounted to the summit of the highest rock, and from thence gazed round in every direction.

But it was not upon Corsica, the very houses of which he could distinguish; nor on Sardinia; nor on the isle of Elba, with its historical associations; nor upon the almost imperceptible line that to the experienced eye of a sailor alone revealed the coast of Genoa the proud, and Leghorn the commercial, that he gazed. It was at the brigantine that had left in the morning, and the tartane that had just set sail, that Edmond fixed his eyes. The first was just disappearing in the straits of Bonifacio; the other, following an opposite direction, was about to round the island of Corsica. This sight reassured him. He then looked at the objects near him. He saw himself on the highest point of the isle, a statue on this vast pedestal of granite, nothing human appearing in sight, whilst the blue ocean beat against the base of the island, and covered it with a fringe of foam. Then he descended with cautious and slow step, for he dreaded lest an accident similar to that he had so adroitly feigned should happen in reality.

Dantès, as we have said, had traced back the marks in the rock; and he had noticed that they led to a small creek, hidden like the bath of some ancient nymph. This creek was sufficiently wide at its mouth, and deep in the centre, to admit

214

of the entrance of a small vessel of the speronare class, which would be perfectly concealed from observation.

Then following the clue that in the hands of the Abbé Faria had been so skilfully used to guide him through the Dædalian labyrinth of probabilities, he thought that the Cardinal Spada, anxious not to be watched, had entered the creek, concealed his little bark, followed the line marked by the notches in the rock, and at the end of it had buried his treasure. It was this idea that had brought Dantès back to the circular rock. One thing only perplexed Edmond, and destroyed his theory. How could this rock, which weighed several tons, have been lifted to this spot without the aid of many men? Suddenly an idea flashed across his mind. Instead of raising it, thought he, they have lowered it. And he sprang from the rock in order to inspect the base on which it had formerly stood.

He soon perceived that a slope had been formed; and the rock had slid along this until it stopped at the spot it now occupied. A large stone had served as a wedge; flints and pebbles had been inserted around it, so as to conceal the orifice; this species of masonry had been covered with earth, and grass and weeds had grown there; moss had clung to the stones, myrtle-bushes had taken root, and the old rock seemed fixed to the earth.

Dantès raised the earth carefully, and detected, or fancied he detected, the ingenious artifice. He attacked this wall, cemented by the hand of time, with his pickaxe. After ten minutes' labour the wall gave way, and a hole large enough to insert the arm was opened. Dantès went and cut the strongest olive-tree he could find, stripped off its branches, inserted it in the hole, and used it as a lever. But the rock was too heavy, and too firmly wedged, to be moved by any one man, were he Hercules himself. Dantès reflected that he must attack this wedge. But how? He cast his eyes around and saw the horn full of powder, which his friend Jacopo had left him. He smiled; the infernal invention would serve him for this purpose. With the aid of his pickaxe, Dantès dug between the upper rock and the one that supported it a mine similar to those formed by pioneers when they wish to spare human labour, filled it with powder, then made a match by rolling his handkerchief in saltpetre. He lighted it and retired.

The explosion was instantaneous; the upper rock was lifted from its base by the terrific force of the powder; the lower one flew into pieces; thousands of insects escaped from the aperture Dantès had previously formed, and a huge snake, like the guardian demon of the treasure, rolled himself along with a sinuous motion, and disappeared.

Dantès approached the upper rock which, now without any support, leant towards the sea. The intrepid treasureseeker walked round it, and selecting the spot from whence it appeared most easy to attack it, placed his lever in one of the crevices, and strained every nerve to move the mass.

The rock already shaken by the explosion, tottered on its base. Dantès redoubled his efforts, he seemed like one of the ancient Titans, who uprooted the mountains to hurl against the father of the gods. The rock yielded, rolled, bounded, and finally disappeared in the ocean.

On the spot it had occupied, was visible a circular place, and which exposed an iron ring let into a square flag-stone. Dantès uttered a cry of joy and surprise; never had a first attempt been crowned with more perfect success. He would fain have continued, but his knees trembled, his heart beat so violently, and his eyes became so dim, that he was forced to pause. This feeling lasted but for a moment. Edmond inserted his lever in the ring, and, exerting all his strength, the flag-stone yielded, and disclosed a kind of stair that descended until it was lost in the obscurity of a subterraneous grotto. Any one else would have rushed on with a cry of joy. Dantès turned pale, hesitated, and reflected.

"Come," said he to himself, "be a man. I am accustomed to adversity. I must not be cast down by the discovery that I have been deceived. What, then, would be the use of all I have suffered? The heart breaks when, after having been elated by flattering hopes, it sees all these illusions destroyed. Faria has dreamed this; the Cardinal Spada buried no treasures here; perhaps he never came here, or if he did Cæsar Borgia, the intrepid adventurer, the stealthy and indefatigable plunderer, has followed him, discovered his traces, pursued them as I have done, like me, raised the stone, and descending before me has left me nothing." He remained motionless and pensive, his eyes fixed on the sombre aperture that was open at his feet.

"Now that I expect nothing, now that I no longer entertain the slightest hopes, the end of this adventure becomes a simple matter of curiosity."

And he remained again motionless and thoughtful.

"Yes, yes, this is an adventure worthy a place in the lights and shades of the life of this royal bandit. This fabulous event has formed but a link of a vast chain. Yes, Borgia has been here, a torch in one hand, a sword in the other, whilst within twenty paces, at the foot of this rock, perhaps two guards kept watch on land and sea, whilst their master descended as I am about to descend, dispelling the darkness before his terrible advance.

"But what was the fate of these guards who thus possessed his secret?" asked Dantès of himself.

"The fate," replied he, smiling, "of those who buried Alaric."

"Yet, had he come," thought Dantès, "he would have found the treasure; and Borgia, he who compared Italy to an artichoke, which he could devour leaf by leaf, knew too well the value of time to waste it in replacing this rock."

"I will go down."

Then he descended; a smile on his lips, and murmuring that last word of human philosophy, "Perhaps!" But instead of the darkness, and the thick and mephitic atmosphere he had expected to find, Dantès saw a dim and bluish light, which, as well as the air he entered, not merely by the aperture he had just formed, but by the interstices and crevices of the rock which were visible from without, and through which he could distinguish the blue sky and the waving branches of the evergreen oaks, and the tendrils of the creepers that grew from the rocks.

After having stood a few minutes in the cavern, the atmosphere of which was rather warm than damp, Dantès' eye, habituated as it was to darkness, could pierce even to the remotest angles of the cavern, which was of granite that sparkled like diamonds.

"Alas!" said Edmond, smiling, "these are the treasures the cardinal has left; and the good abbé, seeing in a dream these glittering walls, has indulged in fallacious hopes."

But he called to mind the words of the will which he knew by heart: "In the farthest angle of the second opening," said the cardinal's will. He had only found the first grotto, he had now to seek the second.

Dantès commenced his search. He reflected that this second grotto must, doubtless, penetrate deeper into the isle; he examined the stones, and sounded one part of the wall where he fancied the opening existed, masked for precaution's sake.

The pickaxe sounded for a moment with a dull sound that covered Dantès' forehead with large drops of perspiration. At last it seemed to him that one part of the wall gave forth a more hollow and deeper echo; he eagerly advanced, and with the quickness of perception that no one but a prisoner possesses, saw that it was there, in all probability, the opening must be.

However, he, like Cæsar Borgia, knew the value of time; and, in order to avoid a fruitless toil, he sounded all the other walls with his pickaxe, struck the earth with the butt of his gun, and finding nothing that appeared suspicious, returned to that part of the wall whence issued the consoling sound he had before heard.

He again struck it, and with greater force.

Then a singular sight presented itself.   As he struck the wall a species of stucco similar to that used as the ground of arabesques detached itself, and fell to the ground in flakes, exposing a large white stone.   The aperture of the rock had been closed with stones, then this stucco had been applied, and painted to imitate granite.

Dantès struck with the sharp end of his pickaxe, which entered some way between the interstices of the stone.   It was there he must dig.   But by some strange phenomenon of the human organisation, in proportion as the proofs that Faria had not been deceived became stronger, so did his heart give way, and a feeling of discouragement steal over him.   This last proof, instead of giving him fresh strength, deprived him of it; the pickaxe descended, or rather fell; he placed it on the ground, passed his hand over his brow, and remounted the stairs, alleging to himself as an excuse a desire to be assured that no one was watching him, but in reality because he felt he was ready to faint.   The isle was deserted, and the sun seemed to cover it with its fiery glance; afar off a few small fishing-boats studded the bosom of the blue ocean.

Dantès had tasted nothing, but he thought not of hunger at such a moment; he hastily swallowed a few drops of rum, and again entered the cavern.   The pickaxe that had seemed so heavy was now like a feather in his grasp; he seized it, and again attacked the wall.   After several blows he perceived that the stones were not cemented, but merely placed one upon the other, and covered with stucco; he inserted the point of his pickaxe, and using the handle as a lever, soon saw with joy the stone turn as if on hinges, and fall at his feet.   He had nothing more to do now but with the iron tooth of the pickaxe to draw the stones towards him one by one.   The first aperture was sufficiently large to enter, but by waiting, he could still cling to hope, and retard the certainty of deception.

At last, after fresh hesitation, Dantès entered the second grotto.   The second grotto was lower and more gloomy than the former; the air that could only enter by the newly formed opening had that mephitic smell Dantès was surprised not to find in the first.   He waited in order to allow pure air to displace the foul atmosphere, and then entered.   At the left of the opening was a dark and deep angle.   But to Dantès' eye there was no darkness.   He glanced round this second grotto, it was, like the first, empty.

The treasure, if it existed, was buried in this corner.   The time had at length arrived; two feet of earth removed, and Dantès' fate would be decided.   He advanced towards the angle, and summoning all his resolution, attacked the ground with the pickaxe.   At the fifth or sixth blow the pickaxe struck against an iron substance.   Never did funeral knell never did alarm-bell produce a greater effect on the hearer. Had Dantès found nothing, he could not have become more ghastly pale. He again struck his pickaxe into the earth, and encountered the same resistance, but not the same sound.

"It is a casket of wood bound with iron," thought he.

At this moment a shadow passed rapidly before the opening; Dantès seized his gun, sprang through the opening, and mounted the stair. A wild goat had passed before the mouth of the cave, and was feeding at a little distance.

This would have been a favourable occasion to secure his dinner; but Dantès feared lest the report of his gun should attract attention.

He reflected an instant, cut a branch of a resinous tree, lighted it at the fire at which the smugglers had prepared their breakfast, and descended with this torch. He wished to see all. He approached the hole he had formed with the torch, and saw that his pickaxe had in reality struck against iron and wood. He planted his torch in the ground and resumed his labour. In an instant a space three feet long by two feet broad was cleared, and Dantès could see an oaken coffer bound with cut steel; in the midst of the lid he saw engraved on a silver plate, which was still untarnished, the arms of the Spada family, viz., a sword *pale* on an oval shield, like all the Italian armorial bearings, and surmounted by a cardinal's hat; Dantès easily recognised them, Faria had so often drawn them for him. There was no longer any doubt, the treasure was there; no one would have been at such pains to conceal an empty casket.

In an instant he had cleared every obstacle away, and he saw successively the lock, placed between two padlocks, and the two handles at each end, all carved as things were carved at that epoch when art rendered the commonest metals precious. Dantès seized the handles, and strove to lift the coffer; it was impossible. He sought to open it; lock and padlock were closed; these faithful guardians seemed unwilling to surrender their trust. Dantès inserted the sharp end of the pickaxe between the coffer and the lid, and pressing with all his force on the handle, burst open the fastenings. The hinges yielded in their turn and fell, still holding in their grasp fragments of the planks, and all was open.

A vertigo seized Edmond, he cocked his gun and laid it beside him. He then closed his eyes as children do in order to perceive in shining night of their own imagination more stars than are visible in the firmament; then he reopened them, and stood motionless with amazement.

Three compartments divided the coffer. In the first, blazed piles of golden coin. In the second, bars of unpolished gold, which possessed nothing attractive save their value, were ranged. In the third, Edmond grasped handsful of diamonds, pearls, and rubies, which, as they fell on one another, sounded like hail against glass.

After having touched, felt, examined these treasures, Edmond rushed through the caverns like a man seized with frenzy; he leapt on a rock, from whence he could behold the sea. He was alone. Alone with these countless, these unheard-of treasures! Was he awake, or was it but a dream?

He would fain have gazed upon his gold, and yet he had not strength enough; for an instant he leaned his head in his hands as if to prevent his senses from leaving him, and then rushed madly about the rocks of Monte-Cristo, terrifying the wild goats and scaring the sea-fowls with his wild cries and gestures; then he returned, and still unable to believe the evidence of his senses, rushed into the grotto, and found himself before this mine of gold and jewels. This time he fell on his knees, and, clasping his hands convulsively, uttered a prayer intelligible to God alone. He soon felt himself calmer and more happy, for now only he began to credit his felicity.

He then set himself to count his fortune. There were a thousand ingots of gold, each weighing from two to three pounds; then he piled up twenty-five thousand crowns, each worth about four pounds sterling of our money, and bearing the effigies of Alexander VI and his predecessors; and he saw that the compartment was not half empty. And he measured ten double handsful of precious stones, many of which, mounted by the most famous workmen, were valuable for their execution. Dantès saw the light gradually disappear; and fearing to be surprised in the cavern, left it, his gun in his hand. A piece of biscuit and a small quantity of rum formed his supper, and he snatched a few hours' sleep, lying over the mouth of the cave.

This night was one of those delicious, and yet terrible ones, of which he had already passed two or three in his lifetime.

CHAPTER XXV

DAYLIGHT, for which Dantès had so eagerly and impatiently waited, again dawned upon the desert shores of Monte-Cristo. With the first dawn of day Dantès resumed his researches. Again he climbed the rocky height he had ascended the previous evening, and strained his view to catch every peculiarity of the landscape; but it wore the same wild barren aspect when seen by the rays of the morning sun which it had done when surveyed by the fading glimmer of eve. Returning to the entrance of the cave, he raised the stone that covered it; and descending to the place that contained the treasure, filled his pockets with precious stones, put the box together as well and securely as he could, sprinkled fresh sand over the spot from which it had been taken, and then carefully trod down the ground to give it every where a similar appearance; then quitting the grotto, he replaced the stone, heaping on it broken masses of rocks and rough fragments of crumbling granite, filling the interstices with earth, into which was skilfully mingled a quantity of rapidly growing plants, such as the wild myrtle and flowering thorn; then carefully watering these new plantations, he scrupulously effaced every trace of foot-mark, leaving the approach to the cavern as savage-looking and untrodden as he had found it. This done, he impatiently awaited the return of his companions. To wait at Monte-Cristo for the purpose of watching over the almost incalculable riches that had thus fallen into his possession satisfied not the cravings of his heart, which yearned to return to dwell among mankind, and to assume the rank, power, and influence, unbounded wealth alone can bestow.

On the sixth day the smugglers returned. From a distance Dantès recognised the cut and manner of sailing of La Jeune Amélie, and dragging himself with affected difficulty towards the landing-place he met his companions with an assurance that, although considerably better than when they quitted him, he still suffered acutely from his late accident. He then inquired how they had fared in their trip.

To this question the smugglers replied that although successful in landing their cargo in safety, they had scarcely done so when they received intelligence that a guard-ship had just quitted the port of Toulon, and was crowding all sail towards them; this obliged them to make all the speed they could to evade the enemy; when they could but lament the absence of Dantès, whose superior skill in the management of a vessel would have availed them so materially. In fact the chasing vessel had almost overtaken them, when, fortunately, night came on and enabled them to double the Cape of Corsica, and so elude all further pursuit.

Upon the whole, however, the trip had been sufficiently successful to satisfy all concerned; while the crew, and particular Jacopo, expressed great regrets at Dantès not having been an equal sharer with themselves in the profits, amounting to no less a sum than fifty piastres each.

Edmond preserved the most admirable self-command, not suffering the faintest indication of a smile to escape him at the enumeration of all the benefits he would have reaped had he been able to quit the isle; but as La Jeune Amélie had merely come to Monte-Cristo to fetch him away, he embarked that same evening, and proceeded with the captain to Leghorn. Arrived at Leghorn, he repaired to the house of a Jew, a dealer in precious stones, to whom he disposed of four of his smallest diamonds for five thousand francs each.

Dantès half feared that such valuable jewels in the hands of a poor sailor like himself might excite suspicion; but the cunning purchaser asked no troublesome questions concerning a bargain by which he gained at least four thousand francs.

The following day Dantès presented Jacopo with an entirely new vessel, accompanying the gift by a donation of one hundred piastres, that he might provide himself with a suitable crew and other requisites for his outfit; upon conditions of his going direct to Marseilles, for the purpose of inquiring after an old man named Louis Dantès, residing in the Allées de Méillan, and also a young female called Mercédès, an inhabitant of the Catalan village.

Jacopo could scarcely believe his senses at receiving this munificent present, which Dantès hastened to account for by saying that he had merely been a sailor for whim and a desire to spite his friends, who did not allow him as much money as he liked to spend; but that on his arrival at Leghorn, he had come into possession of a large fortune, left him by an uncle, whose sole heir he was. The superior education of Dantès gave an air of such extreme probability to this statement, that it never once occurred to Jacopo to doubt its accuracy.

The term for which Edmond had engaged to serve on board La Jeune Amélie having expired, Dantès took leave of the captain, who at first tried all his powers of persuasion to induce him to remain one of the crew, but having been told the history of the legacy he ceased to importune him further.

The succeeding morning Jacopo set sail for Marseilles, with directions from Dantès to rejoin him at the island of Monte-Cristo.

Having seen Jacopo fairly out of the harbour, Dantès proceeded to make his final adieus on board La Jeune Amélie; distributing so liberal a gratuity among her crew as procured him unanimous good wishes and expressions of cordial interest in all that concerned him; to the captain he promised to write when he had made up his mind as to his future plans: this leave-taking over, Dantès departed for Genoa. At the moment of his arrival a small yacht was being tried in the bay; this yacht had been built by order of an Englishman, who, having heard that the Genoese excelled all other builders along the shores of the Mediterranean in the construction of fast-sailing vessels, was desirous of possessing a specimen of their skill; the price agreed upon between the Englishman and Genoese builder was forty thousand francs.

Dantès, struck with the beauty and capability of the little vessel, applied to its owner to transfer it to him, offering sixty thousand francs, upon condition of being allowed to take immediate possession of it; the proposal was too advantageous to be refused; the more so, as the person for whom the yacht was intended had gone upon a tour through Switzerland, and was not expected back in less than three weeks or a month, by which time the builder reckoned upon being able to complete another.

A bargain was therefore struck. Dantès led the owner of the yacht to the dwelling of a Jew; retired with the latter individual for a few minutes to a small back parlour, and upon their return from thence the Jew counted out to the shipbuilder the sum of sixty thousand francs in bright golden money.

The delighted builder then offered his services in providing a suitable crew for the little vessel, but this Dantès declined, with many thanks; saying he was accustomed to cruise about quite alone, and his principal pleasure consisted in managing his yacht himself; the only thing the builder could oblige him in would be to contrive a sort of secret closet, in the cabin at his bed's head; the closet to contain three divisions, so constructed as to be concealed from all but himself. The builder cheerfully undertook the commission, and promised to have these secret places completed by the next day; Dantès furnishing the size and plan upon which he desired they should be arranged.

The following day Dantès sailed, with his yacht from the port of Genoa, amid the gaze of an immense crowd drawn together by curiosity to see the rich Spanish nobleman who preferred managing his vessel himself; but their wonder was soon exchanged for admiration at the perfect skill with which Dantès handled the helm, and without quitting it, making his little vessel perform every movement he chose to direct; his bark seemed indeed replete with all but human intelligence, so promptly did it obey the slightest impulse given; and Dantès required but a short trial of his beautiful craft to acknowledge that it was not without truth the Genoese had attained their high reputation in the art of ship-building.

The spectators followed the little vessel with their eyes so long as it remained visible, they then turned their conjectures upon her probable destination; some insisted she was making for Corsica, others the Isle of Elba; bets were offered to any amount that she was bound for Spain; while Africa was positively reported by many persons as her intended course, but no one thought of Monte-Cristo.

Yet, thither it was that Dantès guided his vessel, and at Monte-Cristo he arrived at the close of the second day; his bark had proved herself a first-class sailer, and had come the distance from Genoa in thirty-five hours. Dantès had carefully noted the general appearance of the shore, and instead of landing at the usual place he dropped anchor in the little creek.

The isle was utterly deserted, nor did it seem as though human foot had trodden on it since he quitted it; his treasure was just as he had left it.

Early on the following morning he commenced the removal of his riches, and ere night-fall the whole of his immense wealth was safely deposited in the secret compartments of his hidden closet.

A week passed by. Dantès employed it in manœuvring his yacht round the island, studying it as a skilful horseman would the animal he destined for some important service, till at the end of that time he was perfectly conversant with its good and bad qualities. The former Dantès proposed to augment, the latter to remedy.

Upon the eighth day of his being on the island he discerned a small vessel crowding all sail towards Monte-Cristo. As it neared, he recognised it as the bark he had given to Jacopo; he immediately signalled it; his signal was returned, and in two hours afterwards the bark lay at anchor beside the yacht.

A mournful answer awaited each of Edmond's eager inquiries as to the information Jacopo had obtained.

Old Dantès was dead, and Mercédès had disappeared.

Dantès listened to these melancholy tidings with outward calmness; but leaping lightly ashore, he signalled his desire to be quite alone. In a couple of hours he returned. Two of the men from Jacopo's bark came on board the yacht to assist in navigating it, and he commanded she should be steered direct to Marseilles.

For his father's death, he was in some manner prepared; but how to account for the mysterious disappearance of Mercédès he knew not.

Without divulging his secret, Dantès could not give sufficiently clear instructions to an agent—there were, besides, other particulars he was desirous of ascertaining, and those were of a nature he alone could investigate in a manner satisfactory to himself. His looking-glass had assured him during his stay at Leghorn that he ran no risk of recognition; added to which, he had now the means of adopting any disguise he thought proper. One fine morning then, his yacht, followed by the little bark, boldly entered the port of Marseilles, and anchored exactly opposite the memorable spot, from whence, on the never-to-be-forgotten night of his departure for the Château d'If, he had been put on board the vessel destined to convey him thither.

Still Dantès could not view without a shudder the approach of a gendarme who accompanied the officers, deputed to demand his bill of health, ere the yacht was permitted to hold communication with the shore; but with that perfect self-possession he had acquired during his acquaintance with Faria, Dantès coolly presented an English passport he had obtained from Leghorn, and with that prompt attention which all such English documents receive, he was informed there existed no obstacle to his immediate debarkation.

The first object that attracted the attention of Dantès as he landed on the Canebière was one of the crew belonging to the Pharaon. Edmond hailed the appearance of this man, who had served under himself, as a sure test of the safe and perfect change time had worked in his own appearance; going straight towards him, he commenced a variety of questions on different subjects, carefully watching the man's countenance as he did so; but not a word or look implied his having the slightest idea of ever having seen before the individual with whom he was then conversing.

Giving the sailor a piece of money in return for his civility, Dantès proceeded onwards; but ere he had gone many steps, he heard the man loudly calling him to stop. Dantès instantly turned to meet him.

"I beg your pardon, sir," said the honest fellow, in almost breathless haste; "but I believe you made a mistake, you intended to give me a two-franc piece, and see, you gave me a double Napoleon."

"Thank you, my good friend; I see that I made a trifling mistake as you say, but by way of rewarding your honest spirit, I give you another double Napoleon that you may drink to my health, and be able to ask your messmates to join you."

So extreme was the surprise of the sailor, that he was unable

C.M.—H.

even to thank Edmond, whose receding figure he continued to gaze after in speechless astonishment; at length, when Dantès had wholly disappeared, he drew a deep breath, and with another look at his gold he returned to the quay saying to himself, "Ah! that's one of them nabob gentlemen from Ingy no doubt, nobody else could afford to chuck gold about like that. Well! he said I was to drink to his health, and so I will with all my heart."

Dantès meanwhile continued his route, each step he trod oppressed his heart with fresh emotion; his first and most indelible recollections were there, not a tree, not a street that he passed but seemed filled with dear and cherished reminiscences. And thus he proceeded onwards till he arrived at the end of Rue de Noäilles, from whence a full view of the Allées de Meillan was obtained; at this spot, so pregnant with fond and filial remembrances, his heart beat almost to bursting, his knees tottered under him, a misty vapour floated over his sight, and had he not clung for support to one of the trees, he would inevitably have fallen to the ground and been crushed beneath the many vehicles continually passing there. Recovering himself, however, he wiped the perspiration from his brows, and stopped not again till he found himself at the door of the house in which his father had lived.

The nasturtiums and other plants which his parent had delighted to train before his window had all disappeared from the upper part of the house; leaning against a tree he remained long gazing on those windows at which the busy hand of the active old man might be daily seen training and arranging his floral treasures. But Edmond remembered he had come thither for other reasons than to indulge a grief, now alas! unavailing; and, stifling the deep sigh that rose to his lips, he advanced to the door and inquired whether there were any chambers to be let in the house; though answered in the negative, he begged so earnestly to be permitted to visit those on the fifth floor, that, in despite of the *concierge's* oft-repeated assurance of their being occupied, Dantès succeeded in inducing the man to go up to the present possessors of these coveted rooms, and ask permission for a gentleman to be allowed to look at them. The tenants of the humble lodging, once the scene of all Dantès' early joys, consisted of a young couple who had been scarcely married a week, and the sight of a wedded happiness he was doomed never to experience drove a bitter pang through his heart. Nothing in the two small chambers forming the apartments remained as it had been in the time of the elder Dantès, the very paper was different, while the articles of antiquated furniture with which the rooms had been filled in Edmond's time had all disappeared. The four walls alone remained as he had left them. The bed belonging to the present occupants was placed as the former owner of the chamber had been accustomed to have his; and, spite of his efforts to prevent it, the eyes of Edmond were suffused in tears, as he reflected that on that spot his beloved parent had expired vainly calling for his son. The young couple gazed with astonishment at the sight of their visitor's emotion, and wondered to see the large tears silently chase each other down his otherwise stern and immovable features; but they felt the sacredness of his grief, and kindly refrained from questioning him as to its cause, while, with instinctive delicacy, they left him to indulge his sorrow alone. When he withdrew from the scene of his painful recollections they both accompanied him down-stairs, reiterating their hope that he would come again whenever he pleased, and assuring him their poor dwelling should ever be open to him. As Edmond passed the door of similar rooms on the fourth floor, he paused to inquire whether Caderousse, the tailor, still dwelt there; but he received for reply, that the individual in question had got into difficulties, and at the present time kept a small inn on the route from Bellegarde to Beaucaire.

Having obtained the address of the person to whom the house in the Allées de Meillan belonged, Dantès next proceeded thither, and, under the name of Lord Wilmore (the same appellation as that contained in his passport), purchased the small dwelling for the sum of 25,000 francs, at least 10,000 more than it was worth; but had its owner asked ten times the sum he did, it would unhesitatingly have been given. The very same day the occupants of the apartments on the fifth floor of the house, now become the property of Dantès, were duly informed by the notary who had arranged the necessary transfer of deeds, &c., that the new landlord gave them their choice of any of the rooms in the house without the least augmentation of rent, upon condition of their giving instant possession of the two small chambers they at present inhabited.

This strange event served to find food for wonder and curiosity in the neighbourhood of the Allées de Meillan and a multitude of various conjectures were afloat as to the probable cause of the house being so suddenly and mysteriously disposed of; but each surmise seemed to wander farther and farther from the real truth.

But that which raised public astonishment to a climax and set all speculations at defiance was, the circumstance of the same stranger who had in the morning visited the Allées de Meillan, being seen in the evening walking in the little village of the Catalans, and afterwards observed to enter a poor fisherman's hut, and to pass more than an hour in inquiring after persons who had been dead, or gone away for more than fifteen or sixteen years. But on the following day, the family from whom all these particulars had been asked received a handsome present, consisting of an entirely new fishing-boat, with a full supply of excellent nets.

The delighted recipients of these munificent gifts would gladly have poured out their thanks to their generous benefactor; but they had seen him, upon quitting the hut, merely give some orders to a sailor, and then springing lightly on horseback, quit Marseilles by the Porte d'Aix.

CHAPTER XXVI

THE AUBERGE OF PONT DU GARD

Such of my readers as have made a pedestrian excursion to the south of France may perchance have noticed, midway between the town of Beaucaire and the village of Bellegarde a small roadside inn, from the front of which hung, creaking and flapping in the wind, a sheet of tin covered with a caricature resemblance of the Pont du Gard. This modern place of entertainment stood on the left-hand side of the grand route, turning its back upon the Rhone. It also boasted of what in Languedoc is styled a garden, consisting of a small plot of ground, a full view of which might be obtained from a door immediately opposite the grand portal by which travellers were ushered in to partake of the hospitality of mine host of the Pont du Gard. This plaisance or garden, scorched up beneath the ardent sun of a latitude of thirty degrees, permitted nothing to thrive or scarcely live in its arid soil; a few dingy olives and stunted fig-trees struggled hard for existence, but their withered, dusty foliage abundantly proved how unequal was the conflict : between these sickly shrubs, grew a scanty supply of garlic, tomatoes, and eschalots, while, lone and solitary, like a forgotten sentinel, a tall pine raised its melancholy head in one of the corners of this unattractive spot, and displayed its flexible stem and fanshaped summit dried and cracked by the withering influence of the mistral, that scourge of Provence.

In the surrounding plain, which more resembled a dusty lake than solid ground, were scattered a few miserable stalks of wheat, the effect no doubt of a curious desire on the part of the agriculturists of the country, to see whether such a thing as the raising of grain in those parched regions was practicable; the scanty produce, however, served to accommodate the numerous grasshoppers who follow the unfortunate invader of this bare soil with untiring persecution, resting themselves after their chase upon the stunted specimens of horticulture, while they filled the ear with their sharp shrill cry.

For nearly the last eight years the small auberge we have just been describing had been kept by a man and his wife, with two servants, one a strong, sturdy wench, answering to the name of Trinette, officiated in the capacity of chambermaid, while the other, a shock-headed country lad, named Pacaud, undertook the management of the outer-door work, and contented himself with the title of *garçon d'écurie*, or ostler as we should style it in England; but alas! the occupation of each domestic was but nominal, for a canal recently made between Beaucaire and Aiguemortes had proved a most successful speculation, and had transferred the mode of sending merchandise and luggage from the heavy wagons to the towed barge, while travellers forsook the diligence to glide over the smooth waters by the more agreeable aid of the steam-boat. And as though to add to the daily misery which this prosperous canal inflicted on the unfortunate aubergiste, whose utter ruin it was fast accomplishing, it was situated not a hundred steps from the forsaken inn, of which we have given so faithful a description.

The aubergiste himself was a man of from forty to fifty-five years of age, tall, strong, and bony, a perfect specimen of the natives of those southern latitudes; he had the dark, sparkling, and deep-set eye, curved nose, and teeth white as those of a carnivorous animal; his hair, which, spite of the light touch time had as yet left on it, seemed as though it refused to assume any other colour than its own, was like his beard, which he wore under his chin, thick and curly, and but slightly mingled with a few silvery threads. His naturally murky complexion had assumed a still further shade of brown from the habit the unfortunate man had acquired of stationing himself from early morn till latest eve at the threshold of his door in eager hope that some traveller, either equestrian or pedestrian, might bless his eyes, and give him the delight of once more seeing a guest enter his doors; but his patience and his expectations were alike useless; yet there he stood, day after day, exposed to the meridional rays of a burning sun, with no other protection for his head than a red handkerchief twisted around it, after the manner of the Spanish muleteers. This anxious, careworn aubergiste was no other than our *cidevant* acquaintance, Caderousse. His wife, on the contrary, whose maiden name had been Madeline Radelle, was pale, meagre, and sickly-looking. Born in the neighbourhood of Arles, she had shared in the beauty for which its females are proverbial; but that beauty had gradually withered beneath the devastating influence of one of those slow fevers so prevalent in the vicinity of the waters of Aiguemortes and the marshes of Camargue. She remained nearly always in her chamber, situated on the first floor; sitting shivering in her chair or extended languid and feeble on her bed, while her husband kept his daily watch at the door—a duty he performed with so much the greater willingness, as it saved him the necessity of listening to the endless plaints and murmurs of his helpmate, who never saw him without breaking out into bitter invectives against fate and the unmerited hardships she was called upon to endure; to all of which her husband would calmly return an unvarying reply, couched in these philosophic words:—

"Cease to grieve about it, La Carconte. It is God's pleasure that you should suffer, and whether you like it or not you must bear it."

The sobriquet of La Carconte had been bestowed on Madeleine Radelle from the circumstance of her having been born in a village so called, situated between Salon and Lanbèse, and as a custom existed among the inhabitants of that part of France where Caderousse lived of styling every person by some particular and distinctive appellation, her husband had bestowed on her the name of La Carconte in place of her sweet and euphonious name of Madeleine, which, in all probability, his rude guttural language would not have enabled him to pronounce.

Still, let it not be supposed that amid this affected resignation to the will of Providence, the unfortunate aubergiste did not writhe under the double misery of seeing the hateful canal carry off alike his customers and profits, and the daily implication of his peevish partner's murmurs and lamentations.

Like other dwellers of the south, he was a man of sober habits and moderate desires, but fond of external show, vain, and addicted to display. During the days of his prosperity, not a *fête*, festivity, or ceremonial, took place without himself and wife being among the spectators. He dressed in the picturesque costume worn upon grand occasions by the inhabitants of the south of France, bearing equal resemblance to the style adopted both by the Catalans and Andalusians; while La Carconte displayed the charming fashion prevalent among the females of Arles, a mode of attire borrowed equally from Greece and Arabia. But, by degrees, watch-chains, necklaces, many-coloured scarfs, embroidered boddices, velvet vests, elegantly worked stockings, striped gaiters, and silver buckles for the shoes, all disappeared; and Gaspard Caderousse, unable to appear abroad in his pristine splendour, had given up any further participation in these pomps and vanities, both for himself or wife, although a bitter feeling of envious discontent filled his mind as the sound of mirth and merry music from the joyous revellers reached even the miserable hostelry to which he still clung, more for the shelter than the profit it afforded.

On the present day, Caderousse was, as usual, at his place of observation before the door, his eyes glancing listlessly from a piece of closely-shaven grass—on which some fowls were industriously, though fruitlessly, endeavouring to turn up some grain or insect suited to their palate—to the deserted road, the two extremities of which pointed respectively north and south, when he was roused from his daily speculations as to the possibility of the auberge of the Pont du Gard ever again being called upon to exercise its hospitable capabilities to any chance visitant by the shrill voice of his wife summoning him to her presence with all speed. Murmuring at the disagreeable interruption to his not very agreeable thoughts, he, however, proceeded to the floor in which was situated the chamber of his better half,—taking care, however, preparatory to so doing, to set the entrance-door wide open, that, in the event of that *rara avis*, a traveller, passing by, it should be made perfectly clear to his comprehension that no ceremony was requisite in entering.

At the moment Caderousse quitted his sentry-like watch before the door, the road on which he so eagerly strained his sight was void and lonely as a desert at mid-day. There it lay stretched out, one interminable line of dust and sand, with its sides bordered by tall, meagre trees, altogether presenting so uninviting an appearance, that no one in their senses could have imagined that any traveller, at liberty to regulate his hours for journeying, would choose to expose himself to the scorch of a meridian sun in such a formidable sahara. Nevertheless, had Caderousse but retained his post a few minutes longer, he might have caught a dim outline of something approaching from the direction of Bellegarde: as the moving object drew nearer, he would easily have perceived it consisted of a man and horse, between whom the kindest and most amiable understanding appeared to exist. The horse was of Hungarian breed, and ambled along with that easy pace peculiar to that race of animals. His rider was a priest, dressed in black, and wearing a three-cornered hat; and, spite of the ardent rays of a noonday sun, the pair came on at a tolerably smart trot.

Having arrived before the auberge du Pont du Gard, the horse stopped, but whether for his own pleasure or that of his rider would have been difficult to say. However that might have been, the measure appeared reciprocally agreeable, since no demur was observable in either. The priest, dismounting, led his steed by the bridle in search of some place to which he could secure him. Availing himself of a handle that projected from a half-fallen door, he tied the animal safely, patted him kindly, and, having drawn a red cotton handkerchief from his pocket, wiped away the perspiration that streamed from his brow; then, advancing to the door, struck thrice with the end of his iron-shod stick. At this unusual sound, a huge black dog came rushing to meet the daring assailant of his ordinarily tranquil abode, snarling and displaying his sharp, white teeth with a determined hostility that abundantly proved how little he was accustomed to society. At that moment a heavy footstep was heard descending the wooden staircase that led from the upper floor, and, with many bows and courteous smiles, mine host of the Pont du Gard welcomed the blessing Heaven had sent him in the shape of a weary traveller; while, retreating into the house with backward step, he besought his guest would honour him by entering also.

"You are welcome, sir, most welcome!" repeated the astonished Caderousse, in his blandest tones. "Now, then, Margontin," cried he, speaking to the dog, "will you be quiet? Pray don't heed him, sir!—he only barks, he never bites! I make no doubt a glass of good wine would be acceptable this dreadfully hot day!" Then perceiving for the first time the description of traveller he had to entertain, Caderousse hastily exclaimed, "A thousand pardons, your reverence! I really did not observe whom I had the honour to receive under my poor roof. What would you please to have, M. l'Abbé? What refreshment can I offer you? All I have is at your service."

The priest gazed on the individual addressing him with a long and searching gaze—there even seemed like a disposition on his part to court a similar scrutiny on the part of the aubergiste; then, remarking in the countenance of the latter no other expression than extreme surprise at his own want of attention to an inquiry so courteously worded, he deemed it as well to terminate this dumb show, and, therefore, said, speaking with a strong Italian accent,—

"You are, I presume, M. Caderousse?"

"Your reverence is quite correct," answered the host, even more surprised at the question than he had been by the silence which had prefaced it; "I am Gaspard Caderousse, at your service."

"Gaspard Caderousse!" rejoined the priest. "Yes, that agrees both with the baptismal appellation and surname of the individual I allude to. You formerly lived, I believe, in the Allées de Meillan, on the fourth floor of a small house situated there?"

"I did."

"Where you followed the business of a tailor?"

"True, I was a tailor, till the trade fell off so as not to afford me a living. Then it is so very hot at Marseilles, that really I could bear it no longer; and it is my idea that all the respectable inhabitants will be obliged to follow my example and quit it. But, talking of heat, is there nothing I can offer you by way of refreshment?"

"Yes; let me have a bottle of your best wine, and then, with your permission, we will resume our conversation from where we left off."

"As you please, M. l'Abbé," said Caderousse, who, anxious not to lose the present opportunity of finding a customer for one of the few bottles of vin de Cahors still remaining in his possession, hastily raised a trap-door in the floor of the apartment they were in, which served both as parlour and kitchen.

Upon his issuing forth from his subterranean retreat at the expiration of five minutes, he found the abbé seated on a species of stool, leaning his elbow on a table, while Margontin, whose animosity seemed appeased by the traveller having pronounced the unusual command for refreshments, had crept up to him, and had established himself very comfortably between his knees, his long, skinny neck resting on his lap, while his dim eye was fixed earnestly on the traveller's face.

"Are you quite alone?" inquired the guest, as Caderousse placed before him the bottle of wine and a glass.

"Quite, quite alone," replied the man—"or, at least, all but so, M. l'Abbé; for my poor wife, who is the only person in the house besides myself, is laid up with illness, and unable to render me the least assistance, poor thing!"

"You are married, then?" said the priest, with a species of interest, glancing round as he spoke at the scanty style of the accommodations and humble fittings-up of the apartment.

"Ah, M. l'Abbé," said Caderousse, with a sigh, "it is easy to perceive I am not a rich man; but in this world a man does not thrive the better for being honest."

The abbé fixed on him a searching, penetrating glance.

"I can certainly say that much for myself," repeated the aubergiste, fairly sustaining the scrutiny of the abbé's gaze, "I can boast with truth of being an honest man;" and continued he, significantly shaking his head, "that is more than every one can say nowadays."

"So much the better for you if what you assert be true," said the abbé; "for I am firmly persuaded that, sooner or later, the good will be rewarded, and the wicked punished."

"Such words as those belong to your profession, M. l'Abbé," answered Caderousse, "and you do well to repeat them; but," added he, with a bitter expression of countenance, "you cannot make people believe them in opposition to what passes before them every day, when the reverse takes place, and it is the wicked man who prospers, and the honest deserving man who suffers."

"You are wrong to speak thus," said the abbé; "and, perhaps, I may in my own person be able to prove to you how completely you are in error in coming to so mischievous and dangerous a conclusion."

"What mean you?" inquired Caderousse, with a look of surprise.

"In the first place, it is requisite I should be satisfied you are the person I am in search of!"

"What proofs do you require?"

"Did you in the year 1814 or 1815 know any thing of a young sailor named Edmond Dantès?"

"Did I? I should think I did. Poor dear Edmond! Why, Edmond Dantès and myself were intimate friends!" exclaimed Caderousse, whose countenance assumed an almost purple hue, as he caught the penetrating gaze of the abbé fixed on him, while the clear, calm eye of the questioner seemed to cover him with confusion.

"You remind me," said the priest, "that the young man, concerning whom I asked you, was said to bear the name of Edmond."

"Said to bear the name!" repeated Caderousse, becoming excited and eager. "Why, he was so called as truly as I myself bore the appellation of Gaspard Caderousse; but, M. l'Abbé, tell me I pray, what has become of poor Edmond. Did you know him? Is he alive and at liberty? Is he prosperous and happy?"

"He died a more wretched, hopeless, heart-broken prisoner than the felons who pay the penalty of their crimes at the galleys of Toulon!"

A deadly paleness succeeded the deep suffusion which had before spread itself over the countenance of Caderousse, who turned away, but not so much so as to prevent the priest's observing him wiping away the tears from his eyes with a corner of the red handkerchief twisted round his head.

"Poor fellow! poor fellow!" murmured Caderousse. "Well, there, M. l'Abbé, is another proof that good people are never rewarded on this earth, and that none but the wicked prosper. Ah," continued Caderousse, speaking in the highly-coloured language of the South, "the world grows worse and worse. Why does not God if he really hates the wicked as he is said to do, send down brimstone and fire and consume them altogether."

"You speak as though you had loved this young Dantès!" observed the abbé, without taking any notice of his companion's vehemence.

"And so I did," replied Caderousse, "though once I confess I envied him his good fortune; but I swear to you, M. l'Abbé, I swear to you, by every thing a man holds dear, I have since then deeply and sincerely lamented his unhappy fate."

There was a brief silence, during which the fixed, searching eye of the abbé was employed in scrutinising the agitated features of the aubergiste.

"You knew the poor lad, then?" continued Caderousse.

"Nay, I was merely called to see him when on his dying bed, that *I* might administer to him the consolations of religion."

"And of what did he die?" asked Caderousse, in a choking voice.

"Of what think you do young and strong men die in prison, when they have scarcely numbered their thirtieth year, unless it be of the horrors of that prison which has spread its stony walls against their breathing the air of heaven, or participating in the secret affections a gracious Creator permitted to find growth within the human breast? Edmond Dantès died in prison of sorrow and a broken heart."

Caderousse wiped away the large drops of perspiration that gathered on his brow.

"But the strangest part of the story is," resumed the abbé "that Dantès, even in his dying moments, swore by his crucified Redeemer, that he was utterly ignorant of the cause of his imprisonment."

"And so he was!" murmured Caderousse. "How should he have been otherwise? Ah, M. l'Abbé, the poor fellow told you the truth."

"And for that reason he besought me to try and clear up a mystery he had never been able to penetrate, and to clear his memory should any foul spot or stain have fallen on it."

And here the look of the abbé, becoming more and more fixed, seemed to rest with ill-concealed satisfaction on the gloomy depression which seemed rapidly spreading over the countenance of Caderousse.

"A rich Englishman," continued the abbé, "who had been his companion in misfortune, but had been released from prison during the second restoration, was possessed of a diamond of immense value: this precious jewel he bestowed on Dantès upon himself quitting the prison, as a mark of his gratitude for the kindness and brotherly care with which Dantès had nursed him in a severe illness he underwent during his confinement. Instead of employing this diamond in attempting to bribe his gaolers, who might only have taken it and then betrayed him to the governor, Dantès carefully preserved it, that in the event of his getting out of prison he might have wherewithal to live, for the produce of such a diamond would have quite sufficed to make his fortune."

"Then, I suppose," asked Caderousse, with eager glowing looks, "that it was a stone of immense value?"

"Why every thing is relative," answered the abbé. "To one in Edmond's position the diamond certainly was of great value. It was estimated at 50,000 francs."

"Bless me!" exclaimed Caderousse, "What a sum! 50,000 francs! Surely the diamond was as large as a nut to be worth all that?"

"No," replied the abbé, "it was not of such a size as that; but you shall judge for yourself, I have it with me."

The sharp gaze of Caderousse was instantly directed towards the priest's garments, as though hoping to discover the talked-of treasure.

Calmly drawing forth from his pocket a small box covered with black shagreen, the abbé opened it, and displayed to the delighted eyes of Caderousse, the sparkling jewel it contained, set in a ring of admirable workmanship.

"And that diamond," cried Caderousse, almost breathless with eager admiration, "you say is worth 50,000 francs?"

"It is, without the setting, which is also valuable," replied the abbé, as he closed the box, and returned it to his pocket, while its brilliant hues seemed still to dance before the eyes of the fascinated aubergiste.

"But how comes this diamond in your possession M. l'Abbé? Did Edmond make you his heir?"

"No, merely his testamentary executor. When dying the unfortunate youth said to me, ' I once possessed four dear and faithful friends, besides the maiden to whom I was betrothed; and I feel convinced they have all unfeignedly grieved over my loss. The name of one of the four friends I allude to is Caderousse.'"

The aubergiste shivered as though he felt the dead cold hand of the betrayed Edmond grasping his own.

"'Another of the number,' continued the abbé, without seeming to notice the emotion of Caderousse, 'is called Danglars; and the third, spite of being my rival, entertained a very sincere affection for me.'"

A fiendish smile played over the features of Caderousse, who was about to break in upon the abbé's speech, when the latter, waving his hand, said,—

"Allow me to finish first, and then if you have any observations to make, you can do so afterwards.

"'The third of my friends, although my rival, was much attached to me—his name was Fernand; that of my betrothed was——' Stay, stay," continued the abbé, " I have forgotten what he called her."

"Mercédès!" cried Caderousse, eagerly.

"True," said the abbé, with a stifled sigh. "Mercédès it was."

"Go on," urged Caderousse.

"Bring me a *carafe* of water," said the abbé.

Caderousse quickly performed the stranger's bidding; and after pouring some into a glass, and slowly swallowing its contents, the abbé, resuming his usual placidity of manner, said, as he placed his empty glass on the table,—

"Where did we leave off?"

"Oh, that the betrothed of Edmond was called Mercédès!"

"To be sure. 'Well, then,' said Dantès—for you understand I repeat his words just as he uttered them—'you will go to Marseilles.' Do you understand?''

"Perfectly.''

"'For the purpose of selling this diamond; the produce of which you will divide into five equal parts, and give an equal portion to the only persons who have loved me upon earth.'''

"But why into five parts?'' asked Caderousse, "you only mentioned four persons.''

"Because the fifth is dead, as I hear. The fifth sharer in Edmond's bequest was his own father.''

"Too true, too true!'' ejaculated Caderousse, almost suffocated by the contending passions which assailed him. "The poor old man did die!''

"I learned so much at Marseilles,'' replied the abbé, making a strong effort to appear indifferent; "but from the length of time that has elapsed since the death of the elder Dantès, I was unable to obtain any particulars of his end. You possibly may be capable of furnishing me with such minute circumstances as may serve to substantiate the decease of the elder Dantès.''

"I do not know who could if I could not,'' said Caderousse. "Why, I lived almost on the same floor with the poor old man. Ah, yes! about a year after the disappearance of his son the old man died!''

"Of what did he die?''

"Why, the doctors called his complaint an internal inflammation, I believe, his acquaintances said he died of grief; but I, who saw him in his dying moments, I say he died of——''

"Of what?'' asked the priest, anxiously and eagerly.

"Why, of downright starvation.''

"Starvation!'' exclaimed the abbé, springing from his seat. "Why, the vilest animals are not suffered to die by such a death as that. The very dogs that wander houseless and homeless in the streets, find some pitying hand to cast them a mouthful of bread; and that a man, a Christian, should be allowed to perish of hunger in the midst of other men equally Christians with himself, is too horrible for beliefs. Oh, it is impossible—utterly impossible.''

"What I have said, I have said,'' answered Caderousse.

"And you are a fool for having said any thing about it,'' said a voice from the top of the stairs. "Why should you meddle with what does not concern you?''

The two male speakers turned round quickly, and perceived the sickly countenance of La Carconte leaning over the rail of the staircase; attracted by the sound of voices, she had feebly dragged herself down the stairs, and, seated on the lower step, she had listened to the foregoing conversation.

"Mind your own business, wife,'' replied Caderousse,

sharply. "This gentleman asks me for information, which common politeness will not permit me to refuse."

"Politeness! you simpleton!" retorted La Carconte. "What have you to do with politeness I should like to know? Better study a little common prudence. How do you know the motives that person may have for trying to extract all he can from you?"

"I pledge you my sacred word, madame," said the abbé, "that my intentions are free from all thoughts of harm or injury to you or yours; and that your husband can incur no risk provided he answers me candidly."

"Ah, that's all very fine," retorted the woman. "Nothing is easier than to begin with fair promises and assurances of nothing to fear; but when poor, silly folks like my husband there have been persuaded to tell all they know, the promises and assurances of safety are quickly forgotten; and at some moment when nobody is expecting it, behold trouble, and misery, and all sorts of persecutions, are heaped on the unfortunate wretches who cannot even see whence all their afflictions come."

"Nay, nay, my good woman, make yourself perfectly easy. I beg of you, whatever evils may befall you, they will not be occasioned by my instrumentality, that I solemnly promise you."

Some inarticulate sounds escaped La Carconte, then letting her head, which she had raised during the excitement of conversation, again droop on to her lap, she commenced her usual aguish trembling, the result of her feverish attack, leaving the two speakers to resume the conversation, but still remaining herself so placed, as to be able to hear every word they uttered.

Again the abbé had been obliged to swallow a draught of water to calm the emotions that threatened to overpower him. When he had sufficiently recovered himself, he said,—

"It appears, then, that the miserable old man you were telling me of was forsaken by every one. Surely had not such been the case, he would not have perished by so dreadful a death as you described."

"Why, he was not altogether forsaken," continued Caderousse; "for Mercédès the Catalan and M. Morrel were very kind to him; but somehow the poor old man had contracted a profound hatred of Fernand—the very person," added Caderousse, with a bitter smile, "that you named just now as being one of Dantès' faithful and attached friends."

"And was he not so?" asked the abbé.

"Gaspard! Gaspard!" murmured the woman, from her seat on the stairs, "mind what you are saying!"

Caderousse made no reply to these words, though evidently irritated and annoyed by the interruption, but, addressing the abbé, said,—

"Can a man be faithful to another whose wife he covets and desires for himself? But Dantès was so honourable and true in his own nature, that he believed every body's professions of friendship. Poor Edmond! he was cruelly deceived; but it was a happy thing he never knew it, or he might have found it more difficult, when on his death-bed, to pardon his enemies. And, whatever people may say," continued Caderousse, in his native language, which was not altogether devoid of rude poetry, "I cannot help being more frightened at the idea of the malediction of the dead than the hatred of the living."

"Weak-minded coward!" exclaimed La Carconte.

"Do you then know in what manner Fernand injured Dantès?" inquired the abbé of Caderousse.

"Do I? No one better."

"Speak out, then; say what it was!"

"Gaspard!" cried La Carconte, "I cannot force you to do otherwise than as you please, but, if you are guided by me, you will have nothing to say on this subject."

"Well, well, wife," replied Caderousse, "I do not know but what you are right! I shall follow your advice."

"Then you are determined not to reveal the circumstances you alluded to?" said the abbé.

"Why, what good would it do?" asked Caderousse. "If the poor lad were living, and came to me to beg I would candidly tell which were his true and which his false friends, why, perhaps, I should not hesitate. But you tell me he is no more, and therefore can have nothing to do with hatred or revenge; so let all such feelings be buried with him."

"You prefer, then," said the abbé, "allowing me to bestow on men you say are false and treacherous, the reward intended for faithful friendship?"

"That is true enough," returned Caderousse. "You say truly the gift of poor Edmond was not meant for such traitors as Fernand and Danglars; besides, what would it be to them? no more than a drop of water in the ocean."

"And remember, husband," chimed in La Carconte, "that to breathe one syllable against those two individuals would be to raise up against yourself two formidable enemies, who at a word could level you with the dust!"

"How so?" inquired the abbé. "Are these persons, then, so rich and powerful?"

"Do you not know their history?"

"I do not. Pray relate it me!"

Caderousse seemed to reflect for a few instants, then said,—

"No, truly, it would take up too much time."

"Well, my good friend," returned the abbé, in a tone that indicated utter indifference on his part, "you are at liberty either to speak or be silent, just as you please; for my own part, I respect your scruples and admire your sentiments. So let the matter end. I shall do my duty as conscientiously as I can, and fulfil my promise to the dying man. My first business will be to dispose of this diamond."

So saying, the abbé again drew the small box from his pocket, opened it, and contrived to hold it in such a light that a bright flash of brilliant hues passed before the dazzled gaze of Caderousse.

"Wife, wife!" cried he, in a voice almost hoarse with eager emotion, "come hither and behold this rich diamond!"

"Diamond!" exclaimed La Carconte, rising and descending to the chamber with a tolerably firm step, "what diamond are you talking about?"

"Why, did you not hear all we said?" inquired Caderousse. "It is a beautiful diamond left by poor Edmond Dantès, to be sold, and the money divided among his father, Mercédès, his betrothed bride, Fernand, Danglars, and myself. The jewel is worth, at least, 50,000 francs."

"Oh, what a splendid diamond!" cried the astonished woman.

"The fifth part of the produce of this stone belongs to us, then, does it not?" asked Caderousse, still devouring the glittering gem with his eyes.

"It does," replied the abbé; "with the addition of an equal division of that part intended for the elder Dantès, which I conceive myself at liberty to share equally with the four surviving persons."

"And wherefore among us four?" inquired Caderousse.

"As being the friends Edmond esteemed most faithful and devoted to him."

"I don't call those friends who betray and ruin you," murmured the wife, in her turn, in a low, muttering voice.

"Of course not!" rejoined Caderousse, quickly, "no more do I; and that was what I was observing to this gentleman just now. I said I looked upon it as a sacrilegious profanation to reward treachery, perhaps crime."

"Remember," answered the abbé, calmly, as he replaced the jewel and its case in the pocket of his cassock, "it is your fault, not mine, that I do so. You will have the goodness to furnish me with the address of both Fernand and Danglars, in order that I may execute Edmond's last wishes!"

The agitation of Caderousse became extreme, and large drops of perspiration rolled from his heated brows. As he saw the abbé rise from his seat and go towards the door, as though to ascertain if his horse were sufficiently refreshed to continue his journey, Caderousse and his wife exchanged looks of deep meaning with each other.

"There, you see, wife," said the former, "this splendid diamond might all be ours if we chose!"

"Do you believe it?"

"Why, surely a man of his holy profession would not deceive us!"

"Well," replied La Carconte, "do as you like. For my part, I wash my hands of the affair."

So saying, she once more climbed the staircase leading to her chamber, her frame shuddering with aguish chills, and her teeth rattling in her head, spite of the intense heat of the weather. Arrived at the top stair, she turned round, and called out in a warning tone to her husband,—

"Gaspard, consider well what you are about to do!"

"I have both reflected and decided," answered he.

La Carconte then entered her chamber, the flooring of which creaked beneath her heavy, uncertain tread, as she proceeded towards her arm-chair, into which she fell as though exhausted.

"Well," asked the abbé, as he returned to the apartment below, "what have you made up your mind to do?"

"To tell you all I know," was the reply.

"I certainly think you act wisely in so doing," said the priest. "Not because I have the least desire to learn anything you may desire to conceal from me, but simply that if, through your assistance, I could distribute the legacy according to the wishes of the testator, why so much the better, that is all."

"I trust, indeed, such will be the case," and that poor Edmond's dying bequest will be given only to such as you shall be convinced are his faithful and attached friends," replied Caderousse, his eyes sparkling and his face flushed with the hope of obtaining all himself.

"Now, then, begin if you please," said the abbé, "I am all attention."

"Stop a minute," answered Caderousse, "we might be interrupted in the most interesting part of my recital, which would be a pity, and it is as well that your visit hither should be made known only to ourselves."

With these words he went stealthily to the door which he closed, and by way of still greater precaution, bolted and barred it as he was accustomed to do at night. During this time the abbé had chosen his place for listening to the painful recital he expected Caderousse's would move; he removed his seat into a corner of the room, where he himself would be in deep shadow, while the light would be fully thrown on the narrator, then, with head bent down and hands clasped or rather clenched together, he prepared to give his whole attention to Caderousse, who seated himself on the little stool, exactly opposite to him.

"Remember, I did not urge you to this," said the trembling voice of La Carconte, as though through the flooring of her chamber, she viewed the scene that was enacting below.

"Enough, enough!" replied Caderousse, "say no more about it; I will take all the consequences upon myself."

He then commenced as follows:

CHAPTER XXVII

THE RECITAL

"First," said Caderousse, "sir, you must make me a promise."

"What is that?" inquired the abbé.

"Why, if you ever make use of the details I am about to give you, that you will never let any one know that it was I who supplied them, for the persons of whom I am about to talk are rich and powerful, and if they only laid the tips of their fingers on me, I should break to pieces like glass."

"Make yourself easy, my friend," replied the abbé; "I am a priest, and confessions die in my breast; recollect our only desire is to carry out in a fitting manner the last wishes of our friend. Speak, then, without reserve as without hatred; tell the truth, the whole truth; I do not know, never may know, the persons of whom you are about to speak; besides, I am an Italian and not a Frenchman, and belong to God and not to man, and I retire to my convent, which I have only quitted to fulfil the last wishes of a dying man."

This last assurance seemed to give Caderousse courage.

"Well, then, under these circumstances," said Caderousse, "I will; indeed I ought to undeceive you as to the friendship which poor Edmond believed so sincere and unquestionable."

"Begin with his father, if you please," said the abbé; "Edmond talked to me a great deal about the old man, for whom he had the deepest love."

"The history is a sad one, sir," said Caderousse, shaking his head; "perhaps you know all the earlier part of it?"

"Yes," answered the abbé. "Edmond related to me every thing until the moment when he was arrested in a small cabaret close to Marseilles."

"At La Réserve! oh! yes! I can see it all before me this moment."

"Was it not his betrothal feast?"

"It was; and the feast that began so gaily had a very sorrowful ending; a commissary of police, followed by four soldiers entered, and Dantès was arrested."

"Yes, and up to this point I know all," said the priest. "Dantès himself only knew that which personally concerned him, for he never beheld again the five persons I have named to you, nor heard mention of any one of them."

"Well, when Dantès was arrested, M. Morrel hastened to obtain the particulars, and they were very sad. The old man returned alone to his home, folded up his wedding suit with tears in his eyes, and paced up and down his chamber the whole day, and would not go to bed at all, for I was underneath him and heard him walking the whole night; and for myself, I assure you I could not sleep either, for the grief of the poor father gave me great uneasiness, and every step he took went to my heart as really as if his foot had pressed against my breast.

"The next day Mercédès came to implore the protection of M. de Villefort, she did not obtain it however, and went to visit the old man; when she saw him so miserable and heart-broken, having passed a sleepless night and not touched food since the previous day, she wished him to go with her that she might take care of him; but the old man would not consent.

"'No,' was the old man's reply, 'I will not leave this house, for my poor dear boy loves me better than anything in the world; and if he gets out of prison he will come and see me the first thing, and what would he think if I did not wait here for him?'

"I heard all this from the window, for I was anxious that Mercédès should persuade the old man to accompany her, for his footsteps over my head night and day did not leave me a moment's repose."

"But did you not go up-stairs and try to console the poor old man?" asked the abbé.

"Ah! sir," replied Caderousse, "we cannot console those who will not be consoled, and he was one of these; besides, I know not why, but he seemed to dislike seeing me. One night, however, I heard his sobs, and I could not resist my desire to go up to him; but when I reached his door he was no longer weeping but praying: I cannot now repeat to you, sir, all the eloquent words and imploring language he made use of; it was more than piety, it was more than grief: and I, who am no canter and hate the Jesuits, said then to myself, 'It is really well, and I am very glad that I have not any children, for if I were a father and felt such excessive grief as the old man does, and did not find in my memory or heart all he is now saying, I should throw myself into the sea at once, for I could not bear it.'"

"Poor father!" murmured the priest.

"From day to day he lived on alone, and more and more solitary. M. Morrel and Mercédès came to see him, but his door was closed, and although I was certain he was at home he would not make any answer. One day, when, contrary to his custom, he had admitted Mercédès, and the poor girl, in spite of her own grief and despair, endeavoured to console him, he said to her,—

"'Be assured, my dear daughter, he is dead; and instead of expecting him it is he who is awaiting us; I am quite happy, for I am the oldest, and of course shall see him first.'

"However well disposed a person may be, why you see we leave off after a time seeing persons who are in sorrow, they make one melancholy, and so at last, old Dantès was left all to himself, and I only saw from time to time strangers go up to him and come down again with some bundle they tried to hide; but I guessed what these bundles were, and he sold by degrees what he had to pay for his subsistence.

"At length, the poor old fellow reached the end of all he had, he owed three quarters' rent, and they threatened to turn him out, he begged for another week which was granted to him. I know this, because the landlord came into my apartment when he left his. For the three first days I heard him walking about as usual, but on the fourth I heard him no longer. I then resolved to go up to him at all risks. The door was closed, but I looked through the key-hole and saw him so pale and haggard, that believing him very ill I went and told Mr. Morrel, and then ran on to Mercédès. They both came immediately. M. Morrel bringing a doctor, and the doctor said it was an affection of the stomach, and ordered him a limited diet. I was there too, and I never shall forget the old man's smile at this prescription. From that time he opened his door, he had an excuse for not eating any more as the doctor had put him on a diet."

The abbé uttered a kind of groan.

"The story interests you, does it not, sir?" inquired Caderousse.

"Yes," replied the abbé, "it is very affecting."

"Mercédès came again, and she found him so altered that she was even more anxious than before to have him taken to her own abode. This was M. Morrel's wish also, who would fain have conveyed the old man against his consent; but the old man resisted and cried so, that they were actually frightened. Mercédès remained, therefore, by his bed-side, and M. Morrel went away making a sign to the Catalane that he had left his purse on the chimney-piece. But availing himself of the doctor's order, the old man would not take any sustenance; at length (after nine days' despair and fasting), the old man died, cursing those who had caused his misery, and saying to Mercédès,—

"'If you ever see my Edmond again, tell him I die blessing him.'"

The abbé rose from his chair, made two turns round the chamber, and pressed his trembling hand against his parched throat.

"And you believe he died——"

"Of hunger, sir, of hunger," said Caderousse; "I am as certain of it as that we two are Christians."

The abbé with a shaking hand seized a glass of water that was standing by him half full, swallowed it at one gulp, and then resumed his seat with red eyes and pale cheeks.

"This was, indeed, a horrid event," said he, in a hoarse voice.

"The more so, sir, as it was men's and not God's doing."

"Tell me of those men," said the abbé, "and remember too," he added, in a voice that was nearly menacing in its tone, "you have promised to tell me every thing. Tell me, therefore, who are these men who have killed the son with despair, and the father with famine?"

"Two men jealous of him, sir, one from love, and the other ambition—Fernand and Danglars."

"Say, how was this jealousy manifested?"

"They denounced Edmond as a Bonapartist agent."

"Which of the two denounced him? which was the real delinquent?"

"Both sir; one with a letter, and the other put it in the post."

"And where was this letter written?"

"At La Réserve, the day before the festival of the betrothing."

"'Twas so then—'twas so then," murmured the abbé, "oh! Faria! Faria! how well did you judge men and things!"

"What did you please to say, sir?" asked Caderousse.

"Nothing, nothing," replied the priest, "go on."

"It was Danglars who wrote the denunciation with his left hand, that his writing might not be recognised, and Fernand who put it in the post."

"But," exclaimed the abbé, suddenly, "you were there yourself."

"I!" said Caderousse, astonished, "who told you I was there?"

The abbé saw he had overshot the mark, and he added quickly,—

"No one; but in order to have known every thing so well, you must have been an eye-witness."

"True! true!" said Caderousse, in a choking voice, "I was there."

"And did you not remonstrate against such infamy?" asked the abbé; "if not you were an accomplice."

"Sir," replied Caderousse, "they had made me drink to such an excess that I nearly lost all perception. I had only an indistinct understanding of what was passing around me, I said all that a man in such a state could say; but they both assured me that it was a jest they were carrying on and perfectly harmless."

"Next day—next day, sir, you must have seen plain enough what they had been doing, yet you said nothing, though you were present when Dantès was arrested."

"Yes, sir, I was there, and very anxious to speak; but Danglars restrained me.

"'If he should really be guilty,' said he, 'and did really put into the isle of Elba; if he is really charged with a letter for the Bonapartist committee at Paris, and if they find this letter upon him, those who have supported him will pass for his accomplices.'

"I confess I had my fears in the state in which politics then were, and I held my tongue: it was cowardly I confess, but it was not criminal."

"I comprehend, you allowed matters to take their course, that was all."

"Yes, sir," answered Caderousse, "and my remorse preys on me night and day. I often ask pardon of God, I swear to you, because this action, the only one with which I have seriously to reproach myself with in all my life, is no doubt the cause of my abject condition. I am expiating a moment of selfishness, and thus it is I always say to Carconte when she complains, 'Hold your tongue, woman, it is the will of God.'"

And Caderousse bowed his head with every sign of real repentance.

"Well, sir," said the abbé, "you have spoken unreservedly and thus to accuse yourself is to deserve pardon."

"Unfortunately Edmond is dead, and has not pardoned me."

"He was ignorant," said the abbé.

"But he knows it all now," interrupted Caderousse; "they say the dead know every thing."

There was a brief silence, the abbé rose and paced up and down pensively, and then resumed his seat.

"You have two or three times mentioned a M. Morrel," he said; "who was he?"

"The owner of the Pharaon and patron of Dantès."

"And what part did he play in this sad drama?" inquired the abbé.

"The part of an honest man, full of courage and real regard. Twenty times he interceded for Edmond; when the emperor returned, he wrote, implored, threatened, and so energetically, that on the second restoration he was persecuted as a Bonapartist. Ten times, as I told you, he came to see Dantès' father, and offered to receive him in his own house; and the night or two before his death, as I have already said, he left his purse on the mantel-piece, with which they paid the old man's debts and buried him decently, and then Edmond's father died as he had lived, without doing harm to any one. I have the purse still by me, a large one made of red silk."

"And," asked the abbé, "is M. Morrel still alive?"

"Yes," replied Caderousse.

"In this case," replied the abbé, "he should be rich, happy."

Caderousse smiled bitterly.

"Yes, happy as myself," said he.

"What! M. Morrel unhappy?" exclaimed the abbé.

"He is reduced almost to the last extremity—nay, he is almost at the point of dishonour."

"How?"

"Yes," continued Caderousse, "and in this way after five-and-twenty years of labour, after having acquired a most honourable name in the trade of Marseilles, M. Morrel is utterly ruined. He has lost five ships in two years, has suffered by the bankruptcy of three large houses, and his only hope now is in that very Pharaon which poor Dantès commanded, and which is expected from the Indies with a cargo of cochineal and indigo. If this ship founders like the others, he is a ruined man."

"And has the unfortunate man wife or children?" inquired the abbé.

"Yes, he has a wife, who in all this, behaved like an angel; he has a daughter, who was about to marry the man she loved, but whose family now will not allow him to wed the daughter of a ruined man; he has besides a son, a lieutenant in the army, and, as you may suppose, all this instead of soothing, doubles his grief. If he were alone in the world he would blow out his brains, and there would be an end."

"Horrible!" ejaculated the priest.

"And it is thus Heaven recompenses virtue, sir," added Caderousse. "You see, I, who never did a bad action but that I have told you of, I am in destitution after having seen my poor wife die of a fever, unable to do any thing in the world for her, I shall die of hunger as old Dantès did, whilst Fernand and Danglars are rolling in wealth."

"How is that?"

"Because all their malpractices have turned to luck, while honest men have been reduced to misery."

"What has become of Danglars, the instigator, and therefore the most guilty?"

"What has become of him? why he left Marseilles, and was taken, on the recommendation of M. Morrel, who did not know his crime, as cashier into a Spanish bank. During the war with Spain, he was employed in the commissariat of the French army, and made a fortune; then with that money he speculated in the funds, and trebled or quadrupled his capital; and, having first married his banker's daughter, who left him a widower, he has married a second time, a widow, a Madame de Nargonne, daughter of M. de Servieux, the king's chamberlain, who is in high favour at court.   He is a millionaire, and they have made him a count, and now he is Le Comte Danglars, with a hotel in the Rue de Mont Blanc, with ten horses in his stables, six footmen in his anti-chamber, and I know not how many hundreds of thousands in his strong-box."

"Ah!" said the abbé, with a peculiar tone, "he is happy."

"Happy! who can answer for that?   Happiness or unhappiness is the secret known but to oneself, and the walls—walls have ears, but no tongue—but if a large fortune produces happiness, Danglars is happy."

"And Fernand?"

"Fernand! why that is another history."

"But how could a poor Catalan fisher-boy, without education and resources, make a fortune?   I confess this staggers me."

"And it has staggered every body, there must have been in his life some strange secret no one knows."

"But then, by what visible steps has he attained this high fortune or high position?"

"Both, sir, he has both fortune and position, both."

"This must be impossible."

"It would seem so, but listen and you will understand.

"Some days before the return of the emperor Fernand was drawn in the conscription.   The Bourbons left him quietly enough at the Catalans, but Napoleon returned, an extraordinary muster was determined on, and Fernand was compelled to join.   I went, too, but as I was older than Fernand and had just married my poor wife, I was only sent to the coast.   Fernand was enrolled in the active troop, went to the frontier with his regiment, and was at the battle of Ligny. The night after that battle he was sentry at the door of a general, who carried on a secret correspondence with the enemy.   That same night the general was to go over to the English.   He proposed to Fernand to accompany him, Fernand agreed to do so, deserted his post and followed the general.

"That which would have brought Fernand to a courtmartial if Napoleon remained on the throne, served for his recommendation to the Bourbons.   He returned to France with the epaulette of sub-lieutenant, and as the protection of the general, who is in the highest favour, was accorded to him, he was a captain in 1823 during the Spanish war, that is to say, at the time when Danglars made his early speculations.   Fernand was a Spaniard, and being sent to Spain to ascertain the feeling of his fellow-countrymen, found Danglars there, became on very intimate terms with him, procured his general support from the royalists of the capital and the provinces, received promises and made pledges on his own part, guided his regiment by paths known to himself alone in gorges of the mountains kept by the royalists, and in fact, rendered such services in this brief campaign, that after the taking of Trocadero he was made colonel, and received the title of count, and the cross of an officer of the Legion of Honour.

"Destiny! destiny!" murmured the abbé.

"Yes, but listen, this was not all. The war with Spain being ended, Fernand's career was checked by the long peace which seemed likely to endure throughout Europe. Greece only had risen against Turkey, and had begun her war of independence; all eyes were turned towards Athens, it was the fashion to pity and support the Greeks. The French government without protecting them, openly, as you know, tolerated partial migrations. Fernand sought and obtained leave to go and serve in Greece, still having his name kept in the ranks of the army. Some time after, it was stated that the Comte de Morcerf, this was the name he bore, had entered the service of Ali Pasha, with the rank of instructor-general. Ali Pasha was killed, as you know, but before he died he recompensed the services of Fernand, by leaving him a considerable sum, with which he returned to France, when his rank of lieutenant-general was confirmed."

"So that now――" inquired the abbé.

"So that now," continued Caderousse, "he possesses a magnificent mansion, No. 27 Rue du Helder, Paris."

The abbé opened his mouth, remained for a moment like a man who hesitates, then making an effort over himself, he said,—

"And Mercédès, they tell me that she has disappeared?"

"Disappeared," said Caderousse, "yes, as the sun disappears to rise the next day with still more splendour."

"Has she made a fortune also?" inquired the abbé, with an ironical smile.

"Mercédès is at this moment one of the greatest ladies in Paris," replied Caderousse.

"Go on," said the abbé, "it seems as if I were hearing the recital of a dream. But I have seen things so extraordinary, that those you mention to me seem less astonishing."

"Mercédès was at first in the deepest despair at the blow which deprived her of Edmond. I have told you of her attempts to propitiate M. de Villefort, her devotion to the father of Dantès. In the midst of her despair a fresh trouble overtook her, this was the departure of Fernand, of Fernand whose crime she did not know, and whom she regarded as her brother. Fernand went and Mercédès remained alone. Three months passed and found her all tears, no news of Edmond, no news of Fernand, nothing before her, but an old man who was dying with despair. One evening, after having been seated, as was her custom, all day at the angle of two roads that lead to Marseilles from the Catalans, she returned to her home more depressed than ever, neither her lover nor her friend returned by either of these roads, and she had no intelligence of one or the other. Suddenly, she heard a step she knew, turned round anxiously, the door opened, and Fernand, dressed in the uniform of a sub-lieutenant, stood before her. It was not the half of that she bewailed, but it was a portion of her past life that returned to her.

"Mercédès seized Fernand's hands with a transport, which he took for love, but which was only joy at being no longer alone in the world, and seeing at last a friend after long hours of solitary sorrow. And then, it must be confessed, Fernand had never been hated, he was only not precisely loved. Another possessed all Mercédès' heart, that other was absent, had disappeared, perhaps was dead. At this last idea Mercédès burst into a flood of tears, and wrung her hands in agony: but this idea which she had always repelled before, when it was suggested to her by another came now in full force upon her mind, and then too, old Dantès incessantly said to her, 'Our Edmond is dead, if he were not he would return to us.' The old man died, as I have told you; had he lived, Mercédès, perchance, had not become the wife of another, for he would have been there to reproach her infidelity. Fernand saw this, and when he learned the old man's death he returned. He was now a lieutenant. At his first coming he had not said a word of love to Mercédès, at the second he reminded her that he loved her. Mercédès begged for six months more to expect and bewail Edmond."

"So that," said the abbé, with a bitter smile, "that makes eighteen months in all, what more could the most devoted lover desire?"

Then he murmured the words of the English poet,—

"'Frailty, thy name is woman.'"

"Six months afterwards," continued Caderousse, "the marriage took place in the church of Accoules."

"The very church in which she was to have married Edmond," murmured the priest, "there was only a change of bridegroom."

"Well, Mercédès was married," proceeded Caderousse, "but although in the eyes of the world she appeared calm, she nearly fainted as she passed La Réserve, where, eighteen months before, the betrothal had been celebrated with him whom she would have seen she still loved had she looked at the bottom of her heart. Fernand, more happy, but not more at his ease,—for I saw at this time he was in constant dread of Edmond's return—Fernand was very anxious to get his wife away and to depart himself. There were too many dangers and recollections associated with the Catalans, and eight days after the wedding they left Marseilles."

"Did you ever see Mercédès again?" inquired the priest.

"Yes, during the war of Spain at Perpignan, where Fernand had left her: she was attending to the education of her son."

The abbé started.

"Her son?" said he.

"Yes," replied Caderousse, "little Albert."

"But, then, to be able to instruct her child," continued the abbé, "she must have received an education herself. I understood from Edmond that she was the daughter of a simple fisherman, beautiful, but uneducated."

"Oh!" replied Caderousse, "did he know so little of his lovely betrothed? Mercédès might have been a queen, sir, if the crown were to be placed on the heads of the loveliest and most intelligent. Fernand's fortune already became greater, and she became greater with his growing fortune. She learned drawing, music, every thing. Besides, I believe, between ourselves, she did this in order to distract her mind, that she might forget, and she only filled her head thus in order to alleviate the weight on her heart. But now every thing must be told," continued Caderousse; "no doubt, fortune and honours have comforted her. She is rich, a countess, and yet——"

Caderousse paused.

"Yet what?" asked the abbé.

"Yet, I am sure she is not happy," said Caderousse.

"What makes you believe this?"

"Why, when I have found myself very wretched, I have thought my old friends would perhaps assist me. So I went to Danglars, who would not even receive me. I called on Fernand, who sent me a hundred francs by his valet-de-chambre."

"Then you did not see either of them?"

"No, but Madame de Morcerf saw me."

"How was that?"

"As I went away, a purse fell at my feet—it contained five-and-twenty louis; I raised my head quickly, and saw Mercédès, who shut the blind directly."

"And M. de Villefort?" asked the abbé.

"Oh! he was never a friend of mine, I did not know him, and I had nothing to ask of him."

"Do you not know what became of him, and the share he had in Edmond's misfortunes?"

"No. I only know that some time after having arrested him, he married Mademoiselle de Saint-Méran, and soon after left Marseilles; no doubt but he has been as lucky as the rest, no doubt he is as rich as Danglars, as high in station as Fernand. I only, as you see, have remained poor, wretched, and forgotten!"

"You are mistaken, my friend," replied the abbé; "God may seem sometimes to forget for a while, whilst His justice reposes, but there always comes a moment when He remembers —and behold! a proof."

As he spoke, the abbé took the diamond from his pocket, and giving it to Caderousse, said,—

"Here, my friend, take this diamond, it is yours."

"What! for me only?" cried Caderousse; "ah! sir, do not jest with me!"

"This diamond was to have been shared amongst his friends. Edmond had one friend only, and thus it cannot be divided. Take the diamond then, and sell it: it is worth fifty thousand francs (2000*l*.), and I repeat my wish that this sum may suffice to release you from your wretchedness."

"Oh, sir," said Caderousse, putting out one hand timidly, and with the other wiping away the perspiration which bedewed his brow,—"oh, sir, do not make a jest of the happiness or despair of a man!"

"I know what happiness and what despair are, and I never make a jest of such feelings. Take it then, but in exchange——"

Caderousse, who touched the diamond, withdrew his hand. The abbé smiled.

"In exchange," he continued, "give me the red silk purse that M. Morrel left on old Dantès' chimney-piece, and which you tell me is still in your hands."

Caderousse, more and more astonished, went towards a large oaken cupboard, opened it, and gave the abbé a long purse of faded red silk, round which were two copper runners that had once been gilt. The abbé took it, and in return gave Caderousse the diamond.

"Oh! you are a man of God, sir," cried Caderousse; "for no one knew that Edmond had given you this diamond, and you might have kept it."

"Which," said the abbé to himself, "you would have done." The abbé rose, took his hat and gloves.

"Well," he said, "all you have told me is perfectly true then, and I may believe it in every particular?"

"See, M. l'Abbé," replied Caderousse, "in this corner is a crucifix in holy wood—here on this shelf is the gospel of my wife; open this book and I will swear upon it with my hand on the crucifix; I will swear to you by my soul's salvation, my faith as a Christian, I have told every thing to you as it occurred, and as the angel of men will tell it to the ear of God at the day of the last judgment!"

"'Tis well," said the abbé, convinced by his manner and tone that Caderousse spoke the truth. "'Tis well, and may this money profit you! Adieu! I go far from men who thus so bitterly injure each other."

The abbé with difficulty got away from the enthusiastic thanks of Caderousse, opened the door himself, got out and mounted his horse, once more saluted the innkeeper, who kept uttering his loud farewells, and then returned by the road he had travelled in coming. When Caderousse turned round, he saw behind him La Carconte paler and trembling more than ever.

"Is, then, all that I have heard really true?" she inquired.

"What! that he has given the diamond to us only?" inquired Caderousse, half bewildered with joy.

"Yes!"

"Nothing more true! See! here it is."

The woman gazed at it a moment, and then said, in a gloomy voice,

"Suppose it's false?"

Caderousse started and turned pale.

"False!" he muttered. "False! why should that man give me a false diamond?"

"To possess your secret without paying for it, you blockhead!"

Caderousse remained for a moment aghast under the weight of such an idea.

"Oh!" he said, taking up his hat, which he placed on the red handkerchief tied round his head, "we will soon learn that."

"In what way?"

"Why, it is the fair of Beaucaire, there are always jewellers from Paris there, and I will shew it to them. Take care of the house, wife, and I shall be back in two hours."

Caderousse left the house in haste, and ran rapidly in a direction contrary to that which the unknown had taken.

"Fifty thousand francs!" muttered La Carconte, when left alone; "it is a large sum of money, but it is not a fortune."

CHAPTER XXVIII

THE PRISON REGISTER

The day after that on which the scene had passed on the road between Bellegarde and Beaucaire we have just related, a man of about thirty or two-and-thirty, dressed in a bright blue frock-coat, nankeen trousers, and a white waistcoat, having the appearance and accent of an Englishman, presented himself before the mayor of Marseilles.

"Sir," said he, " I am chief clerk of the house of Thomson and French of Rome. We are, and have been these ten years, connected with the house of Morrel and Son of Marseilles. We have a hundred thousand francs (4000*l*.) or thereabouts engaged in speculation with them, and we are a little uneasy at reports that have reached us that the firm is on the eve of ruin. I have come, therefore, express from Rome to ask you for information as to this house."

"Sir," replied the mayor, "I know very well that during the last four or five years misfortune seems to pursue M. Morrel. He has lost four or five vessels and suffered by three or four bankruptcies; but it is not for me, although I am a creditor myself to the amount of ten thousand francs (400*l*.) to give any information as to the state of his finances. Ask of me, as mayor, what is my opinion of M. Morrel, I shall say he is a man honourable to the last degree, and who has up to this time fulfilled every engagement with scrupulous punctuality. This is all I can say, sir; if you wish to learn more, address yourself to M. de Boville, the Inspector of Prisons, No. 15 Rue de Nouailles; he has, I believe, two hundred thousand francs placed in the hands of Morrel, and if there be any grounds for apprehension, as this is a greater amount than mine, you will most probably find him better informed than myself."

The Englishman seemed to appreciate this extreme delicacy, made his bow, and went away, walking with that step peculiar to the sons of Great Britain, towards the street mentioned. M. de Boville was in his private room, and the Englishman, on perceiving him, made a gesture of surprise, which seemed to indicate that it was not the first time he had been in his presence. As to M. de Boville, he was in such a state of despair that it was evident all the faculties of his mind, absorbed in the thought which occupied him at the moment, did not allow either his memory or his imagination to stray to the past. The Englishman, with the coolness of his nation, addressed him in terms nearly similar to those with which he had accosted the mayor of Marseilles.

"Oh, sir," exclaimed M. de Boville, "your fears are unfortunately but too well founded, and you see before you a man in despair. I had two hundred thousand francs placed in the hand of Morrel and Son; these two hundred thousand francs were my daughter's dowry, who was to be married in a fortnight, and these two hundred thousand francs were payable, half on the 15th of this month, and the other half on the 15th of next month. I had informed M. Morrel of my desire to have these payments punctually, and he has been here within the last half-hour to tell me that if his ship the Pharaon did not come into port on the 15th he would be wholly unable to make this payment."

"But," said the Englishman, "this looks very much like a suspension of payments!"

"Say, sir, that it resembles a bankruptcy!" exclaimed M. de Boville, despairingly.

The Englishman appeared to reflect a moment, and then said,—

"Thus, then, sir, this credit inspires you with considerable apprehensions!"

"To say truth, I consider it lost."

"Well, then, I will buy it of you."

"You?"

"Yes, I!"

"But at a tremendous discount, of course?"

"No; for two hundred thousand francs. Our house," added the Englishman, with a laugh, "does not do things in that way."

"And you will pay——"

"Ready money."

And the Englishman drew from his pocket a bundle of bank-notes, which might have been twice the sum M. de Boville feared to lose. A ray of joy passed across M. de Boville's countenance, yet he made an effort over himself, and said,—

"Sir, I ought to tell you that in all probability you will not have six per cent of this sum."

"That's no affair of mine," replied the Englishman, "that is the affair of the house of Thomson and French, in whose name I act. They have, perhaps, some motive to serve in hastening the ruin of a rival firm. But all I know, sir, is, that I am ready to hand you over this sum in exchange for your assignment of the debt. I only ask a brokerage."

C.M.—I.

"Of course, that is perfectly just," cried M. de Boville. "The commission is usually one and a half; will you have two —three—five per cent, or even more?   Say!"

"Sir," replied the Englishman, laughing, "I am like my house, and do not do such things—no, the commission I ask is quite different."

"Name it, sir, I beg."

"You are the inspector of prisons?"

"I have been so these fourteen years."

"You keep the registers of entries and departures?"

"I do."

"To these registers there are added notes relative to the prisoners?"

"There are special reports on every prisoner."

"Well, sir, I was educated at Rome by a poor devil of an abbé, who disappeared suddenly.   I have since learned that he was confined in the Château d'If, and I should like to learn some particulars of his death."

"What was his name?"

"The Abbé Faria."

"Oh, I recollect him perfectly," cried M. de Boville, "he was crazy."

"So they said."

"Oh, he was, decidedly."

"Very possibly, but what sort of madness was it?"

"He pretended to know of an immense treasure, and offered vast sums to government if they would liberate him."

"Poor devil! and he is dead?"

"Yes, sir; five or six months ago, last February."

"You have a good memory, sir, to recollect dates so well!"

"I recollect this, because the poor devil's death was accompanied by a singular circumstance."

"May I ask what that was?" said the Englishman, with an expression of curiosity which a close observer would have been astonished at discovering in his phlegmatic countenance.

"Oh dear, yes, sir; the abbé's dungeon was forty or fifty feet distant from that of an old agent of Bonaparte's—one of those who had the most contributed to the return of the usurper in 1815, a very resolute and very dangerous man."

"Indeed!" said the Englishman.

"Yes," replied M. de Boville; "I myself had occasion to see this man in 1816 or 1817, and we could only go into his dungeon with a file of soldiers: that man made a deep impression on me; I shall never forget his countenance!"

The Englishman smiled imperceptibly.

"And you say, sir," he said, "that the two dungeons——"

"Were separated by a distance of fifty feet; but it appears that this Edmond Dantès——"

"This dangerous man's name was——"

"Edmond Dantès. It appears, sir, that this Edmond Dantès had procured tools, or made them, for they found a passage by which the prisoners communicated."

"This passage was formed, no doubt, with an intention of escape?"

"No doubt; but unfortunately for the prisoners, the Abbè Faria had an attack of catalepsy, and died."

"That must have cut short the projects of escape."

"For the dead man, yes," replied M. de Boville, "but not for the survivor: on the contrary, this Dantès saw a means of accelerating his escape. He, no doubt, thought that prisoners who died in the Château d'If were interred in a burial-ground as usual, and he conveyed the dead man into his own cell, assumed his place in the sack in which they had sewn up the defunct, and awaited the moment of interment."

"It was a bold step, and one that indicated some courage," remarked the Englishman.

"As I have already told you, sir, he was a very dangerous man; and fortunately, by his own act disembarrassed the government of the fears it had on his account."

"How was that?"

"How? do you not comprehend?"

"No."

"The Château d'If has no cemetery, and they simply throw the dead into the sea after having fastened a thirty-six pound bullet to their feet."

"Well?" observed the Englishman, as if he were slow of comprehension.

"Well, they fastened a thirty-six pound bullet to his feet and threw him into the sea."

"Really!" exclaimed the Englishman.

"Yes, sir," continued the inspector of prisons. "You may imagine the amazement of the fugitive when he found himself flung headlong beneath the rocks! I should like to have seen his face at this moment."

"That would have been difficult."

"No matter," replied De Boville, in supreme good-humour at the certainty of recovering his two hundred thousand francs, —"no matter, I can fancy it."

And he shouted with laughter.

"So can I," said the Englishman, and he laughed too; but he laughed as the English do, with clenched teeth.

"And so," continued the Englishman, who first regained his composure, "he was drowned?"

"Unquestionably."

"So that the governor got rid of the fierce and crazy prisoner at the same time?"

"Precisely."

"But some official document was drawn up as to this affair, I suppose?" inquired the Englishman.

"Yes, yes, the mortuary deposition. You understand, Dantès' relations, if he had any, might have some interest in knowing if he were dead or alive."

"So that now, if there were anything to inherit from him, they may do so with easy conscience. He is dead, and no mistake about it?"

"Oh, yes; and they may have the fact attested whenever they please."

"So be it," said the Englishman. "But to return to these registers."

"True, this story has diverted our attention from them. Excuse me."

"Excuse you for what? for the story? By no means, it really seems to me very curious."

"Yes, indeed. So, sir, you wish to see all relating to the poor abbé, who really was gentleness itself."

"Yes, you will much oblige me."

"Go into my study here, and I will shew it to you"

And they both entered M. de Boville's study.

All was here arranged in perfect order; each register had its number, each file of paper its place. The inspector begged the Englishman to seat himself in an arm-chair, and placed before him the register and documents relative to the Château d'If, giving him all the time he desired to examine it, whilst De Boville seated himself in a corner, and began to read his newspaper.

The Englishman easily found the entries relative to the Abbé Faria; but it seemed that the history which the inspector had related interested him greatly, for, after having perused the first documents he turned over the leaves until he reached the deposition respecting Edmond Dantès. There he found every thing arranged in due order,—the denunciation, examination, Morrel's petition, M de Villefort's marginal notes. He folded up the denunciation quietly, and put it as quietly in his pocket; read the examination, and saw that the name of Noirtier was not mentioned in it; perused, too, the application, dated 10th April, 1815, in which Morrel, by the deputy-procureur's advice, exaggerated with the best intentions (for Napoleon was then on the throne) the services Dantès had rendered to the imperial cause,—services which Villefort's certificates rendered indispensable. Then he saw through all. This petition to Napoleon, kept back by Villefort, had become, under the second restoration, a terrible weapon against him in the hands of the procureur due roi. He was no longer astonished when he searched on to find in the register this note placed in a bracket against his name:—

EDMOND DANTÈS, { An inveterate Bonapartist; took an active part in the return from the Isle of Elba.

To be kept in complete solitary confinement, and to be strictly watched and guarded.

Beneath these lines was written in another hand,—
"See note above—nothing can be done."

He compared the writing in the bracket with the writing of the certificate placed beneath Morrel's petition, and discovered that the note in the bracket was the same writing as the certificate,—that is to say, were in Villefort's hand-writing.

As to the note which accompanied this, the Englishman understood that it might have been added by some inspector, who had taken a momentary interest in Dantès' situation, but who had, from the remarks we have quoted, found it impossible to give any effect to the interest he experienced.

As we have said, the inspector, from discretion, and that he might not disturb the Abbé Faria's pupil in his researches, had seated himself in a corner, and was reading "Le Drapeau Blanc."

He did not see the Englishman fold up and place in his pocket the denunciation written by Danglars under the arbour of La Réserve, and which had the post-mark of Marseilles, 2d March, delivery 6 o'clock P.M.

But it must be said that if he had seen it he attached so small importance to this scrap of paper and so great importance to his 200,000 francs, that he would not have opposed what the Englishman did, how incorrect soever it might be.

"Thanks!" said the latter, closing the register with a noise, "I have all I want; now it is for me to perform my promise. Give me a simple assignment of your debt; acknowledge therein the receipt of the cash, and I will hand you over the money."

He rose, gave his seat to M. de Boville, who took it without ceremony, quickly drew out the required assignment, whilst the Englishman was counting out the bank-notes on the other side of the desk.

CHAPTER XXIX

THE HOUSE OF MORREL AND SON

ANY one who had quitted Marseilles a few years previously well acquainted with the interior of Morrel's house, and had returned at this date, would have found a great change.

Instead of that air of life, of comfort, and of happiness that exhales from a flourishing and prosperous house,—instead of the merry faces seen at the windows, of the busy clerks hurrying to and fro in the long corridors,—instead of the court filled with bales of goods, re-echoing the cries and the jokes of the porters, he would have at once perceived an air of sadness and gloom. In the deserted corridor and the empty office, out of all the numerous clerks that used to fill the office, but two remained. One was a young man of three or four and twenty, who was in love with M. Morrel's daughter, and had remained with him, spite of the efforts of his friends to induce him to withdraw; the other was an old one-eyed cashier, named Coclès, a nickname given him by the young men who used to inhabit this vast bee-hive, now almost deserted, and which had so completely replaced his real name that he would not, in all probability, have replied to any one who addressed himself by it.

Coclès remained in M. Morrel's service, and a most singular change had taken place in his situation, he had at the same time risen to the rank of cashier and sunk to the rank of a servant. He was, however, the same Coclès, good, patient, devoted, but inflexible on the subject of arithmetic, the only point on which he would have stood firm against the world, even against M. Morrel, and strong in the multiplication-table which he had at his fingers' ends, no matter what scheme or what trap was laid to catch him. In the midst of the distress of the house Coclès was the only one unmoved. But this did not arise from a want of affection, but, on the contrary, from a firm conviction, like the rats that leave by degrees the vessel doomed to perish at sea: so that these egotistical guests have completely abandoned the ship at the moment when the vessel weighs anchor. So all these numerous clerks had by degrees deserted the bureaus and warehouse. Coclès had seen them go without thinking of inquiring the cause of their departure: every thing was, as we have said, a question of arithmetic to Coclès, and during twenty years he had always seen all payments made with such exactitude, that it seemed as impossible to him that the house should stop payment as it would to a miller that the river that had so long turned his mill should cease to flow.

Nothing had as yet occurred to shake Coclès' belief; the last month's payment had been made with the most scrupulous exactitude; Coclès had detected an error of fourteen sous to the prejudice of Morrel, and the same evening he had brought them to M. Morrel, who, with a melancholy smile, threw them into an almost empty drawer, saying,—

"Thanks, Coclès, you are the pearl of cashiers."

Coclès retired perfectly happy, for this eulogium from M. Morrel, himself the pearl of the honest men of Marseilles, flattered him more than a present of fifty pounds. But since the end of the month M. Morrel had passed many an anxious hour. In order to meet the end of the month he had collected all his resources, and, fearing lest the report of his distress should get bruited abroad at Marseilles when he was known to be reduced to such an extremity, he went to the fair of Beaucaire to sell his wife and daughter's jewels and a portion of his plate. By this means the end of the month was passed, but his resources were now exhausted. Credit, owing to the reports afloat, was no longer to be had; and to meet the 4000*l.* due on the 15th of the present month to M. de Boville, and the 4000*l.* due on the 15th of the next month, M. Morrel had, in reality, no hope but the return of the Pharaon, whose departure he had learnt from a vessel which had weighed anchor at the same time, and which had already arrived in harbour.

But this vessel which, like the Pharaon, came from Calcutta, had arrived a fortnight, whilst no intelligence had been received of the Pharaon.

Such was the state of things when, the day after his interview with M. de Boville, the confidential clerk of the house of Thomson and French, of Rome, presented himself at M. Morrel's. Emmanuel received him; the young man whom every fresh visage alarmed, for each fresh visage announced a fresh creditor, who in his alarm came to question the head of the house. The young man, wishing to spare his employer the pain of this interview, questioned the new-comer; but the stranger declared he had nothing to say to M. Emmanuel, and that his business was with M. Morrel in person.

Emmanuel sighed, and summoned Coclès. Coclès appeared, and the young man bade him conduct the stranger to M. Morrel's apartment. Coclès went first, and the stranger followed him. On the staircase they met a beautiful girl, of sixteen or seventeen, who looked with anxiety at the stranger.

"M. Morrel is in his room, is he not, Mademoiselle Julie?" said the cashier.

"Yes; I think so, at least," said the young girl, hesitatingly. "Go and see, Coclès, and if my father is there, announce this gentleman."

"It will be useless to announce me, Mademoiselle," returned the Englishman. "M. Morrel does not know my name; this worthy gentleman has only to announce the confidential clerk of the house of Thomson and French, of Rome, with whom your father does business."

The young girl turned pale, and continued to descend, whilst the stranger and Coclès continued to mount the staircase. She entered the office where Emmanuel was, whilst Coclès, by the aid of a key he possessed, opened a door in the corner of a landing-place on the second staircase, conducted the stranger into an ante-chamber, opened a second door, which he closed behind him, and after having left the clerk of the house of Thomson and French alone, returned and signed to him that he could enter.

The Englishman entered, and found Morrel seated at a table, turning over the formidable columns of his ledger, which contained the list of his liabilities. At the sight of the stranger M. Morrel closed the ledger, rose, and offered a seat to the stranger, and when he had seen him seated resumed his own chair.

Fourteen years had changed the worthy merchant, who, in his thirty-sixth year at the opening of this history, was now in his fiftieth; his hair had turned white, and time and sorrow had ploughed deep furrows on his brow, and his look, once so firm and penetrating, was now irresolute and wandering, as if he feared being forced to fix his attention on an idea or a man. The Englishman looked at him with an air of curiosity, evidently mingled with interest.

"Monsieur," said Morrel, whose uneasiness was increased by this examination, "you wish to speak to me."

"Yes, monsieur; you are aware from whom I come?"

"The house of Thomson and French; at least, so my cashier tells me."

"He has told you rightly. The house of Thomson and French had 3 or 400,000 francs (12 to 16,000*l.*) to pay this month in France, and, knowing your strict punctuality, have collected all the bills bearing your signature and charged me as they became due to present them and to employ the money otherwise."

Morrel sighed deeply and passed his hand over his forehead which was covered with perspiration.

"So then, sir," said Morrel, "you hold bills of mine?"

"Yes, and for a considerable sum."

"What is the amount?" asked Morrel, with a voice he strove to render firm.

"Here is," said the Englishman, taking a quantity of papers from his pocket, "an assignment of 200,000 francs to our house by M. de Boville, the inspector of prisons, to whom they are due.   You acknowledge, of course, you owe this sum to him?"

"Yes, he placed the money in my hands at four and a half per cent. nearly five years ago."

"When are you to pay?"

"Half the 15th of this month, half the 15th of next."

"Just so; and now here are 32,500 francs payable shortly, they are all signed by you and assigned to our house by the holders."

"I recognise them," said Morrel, whose face was suffused as he thought that for the first time in his life he would be unable to honour his own signature.   "Is this all?"

"No, I have for the end of the month these bills which have been assigned to us by the house of Pascal and the house of Wild and Turner of Marseilles amounting to nearly 55,000 francs (2,200*l.*); in all, 287,500 francs (11,500*l.*)."

It is impossible to describe what Morrel suffered during this enumeration.

"Two hundred and eighty-seven thousand five hundred francs," repeated he.

"Yes, sir," replied the Englishman.

"I will not," continued he, after a moment's silence, "conceal from you, that whilst your probity and exactitude up to this moment are universally acknowledged, yet the report is current in Marseilles that you are not able to meet your engagements."

At this almost brutal speech Morrel turned deathly pale.

"Sir," said he, "up to this time, and it is now more than four-and-twenty years since I received the direction of this house from my father, who had himself conducted it for five-and-thirty years, and never has any thing bearing the signature of Morrel and Son been dishonoured."

"I know that," replied the Englishman.   "But as a man of honour should answer another, tell me fairly, shall you pay these with the same punctuality?"

Morrel shuddered, and looked at the man, who spoke with more assurance than he had hitherto shewn.

"To questions frankly put," said he, "a straightforward answer should be given.   Yes, I shall pay, if, as I hope, my vessel arrives safely; for its arrival will again procure me the credit which the numerous accidents, of which I have been the victim, have deprived me; but if the Pharaon should be lost, and this last resource be gone——"

C.M.—I*

The poor man's eyes filled with tears.

"Well," said the other, "if this last resource fail you?"

"Well," returned Morrel, "it is a cruel thing to be forced to say, but, already used to misfortune, I must habituate myself to shame. I fear I shall be forced to suspend my payments."

"Have you no friends who could assist you?"

Morrel smiled mournfully.

"In business, sir," said he, "one has no friends, only correspondents."

"It is true," murmured the Englishman; "then you have but one hope."

"But one."

"The last?"

"The last."

"So that if this fail——"

"I am ruined,—completely ruined!"

"As I came here a vessel was entering the port."

"I know it, sir; a young man, who still adheres to my fallen fortunes, passes a part of his time in a belvidere at the top of the house, in hopes of being the first to announce good news to me: he has informed me of the entrance of this ship."

"And it is not yours?"

"No, it is a vessel of Bordeaux, La Gironde; it comes from India also, but it is not mine."

"Perhaps it has spoken the Pharaon, and brings you some tidings of it?"

"Shall I tell you plainly one thing, sir? I dread almost as much to receive any tidings of my vessel as to remain in doubt. Incertitude is still hope."

Then in a low voice Morrel added,—

"This delay is not natural. The Pharaon left Calcutta the 5th of February; it ought to have been here a month ago."

"What is that?" said the Englishman. "What is the meaning of this noise?"

"Oh! oh!" cried Morrel, turning pale; "what is this?"

A loud noise was heard on the stairs of people moving hastily and half-stifled sobs. Morrel rose and advanced to the door; but his strength failed him, and he sank into a chair. The two men remained opposite one another. Morrel trembling in every limb, the stranger gazing at him with an air of profound pity. The noise had ceased; but it seemed that Morrel expected something,—something had occasioned the noise, and something must follow.

The stranger fancied he heard footsteps on the stairs, and that the steps, which were those of several persons, stopped at the door. A key was inserted in the lock of the first door, and the creaking of hinges was audible.

"There are only two persons who have the key of the door," murmured Morrel, "Coclès and Julie."

At this instant the second door opened, and the young girl, her eyes bathed with tears, appeared.

Morrel rose tremblingly, supporting himself by the arm of the chair. He would have spoken, but his voice failed him.

"Oh, father!" said she, clasping her hands, "forgive your child for being the messenger of ill."

Morrel again changed colour. Julie threw herself into his arms.

"Oh, father, father!" murmured she, "courage!"

"The Pharaon has then perished?" said Morrel, in a hoarse voice.

The young girl did not speak; but she made an affirmative sign with her head as she lay on her father's breast.

"And the crew?" asked Morrel.

"Saved," said the girl; "saved by the crew of the vessel that has just entered the harbour."

Morrel raised his two hands to heaven with an expression of resignation and sublime gratitude.

"Thanks, my God," said he, "at least you strike but me alone."

Spite of his phlegm a tear moistened the eye of the Englishman.

"Come in, come in," said Morrel, "for I presume you are all at the door."

Scarcely had he uttered these words than Madame Morrel entered weeping bitterly, Emmanuel followed her, and in the antechamber were visible the rough faces of seven or eight half-naked sailors.

At the sight of these men the Englishman started and advanced a step; then restrained himself, and retired into the farthest and most obscure corner of the apartment.

Madame Morrel sat down by her husband and took one of his hands in hers, Julie still lay with her head on his shoulder, Emmanuel stood in the centre of the chamber, and seemed to form the link between Morrel's family and the sailors at the door.

"How did this happen?" said Morrel.

"Draw nearer, Penelon," said the young man, "and relate all."

An old seaman, bronzed by the tropical sun, advanced twirling the remains of a hat between his hands.

"Good day, M. Morrel!" said he, as if he had just quitted Marseilles the previous evening, and had just returned from Aix or Toulon.

"Good day, Penelon!" returned Morrel, who could not refrain from smiling through his tears, "where is the captain?"

"The captain, M. Morrel,—he has stayed behind sick at Palma, but, please God, it won't be much, and you will see him in a few days all alive and hearty."

"Well, now tell your story, Penelon."

Penelon rolled his quid in his cheek, placed his hand before his mouth, turned his head, and sent a long jet of tobacco-juice into the antechamber, advanced his foot, and began,—

"You see, M. Morrel," said he, "we were somewhere between Cape Blanc and Cape Bogador, sailing with a fair breeze south-south-west after a week's calm, when Captain Gaumard comes up to me,—I was at the helm I should tell you,—and says, 'Penelon, what do you think of those clouds that are arising there?'

"I was just then looking at them myself. 'What do I think, captain? why I think that they are rising faster than they have any business, and that they would not be so black if they did not mean mischief.'

"'That's my opinion, too,' said the captain, 'and I'll take precautions accordingly. We are carrying too much canvass. Holloa! all hands to slacken sail and lower the flying jib.'

"It was time; the squall was on us and the vessel began to heel.

"'Ah,' said the captain, 'we have still too much canvass set, all hands to lower the mainsail!' five minutes after it was down, and we sailed under mizen-topsails and top-gallant-sails.

"'Well, Penelon,' said the captain, 'what makes you shake your head?'

"'Why,' I says, 'I don't think that we shall stop here.'

"'I think you are right,' answered he; 'we shall have a gale.'

"'A gale! more than that, we shall have a tempest, or I know nothing about it.'

"You could see the wind coming like the dust at Montre-don: luckily the captain understood his business.

"'All hands take in two reefs in the topsails,' cried the captain; 'let go the bowlines, brace to, lower the top-gallant-sails, haul out the reef-tackles on the yards.'"

"That was not enough for those latitudes," said the Englishman; "I should have taken four reefs in the topsails, and lowered the mizen."

His firm, sonorous, and unexpected voice made every one start. Penelon put his hand over his eyes, and then stared at the man who thus criticised the manœuvres of his captain.

"We did better than that, sir," said the old sailor, with a certain respect; "we put the helm to the wind to run before the tempest; ten minutes after we struck our topsails and scudded under bare poles."

"The vessel was very old to risk that," said the Englishman.

"Eh, it was that that wrecked us, after having been tossed about for twelve hours, we sprung a leak. 'Penelon,' said the captain, ' I think we are sinking, give me the helm, and go down into the hold.'

"I gave him the helm, and descended; there was already three feet water. I cried, 'All hands to the pumps!' but it was too late, and it seemed the more we pumped the more came in.

"'Ah!' said I, after four hours' work, 'since we are sinking, let us sink, we can die but once.'

"'That's the example you set, Penelon,' cries the captain, 'very well, wait a minute.'

"He went into his cabin and came back with a brace of pistols.

"'I will blow the brains out of the first man who leaves the pump,' said he."

"Well done!" said the Englishman.

"There's nothing gives you so much courage as good reasons," continued the sailor; "and during that time the wind had abated, and the sea gone down, but the water kept rising; not much, only two inches an hour, but still it rose. Two inches an hour does not seem much, but in twelve hours that makes two feet, and three we had before, that makes five.

"'Come,' said the captain, 'we have done all in our power, and M. Morrel will have nothing to reproach us with; we have tried to save the ship, let us now save ourselves. To the boats, my lads, as quick as you can.'

"Now," continued Penelon, "you see, M. Morrel, a sailor is attached to his ship, but still more to his life; so we did not wait to be told twice; the more so, that the ship was sinking under us, and seemed to say, Get along, save yourselves."

"We soon launched the boat, and all eight of us got into it. The captain descended the last, or, rather, he did not descend, he would not quit the vessel, so I took him round the waist, and threw him into the boat, and then I jumped after him. It was time, for just as I jumped, the deck burst with a noise like the broadside of a man-of-war. Ten minutes after she pitched forward, then the other way, spun round and round, and then good-by to the Pharaon. As for us, we were three days without anything to eat or drink, so that we began to think of drawing lots who should feed the rest, when we saw La Gironde; we made signals of distress, she perceived us, made for us, and took us all on board. There now, M. Morrel, that's the whole truth, on the honour of a sailor; is not it true, you fellows there?"

A general murmur of approbation shewed that the narrator had faithfully detailed their misfortunes and sufferings.

"Well, well," said Morrel, " I know there was no one in fault but destiny. It was the will of God that this should happen, blessed be His name. What wages are due to you?"

"Oh, don't let us talk of that, M. Morrel."

"On the contrary, let us speak of it."

"Well, then, three months," said Penelon.

"Coclès! pay 200 francs to each of these good fellows," said Morrel. "At another time," added he, "I should have said, give them, besides, 200 francs over as a present; but times are changed, and the little money that remains to me is not my own."

Penelon turned to his companions, exchanged a few words with them.

"As for that, M. Morrel," said he, again turning his quid. "As for that——"

"As for what?"

"The money."

"Well——"

"Well, we all say that fifty francs will be enough for us at present, and that we will wait for the rest."

"Thanks, my friends, thanks!" cried Morrel, gratefully; "take it—take it, and if you can find another employer, enter his service, you are free to do so."

These last words produced a prodigious effect on the seamen, Penelon nearly swallowed his quid, fortunately he recovered.

"What! M. Morrel," said he, in a low voice, "you send us away, you are then angry with us?"

"No, no," said M. Morrel, "I am not angry, on the contrary, I do not send you away; but I have no more ships, and therefore I do not want any sailors."

"No more ships," returned Penelon, "well, then, you'll build some; we'll wait for you."

"I have no money to build ships with, Penelon," said the poor owner mournfully, "so I cannot accept your kind offer."

"No more money? then you must not pay us, we can go, like the Pharaon, under bare poles."

"Enough! enough!" cried Morrel, almost overpowered, "leave me, I pray you, we shall meet again in a happier time. Emmanuel, accompany them, and see that my orders are executed."

"At least, we shall see each other again, M. Morrel?" asked Penelon.

"Yes, I hope so at least; now go."

He made a sign to Coclès, who marched first, the seamen followed him, and Emmanuel brought up the rear.

"Now," said the owner, to his wife and daughter, "leave me, I wish to speak with this gentleman."

And he glanced towards the clerk of Thomson and French, who had remained motionless in the corner during this scene, in which he had taken no part, except the few words we have mentioned. The two females looked at this person, whose presence they had entirely forgotten and retired; but as she left the apartment, Julie gave the stranger a supplicating glance, to which he replied by a smile, that an indifferent spectator would have been surprised to see on his stern features.

The two men were left alone.

"Well, sir," said Morrel, sinking into a chair, "you have heard all, and I have nothing further to tell you."

"I see," returned the Englishman, "that a fresh and unmerited misfortune has overwhelmed you, and this only increases my desire to serve you."

"Oh! sir," cried Morrel.

"Let me see," continued the stranger, "I am one of your largest creditors."

"Your bills, at least, are the first that will fall due."

"Do you wish for time to pay?"

"A delay would save my honour, and consequently my life."

"How long a delay do you wish for?"

Morrel reflected.

"Two months," said he.

"I will give you three," replied the stranger.

"But," asked Morrel, "will the house of Thomson and French consent?"

"Oh! I take every thing on myself. To-day is the 5th of June."

"Yes."

"Well, renew these bills up to the 5th of September, and on the 5th of September at eleven o'clock (the hand of the clock pointed to eleven), I shall come to receive the money."

"I shall expect you," returned Morrel, "and I will pay you, or I shall be dead."

These last words were uttered in so low a tone that the stranger could not hear them. The bills were renewed, the old ones destroyed, and the poor ship-owner found himself with three months before him to collect his resources. The Englishman received his thanks with the phlegm peculiar to his nation, and Morrel overwhelming him with grateful blessings conducted him to the staircase.

The stranger met Julie on the stairs; she affected to be descending, but, in reality, she was waiting for him.

"Oh, sir—" said she, clasping her hands.

"Mademoiselle," said the stranger, "one day you will receive a letter, signed 'Sinbad the Sailor'; do exactly what the letter bids you, however strange it may appear."

"Yes, sir," returned Julie.

"Do you promise?"

"I swear to you I will"

"It is well. Adieu, mademoiselle!—remain as pure and virtuous as you are at present, and I have great hopes that Heaven will reward you by giving you Emmanuel for a husband."

Julie uttered a faint cry, blushed like a rose, and leaned against the baluster.

The stranger waved his hand, and continued to descend. In the court he found Penelon; who, with a rouleau of a hundred francs in either hand, seemed unable to make up his mind to retain them.

"Come with me, my friend," said the Englishman, "I wish to speak to you."

CHAPTER XXX

THE delay afforded by the agent of the house of Thomson and French, at the moment when Morrel expected it least, appeared to the poor ship-owner one of those returns of good fortune, which announce to a man that fate is at length weary of wasting her spite upon him. The same day he related to his wife, to Emmanuel, and his daughter, what had occurred to him, and a ray of hope, if not tranquillity, returned to the family. Unfortunately, however, Morrel had not only engagements with the house of Thomson and French, who had shewn themselves so considerate towards him; and, as he had said, in business he had correspondents and not friends. When he reflected deeply, he could by no means account for this generous conduct on the part of Thomson and French towards him, and could only attribute it to the selfish reflection of the firm: "We had better support a man who owes us nearly 300,000 francs, and have that 300,000 francs at the end of three months than hasten his ruin, and have six or eight per cent. of capital."

Unfortunately, whether from hate or blindness, all Morrel's correspondents did not reflect similarly, and some made even a contrary reflection. The bills signed by Morrel were thus presented at his office with scrupulous exactitude, and, thanks to the delay granted by the Englishman, were paid by Coclès with equal punctuality. Coclès thus remained in his accustomed tranquillity. It was Morrel alone who remembered with alarm, that if he had to repay on the 15th the 50,000 francs of M. de Boville, and on the 30th the 32,500 francs of bills, for which, as well as the debt due to the inspector of prisons he had time granted, he must be a ruined man.

The opinion of all the commercial men was, that under the reverses which had successively weighed down Morrel, it was impossible for him to stand against it. Great, therefore, was the astonishment, when they saw the end of the month come, and he fulfilled all his engagements with his usual punctuality. Still confidence was not restored to all minds, and the general voice postponed only until the end of the month the complete ruin of the unfortunate ship-owner. The month passed amidst unheard-of efforts on the part of Morrel, to get in all his resources. Formerly, his paper at any date was taken with confidence and was even in request. Morrel now tried to negotiate bills at ninety days only, and found all the banks closed. Fortunately, Morrel had some monies coming in on which he could rely, and as they reached him he found himself in a condition to meet his engagements when the end of July came.

The agent of Thomson and French had not been again seen at Marseilles: the day after, or two days after his visit to Morrel, he had disappeared, and as in that city he had had no intercourse but with the mayor, the inspector of prisons, and M. Morrel, his appearance left no other trace than the different remembrances of him which these three persons retained. As to the sailors of the Pharaon, it seemed that they must have found some engagement, for they had disappeared also.

Captain Gaumard, recovered from his illness, had returned from Palma. He hesitated to present himself at Morrel's, but the owner hearing his arrival, went to him. The worthy ship-owner knew from Penelon's recital of the captain's brave conduct during the storm, and tried to console him. He brought him also the amount of his wages, which Captain Gaumard had not dared to apply for. As he descended the staircase, Morrel met Penelon who was going up. Penelon had, it would seem, made good use of his money, for he was newly clad; when he saw his employer, the worthy tar seemed much embarrassed, drew on one side into the corner of the landing-place, passed his quid from one cheek to the other, stared stupidly with his great eyes, and only acknowledged the squeeze of the hand which Morrel as usual gave him by a slight pressure in return. Morrel attributed Penelon's embarrassment to the elegance of his attire, it was evident the good fellow had not gone to such an expense on his own account; he was no doubt engaged on board some other vessel, and thus his bashfulness arose from the fact of his not having, if we may so express ourselves, worn mourning for the Pharaon longer. Perhaps, he had come to tell Captain Gaumard of his good luck, and to offer him employment from his new master.

"Worthy fellow," said Morrel, as he went away, "may your new master love you as I loved you, and be more fortunate than I have been!"

August rolled by in increasing efforts on the part of Morrel to renew his credit or revive the old. On the 20th of August it was known at Marseilles, that he had taken a place in the mail-coach, and then it was said that it was at the end of the month the docket was to be struck and Morrel had gone away before, that he might not be present at this cruel act; but had left his chief clerk Emmanuel, and his cashier Coclès to meet it. But contrary to all expectation, when the 31st of August came the house opened as usual, and Coclès appeared behind the grating of the counter, examined all bills presented with the same scrutiny, and, from first to last, paid all with the same precision. There came in, moreover, two repayments which M. Morrel had anticipated, and which Coclès paid as punctually as those bills which the shipowner had accepted. All this was incomprehensible, and then with the tenacity peculiar to prophets of bad news, the failure was put off until the end of September.

On the 1st Morrel returned, he was awaited by his family with extreme anxiety, for from this journey to Paris they hoped a last means of safety would arrive. Morrel had thought of Danglars, who was now immensely rich, and had lain under great obligations to Morrel in former days, since to him it was owing that Danglars entered the service of the Spanish banker, with whom had commenced his vast wealth. It was said at this moment that Danglars was worth from 200,000*l.* to 300,000*l.*, and had unlimited credit. Danglars then, without taking a crown from his pocket, could save Morrel; he had but to pass his word for a loan and Morrel was saved. Morrel had long thought of Danglars, but there are those instinctive revoltings impossible to control, and Morrel had delayed as long as possible, before he had recourse to this last resource. And Morrel was right, for he returned home borne down by all the humiliation of a refusal. Yet on his arrival Morrel did not utter a complaint nor say one harsh word, he embraced his weeping wife and daughter, pressed Emmanuel's hand with friendly warmth, and then going to his private room on the second floor, had sent for Coclès.

"Then," said the two women to Emmanuel, "we are indeed ruined."

It was agreed in a brief council held amongst them, that Julie should write to her brother, who was in garrison at Nismes, to come to them as speedily as possible. The poor woman felt instinctively, that they required all their strength to support the blow that impended. Besides, Maximilian Morrel, though hardly two-and-twenty, had great influence over his father. He was a strong-minded, upright young man. At the time when he decided on his profession his father had no desire to choose for him, but had consulted young Maximilian's taste. He had at once declared for a military life, and had in consequence studied hard, passed brilliantly through the Ecole Polytechnique, and left it as sub-lieutenant of the 53d of the line. For a year he had held this rank, and expected promotion on the first vacancy. In his regiment, Maximilian Morrel was noted as the most rigid observer, not only of the obligations imposed on a soldier, but also of the duties of a man, and he thus gained the name of "the stoic." We need hardly say, that many of those who gave him this epithet repeated it because they had heard it, and did not even know what it meant. This was the young man whom his mother and sister called to their aid to sustain them under the grave circumstances which they felt they would soon have to endure. They had not mistaken the gravity of this event, for the moment after Morrel had entered his cabinet with Coclès, Julie saw the latter leave it pale, trembling, and his features betraying the utmost consternation. She would have questioned him as he passed by her, but the worthy creature hastened down the staircase with unusual precipitation, and only raised his hands to heaven and exclaimed,——

"O mademoiselle! mademoiselle! what a dreadful misfortune! Who could ever have believed it?"

A moment afterwards Julie saw him go up-stairs carrying two or three heavy ledgers, a pocket-book, and a bag of money.

Morrel examined the ledgers, opened the pocket-book, and counted the money. All his funds amounted to 6,000 or 8,000 francs, his expectancies up to the 5th to 4,000 or 5,000, which making the best of every thing, gave him 14,000 francs to meet bills amounting to 287,500 francs. He could not make such a proposal. However, when Morrel went down to his dinner, he appeared very composed. This calmness was the more alarming to the two women than the deepest dejection would have been. After dinner Morrel usually went out, and used to take his coffee at the club of the Phocéens, and read the "Semaphore"; but this day he did not leave the house, but returned to his office.

As to Coclès, he seemed completely bewildered. For part of the day he went into the court-yard, seated himself on a stone with his head bare, and exposed to a sun of thirty degrees.

Emmanuel tried to comfort the females, but his eloquence faltered. The young man was too well acquainted with the business of the house, not to feel that a great catastrophe hung over the Morrel family.

Night came, the two women had watched hoping that when he left his room Morrel would come to them, but they heard him pass before their door, and trying to conceal the noise of his footsteps. They listened, he went into his sleeping-room, and fastened the door inside. Madame Morrel sent her daughter to bed, and half an hour after Julie had retired, she rose, took off her shoes, and went stealthily along the passage, to see through the keyhole what her husband was doing. In the passage she saw a retreating shadow, it was Julie, who, uneasy herself, had anticipated her mother. The young lady went towards Madame Morrel,——

"He is writing," she said.

They had understood each other without speaking. Madame Morrel looked again through the key-hole, Morrel was writing; but Madame Morrel remarked what her daughter had not observed, that her husband was writing on stamped paper. The terrible idea that he was writing his will flashed across her, she shuddered, and yet had not strength to utter a word.

Next day M. Morrel seemed as calm as ever, went into his office as usual, came to his breakfast punctually, and then, after dinner, he placed his daughter beside him, took her head in his arms, and held her for a long time against his bosom. In the evening, Julie told her mother, that although so calm in appearance, she had remarked, that her father's heart beat violently.

The two next days passed almost similarly. On the evening of the 4th of September, M. Morrel asked his daughter for the key of his cabinet. Julie trembled at this request, which seemed to her of bad omen. Why did her father ask for this key which she always kept, and which was only taken from her in childhood as a punishment? The young girl looked at Morrel.

"What have I done wrong, father," she said, "that you should take this key from me?"

"Nothing, my dear," replied the unhappy man, the tears starting to his eyes at this simple question,—"nothing, only I want it."

Julie made a pretence to feel for the key.

"I must have left it in my room," she said.

And she went out, but instead of going to her apartment she hastened to consult Emmanuel.

"Do not give this key to your father," said he, "and to-morrow morning if possible, do not quit him for a moment."

She questioned Emmanuel, but he knew nothing, or would not say it if he did.

During the night, between the 4th and 5th of September, Madame Morrel remained listening for every sound, and until three o'clock in the morning she heard her husband pacing the room in great agitation. It was three o'clock when he threw himself on the bed. The mother and daughter passed the night together. They had expected Maximilian since the previous evening. At eight o'clock in the morning Morrel entered their chamber. He was calm, but the agitation of the night was legible in his pale and careworn visage. They did not dare to ask him how he had slept.

Morrel was kinder to his wife, more affectionate to his daughter, than he had ever been. He could not cease gazing at and kissing the sweet girl. Julie, mindful of Emmanuel's request, was following her father when he quitted the room, but he said to her quickly,——

"Remain with your mother, dearest."

Julie wished to accompany him.

"I wish you to do so," he said.

This was the first time Morrel had ever so spoken, but he said it in a tone of paternal kindness, and Julie did not dare refuse compliance. She remained at the same spot standing, mute and motionless. An instant afterwards the door opened, she felt two arms encircle her, and a mouth pressed her forehead. She looked up and uttered an exclamation of joy.

"Maximilian! my dearest brother!" she cried.

At these words Madame Morrel rose, and threw herself into her son's arms.

"Mother!" said the young man, looking alternately at Madame Morrel and her daughter, "what has occurred—what has happened? your letter has frightened me, and I have come hither with all speed."

"Julie," said Madame Morrel, making a sign to the young man, "go and tell your father that Maximilian has just arrived."

The young lady rushed out of the apartment, but on the first step of the staircase she found a man holding a letter in his hand.

"Are you not Mademoiselle Julie Morrel?" inquired the man with a strong Italian accent.

"Yes, sir," replied Julie, with hesitation; "what is your pleasure? I do not know you."

"Read this letter," he said, handing it to her.

Julie hesitated.

"It concerns the best interests of your father," said the messenger.

The young girl hastily took the letter from him. She opened it quickly and read,—

"Go this moment to the Allées de Meillan, enter the house No. 15, ask the porter for the key of the room on the fifth floor, enter the apartment, take from the corner of the mantel-piece a purse netted in red silk, and give it to your father. It is important that he should receive it before eleven o'clock. You promised to obey me implicitly. Remember your oath.

"SINBAD THE SAILOR."

The young girl uttered a joyful cry, raised her eyes, looked round to question the messenger, but he had disappeared.

She cast her eyes again over the note to peruse it a second time, and saw there was a postscript. She read,—

"It is important that you should fulfil this mission in person and alone, if you go accompanied by any other person, or should any one else present themselves, the porter will reply that he does not know anything about it."

This postscript was a great check to the young girl's joy. Was there nothing to fear? was there not some snare laid for her? Her innocence had kept her in ignorance of the dangers that might assail a young girl of her age; but there is no need to know danger in order to fear it: indeed, it may be observed, that it is usually unknown perils that inspire the greatest terror.

Julie hesitated, and resolved to take counsel. Yet, by a singular feeling, it was neither to her mother nor her brother that she applied, but to Emmanuel.

She hastened down and told him what had occurred on the day when the agent of the house of Thomson and French had come to her father's, related the scene on the staircase, repeated the promise she had made, and shewed him the letter.

"You must go, then, mademoiselle," said Emmanuel.

"Go there!" murmured Julie.

"Yes, I will accompany you."

"But did you not read that I must be alone?" said Julie.

"And you shall be alone," replied the young man. "I will await you at the corner of the Rue du Musée, and if you are so long absent as to make me uneasy, I will hasten to rejoin you, and woe to him of whom you shall have cause to complain to me!"

"Then, Emmanuel," said the young girl, with hesitation, "it is your opinion that I should obey this invitation?"

"Yes. Did not the messenger say your father's safety was in it?"

"But what danger threatens him, then, Emmanuel?" she asked.

Emmanuel hesitated a moment, but his desire to make Julie decide immediately made him reply.

"Listen," he said, "to-day is the 5th of September—is it not?"

"Yes."

"To-day, then, at eleven o'clock, your father has nearly 300,000 francs to pay?"

"Yes, we know that."

"Well, then," continued Emmanuel, "we have not 15,000 francs in the house."

"What will happen then?"

"Why, if to-day before eleven o'clock your father has not found some one who will come to his aid, he will be compelled at twelve o'clock to declare himself a bankrupt."

"Oh, come, then, come!" cried she, hastening away with the young man.

During this time, Madame Morrel had told her son every thing. The young man knew quite well that after the succession of misfortunes which had befallen his father, great changes had taken place in the style of living and house-keeping, but he did not know that matters had reached such a point. He was thunderstruck. Then, rushing hastily out of the apartment, he ran upstairs, expecting to find his father in his cabinet, but he rapped there in vain. Whilst he was yet at the door of the cabinet he heard the bedroom door open, turned and saw his father. Instead of going direct to his cabinet, M. Morrel had returned to his bed-chamber, which he was only this moment quitting.

Morrel uttered a cry of surprise at the sight of his son, of whose arrival he was ignorant. He remained motionless on the spot, pressing with his left hand something he had concealed under his coat. Maximilian sprung down the staircase and threw his arms round his father's neck; but suddenly he recoiled, and placed his right hand on Morrel's breast.

"Father!" he exclaimed, turning pale as death, "what are you going to do with the brace of pistols under your coat?"

"Oh, this is what I feared!" said Morrel.

"Father, father! in Heaven's name," exclaimed the young man, "what are these weapons for?"

"Maximilian," replied Morrel, looking fixedly at his son, "you are a man and a man of honour. Come, and I will explain to you."

And with a firm step, Morrel went up to his cabinet, whilst Maximilian followed him, trembling as he went. Morrel opened the door and closed it behind his son; then crossing the ante-room, went to his desk on which he placed the pistols, and pointed with his finger to an open ledger. In this ledger was made out an exact balance-sheet of affairs. Morrel had to pay, within half-an-hour, 287,500 francs. All he possessed was 15,257 francs.

"Read!" said Morrel.

The young man was overwhelmed as he read. Morrel said not a word. What could he say? What need he add to such a desperate proof in figures?

"And have you done all that is possible, father, to meet this disastrous result?" asked the young man, after a moment's pause.

"I have," replied Morrel.

"You have no money coming in on which you can rely?"

"None."

"You have exhausted every resource?"

"All."

"And in half an hour," said Maximilian, in a gloomy voice, "our name is dishonoured!"

"Blood washes out dishonour," said Morrel.

"You are right, father: I understand you."

Then extending his hand towards one of the pistols, he said,——

"There is one for you and one for me—thanks!"

Morrel checked his hand.

"Your mother—your sister! Who will support them?"

A shudder ran through the young man's frame.

"Father," he said, "do you reflect that you are bidding me to live?"

"Yes, I do bid you," answered Morrel, "it is your duty. You have a calm, strong mind, Maximilian. Maximilian, you are no ordinary man: I desire nothing,—I command nothing. I only say to you, examine my position as if it were your own, and then judge for yourself."

The young man reflected an instant, then an expression of sublime resignation appeared in his eyes, and, with a slow and sad gesture, he took off his two epaulettes, the marks of his rank.

"Be it so then, my father," he said, extending his hand to Morrel, "die in peace, my father, I will live."

Morrel was about to cast himself on his knees before his son, but Maximilian caught him in his arms, and those two noble hearts were pressed against each other for a moment.

"You know it is not my fault," said Morrel.

Maximilian smiled.

"I know father you are the most honourable man I have ever known."

"Good, my son, and now all is said; go now and rejoin your mother and sister."

"My father," said the young man, bending his knee, "bless me!"

Morrel took his head between his two hands, drew him towards him, and kissing his forehead several times, said, "Oh! yes, yes, I bless you in my own name, and in the name of three generations of irreproachable men, who say by my voice,—the edifice which misfortune has destroyed Providence may build up again. On seeing me die such a death, the most inexorable will have pity on you; to you perhaps they will accord the time they have refused to me; try that the word of disgrace be never pronounced; go to work, labour, young man, struggle ardently and courageously; live, yourself, your mother and sister, with the most rigid economy, so that from day to day the property of those whom I leave in your hands may augment and fructify. Reflect how glorious a day it will be, how grand, how solemn that day of complete restoration—on which you will say in this very office, 'My father died because he could not do what I have this day done; but he died calmly and peaceably, because in dying he knew what I should do.'"

"My father! my father!" cried the young man, "why should you not live?"

"If I live all would be changed; if I live, interest would be converted into doubt, pity into hostility; if I live I am only a man who has broken his word, failed in his engagements—in fact, only a bankrupt. If, on the contrary, I die, remember, Maximilian, my corpse is that of an honest but unfortunate man. Living, my best friends would avoid my house; dead, all Marseilles will follow me in tears to my last home. Living, you would feel shame at my name; dead, you may raise your head and say, 'I am the son of him you killed, because, for the first time, he has been compelled to fail in his word.'"

The young man uttered a groan, but appeared resigned.

"And now," said Morrel, "leave me alone, and endeavour to keep your mother and sister away."

"Will you not see my sister once more?" asked Maximilian.

A last but final hope was concealed by the young man in the effect of this interview, and therefore he had suggested it.

Morrel shook his head.

"I saw her this morning, and bade her adieu."

"Have you no particular commands to leave with me, my father?" inquired Maximilian in a faltering voice.

"Yes, my son, and a sacred command."

"Say it, my father."

"The house of Thomson and French is the only one, who, from humanity—or it may be selfishness—it is not for me to read men's hearts—have had any pity for me. His agent, who will in ten minutes present himself to receive the amount of a bill of 287,500 francs, I will not say granted, but offered me three months. Let this house be the first re-paid, my son, and respect this man."

"Father, I will," said Maximilian.

"And now once more adieu," said Morrel, "go, leave me, I would be alone; you will find my will in the secretaire in my bed-room."

The young man remained standing, and motionless, having but the force of will, and not the power of execution.

"Hear me, Maximilian," said his father. "Suppose I was a soldier like you, and ordered to carry a certain redoubt, and you knew I must be killed in the assault, would you not say to me as you said just now, "Go, father, for you are dishonoured by delay, and death is preferable to shame!"

"Yes, yes!" said the young man—"yes," and once again embracing his father with convulsive pressure, he said, "Be it so, my father."

And he rushed out of the cabinet.

When his son had left him, Morrel remained an instant standing with his eyes fixed on the door—then putting forth his arm, he pulled the bell.

After a moment's interval, Coclès appeared.

It was no longer the same man—the fearful convictions of the three last days had crushed him. This thought—the house of Morrel is about to stop payment—bent him to the earth more than twenty years would otherwise have done.

"My worthy Coclès," said Morrel, in a tone impossible to describe, "do you remain in the ante-chamber; when the gentleman who came three months ago, the agent of the house of Thomson and French, arrives, announce his arrival to me."

Coclès made no reply; he made a sign with his head, went into the ante-room, and seated himself.

Morrel fell back in his chair, his eyes fixed on the clock; there were seven minutes left, that was all; the hand moved on with incredible rapidity; it seemed to him as if he saw it progress.

What then passed, at this final moment of time in the mind of this man, who, still young, had by a course of reasoning, false perhaps, but at least specious, was about to separate himself from all he loved in the world, and quit life which possessed for him all domestic delights,—it is impossible to express:—to form the slightest idea of his feelings, he must have been seen with his brow bathed in perspiration, yet resigned; his eyes moistened with tears, and yet raised to Heaven.

The clock hand moved on; the pistols were cocked, he stretched forth his hand, took one up, and murmured his daughter's name.

Then he laid down the mortal weapon, took up his pen, and wrote a few words. It seemed to him as if he had not taken a sufficient farewell of his beloved daughter.

Then he turned again to the clock; he no longer counted by minutes, but by seconds. He took up the deadly weapon again, his mouth half-opened and his eyes fixed on the clock, and then shuddered at the click of the trigger as he cocked the pistol.

At this moment of mortal agony, a damp colder than death passed over his brow, an agony stronger than death clutched at his heart strings.

He heard the door of the staircase creak on its hinges. The clock gave its warning to strike eleven. The door of his cabinet opened—Morrel did not turn round, he expected these words of Coclès—

"The agent of Thomson and French."

He placed the muzzle of the pistol between his teeth. Suddenly he heard a cry,—it was his daughter's voice. He turned and saw Julie, the pistol fell from his hands.

"My father!" cried the young girl, out of breath and half dead with joy. "Saved!—you are saved!" And she threw herself into his arms, holding in her extended hand a red netted silk purse.

"Saved!—my child!" said Morrel, "what do you mean?"

"Yes, saved—saved! see, see!" said the young girl.

Morrel took the purse, and started as he did so, for a vague remembrance reminded him that it once belonged to himself, at one end was the bill for the 287,500 francs *receipted*, at the other was a diamond as large as a hazel nut, with these words on a small slip of parchment:—

"JULIE'S DOWRY."

Morrel passed his hand over his brow; it seemed to him a dream. At this moment the clock struck eleven. The sound vibrated as if each stroke of the hammer struck on Morrel's heart.

"Explain, my child," he said; "explain where did you find this purse?"

"In a house in the Allées de Meillan, No. 15, on the corner of a mantel-piece, in a small room on the fifth floor."

"But!" cried Morrel, "this purse is not yours."

Julie handed to her father the letter she had received in the morning.

"And did you go alone?" asked Morrel, after he had read it.

"Emmanuel accompanied me, father. He was to have waited for me at the corner of the Rue de Musée, but, strange to say, he was not there when I returned."

"Monsieur Morrel!" exclaimed a voice on the stairs. "Monsieur Morrel!"

"It is his voice!" said Julie.

At this moment Emmanuel entered, his countenance full of animation and joy.

"The Pharaon!" he cried; "the Pharaon!"

"What!—what! the Pharaon! are you mad, Emmanuel? You know the vessel is lost."

"The Pharaon, sir—they signal the Pharaon! The Pharaon is entering the harbour!"

Morrel fell back in his chair, his strength was failing him; his understanding weakened by such events refused to comprehend such incredible, unheard-of, fabulous facts.

But his son came in.

"Father!" cried Maximilian, "how could you say the Pharaon was lost? The watch-tower has signalled her, and they say she is now coming into port."

"My dear friends!" said Morrel, "if this were so, it must be a miracle of Heaven! Impossible! impossible!"

But what was real and not less incredible was the purse he held in his hand; the acceptance receipted—the splendid diamond.

"Ah! sir," exclaimed Coclès, "what can it mean?—the Pharaon?"

"Come, my dear," said Morrel, rising from his seat, "let us go and see, and Heaven have pity upon us if it be false intelligence."

They all went out, and on the stairs met Madame Morrel, who had been afraid to go up into the cabinet. In an instant they were at the Cannebière. There was a crowd on the pier. All the crowd gave way before Morrel.

"The Pharaon! the Pharaon!" said every voice.

And, wonderful to say, in front of the tower of Saint-Jean, was a ship bearing on her stern these words printed in white letters, "The Pharaon, Morrel and Son, of Marseilles." It was precisely resembling the other Pharaon, and loaded as that had been with cochineal and indigo. It cast anchor, brailed all sails, and on the deck was Captain Gaumard giving orders, and Maître Penelon making signals to M. Morrel.

To doubt any longer was impossible; there was the evidence of the senses and ten thousand persons, who came to corroborate the testimony.

As Morrel and his son embraced on the pier-head, in the presence and applause of the whole city witnessing this prodigy, a man with his face half covered by a black beard, and who, concealed behind the sentry-box, watched the scene with delight, uttered these words in a low tone, "Be happy, noble heart, be blessed for all the good thou hast done and wilt do hereafter, and let my gratitude rest in the shade with your kindness."

And with a smile in which joy and happiness were revealed, he left his hiding-place, and without being observed descended one of those flight of steps which serve for debarkation, and hailing three times, shouted, "Jacopo! Jacopo! Jacopo!"

Then a shallop came to shore, took him on board, and conveyed him to a yacht splendidly fitted up, on whose deck he sprung with the activity of a sailor; thence he once again looked towards Morrel, who weeping with joy was shaking hands most cordially with all the crowd around him, and thanking with a look the unknown benefactor whom he seemed to be seeking in the skies.

"And now," said the unknown, "farewell kindness, humanity, and gratitude! Farewell to all the feelings that expand the heart! I have been Heaven's substitute to recompense the good—now the God of Vengeance yields to me his power to punish the wicked!"

At these words he gave a signal, and, as if only awaiting this signal, the yacht instantly put out to sea.

CHAPTER XXXI

ITALY: SINBAD THE SAILOR

TOWARDS the commencement of the year 1838, two young men belonging to the first society of Paris, the Viscount Albert de Morcerf and the Baron Franz d'Epinay, were at Florence. They had agreed to see the carnival at Rome that year, and that Franz, who for the last three or four years had inhabited Italy, should act as *cicerone* to Albert.

As it is no inconsiderable affair to spend the carnival at Rome, especially when you have no great desire to sleep on the Place du Peuple, or the Campo Vaccino, they wrote to Maître Pastrini, the proprietor of the Hôtel de Londres, Place d'Espagne, to reserve comfortable apartments for them. Maître Pastrini replied that he had only two rooms and a cabinet *al secondo piano*, which he offered at the low charge of a louis per diem. They accepted his offer; but wishing to make the best use of the time that was left Albert started for Naples. As for Franz he remained at Florence. After having passed several days here, when he had walked in the Eden called the Casines, when he had passed two or three evenings at the houses of the nobles of Florence, he took a fancy into his head, after having already visited Corsica, the cradle of Bonaparte, to visit Elba, the halting-place of Napoleon.

One evening he loosened a bark from the iron ring that secured it to the port of Leghorn, laid himself down, wrapped in his cloak, at the bottom, and said to the crew,——

"To the isle of Elba."

The bark shot out of the harbour like a bird, and the next morning Franz disembarked at Porto-Ferrajo. He traversed the island, after having followed the traces which the footsteps of the giant have left, and re-embarked for Marciana. Two hours after he again landed at Pianosa, where he was assured red partridges abounded. The sport was bad; Franz only succeeded in killing a few partridges, and, like every unsuccesful sportsman, he returned to the boat very much out of temper.

"Ah, if your excellency chose," said the captain, "you might have capital sport."

"Where?"

287

"Do you see that island?" continued the captain, pointing to a conical pile that 'rose from out the azure main.'

"Well; what is this island?"

"The island of Monte-Cristo."

"But I have no permission to shoot over this island."

"Your excellency does not require a permission, for the island is uninhabited."

"Ah, indeed!" said the young man. "A desert island in the midst of the Mediterranean must be a curiosity."

"It is very natural; this isle is a mass of rocks, and does not contain an acre of land capable of cultivation."

"To whom does this island belong?"

"To Tuscany."

"What game shall I find there?"

"Thousands of wild goats."

"Who live upon the stones, I suppose," said Franz, with an incredulous smile.

"No; but by browsing the shrubs and trees that grow out of the crevices of the rocks."

"Where can I sleep?"

"On shore in the grottoes, or on board in your cloak; besides, if your excellency pleases, we can leave as soon as the chase is finished—we can sail as well by night as by day, and if the wind drops we can use our oars."

As Franz had sufficient time, and besides had no longer his apartments at Rome to seek after, he accepted the proposition. Upon his answer in the affirmative, the sailors exchanged a few words together in a low tone.

"Well?" asked he, "what, is there any difficulty to be surmounted?"

"No," replied the captain, "but we must warn your excellency that the island is contumacious."

"What do you mean?"

"That Monte-Cristo, although uninhabited, yet serves occasionally as a refuge for the smugglers and pirates who come from Corsica, Sardinia, and Africa, and that if any thing betrays that we have been there, we shall have to perform quarantine for six days on our return to Leghorn."

"The devil! that is quite another thing;—rather a long time too."

"But who will say your excellency has been to Monte-Cristo?"

"Oh, I shall not," cried Franz.

"Nor I, nor I," chorused the sailors.

"Then steer for Monte-Cristo."

The captain gave his orders, the helm was put up, and the bark was soon sailing in the direction of the island.

Franz waited until all was finished, and when the sail was

filled, and the four sailors had taken their place—three forward and one at the helm—he resumed the conversation.

"Gaetano," said he to the captain, "you tell me Monte-Cristo serves as a refuge for pirates, who are, it seems to me, a very different kind of game from the goats."

"Yes, your excellency, and it is true."

"I knew there were smugglers, but I thought that since the capture of Algiers, and the destruction of the regency, pirates only existed in the romances of Cooper and Captain Marryat."

"Your excellency is mistaken; there are pirates like the bandits who were believed to have been exterminated by Pope Leo XII, and who yet every day rob travellers at the gates of Rome. Has not your excellency heard that the French *chargé d'affaires* was robbed six months ago within five hundred paces of Velletri?"

"Oh yes, I heard that."

"Well, then, if like us, your excellency lived at Leghorn, you would hear, from time to time, that a little merchant-vessel, or an English yacht that was expected at Bastia, at Porto-Ferrajo, or at Civita Vecchia, has not arrived, no one knows what has become of it, but, doubtless, it has struck on a rock and foundered. Now this rock it has met has been a long and narrow boat manned by six or eight men, who have surprised and plundered it some dark and stormy night, near some desert and gloomy isle, as bandits plunder a carriage at the corner of a wood."

"But," asked Franz, who lay wrapped in his cloak at the bottom of the bark, "why do not those who have been plundered complain to the French, Sardinian, or Tuscan governments?"

"Why?" said Gaetano, with a smile.

"Yes, why?"

"Because, in the first place, they transfer from the vessel to their own boat whatever they think worth taking, then they bind the crew hand and foot, they attach to every one's neck a four-and-twenty pound ball, a large hole is pierced in the vessel's bottom, and then they leave her. At the end of ten minutes the vessel begins to roll, labour, and then sink; then one of the sides plunges, and then the other; it rises and sinks again; suddenly a noise like the report of a cannon is heard—it is the air blowing up the deck; soon the water rushes out of the scupper-holes like a whale spouting, the vessel gives a last groan, spins round and round, and disappears, forming a vast whirlpool in the ocean, and then all is over; so that in five minutes nothing but the eye of God can see the vessel where she lies at the bottom of the sea. Do you understand now," said the captain, "why no complaints are made to the government, and why the vessel does not arrive at the port?"

It is probable that if Gaetano had related this previous to
proposing the expedition, Franz would have hesitated ere he
accepted it, but now that they had started, he thought it would
be cowardly to draw back; he was one of those men who do not
rashly court danger, but if danger present itself, combat it with
the most unalterable *sang froid*; he was one of those calm and
resolute men who look upon a danger as an adversary in a duel,
who, calculating his movements, study his attacks; who retreat
sufficiently to take breath, but not to appear cowardly; who,
understanding all their advantages, kill at a single blow.

"Bah!" said he, "I have travelled through Sicily and
Calabria, I have sailed two months in the Archipelago, and yet
I never saw even the shadow of a bandit or a pirate."

"I did not tell your excellency this to deter you from your
project," replied Gaetano, "but you questioned me, and I have
answered, that's all."

"Yes, and your conversation is most interesting, and as I
wish to enjoy it as long as possible, steer for Monte-Cristo."

The wind blew strongly, the bark sailed six or seven knots
an hour, and they were rapidly reaching the end of their
voyage; as they approached, the isle became larger, and they
could already distinguish the rocks heaped on one another, like
bullets in an arsenal, in whose crevices they could see the green
bushes and trees that were growing. As for the sailors,
although they appeared perfectly tranquil, yet it was evident
that they were on the alert, and that they carefully watched
the glassy surface over which they were sailing, and on which
a few fishing-boats, with their white sails, were alone visible.
They were within fifteen miles of Monte-Cristo when the sun
began to set behind Corsica, whose mountains appeared
against the sky, and shewing their rugged peaks in bold relief;
this mass of stones, like the giant Adamastor, rose threaten-
ingly before the bark, from which it shaded the sun that gilded
its lower parts; by degrees the shadow rose from the sea and
seemed to drive before it the last rays of the expiring day; at
last the reflexion rested on the summit of the mountain, where
it paused an instant, like the fiery crest of a volcano, then the
shadow gradually covered the summit as it had covered the
base, and the isle now only appeared to be a grey mountain
that grew continually darker; half an hour after and the night
was quite dark.

Fortunately the mariners were used to these latitudes, and
knew every rock in the Tuscan Archipelago; for in the midst of
this obscurity Franz was not without uneasiness. Corsica
had long since disappeared, and Monte-Cristo itself was
invisible, but the sailors seemed, like the lynx, to see in the
dark, and the pilot, who steered, did not evince the slightest
hesitation.

An hour had passed since the sun had set, when Franz fancied he saw, at a quarter of a mile to the left, a dark mass, but it was impossible to make out what it was, and fearing to excite the mirth of the sailors, by mistaking a floating cloud for land, he remained silent; suddenly, a great light appeared on the strand; land might resemble a cloud, but the fire was not a meteor.

"What is this light?" asked he.

"Silence!" said the captain.   "It is a fire."

"But you told me the isle was uninhabited?"

"I said there were no fixed habitations on it, but I said also that it served sometimes as a harbour for smugglers."

"And for pirates?"

"And for pirates," returned Gaetano, repeating Franz's words.   "It is for that reason I have given orders to pass the isle, for, as you see, the fire is behind us."

"But this fire?" continued Franz.   "It seems to me rather to assure than alarm us: men who did not wish to be seen would not light a fire."

"Oh, that goes for nothing," said Gaetano.   "If you can guess the position of the isle in the darkness, you will see that the fire cannot be seen from the side, or from Pianosa, but only from the sea."

"You think, then, that this fire announces unwelcome neighbours?"

"That is what we must ascertain," returned Gaetano, fixing his eyes on this terrestrial star.

"How can you ascertain?"

"You shall see."

Gaetano consulted with his companions, and after five minutes' discussion, a manœuvre was executed which caused the vessel to tack about, they returned the way they had come, and in a few minutes the fire disappeared, hidden by a rise in the land.

The pilot again changed the course of the little bark, which rapidly approached the isle, and was soon within fifty paces of it.   Gaetano lowered the sail, and the bark remained stationary. All this was done in silence, and since their course had been changed not a word was spoken.

Gaetano, who had proposed the expedition, had taken all the responsibility on himself, the four sailors fixed their eyes on him, whilst they prepared their oars and held themselves in readiness to row away, which, thanks to the darkness, would not be difficult.   As for Franz, he examined his arms with the utmost coolness: he had two double-barrelled guns and a rifle; he loaded them, looked at the locks, and waited quietly.

During this time the captain had thrown off his vest and shirt, and secured his trousers round his waist; his feet were naked, so he had no shoes and stockings to take off; after these preparations he placed his finger on his lips, and lowering himself noiselessly into the sea, swam towards the shore with such precaution that it was impossible to hear the slightest sound, he could only be traced by the phosphorescent line in his wake. This track soon disappeared; it was evident that he had touched the shore. Every one on board remained motionless during half an hour, when the same luminous track was again observed, and in two strokes he had regained the bark.

"Well!" exclaimed Franz and the sailors altogether.

"They are Spanish smugglers," said he; "they have with them two Corsican bandits."

"And what are these Corsican bandits doing here with Spanish smugglers?"

"Alas!" returned the captain, with an accent of the most profound pity, "we ought always to help one another. Very often the bandits are hard pressed by gendarmes or carabineers; well, they see a bark, and good fellows like us on board, they come and demand hospitality of us; you can't refuse help to a poor hunted devil, we receive them, and for greater security we stand out to sea. This costs us nothing, and saves the life, or at least the liberty of a fellow-creature, who on the first occasion returns the service by pointing out some safe spot where we can land our goods without interruption."

"Ah!" said Franz, "then you are a smuggler occasionally, Gaetano."

"Your excellency, we must live somehow," returned the other smiling, in a way impossible to describe.

"Then you know the men who are now on Monte-Cristo?"

"Oh, yes, we sailors are like free-masons, and recognise each other by signs!"

"And do you think we have nothing to fear if we land?"

"Nothing at all! smugglers are not thieves."

"But these two Corsican bandits?" said Franz, calculating the chances of peril.

"It is not their faults that they are bandits, but that of the authorities."

"How so?"

"Because they are pursued for having made a *peau*, as if it was not in a Corsican's nature to revenge himself."

"What do you mean by having made a *peau*?—having assassinated a man?" said Franz, continuing his investigation.

"I mean that they have killed an enemy, which is a very different thing," returned the captain.

"Well," said the young man, "let us demand hospitality of these smugglers and bandits. Do you think they will grant it?"

"Without doubt."

"How many are they?"

"Four, and the two bandits make six."

"Just our number, so that if they prove troublesome we shall be able to check them; so, for the last time, steer to Monte-Cristo."

"Yes, but your excellency will permit us to take all due precautions."

"By all means, be as wise as Nestor, and as prudent as Ulysses,—I do more than permit, I exhort you."

"Silence, then!" said Gaetano.

Every one obeyed.

For a man who, like Franz, viewed his position in its true light, it was a grave one. He was alone in the darkness with sailors whom he did not know, and who had no reason to be devoted to him; who knew that he had in his belt several thousand francs, and who had often examined his arms, which were very beautiful, if not with envy, at least with curiosity. On the other hand, he was about to land, without any other escort than these men, on an island whose name was religious, but which did not seem to Franz likely to afford him much hospitality, thanks to the smugglers and bandits. The history of the scuttled vessels which had appeared improbable during the day seemed very probable at night; placed as he was between two imaginary dangers, he did not quit the crew with his eyes, or his gun with his hand.

However, the sailors had again hoisted the sail, and the vessel was once more cleaving the waves. Through the darkness, Franz, whose eyes were now more accustomed to it, distinguished the granite giant by which the bark was sailing, and then, turning an angle of the rock, he saw the fire more brilliant than ever, round which five or six persons were seated.

The blaze illumined the sea for a hundred paces round. Gaetano skirted the light, carefully keeping the bark out of its rays, then, when they were opposite the fire, he entered into the centre of the circle, singing a fishing song, of which his companions sung the chorus.

At the first words of the song, the men seated round the fire rose and approached the landing-place, their eyes fixed on the bark, of which they evidently sought to judge the force and divine the intention. They soon appeared satisfied, and returned (with the exception of one who remained at the shore) to their fire, at which a whole goat was roasting.

When the bark was within twenty paces of the shore the man on the beach made with his carbine the movement of a sentinel who sees a patrol, and cried, "Who goes there?" in Sardinian. Franz coolly cocked both barrels. Gaetano then exchanged a few words with the man, which the traveller did not understand, but which evidently concerned him.

"Will your excellency give your name or remain incognito?" asked the captain.

"My name must rest unknown,—merely say I am a Frenchman travelling for pleasure."

As soon as Gaetano had transmitted this answer, the sentinel gave an order to one of the men seated round the fire, who rose and disappeared among the rocks. Not a word was spoken, every one seemed occupied, Franz with his disembarkment, the sailors with their sails, the smugglers with their goat; but in the midst of all this carelessness it was evident that they mutually observed each other.

The man who had disappeared returned suddenly on the opposite side to that by which he had left, he made a sign with his head to the sentinel, who, turning to the bark uttered these words, "S'accommodi." The Italian s'accommodi is untranslatable; it means at once, "Come, enter, you are welcome, make yourself at home, you are the master." It is like that Turkish phrase of Molière's that so astonished le bourgeois gentilhomme by the number of things it contained.

The sailors did not wait for a second invitation; four strokes of the oar brought them to the land, Gaetano sprang to shore, exchanged a few words with the sentinel, then his comrades descended, and lastly came Franz's turn. One of his guns was swung over his shoulder, Gaetano had the other, and a sailor held his rifle, his dress, half artist, half dandy, did not excite any suspicion, and consequently no disquietude. The bark was moored to the shore, and they advanced a few paces to find a comfortable bivouack; but, doubtless, the spot they chose did not suit the smuggler who filled the post of sentinel, for he cried out,—

"Not that way, if you please."

Gaetano faltered an excuse, and advanced to the opposite side whilst two sailors kindled torches at the fire to light them on their way. They advanced about thirty paces, and then stopped at a small esplanade surrounded with rocks, in which seats had been cut not unlike sentry-boxes. Around in the crevices of the rocks grew a few dwarf oaks and thick bushes of myrtles. Franz lowered a torch, and saw, by the light of a mass of cinders, that he was not the first to discover this retreat, which was, doubtless, one of the halting places of the wandering visitors of Monte-Cristo. As for his anticipation of events, once on terra firma, once that he had seen the indifferent, if not friendly appearance of his hosts, his pre-occupation had disappeared, or rather, at sight of the goat, had turned to appetite.

He mentioned this to Gaetano, who replied that nothing

could be more easy than to prepare a supper when they had in their boat bread, wine, half-a-dozen partridges, and a good fire to roast them by.

"Besides," added he, "if the smell of their roast meat tempts you, I will go and offer them two of our birds for a slice."

"You seem born for negotiation," returned Franz; "go and try."

During this time the sailors had collected dried sticks and branches, with which they made a fire.

Franz waited impatiently, smelling the odour of the goat, when the captain returned with a mysterious air.

"Well," said Franz, "any thing new?—do they refuse?"

"On the contrary," returned Gaetano; "the chief, who was told you were a young Frenchman, invites you to sup with him."

"Well," observed Franz, "this chief is very polite, and I see no objection;—the more so, as I bring my share of the supper."

"Oh, it is not that,—he has plenty, and to spare, for supper; but he attaches a singular condition to your presentation at his house."

"His house! has he built one here then?"

"No, but he has a very comfortable one all the same, so they say."

"You know this chief, then?"

"I have heard talk of him."

"Ill or well?"

"Both."

"The devil!—and what is this condition?"

"That you are blindfolded, and do not take off the bandage until he himself bids you."

Franz looked at Gaetano to see, if possible, what he thought of this proposal.

"Ah!" replied he, guessing Franz's thought, "I know this merits reflection."

"What should you do in my place?"

"I who have nothing to lose,—I should go."

"You would accept?"

"Yes, were it only out of curiosity."

"There is something very curious about this chief then?"

"Listen," said Gaetano, lowering his voice, "I do not know if what they say is true——"

He stopped to look if any one was near.

"What do they say?"

"That this chief inhabits a cavern to which the Pitti Palace is nothing."

"What nonsense!" said Franz, reseating himself.

"It is no nonsense, it is quite true. Cama the pilot of the Saint Ferdinand, went in once, and he came back amazed, vowing that such treasures were only to be heard of in fairy tales."

"Do you know," observed Franz, "that with such stories you would make me enter the enchanted cavern of Ali Baba?"

"I tell you what I have been told."

"Then you advise me to accept?"

"Oh, I don't say that, your excellency will do as you please; I should be sorry to advise you in the matter."

Franz reflected a few moments, felt that a man so rich could not have any intention of plundering him of what little he had, and seeing only the prospect of a good supper, he accepted. Gaetano departed with the reply. Franz was prudent, and wished to learn all he possibly could concerning his host; he turned towards the sailor, who, during this dialogue, had sat gravely plucking the partridges, with the air of a man proud of his office, and asked him how these men had landed, as no vessel of any kind was visible.

"Never mind that," returned the sailor, "I know their vessel."

"Is it a very beautiful vessel?"

"I would not wish for a better to sail round the world."

"Of what burden is she?"

"About a hundred tons; but she is built to stand any weather. She is what the English call a yacht."

"Where was she built?"

"I know not, but my own opinion is, she is a Genoese."

"And how did a leader of smugglers," continued Franz, "venture to build a vessel designed for such a purpose at Genoa?"

"I did not say that the owner was a smuggler," replied the sailor.

"No, but Gaetano did, I thought."

"Gaetano had only seen the vessel from a distance, he had not then spoken to any one."

"And if this person be not a smuggler, who is he?"

"A wealthy signor, who travels for his pleasure."

"Come," thought Franz, "he is still more mysterious, since the two accounts do not agree. What is his name?"

"If you ask him he says, Sinbad the Sailor, but I doubt its being his real name."

"Sinbad the Sailor?"

"Yes."

"And where does he reside?"

"On the sea."

"What country does he come from?"

"I do not know."

"Have you ever seen him?"

"Sometimes."

"What sort of man is he?"

"Your excellency will judge for yourself."

"Where will he receive me?"

"No doubt in the subterranean palace Gaetano told you of."

"Have you never had the curiosity, when you have landed and found this island deserted, to seek for this enchanted palace?"

"Oh, yes, more than once, but always in vain; we examined the grotto all over, but we never could find the slightest trace of any opening; they say that the door is not opened by a key, but a magical word."

"Decidedly," muttered Franz, "this is an adventure of the Arabian Nights."

"His excellency waits for you," said a voice, which he recognised as that of the sentinel.

He was accompanied by two of the yacht's crew. Franz drew his handkerchief from his pocket and presented it to the man who had spoken to him. Without uttering a word they bandaged his eyes with a care that shewed their apprehensions of his committing some indiscretion. Afterwards he was made to promise he would not make the least attempt to raise the bandage. He promised. Then his two guides took his arms, and he advanced guided by them, and preceded by the sentinel. After advancing about thirty paces he smelt the appetising odour of the kid that was roasting, and knew thus that he was passing the bivouack; they then led him on about fifty paces farther, evidently advancing towards the shore, where they would not allow Gaetano to penetrate,—a refusal he could now comprehend. Presently, by a change in the atmosphere, he comprehended that they were entering a cave; after going on for a few seconds more he heard a crackling, and it seemed to him as though the atmosphere again changed, and became balmy and perfumed. At length his feet touched on a thick and soft carpet, and his guides let go their hold of him. There was a moment's silence, and then a voice, in excellent French, although with a foreign accent, said,—

"Welcome, sir. I beg you will remove your bandage."

It may be supposed, then, Franz did not wait for a repetition of this permission, but took off the handkerchief, and found himself in the presence of a man from thirty-eight to forty years of age, dressed in a Tunisian costume, that is to say, a red cap with a long blue silk tassel, a vest of black cloth embroidered with gold, pantaloons of deep red, large and full gaiters of the same colour, embroidered with gold, like the vest, and yellow slippers; he had a splendid cachemire round

C.M.—J*

his waist, and a small sharp and crooked cangiar was passed through his girdle. Although of a paleness that was almost livid, this man had a remarkably handsome face; his eyes were penetrating and sparkling; a nose, quite straight and projecting direct from the brow, gave out the Greek type in all its purity, whilst his teeth, as white as pearls, were set off to admiration by the black moustache that encircled them.

This pallor was so peculiar that it seemed as though it were that which would be exhibited by a man who had been inclosed for a long time in a tomb, and who was unable to resume the healthy glow and hue of the living. He was not particularly tall, but extremely well made, and, like the men of the south, had small hands and feet. But what astonished Franz, who had treated Gaetano's description as a fable, was the splendour of the apartment in which he found himself. The entire chamber was lined with crimson brocade, worked with flowers of gold. In a recess was a kind of divan, surmounted with a stand of Arabian swords in silver scabbards, and the handles resplendent with gems; from the ceiling hung a lamp of Venice glass, of beautiful shape and colour, whilst the feet rested on a Turkey carpet, in which they sunk to the instep; tapestry hung before the door by which Franz had entered, and also in front of another door, leading into a second apartment, which seemed to be brilliantly lighted up. The host gave Franz time for his surprise, and, moreover, rendered him look for look, not even taking his eyes off him.

"Sir," he said, after some pause, "a thousand excuses for the precaution taken in your introduction hither; but as, during the greater portion of the year, this island is deserted, if the secret of this abode were discovered I should, doubtless, find on my return my temporary retirement in a great state of disorder, which would be exceedingly annoying, not for the loss it occasioned me, but because I should not have the certainty I now possess of separating myself from all the rest of mankind at pleasure. Let me now endeavour to make you forget this temporary unpleasantness, and offer you what no doubt you did not expect to find here, that is to say, a tolerable supper and pretty comfortable beds."

"*Ma foi!* my dear sir," replied Franz, "make no apologies. I have always observed that they bandage people's eyes, who penetrate enchanted palaces, for instance, those of Raoul in the *Huguenots*, and really I have nothing to complain of, for what I see is a sequel to the wonders of the Arabian Nights."

"Alas! I may say with Lucullus, if I could have anticipated the honour of your visit I would have prepared for it. But such as is my hermitage, it is at your disposal; such as is my supper, it is yours to share, if you will. Ali, is the supper ready?"

At this moment the tapestry moved aside, and a Nubian, black as ebony, and dressed in a plain white tunic, made a sign to his master that all was prepared in the *salle-à-manger*.

"Now," said the unknown to Franz, "I do not know if you are of my opinion, but I think nothing is more annoying than to remain two or three hours *tête-à-tête* without knowing by name or appellation how to address one another. Pray observe, that I too much respect the laws of hospitality to ask your name or title. I only request you to give me one by which I may have the pleasure of addressing you. As for myself, that I may put you at your ease, I tell you that I am generally called 'Sinbad the Sailor.'"

"And I," replied Franz, "will tell you, as I only require his wonderful lamp to make me precisely like Aladdin, that I see no reason why at this moment I should not be called Aladdin. That will keep us from going away from the East, whither I am tempted to think I have been conveyed by some good genius."

"Well, then, Signor Aladdin," replied the singular Amphitryon, "you heard our repast announced, will you now take the trouble to enter the *salle-à-manger*, your humble servant going first to shew you the way?"

At these words, moving aside the tapestry, Sinbad preceded his guest. Franz proceeded from one enchantment to another; the table was splendidly covered, and, once convinced of this important point, he cast his eyes around him. The *salle-à-manger* was scarcely less striking than the boudoir he had just left; it was entirely of marble, with antique bas-reliefs of priceless value; and at the four corners of this apartment, which was oblong, were four magnificent statues, having baskets on their heads. These baskets contained four pyramids of most splendid fruit; there were the pine-apples of Sicily, pomegranates of Malaga, oranges from the Balearic Isles, peaches from France, and dates from Tunis.

The supper consisted of a roast pheasant, garnished with Corsican blackbirds; a boar's ham *à la gelée*, a quarter of a kid *à la tartare*, a glorious turbot, and a gigantic lobster. Between these large dishes were smaller ones, containing various dainties. The dishes were of silver, and the plates of Japanese china.

Franz rubbed his eyes in order to assure himself that this was not a dream. Ali alone was present to wait at table, and acquitted himself so admirably, that the guest complimented his host thereupon.

"Yes," replied he, whilst he did the honours of the supper with much ease and grace,—"yes, he is a poor devil who is much devoted to me, and does all he can to prove it. He remembers I saved his life, and as he has a regard for his head he feels some gratitude towards me for having kept it on his shoulders."

Ali approached his master, took his hand and kissed it.

"Would it be impertinent, Signor Sinbad," said Franz, "to ask the particulars of this kindness?"

"Oh! they are simple enough," replied the host. "It seems the fellow had been caught wandering nearer to the harem of the Bey of Tunis than etiquette permits to one of his colour, and he was condemned by the Bey to have his tongue cut out, and his hand and head cut off; the tongue the first day, the hand the second, and the head the third. I always had a desire to have a mute in my service, so learning the day his tongue was cut out, I went to the Bey, and proposed to give him for Ali a splendid double-barrelled gun, which I knew he was very desirous of having. He hesitated a moment, he was so very desirous to complete the poor devil's punishment. But when I added to the gun an English cutlass with which I had shivered his highness's yataghan to pieces, the Bey yielded, and agreed to forgive the hand and head, but on condition he never again set foot in Tunis. This was a useless clause in the bargain, for whenever the coward sees the first glimpse of the shores of Africa, he runs down below, and can only be induced to appear again when we are out of sight of one quarter of the globe."

Franz remained a moment mute and pensive, hardly knowing what to think of the half-kindness, half-cruelty, with which his host related the brief narrative.

"And, like the celebrated sailor whose name you have assumed," he said, by way of changing the conversation, "you pass your life in travelling?"

"Yes! I made a vow at a time when I little thought I should ever be able to accomplish it," said the unknown, with a singular smile; "and I made some others also, which I hope I may fulfil in due season."

Although Sinbad pronounced these words with much calmness, his eyes darted gleams of singular ferocity.

"You have suffered a great deal, sir?" said Franz, inquiringly.

Sinbad started and looked fixedly at him, as he replied, "What makes you suppose so?"

"Every thing!" answered Franz,—"your voice, your look, your pallid complexion, and even the life you lead."

"I! I live the happiest life possible, the real life of a pacha. I am king of all creation. I am pleased with one place, and stay there; I get tired of it, and leave it; I am free as a bird, and have wings like one; my attendants obey me at a signal.

Sometimes I amuse myself by carrying off from human justice some bandit it is in quest of, some criminal whom it pursues. Then I have my mode of dispensing justice, silent and sure, without respite or appeal, which condemns or pardons, and which no one sees. Ah! if you had tasted of my life, you would not desire any other, and would never return to the world unless you had some great project to accomplish there."

"A vengeance, for instance!" observed Franz.

The unknown fixed on the young man one of those looks which penetrate into the depth of the heart and thoughts.

"And why a vengeance?" he asked.

"Because," replied Franz, "you seem to me like a man who, persecuted by society, has a fearful account to settle with it."

"Ah!" responded Sinbad, laughing with his singular laugh, which displayed his white and sharp teeth. "You have not guessed rightly! Such as you see me I am, a sort of philosopher, and one day perhaps I shall go to Paris to rival M. Appert, and the little man in the blue cloak."

"And will that be the first time you ever took that journey?"

"Yes it will! I must seem to you by no means curious, but I assure you that it is not my fault I have delayed it so long —it will happen one day or the other."

"And do you propose to make this journey very shortly?"

"I do not know, it depends on circumstances which depend on certain arrangements!"

"I should like to be there at the time you come, and I will endeavour to repay you as far as lies in my power for your liberal hospitality displayed to me at Monte-Cristo."

"I should avail myself of your offer with pleasure," replied the host, "but, unfortunately, if I go there it will be in all probability incognito."

The supper appeared to have been supplied solely for Franz, for the unknown scarcely touched one or two dishes of the splendid banquet to which his guest did ample justice. Then Ali brought on the dessert, or rather took the baskets from the hands of the statues and placed them on the table. Between the two baskets he placed a small silver cup, closed with a lid of the same. The care with which Ali placed this cup on the table roused Franz's curiosity. He raised the lid and saw a kind of greenish paste, something like preserved angelica, but which was perfectly unknown to him. He replaced the lid, as ignorant of what the cup contained as he was before he had looked at it, and then casting his eyes towards his host he saw him smile at his disappointment.

"You cannot guess," said he, "what there is in that small vase, can you?"

"No, I really cannot!"

"Well, then, that kind of green preserve is nothing less than the ambrosia which Hebe served at the table of Jupiter!"

"But," replied Franz, "this ambrosia, no doubt in passing through mortal hands, has lost its heavenly appellation and assumed a human name; in vulgar phrase, what may you term this composition, for which, to say the truth, I do not feel any particular desire?"

"Ah! thus it is that our material origin is revealed," cried Sinbad; "we frequently pass so near to happiness without seeing, without regarding it, or if we do see and regard it, yet without recognising it. Are you a man for the substantials, and is gold your God? taste this, and the mines of Peru, Guzerat, and Golconda, are opened to you. Are you a man of imagination—a poet? taste this, and the boundaries of possibility disappear; the fields of infinite space open to you, you advance free in heart, free in mind, into the boundless realms of unfettered reverie. Are you ambitious, and do you seek after the greatnesses of the earth? taste this, and in an hour you will be a king, not a king of a petty kingdom hidden in some corner of Europe like France, Spain, or England, but king of the world, king of the universe, king of creation; without bowing at the feet of Satan, you will be king and master of all the kingdoms of the earth. Is it not tempting what I offer you, and is it not an easy thing since it is only to do thus?—look!"

At these words he uncovered the small cup which contained the substance so lauded, took a tea-spoonful of the magic sweetmeat, raised it to his lips and swallowed it slowly, with his eyes half shut and his head bent backwards.

Franz did not disturb him whilst he absorbed his favourite *bonne bouche*, but when he had finished he inquired,—

"What, then, is this precious stuff?"

"Did you ever hear," he replied, "of the Old Man of the Mountain who attempted to assassinate Philippe Augustus?"

"Of course I have!"

"Well! you know he reigned over a rich valley which was overhung by the mountain whence he derived his picturesque name. In this valley were magnificent gardens planted by Hassen-ben-Sabah, and in these gardens isolated pavilions. Into these pavilions he admitted the elect; and there, says Marco Polo, gave them to eat a certain herb, which transported them to paradise, in the midst of ever-blooming shrubs, ever-ripe fruit, and ever-lovely virgins. But what these happy persons took for reality was but a dream; but it was a dream so soft, so voluptuous, so enthralling, that they sold themselves body and soul to him who gave it to them, and obedient to his orders as those of a deity, struck down the marked victim, died in torture without a murmur; believing that the death they underwent was but a quick transition to that life of delights of which the holy herb, now before you, had given them a slight foretaste."

"Then," cried Franz, "it is hashish! I know that—by name at least."

"That is it precisely, Signor Aladdin; it is hashish—the purest and most unadulterated hashish of Alexandria,—the hashish of Abou-Gor, the celebrated maker, the only man, the man to whom there should be built a palace, inscribed with these words, ' A grateful world to the dealer in happiness.'"

"Do you know," said Franz, "I have a very great inclination to judge for myself of the truth or exaggeration of your eulogies!"

"Judge for yourself, Signor Aladdin—judge, but do not confine yourself to one trial. Like every thing else, we must habituate the senses to a fresh impression, gentle or violent, sad or joyous. There is a struggle in nature against this divine substance,—in nature which is not made for joy and clings to pain. Nature subdued must yield in the combat, the dream must succeed to reality, and then the dream reigns supreme, then the dream becomes life, and life becomes the dream. But what changes occur! It is only by comparing the pains of actual being with the joys of the assumed existence, that you would desire to live no longer, but to dream thus for ever! When you return to this mundane sphere from your visionary world, you would seem to leave a Neapolitan spring for a Lapland winter—to quit paradise for earth—heaven for hell! Taste the hatchis, guest of mine,—taste the hashish!"

Franz's only reply was to take a tea-spoonful of the marvellous preparation, about as much in quantity as his host had eaten, and lift it to his mouth.

"Diable!" he said, after having swallowed the divine preserve. "I do not know if the result will be as agreeable as you describe, but the thing does not appear to me as succulent as you say."

"Because your palate has not yet attained the sublimity of the substances it flavours. Tell me, the first time you tasted oysters, tea, porter, truffles, and sundry other dainties which you now adore, did you like them? Could you comprehend how the Romans stuffed their pheasants with assafœtida, and the Chinese eat swallows' nests? Eh? no! Well, it is the same with hashish; only eat it for a week, and nothing in the world will seem to you to equal the delicacy of its flavour, which now appears to you sleepy and distasteful. Let us now go into the chamber beside you, which is your apartment, and Ali will bring us coffee and pipes."

They both arose, and whilst he who called himself Sinbad, —and whom we have occasionally named so, that we might, like his guest, have some title by which to distinguish him,— gave some orders to the servant, Franz entered into the adjoining apartment. It was simply yet richly furnished. It was round, and a large divan completely encircled it. Divan, walls, ceiling, floor, were all covered with magnificent skins, as soft and downy as the richest carpets; there were skins of the lions of Atlas, with their large manes, skins of the Bengal tigers, with their striped hides; skins of the panthers of the Cape spotted beautifully, like those that appeared to Dante; skins of the bears of Siberia, the foxes of Norway, &c.; and all these skins were strewn in profusion one on the other, so that it seemed like walking over the most mossy turf, or reclining on the most luxurious bed.

Both laid themselves down on the divan: chibouques, with jasmine tubes and amber mouth-pieces, were within reach, and all prepared so that there was no need to smoke the same pipe twice. Each of them took one, which Ali lighted, and then retired to prepare the coffee. There was a moment's silence, during which Sinbad gave himself up to thoughts that seemed to occupy him incessantly, even in the midst of his conversation, and Franz abandoned himself to that mute reverie, into which we always sink when smoking excellent tobacco, which seems to remove with its fume all the troubles of the mind, and to give the smoker in exchange all the visions of the soul. Ali brought in the coffee.

"How do you take it?" inquired the unknown, "*à la Française* or *à la Turque*, strong or weak, sugar or none, cool or boiling? As you please, it is ready in all ways."

"I will take it *à la Turque*," replied Franz.

"And you are right," said his host, "it shews you have a tendency for an Oriental life. Ah! those Orientals! they are the only men who know how to live. As for me," he added, with one of those singular smiles which did not escape the young man, "when I have completed my affairs in Paris, I shall go and die in the East, and should you wish to see me again, you must seek me at Cairo, Bagdad, or Ispahan."

"*Ma foi!*" said Franz, "it would be the easiest thing in the world, for I feel eagle's wings springing out at my shoulders, and with these wings I could make a tour of the world in four-and-twenty hours."

"Ah! ah! it is the hashish that is operating. Well, unfurl your wings and fly into superhuman regions; fear nothing, there is a watch over you, and if your wings, like those of Icarus, melt before the sun, we are here to receive you."

He then said some Arabian words to Ali, who made a sign of obedience and withdrew, but not to any distance. As to

Franz, a strange transformation had taken place in him. All the bodily fatigue of the day, all the pre-occupation of mind which the events of the evening had brought on disappeared, as they would at that first feeling of sleep, when we are still sufficiently conscious to be aware of the coming of slumber. His body seemed to acquire an airy lightness, his perception brightened in a remarkable manner, his senses seemed to redouble their power, the horizon continued to expand; but it was not that gloomy horizon over which a vague alarm prevails, and which he had seen before he slept; but a blue, transparent, unbounded horizon, with all the blue of the ocean, all the spangles of the sun, all the perfumes of the summer breeze; then in the midst of the songs of his sailors,—songs so clear and sounding, that they would have made a divine harmony had their notes been taken down,—he saw the isle of Monte-Cristo, no longer as a threatening rock in the midst of the waves, but as an oasis lost in the desert: then as the bark approached the songs became louder, for an enchanting and mysterious harmony rose to heaven from this island, as if some fay like Lorelay, or some enchanter like Amphion, had decreed to attract thither a soul or build there a city.

At length the bark touched the shore, but without effort, without shock, as lips touch lips, and he entered the grotto amidst continued strains of most delicious melody. He descended, or rather seemed to descend, several steps, inspiring the fresh and balmy air, like that which may be supposed to reign around the grotto of Circe, formed from such perfumes as set the mind a-dreaming, and such fires as burn the very senses; and he saw again all he had seen before his sleep, from Sinbad his singular host to Ali the mute attendant; then all seemed to fade away and become confused before his eyes, like the last shadows of the magic lantern before it is extinguished, and he was again in the chamber of statues, lighted only by one of those pale and antique lamps which watch in the dead of the night over the sleep of pleasure. They were the same statues, rich in form, in attraction, and poesy, with eyes of fascination, smiles of love, and "bright and flowing hair." They were Phyrne, Cleopatra, Messalina, those three celebrated courtesans; then amongst them glided like a pure ray, like a Christian angel in the midst of Olympus, one of those chaste figures, those calm shadows, those soft visions, which seemed to veil its virgin brow before these marble wantons. Then these three statues advanced towards him with looks of love, and approached the couch on which he was reposing, their feet hidden in their long tunics, their throats bare, hair flowing like waves, and assuming attitudes which the gods could not resist, but which saints withstood, and looks inflexible and ardent like the serpent's on the bird, and then he gave way before these looks as painful as a powerful grasp and as delightful as a kiss.

It seemed to Franz that he closed his eyes, and thought that in the last look he gave he saw the modest statue completely veiled, and then with his eyes closed upon all nature his senses awoke to impassable impressions, and he was under the painful yet delicious enthralment produced by the hashish, whose enchantment had brought up this marvellous and thrilling vision.

CHAPTER XXXII

THE WAKING

WHEN Franz returned to himself, exterior objects seemed a second portion of his dream, he thought himself in a sepulchre, into which scarcely penetrated (and then like a look of pity) a ray of the sun; he stretched forth his hand and touched stone, he rose to his seat and found himself lying on his bournous in a bed of dry heather, very soft and odoriferous. The vision had entirely fled, and as if the statues had been but shadows coming from their tomb during his dream, they vanished at his waking.

He advanced several paces towards the point whence the light came, and to all the excitement of his dream succeeded the calmness of reality. He found that he was in a grotto, went towards the opening, and through a kind of fanlight saw a blue sea and an azure sky. The air and water were shining in the beams of the morning sun, on the shore the sailors were sitting chatting and laughing, and at ten yards from them the bark was at anchor, undulating gracefully on the water. There for some time he enjoyed the fresh breeze which played on his brow, and listened to the dash of the waves on the beach leaving against the rocks a lace of foam as white as silver. He was for some time without reflection or thought for the divine charm which is in the things of nature, especially after a fantastic dream: then gradually this view of outward matters so calm, so pure, so grand, reminded him of the illusiveness of a dream, and remembrance became busy again in his memory. He recalled his arrival on the island, his presentation to a smuggler chief, a subterranean palace full of splendour, an excellent supper, and a spoonful of hashish. It seemed, however, even in the very face of open day, that at least a year had elapsed since all these things had passed; so deep was the impression made in his mind by the dream, and so strong a hold had it taken of his imagination. Thus every now and then his fancy placed amidst the sailors, or seated on a rock, saw undulating in the vessel, one of those shadows which had shared his dreams with their looks and their kisses. Otherwise his head was perfectly clear and his limbs entirely reposed, he was free from the slightest headache; on the contrary, he felt a certain degree of lightness, a faculty of absorbing the pure air, and enjoying the bright sunshine more vividly than ever.

He went gaily up to the sailors, who rose as soon as they perceived him, and the patron accosting him said,—

"The Signor Sinbad has left his compliments for your excellency, and desired us to express the regret he feels at not being able to take his leave in person, but he trusts you will excuse him, as very important business calls him to Malaga."

"So then, Gaetano," said Franz, "this is then all reality, there exists a man who had received me in this isle, entertained me right royally, and has departed whilst I was asleep."

"He exists as certainly as that you may see his small yacht with all her sails spread; and if you will use your glass, you will, in all probability, recognise your host in the midst of his crew."

So saying, Gaetano pointed in a direction in which a small vessel was making sail towards the southern point of Corsica.

Franz adjusted his telescope and directed it towards the bark.

Gaetano was not mistaken. At the stern the mysterious stranger was standing up looking towards the shore, and holding a spy-glass in his hand; he was attired as he had been on the previous evening, and waved his pocket-handkerchief to his guest in token of adieu.

Franz returned the salute by shaking his handkerchief as an exchange of signals.

After a second, a slight cloud of smoke was seen at the stern of the vessel, which rose gracefully as it expanded in the air, and then Franz heard a slight report.

"There! do you hear?" observed Gaetano, "he is bidding you adieu!"

The young man took his carbine and fired it in the air, but without any idea that the noise could be heard at the distance which separated the yacht from the shore.

"What are your excellency's orders?" inquired Gaetano.

"In the first place, light me a torch."

"Ah, yes! I understand," replied the patron, "to find the entrance to the enchanted apartment. With much pleasure, your excellency, if it would amuse you, and I will get you the torch you ask for. But I, too, have had the idea you have, and two or three times the same fancy has come over me; but I have always given it up. Giovanni, light a torch," he added, "and give it to his excellency."

Giovanni obeyed, Franz took the lamp, and entered the

subterranean grotto followed by Gaetano. He recognised the place where he had awoke by the bed of heather that was there, but it was in vain that he carried his torch all around the exterior surface of the grotto, he saw nothing, unless that by traces of smoke others had before him attempted the same thing, and like him in vain. Yet he did not leave a foot of this granite wall, as impenetrable as futurity, without strict scrutiny: he did not see a fissure without introducing the blade of his hunting sword in it, nor a projecting point on which he did not lean and press in the hopes it would give way: all was vain, and he lost two hours in his attempts, which were at last utterly useless.

At the end of this time he gave up his research, and Gaetano smiled.

When Franz appeared again on the shore, the yacht only seemed like a small white speck in the horizon, he looked again through his glass, but even then he could not distinguish any thing. Gaetano reminded him that he had come for the purpose of shooting goats, which he had utterly forgotten. He took his fowling-piece and began to hunt over the isle with the air of a man who is fulfilling a duty rather than enjoying a pleasure, and at the end of a quarter of an hour he had killed a goat and two kids. These animals, though wild and agile as chamois, were too much like domestic goats, and Franz could not consider them as game.

Moreover, other ideas much more powerful occupied his mind. Since the evening before, he had really been the hero of one of the tales of the *Thousand and One Nights*, and he was irresistibly attracted towards the grotto. Then in spite of the failure of his first search he began a second, after having told Gaetano to roast one of the two kids. The second visit was a long one, and when he returned the kid was roasted and the repast ready.

Franz was sitting on the spot where he was on the previous evening when his mysterious host had invited him to supper, and he saw the little yacht, now like a sea-gull on the wave, continuing her flight towards Corsica.

"Why," he remarked to Gaetano, "you told me that Signor Sinbad was going to Malaga, whilst it seems he is in the direction of Porto-Vecchio."

"Don't you remember," said the patron, "I told you that amongst the crew there were two Corsican brigands?"

"True! and he is going to land them," added Franz.

"Precisely so," replied Gaetano. "Ah! he is an individual who fears neither God nor the devil they say, and would at any time run fifty leagues out of his course to do a poor devil a service."

"But such services as these might involve him with the

authorities of the country in which he practises this kind of philanthropy," said Franz.

"And what cares he for that?" replied Gaetano, with a laugh, "or any authorities? he smiles at them: let them try to pursue him—why, in the first place, his yacht is not a ship, but a bird, and he would beat any frigate three knots in every nine; and if he were to throw himself on the coast, why, a'n't he certain of finding friends every where?"

It was perfectly clear that the Signor Sinbad, Franz's host, had the honour of being on excellent terms with the smugglers and bandits along the whole coast of the Mediterranean, which placed him in a position singular enough.

As to Franz, he had no longer any inducement to remain at Monte-Cristo. He had lost all hope of detecting the secret of the grotto, he consequently despatched his breakfast, and his bark being ready he hastened on board, and they were soon under way.

At the moment the bark began her course they lost sight of the yacht, as it disappeared in the gulf of Porto-Vecchio. With it was effaced the last trace of the preceding night, and then supper, Sinbad, hashish, statues, all became a dream for Franz. The bark went on all day and all night, and next morning when the sun rose, they had lost sight of Monte-Cristo.

When Franz had once again set foot on shore, he forgot, for the moment, at least, the events which had just passed, whilst he finished his affairs of pleasure at Florence, and then thought of nothing but how he should rejoin his companion, who was awaiting him at Rome.

He set out, and on the Saturday evening reached the Place de la Douane by the mail-coach. An apartment, as we have said, had been retained beforehand, and thus he had but to go to the hotel of Maître Pastrini; but this was not so easy a matter, for the streets were thronged with people, and Rome was already a prey to that low and feverish murmur which precedes all great events, and at Rome there are four great events in every year—the Carnival, the Holy Week, the Fête Dieu, and the Saint Peter. All the rest of the year the city is in that state of dull apathy, between life and death, which renders it similar to a kind of station between this world and the next: a sublime spot, a resting-place full of poetry and character, and at which Franz had already halted five or six times, and at each time found it more marvellous and striking. At last he made his way through this mob, which was continually increasing and more agitated, and reached the hotel. On his first inquiry, he was told with the impertinence peculiar to hackney-coachmen who are hired and innkeepers with their house full, that there was no room for him at the Hôtel de

Londres. Then he sent his card to Maître Pastrini, and demanded Albert de Morcerf. This plan succeeded, and Maître Pastrini himself ran to him, excusing himself for having made his excellency wait, scolding the waiters, taking the candlestick in his hand from the cicerone, who was ready to pounce on the traveller, and was about to lead him to Albert when Morcerf himself appeared.

The apartment consisted of two small rooms and a closet. The two rooms looked on to the street, a fact which Maître Pastrini commented upon as an inappreciable advantage. The remainder of the story was hired by a very rich gentleman, who was supposed to be a Sicilian or Maltese; but the host was unable to decide to which of the two nations the traveller belonged.

"Very good, Maître Pastrini," said Franz, "but we must have some supper instantly, and a carriage for to-morrow and the following days."

"As to supper," replied the landlord, "you shall be served immediately; but as for the carriage——"

"What as to the carriage?" exclaimed Albert, "come, come, Maître Pastrini, no joking, we must have a carriage."

"Sir," replied the host, "we will do all in our power to procure you one,—this is all I can say."

"And when shall we know?" inquired Franz.

"To-morrow morning," answered the innkeeper.

"Oh! the devil! then we shall pay the more, that's all, I see plainly enough   At Drake and Aaron's one pays twenty-five francs for common days, and thirty or thirty-five francs a-day more for Sundays and fêtes, add five francs a-day more for extras, that will make forty, and there's an end of it."

"I am afraid if we offer them double that we shall not procure a carriage."

"Then they must put horses to mine, it is a little the worse for the journey, but that's no matter."

"There are no horses."

Albert looked at Franz like a man who hears a reply he does not understand.

"Do you understand that, my dear Franz? no horses!" he said; "but can't we have post-horses?"

"They have been all hired this fortnight, and there are none left, but those absolutely requisite for posting."

"What are we to say to this?" asked Franz.

"I say, that when a thing completely surpasses my comprehension, I am accustomed not to dwell on that thing but to pass to another.   Is supper ready, Maître Pastrini?"

"Yes, your excellency."

"Well, then, let us sup."

"But the carriage and horses?" said Franz.

"Be easy, my dear boy, they will come in due season; it is only a question of how much shall be charged for them."

Morcerf then, with that delightful philosophy which believes that nothing is impossible to a full purse and well-lined pocket-book, supped, went to bed, slept soundly, and dreamed he was racing all over Rome at Carnival time in a coach with six horses.

CHAPTER XXXIII

ROMAN BANDITS

THE next morning Franz woke first, and instantly rang the bell. The sound had not yet died away when Maître Pastrini himself entered.

"Well, excellency," said the landlord triumphantly, and without waiting for Franz to question him, "I feared yesterday when I would not promise you anything that you were too late,—there is not a single carriage to be had,—that is, for the three last days."

"Yes," returned Franz, "that is for the very three days it is most necessary."

"What is the matter?" said Albert, entering, "no carriage to be had?"

"Just so," returned Franz, "you have guessed it."

"Well! your Eternal City is a devilish nice city."

"That is to say, excellency," replied Pastrini, who was desirous to keep up the dignity of the capital of the Christian world in the eyes of his guests, "that there are no carriages to be had from Sunday to Tuesday evening, but from now till Sunday you can have fifty if you please."

"Ah! that is something," said Albert, "to-day is Thursday, and who knows what may arrive between this and Sunday?"

"Ten or twelve thousand travellers will arrive," replied Franz, "which will make it still more difficult."

"My friend," said Morcerf, "let us enjoy the present without gloomy forebodings for the future."

"At least we can have a window?"

"Where?"

"Looking on the Rue du Cours."

"Ah, a window!" exclaimed Maître Pastrini,—"utterly impossible; there was only one left on the fifth floor of the Doria Palace, and that has been let to a Russian prince for twenty sequins a-day."

The two young men looked at each other with an air of stupefaction.

"Well," said Franz to Albert, "do you know what is the best thing we can do? It is to pass the Carnival at Venice;

there we are sure of obtaining gondolas if we cannot have carriages."

"Ah! the devil! no," cried Albert; "I came to Rome to see the Carnival, and I will, though I see it on stilts."

"Bravo! an excellent idea; we will disguise ourselves as monster pulchinellos or shepherds of the Landes, and we shall have complete success."

"Do your excellencies still wish for a carriage from now to Sunday morning?"

"*Parbleu!*" said Albert, "do you think we are going to run about on foot in the streets of Rome like lawyers' clerks?"

"I hasten to comply with your excellencies' wishes; only, I tell you beforehand, the carriage will cost you six piastres a-day."

"And as I am not a millionnaire, like the gentleman in the next apartments," said Franz, "I warn you, that as I have been four times before at Rome, I know the prices of all the carriages; we will give you twelve piastres for to-day, to-morrow, and the day after, and then you will make a good profit."

"But, excellency——" said Pastrini, still striving to gain his point.

"Now go," returned Franz, "or I shall go myself and bargain with your *afflitatore*, who is mine also; he is an old friend of mine, who has plundered me pretty well already, and in the hope of making more out of me, he will take a less price than the one I offer you; you will lose the preference, and that will be your fault."

"Do not give yourself the trouble, excellency," returned Maître Pastrini, with that smile of the Italian speculator who avows himself defeated; "I will do all I can, and I hope you will be satisfied."

"Ah, now we understand each other."

"When do you wish the carriage to be here?"

"In an hour."

"In an hour it will be at the door."

An hour after the vehicle was at the door; it was a hack conveyance, which was elevated to the rank of a private carriage in honour of the occasion, but, in spite of its humble exterior, the young men would have thought themselves happy to have secured it for the three last days of the Carnival.

"Excellency," cried the cicerone, seeing Franz approach the window, "shall I bring the carriage nearer the palace?"

Accustomed as Franz was to the Italian phraseology, his first impulse was to look round him, but these words were addressed to him. Franz was the "excellency," the vehicle was the "carriage," and the Hôtel de Londres was the "palace."

Franz and Albert descended, the carriage approached the palace, their excellencies stretched their legs along the seats, the cicerone sprang into the seat behind.

"Where do your excellencies wish to go?" asked he.

"To Saint Peter's first, and then to the Colosseum," returned Albert.

But Albert did not know that it takes a day to see Saint Peter's, and a month to study it. The day was passed at Saint Peter's alone. Suddenly the daylight began to fade away, Franz took out his watch—it was half-past four. They returned to the hotel, at the door Franz ordered the coachman to be ready at eight. He wished to shew Albert the Colosseum by moonlight, as he had shewn him Saint Peter's by daylight. When we shew a friend a city one has already visited, we feel the same pride as when we point out a woman whose lover we have been. He was to leave the city by the Porte del Popolo, skirt the outer wall, and re-enter by the Porte San Giovanni; thus they would behold the Colosseum without being in some measure prepared by the sight of the Capitol, the Forum, the Arch of Septimus Severus, the Temple of Antoninus and Faustina, and the Via Sacra.

They sat down to dinner. Maître Pastrini had promised them a banquet; he gave them a tolerable repast. At the end of the dinner he entered in person. Franz concluded he came to hear his dinner praised, and began accordingly, but at the first words he interrupted him.

"Excellency," said he, "I am delighted to have your approbation, but it was not for that I came."

"Did you come to tell us you have procured a carriage?" asked Albert, lighting his cigar.

"No, and your excellencies will do well not to think of that any longer; at Rome things can or cannot be done: when you are told any thing cannot be done, there is an end of it."

"It is much more convenient at Paris,—when any thing cannot be done, you pay double, and it is done directly."

"That is what all the French say," returned Maître Pastrini, somewhat piqued; "for that reason I do not understand why they travel."

"But," said Albert, emitting a volume of smoke, and balancing his chair on its hind legs, "only madmen or blockheads, like we are, travel. Men in their senses do not quit their hotel in the Rue du Helder, their walk on the Boulevard de Gand, and the Café de Paris."

It is, of course, understood, that Albert resided in the aforesaid *rue*, appeared every day on the fashionable walk, and dined frequently at the only *café* where you can really dine, that is, if you are on good terms with its frequenters.

Maître Pastrini remained silent a short time; it was evident that he was musing over this answer, which did not seem very clear.

"But," said Franz, in his turn interrupting his host's meditations, "you had some motive for coming here, may I beg to know what it was?"

"Ah, yes; you have ordered your carriage at eight o'clock precisely?"

"I have."

"You intend visiting *Il Colosseo*."

"You mean the Colosseum?"

"It is the same thing. You have told your coachman to leave the city by the Porte del Popolo, to drive round the walls, and re-enter by the Porte San Giovanni?"

"These are my words exactly."

"Well, this route is impossible."

"Impossible!"

"Very dangerous, to say the least."

"Dangerous! and why?"

"On account of the famous Luigi Vampa."

"Pray who may this famous Luigi Vampa be?" inquired Albert; "he may be very famous at Rome, but I can assure you he is quite unknown at Paris."

"What! do you not know him?"

"I have not that honour."

"You have never heard his name?"

"Never."

"Well, then, he is a bandit, compared to whom the Decesaris and the Gasparones were mere children."

"Now then, Albert," cried Franz, "here is a bandit for you at last."

"I forewarn you, Maître Pastrini, that I shall not believe one word of what you are going to tell us; having told you this, begin."

"Once upon a time——"

"Well, go on."

Maître Pastrini turned round to Franz, who seemed to him the more reasonable of the two; we must do him justice,—he had had a great many Frenchmen in his house, but had never been able to comprehend them.

"Excellency," said he, gravely, addressing Franz, "if you look upon me as a liar, it is useless for me to say any thing; it was for your interest I——"

"Albert does not say you are a liar, Maître Pastrini," said Franz; "but that he will not believe what you are going to tell us,—but I will believe all you say; so proceed."

"But if your excellency doubt my veracity——"

"Maître Pastrini," returned Franz, "you are more susceptible than Cassandra, who was a prophetess, and yet no one believed her; whilst you, at least, are sure of the credence of half your auditory. Come, sit down, and tell us all about M. Vampa."

"I had told your excellency he is the most famous bandit we have had since the days of Mastrilla."

"Well, what has this bandit to do with the order I have given the coachman, to leave the city by the Porte del Popolo and to re-enter by the Porte San Giovanni?"

"This," replied Maître Pastrini, "that you will go out by one, but I very much doubt your returning by the other."

"Why?" asked Franz.

"Because after nightfall you are not safe fifty yards from the gates."

"On your honour, is that true?" cried Albert.

"M. le Comte," returned Maître Pastrini, hurt at Albert's repeated doubts of the truth of his assertions, "I do not say this to you, but to your companion, who knows Rome, and knows, too, that these things are not to be laughed at."

"My dear fellow," said Albert, turning to Franz, "here is an admirable adventure; we will fill our carriage with pistols, blunderbusses, and double-barrelled guns. Luigi Vampa comes to take us, and we take him—we bring him back to Rome, and present him to His Holiness the Pope, who asks how he can repay so great a service; then we merely ask for a carriage and a pair of horses, and we see the Carnival in the carriage, and doubtless the Roman people will crown us at the Capitol, and proclaim us, like Curtius and Horatius Cocles, the preservers of the country."

Whilst Albert proposed this scheme, Maître Pastrini's face assumed an expression impossible to describe.

"And pray," asked Franz, "where are these pistols, blunderbusses, and other deadly weapons with which you intend filling the carriage?"

"Not out of my armoury, for at Terracina I was plundered even of my hunting-knife."

"I shared the same fate at Aquependente."

"Do you know, Maître Pastrini," said Albert, lighting a second cigar at the first, "that this practice is very convenient for robbers, and that it seems to have been an arrangement between them."

Doubtless Maître Pastrini found this pleasantry compromising, for he only answered half the question, and then he spoke to Franz, as the only one likely to listen with attention.

"Your excellency knows that it is not customary to defend yourself when attacked by bandits."

"What!" cried Albert, whose courage revolted at the idea of being plundered tamely, "not make any resistance!"

"No, for it would be useless; what could you do against a dozen bandits who spring out of some pit, ruin, or aqueduct, and level their pieces at you?"

"Eh, *parbleu!*—they should kill me."

The innkeeper turned to Franz with an air that seemed to say, "Your friend is decidedly mad."

"My dear Albert," returned Franz, "your answer is sublime, and worthy the '*Let him die*' of Corneille, only when Horace made that answer, the safety of Rome was concerned; but as for us, it is only to gratify a whim, and it would be ridiculous to risk our lives for so foolish a motive."

Albert poured himself out a glass of *Lachryma Christi*, which he sipped at intervals, muttering some unintelligible words.

"Well, Maître Pastrini," said Franz, "now that my companion is quieted, and you have seen how peaceful my intentions are, tell me who is this Luigi Vampa. Is he a shepherd or a nobleman?—young or old?—tall or short? Describe him, in order that, if we meet him by chance, like Jean Sbogar or Lara, we may recognise him."

"You could not apply to any one better able to inform you on all these points, for I knew him when he was a child; and one day that I fell into his hands going from Ferentino to Alatri, he, fortunately for me, recollected me, and set me free, not only without ransom, but made me a present of a very splendid watch, and related his history to me."

"Let us see the watch," said Albert.

Maître Pastrini drew from his fob a magnificent Bréguet, bearing the name of its maker, of Parisian manufacture, and a count's coronet.

"Here it is," said he.

"*Peste!*" returned Albert, "I compliment you on it; I have its fellow;" he took his watch from his waistcoat pocket, "and it cost me 3,000 francs (120*l.*)."

"Let us hear the history," said Franz, motioning Maître Pastrini to seat himself.

"Your excellencies permit it?" asked the host.

"*Pardieu!*" cried Albert, "you are not a preacher, to remain standing."

The host sat down after having made each of them a respectful bow, which meant to say he was ready to tell them all they wished to know concerning Luigi Vampa.

"You tell me," said Franz, at the moment Maître Pastrini was about to open his mouth, "that you knew Luigi Vampa when he was a child—he is still a young man, then?"

"A young man! he is only two-and-twenty;—he will gain himself a reputation."

"What do you think of that, Albert?—at two-and-twenty to be thus famous?"

"Yes, and at his age, Alexander, Cæsar, and Napoleon, who have all made some noise in the world, were not so advanced."

"So," continued Franz, "the hero of this history is only two-and-twenty?"

"Scarcely so much."

"Is he tall or short?"

"Of the middle height—about the same stature as his excellency," returned the host, pointing to Albert.

"Thanks for the comparison," said Albert, with a bow.

"Go on, Maître Pastrini," continued Franz, smiling at his friend's susceptibility. "To what class of society does he belong?"

"He was a shepherd boy attached to the farm of the Comte de San-Felice, situated between Palestrina and the Lake of Gabri; he was born at Pampinara, and entered the count's service when he was five years old; his father was also a shepherd, who owned a small flock, and lived by the wool and the milk which he sold at Rome. When quite a child, the little Vampa was of a most extraordinary disposition. One day, when he was seven years old, he came to the curé of Palestrina, and prayed him to teach him to read; it was somewhat difficult, for he could not quit his flock; but the good curé went every day to say mass at a little hamlet too poor to pay a priest, and which, having no other name, was called Borgo; he told Luigi that he might meet him on his return, and that then he would give him a lesson, warning him that it would be short, and that he must profit as much as possible by it. The child accepted joyfully.

"Every day Luigi led his flock to graze on the road that leads from Palestrina to Borgo; every day at nine o'clock in the morning, the priest and the boy sat down on a bank by the wayside, and the little shepherd took his lesson out of the priest's breviary. At the end of three months he had learned to read. This was not enough—he must now learn to write.

"The priest had made, by a teacher of writing at Rome, three alphabets—one large, one middling, and one small, and pointed out to him, that by the help of a sharp instrument he could trace the letters on a slate, and thus learn to write.

"The same evening, when the flock was safe at the farm, the little Luigi hastened to the smith of Palestrina, took a large nail, forged it, sharpened it, and formed a sort of style. The next morning he had collected a quantity of slates and commenced. At the end of three months he had learned to write. The curé, astonished at his quickness and intelligence, made him a present of pens, paper, and a penknife. This was a fresh labour, but nothing compared to the first; at the end of a week he wrote as well with the pen as with the style.

"The curé related this anecdote to the Comte de San-Felice, who sent for the little shepherd, made him read and write before him, ordered his attendant to let him eat with the domestics, and to give him two piastres a-month. With this Luigi purchased books and pencils.

"He applied to every thing his imitative powers, and, like Giotto, when young, he drew on his slate sheep, houses, and trees. Then with his knife he began to carve all sorts of objects in wood; it was thus that Pinelli, the famous sculptor, had commenced.

"A girl of six or seven—that is, a little younger than Vampa—tended sheep on a farm near Palestrina; she was an orphan, born at Valmontone, and was named Teresa.

"The two children met, sat down near each other, let their flocks mingle together, played, laughed, and conversed together; in the evening they separated the flocks of the Comte de San-Felice from those of the Baron de Cervetri, and the children returned to their respective farms, promising to meet the next morning. The next day they kept their word, and thus grew up. Vampa was twelve, and Teresa eleven. And yet their natural disposition revealed itself.

"Besides his taste for the fine arts, which Luigi had carried as far as he could in his solitude, he was sad by fits, ardent by starts, angry by caprice, and always sarcastic. None of the lads of Pampinara, or of Palestrina, or of Valmontone, had been able to gain any influence over him, or even to become his companion. His disposition (always inclined to exact concessions rather than to make them) kept him aloof from all friendships. Teresa alone ruled, by a look, a word, a gesture, this impetuous character, which yielded beneath the hand of a woman, and which beneath the hand of a man might have broken, but would never have bent or yielded.

"Teresa was, on the contrary, lively and gay, but coquettish to excess. The two piastres that Luigi received every month from the Comte de San-Felice's steward, and the price of all the little carvings in wood he sold at Rome, were expended in earrings, necklaces, and gold hair-pins. So that, thanks to her friend's generosity, Teresa was the most beautiful and the best attired peasant near Rome.

"The two children grew up together, passing all their time with each other, and giving themselves up to the wild ideas of their different characters. Thus, in all their dreams, their wishes, and their conversations, Vampa saw himself the captain of a vessel, general of an army, or governor of a province. Teresa saw herself rich, superbly attired, and attended by a train of liveried domestics. Then, when they had thus passed the day in building castles in the air, they separated their flocks, and descended from the elevation of their dreams to the reality of their humble position.

"One day the young shepherd told the count's steward he had seen a wolf come out of the Sabine mountains, and prowl around his flock. The steward gave him a gun; this was what Vampa longed for. This gun had an excellent barrel, made at Breschia, and carrying a ball with the precision of an English rifle; but one day the count broke the stock, and had then cast the gun aside. This, however, was nothing to a sculptor like Vampa; he examined the ancient stock, calculated what change it would require to adapt the gun to his shoulder, and made a fresh stock so beautifully carved that it would have fetched fifteen or twenty piastres, had he chosen to sell it. But nothing could be farther from his thoughts. For a long time a gun had been the young man's greatest ambition. In every country where independence has taken the place of liberty, the first desire of a manly heart is to possess a weapon which at once renders him capable of defence or attack, and by rendering its owner terrible, makes him often redoubted.

"From this moment Vampa devoted all his leisure time in perfecting himself in the use of this precious weapon; he purchased powder and ball, and every thing served him for a mark—the trunk of some old and moss-grown olive-tree, that grew on the Sabine mountains; the fox, as he quitted his earth on some marauding excursion; the eagle that soared above their heads; and thus he soon became so expert, that Teresa overcame the terror she at first felt at the report, and amused herself by watching him direct the ball wherever he pleased, with as much accuracy as if placed by the hand.

"One evening a wolf emerged from a pine-wood near which they were usually stationed, but the wolf had scarcely advanced ten yards ere he was dead. Proud of this exploit, Vampa took the dead animal on his shoulders, and carried him to the farm.

"All these circumstances had gained Luigi considerable reputation. The man of superior abilities always finds admirers, go where he will. He was spoken of as the most adroit, the strongest, and the most courageous *contadino* for ten leagues round; and although Teresa was universally allowed to be the most beautiful girl of the Sabines, no one had ever spoken to her of love, because it was known that she was beloved by Vampa. And yet the two young people had never declared their affection; they had grown together like two trees whose roots are mingled, whose branches intertwine, and whose perfume rises together to the heavens. Only their wish to see each other had become a necessity, and they would have preferred death to a day's separation. Teresa was sixteen and Vampa eighteen.

"About this time a band of brigands, that had established itself in the Lepini mountains, began to be much spoken of. The brigands have never been really extirpated from the neighbourhood of Rome. Sometimes it wants a chief, but when a chief presents himself he rarely wants a band.

"The celebrated Cucumetto, pursued in the Abruzzo, driven out of the kingdom of Naples, where he had carried on a regular war, had crossed the Garigliano, like Manfred, and had come between Sonnino and Juperno, to take refuge on the banks of the Amasine. He it was who strove to reorganise a band, and who followed the footsteps of Decesaris and Gasperone, whom he hoped to surpass. Many young men of Palestrina, Frascati, and Pampinara disappeared. Their disappearance, at first, caused much inquietude; but it was soon known they had joined the band of Cucumetto. After some time Cucumetto became the object of universal attention; the most extraordinary traits of ferocious daring and brutality were related of him. One day he carried off a young girl, the daughter of a surveyor of Frosinone. The bandits' laws are positive, a young girl belongs first to him who carries her off, then the rest draw lots for her, and she is abandoned to their brutality until death relieves her sufferings. When their parents are sufficiently rich to pay a ransom, a messenger is sent to treat concerning it; the prisoner is hostage for the security of the messenger; should the ransom be refused, the prisoner is irrecoverably lost. The young girl's lover was in Cucumetto's troop; his name was Carlini. When she recognised her lover the poor girl extended her arms to him, and believed herself safe; but Carlini felt his heart sink, for he but too well knew the fate that awaited her. However, as he was a favourite with Cucumetto, as he had for three years faithfully served him, and as he had saved his life by shooting a dragoon who was about to cut him down, he hoped he would have pity on him. He took him apart, whilst the young girl, seated at the foot of a huge pine that stood in the centre of the forest, formed with her picturesque headdress a veil to hide her face from the lascivious gaze of the bandits. There he told him all, his affection for the prisoner, their promises of mutual fidelity, and how every night, since he had been near, they had met in a ruin.

"It so happened that night that Cucumetto had sent Carlini to a neighbouring village, so that he had been unable to go to the place of meeting. Cucumetto had been there, however, by accident, as he said, and had carried the maiden off.

"Carlini besought his chief to make an exception in Rita's favour, as her father was rich and could pay a large ransom. Cucumetto seemed to yield to his friend's entreaties, and bade him find a shepherd to send to Rita's father at Frosinone. Carlini flew joyfully to Rita, telling her she was saved, and bidding her write to her father to inform him what had occurred, and that her ransom was fixed at three hundred piastres. Twelve hours' delay was all that was granted, that is, until nine the next morning.

"The instant the letter was written, Carlini seized it, and hastened to the plain to find a messenger. He found a young shepherd watching his flock. The natural messengers of the bandits are the shepherds, who live between the city and the mountains, between civilised and savage life. The boy undertook the commission, promising to be at Frosinone in less than an hour. Carlini returned, anxious to see his mistress, and announce the joyful intelligence. He found the troop in the glade, supping off the provisions exacted as contributions from the peasants; but his eye vainly sought Rita and Cucumetto amongst them. He inquired where they were, and was answered by a burst of laughter. A cold perspiration burst from every pore, and his hair stood on end. He repeated his question. One of the bandits rose, and offered him a glass filled with wine of Orvietto, saying,—

"'To the health of the brave Cucumetto and the fair Rita.'

"At this moment Carlini heard the cry of a woman; he divined the truth, seized the glass, broke it across the face of him who presented it, and rushed towards the spot whence the cry came. After a hundred yards he turned the corner of a thicket, he found Rita senseless in the arms of Cucumetto. At the sight of Carlini, Cucumetto rose, a pistol in each hand. The two brigands looked at each other for a moment; the one with a smile of lasciviousness on his lips, the other with the pallor of death on his brow. It seemed that something terrible was about to pass between these two men, but by degrees Carlini's features relaxed, his hand which had grasped one of the pistols in his belt fell to his side. Rita lay between them. The moon lighted the group.

"'Well,' said Cucumetto, 'have you executed your commission?'

"'Yes, captain,' returned Carlini. 'At nine o'clock to-morrow Rita's father will be here with the money.'

"'It is well; in the meantime we will have a merry night; this young girl is charming, and does credit to your taste. Now, as I am not egotistical, we will return to our comrades and draw lots for her.'

"'You have determined then to abandon her to the common law?' said Carlini.

"'Why should an exception be made in her favour?'

"'I thought that my entreaties——'

"'What right have you any more than the rest to ask for an exception?'

"'It is true.'

"'But never mind,' continued Cucumetto, laughing, 'sooner or later your turn will come.'

"Carlini's teeth clenched convulsively.

"'Now then,' said Cucumetto, advancing towards the other bandits, 'are you coming?'

"'I follow you.'

"Cucumetto departed without losing sight of Carlini, for, doubtless, he feared lest he should strike him unawares; but nothing betrayed a hostile design on Carlini's part. He was standing, his arms folded, near Rita, who still was insensible. Cucumetto fancied for a moment the young man was about to take her in his arms and fly; but this mattered little to him now, Rita had been his, and as for the money, three hundred piastres distributed amongst the band was so small a sum that he cared little about it. He continued to follow the path to the glade; but, to his great surprise, Carlini arrived almost as soon as himself.

"'Let us draw lots!—let us draw lots!' cried all the brigands when they saw the chief.

"Their demand was fair, and the chief inclined his head in sign of acquiescence. The eyes of all shone fiercely as they made their demand, and the red light of the fire made them look like demons. The names of all, including Carlini, were placed in a hat, and the youngest of the band drew forth a ticket; the ticket bore the name of Diavolaccio. He was the man who had proposed to Carlini the health of their chief, and to whom Carlini replied by breaking the glass across his face. A large wound, extending from the temple to the mouth, was bleeding profusely. Diavolaccio, seeing himself thus favoured by fortune, burst into a loud laugh.

"'Captain,' said he, 'just now Carlini would not drink your health when I proposed it to him; propose mine to him, and let us see if he will be more condescending to you than to me.'

"Every one expected an explosion on Carlini's part; but,

to their great surprise, he took a glass in one hand and a flask in the other, and filling it,—

"'Your health, Diavolaccio,' said he calmly, and he drank it off without his hand trembling in the least. Then sitting down by the fire, 'My supper,' said he, 'my expedition has given me an appetite.'

"'Well done, Carlini,' cried the brigands. 'That is acting like a good fellow;' and they all formed a circle round the fire, whilst Diavolaccio disappeared.

"Carlini ate and drank as if nothing had happened. The bandits looked on with astonishment at this singular conduct until they heard footsteps. They turned round, and saw Diavolaccio bearing the young girl in his arms. Her head hung back, and her long hair swept the ground. As they entered the circle, the bandits could perceive, by the fire-light, the unearthly pallor of the young girl and of Diavolaccio. This apparition was so strange, and so solemn that every one rose, with the exception of Carlini, who remained seated, and ate and drank calmly. Diavolaccio advanced amidst the most profound silence, and laid Rita at the captain's feet. Then every one could understand the cause of the unearthly pallor of the young girl and the bandit. A knife was plunged up to the hilt in Rita's left breast. Every one looked at Carlini, the sheath at his belt was empty.

"'Ah, ah!' said the chief, 'I now understand why Carlini stayed behind.'

"All savage natures appreciate a desperate deed. No other of the bandits would, perhaps, have done the same, but they all understood what Carlini had done.

"'Now then,' cried Carlini, rising in his turn, and approaching the corpse, his hand on the butt of one of his pistols, 'does any one dispute the possession of this woman with me?'

"'No,' returned the chief, 'she is thine.'

"Carlini raised her in his arms and carried her out of the circle of light caused by the fire. Cucumetto placed his sentinels for the night, and the bandits wrapped themselves in their cloaks and lay down before the fire.

"At midnight the sentinel gave the alarm, and in an instant all were on the alert. It was Rita's father, who brought his daughter's ransom in person.

"'Here!' said he to Cucumetto,—'here are three hundred piastres, give me back my child.'

"But the chief, without taking the money, made a sign to him to follow him. The old man obeyed, they both advanced beneath the trees, through whose branches streamed the moonlight; Cucumetto stopped at last, and pointed to two persons grouped at the foot of a tree.

"'There!' said he, 'demand thy child of Carlini, he will tell thee what has become of her;' and he returned to his companions.

"The old man remained motionless, he felt that some great and unforeseen misfortune hung over his head. At length he advanced towards the group, which he could not comprehend. As he approached, Carlini raised his head, and the forms of two persons became visible to the old man's eyes. A female lay on the ground, her head resting on the knees of a man, who was seated by her; as he raised his head, the female's face became visible. The old man recognised his child, and Carlini recognised the old man.

"'I expected thee,' said the bandit to Rita's father.

"'Wretch!' returned the old man, 'what hast thou done?' and he gazed with terror on Rita, pale, and bloody; a knife buried in her bosom. A ray of moonlight poured through the trees, and lighted up the face of the dead.

"'Cucumetto had violated thy daughter,' said the bandit, 'I loved her, therefore I slew her; for she would have served as the sport of the whole band.'

"The old man spoke not, and grew pale as death.

"'Now,' continued Carlini, 'if I have done wrongly, avenge her;' and withdrawing the knife from the wound in Rita's bosom, he held it out to the old man with one hand, whilst with the other he tore open his vest.

"'Thou hast done well!' returned the old man, in a hoarse voice; 'embrace me, my son!'

"Carlini threw himself, sobbing like a child, into the arms of his mistress's father. These were the first tears the man of blood had ever wept.

"'Now,' said the old man, 'aid me to bury my child.'

"Carlini fetched two pickaxes; and the father and the lover began to dig at the foot of a huge oak, beneath which the young girl was to repose. When the grave was formed, the father embraced her first and then the lover; afterwards, one taking the head, the other the feet, they placed her in the grave. Then they knelt on each side of the grave, and said the prayers of the dead. Then, when they had finished, they cast the earth over the corpse, until the grave was filled. Then, extending his hand, the old man said,—

"'I thank you, my son; and now leave me alone.'

"'Yet——' replied Carlini.

"'Leave me, I command you!'

"Carlini obeyed, rejoined his comrades, folded himself in his cloak, and soon appeared as deep asleep as the rest. It had been resolved the night before to change their encampment. An hour before daybreak Cucumetto aroused his men, and gave the word to march. But Carlini would not quit the forest without knowing what had become of Rita's father. He went towards the place where he had left him. He found the old man suspended from one of the branches of the oak which shaded his daughter's grave. He then took an oath of bitter vengeance over the dead body of the one and the tomb of the other. But he was unable to complete this oath, for two days afterwards, in a rencontre with the Roman carbineers, Carlini was killed. There was some surprise, however, that, as he was with his face to the enemy, he should have received a ball between his shoulders. That astonishment ceased when one of the brigands remarked to his comrades that Cucumetto was stationed ten paces in Carlini's rear when he fell.

"On the morning of the departure from the forest of Frosinone he had followed Carlini in the darkness, had heard his oath of vengeance, and, like a wise man, anticipated it. They told ten other stories of this bandit chief, each more singular than the other. Thus, from Fondi to Perouse, every one trembles at the name of Cucumetto. These narratives were frequently the themes of conversation between Luigi and Teresa. The young girl trembled very much at all these tales; but Vampa reassured her with a smile, rapping the butt of his good fowling-piece, which threw its ball so well, and if that did not restore her courage, he pointed to a crow perched on some dead branch, took an aim, touched the trigger, and the bird fell dead at the foot of the tree.

"Time passed on, and the two young people had settled to be married when Vampa should be twenty and Teresa nineteen years of age. They were both orphans, and had only their employers' leave to ask, which had been already sought and obtained. One day when they were talking over their plans for the future, they heard two or three reports of fire-arms, and then, suddenly, a man came out of the wood, near which the two young persons used to graze their flocks, and hurried towards them. When he came within hearing he exclaimed,—

"'I am pursued; can you conceal me?'

"They knew full well that this fugitive must be a bandit; but there is an innate sympathy between the Roman brigand and the Roman peasant, and the latter is always ready to aid the former. Vampa, without saying a word, hastened to the stone that closed up the entrance to their grotto, drew it away, made a sign to the fugitive to take refuge there, in a retreat unknown to every one, closed the stone upon him, and then went and resumed his seat by Teresa. Instantly afterwards four carbineers, on horseback, appeared on the edge of the wood, three of them appeared to be looking for the fugitive, whilst the fourth dragged a brigand prisoner by the neck. The three carbineers scutinised on all sides, saw the young peasants, and, galloping up, interrogated them. They had seen no one.

"'That is very annoying,' said the brigadier, 'for the man we are looking for is the chief.'

"'Cucumetto?' cried Luigi and Teresa at the same moment.

"'Yes,' replied the brigadier.

"'And, as his head is valued at a thousand Roman crowns, there would have been five hundred for you if you had helped us to catch him.'

"The two young persons exchanged looks. The brigadier had a moment's hope. Five hundred Roman crowns are three thousand francs, and three thousand francs are a fortune for two poor orphans who are going to be married.

"'Yes, it is very annoying,' said Vampa, 'but we have not seen him.'

"Then the carbineers scoured the country in different directions, but in vain. Then after a time they disappeared. Vampa then removed the stone, and Cucumetto came out. He had seen through the crevices in the granite the two young peasants talking with the carbineers, and guessed the subject of their parley. He had read in the countenances of Luigi and Teresa their steadfast resolution not to surrender him, and he drew from his pocket a purse full of gold, which he offered to them. But Vampa raised his head proudly; as to Teresa, her eyes sparkled when she thought of all the fine gowns and gay jewellery she could buy with this purse of gold.

"Cucumetto was a cunning fiend, and had assumed the form of a brigand instead of a serpent, and this look of Teresa revealed to him that she was a worthy daughter of Eve, and he returned to the forest, pausing several times on his way, under the pretext of saluting his protectors. Several days elapsed, and they neither saw nor heard of Cucumetto. The time of the Carnival was at hand. The Comte de San-Felice announced a grand masqued ball, to which all that were distinguished in Rome were invited.

"Teresa had a great desire to see this ball. Luigi asked permission of his protector the steward, that she and he might be present amongst the servants of the house. This was granted.

"The ball was given by the count for the particular pleasure of his daughter Carmela, whom he adored. Carmela was precisely the age and figure of Teresa, and Teresa was as handsome as Carmela. On the evening of the ball Teresa was attired in her best, her most brilliant hair ornaments, and gayest glass beads—she was in the costume of the women of Frascati.

Luigi wore the very picturesque garb of the Roman peasant at holyday time. They both mixed, as they had leave to do, with the servants and peasants.

"The fête was magnificent, not only was the villa brilliantly illuminated, but thousands of coloured lanterns were suspended from the trees in the garden; and very soon the palace overflowed to the terraces, and the terraces to the garden-walks. At each cross-path was an orchestra, and tables spread with refreshments; the guests stopped, formed quadrilles, and danced in every part of the grounds they pleased.

"Carmela was attired like a woman of Sonnino. Her cap was embroidered with pearls, the pins in her hair were of gold and diamonds, her girdle was of Turkey silk, with large embroidered flowers, her bodice and skirt were of cachemere, her apron of Indian muslin, and the buttons of her corslet were of jewels.

"Two of her companions were dressed, the one as a woman of Nettuno, and the other as a woman of La Riccia. Four young men of the richest and noblest families of Rome accompanied them with that Italian freedom which has not its parallel in any other country of the world. They were attired as peasants of Albano, Velletri, Civita Castellana, and Sora. We need hardly add that these peasant costumes, like those of the females, were brilliant with gold and jewels.

"Carmela wished to make an uniform quadrille, but there was one lady wanting. Carmela looked all around her, but not one of the guests had a costume similar to her own, or those of her companions.

"The Comte de San-Felice pointed out to her in the group of peasants Teresa, who was hanging on Luigi's arm.

"'Will you allow me, father?' said Carmela.

"'Certainly,' replied the comte, "are we not in Carnival time?"

Carmela turned towards the young man who was talking with her, and saying a few words to him, pointed with her finger to Teresa. The young man followed with his eyes the lovely hand which made this indication, bowed in obedience, and then went to Teresa, and invited her to dance in a quadrille, directed by the count's daughter. Teresa felt something like a flame pass over her face, she looked at Luigi, who could not refuse his assent. Luigi slowly relinquished Teresa's arm, which he had held beneath his own, and Teresa, accompanied by her elegant cavalier, took her appointed place with much agitation in the aristocratic quadrille.

"Certainly, in the eyes of an artist, the exact and strict costume of Teresa had a very different character from that of Carmela and her companions; and Teresa was frivolous and coquettish, and thus the embroidery and muslins, the cache-mere waist-girdles, all dazzled her, and the reflection of sapphires and diamonds almost turned her giddy brain.

"Luigi felt a sensation hitherto unknown arising in his mind. It was like an acute pain which gnawed at his heart, and then passed thrillingly throughout his frame, chasing through his veins and pervading his entire body. He followed, with his eye, each movement of Teresa and her cavalier; when their hands touched, he felt as though he should swoon; every pulse beat with violence, and it seemed as though a bell were ringing in his ears. When they spoke, although Teresa listened timidly and with downcast eyes to the conversation of her cavalier, as Luigi could read in the ardent looks of the good-looking young man that his language was that of praise, it seemed as if the whole world was turning round with him, and all the voices of hell were whispering in his ears ideas of murder and assassination. Then, fearing that his paroxysm might get the better of him, he clutched with one hand the branch of a tree against which he was leaning, and with the other convulsively grasped the dagger with a carved handle, which was in his belt, and which, unwittingly, he drew from the scabbard from time to time.

"Luigi was jealous! He felt that, influenced by her ambition and coquettish disposition, Teresa might escape him.

"The young peasant girl, at first timid and scared, soon recovered herself. We have said that Teresa was handsome, but this is not all; Teresa was replete with all those wild graces which are so much more potent than our affected and studied elegances. She had almost all the honours of the quadrille, and if she were envious of the Comte de San-Felice's daughter, we will not undertake to say that Carmela was not jealous of her. And with overpowering compliments, her handsome cavalier led her back to the place whence he had taken her and where Luigi awaited her.

"Twice or thrice during the dance the young girl had glanced at Luigi, and each time she saw he was pale and his features agitated; once even the blade of his knife, half drawn from its sheath, had dazzled her eyes with sinister glare. Thus, it was almost trembling that she resumed her lover's arm.

"The quadrille had been most perfect, and it was evident there was a great demand for a second edition, Carmela alone objecting to it, but the Comte de San-Felice begged his daughter so earnestly that she acceded to it. One of the cavaliers then hastened to invite Teresa, without whom it was impossible the quadrille could be formed, but the young girl had disappeared.

"The truth was, that Luigi had not felt the strength to support another such trial, and, half by persuasion and half by force, he had removed Teresa towards another part of the garden. Teresa had yielded in spite of herself, but when she looked at the agitated countenance of the young man, she understood by his silence and trembling voice that something strange was passing within him. She herself was not exempt from internal emotion, and without having done anything wrong, yet fully comprehended that Luigi was right in reproaching her. Why, she did not know, but yet she did not the less feel that these reproaches were merited. However, to Teresa's great astonishment Luigi remained mute, and not a word escaped his lips the rest of the evening. When the chill of the night had driven away the guests from the gardens, and the gates of the villa were closed on them for the fête in-doors, he took Teresa quite away, and as he left her at her home, he said,—

"'Teresa, what were you thinking of as you danced opposite the young Comtesse de San-Felice?'

"'I thought,' replied the young girl, with all the frankness of her nature, 'that I would give half my life for a costume such as she wore.'

"'And what said your cavalier to you?'

"'He said it only depended on myself to have it, and I had only one word to say.'

"'He was right,' said Luigi. 'Do you desire it as ardently as you say?'

"'Yes.'

"'Well, then, you shall have it!'

"The young girl, much astonished, raised her head to look at him, but his face was so gloomy and terrible that her words froze to her lips.

"As Luigi spoke thus, he left her. Teresa followed him with her eyes into the darkness as long as she could, and when he had quite disappeared, she entered her apartment with a sigh.

"That night a great accident happened, no doubt from the imprudence of some servant who had neglected to extinguish the lights. The Villa de San-Felice took fire in the rooms adjoining the very apartment of the lovely Carmela. Awoke in the night by the light of the flames, she had sprung out of bed, wrapped herself in a dressing-gown, and attempted to escape by the door but the corridor by which she hoped to fly was already a prey to the flames. She had then returned to her room, calling for help as loudly as she could, when suddenly, her window, which was twenty feet from the ground, was opened, a young peasant jumped into the chamber, seized her in his arms, and with superhuman skill and strength, conveyed

her to the turf of the grass-plot, where she fainted. When she
recovered, her father was by her side. All the servants
surrounded her, offering her assistance. An entire wing of the
villa was burnt down; but what was that as Carmela was safe
and uninjured? Her preserver was every where sought for,
but her deliverer did not appear; he was inquired for every
where, but no one had seen him. Carmela was greatly
troubled that she had not recognised him.

"As the count was immensely rich, excepting the danger
Carmela had run, and, as appeared to him, the marvellous
manner in which she had escaped, which was rather a favour of
Providence than a real misfortune, the loss occasioned by the
conflagration was to him but a trifle.

"The next day, at the usual hour, the two young peasants
were on the borders of the forest. Luigi arrived first. He
came towards Teresa in high spirits, and seemed to have
completely forgotten the events of the previous evening.
The young girl was very pensive, but seeing Luigi so
cheerful, she, on her part, assumed a smiling air, which
was natural to her when no excitement of passion came to
disturb her.

"Luigi took her arm beneath his own, and led her to the
door of the grotto. Then he paused. The young girl,
perceiving that there was something extraordinary, looked at
him steadfastly.

"'Teresa,' said Luigi, 'yesterday evening you told me you
would give all the world to have a costume similar to that of
the count's daughter.'

"'Yes,' replied Teresa, with astonishment; 'but I was mad
to utter such a wish.'

"'And I replied, "Very well, you shall have it."'

"'Yes,' replied the young girl, whose astonishment
increased at every word uttered by Luigi, 'but of course your
reply was only to please me.'

"'I have promised no more than I have given you,
Teresa,' said Luigi, proudly. 'Go into the grotto, and dress
yourself.'

"At these words he drew away the stone, and shewed
Teresa the grotto, lighted up by two wax-lights which
burnt on each side of a splendid mirror; on a rustic table
made by Luigi, were spread out the pearl necklace and the
diamond pins, and on a chair at the side was laid the rest of
the costume.

"Teresa uttered a cry of joy, and, without inquiring whence
this attire came, or even thanking Luigi, darted into the grotto
transformed into a dressing-room.

"Luigi pushed the stone behind her, for he saw on the crest
of a small adjacent hill which prevented him from seeing

Palestrina from where he was, a traveller on horseback, who stopped a moment, as if uncertain of his road, and thus presented, in the blue sky, that perfect outline peculiar to the distances of southern climes.

"When he saw Luigi, he put his horse into a gallop, and advanced towards him. Luigi was not mistaken. The traveller who was going from Palestrina to Tivoli, had mistaken his way: the young man directed him; but as at a quarter of a mile distance the road again divided into three ways, and on reaching these the traveller might again stray from his route, he begged Luigi to be his guide. Luigi threw his cloak on the ground, placed his carbine on his shoulder, and freed from his heavy covering, preceded the traveller with the rapid step of a mountaineer, which a horse can scarcely keep up with. In ten minutes Luigi and the traveller reached the cross roads alluded to by the young shepherd. On arriving there, with an air as majestic as that of an emperor, he stretched his hand towards that one of the roads which the traveller was to follow.

"'That is your road, excellency, and now you cannot again mistake.'

"'And here is your recompense,' said the traveller, offering the young herdsman some pieces of small money.

"'Thank you,' said Luigi, drawing back his hand; 'I render a service, I do not sell it.'

"'Well,' replied the traveller, who seemed used to this difference between the servility of a man of the cities and the pride of the mountaineer, 'if you refuse pay, you will, perhaps, accept of a present.'

"'Ah, yes, that is another thing.'

"'Then,' said the traveller, 'take these two Venice sequins and give them to your bride, to make herself a pair of earrings.'

"'And then do you take this poniard,' said the young herdsman; 'you will not find one better carved between Albana and Civita-Castellana.'

"'I accept it,' answered the traveller, 'but then the obligation will be on my side, for this poniard is worth more than two sequins.'

"'For a dealer, perhaps; but for me, who engraved it myself, it is hardly worth a piastre.'

"'What is your name?' inquired the traveller.

"'Luigi Vampa,' replied the shepherd, with the same air as he would have replied, Alexander, king of Macedon.

"'And yours?'

"'I,' said the traveller, 'am called Sinbad the Sailor.'"
Franz d'Epinay started with surprise.

"Sinbad the Sailor?" he said.

"Yes," replied the narrator; "that was the name which the traveller gave to Vampa as his own."

"Well, and what have you to say against this name?" inquired Albert; "it is a very pretty name, and the adventures of the gentleman of that name amused me very much in my youth, I must confess."

Franz said no more. The name of Sinbad the Sailor, as may be well supposed, awakened in him a world of recollections, as had the name of the Count of Monte-Cristo on the previous evening.

"Proceed!" said he to the host.

"Vampa put the two sequins haughtily into his pocket, and slowly returned by the way he had gone. As he came within two or three hundred paces of the grotto, he thought he heard a cry. He listened to know whence this sound could proceed. A moment afterwards and he heard his own name pronounced distinctly. The cry proceeded from the grotto. He bounded like a chamois, cocking his carbine as he went, and in a moment reached the summit of a hill opposite to that on which he had perceived the traveller. Thence cries of help came more distinctly on his ear. He cast his eyes around him, and saw a man carrying off Teresa, as did the Centaur Nessus, Dejanira. This man, who was hastening towards the wood, was already three-quarters of the way on the road from the grotto to the forest. Vampa measured the distance, the man was at least two hundred paces in advance of him, and there was not a chance of overtaking him. The young shepherd stopped, as if his feet had been rooted to the ground; then he put the butt of his carbine to his shoulder, took aim at the ravisher, followed him for a second in his track, and then fired. The ravisher stopped suddenly, his knees bent under him, and he fell with Teresa in his arms. The young girl rose instantly, but the man lay on the earth struggling in the agonies of death. Vampa then rushed towards Teresa; for at ten paces from the dying man, her legs had failed her, and she had dropped on her knees, so that the young man feared the ball that had brought down his enemy had also wounded his betrothed. Fortunately, she was un-scathed, and it was fright alone that had overcome Teresa. When Luigi had assured himself that she was safe and un-harmed, he turned towards the wounded man. He had just expired with clenched hands, his mouth in a spasm of agony, and his hair on end in the sweat of death. His eyes remained open and menacing. Vampa approached the carcass and recognised Cucumetto. From the day on which the bandit had been saved by the two young peasants he had been enamoured of Teresa, and had sworn she should be his. From that time he had watched them, and profiting by the

moment when her lover had left her alone, whilst he guided
the traveller on his way, had carried her off, and believed he
at length had her in his power, when the ball, directed by the
unerring skill of the young herdsman, had pierced his heart.
Vampa gazed on him for a moment without betraying the
slightest emotion; whilst, on the contrary, Teresa, shuddering
in every limb, dared not approach the slain ruffian but by
degrees, and threw a hesitating glance at the dead body over
the shoulder of her lover. Suddenly Vampa turned towards
his mistress:—

"'Ah! ah!' said he; 'good, good, you are attired, it is
now my turn to dress myself.'

"Teresa was clothed from head to foot in the garb of the
Comte de San-Felice's daughter. Vampa took Cucumetto's
body in his arms and conveyed it to the grotto, whilst in her
turn Teresa remained outside. If a second traveller had
passed, he would have seen a strange thing; a shepherdess
watching her flock clad in a cachemire gown, with earrings
and necklace of pearls, diamond pins and buttons of sapphires,
emeralds and rubies. He would, no doubt, have believed
that he had returned to the times of Florian, and would have
declared, on reaching Paris, that he had met a shepherdess of
the Alps seated at the foot of the Sabine Hill. At the end of a
quarter of an hour Vampa quitted the grotto: his costume
was no less elegant than that of Teresa. He wore a vest of
garnet-coloured velvet, with buttons of cut gold; a silk waistcoat covered with embroidery; a Roman scarf tied round his
neck; a cartouche-box worked with gold, and red and green
silk; sky-blue velvet breeches, fastened above the knee with
diamond buckles; garters of deer-skin, worked with a thousand
arabesques, and a hat whereon hung ribands of all colours;
two watches hung from his girdle, and a splendid poniard was
in his belt. Teresa uttered a cry of admiration. Vampa in
this attire resembled a painting by Leopold Robert or Schnetz.
He had assumed the entire costume of Cucumetto. The young
man saw the effect produced on his betrothed, and a smile of
pride passed over his lips.

"'Now,' he said to Teresa, 'are you ready to share my
fortune, whatever it may be?'

"'Oh, yes!' exclaimed the young girl, enthusiastically.

"'And follow me wherever I go?'

"'To the world's end.'

"'Then take my arm and let us on, we have no time to lose.'

"The young girl did so without questioning her lover as to
where he was conducting her, for he appeared to her at this
moment as handsome, proud, and powerful, as a god. They
went towards the forest, and soon entered it. We need
scarcely say that all the paths of the mountain were known to

Vampa; he, therefore, went forward without a moment's hesitation, although there was no beaten track; but he knew his path by looking at the trees and bushes; and thus they kept on advancing for nearly an hour and a half. At the end of this time they had reached the thickest of the forest. A torrent, whose bed was dry, led into a deep gorge. Vampa took this wild road which enclosed between two ridges, and shadowed by the tufted umbrage of the pines, seemed, but for the difficulties of its descent, that path to Avernus of which Virgil speaks. Teresa had become alarmed at the wild and deserted look of the plain around her, and pressed closely against her guide, not uttering a syllable; but as she saw him advance with even step and composed countenance, she endeavoured to repress her emotion. Suddenly, about ten paces from them, a man advanced from behind a tree and aimed at Vampa.

" 'Not another step,' he said, 'or you are a dead man.'

" 'What then?' said Vampa, raising his hand with a gesture of disdain, whilst Teresa, no longer able to restrain her alarm, clung closely to him: 'do wolves rend each other?'

" 'Who are you?' inquired the sentinel.

" 'I am Luigi Vampa, shepherd of the farm of San-Felice.'

" 'What do you want?'

" 'I would speak with your companions who are in the recess at Rocca Bianca.'

" 'Follow me, then,' said the sentinel; 'or, as you know your way, go first.'

"Vampa smiled disdainfully at this precaution of the bandit, went before Teresa, and continued to advance with the same firm and easy step as before. At the end of ten minutes the bandit made them a sign to stop. The two young persons obeyed. Then the bandit thrice imitated the cry of a crow; a croak answered this signal.

" 'Good!' said the sentry; 'you may now advance.'

"Luigi and Teresa again set forward: as they advanced, Teresa clung tremblingly to her lover, as she saw through the trees arms appear and the barrels of carbines shine. The retreat of Rocca Bianca was at the top of a small mountain, which no doubt in former days had been a volcano,—an extinct volcano before the days when Remus and Romulus had deserted Alba to come and found the city of Rome. Teresa and Luigi reached the summit, and all at once found themselves in the presence of twenty bandits.

" 'Here is a young man who seeks and wishes to speak to you,' said the sentinel.

" 'What has he to say?' inquired the man who was in command in the chief's absence.

" 'I wish to say, that I am tired of a shepherd's life,' was Vampa's reply.

" 'Ah, I understand,' said the lieutenant; 'and you seek admittance into our ranks?'

" 'Welcome!' cried several bandits of Ferrusino, Pampinara, and Anagni, who had recognised Luigi Vampa.

" 'Yes, but I come to ask something more than to be your companion.'

" 'And what may that be?' inquired the bandits, with astonishment.

" 'I come to ask to be your captain,' said the young man.

"The bandits shouted with laughter.

" 'And what have you done to aspire to this honour?' demanded the lieutenant.

" 'I have killed your chief, Cucumetto, whose dress I now wear; and I set fire to the Villa San-Felice to procure a wedding-dress for my betrothed.'

"An hour afterwards Luigi Vampa was chosen captain *vice* Cucumetto deceased."

"Well, my dear Albert," said Franz, turning towards his friend, "what think you of citizen Luigi Vampa?"

"I say he is a myth," replied Albert, "and never had an existence."

"And what may a myth be?" inquired Pastrini.

"The explanation would be too long, my dear landlord," replied Franz.

"And you say that Maître Vampa exercises his profession at this moment in the environs of Rome?"

"And with a boldness of which no bandit before him ever gave an example."

"Then the police have vainly tried to lay hands on him?"

"Why, you see, he has a good understanding with the shepherds in the plains, the fishermen of the Tiber, and the smugglers of the coast. They seek for him in the mountains, and he is on the waters; they follow him on the waters, and he is on the open sea; then they pursue him, and he has suddenly taken refuge in the isle of Giglio, of Guanouti, or Monte-Cristo; and when they hunt for him there he reappears suddenly at Albano, Tivoli, or La Riccia."

"And how does he behave towards travellers?"

"Alas! his plan is very simple. It depends on the distance he may be from the city, whether he gives eight hours, twelve hours, or a day wherein to pay their ransom; and when that time has elapsed he allows another hour's grace. At the sixtieth minute of this hour, if the money is not forthcoming, he blows out the prisoner's brains with a pistol-shot, or plants his dagger in his heart, and that settles the account."

"Well, Albert," inquired Franz of his companion, "are you still disposed to go to the Colosseum by the outer Boulevards?"

"Perfectly," said Albert, "if the way be picturesque."

The clock struck nine as the door opened and a coachman appeared.

"Excellencies," said he, "the coach is ready."

"Well, then," said Franz, "let us to the Colosseum."

"By the Porto del Popolo or by the streets, your excellencies?"

"By the streets, *morbleu!* by the streets," cried Franz.

"Ah, my dear fellow!" said Albert, rising and lighting his third cigar; "really, I thought you had more courage."

So saying, the two young men went down the staircase and got into the carriage.

CHAPTER XXXIV

THE COLOSSEUM

FRANZ had so managed his route, that during the ride to the Colosseum they passed not a single ancient ruin, so that no gradual preparation was made on the mind for the colossal proportions of the gigantic building they came to admire. The road selected was a continuation of the Via Sistina; then, by cutting off the right angle of the street in which stands Sainte Marie Majeure, and proceeding by the Via Urbana and San Pietro in Vincoli, the travellers would find themselves directly opposite the Colosseum. This itinerary possessed another great advantage, that of leaving Franz at full liberty to indulge his deep reverie upon the subject of the story recounted by Maître Pastrini, in which his mysterious host of the isle of Monte-Cristo was so strangely mixed up. Seated with folded arms in a corner of the carriage, he continued to ponder over the singular history he had so lately listened to, and to ask himself an interminable number of questions touching its various circumstances, without, however, arriving at a satisfactory reply to any of them. One fact more than the rest brought his friend "Sinbad the Sailor" back to his recollection, and that was the mysterious sort of intimacy that seemed to exist between the brigands and sailors; and Pastrini's account of Vampa's having found refuge on board the vessels of smugglers and fishermen, reminded Franz of the two Corsican bandits he had found supping so amicably with the crew of the little yacht which had even deviated from its course and touched at Porto-Vecchio for the sole purpose of landing them. The very name assumed by his host of Monte-Cristo, and again repeated by the landlord of the Hôtel de Londres, abundantly proved to him, that his island friend was playing his philanthropic part equally on the shores of Piombino, Civita Vecchia, Ostia, and Gaëta, as on those of Corsica, Tuscany, and Spain; and further, Franz bethought him of having heard his singular entertainer speak both of Tunis and Palermo, proving thereby how largely his circle of acquaintances extended.

But however the mind of the young man might be absorbed in these reflections, they were at once dispersed at the sight of the dark frowning ruins of the stupendous Colosseum, through the various openings of which the pale moonlight played and flickered like the unearthly gleam from the eyes of the wandering dead. The carriage stopped near the Meta Sudans, the door was opened, and the young men eagerly alighting, found themselves opposite a cicerone, who appeared to have sprung up from the ground, so unexpected was his appearance.

The usual guide from the hotel having followed them, they had paid two conductors; nor is it possible, at Rome, to avoid this abundant supply of guides; besides the ordinary cicerone who seizes upon you directly you set foot in your hotel, and never quits you while you remain in the city, there is also a special cicerone belonging to each monument,—nay, almost to each part of a monument. It may, therefore, be easily imagined there is no scarcity of guides at the Colosseum, that wonder of all ages, which Martial thus eulogises:—"Let Memphis cease to boast the barbarous miracles of her pyramids, nor the wonders of Babylon be talked of among us; all must bow to the superiority of the gigantic labour of the Cæsars, and the many voices of Fame spread far and wide the surpassing merits of this incomparable monument."

As for Albert and Franz, they essayed not to escape from their ciceronian tyrants. And, indeed, it would have been so much the more difficult to break their bondage, as the guides alone are permitted to visit these monuments with torches in their hands; thus, then, the young men made no attempt at resistance, but blindly and confidingly surrendered themselves into the care and custody of their conductors. Albert had already made seven or eight similar excursions to the Colosseum, while his less favoured companion trod for the first time in his life the classic ground forming the monument of Flavius Vespasian, and to his credit be it spoken, his mind, even amid the glib loquacity of the guides, was duly and deeply touched with awe and enthusiastic admiration of all he saw; and certainly no adequate notion of these stupendous ruins can be formed save by such as have visited them, and more especially by moonlight; at which time the vast proportions of the building appear twice as large as when viewed by the mysterious beams of a southern moonlit sky, whose rays are sufficiently clear and vivid to gild the horizon with a glow equal to the soft twilight of an Eastern clime. Scarcely, therefore, had the reflective Franz walked a hundred steps beneath the interior porticoes of the ruin, than, abandoning Albert to the guides who would by no means yield their prescriptive right of carrying their victims through the routine regularly laid down, and as regularly followed by them, but dragged the unconscious visitor to the various objects with a pertinacity that admitted of no appeal; beginning, as a matter of course, with the "Fosse des Lions," and finishing with the "Podium des Cesars," to escape a jargon and mechanical survey of the wonders by which he was surrounded, Franz ascended a half-dilapidated staircase, and leaving them to follow their monotonous round, seated himself at the foot of a column, and immediately opposite a large chasm, which permitted him to enjoy a full and undisturbed view of the gigantic dimensions of this majestic ruin.

Franz had remained for nearly a quarter of an hour perfectly hidden by the shadow of the vast column at whose base he had found a resting-place, and from whence his eyes followed the motions of Albert and his guides, who, holding torches in their hands had emerged from a vomitarium placed at the opposite extremity of the Colosseum, and then again disappeared down the steps conducting to the seats reserved for the Vestal virgins, resembling as they glided along, some restless shades following the flickering glare of so many ignes-fatui, when all at once his ear caught a sound resembling that of a stone rolling down the staircase opposite the one by which he had himself ascended; there was nothing remarkable in the circumstance of a morsel of granite giving way and falling heavily below; but it seemed to him that the substance that fell gave way beneath the pressure of a foot; and also that some one, who endeavoured as much as possible to prevent his footsteps from being heard, was approaching the spot where he sat. Conjecture soon became certainty, for the figure of a man was distinctly visible to Franz, gradually emerging from the staircase opposite, upon which the moon was at that moment pouring a full tide of silvery brightness.

The stranger thus presenting himself was probably a person, who, like Franz, preferred the enjoyment of solitude and his own thoughts to the frivolous gabble of the guides; and his appearance had nothing extraordinary in it; but the hesitation with which he proceeded onwards, stopping and listening with anxious attention at every step he took, convinced Franz he expected the arrival of some person. By a sort of instinctive impulse, Franz withdrew as much as possible behind his pillar. About ten feet from the spot where himself and the stranger were placed, the roof had given way, leaving a large round aperture, through which might be seen the blue vault of heaven thickly studded with stars. Around this opening which had, possibly for ages, permitted a free entrance to the brilliant moonbeams that now illumined the vast pile, grew a quantity of creeping plants, whose delicate green branches stood out in bold relief against the clear azure of the firmament, while large masses of thick, strong fibrous shoots forced their way through the chasm and hung floating to and fro like so many wavering strings.

The person whose mysterious arrival had attracted the attention of Franz stood in a kind of half light, that rendered it impossible to distinguish his features, although his dress was easily made out; he wore a large brown mantle, one fold of which thrown over his left shoulder served likewise to mask the lower part of his countenance, while the upper part was completely hidden by his broad-brimmed hat; the lower part of his dress was more distinctly visible by the bright rays of the moon, which, entering through the broken ceiling, shed their refulgent beams on feet cased in elegantly made boots of polished leather, over which descended fashionably cut trousers of black cloth.

From the imperfect means Franz had of judging, he could only come to one conclusion,—that the individual whom he was thus watching certainly belonged to no inferior station of life. Some few minutes had elapsed and the stranger began to show manifest signs of impatience, when a slight noise was heard outside the aperture in the roof, and almost immediately a dark shadow seemed to obstruct the flood of light that had entered from it, and the figure of a man was clearly seen gazing with eager scrutiny on the immense space beneath him; then as his eye caught sight of the individual in the mantle, he grasped a floating mass of thickly matted boughs, and glided down by their help to within three or four feet of the ground, and then leaped lightly on his feet; the man who had performed this daring act with so much indifference wore the costume of Transtevere.

"I beg your excellency's pardon for keeping you waiting," said the man, in the Roman dialect, "but I don't think I'm many minutes after my time, ten o'clock has just struck by the clock of Saint-Jean-de-Latran."

"Say not a word about being late," replied the stranger, in purest Tuscany; "'tis I who am too soon; but even if you had caused me to wait a little while, I should have felt quite sure that the delay was not occasioned by any fault of yours."

"Your excellency is perfectly right in so thinking," said the man; "I came here direct from the Château Saint-Ange, and I had an immense deal of trouble before I could get to speak to Beppo."

"And who is Beppo?"

"Oh! Beppo is employed in the prison, and I give him so much a-year to let me know what is going on within his holiness's château."

"Indeed! you are a provident person, I see."

"Why, you see no one knows what may happen, perhaps some of these days I may be entrapped like poor Peppino, and may be very glad to have some little nibbling mouse to gnaw the meshes of my net, and so help me out of prison."

"Briefly, what news did you glean?"

"That two executions of considerable interest will take place the day after to-morrow at two o'clock, as is customary at Rome at the commencement of all great festivals; one of the culprits will be *mazzolato*, he is an atrocious villain, who murdered the priest who brought him up, and deserves not the smallest pity; the other sufferer is sentenced to be *decapitato*, and he, your excellency, is poor Peppino."

"The fact is that you have inspired not only the pontificial government, but also the neighbouring states, with such extreme fear, that they are glad of an opportunity of making an example."

"But Peppino did not even belong to my band, he was merely a poor shepherd, whose only crime consisted in furnishing us with provisions."

"Which makes him your accomplice to all intents and purposes; but mark the distinction with which he is treated, instead of being knocked on the head as you would be if once they caught hold of you, he is simply sentenced to be guillotined, by which means, too, the amusements of the day are diversified, and there is a spectacle to please every spectator."

"Without reckoning the wholly unexpected one I am preparing to surprise them with."

"My good friend," said the man in the cloak, "excuse me for saying that you seem to me precisely in the mood to commit some wild or extravagant act."

"Perhaps I am; but one thing I have resolved on, and that is, to stop at nothing to restore a poor devil to liberty, who has got into this scrape solely from having served me; I should hate and despise myself as a coward, did I desert the brave fellow in his present extremity."

"And what do you mean to do?"

"To surround the scaffold with twenty of my best men, who, at a signal from me, will rush forward directly Peppino is brought for execution, and by the assistance of their stilettos drive back the guard and carry off the prisoner."

"That seems to me as hazardous as uncertain, and convinces me my scheme is far better than yours."

"And what is your excellency's project?"

"Just this! I will so advantageously bestow 2000 piastres, that the person receiving them shall obtain a respite till next year for Peppino; and during that year, another skilfully placed 1000 piastres shall afford him the means of escaping from his prison."

"And do you feel sure of succeeding?"

"*Pardieu!*" exclaimed the man in the cloak, suddenly expressing himself in French.

"What did your excellency say?" inquired the other.

"I said, my good fellow, that I would do more single-handed by the means of gold than you and all your troop could effect with stilettos, pistols, carbines, and blunderbusses included; leave me then to act, and have no fears for the result."

"At least there can be no harm in myself and party being in readiness, in case your excellency should fail."

"None, whatever; take what precautions you please if it is any satisfaction to you to do so; but rely upon my obtaining the reprieve I seek."

"Remember the execution is fixed for the day after tomorrow, and that you have but one day to work in."

"And what then? Is not a day divided into twenty-four hours, each hour into sixty minutes, and every minute subdivided into sixty seconds? Now in 86,400 seconds very many things can be done."

"And how shall I know whether your excellency has succeeded or not?"

"Oh! that is very easily arranged, I have engaged the three lower windows at the Café Rospoli; should I have obtained the requisite pardon for Peppino, the two outside windows will be hung with yellow damasks, and the centre with white, having a large cross in red marked on it."

"And whom will you employ to carry the reprieve to the officer directing the execution?"

"Send one of your men disguised as a penitent friar, and I will give it to him; his dress will procure him the means of approaching the scaffold itself, and will deliver the official order to the officer, who in his turn will hand it to the executioner; in the meantime, it will be as well to acquaint Peppino with what we have determined on, if it be only to prevent him dying of fear or losing his senses, because in either case a very useless expense will have been incurred."

"Your excellency," said the man, "you are fully persuaded of my entire devotion to you, are you not?"

"Nay, I flatter myself that there can be no doubt of it," replied the cavalier in the cloak.

"Well, then, only fulfil your promise of rescuing Peppino, and henceforward you shall receive not only devotedness, but the most absolute obedience from myself and those under me that one human being can render to another."

"Have a care how far you pledge yourself, my good friend, for I may remind you of your promises at some, perhaps not very distant, period, when I, in my turn, may require your aid and influence."

"Let that day come sooner or later, your excellency will find me what I have found you in this my heavy trouble; and if from the other end of the world you but write me word to do such or such a thing, conclude it done, for done shall it be on the word and faith of——"

"Hush!" interrupted the stranger; "I hear a noise."

" 'Tis some travellers, who are visiting the Colosseum by torchlight."

" 'Twere better we should not be seen together; those guides are nothing but spies, and might possibly recognise you; and however I may be honoured by your friendship, my worthy friend, if once the extent of our intimacy were known, I am sadly afraid both my reputation and credit would suffer thereby."

"Well, then, if you obtain the reprieve?"

"The middle window at the Café Rospoli will be hung with white damask bearing on it a red cross."

"And if you fail?"

"Then, all three windows will have yellow draperies."

"And then?"

"And then, my good fellow, use your daggers in any way you please; and I further promise you to be there as a spectator of your prowess."

"All is then understood between us. Adieu, your excellency, depend upon me as firmly as I do upon you."

Saying these words, the Transtevere disappeared down the staircase, while his companion, muffling his features more closely than before in the folds of his mantle, passed almost close to Franz, and descended to the arena by an outward flight of steps. The next minute Franz heard himself called by Albert, who made the lofty building re-echo with the sound of his friend's name. Franz, however, did not obey the summons till he had satisfied himself the two individuals, whose conversation he had thus surprised, were at a sufficient distance to prevent his encountering them in his descent, not wishing that they should suspect having had a witness to their discourse, who, if unable to recognise their faces, had at least heard every word that passed. In ten minutes from the parting of the strangers, Franz was on the road to the Hôtel d'Espagne, listening with mortifying indifference to the learned dissertation delivered by Albert, after the manner of Pliny and Calpurnius, touching the iron-pointed nets used to prevent the ferocious beasts from springing on the spectators. Franz let him proceed without interruption; in fact, he heard not what he said; he longed to be alone, and able undisturbedly to ponder over all that had occurred.

One of the two men whose mysterious rendezvous in the Colosseum he had so unintentionally witnessed was an entire stranger to him, but not so the other; and though Franz had been unable to distinguish his features, from his being either wrapped in his mantle or obscured by the shadow, the tones of his voice had made too powerful an impression on him the first time he heard them for him ever again to forget them, hear them when or where he might. It was more especially when speaking in a manner half jesting, half bitter, that Franz's ear recalled most vividly the deep sonorous, yet well-pitched voice, that had spoken to him in the grotto of Monte-Cristo, and which he heard for the second time amid the darkness and ruined grandeur of the Colosseum! And the more he thought, the more entire was his conviction, that the individual in the mantle was no other than his former host and entertainer "Sinbad the Sailor."

Under any other circumstances Franz would have found it impossible to resist his extreme curiosity to know more of so singular a personage, and with that intent have sought to renew their short acquaintance; but in the present instance, the confidential nature of the conversation he had overheard made him, with propriety, judge that his appearance at such a time would be anything but agreeable. As we have seen, therefore, he permitted his former host to retire without attempting a recognition; but fully promising himself a rich indemnity for his present forbearance should chance afford him another opportunity.

In vain did Franz endeavour to forget the many perplexing thoughts which assailed him; in vain did he court the refreshment of sleep. Slumber refused to visit his eyelids, and his night was passed in feverish contemplation of the chain of circumstances tending to prove the individuality of the mysterious visitant to the Colosseum and the inhabitant of the grotto of Monte-Cristo; and the more he thought, the firmer grew his opinion on the subject. Worn out at length, he fell asleep at daybreak, and did not awake till late. Like a geniune Frenchman, Albert had employed his time in arranging for the evening's diversion, he had sent to engage a box at the Teatro Argentino; and Franz having a number of letters to write, relinquished the carriage to Albert for the whole of the day.

At five o'clock Albert returned delighted with his day's work; he had been occupied in leaving his letters of introduction, and had received in return more invitations to balls and soirées than it would be possible for him to fulfil; besides this, he had seen (as he called it) all the remarkable sights at Rome. Yes, in a single day he had accomplished what his more reflective companion would have taken weeks to effect. Neither had he neglected to ascertain the name of the piece to be played that night at the Teatro Argentino, and also what performers appeared in it.

The Opera of Parisina was announced for representation, and the principal actors were Coselli, Moriani, and La Spech. The young men therefore had reason to consider themselves fortunate in having the opportunity of hearing one of the best works by the composer of "Lucia di Lammermoor," supported by three of the most renowned vocalists of Italy. Albert had never been able to endure the Italian theatres, with their orchestras from which it is impossible to see, and the absence of balconies or open boxes; all these defects pressed hard on a man who had had his stall at the Opera buffa, and his share in the omnibus box at the Italian Opera. Still, in despite of this, Albert displayed his most dazzling and effective costume each time he visited the theatres; but alas! his *recherché* toilette was wholly thrown away; and one of the most worthy representatives of Parisian fashion had to carry with him the mortifying reflection of having nearly overrun Italy without meeting with a single adventure.

Sometimes Albert would effect to make a joke of his want of success, but internally he was deeply wounded, and his self-love immensely piqued to think that Albert de Morcerf, the most admired and most sought after of any young person of his day, should thus be passed over, and merely have his labour for his pains. And the thing was so much the more annoying, as, according to the characteristic modesty of a Frenchman, Albert had quitted Paris with the full conviction that he had only to shew himself in Italy to carry all before him, and that upon his return he should astonish the Parisian world with the recital of his numerous love-affairs.

Alas! poor Albert, none of those interesting adventures fell in his way; the lovely Genoese, Florentine, and Neapolitan females were all faithful, if not to their husbands, at least to their lovers, and thought not of changing even for the splendid appearance of Albert de Morcerf; and all he gained was the painful conviction, that the ladies of Italy have this advantage over those of France, that they are faithful even in their infidelity. Yet he could not restrain a hope, that in Italy, as elsewhere, there might be an exception to the general rule. Albert, besides being an elegant, well-looking young man, was also possessed of considerable talent and ability; moreover, he was a viscount, a recently created one certainly; but in the present day it is not necessary to go as far back as Noah in tracing a descent, and a genealogical tree is equally estimated, whether dated from 1399 or merely 1815; but to crown all these advantages, Albert de Morcerf commanded an income of 50,000 livres (2,000*l.*), a more than sufficient sum to render him a personage of considerable importance in Paris. It was, therefore, no small mortification to him to have visited most of the principal cities in Italy, without having excited the most trifling observation. Albert, however, hoped to indemnify himself for all these slights and indifferences during the Carnival, knowing full well that among the different states and kingdoms in which this festivity is celebrated, Rome is the spot where even the wisest and gravest throw off the usual rigidity of their lives, and deign to mingle in the follies of this time of liberty and relaxation.

The carnival was to commence on the morrow; therefore Albert had not an instant to lose in setting forth the programme of his hopes, expectations, and claims to notice. With this design, he had engaged a box in the most conspicuous part of the theatre, and exerted himself to set off his personal attractions by the aid of the most *recherché* and elaborate toilette. The box taken by Albert was in the first circle; although each of the three tiers of boxes is deemed equally aristocratic, and is, for this reason, generally styled the "nobility's boxes," and although the box engaged for the two friends was sufficiently capacious to contain at least a dozen persons, it had cost less than would be paid at some of the French theatres for one admitting merely four occupants.

Another motive had influenced Albert's selection of his seat:—who knew but that thus advantageously placed, he could not fail to attract the notice of some fair Roman; and an introduction might ensue that would procure him the offer of a seat in a carriage, or a place in a princely balcony, from which he might behold the gaieties of the Carnival?

These united considerations made Albert more lively and anxious to please than he had hitherto been. Totally disregarding the business of the stage, he leaned from his box and began attentively scrutinising the beauty of each pretty woman, aided by a powerful lorgnette; but alas! this attempt to attract similar notice wholly failed; not even curiosity had been excited; and it was but too apparent, that the lovely creatures, into whose good graces he was desirous of stealing, were all so much engrossed with themselves, their lovers, or their own thoughts, that they had not so much as remarked him or the pointing of his glass.

The truth was, that the anticipated pleasures of the Carnival, with the "holy week," that was to succeed it, so filled every fair breast, as to prevent the least attention being bestowed even on the business of the stage; the actors made their entries and exits unobserved or unthought of; at certain conventional moments, the spectators would suddenly cease their conversation, or rouse themselves from their musings to listen to some brilliant effort of Moriani's, a well-executed recitative by Coselli, or to join in loud applause at the wonderful powers of La Spech; but that momentary excitement over, they quickly relapsed into their former state of pre-occupation or interesting conversation. Towards the close of the first act, the door of a box which had been hitherto vacant was opened; a lady entered to whom Franz had been introduced in Paris, where, indeed, he had imagined she still was. The quick eye of Albert caught the involuntary start with which his friend beheld the new arrival, and turning to him, he said hastily,—

"Do you know the woman who has just entered the box?"

"Yes, what do you think of her?"

"Oh, she is perfectly lovely—what a complexion? And such magnificent hair! Is she French?"

"No, a Venetian."

"And her name is——"

"Countess G——."

"Ah! I know her by name," exclaimed Albert, "she is said to possess as much wit and cleverness as beauty! I was to have been presented to her when I met her at Madame Villefort's ball."

"Shall I assist you in repairing your negligence?" asked Franz.

"My dear fellow, are you really on such good terms with her as to venture to take me to her box?"

"Why, I have only had the honour of being in her society and conversing with her three or four times in my life; but you know that even such an acquaintance as that might warrant my doing what you ask."

At this instant, the countess perceived Franz, and graciously waved her hand to him, to which he replied by a respectful inclination of the head.

"Upon my word," said Albert, "you seem to be on excellent terms with the beautiful countess!"

"You are mistaken in thinking so," returned Franz, calmly, "but you merely fall into the same error which leads so many of our countrymen to commit the most egregious blunders, I mean that of judging the habits and customs of Italy and Spain by our Parisian notions; believe me, nothing is more fallacious than to form any estimate of the degree of intimacy you may suppose existing among persons by the familiar terms they seem upon; there is a similarity of feeling at this instant between ourselves and the countess,—nothing more."

"Is there, indeed, my good fellow? Pray tell me is it sympathy of heart?"

"No, of taste!" continued Franz, gravely.

"And in what manner has this congeniality of mind been evinced?"

"By the Countess's visiting the Colosseum, as we did last night, by moonlight, and nearly alone."

"You were with her then?"

"I was!"

"And what did you say to her?"

"Oh! we talked mutually of the illustrious dead of whom that magnificent ruin is a glorious monument!"

"Upon my word!" cried Albert, "you must have been a very entertaining companion alone, or all but alone, with a beautiful woman in such a place of sentiment as the Colosseum, and yet to find nothing better to talk about than the dead! All I can say is, if I should ever get such a chance, the living should be my theme."

"And you will probably find your theme ill-chosen."

"But," said Albert, breaking in upon his discourse, "never mind the past, let us only remember the present! Are you not going to keep your promise of introducing me to the fair subject of our remarks?"

"Certainly, directly the curtain falls on the stage!"

"What a confounded time this first act is about! I believe on my soul, that they never mean to finish it!"

"Oh, yes! they will! only listen to that charming finale! How exquisitely Coselli sings his part!"

"But what an awkward, inelegant fellow he is!"

"Well, then, what do you say to La Spech? Did you ever see any thing more perfect than her acting?"

"Why, you know, my dear fellow, when one has been accustomed to Malibran and Sontag, these kind of singers don't make the same impression on you they perhaps do on others."

"At least, you must admire Moriani's style and execution."

"I never fancied men of his dark, ponderous appearance singing with a voice like a woman's."

"My good friend," said Franz, turning to him, while Albert continued to point his glass at every box in the theatre, "you seem determined not to approve, you are really too difficult to please."

The curtain at length fell on the performances, to the infinite satisfaction of the Viscount de Morcerf, who seized his hat, rapidly passed his fingers through his hair, arranged his cravat and wristbands, and signified to Franz that he was waiting for him to lead the way.

Franz, who had mutely interrogated the countess, and received from her a gracious smile in token that he would be welcome, sought not to retard the gratification of Albert's eager impatience, but commenced at once the tour of the house, closely followed by Albert, who availed himself of the few minutes it occupied to reach the opposite side of the theatre to settle the height and smoothness of his collar and to arrange the lappets of his coat; this important task was just completed as they arrived at the countess's box; at the knock the door was immediately opened, and the young man, who was seated beside the countess in the front of the *loge*, in obedience to the Italian custom, instantly rose and surrendered his place to the strangers, who, in turn, would be expected to retire upon the arrival of other visitors.

Franz presented Albert as one of the most distinguished young men of the day, both as regarded his position in society and extraordinary talents; nor did he say more than the truth, for in Paris and the circle in which the viscount moved he was looked upon and cited as a model of perfection. Franz added that his companion, deeply grieved at having been prevented the honour of being presented to the countess during her sojourn in Paris, was most anxious to make up for it, and had requested him (Franz) to remedy the past misfortune by conducting him to her box, and concluded by asking pardon for his presumption in having taken upon himself to do so. The countess in reply bowed gracefully to Albert, and extended her hand with cordial kindness to Franz; then, inviting Albert to take the vacant seat beside her, she recommended Franz to take the next best, if he wished to view the ballet, and pointed to the one behind her own chair. Albert was soon deeply engrossed in discoursing upon Paris and Paris matters, speaking to the countess of the various persons they both knew there. Franz perceived how completely he was in his element; and, unwilling to interfere with the pleasure he so evidently felt, took up Albert's enormous lorgnette, and began in his turn to survey the audience. Sitting alone, in the front of a box immediately opposite, but situated on the third row, was a female of exquisite beauty, dressed in a Greek costume, which it was evident, from the ease and grace with which she wore it, was her national attire. Behind her, but in deep shadow, was the outline of a male figure; but the features of this latter personage it was not possible to distinguish. Franz could not forbear breaking in upon the apparently interesting conversation passing between the countess and Albert to inquire of the former if she knew who was the fair Albanaise opposite, since beauty, such as hers, was well worthy of being remarked by either sex.

"All I can tell you about her," replied the countess, "is, that she has been at Rome since the beginning of the season; for I saw her where she now sits the very first night of the theatre's opening, and since then she has never missed a performance. Sometimes accompanied by the individual who is with her, and at others merely attended by a black servant."

"And what do you think of her personal appearance?"

"Oh, I consider her perfectly lovely,—she is just my idea of what Medora must have been."

Franz and the countess exchanged a smile, and then the latter resumed her conversation with Albert, while Franz returned to his previous survey of the house and company. The curtain rose on the ballet, which was one of those excellent specimens of the Italian school, admirably arranged and put on the stage by Henri, who has established for himself a great reputation throughout Italy for his taste and skill in the chorographic art,—one of those masterly productions of grace, method, and elegance, in which the whole corps de ballet, from the principal dancers to the humblest supernumerary, are all engaged on the stage at the same time; and a hundred and fifty persons may be seen exhibiting the same attitude, or elevating the same arm or leg with a simultaneous movement, that would lead you to suppose but one mind, one act of volition influenced the moving mass: the ballet was called " Poliska." However much the ballet might have claimed his attention, Franz was too deeply occupied with the beautiful Greek to take any note of it, while she seemed to experience an almost childlike delight in watching it; her eager, animated looks, contrasting strongly with the utter indifference of her companion, who, during the whole time the piece lasted, never even moved, spite of the furious crashing din produced by the trumpets, cymbals, and Chinese bells, made to produce their loudest sound from the orchestra. The apathetic companion of the fair Greek took no heed of the deafening sounds that prevailed; but was, as far as appearances might be trusted, enjoying soft repose and bright celestial dreams. The ballet at length came to a close, and the curtain fell amid the loud unanimous plaudits of an enthusiastic and delighted audience.

Owing to the very judicious plan of dividing the two acts of the opera with a ballet, the pauses between the performances are very short; the singers in the opera having time to repose themselves and change their costume, when necessary, while the dancers are executing their pirouettes and exhibiting their graceful steps. The overture to the second act began; and at the first sound of the leader's bow across his violin Franz observed the sleeper slowly arise and approach the Greek girl, who turned round to say a few words to him, and then leaning forward again on her box, she became as absorbed as before in what was going on. The countenance of the person who had addressed her remained so completely in the shade that though Franz tried his utmost he could not distinguish a single feature. The curtain drew up, and the attention of Franz was attracted by the actors, and his eyes quitted their gaze at the box containing the Greek girl and her strange companion to watch the business of the stage.

Most of my readers are aware that the second act of

Parisina opens with the celebrated and effective duet, in which Parisina, while sleeping, betrays to Azzo the secret of her love for Ugo. The injured husband goes through all the workings of jealousy, until conviction seizes on his mind, and then, in a frenzy of his rage and indignation, he awakens his guilty wife to tell her he knows her guilt and to threaten her with his vengeance. This duet is one of the finest conceptions that has ever emanated from the fruitful pen of Donizetti. Franz now listened to it for the third time, yet its notes, so tenderly expressive and fearfully grand, as the wretched husband and wife give vent to their different griefs and passions, thrilled through the soul of Franz with an effect equal to his first emotions upon hearing it. Excited beyond his usual calm demeanour Franz rose with the audience, and was about to join the loud enthusiastic applause that followed, but suddenly his purpose was arrested, his hands fell by his sides, and the half-uttered "bravos" expired on his lips.

The occupant of the box, in which the Greek girl sat, appeared to share the universal animation that prevailed, for he left his seat to stand up in the front, so that his countenance being fully revealed, Franz had no difficulty in recognising him as the mysterious inhabitant of Monte-Cristo, and the very same individual he had encountered the preceding evening in the ruins of the Colosseum, and whose voice and figure had seemed so familiar to him. All doubt of his identity was now at an end; his singular host evidently resided at Rome. The surprise and agitation occasioned by this full confirmation of Franz's former suspicion had, no doubt, imparted a corresponding expression to his features; for the countess, after gazing with a puzzled look on his speaking countenance, burst into a fit of laughter, and begged to know what had happened.

"Madame la Comtesse," returned Franz, totally unheeding her raillery, "I asked you a short time since if you knew any particulars respecting the Albanian lady opposite, I must now beseech you to inform me who and what is her husband?"

"Nay," answered the countess, "I know no more of him than yourself."

"Perhaps you never before remarked him?"

"What a question! so truly French! Do you not know that we Italians have eyes only for the man we love?"

"True," replied Franz.

"All I can say," continued the countess, taking up the lorgnette, and directing it to the box in question, "is that the gentleman, whose history I am unable to furnish, seems to me as though he had just been dug up; he looks more like a corpse permitted by some friendly gravedigger to quit his tomb for a while, and revisit this earth of ours, than any thing human. How ghastly pale he is!"

C.M.—L

"Oh, he is always as colourless as you now see him," said Franz.

"Then you know him?" almost screamed the countess. "Oh! pray do, for heaven's sake, tell us all about——is he a vampire or a resuscitated corpse, or what?"

"I fancy I have seen him before; and I even think he recognises me."

"And I can well understand," said the countess, shrugging up her beautiful shoulders, as though an involuntary shudder passed through her veins, "that those who have once seen that man will never be likely to forget him."

The sensation experienced by Franz was evidently not peculiar to himself,—another, and wholly uninterested person, felt the same unaccountable awe and misgiving.

"Well," inquired Franz, after the countess had a second time directed her lorgnette at the *loge* of their mysterious *vis-à-vis*, "what do you think of our opposite neighbour?"

"Why, that he is no other than Lord Ruthven himself in a living form."

This fresh allusion to Byron drew a smile to Franz's countenance; although he could but allow that if anything was likely to induce belief in the existence of vampires, it would be the presence of such a man as the mysterious personage before him.

"I must positively find out who and what he is," said Franz, rising from his seat.

"No, no!" cried the countess; "you must not leave me. I depend upon you to escort me home. Oh, indeed, I cannot permit you to go."

"Is it possible," whispered Franz, "that you entertain any fear?"

"I'll tell you," answered the countess. "Byron had the most perfect belief in the existence of vampires, and even assured me he had seen some. The description he gave me perfectly corresponds with the features and character of the man before us. Oh! it is the exact personification of what I have been led to expect. The coal-black hair, large bright glittering eyes, in which a wild, unearthly fire seems burning, —the same ghastly paleness. Then observe, too, that the very female he has with him is altogether unlike all others of her sex. She is a foreigner—a stranger. Nobody knows who she is or where she comes from. No doubt she belongs to the same horrible race he does, and is, like himself, a dealer in magical arts. I entreat of you not to go near him—at least to-night: and if to-morrow your curiosity still continues as great, pursue your researches if you will; but to-night you neither can or shall. For that purpose I mean to keep you all to myself."

Franz protested he could not defer his pursuit till the following day for many reasons.

"Listen to me," said the countess, "and do not be so headstrong. I am going home. I have a party at my house to-night, and therefore cannot possibly remain till the conclusion of the opera. Now, I cannot for one instant believe you so devoid of gallantry as to refuse a lády your escort when she even condescends to ask you for it."

There was nothing else left for Franz to do but to take up his hat. open the door of the *loge*, and offer the countess his arm.

It was quite evident, by the countess's manner, that her uneasiness was not feigned; and Franz himself could not resist a species of superstitious dread—so much the stronger in him, as it arose from a variety of corroborating recollections, while the terror of the countess sprung from an instinctive feeling, originally created in her mind by the wild tales she had listened to till she believed them. Franz could even feel her arm tremble as he assisted her into the carriage.

Upon arriving at her hotel, Franz perceived that she had deceived him when she spoke of expecting company; on the contrary, her own return before the appointed hour seemed greatly to astonish the domestics.

"Excuse my little subterfuge," said the countess, in reply to her companion's half-reproachful observation on the subject; "but that horrid man had made me feel quite uncomfortable, and I longed to be alone that I might compose my startled mind."

Franz essayed to smile.

"Nay," said she, "smile not; it ill accords with the expression of your countenance, and I am sure it springs not from your heart. However, promise me one thing."

"What is it?"

"Promise me! I say."

"I will do anything you desire, except relinquish my determination of finding out who this man is. I have more reasons than you can imagine for desiring to know who he is, from whence he came, and whither he is going."

"Where he comes from I am ignorant; but I can readily tell you where he is going to, and that is down below without the least doubt."

"Let us only speak of the promise you wished me to make," said Franz.

"Well, then, you must give me your word to return immediately to your hotel, and make no attempt to follow this man to-night. There are certain affinities between the persons we quit and those we meet afterwards. For heaven's sake do not serve as a conductor between that man and me. Pursue your chase after him to-morrow as eagerly as you please; but never bring him near me if you would not see me die of terror. And now, good night; retire to your apartments, and try to sleep away all recollections of this evening. For my own part, I am quite sure I shall not be able to close my eyes." So saying, the countess quitted Franz, leaving him unable to decide whether she were merely amusing herself at his expense, or that her fears and agitation were genuine.

Upon his return to the hotel, Franz found Albert in his dressing-gown and slippers, listlessly extended on a sofa, smoking a cigar.

"My dear fellow!" cried he, springing up, "is it really you? Why, I did not expect to see you before to-morrow."

"My dear Albert!" replied Franz, " I am glad of this opportunity to tell you once and for ever that you entertain a most erroneous notion concerning Italian females. I should have thought the continual failures you have met with in all your own love-affairs might have taught you better by this time."

"Upon my soul! these women would puzzle the very devil to read them aright. Why, here—they give you their hand— they press yours in return—they keep up a whispering conversation—permit you to accompany them home! Why, if a Parisian were to indulge in a quarter of these marks of flattering attention, her reputation would be gone for ever."

"And the very reason why the females of this fine country put so little restraint on their words and actions is because they live so much in public, and have really nothing to conceal. Besides, you must have perceived that the countess was really alarmed."

"At what? at the sight of that respectable gentleman sitting opposite to us in the same *loge* as the lovely Greek girl? Now, for my part, I met them in the lobby after the conclusion of the piece; and, hang me, if I can guess where you took your notions of the other world from! I can assure you that this hobgoblin of yours is a deuced fine-looking fellow—admirably dressed; indeed I feel quite sure, from the cut of his clothes, they are made by a first-rate Paris tailor—probably Blin or Humann. He was rather too pale, certainly; but then, you know, paleness is always looked upon as a strong proof of aristocratical descent and distinguished breeding."

Franz smiled; for he well remembered that Albert particularly prided himself on the entire absence of colour in his own complexion.

"Well, that tends to confirm my own ideas," said Franz, "that the countess's suspicions were destitute alike of sense and reason. Did he speak in your hearing? and did you catch any of his words?"

"I did; but they were uttered in the Romaic dialect. I

knew that from the mixture of Greek words. I don't know whether I ever told you that when I was at college I was rather—rather 'strong in Greek.'"

"He spoke the Romaic language, did he?"

"I think so."

"That settles it," murmured Franz. "'Tis he, past all doubt."

"What do you say?"

"Nothing, nothing. But tell me, what were you thinking about when I came in?"

"Oh, I was arranging a little surprise for you."

"Indeed! Of what nature?"

"Why, you know, it is quite impossible to procure a carriage."

"Certainly; and I also know that we have done all that human means afforded to endeavour to get one."

"Now, then, in this difficulty a bright idea has flashed across my brain."

Franz looked at Albert as though he had not much confidence in the suggestions of his imagination.

"I tell you what, M. Franz!" cried Albert, "you deserve to be called out for such a misgiving and incredulous glance as that you were pleased to bestow on me just now."

"And I promise to give you the satisfaction of a gentleman if your scheme turns out as ingenious as you assert."

"Well, then, hearken to me."

"I listen."

"You agree, do you not, that obtaining a carriage is out of the question?"

"I do."

"Neither can we procure horses?"

"True; we have offered any sums, but have failed."

"Well, now, what do you say to a cart? I dare say such a thing might be had."

"Very possibly."

"And a pair of oxen?"

"As easily found as the cart."

"Then you see, my good fellow, with a cart and couple of oxen our business can be managed. The cart must be tastefully ornamented; and if you and I dress ourselves as Neapolitan reapers, we may get up a striking tableau, after the manner of that splendid picture by Leopold Robert. It would add greatly to the effect if the countess would join us in the costume of a peasant from Puzzoli or Sorento. Our group would then be quite complete, more especially as the countess is quite beautiful enough to represent the mother with child."

"Well," said Franz, "this time, M. Albert, I am bound to give you credit for having hit upon a most capital idea."

"And quite a national one, too," replied Albert, with gratified pride. "A mere masque borrowed from our own festivities. Ha! ha! Messieurs les Romains, you thought to make us unhappy strangers trot at the heels of your processions, like so many lazzaroni, because no carriages or horses are to be had in your beggarly city. But you don't know us; when we can't have one thing we invent another."

"And have you communicated your triumphant idea to any person?"

"Only to our host. Upon my return home I sent to desire he would come to me, and I then explained to him what I wished to procure. He assured me that nothing would be easier than to furnish all I desired. One thing I was sorry for: when I bade him have the horns of the oxen gilded, he told me there would not be time, as it would require three days to effect that; so you see we must do without this little superfluity."

"And where is he now?"

"Who?"

"Our host."

"Gone out in search of our equipage: by to-morrow it might be too late."

"Then he will be able to give us an answer to-night?"

"Oh, I expect him every minute."

At this instant the door opened, and the head of Maître Pastrini appeared.

"*Permesso?*" inquired he.

"Certainly—certainly," cried Franz. "Come in, mine host."

"Now, then," asked Albert, eagerly; "have you found the desired cart and oxen?"

"Better than that!" replied the Maître Pastrini, with the air of a man perfectly well satisfied with himself.

"Take care, my worthy host," said Albert, "*better* is a sure enemy to *well.*"

"Let your excellencies only leave the matter to me," returned Maître Pastrini, in a tone indicative of unbounded self-confidence.

"But what *have* you done?" asked Franz. "Speak out, there's a worthy fellow."

"Your excellencies are aware," responded the landlord, swelling with importance, "that the Count of Monte-Cristo is living on the same floor with yourselves?"

"I should think we did know it," exclaimed Albert, "since it is owing to that circumstance that we are packed into these small rooms, like two poor students in the back streets of Paris."

"Well, then, the Count of Monte-Cristo, hearing of the

dilemma in which you are placed, has sent to offer you seats in his carriage and two places at his windows in the Rospoli Palace."

The friends looked at each other with unutterable surprise.

"But do you think," asked Franz, "that we ought to accept such offers from a perfect stranger?"

"What sort of person is this Count of Monte-Cristo?" asked Franz of his host.

"A very great nobleman, but whether Maltese or Sicilian I cannot exactly say; but this I know, that he is noble as a Borghese and rich as a gold-mine."

"It seems to me," said Franz, speaking in an under tone to Albert, "that if this individual merited the high panegyrics of our landlord, he would have conveyed his invitation through another channel, and not permitted it to be brought to us in this unceremonious way. He would have written—or——"

At this instant some one knocked at the door.

"Come in!" said Franz.

A servant, wearing a livery of considerable style and richness, appeared at the threshold, and placing two cards in the landlord's hands, who forthwith presented them to the two young men, he said, "Please to deliver these, from M. le Comte de Monte-Cristo, to M. le Vicomte Albert de Morcerf and M. Franz Epinay. M. le Comte de Monte-Cristo," continued the servant, "begs these gentlemen's permission to wait upon them as their neighbour, and he will be honoured by an intimation of what time they will please to receive him."

"Faith, Franz," whispered Albert, "there is not much to find fault with here."

"Tell the count," replied Franz, "that we will do ourselves the pleasure of calling on him."

The servant bowed and retired.

"That is what I call an elegant mode of attack," said Albert. "You were quite correct in what you stated, Maître Pastrini. The Count of Monte-Cristo is unquestionably a man of first-rate breeding and knowledge of the world."

"Then you accept his offer?" said the host.

"Of course we do," replied Albert. "Still I must own I am sorry to be obliged to give up the cart and the group of reapers —it would have produced such an effect! And were it not for the windows at the Rospoli Palace, by way of recompense for the loss of our beautiful scheme, I don't know but what I should have held on by my original plan. What say you, Franz?"

"Oh, I agree with you; the windows in the Rospoli Palace alone decided me."

The truth was, that the mention of two places in the Rospoli Palace had recalled to Franz's mind the conversation he had overheard the preceding evening in the ruins of the Colosseum between the mysterious unknown and the Transtevere, in which the stranger in the cloak had undertaken to obtain the freedom of a condemned criminal; and if this muffled up individual proved (as Franz felt sure he would) the same as the person he had just seen in the Teatro Argentino, then he should be able to establish his identity,* and also to prosecute his researches respecting him with perfect facility and freedom. Franz passed the night in confused dreams respecting the two meetings he had already had with his mysterious tormentor, and in waking speculations as to what the morrow would produce. The next day must clear up every doubt, and unless his near neighbour and would-be friend, the Count of Monte-Cristo, possessed the ring of Gyges, and by its power were able to render himself invisible, it was very certain he could not escape this time. Eight o'clock found Franz up and dressed, while Albert, who had not the same motives for early rising, was still profoundly asleep. The first act of Franz was to summon his landlord, who presented himself with his accustomed obsequiousness.

"Pray, Maître Pastrini," asked Franz, "is not some execution appointed to take place to-day?"

"Yes, your excellence; but if your reason for inquiry is, that you may procure a window to view it from, you are much too late."

"Oh no!" answered Franz, "I had no such intention; and even if I had felt a wish to witness the spectacle, I might have done so from Monte Pincio,—could I not?"

"Ah!" exclaimed mine host, "I did not think it likely your excellence would have chosen to mingle with such a rabble as are always collected on that hill, which indeed they consider as exclusively belonging to themselves."

"Very possibly I may not go," answered Franz; "but in case I feel disposed, give me some particulars of to-day's executions."

"What particulars would your excellence like to hear?"

"Why, the number of persons condemned to suffer, their names, and description of the death they are to die."

"That happens just lucky, your excellence! Only a few minutes ago they brought me the *tavolettas*."

"What are they?"

"Sort of wooden tablets hung up at the corners of streets the evening before an execution, on which is pasted up a paper containing the names of the condemned persons, their crimes, and mode of punishment; the reason for so publicly announcing all this is that all good and faithful Catholics may offer up their prayers for the unfortunate culprits, and above all, beseech of Heaven to grant them a sincere repentance."

"And these tablets are brought to you, that you may add your prayers to those of the faithful, are they?" asked Franz, somewhat incredulously.

"Oh dear no, your excellence; I have not time for any body's affairs but my own and those of my honourable guests; but I make an agreement with the man who pastes up the papers, and he brings them to me as he would the play-bills, that in case any person staying at my hotel should like to witness an execution, he may obtain every requisite information concerning the time and place, &c."

"Upon my word, that is most delicate attention on your part, Maître Pastrini," cried Franz.

"Why, your excellence," returned the landlord, chuckling and rubbing his hands with infinite complacency, " I think I may take upon myself to say I neglect nothing to deserve the support and patronage of the noble visitors to this poor hotel."

"I see that plainly enough, my most excellent host, and you may rely upon my repeating so striking a proof of your attention to your guests wherever I go. Meanwhile, oblige me by a sight of one of these *tavolettas*."

"Nothing can be easier than to comply with your excellence's wish," said the landlord, opening the door of the chamber, " I have caused one to be placed on the landing, close by your apartment." Then taking the tablet from the wall, he handed it to Franz, who read as follows:—

"'The public is informed, that on Wednesday, February 23d, being the first day of the Carnival, two executions will take place in the Place del Popolo, by order of the Tribunal de la Rota, of two individuals, named Andrea Rondola and Peppino, otherwise called Rocca Priori; the former found guilty of the murder of a venerable and exemplary priest, named Don César Torlini, canon of the church of Saint-Jean-de-Latran, and the latter convicted of being an accomplice of the atrocious and sanguinary bandit Luigi Vampa and his troop. The first-named malefactor will be *mazzolato*, the second culprit *decapitato*. The prayers of all good Christians are entreated for these unfortunate men, that it may please God to awaken them to a sense of their guilt, and to grant them a hearty and sincere repentance for their crimes.'"

This was precisely what Franz had heard the evening before in the ruins of the Colosseum. No part of the programme differed—the names of the condemned persons—their crimes and mode of punishment—all agreed with his previous information. In all probability, therefore, the Transtevere was no other than the bandit Luigi Vampa himself, and the man shrouded in the mantle the same he had known as "Sinbad the Sailor," but who, no doubt, was still pursuing his philanthropic expedition in Rome as he had already done at

Porto-Vecchio and Tunis.   Time was getting on, however, and Franz deemed it advisable to awaken Albert; but at the moment he prepared to proceed to his chamber, his friend entered the saloon in perfect costume for the day.   The anticipated delights of the Carnival had so run in his head as to make him leave his pillow long before his usual hour.

"Now, my excellent Maître Pastrini," said Franz, addressing his landlord, "since we are both ready, do you think we may proceed at once to visit the Count of Monte-Cristo?"

"Most assuredly," replied he.   "The Count of Monte-Cristo is always an early riser; and I can answer for his having been up these two hours."

"Then you really consider we shall not be intruding if we pay our respects to him directly?"

"Oh, I am quite sure.   I will take all the blame on myself if you find I have led you into an error."

"Well, then, if it be so; are you ready, Albert?"

"Perfectly!"

"Let us go and return our best thanks for his courtesy."

"Yes, let us do so."

The landlord preceded the friends across the landing, which was all that separated them from the apartments of the count, rang at a bell, and upon the door being opened by a servant, said,—

"*I Signori Francesi.*"

The domestic bowed respectfully, and invited them to enter.   They passed through two rooms, furnished with a style and luxury they had not calculated on finding under the roof of Maître Pastrini, and were shewn into an elegantly fitted-up salon.   The richest Turkey carpets covered the floor, and the softest and most inviting couches, *bergères*, and sofas, offered their high-piled and yielding cushions to such as desired repose or refreshment.   Splendid paintings by the first masters were ranged against the walls, intermingled with magnificent trophies of war, while heavy curtains of costly tapestry were suspended before the different doors of the room.

"If your excellences will please to be seated," said the man, "I will let M. le Comte know you are here."

And with these words he disappeared behind one of the tapestried *portières*.   As the door opened, the sound of a *guzla* reached the ears of the young men, but was almost immediately lost, for the rapid closing of the door merely allowed one rich swell of harmony to enter the saloon.   Franz and Albert looked inquiringly at each other, then at the gorgeous fittings-up of the apartment.   All seemed even more splendid at a second view than it had done at their first rapid survey.

"Well," said Franz to his friend, "what think you of all this?"

"Why, upon my soul, my dear fellow, it strikes me our elegant and attentive neighbour must either be some successful stock-jobber who has speculated in the fall of the Spanish funds or some prince travelling incog."

"Hush! hush!" replied Franz, "we shall ascertain who and what he is—he comes!"

As Franz spoke he heard the sound of a door turning on its hinges, and almost immediately afterwards the tapestry was drawn aside, and the owner of all these riches stood before the two young men. Albert instantly rose to meet him, but Franz remained in a manner spell-bound on his chair, for in the person of him who had just entered he recognised not only the mysterious visitant to the Colosseum, and the occupant of the *loge* at the Salle Argentino, but also his singular host of Monte-Cristo.

CHAPTER XXXV

LA MAZZOLATA

"GENTLEMEN," said the Count of Monte-Cristo as he entered, "I pray you excuse me for suffering my visit to be anticipated; but I feared to disturb you by presenting myself earlier at your apartments; besides, you sent me word you would come to me, and I have held myself at your disposal."

"Franz and I have to thank you a thousand times, M. le Comte," returned Albert; "you extricate us from a great dilemma, and we were on the point of inventing some very fantastic vehicle when your friendly invitation reached us."

"Indeed!" returned the count, motioning the two young men to sit down. "It was the fault of that blockhead Pastrini, that I did not sooner assist you in your distress. He did not mention a syllable of your embarrassment to me, when he knows that, alone and isolated as I am, I seek every opportunity of making the acquaintance of my neighbours. As soon as I learned I could in any way assist you, I most eagerly seized the opportunity of offering my services."

The two young men bowed. Franz had, as yet, found nothing to say; he had adopted no determination; and as nothing in the count's manner manifested the wish that he should recognise him, he did not know whether to make any allusion to the past or wait until he had more proof; besides, although sure it was he who had been in the box the previous evening, he could not be equally positive that he was the man he had seen at the Colosseum. He resolved, therefore, to let things take their course without making any direct overture to the count. Besides, he had this advantage over him, he was master of his secret, whilst he had no hold on Franz, who had nothing to conceal.

However, he resolved to lead the conversation to a subject which might possibly clear up his doubts.

"M. le Comte," said he, "you have offered us places in your carriage, and at your windows of the Rospoli Palace. Can you tell us where we can obtain a sight of the Place del Popolo?"

"Ah!" said the count negligently, looking attentively at Morcerf, "Is there not something like an execution upon the Place del Popolo?"

"Yes," returned Franz, finding that the count was coming to the point he wished.

"Stay, I think I told my steward yesterday to attend to this. Perhaps I can render you this slight service also."

He extended his hand and rang the bell thrice.

"Did you ever occupy yourself," said he to Franz, "with the employment of time and the means of simplifying the summoning your servants? I have:—when I ring once, it is for my valet; twice, for my maître d'hôtel; thrice, for my steward: thus I do not waste a minute or a word. Here he is!" A man of about five-and-forty to fifty entered, exactly resembling the smuggler who had introduced Franz into the cavern, but he did not appear to recognise him. It was evident he had his orders.

"M. Bertuccio," said the count, "have you procured me windows looking on the Place del Popolo, as I ordered you yesterday?"

"Yes, excellency," returned the steward, "but it was very late."

"Did I not tell you I wished for one?" replied the count, frowning.

"And your excellency has one, which was let to Prince Lobanieff, but I was obliged to pay a hundred——"

"That will do—that will do, Monsieur Bertuccio, spare these gentlemen all such domestic arrangements. You have the window, that is sufficient. Give orders to the coachman, and be in readiness on the stairs to conduct us to it."

The steward bowed, and was about to quit the room.

"Ah!" continued the count, "be good enough to ask Pastrini if he has received the *tavoletta*, and if he can send us an account of the execution."

"There is no need to do that," said Franz, taking out his tablets, "for I saw the account, and copied it down."

"Very well, you can retire, Maître Bertuccio; let us know when breakfast is ready. These gentlemen," added he, turning to the two friends, "will, I trust, do me the honour to breakfast?"

"But, M. le Comte," said Albert, "we shall abuse your kindness."

"Not at all; on the contrary, you will give me great pleasure. You will, one or other of you, perhaps both, return it to me at Paris. Maître Bertuccio, lay covers for three."

He took Franz's tablets out of his hand.

"'We announce,'" he read, in the same tone with which he would have read a newspaper, "'that to-day, the 23d of February, will be executed Andrea Rondolo, guilty of murder on the person of the respectable and venerated Don César Torlini, canon of the church Saint-Jean-de-Latran, and Peppino called Rocca Priori, convicted of complicity, with the detestable bandit Luigi Vampa and the men of his troop.' Hum! 'The first will be *mazzolato*, the second *decapitato*.' Yes," continued the count, "it was at first arranged in this way, but I think since yesterday some change has taken place in the order of the ceremony."

"Really!" said Franz.

"Yes, I passed the evening at the Cardinal Rospigliosi's, and there mention was made of something like a pardon for one of the two men."

"For Andrea Rondolo?" asked Franz.

"No," replied the count, carelessly, "for the other (he glanced at the tablets as if to recall the name), for Peppino, called Rocca Priori. You are thus deprived of seeing a man guillotined, but the *mazzolato* still remains, which is a very curious punishment when seen for the first time, and even the second, whilst the other, as you must know, is very simple. The *mandaïa* never fails, never trembles, never strikes thirty times ineffectually, like the soldier who beheaded the Comte de Chalais, and to whose tender mercy Richelieu had doubtless recommended the sufferer. Ah!" added the count, in a contemptuous tone, "do not tell me of European punishments, they are in the infancy, or rather the old age of cruelty."

"Really, M. le Comte," replied Franz, "one would think that you had studied the different tortures of all the nations of the world."

"There are, at least, few that I have not seen," said the count, coldly.

"And you took pleasure in beholding these dreadful spectacles?"

"My first sentiment was horror, the second indifference, the third curiosity."

"Curiosity! that is a terrible word."

"Why so? In life, our greatest preoccupation is death; is it not, then, curious to study the different ways by which the soul and body can part, and how, according to their different characters, temperaments, and even the different customs of their countries, individuals bear the transition from life to death, from existence to annihilation? As for myself, I can assure you of one thing, the more men you see die, the easier it becomes to die; and in my opinion, death may be a torture, but it is not an expiation."

"I do not quite understand you," replied Franz, "pray explain your meaning, for you excite my curiosity to the highest pitch."

"Listen," said the count, and deep hatred mounted to his face, as the blood would to the face of any other. "If a man had by unheard-of and excruciating tortures destroyed your father, your mother, your mistress; in a word, one of those beings, who when they are torn from you, leave a desolation, a wound that never closes, in your breast, do you think the reparation that society gives you sufficient by causing the knife of the guillotine to pass between the base of the occiput and the trapezal muscles of the murderer, because he who has caused us years of moral sufferings undergoes a few moments of physical pain?"

"Yes, I know," said Franz, "that human justice is insufficient to console us, she can give blood in return for blood, that is all; but you must demand from her only what it is in her power to grant."

"I will put another case to you," continued the count, "that where society attacked by the death of a person, avenges death by death. But are there not a thousand tortures by which a man may be made to suffer without society taking the least cognisance of them or offering him even the insufficient means of vengeance of which we have just spoken? Are there not crimes for which the empalement of the Turks, the augers of the Persians, the stake and the brand of the Iroquois Indians, are inadequate tortures, and which are unpunished by society? Answer me, do not these crimes exist?"

"Yes," answered Franz, "and it is to punish them that duelling is tolerated."

"Ah, duelling!" cried the count, "a pleasant manner, upon my soul, of arriving at your end when that end is vengeance! A man has carried off your mistress, a man has seduced your wife, a man has dishonoured your daughter; he has rendered the whole life of one who had the right to expect from Heaven that portion of happiness God has promised to every one of His creatures an existence of misery and infamy; and you think you are avenged because you send a ball through the head, or pass a sword through the breast, of that man who has planted madness in your brain and despair in your heart. Without recollecting that it is often he who comes off victorious from the strife, absolved of all crime in the eyes of the world! No, no," continued the count, "had I to avenge myself, it is not thus I would take revenge."

"Then you disapprove of duelling! you would not fight a duel?" asked Albert in his turn, astonished at this strange theory.

"Oh yes," replied the count; "understand me, I would fight a duel for a trifle, for an insult, for a blow: and the more so, that, thanks to my skill in all bodily exercises, and the indifference to danger I have gradually acquired, I should be almost certain to kill my man. Oh! I would fight for such a cause; but in return for a slow, profound, eternal torture, I would give back the same were it possible: an eye for an eye, a tooth for tooth, as the Orientals say;—our masters in every thing; those favoured creatures who have formed for themselves a life of dreams and a paradise of realities."

"But," said Franz to the count, "with this theory, which renders you at once judge and executioner of your own cause, it would be difficult to adopt a course that would for ever prevent your falling under the power of the law. Hatred is blind; rage carries you away; and he who pours out vengeance runs the risk of tasting a bitter draught."

"Yes, if he be poor and inexperienced, not if he be rich and skilful; besides, the worst that could happen to him would be the punishment of which we have already spoken, and which the philanthropic French Revolution has substituted for being torn to pieces by horses or broken on the wheel. What matters this punishment as long as he is avenged? On my word, I almost regret that in all probability this miserable Peppino will not be *decapitato*, as you might have had an opportunity then of seeing how short a time the punishment lasts, and whether it is worth even mentioning; but, really, this is a most singular conversation for the Carnival, gentlemen; how did it arise? Ah! I recollect, you asked for a place at my window; you shall have it; but let us first sit down to table, for here comes the servant to inform us breakfast is ready."

As he spoke a servant opened one of the four doors of the salon, saying,—

"*Al suo commodo!*"

The two young men rose and entered the breakfast-room.

During the meal, which was excellent and admirably served, Franz looked repeatedly at Albert in order to remark the impression which he doubted not had been made on him by the words of their entertainer, but whether with his usual carelessness he had paid but little attention to him, whether the explanation of the Count of Monte-Cristo with regard to duelling had satisfied him, or whether the events which Franz knew of had a double effect on him alone, he remarked that his companion did not pay the least regard to them, but on the contrary ate like a man who for the last four or five months had been condemned to partake of Italian cookery,—that is, the worst in the world. As for the count he just touched the dishes; he seemed as if he fulfilled the duties of an entertainer by sitting down with his guests, and awaited their departure to be served with some strange or more delicate food. This brought back to Franz, in spite of himself, the recollection of the terror with which the count had inspired the Countess G——, and her firm conviction that the man in the opposite box was a vampire.

At the end of the breakfast Franz took out his watch.

"Well," said the count, "what are you doing?"

"You must excuse us, M. le Comte," returned Franz, "but we have still much to do."

"What may that be?"

"We have no disguises, and it is absolutely necessary to procure them."

"Do not concern yourself about that; we have, I think, a private room in the Place del Popolo; I will have whatever costumes you choose brought to us and you can dress there."

"After the execution?" cried Franz.

"Before or after, which you please."

"Opposite the scaffold?"

"The scaffold forms part of the fête."

"M. le Comte, I have reflected on the matter," said Franz, "I thank you for your courtesy, but I shall content myself with accepting a place in your carriage and at your window at the Rospoli Palace, and I leave you at liberty to dispose of my place at the Place del Popolo."

"But I warn you, you will lose a very curious sight," returned the count.

"You will relate it to me," replied Franz, "and the recital from your lips will make as great an impression on me as if I had witnessed it. I have more than once intended witnessing an execution, but I have never been able to make up my mind; and you, Albert?"

"I," replied the viscount,—"I saw Castaing executed, but I think I was rather intoxicated that day, for I had quitted college the same morning, and we had passed the previous night at a tavern."

"Besides, it is no reason because you have not seen an execution at Paris, that you should not see one anywhere else, when you travel, it is to see every thing. Think what a figure you will make when you are asked, 'How do they execute at Rome?' and you reply, 'I do not know!' And, besides, they say that the culprit is an infamous scoundrel, who killed with a log of wood a worthy canon who had brought him up like his own son. Diable! when a churchman is killed, it should be with a different weapon than a log, especially when he has behaved like a father. If you went to Spain, would you not see the bull-fights? Well, suppose it is a bull-fight you are going to see! Recollect the ancient Romans of the Circus, and the sports where they killed three hundred lions and a hundred men. Think of the eighty thousand applauding spectators, the sage matrons who took their daughters and the charming Vestals who made with the thumb of their white hands the fatal sign that said, 'Come, despatch this man already nearly dead.'"

"Shall you go then, Albert?" asked Franz.

"*Ma foi!* yes; like you I hesitated, but the count's eloquence decides me!"

"Let us go then," said Franz, "since you wish it, but on our way to the Place del Popolo I wish to pass through the Rue de Cours. Is this possible, M. le Comte?"

"On foot, yes! in a carriage, no!"

"I will go on foot, then!"

"Is it important that you should pass through this street?"

"Yes, there is something I wish to see!"

"Well, we will pass by the Rue de Cours. We will send the carriage to wait for us on the Piazza del Popolo, by the Strada del Babuino, for I shall be glad to pass, myself, through the Rue de Cours, to see if some orders I have given have been executed."

"Excellency," said a servant, opening the door, "a man in the dress of a penitent wishes to speak to you."

"Ah! yes!" returned the count, "I know who he is, gentlemen; will you return to the salon? you will find on the centre table some excellent Havanna cigars. I will rejoin you directly."

The young men rose and returned into the salon, whilst the count, again apologising, left by another door. Albert, who was a great smoker, and who had considered it no small sacrifice to be deprived of the cigars of the Café de Paris, approached the table and uttered a cry of joy at perceiving some veritable *pueros*.

"Well," asked Franz, "what think you of the Count of Monte-Cristo?"

"What do I think?" said Albert, evidently surprised at such a question from his companion; "I think that he is a delightful fellow, who does the honours of his table admirably; who has travelled much, read much, is like Brutus of the Stoic school, and moreover," added he, sending a volume of smoke up towards the ceiling, "that he has excellent cigars."

Such was Albert's opinion of the count, and as Franz well knew that Albert professed never to form an opinion except upon long reflection, he made no attempt to change it.

"But," said he, "did you remark one very singular thing?"

"What?"

"How attentively he looked at you."

"At me?"

"Yes."

Albert reflected.

"Ah!" replied he, sighing, "that is not very surprising, I have been more than a year absent from Paris, and my clothes are of a most antiquated cut; the count takes me for a provincial. The first opportunity you have, undeceive him, I beg, and tell him I am nothing of the kind."

Franz smiled: an instant after, the count entered.

"I am now quite at your service, gentlemen," said he. "The carriage is going one way to the Place del Popolo, and we will go another; and if you please, by the Rue du Cours. Take some more of these cigars, M. de Morcerf."

"With all my heart," returned Albert, "these Italian cigars are horrible. When you come to Paris, I will return all this."

"I will not refuse. I intend going there soon, and since you allow me, I will pay you a visit. Come! we have not any time to lose, it is half-past twelve, let us set off."

All three descended: the coachman received his master's orders and drove down the Via del Babuino. Whilst the three gentlemen walked towards the Place d'Espagne and the Via Frattina, which led directly between the Fiano and Rospoli Palaces, all Franz's attention was directed towards the windows of that last palace, for he had not forgotten the signal agreed upon between the man in the mantle and the Transtevere peasant.

"Which are your windows?" asked he of the count, with as much indifference as he could assume.

"The three last," returned he, with a negligence evidently unaffected; for he could not imagine with what intention the question was put.

Franz glanced rapidly towards the three windows. The side windows were hung with yellow damask, and the centre one with white damask and a red cross. The man in the mantle had kept his promise to the Transtevere, and there could now be no doubt that he was the count. The three windows were still untenanted. Preparations were making on every side; chairs were placed, scaffolds were raised, and windows were hung with flags. The masks could not appear; the carriages could not move about; but the masks were visible behind the windows, the carriages, and the doors.

Franz, Albert, and the count, continued to descend the Rue du Cours: as they approached the Place del Popolo, the crowd became more dense, and above the heads of the multitude two objects were visible; the obelisk surmounted by a cross, which marks the centre of the place, and before the obelisk, at the point where the three streets, del Babuino, del Corso, and di Ripetta meet, the two uprights of the scaffold, between which glittered the curved knife of the *mandaïa*. At the corner of the street they met the count's steward, who was awaiting his master.

The window, let at an exorbitant price, which the count had doubtless wished to conceal from his guests, was on the second floor of the great palace, situated between the Rue del Babuino and the Monte-Pincio. It consisted as we have said, of a small dressing-room opening into a bedroom, and when the door of communication was shut, the inmates were quite alone. On two chairs were laid as many elegant carnival costumes, in blue and white satin.

"As you left the choice of your costumes to me," said the count to the two friends, "I have had these brought as they will be the most worn this year; and they are most suitable on account of the *confetti* (sweetmeats), as they do not shew the flour."

Franz heard the words of the count but imperfectly, and he perhaps did not fully appreciate this new attention to their wishes; for he was wholly absorbed by the spectacle that the Piazza del Popolo presented, and by the terrible instrument that was in the centre. It was the first time Franz had ever seen a guillotine,—we say guillotine, because the Roman *mandaïa* is formed on almost the same model as the French instrument: the knife, which is shaped like a crescent, that cuts with the convex side, falls from a less height, and that is all the difference. Two men, seated on the movable plank on which the culprit is laid, were eating their breakfasts, whilst waiting for the criminal. Their repast consisted, apparently, of bread and sausages. One of them lifted the plank, took thence a flask of wine, drank some, and then passed it to his companion. These two men were the executioner's assistants. At this sight Franz felt the perspiration start forth upon his brow. The prisoners, transported the previous evening from the Carceri Nuovo to the little church of Sainte-Marie del Popolo, had passed the night, each accompanied by two priests, in a chapel closed by a grating, before which were two sentinels, relieved at intervals. A double line of carabineers, placed on each side of the door of the church, reached to the scaffold, and formed a circle round it, leaving a path about ten feet wide, and around the guillotine a space of nearly a hundred feet. All the rest of the square was paved with heads. Many women held their infants on their shoulders, and thus the children had the best view. The Monte-Pincio seemed a vast amphitheatre filled with spectators: the balconies of the two churches at the corner of the Rue del Babuino and the Rue di Ripetta were crammed: the steps even seemed a partly-coloured sea, that was impelled towards the portico: every niche in the wall held its living statue. What the count said was true,—the most curious spectacle in life is that of death. And yet, instead of the silence and the solemnity demanded by the occasion, a noise of laughter and jest arose from the crowd: it was evident that this execution was, in the eyes of the people, only the commencement of the Carnival. Suddenly the tumult ceased, as if by magic: the doors of the church opened. A brotherhood of penitents, clothed from head to foot in robes of grey sackcloth, with holes for the eyes alone, and holding in their hand a lighted taper, appeared first: the chief marched at the head. Behind the penitents came a man of vast stature and proportions. He was naked, with the exception of cloth drawers, at the left side of which hung a large knife in a sheath, and he bore on his right shoulder a heavy mace. This man was the executioner. He had, moreover, sandals bound on his feet by cords. Behind the executioner came, in the order in which they were to die, first Peppino, and then Andrea. Each was accompanied by two priests. Neither had their eyes bandaged. Peppino walked with a firm step, doubtless aware of what awaited him. Andrea was supported by two priests. Each of them kissed, from time to time, the crucifix a confessor held out to them. At this sight alone Franz felt his legs tremble under him: he looked at Albert,—he was white as his shirt, and mechanically cast away his cigar, although he had not half smoked it. The count alone seemed unmoved,—nay, more, a slight colour seemed striving to rise in his pale cheeks. His nostril dilated like a wild beast that scents its prey, and his lips, half opened, disclosed his white teeth, small and sharp like those of a jackal. And yet his features wore an expression of smiling tenderness, such as Franz had never before witnessed in them; his black eyes especially were full of kindness and pity. However, the two culprits advanced, and as they approached, their faces became visible. Peppino was a handsome young man of four or five-and-twenty, bronzed by the sun: he carried his head erect, and seemed to look on which side his liberator would appear. Andrea was short and fat. His visage, marked with brutal cruelty, did not indicate age: he might be thirty. In prison he had suffered his beard to grow,—his head fell on his shoulder,—his legs bent beneath him,—and he seemed to obey a mechanical movement, of which he was unconscious.

"I thought," said Franz to the count, "that you told me there would be but one execution?"

"I told you true," replied he, coldly.

"However, here are two culprits."

"Yes; but only one of these two is about to die!—the other has long years to live."

"If the pardon is to come, there is no time to lose."

"And, see, here it is," said the count.

At the moment when Peppino arrived at the foot of the *mandaïa*, a penitent, who seemed to arrive late, forced his way through the soldiers, and, advancing to the chief of the brotherhood, gave him a folded paper.

The piercing eye of Peppino had noticed all. The chief took the paper, unfolded it, and, raising his hands, "Heaven be praised! and his Holiness also!" said he, in a loud voice. "Here is a pardon for one of the prisoners."

"A pardon!" cried the people with one voice. "A pardon!"

At this cry Andrea raised his head.

"Pardon for whom?" cried he.

Peppino remained breathless.

"A pardon for Peppino, called Rocca Priori," said the principal friar. And he passed the paper to the officer commanding the carabineers, who read and returned it to him.

"For Peppino!" cried Andrea, who seemed aroused from the torpor in which he had been plunged. "Why for him and not for me? We ought to die together. I was promised he should die with me. You have no right to put me to death alone. I will not die alone,—I will not!" And he broke from the priests, struggling and raving like a wild beast, and striving desperately to break the cords that bound his hands.

The executioner made a sign, and his assistant leaped from the scaffold and seized him.

"What is happening?" asked Franz of the count. For as all this occurred in the Roman dialect, he had not perfectly comprehended it.

"Do you not understand," returned the count, "that this human creature who is about to die is furious that his fellow-sufferer does not perish with him? and, were he able, he would rather tear him to pieces with his teeth and nails than let him enjoy the life he himself is about to be deprived of. Oh! man, man!—race of crocodiles!" cried the count, extending his clenched hands towards the crowd; "how well do I recognise you there, and that at all times you are worthy of yourselves!"

All this time Andrea and the two executioners were

struggling on the ground, and he kept exclaiming, "He ought to die! he shall die!—I will not die alone!"

"Look!—look!" cried the count, seizing the young men's hands; "look, for on my soul it is curious. Here is a man who had resigned himself to his fate; who was going to the scaffold to die,—like a coward, it is true,—but he was about to die without resistance. Do you know what gave him strength?—do you know what consoled him? It was, that another partook of his punishment,—that another partook of his anguish,—that another was to die before him! Lead two sheep to the butcher's, two oxen to the slaughter-house, and make one of them understand his companion will not die: the sheep will bleat for pleasure, the ox will bellow with joy. But man, —man whom God created in His own image,—man, upon whom God has laid His first, His sole commandment, to love his neighbour,—man, to whom God has given a voice to express his thoughts,—what is his first cry when he hears his fellow-man is saved? A blasphemy! Honour to man, — this masterpiece of nature, — this king of the creation!" And the count burst into a laugh; but a terrible laugh, that shewed he must have suffered horribly to be able thus to laugh.

However, the struggle still continued, and it was dreadful to witness. The people all took part against Andrea, and twenty thousand voices cried, "Put him to death!—put him to death!"

Franz sprang back; but the count seized his arm, and held him before the window.

"What are you doing?" said he. "Do you pity him? If you heard the cry of 'Mad dog!' you would take your gun,— you would, unhesitatingly, shoot the poor beast, who, after all, was only guilty of having been bitten by another dog. And yet you pity a man who, without being bitten by one of his race, has yet murdered his benefactor; and who, now unable to kill any one, because his hands are bound, wishes to see his companion in captivity perish. No—no: look!— look!"

This recommendation was needless; Franz was fascinated by the horrible spectacle. The two assistants had borne Andrea to the scaffold; and there, spite of his struggles, his bites, and his cries, had forced him to his knees. During this time the executioner had raised his mace, and signed to them to get out of the way: the criminal strove to rise, but, ere he had time, the mace fell on his left temple. A dull and heavy sound was heard, and the man dropped like an ox on his face, and then turned over on his back. The executioner let fall his mace, drew his knife, and with one stroke opened his throat, and, mounting on his stomach, stamped violently on it with his feet. At every stroke a jet of blood sprang from the wound.

This time Franz could sustain himself no longer, but sank, half fainting, into a seat. Albert, with his eyes closed, was standing grasping the window curtains. The count was erect and triumphant, like the Avenging Angel!

CHAPTER XXXVI

THE CARNIVAL AT ROME

WHEN Franz recovered his senses, he saw Albert drinking a glass of water, of which his paleness showed he stood in great need; and the count, who was assuming his carnival costume. He glanced mechanically towards the square ; all had disappeared—scaffold, executioners, victims. Nought remained but the people, full of noise and excitement. The bell of Monte-Citorio, which only sounds on the pope's decease and the opening of the Carnival, was ringing a joyous peal.

"Well," asked he of the count, "what has then happened?"

"Nothing," replied the count; "only, as you see, the Carnival has commenced. Make haste and dress yourself."

"In reality," said Franz, "this horrible scene has passed away like a dream."

"It is but a dream—the nightmare, that has disturbed you."

"Yes, that I have suffered. But the culprit?"

"That is a dream also; only he has remained asleep, whilst you have awakened; and who knows which of you is the most fortunate?"

"But Peppino, what has become of him?"

"Peppino is a lad of sense, who, unlike most men who are furious if they pass unnoticed, was delighted to see that the general attention was directed towards his companion. He profited by this distraction to slip away amongst the crowd, without even thanking the worthy priests who accompanied him. Decidedly man is an ungrateful and egotistical animal. But dress yourself; see, M. de Morcerf sets you the example."

Albert was, in reality, drawing on the satin pantaloons over his black trousers and varnished boots.

"Well, Albert," said Franz, "do you feel much inclined to join the revels? Come, answer frankly!"

"*Ma foi!* no," returned Albert. "But I am really glad to have seen such a sight; and I understand what M. le Comte said, that when you have once habituated yourself to a similar spectacle, it is the only one that causes you any emotion."

"Without reflecting that this is the only moment in which you can study characters," said the count, "on the steps of the scaffold death tears off the mask that has been worn through

life, and the real visage is disclosed. It must be allowed
Andrea was not very handsome,—the hideous scoundrel!
Come, dress yourselves, gentlemen,—dress yourselves."

Franz felt it would be ridiculous not to follow his two companions' example. He assumed his costume, and fastened on
his mask, that scarcely equalled the pallor of his own face.
Their toilette finished, they descended; the carriage awaited
them at the door, filled with sweetmeats and bouquets. They
fell into the line of carriages.

It is difficult to form an idea of the perfect change that had
taken place. Instead of the spectacle of gloomy and silent
death, the Place del Popolo presented a spectacle of gay and
noisy mirth and revelry. A crowd of masks flowed in from all
sides, escaping from the doors, descending from the windows.
From every street and every turn drove carriages filled with
pierrots, harlequins, dominos, marquises, Transteveres, knights,
and peasants—screaming, fighting, gesticulating, whirling eggs
filled with flour, confetti, nosegays—attacking, with their
sarcasms and their missiles, friends and foes, companions and
strangers, indiscriminately, without any one taking offence, or
doing any thing else than laugh. Franz and Albert were like
men who, to drive away a violent sorrow, have recourse to
wine, and who, as they drink and become intoxicated, feel a
thick veil drawn between the past and the present. They saw,
or rather continued to see, the image of what they had witnessed; but, little by little, the general vertigo seized them, and
they felt themselves obliged to take a part in the noise and
confusion. A handful of confetti that came from a neighbouring carriage, and which, whilst it covered Morcerf and his two
companions with dust, pricked his neck and that portion of his
face uncovered by his mask like a hundred pins, plunged him
into the general combat in which all the masks around him
were engaged. He rose in his turn, and seizing handfuls of
confetti and sweetmeats, with which the carriage was filled,
cast them with all the force and address he was master of.

The strife had fairly commenced, and the recollection of
what they had seen half an hour before was gradually effaced
from the young men's minds, so much were they occupied by
the gay and glittering procession they now beheld. As for
the Count of Monte-Cristo, he had never for an instant showed
any appearance of having been moved. Imagine the large and
splendid Rue du Cours, bordered from one end to the other
with lofty palaces, with their balconies hung with carpets, and
their windows with flags; at these balconies three hundred
thousand spectators—Romans, Italians, strangers from all
parts of the world. The united aristocracy of birth, wealth,
and genius; lovely women who, yielding to the influence of the
scene, bend over their balconies, or lean from their windows,

and shower down confetti, that is returned by bouquets. The air seems darkened with confetti that falls, and flowers that rise. In the streets the lively crowd, dressed in the most fantastic costumes. Gigantic cabbages walked gravely about —buffaloes' heads bellowed from men's shoulders—dogs pranced on their hind-legs. In the midst of all this a mask is lifted, and, as in Callot's Temptation of St. Anthony, a lovely face is exhibited, which we would fain follow, but from which we are separated by troops of fiends. This will give but a faint idea of the Carnival at Rome.

At the second turn the count stopped the carriage, and requested permission to quit them, leaving the vehicle at their disposal. Franz looked up; they were opposite the Rospoli Palace. At the centre window, the one hung with white damask with a red cross, was a blue domino, beneath which Franz's imagination easily pictured the beautiful Greek of the Argentina.

"Gentlemen," said the count, springing out, "when you are tired of being actors, and wish to become spectators of this scene, you know you have places at my windows. In the meantime, dispose of my coachman, my carriage, and my servants."

We have forgotten to mention that the count's coachman was attired in a bear-skin, exactly resembling Odry's in *The Bear and the Pacha;* and the two footmen behind were dressed up as green monkeys, with spring masks, with which they made grimaces at every one who passed.

Franz thanked the count for his attention. As for Albert, he was busily occupied throwing bouquets at a carriage full of Roman peasants that was passing near him. Unfortunately for him, the line of carriages moved on again, and whilst he descended the Place del Popolo, the other ascended towards the Palais de Vénise.

"Ah! my dear fellow!" said he to Franz; "you did not see?"

"What?"

"There—that *calèche* filled with Roman peasants."

"No."

"Well, I am convinced they were all charming women."

"How unfortunate you were masked, Albert!" said Franz; "here was an opportunity of making up for past disappointments."

"Oh!" replied he, half laughing, half serious; "I hope the Carnival will not pass without some amends in one shape or the other."

But, in spite of Albert's hope, the day passed unmarked by any incident, except meeting two or three times the *calèche* with the Roman peasants. At one of these encounters, acci-

dentally or purposely, Albert's mask fell off.   He instantly
rose and cast the remainder of the bouquets into the carriage.
Doubtless one of the charming females Albert had divined
beneath their coquettish disguise was touched by his gallantry;
for, in her turn, as the carriage of the two friends passed her,
she threw a bunch of violets into it.   Albert seized it, and as
Franz had no reason to suppose it was addressed to him, he
suffered Albert to retain it.   Albert placed it in his button-
hole, and the carriage went triumphantly on.

"Well," said Franz to him; "here is the commencement of
an adventure."

"Laugh if you please.   I really think so.   So I will not
abandon this bouquet."

"*Pardieu!*" returned Franz, laughing, "in token of your
gratitude."

The jest, however, soon appeared to become earnest; for
when Albert and Franz again encountered the carriage with the
contadini, the one who had thrown the violets to Albert clapped
her hands when she beheld them in his button-hole.

"Bravo! bravo!" said Franz; "things go wonderfully.
Shall I leave you?   Perhaps you would prefer being alone?"

"No," replied he; "I will not be caught like a fool at a first
demonstration by a rendezvous beneath the clock, as they say
at the opera balls.   If the fair peasant wishes to carry matters
any further, we shall find her, or rather she will find us to-
morrow; then she will give me some sign or other, and I shall
know what I have to do."

"On my word," said Franz, "you are wise as Nestor and
prudent as Ulysses, and your fair Circe must be very skilful or
very powerful if she succeed in changing you into a beast of any
kind."

Albert was right; the fair unknown had resolved, doubtless,
to carry the intrigue no farther; for although the young men
made several more turns, they did not again see the calèche,
which had turned up one of the neighbouring streets.   Then
they returned to the Rospoli Palace; but the count and the
blue domino had also disappeared; the two windows, hung
with yellow damask, were still occupied by the persons whom
the count had invited.   At this moment the same bell that had
proclaimed the commencement of the carnival sounded the
retreat.   The file on the Corso broke the line, and in a second
all the carriages had disappeared.   Franz and Albert were
opposite the Via delle Maratte; the coachman, without saying
a word, drove up it, passed along the Place d'Espagne and the
Rospoli Palace, and stopped at the door of the hôtel.

Maître Pastrini came to the door to receive his guests.

Franz's first care was to inquire after the count, and to
express his regret he had not returned in sufficient time to take

him up; but Pastrini reassured him by saying, that the Count of Monte-Cristo had ordered a second carriage for himself, and that it had gone at four o'clock to fetch him at the Rospoli Palace. The count had, moreover, charged him to offer the two friends the key of his box at the Argentina. Franz questioned Albert as to his intentions; but Albert had great projects to put into execution before going to the theatre; and, instead of making any answer, he inquired if Maître Pastrini could procure him a tailor.

"A tailor!" said the host; "and for what?"

"To make us between now and to-morrow two costumes of Roman peasants," returned Albert.

The host shook his head. "To make you two costumes between now and to-morrow? I ask your excellencies' pardon, but this is a demand quite French; for the next week you will not find a single tailor who would consent to sew six buttons on a waistcoat if you paid him a crown a piece for each button."

"Then I must give up the idea?"

"No; we have them ready made. Leave all to me; and, to-morrow, when you wake, you shall find a collection of costumes with which you will be satisfied."

"My dear Albert," said Franz, "leave all to our host; he has already proved himself full of resources: let us dine quietly, and afterwards go and see *"L'Italiana in Algeri."*

"Agreed," returned Albert; "but, recollect, Maître Pastrini, that both my friend and myself attach the greatest importance to having to-morrow the costumes we have asked for."

The host again assured them they might rely on him, and that their wishes should be attended to; upon which Franz and Albert mounted to their apartments, and proceeded to disencumber themselves of their costume. Albert, as he took off his dress, carefully preserved the bunch of violets; it was his sign of recognition for the morrow. The two friends sat down to table; but they could not refrain from remarking the difference between the table of the Count of Monte-Cristo and that of Maître Pastrini. Truth compelled Franz, spite of the dislike he seemed to have taken to the count, to confess that the advantage was not on Pastrini's side.

During dessert the servant inquired at what time they wished for the carriage. Albert and Franz looked at each other, fearing really to abuse the count's kindness. The servant understood them.

"His excellency, the Count of Monte-Cristo, had," he said, "given positive orders that the carriage was to remain at their lordships' orders all the day, and they could, therefore, dispose of it without fear of indiscretion."

They resolved to profit by the count's courtesy, and ordered the horses to be harnessed, whilst they substituted an evening costume for that which they had on, and which was somewhat the worse for the numerous combats they had sustained. This precaution taken, they went to the theatre, and installed themselves in the count's box. During the first act, the Countess G—— entered hers. Her first look was at the *loge* where she had seen the count the previous evening, so that she perceived Franz and Albert in the box of the very person concerning whom she had expressed so strange an opinion to Franz. Her opera-glass was so fixedly directed towards them, that Franz saw it would be cruel not to satisfy her curiosity; and, availing himself of one of the privileges of the spectators of the Italian theatres, which consists in using their boxes as their drawing-room, the two friends quitted their box to pay their respects to the countess. Scarcely had they entered the *loge*, than she motioned to Franz to assume the seat of honour. Albert, in his turn, sat behind.

"Well," said she, hardly giving Franz time to sit down, "it seems you have nothing better to do than to make the acquaintance of this new Lord Ruthven, and you are the best friends in the world."

"Without being so far advanced as that, Madame la Comtesse," returned Franz, "I cannot deny we have abused his good-nature all day."

"All day?"

"Yes, this morning we breakfasted with him; we rode in his carriage all day, and now we have taken possession of his box."

"You know him, then?"

"Yes, and no."

"How so?"

"It is a long story."

"Relate it to me."

"It would frighten you too much."

"Another reason."

"At least wait until the story has a conclusion."

"Very well; I prefer complete histories; but tell me how you made his acquaintance. Did any one introduce you to him?"

"No; it was he who introduced himself to us."

"When?"

"Last night, after we left you."

"Through what medium?"

"The very prosaic one of our landlord."

"He is staying then at the Hôtel de Londres with you?"

"Not only in the same hôtel, but on the same floor."

"What is his name; for, of course, you know?"

"The Count of Monte-Cristo."

"That is not a family name?"

"No, it is the name of the island he has purchased."

"And he is a count?"

"A Tuscan count."

"Well, we must put up with that," said the countess, who was herself of one of the oldest families of Venice. "What sort of a man is he?"

"Ask the Vicomte de Morcerf."

"You hear, M. de Morcerf, I am referred to you," said the countess.

"We should be very hard to please, madame," returned Albert, "did we not think him delightful; a friend of ten years' standing could not have done more for us, or with a more perfect courtesy."

"Come," observed the countess, smiling, "I see my vampire is only some millionaire, who has taken the appearance of Lara in order to avoid being confounded with M. de Rothschild; and have you seen her?"

"Her?"

"The beautiful Greek of yesterday."

"No; we heard, I think, the sound of her *guzla*, but she remained perfectly invisible."

"When you say invisible," interrupted Albert, "it is only to keep up the mystery; for whom do you take the blue domino at the window with the white curtains?"

"Where was this window with white hangings?" said the countess.

"At the Rospoli Palace."

"The count had three windows of the Rospoli Palace?"

"Yes. Did you pass through the Rue du Cours?"

"Yes."

"Well, did you remark two windows hung with yellow damask, and one with white damask with a red cross? Those were the count's windows."

"Why, he must be a nabob! Do you know what those three windows were worth?"

"Two or three hundred Roman crowns?"

"Two or three thousand!"

"The devil!"

"Does his isle produce him such a revenue?"

"It does not bring him a bajocco."

"Then why did he purchase it?"

"For a whim."

"He is an original, then?"

"In reality," observed Albert, "he seemed to me somewhat eccentric; were he at Paris, and a frequenter of the theatres, I should say he was a poor devil, literally mad. This morning he made two or three exits worthy of Didier or Anthony."

At this moment a fresh visitor entered, and, according to custom, Franz gave up his seat to him. This circumstance had, moreover, the effect of changing the conversation; an hour afterwards the two friends returned to their hotel. Maître Pastrini had already set about procuring their disguises for the morrow; and he assured them they would be perfectly satisfied. The next morning, at nine o'clock, he entered Franz's room, followed by a tailor, who had eight or ten costumes of Roman peasants on his arm; they selected two exactly alike, and charged the tailor to sew on each of their hats about twenty yards of riband, and to procure them two of those long silken sashes of different colours with which the lower orders decorate themselves on fête-days. Albert was impatient to see how he looked in his new dress; it was a jacket and breeches of blue velvet, silk stockings with clocks, shoes with buckles, and a silk waistcoat. This picturesque attire set him off to great advantage; and when he had bound the scarf around his waist and when his hat, placed coquettishly on one side, let fall on his shoulder a stream of ribands, Franz was forced to confess that costume has much to do with the physical superiority we accord to certain nations. The Turks, who used to be so picturesque with their long and flowing robes, are they not now hideous with their blue frocks buttoned up to the chin, and their red caps, which make them look like a bottle of wine with a red seal? Franz complimented Albert, who looked at himself in the glass with an unequivocal smile of satisfaction. They were thus engaged when the Count of Monte-Cristo entered.

"Gentlemen," said he, "although a companion is agreeable, perfect freedom is sometimes still more agreeable. I come to say that to-day, and the remainder of the Carnival, I leave the carriage entirely at your disposal. The host will tell you I have three or four more, so that you do not deprive me in any way of it. Employ it, I pray you, for your pleasure or your business."

The young men wished to decline; but they could find no good reason for refusing an offer which was so agreeable to them. The Count of Monte-Cristo remained a quarter of an hour with them conversing on all subjects with the greatest ease. He was, as we have already said, perfectly well acquainted with the literature of all countries. A glance at the walls of his salon proved to Franz and Albert that he was an amateur of pictures. A few words he let fall shewed them he was no stranger to the sciences, and he seemed much occupied with chemistry. The two friends did not venture to return the count the breakfast he had given them: it would have been too absurd to offer him in exchange for his excellent table the very inferior one of Maître Pastrini. They told him so frankly, and he received their excuses with the air of a man who appreciated their delicacy. Albert was charmed with the count's manners;

and he was only prevented from recognising him for a veritable
gentleman by his science. The permission to do what he liked
with the carriage pleased him above all; for the fair peasants
had appeared in a most elegant carriage the preceding evening,
and Albert was not sorry to be upon an equal footing with
them. At half-past one they descended, the coachman and
footman had put on their livery over their disguises, which
gave them a more ridiculous appearance than ever; and which
gained them the applause of Franz and Albert. Albert had
fastened the faded bunch of violets to his button-hole. At the
first sound of the bell they hastened into the Rue du Cours by
the Via Vittoria.

At the second turn, a bunch of fresh violets, thrown from a
carriage filled with pierrots and pierrettes, indicated to Albert
that, like himself and his friend, the peasants had changed
their costume also; and whether it was the result of chance,
or whether a similar feeling had possessed them both, whilst he
had changed his costume they had assumed his.

Albert placed the fresh bouquet in his button-hole; but he
kept the faded one in his hand; and when he again met the
calèche, he raised it to his lips, an action which seemed greatly
to amuse not only the fair lady who had thrown it, but her
joyous companions also. The day was as gay as the preceding
one, perhaps even more animated and noisy; the count
appeared for an instant at his window, but when they again
repassed, he had disappeared. It is almost needless to say
that the flirtation between Albert and the fair peasant continued all day. The evening on his return Franz found a letter
from the embassy to inform him he would have the honour of
being received by his Holiness the next day. At each previous
visit he had made to Rome, he had solicited and obtained the
same favour; and incited as much by a religious feeling as by
gratitude, he was unwilling to quit the capital of the Christian
world without laying his respectful homage at the feet of one
of St. Peter's successors, who has set the rare example of all
virtues. He did not then think of the Carnival; for, in spite
of his condescension and touching kindness, one cannot incline
one's self without awe before the venerable and noble old man
called Gregory XVI. On his return from the Vatican, Franz
carefully avoided the Rue du Cours; he brought away with him
a treasure of pious thoughts, to which the mad gaiety of the
mascherata would have been profanation.

At ten minutes past five Albert entered overjoyed. The
pierrette had reassumed her peasant's costume, and as she
passed had raised her mask. She was charming.

Franz congratulated Albert, who received his congratulations with the air of a man conscious they are merited. He had
recognised, by certain unmistakable signs, that his fair

C.M.—M

incognito belonged to the aristocracy. He had made up his mind to write to her the next day.

Franz remarked, whilst he gave these details, that Albert seemed to have something to ask of him, but that he was unwilling to ask it. He insisted upon it, declaring beforehand that he was willing to make any sacrifice he required. Albert let himself be pressed just as long as friendship required, and then avowed to Franz that he would do him a great favour by suffering him to occupy the carriage alone the next day.

Albert attributed to Franz's absence the extreme kindness of the fair peasant in raising her mask.

Franz was not sufficiently egotistical to stop Albert in the middle of an adventure that promised to prove so agreeable to his curiosity and so flattering to his vanity. He felt assured that the perfect indiscretion of his friend would duly inform him of all that happened; and as during three years that he had travelled all over Italy a similar piece of good fortune had never fallen to his share, Franz was by no means sorry to learn how to act on such an occasion. He therefore promised Albert that he would content himself the morrow with witnessing the Carnival from the windows of the Rospoli Palace.

The next morning he saw Albert pass and repass. He held an enormous bouquet, which he, doubtless, meant to make the bearer of his amorous epistle. This belief was changed into certainty when Franz saw the bouquet (remarkable by a circle of white camelias) in the hand of a charming pierrette dressed in rose-coloured satin.

The evening was no longer joy but delirium. Albert nothing doubted but that the fair unknown would reply in the same manner. Franz anticipated his wishes by telling him the noise fatigued him, and that he should pass the next day in writing and looking over his journal.

Albert was not deceived; for the next evening Franz saw him enter, shaking triumphantly a folded paper he held by one corner.

"Well," said he, "was I mistaken?"

"She has answered you!" cried Franz.

"Read!"

This word was pronounced in a manner impossible to describe. Franz took the letter and read:—

"Tuesday evening, at seven o'clock, descend from your carriage opposite the Via dei Pontefici, and follow the Roman peasant who snatches your *moccoletto* from you. When you arrive at the first step of the church of San Giacomo, be sure to fasten a knot of rose-coloured ribands to the shoulder of your carnival costume, in order that you may be recognised. Until then you will not see me. Constancy and Discretion."

"Well," asked he, when Franz had finished, "what do you think of that?"

"I think that the adventure is assuming a very agreeable appearance."

"I think so, also," replied Albert; "and I very much fear you will go alone to the Duke of Bracciano's ball."

Franz and Albert had received that morning an invitation from the celebrated Roman banker.

"Take care, Albert," said Franz. "All the nobility of Rome will be present; and if your fair *incognita* belong to the higher class of society she must go there."

"Whether she goes there or not my opinion is still the same," returned Albert. "You have read the letter?"

"Yes."

"You know how imperfectly the women of the *mezzo cito* are educated in Italy?"

(This is the name of the lower class.)

"Yes."

"Well; read the letter again. Look at the writing, and find a fault in the language or orthography."

(The writing was in reality charming, and the orthography irreproachable.)

"You are born to good fortune," said Franz, as he returned the letter.

"Laugh as much as you will," replied Albert, "I am in love."

"You alarm me," cried Franz. "I see that I shall not only go alone to the Duke of Bracciano's, but also return to Florence alone."

"If my unknown be as amiable as she is beautiful," said Albert, "I shall fix myself at Rome for six weeks at least. I adore Rome, and I have always had a great taste for archæology."

"Come, two or three more such adventures, and I do not despair of seeing you a member of the Academy."

Doubtless Albert was about to discuss seriously his right to the academic chair, when they were informed dinner was ready. Albert's love had not taken away his appetite. He hastened with Franz to seat himself, free to recommence the discussion after dinner.

After dinner the Count of Monte-Cristo was announced. They had not seen him for two days. Maître Pastrini informed them that business had called him to Civita Vecchia. He had started the previous evening, and had only returned an hour since.

He was charming. Whether he kept a watch over himself, or whether accident did not sound the acrimonious chords that certain circumstances had already touched, he was like every body else. This man was an enigma to Franz. The count must feel sure he recognised him; and yet he had not let fall a single word that indicated he had seen him anywhere. On his side, however, great Franz's desire was to allude to their former interview, the fear of its being disagreeable to the man who had loaded himself and his friend with kindness prevented him from mentioning it.

The count had learned the two friends had sent to secure a box at the Argentina Theatre, and were told they were all let. In consequence he brought them the key of his own—at least such was the apparent motive of his visit.

Franz and Albert made some difficulty, alleging their fear of depriving him of it; but the count replied, that as he was going to the Palli Theatre, the box at the Argentina Theatre would be lost if they did not profit by it. This assurance determined the two friends to accept it.

Franz had become by degrees accustomed to the count's paleness, which had so forcibly struck him the first time he saw him. He could not refrain from admiring the severe beauty of his features, the only defect, or rather the principal quality of which was the pallor. Veritable hero of Byron! Franz could not (we will not say see him, but) even think of him without representing his stern head on the shoulders of Manfred, or beneath the casque of Lara. His forehead was marked by the line that indicates the constant presence of a bitter thought; he had those fiery eyes that seem to penetrate to the heart; and the haughty and disdainful upper lip, that gives to the words it utters a peculiar character that impresses them on the minds of those to whom they are addressed. The count was no longer young. He was at least forty; and yet it was easy to understand he was formed to rule the young men with whom he associated at present. In reality, to complete his resemblance with the fantastic heroes of the English poet, the count seemed to have the power of fascination.

Albert was constantly expatiating on their good fortune in meeting such a man. Franz was less enthusiastic; but the count exercised over him also the ascendancy a strong mind always acquires. He thought several times of the project the count had of visiting Paris; and he had no doubt but that with his eccentric character, his characteristic face, and his colossal fortune, he would produce a great effect there. And yet he did not wish to be at Paris when the count was there.

The evening passed as evenings mostly pass at Italian theatres: that is, not in listening to the music, but in paying visits and conversing. The Countess G—— wished to revive the subject of the count, but Franz announced he had something far newer to tell her; and, in spite of Albert's demonstrations of false modesty, he informed the countess of the great event which had pre-occupied them for the three last days.

As similar intrigues are not uncommon in Italy, if we may credit travellers, the countess did not manifest the least incredulity, but congratulated Albert on his success. They promised, upon separating, to meet at the Duke of Bracciano's ball, to which all Rome was invited. The heroine of the bouquet kept her word: she gave Albert no sign of her existence the morrow and day after.

At length arrived the Tuesday, the last and most tumultuous day of the Carnival. The Tuesday the theatres open at ten o'clock in the morning, as Lent begins after eight at night; the Tuesday all those who through want of money, time or enthusiasm, have not been to see the Carnival before, mingle in the gaiety and contribute to the noise and excitement. From two o'clock till five Franz and Albert followed in the fête, exchanging handfuls of confetti with the other carriages and the pedestrians, who crowded amongst the horses' feet and the carriage-wheels without a single accident, a single dispute, or a single fight.

The fêtes are veritable days of pleasure to the Italians. The author of this history, who has resided five or six years in Italy, does not recollect to have ever seen a ceremony interrupted by one of those events so common in other countries.

Albert was triumphant in his carnival costume. A knot of rose-coloured ribands fell from his shoulder almost to the ground. In order that there might be no confusion, Franz wore his peasant's costume.

As the day advanced the tumult became greater. There was not on the pavement, in the carriages, at the windows, a single tongue that was silent, a single arm that did not move. It was a human storm composed of a thunder of cries, and a hail of sweetmeats, flowers, eggs, oranges, and nosegays. At three o'clock the sound of fireworks, let off on the Place del Popolo and the Palais de Vénise (heard with difficulty amid the din and confusion), announced that the races were about to begin. The races, like the *moccoli,* are one of the episodes peculiar to the last days of the Carnival. At the sound of the fireworks the carriages instantly broke the ranks and retired by the adjacent streets. All these evolutions are executed with an inconceivable address and marvellous rapidity, without the police interfering in the matter.

The pedestrians ranged themselves against the walls; then the trampling of horses and the clashing of steel were heard. A detachment of carabineers, fifteen a-breast, galloped up the Rue du Cours in order to clear it for the *barberi.* When the detachment arrived at the Palaise de Vénise, a second volley of fireworks was again discharged to announce that the street was clear. Almost instantly, in the midst of a tremendous and general outcry, seven or eight horses, excited by the shouts of three hundred thousand spectators, passed by like lightning. Then the Castle of Saint-Angelo fired three cannons to indicate that number three had won. Immediately, without any signal, the carriages moved on, flowing on towards the Corso, down all the streets, like torrents pent up for awhile, which again flow into the parent river; and the immense stream again continued its course between its two banks of granite.

A new source of noise and movement was added to the crowd. The sellers of *moccoletto* entered on the scene. The *moccoli*, or *moccoletto*, are candles which vary in size from the pascal taper to the rushlight, and which cause the actors on the great scene which terminates the Carnival two different sources of thought; 1st. How to preserve their *moccoletto* alight. 2d. How to extinguish the *moccoletto* of others.

The *moccoletto* is like life: man has found but one means of transmitting it, and that one comes from God. But he has discovered a thousand means of taking it away, although the devil has somewhat aided him. The *moccoletto* is kindled by approaching it to a light. But who can describe the thousand means of extinguishing the *moccoletto*?—the gigantic bellows, the monstrous extinguishers, the super-human fans. Every one hastened to purchase *moccoletti*—Franz and Albert among the rest.

The night was rapidly approaching; and already, at the cry of "*moccoletto!*" repeated by the shrill voices of a thousand vendors, two or three stars began to burn among the crowd. It was a signal. At the end of ten minutes fifty thousand lights glittered, descending from the Palais de Vénise to the Place del Popolo, and mounting from the Place del Popolo to the Palais de Vénise. It seemed the fête of Jack-o'-lanterns. It is impossible to form any idea of it, without having seen it. Suppose all the stars had descended from the sky and mingled in a wild dance on the face of the earth; the whole accompanied by cries that were never heard in any other part of the world. The *facchino* follows the prince, the Transtevere the citizen, every one blowing, extinguishing, relighting. Had old Æolus appeared at this moment he would have been proclaimed king of the *moccoli*, and Aquilo the heir-presumptive to the throne.

This flaming race continued for two hours; the Rue du Cours was light as day; the features of the spectators on the third and fourth stories were visible. Every five minutes Albert took out his watch; at length it pointed to seven. The two friends were in the Via dei Pontefici. Albert sprang out, bearing his *moccoletto* in his hand. Two or three masks strove to knock his *moccoletto* out of his hand; but Albert, a first-rate pugilist, sent them rolling in the street one after the other, and continued his course towards the church of San Giacomo. The steps were crowded with masks, who strove to snatch each other's flambeaux. Franz followed Albert with his eyes, and saw him mount the first step. Instantly a mask, wearing the well-known costume of a female peasant, snatched his *moccoletto* from him without his offering any resistance. Franz was too far off to hear what they said, but without doubt nothing hostile passed, for he saw Albert disappear arm-in-arm with the peasant girl.

He watched them pass through the crowd some time, but at length he lost sight of them in the Via Macello. Suddenly the bell that gives the signal for the Carnival sounded, and at the same instant all the *moccoletto* were extinguished as if by enchantment. It seemed as though one immense blast of the wind had extinguished every one. Franz found himself in utter darkness. No sound was audible save that of the carriages that conveyed the masks home; nothing was visible save a few lights that burnt behind the windows.

The Carnival was finished.

CHAPTER XXXVII

THE CATACOMBS OF SAINT-SEBASTIAN

In his whole life, perhaps, Franz had never before experienced so sudden an impression, so rapid a transition from gaiety to sadness, as in this moment. It seemed as though Rome, under the magic breath of some demon of the night, had suddenly changed into a vast tomb. By a chance, which added yet more to the intensity of the darkness, the moon, which was on the wane, did not rise until eleven o'clock, and the streets which the young man traversed were plunged in the deepest obscurity. The distance was short; and at the end of ten minutes his carriage, or rather the count's, stopped before the Hôtel de Londres.

Dinner was waiting; but as Albert had told him that he should not return so soon, Franz sat down without him.

Maître Pastrini, who had been accustomed to see them dine together, inquired into the cause of his absence, but Franz merely replied, that Albert had received on the previous evening an invitation which he had accepted. The sudden extinction of the *moccoletti*, the darkness which had replaced the light, the silence which had succeeded, and the turmoil, had left in Franz's mind a certain depression which was not free from uneasiness. He therefore dined very silently, in spite of the officious attentions of his host, who presented himself two or three times to inquire if he wanted any thing.

Franz resolved to wait for Albert as late as possible. He ordered the carriage, therefore, for eleven o'clock, desiring Maître Pastrini to inform him the moment Albert returned to the hôtel. At eleven o'clock Albert had not come back. Franz dressed himself and went out, telling his host that he was going to pass the night at the Duke of Bracciano's. The house of the Duke of Bracciano is one of the most delightful in Rome: his lady, one of the last heiresses of the Colonnas, does its honours with the most consummate grace, and thus their fêtes have an European celebrity. Franz and Albert had brought to Rome letters of introduction to them; and the first question on Franz's arrival was to ask him where was his travelling companion. Franz replied that he had left him at the moment they were about to extinguish the *moccoli*, and that he had lost sight of him in the Via Macello.

"Then he has not returned?" said the Duke.

"I waited for him until this hour," replied Franz.

"And do you know whither he went?"

"No, not precisely: however, I think it was something very like an assignation."

"Diavolo!" said the Duke, "this is a bad day, or rather a bad night, to be out late; is it not, countess?"

These words were addressed to the Countess G——, who had just arrived and was leaning on the arm of Mr. Torlonia, the duke's brother.

"I think, on the contrary, that it is a charming night," replied the countess, "and those who are here will not complain but of one thing, that of its too rapid flight."

"I am not speaking," said the duke, with a smile, "of the persons who are here: the men run no other danger than that of falling in love with you, and the women of falling ill of jealousy at seeing you so lovely: I alluded to persons who were out in the streets of Rome."

"Ah!" asked the countess, "who is out in the streets of Rome at this hour, unless it be to go to a ball?"

"Our friend Albert de Morcerf, countess, whom I left in pursuit of his unknown about seven o'clock this evening," said Franz, "and whom I have not since seen."

"And don't you know where he is?"

"Not at all."

"Is he armed?"

"He is *en paillasse*."

"You should not have allowed him to go," said the duke to Franz; "you who know Rome better than he does."

"You might as well have tried to stop number three of the *barberi* who gained the prize in the race to-day," replied Franz; "and then, moreover, what could happen to him?"

"Who can tell? the night is gloomy, and the Tiber is very near the Via Macello."

Franz felt a shudder run through his veins at observing the feeling of the duke and the countess so much in unison with his own personal disquietude.

"I informed them at the hôtel that I had the honour of passing the night here, duke," said Franz, "and desired them to come and inform me of his return."

"Ah!" replied the duke, "here, I think, is one of my servants who is seeking you."

The duke was not mistaken; when he saw Franz, the servant came up to him.

"Your excellency," he said, "the master of the Hôtel de

C.M.——M*

Londres has sent to let you know that a man is waiting for you with a letter from the Viscount of Morcerf."

"A letter from the viscount!" exclaimed Franz.

"Yes."

"And who is the man?"

"I do not know."

"Why did he not bring it to me here?"

"The messenger did not say."

"And where is the messenger?"

"He went away directly he saw me enter the ball-room to find you."

"Oh!" said the countess to Franz; "go with all speed,—poor young man! perhaps some accident has happened to him."

"I will hasten," replied Franz.

"Shall we see you again to give us any information?" inquired the countess.

"Yes, if it is not any serious affair, otherwise I cannot answer as to what I may do myself."

"Be prudent, in any event," said the countess.

"Oh! pray, be assured of that."

Franz took his hat and went away in haste. He had sent away his carriage with orders for it to fetch him at two o'clock: fortunately the Palazzo Bracciano, which is on one side in the Rue du Cours and in the other in the Place des Saints Apôtres, is hardly ten minutes' walk from the Hôtel de Londres. As he came near the hotel, Franz saw a man in the centre of the street, he had no doubt that it was the messenger from Albert. The man was wrapped up in a large cloak. He went up to him, but to his extreme astonishment this individual first addressed him.

"What wants your excellency of me?" inquired the man, retreating a step or two as if to keep on his guard.

"Are you not the person who brought me a letter," inquired Franz, "from the Viscount de Morcerf?"

"Your excellency lodges at Pastrini's hotel?"

"I do."

"Your excellency is the travelling companion of the viscount?"

"I am."

"Your excellency's name——"

"Is the Baron Franz d'Epinay."

"Then it is to your excellency that this letter is addressed."

"Is there any answer?" inquired Franz, taking the letter from him.

"Yes,—your friend, at least, hopes so."

"Come up-stairs with me, and I will give it to you."

"I prefer waiting here," said the messenger, with a smile.

"And why?"

"Your excellency will know when you have read the letter."

"Shall I find you, then, here?"

"Certainly."

Franz entered the hôtel. On the staircase he met Maître Pastrini.

"Well?" said the landlord.

"Well—what?" responded Franz.

"You have seen the man who desired to speak with you from your friend?" he asked of Franz.

"Yes, I have seen him," he replied, "and he has handed this letter to me. Light the candle in my apartment, if you please."

The innkeeper gave orders to a servant to go before Franz with a bougie. The young man had found Maître Pastrini looking very much alarmed, and this had only made him the more anxious to read Albert's letter, and thus he went instantly towards the waxlight and unfolded the letter. It was written and signed by Albert. Franz read it twice before he could comprehend what it contained. It was thus conceived:—

"MY DEAR FELLOW,—The moment you have received this, have the kindness to take from my pocket-book, which you will find in the square drawer of the secrétaire, the letter of credit: add your own to it, if it be not sufficient. Run to Torlonia, draw from him instantly four thousand piastres, and give them to the bearer. It is urgent that I should have this money without delay.

"I do not say more, relying on you as you may rely on me.
"Your friend,
"ALBERT DE MORCERF.

"P.S. I now believe in Italian banditti."

Below these lines were written in a strange hand the following in Italian:—

"Se alle sei della mattina le quattro mile piastre non sono nelle mie mani, alle sette il Conte Alberto avrà cessato di vivere.
"LUIGI VAMPA."

"If by six in the morning the four thousand piastres are not in my hands, by seven o'clock the Viscount Albert de Morcerf will have ceased to live."

This second signature explained all to Franz, who now understood the objection of the messenger to coming up into the apartment; the street was safer for him. Albert, then, had fallen into the hands of the famous chief of banditti in whose existence he had for so long time refused to believe.

There was no time to lose. He hastened to open the secrétaire, and found the pocket-book in the drawer, and in it the letter of credit; there was in all six thousand piastres, but of these six thousand Albert had already expended three thousand. As to Franz he had no letter of credit as he lived at Florence, and had only come to Rome to pass seven or eight days; he had brought but a hundred louis, and of these he had not more than fifty left.

Thus seven or eight hundred piastres were wanting to them both to make up the sum that Albert required. True he might in such a case rely on the kindness of M. Torlonia.

He was, therefore, about to return to the Palazzo Bracciano without loss of time when suddenly a luminous idea crossed his mind. He remembered the Count of Monte-Cristo. Franz was about to ring for Maître Pastrini when that worthy presented himself.

"My dear sir," he said hastily, "do you know if the count is within?"

"Yes, your excellency; he has this moment returned."

"Is he in bed?"

"I should say no."

"Then ring at his door, if you please, and request him to be so kind as to give me an audience."

Maître Pastrini did as he was desired, and returning five minutes after he said,

"The count awaits your excellency."

Franz went along the corridor, and a servant introduced him to the count. He was in a small cabinet which Franz had not yet seen, and which was surrounded with divans. The count came towards him.

"Well, what good wind blows you hither at this hour?" said he: "have you come to sup with me? it would be very kind of you."

"No, I have come to speak to you of a very serious matter."

"A serious matter!" said the count, looking at Franz with the earnestness usual to him: "and what may it be?"

"Are we alone?"

"Yes," replied the count, going to the door and returning. Franz gave him Albert's letter.

"Read that," he said. The count read it.

"Ah! ah!" said he.

"Did you see the postscript?"

"I did, indeed.

"'Se alle sei della mattina le quattro mile piastre non sono nelle mie mani, alle sette il Conte Alberto avrà cessato di vivere.

"'LUIGI VAMPA.'"

"What think you of that?" inquired Franz.

"Have you the money he demands?"

"Yes, all but eight hundred piastres."

The count went to his secrétaire, opened it, and pulling out a drawer filled with gold, said to Franz,—

"I hope you will not offend me by applying to anyone but myself."

"You see, on the contrary, I come to you first and instantly," replied Franz.

"And I thank you; have what you will;" and he made a sign to Franz to take what he pleased.

"Is it absolutely necessary, then, to send the money to Luigi Vampa?" asked the young man, looking fixedly in his turn at the count.

"Judge yourself," replied he. "The postscript is explicit."

"I think that if you would take the trouble of reflecting, you could find a way of simplifying the negotiation," said Franz.

"How so?" returned the count, with surprise.

"If we were to go together to Luigi Vampa, I am sure he would not refuse you Albert's freedom."

"What influence can I possibly have over a bandit?"

"Have you not just rendered him one of those services that are never forgotten?"

"What is that?"

"Have you not saved Peppino's life?"

"Ah! ah!" said the count, "who told you that?"

"No matter, I know it."

The count knit his brows and remained silent an instant.

"And if I went to seek Vampa, would you accompany me?"

"If my society would not be disagreeable."

"Be it so; it is a lovely night, and a walk without Rome will do us both good."

"Shall I take my arms?"

"For what purpose?"

"Any money?"

"It is useless. Where is the man who brought the letter?"

"In the street."

"He awaits the answer?"

"Yes."

"I must learn where we are going. I will summon him hither."

"It is useless, he would not come up."

"To your apartments, perhaps: but he will not make any difficulty in entering mine."

The count went to the window of the apartment that looked on to the street, and whistled in a peculiar manner. The man in the mantle quitted the wall, and advanced into the centre of the street.

"*Salite !*" said the count, in the same tone in which he would have given an order to his servant. The messenger obeyed without the least hesitation, but rather with alacrity, and mounting the steps of the passage at a bound, entered the hôtel: five seconds afterwards he was at the door of the cabinet.

"Ah! it is you, Peppino," said the count.

But Peppino, instead of answering, threw himself on his knees, seized the count's hand, and covered it with kisses.

"Ah!" said the count, "you have, then, not forgotten that I saved your life; that is strange, for it is a week ago."

"No, excellency, and I never shall forget it," returned Peppino, with an accent of profound gratitude.

"Never! that is a long time: but it is something that you believe so. Rise and answer."

Peppino glanced anxiously at Franz.

"Oh, you may speak before his excellency," said he. "He is one of my friends.—You allow me to give you this title," continued the count in French; "it is necessary to win this man's confidence."

"You can speak before me," said Franz. "I am a friend of the count's."

"Good," returned Peppino; "I am ready to answer any questions your excellency may address to me."

"How did the Viscount Albert fall into Luigi's hands?"

"Excellency, the Frenchman's carriage passed several times the one in which was Teresa."

"The chief's mistress?"

"Yes: the Frenchman threw her a bouquet, Teresa returned it: all this with the consent of the chief, who was in the carriage."

"What!" cried Franz, "was Luigi Vampa in the carriage with the Roman peasants?"

"It was he who drove, disguised as the coachman," replied Peppino.

"Well?" said the count.

"Well, then the Frenchman took off his mask. Teresa, with the chief's consent, did the same. The Frenchman asked for a rendezvous; Teresa gave him one; only instead of Teresa it was Beppo who was on the steps of the church of San Giacomo."

"What!" exclaimed Franz, "the peasant girl who snatched his moccoletto from him——?"

"Was a lad of fifteen," replied Peppino; "but it was no disgrace to your friend to have been deceived. Beppo has taken in plenty of others."

"And Beppo led him outside the walls?" said the count.

"Exactly so; a carriage was waiting at the end of Via Macello. Beppo got in, inviting the Frenchman to follow him, and he did not wait to be asked twice. He gallantly offered the right-hand seat to Beppo, and sat by him. Beppo told him he was going to take him to a villa, a league from Rome; the Frenchman assured him he would follow him to the end of the world. The coachman went up the Rue di Ripetta and the Porte San Paola; and when they were two hundred yards outside, as the Frenchman became somewhat too forward, Beppo put a brace of pistols to his head, the coachman pulled up and did the same. At the same time four of the band, who were concealed on the banks of the Almo, surrounded the carriage. The Frenchman made some resistance, and nearly strangled Beppo; but he could not resist five armed men, and was forced to yield, they made him get out, walk along the banks of the river, and then brought him to Teresa and Luigi, who were waiting for him in the catacombs of Saint Sebastian."

"Well," said the count, turning towards Franz, "it seems to me that this is a very likely story. What do you say to it?"

"Why, that I should think it very amusing," replied Franz, "if it had happened to any one but poor Albert."

"And, in truth, if you had not found me here," said the count, "it might have proved a gallant adventure, which would have cost your friend dear; but now be assured, his alarm will be the only serious consequence."

"And shall we go and find him?" inquired Franz.

"Oh! decidedly, sir; he is in a very picturesque place. Do you know the catacombs of San Sebastian?"

"I was never in them, but I have often resolved to visit them."

"Well, here is an opportunity made to your hand, and it would be difficult to contrive a better. Have you a carriage?"

"No."

"That is of no consequence; I always have one ready, day and night."

"Always ready?"

"Yes; I am a very capricious being, and I should tell you that sometimes when I rise, or after my dinner, or in the middle of the night, I resolve on starting for some particular point, and away I go."

The count rang, and a footman appeared.

"Order out the carriage," he said, "and remove the pistols which are in the holsters. You need not awaken the coachman. Ali will drive."

In a very short time the noise of wheels was heard, and the carriage stopped at the door. The count took out his watch.

"Half-past twelve," he said; "we might start at five o'clock and be in time, but the delay may cause your friend to pass an uneasy night; and, therefore, we had better go with all speed to extricate him from the hands of the infidels. Are you still resolved to accompany me?"

"More determined than ever."

"Well, then, come along."

Franz and the count went down-stairs, accompanied by Peppino. At the door they found the carriage. Ali was on the bow, in whom Franz recognised the dumb slave of the grotto of Monte-Cristo. Franz and the count got into the carriage. Peppino placed himself beside Ali, and they set off at a rapid pace. Ali had received his instructions, and went down the Rue du Cours, crossed the Camp Vaccino, went up the Strada San Gregorio, and reached the gates of Saint Sebastian; then the porter raised some difficulties; but the Count of Monte-Cristo produced an authority from the governor of Rome to quit or enter the city at any and all hours of the day or night; the portcullis was therefore raised, the porter had a louis for his trouble, and they went on their way. The road which the carriage now traversed was the ancient Appian Way, and bordered with tombs. From time to time, by the light of the moon which began to rise, Franz imagined that he saw something like a sentinel appear from various points of the ruin, and suddenly retreat into the darkness on a signal from Peppino.

A short time before they reached the Circus of Caracalla the carriage stopped, Peppino opened the door, and the count and Franz alighted.

"In ten minutes," said the count to his companion, "we shall arrive there."

He then took Peppino aside, gave him some order in a low voice, and Peppino went away, taking with him a torch, brought with them in the carriage. Five minutes elasped, during which Franz saw the shepherd advance along a narrow path in the midst of the irregular ground which forms the convulsed soil of the plain of Rome, and disappear in the midst of the high red herbage, which seemed like the bristling mane of some enormous lion.

"Now," said the count, "let us follow him."

Franz and the count, in their turn then advanced along the same path, which, at the end of a hundred paces, led them by a declivity to the bottom of a small valley. They then perceived two men conversing in the shade.

"Ought we to advance?" asked Franz of the count; "or should we pause?"

"Let us go on; Peppino will have warned the sentry of our coming."

One of these two men was Peppino, and the other a bandit on the look-out. Franz and the count advanced, and the bandit saluted them.

"Your excellency," said Peppino, addressing the count, "if you will follow me the opening of the catacombs is close at hand."

"Go on, then," replied the count.

They came to an opening behind a clump of bushes, and in the midst of a pile of rocks by which a man could scarcely pass. Peppino glided first into this crevice, but after advancing a few paces the passage widened. Then he paused, lighted his torch, and turned round to see if they came after him. The count first reached a kind of square space, and Franz followed him closely. The earth sloped in a gentle descent, enlarging as they proceeded, still Franz and the count were compelled to advance stooping and scarcely able to proceed two abreast. They went on a hundred and fifty paces thus, and then were stopped by "Who goes there?"

At the same time they saw the reflection of a torch on the barrel of a carbine.

"A friend!" responded Peppino, and advancing alone towards the sentry, he said a few words to him in a low tone, and then he, like the first, saluted the nocturnal visitors, making a sign that they might proceed.

Behind the sentinel was a staircase with twenty steps. Franz and the count descended these, and found themselves in a kind of crossroads, forming a burial-ground. Five roads diverged like the rays of a star, and the walls, dug into niches, placed one above the other in the shape of coffins, shewed that they were at last in the catacombs. In one of the cavities, whose extent it was impossible to determine, some rays of light were visible.   The count laid his hand on Franz's shoulder,—

"Would you like to see a camp of bandits in repose?" he inquired.

"Exceedingly," replied Franz.

"Come with me, then.   Peppino, extinguish the torch."

Peppino obeyed, and Franz and the count were suddenly in utter darkness, only fifty paces in advance of them there played along the wall some reddish beams of light, more visible since Peppino had put out his torch.   They advanced silently, the count guiding Franz as if he had the singular faculty of seeing in the dark.   Franz himself, however, distinguished his way more plainly in proportion as he advanced towards the rays of light which served them for guides,— three arcades, of which the middle served as the door, offered themselves.   These arcades opened on one side to the corridor, in which were the count and Franz, and on the other to a large square chamber, entirely surrounded by niches similar to those of which we have spoken.   In the midst of this chamber were four stones, which had formerly served as an altar, as was evident from the cross which still surmounted them.   A lamp, placed at the base of a pillar, lighted up with its pale and flickering flame the singular scene which presented itself to the eyes of the two visitors concealed in the shadow.   A man was seated with his elbow leaning on the column, and was reading with his back turned to the arcades, through the openings of which the new comers contemplated him.   This was the chief of the band, Luigi Vampa.   Around him, and in groups, according to their fancy, lying in their mantles, or with their backs against a kind of stone bench, which went all round the Columbarium, were to be seen twenty brigands or more, each having his carbine within reach.   At the bottom, silent, scarcely visible, and like a shadow, was a sentinel, who was walking up and down before a kind of opening, which was only distinguishable because in that spot the darkness seemed thicker.   When the count thought Franz had gazed sufficiently on this picturesque tableau, he raised his finger to his lips, to warn him to be silent, and ascending the three steps which led to the corridor of the Columbarium, entered the chamber by the centre arcade, and advanced towards Vampa, who was so intent on the book before him that he did not hear the noise of his footsteps.

"Who goes there?" cried the sentinel, less occupied, and who saw by the lamp's light a shadow which approached his chief.

At this sound Vampa rose quickly, drawing at the same

moment a pistol from his girdle. In a moment all the bandits were on their feet, and twenty carbines were levelled at the count.

"Well," said he, in a voice perfectly calm, and no muscle of his countenance disturbed, "well, my dear Vampa, it appears to me that you receive a friend with a great deal of ceremony!"

"Ground arms!" exclaimed the chief, with an imperative sign of the hand, whilst with the other he took off his hat respectfully; then turning to the singular personage who had caused this scene, he said,—"Your pardon, M. le Comte, but I was so far from expecting the honour of a visit, that I did not really recognise you."

"It seems that your memory is equally short in every thing, Vampa," said the count, "and that not only do you forget people's faces, but also the conditions you make with them."

"What conditions have I forgotten, M. le Comte?" inquired the bandit, with the air of a man who, having committed an error, is anxious to repair it.

"Was it not agreed," asked the count, "that not only my person, but also that of my friends, should be respected by you?"

"And how have I broken that treaty, your excellency?"

"You have this evening carried off and conveyed hither the Viscount Albert de Morcerf. Well," continued the count, in a tone that made Franz shudder, "this young gentleman is one of *my friends*,—this young gentleman lodges in the same hotel as myself,—this young gentleman has been up and down the Corso for eight hours in my private carriage, and yet I repeat to you, you have carried him off, and conveyed him hither, and," added the count, taking the letter from his pocket, "you have set a ransom on him as if he were an indifferent person."

"Why did you not tell me all this, you?" inquired the brigand chief, turning towards his men who all retreated before his look. "Why have you exposed me thus to fail in my word towards a gentleman like the count who has all our lives in his hands? By heavens! if I thought one of you knew that the young gentleman was a friend of his excellency, I would blow his brains out with my own hand!"

"Well," said the count, turning towards Franz, "I told you there was some mistake in this."

"Are you not alone?" asked Vampa, with uneasiness.

"I am with the person to whom this letter was addressed, and to whom I desired to prove that Luigi Vampa was a man of his word.—Come, your excellency, here is Luigi Vampa, who will himself express to you his deep regret at the mistake he has committed."

Franz approached the chief, advancing several steps to meet him.

"Welcome amongst us, your excellency," he said to him; "you heard what the count just said, and also my reply; let me add that I would not for the four thousand piastres at which I had fixed your friend's ransom that this had happened."

"But," said Franz, looking around him uneasily, "where is the viscount?—I do not see him."

"Nothing has happened to him, I hope?" said the count, frowningly.

"The prisoner is there," replied Vampa, pointing to the hollow place in front of which the bandit was on guard, "and I will go myself and tell him he is free."

The chief went towards the place he had pointed out as Albert's prison, and Franz and the count followed him.

"What is the prisoner doing?" inquired Vampa of the sentinel.

"*Ma foi!* captain," replied the sentry, "I do not know, for the last hour I have not heard him stir."

"Come in, your excellency," said Vampa.

The count and Franz ascended seven or eight steps after the chief, who drew back a bolt, and opened a door. Then by the gleam of a lamp, similar to that which lighted the Columbarium, Albert was to be seen wrapped up in a cloak which one of the bandits had lent him, lying in a corner in profound slumber.

"Come!" said the count, smiling with his own peculiar smile, "not so bad for a man who is to be shot at seven o'clock to-morrow morning!"

Vampa looked at Albert with a kind of admiration; he was not insensible to such a proof of courage.

"You are right, M. le Comte," he said; "this must be one of your friends."

Then, going to Albert, he touched him on the shoulder, saying,—

"Will your excellency please to awaken?"

Albert stretched out his arms, rubbed his eyelids, and opened his eyes.

"Ah! ah!" said he, "is it you, captain? You should have allowed me to have slept. I had such a delightful dream: I was dancing the galop at Torlonia's with the Countess G——."

Then he drew from his pocket his watch, which he had preserved that he might see how time sped.

"Half-past one only," said he. "Why the devil do you rouse me at this hour?"

"To tell you that you are free, your excellency."

"My dear fellow," replied Albert, with perfect ease of

mind, "remember, for the future, Napoleon's maxim, 'Never awaken me but for bad news:' if you had let me sleep on, I should have finished my galop, and have been grateful to you all my life. So, then, they have paid my ransom?"

"No, your excellency!"

"Well, then, how am I free?"

"A person to whom I can refuse nothing has come to demand you."

"Come hither?"

"Yes, hither."

"Really! then that person is a most amiable person."

Albert looked round, and perceived Franz.

"What!" said he, "is it you, my dear Franz, whose devotion and friendship are thus displayed?"

"No, not I," replied Franz, "but our neighbour, the Count of Monte-Cristo."

"Ah! ah! M. le Comte," said Albert, gaily, and arranging his cravat and wristbands, "you are really most kind, and I hope you will consider me as your eternally obliged, in the first place for the carriage, and in the next for this!" and he put out his hand to the count, who shuddered as he gave his own, but who nevertheless did give it.

The bandit gazed on the scene with amazement, he was evidently accustomed to see his prisoners tremble before him, and yet here was one whose gay temperament was not for a moment altered; as for Franz, he was enchanted at the way in which Albert had sustained the national honour in the presence of the bandit.

"My dear Albert," he said, "if you will make haste, we shall yet have time to finish the night at Torlonia's. You may conclude your interrupted galop, so that you will owe no ill-will to Signor Luigi, who has, indeed, throughout this whole affair acted like a gentleman."

"You are decidedly right; and we may reach the Palazzo at two o'clock. Signor Luigi," continued Albert, "is there any formality to fulfil before I take leave of your excellency?"

"None, sir," replied the bandit; "you are as free as air."

"Well, then, a happy and merry life to you. Come, gentlemen, come!"

And Albert, followed by Franz and the count, descended the staircase, crossed the square chamber, where stood all the bandits, hat in hand.

"Peppino," said the brigand chief, "give me the torch."

"What are you going to do then?" inquired the count.

"I will shew you the way back myself," said the captain; "that is the least honour I can testify to your excellency."

And taking the lighted torch from the hand of the herdsman, he preceded his guests, not as a servant who performs an act of servility, but like a king who precedes ambassadors. On reaching the door, he bowed.

"And now, M. le Comte," added he, "allow me to repeat my apologies, and I hope you will not entertain any resentment at what has occurred."

"No, my dear Vampa," replied the count; "besides, you compensate for your mistakes in so gentlemanly a way, that one almost feels obliged to you for having committed them."

"Gentlemen!" added the chief, turning towards the young men, "perhaps the offer may not appear very tempting to you, but if you should ever feel inclined to pay me a second visit, wherever I may be, you shall be welcome."

Franz and Albert bowed.

The count went out first, then Albert; Franz paused for a moment.

"Has your excellency any thing to ask me?" said Vampa, with a smile.

"Yes, I have," replied Franz. "I am curious to know what work you were perusing with so much attention as we entered?"

"Cæsar's *Commentaries*," said the bandit; "it is my favourite work."

"Well, are you coming?" asked Albert.

"Yes," replied Franz, "here I am!" and he, in turn, left the caves.

They advanced to the plain.

"Ah, your pardon!" said Albert, turning round; "will you allow me, captain?"

And he lighted his cigar at Vampa's torch.

"Now, M. le Comte," he said, "let us on with all the speed we may. I am enormously anxious to finish my night at the Duke of Bracciano's."

They found the carriage where they had left it. The count said a word in Arabic to Ali, and the horses went off at great speed.

It was just two o'clock by Albert's watch when the two friends entered into the dancing-room.

Their return was quite an event, but as they entered together, all uneasiness on Albert's account ceased instantly.

"Madame," said the Viscount Morcerf, advancing towards the countess, "yesterday you were so condescending as to promise me a galop; I am rather late in claiming this gracious promise, but here is my friend, whose character for veracity you well know, and he will assure you the delay arose from no fault of mine."

And as at this moment the music gave the warning for the waltz, Albert put his arm round the waist of the countess, and disappeared with her in the whirl of dancers. In the meanwhile Franz was considering the singular shudder that had pervaded the Count of Monte-Cristo's frame at the moment when he had been, in some sort, forced to give his hand to Albert.

CHAPTER XXXVIII

THE RENDEZVOUS

ALBERT'S first words to his friend, on the following morning, contained a request that he would accompany him to visit the count; true, he had warmly and energetically thanked him the previous evening, but services such as he had rendered could never be too often acknowledged.

Franz, who seemed attracted by some invisible influence towards the count, in which terror was strangely mingled, felt an extreme reluctance to permit his friend to be exposed alone to the singular fascination the mysterious count seemed to exercise over him, and, therefore, made no objection to Albert's request, but at once accompanied him to the desired spot, and, after a short delay, the count joined them in the saloon.

"M. le Comte," said Albert, advancing to meet him, "permit me to repeat the poor thanks I offered last night, and to assure you that the remembrance of all I owe you will never be effaced from my memory; believe me, while I have life I shall never cease to dwell with grateful recollection on the prompt and important service you rendered me; as also to remember that to you I am indebted even for my life."

"My very good friend and excellent neighbour," replied the count, with a smile, "you really exaggerate my trifling exertions. You owe me nothing but some trifle of 20,000 francs which you have been saved out of your travelling expenses, so that there is not much of a score between us;— but you must really permit me to congratulate you on the ease and unconcern with which you resigned yourself to your fate, and the perfect indifference you manifested as to the turn events might take."

"Upon my word," said Albert, "I deserve no credit for what I could not help, namely, a determination to take every thing as I found it; and to let those bandits see, that although men get into troublesome scrapes all over the world, there is no nation but the French can smile even in the face of grim Death itself. All that, however, has nothing to do with my obligations to you, and I now come to ask you, whether, in my own person, my family, or connexions, I can, in any way, serve you? My father, the Comte de Morcerf, although of

Spanish origin, possesses considerable influence, both at the court of France and Madrid, and I unhesitatingly place the best services of myself, and all to whom my life is dear, at your disposal."

"M. de Morcerf," replied the count, "your offer, far from surprising me, is precisely what I expected from you, and I accept it in the same spirit of hearty sincerity with which it is made;—nay, I will go still further, and say that I had previously made up my mind to ask a great favour at your hands."

"Oh, pray name it."

"I am wholly a stranger to Paris—it is a city I have never yet seen."

"Is it possible," exclaimed Albert, "that you have reached your present age without visiting the finest capital in the world? I can scarcely credit it."

"Nevertheless, it is quite true; still I agree with you in thinking that my present ignorance of the first city in Europe is a reproach to me in every way, and calls for immediate correction; but, in all probability, I should have performed so important, so necessary a duty, as that of making myself acquainted with the wonders and beauties of your justly-celebrated capital, had I known any person who would have introduced me into the fashionable world, but unfortunately I possessed no acquaintance there, and, of necessity, was compelled to abandon the idea."

"So distinguished an individual as yourself," cried Albert, "could scarcely have required an introduction."

"You are most kind; but, as regards myself, I can find no merit I possess, save that as a millionaire. I might have become a partner in the speculations of M. Aguado and M. Rothschild; but as my motive in travelling to your capital would not have been for the pleasure of dabbling in the funds, I stayed away till some favourable chance should present itself of carrying my wish into execution: your offer, however, smooths all difficulties, and I have only to ask you, my dear M. de Morcerf" (these words were accompanied by a most peculiar smile), "whether you undertake, upon my arrival in France, to open to me the doors of that fashionable world, of which I know no more than a Huron or native of Cochin-China?"

"Oh, that I do, and with infinite pleasure!" answered Albert; "and so much the more readily, as a letter received this morning from my father summons me to Paris in consequence of a treaty of marriage (my dear Franz, do not smile, I beg of you) with a family of high standing, and connected with the very élite of Parisian society."

"Connected by marriage, you mean," said Franz, laughingly.

"Well, never mind how it is," answered Albert, "it comes to the same thing in the end. Perhaps by the time you return to Paris, I shall be quite a sober, staid father of a family! A most edifying representative I shall make of all the domestic virtues—don't you think so? But as regards your wish to visit our fine city, my dear count, I can only say, that you may command me and mine to any extent you please."

"Then it is a settled affair," said the count, "and I give you my solemn assurance, that I only waited an opportunity like the present to realise schemes I have long meditated."

Franz doubted not that these schemes were the same concerning which he had dropped some words in the grotto of Monte-Cristo; and while the count gave utterance to the expression, the young man closely examined his features in the hopes that some powerful emotion might render the nature of these projects easily traced upon his expressive countenance: but it was altogether impossible to read the thoughts of the mysterious individual before him, especially when he employed one of those bewildering smiles he so well knew how to call up.

"But tell me now, count," exclaimed Albert, delighted at the idea of having to chaperone so distinguished a person as Monte-Cristo; "tell me truly whether you are in earnest, or if this project of visiting Paris is merely one of those chimerical and uncertain things of which we make so many in the course of our lives; but which like a house built on the sand, is liable to be blown over by the first puff of wind?"

"I pledge you my honour," returned the count, "that I mean to do as I have said; both inclination and positive necessity compel me to visit Paris!"

"When do you propose going thither?"

"Have you made up your mind when you shall be there yourself?"

"Certainly I have; in a fortnight or three weeks' time: that is to say, as fast as I can get there!"

"Nay," said the count; "I will give you three months ere I join you; you see I make an ample allowance for all delays and difficulties."

"And in three months' time," said Albert, "you will be at my house?"

"Shall we make a positive appointment for a particular day and hour?" inquired the count; "only let me warn you that I am proverbial for my punctilious exactitude in keeping my engagements."

"The very thing!" exclaimed Albert; "yes, by all means let us have this rendezvous duly drawn up and attested."

"So be it, then," replied the count, and extending his hand towards an almanack, suspended near the chimney-piece, he said, "to-day is the 21st of February," and drawing out his watch, added, "it is exactly half-past ten o'clock. Now promise me to remember this, and expect me the 21st of May at the same hour in the forenoon."

"Capital!" exclaimed Albert; "and you shall find every thing and every body ready to receive you. I take upon myself to promise that your breakfast shall be smoking hot awaiting your arrival."

"Where do you live?"

"No. 27 Rue du Helder!"

"Have you bachelor's apartments there? I hope my coming will not put you to any inconvenience."

"I reside in my father's mansion, but occupy a pavilion at the farther side of the court-yard, entirely separated from the main building."

"Quite sufficient," replied the count, as taking out his tablets he wrote down "No. 27 Rue du Helder, 21st May, half-past ten in the morning." "Now then," said the count, returning his tablets to his pocket, "make yourself perfectly easy, the hand of your time-piece will not be more accurate in marking the time than myself."

"Shall I see you again ere my departure?" asked Albert.

"That will be according to circumstances; but when do you set off?"

"To-morrow evening, at five o'clock."

"In that case I must say adieu to you; as I am compelled to go to Naples, and shall not return hither before Saturday evening or Sunday morning. And you, M. le Baron," pursued the count, addressing Franz, "do you also depart to-morrow?"

"Yes, I go also."

"And whither do you wend your way? to Paris?"

"No, to Venice; I shall remain in Italy for another year or two."

"Then we shall not meet in Paris?"

"I fear I shall not have that honour."

"Well, since we must part," said the count, holding out a hand to each of the young men; "allow me to wish you both a safe and pleasant journey."

It was the first time the hand of Franz had come in contact with that of the mysterious individual before him, and unconsciously he shuddered at its touch, for it felt cold and icy as that of a corpse.

"Let us understand each other," said Albert; "it is agreed —is it not?—that you are to be in the Rue du Helder on the 21st of May at half-past ten in the morning, and your word of honour passed for your punctuality?"

"All that is settled, and arranged upon honour," replied the count; "rely upon seeing me at the time and place agreed on."

The young men then rose, and courteously bowing to their singular acquaintance, quitted the room.

"What is the matter?" asked Albert of Franz, when they had returned to their own apartments; "you seem more than commonly thoughtful."

"I will confess to you, Albert," replied Franz, "that I am deeply puzzled to unravel the real character of this strange count; and the appointment you have made to meet him in Paris fills me with a thousand apprehensions."

"My dear fellow," exclaimed Albert, "what can there possibly be in that to excite uneasiness? why you must have lost your senses to imagine either harm or danger can spring from it!"

"Whether I am in my senses or not," answered Franz, "such is my view of the evil effects that may arise from a second meeting with this incomprehensible count, that I would give much you had not crossed his path."

"Listen to me, Franz," said Albert; "I am not sorry that our present conversation gives me an opportunity of remarking to you how much I have been struck with the difference of your manner towards the count to that with which you treat your friends in general: to him you are frigid and polite, while to myself, for instance, you are warm and cordial as a friend should be; have you any private reasons for so acting?"

"Possibly."

"Did you ever meet him previously to coming hither?"

"I have."

"And where?"

"Will you promise me not to repeat a single word of what I am about to tell you?"

"I promise you to observe the utmost secrecy."

"And you pledge me your honour that nothing shall induce you to divulge it?"

"I pledge my honour."

"Then listen to me."

Franz then related to his friend the history of his excursion to the isle of Monte-Cristo, and of his finding a party of smugglers there, with whom were two Corsican bandits; he dwelt with considerable force and energy on the almost magical hospitality he had received from the count, and the magnificence of his entertainment in the grotto" of the thousand and one nights"; he recounted with circumstantial exactitude all particulars of the supper; the hashish, the statues, the dream, and reality, and how at his awakening, there remained no proof or trace of all these events, save the small yacht, seen in the distant horizon hastening with spread sails towards Porto-Vecchio. Then he detailed the conversation overheard by him at the Colosseum, between the mysterious visitant Vampa, in which the count had promised to obtain the release of the bandit Peppino—an engagement which, as our readers are aware, he most faithfully fulfilled.

At last he arrived at the adventure of the preceding night; and the embarrassment in which he found himself placed, by not having sufficient cash to complete the sum of 6 or 700 piastres, with the circumstance of his having applied to the count to furnish the money in which he was deficient, an impulse which had led to results so picturesque and satisfactory. Albert listened with the most profound attention.

"Well!" said he, when Franz had concluded, "what do you find to object to in all you have related? the count is fond of travelling, and being rich, possesses a vessel of his own. Go but to Portsmouth or Southampton, and you will find the harbours crowded with the yachts belonging to such of the English as can afford the expense, and have the same liking for this amusement as your mysterious acquaintance of the isle of Monte-Cristo. Now, by way of having a resting-place during his excursions, avoiding the wretched cookery which has been trying its best to poison me during the last four months, while you have manfully resisted its effects for as many years, and obtaining a bed on which it is impossible to slumber, Monte-Cristo has furnished for himself a temporary abode where you first found him; but, to prevent the possibility of the Tuscan government taking a fancy to his enchanted palace, and thereby depriving him of the advantages naturally expected from so large an outlay of capital, he has wisely enough purchased the island, and assumed the title of its count. Just ask yourself, my good fellow, whether there are not many persons of our acquaintance who assume the names of lands and properties they never in their lives were master of?"

"But," said Franz, "how do you account for the circumstance of the Corsican bandits being among the crew of his vessel?"

"Why, really, the thing seems to me simple enough. Nobody knows better than yourself, that the bandits of Corsica are not rogues or thieves, but purely and simply fugitives, driven by some sinister motive from their native town or village, and that their fellowship involves no disgrace or stigma; for my own part, I protest that should I ever visit Corsica, my first visit, ere even I presented myself to the mayor or *préfet*, should be to the bandits of Colomba, if I could only manage to find them; for, on my conscience, they are a race of men I admire greatly."

"Still," persisted Franz, "I suppose you will allow that such men as Vampa and his band are regular villains, who have no other motive than plunder when they seize your person.

How do you explain the influence the count evidently possessed over those ruffians?"

"My good friend, as in all probability I owe my present safety to that influence, it would ill become me to search too closely into its source; therefore, instead of condemning him for his intimacy with outlaws, you must give me leave to excuse any little irregularity there may be in such a connexion; not altogether for preserving my life, for my own idea is, that it never was in much danger; but certainly, for saving me 4,000 piastres, which, being translated, means neither more nor less than 24,000 livres of our money,—a sum at which, most assuredly, I should never have been estimated in France; proving most indisputably," added Albert, with a laugh, "that no prophet is honoured in his own country."

"Talking of countries," replied Franz, "can you tell me what country produced this mysterious person, what is his native tongue, his means of existence, and from whence does he derive his immense fortune, and what were those events of his early life,—a life as marvellous as unknown,—that have tinctured his succeeding years with so dark and gloomy a misanthropy? Certainly these are questions that, in your place, I should like to have answered."

"My dear Franz," replied Albert, "when, upon receipt of my letter, you found the necessity of asking the count's assistance, you promptly went to him, saying, 'My friend, Albert de Morcerf is in danger; help me to deliver him.' Was not that nearly what you said?"

"It was."

"Well, then, did he ask you, 'Who is M. Albert de Morcerf? how does he come by his name—his fortune? what are his means of existence? what is his birth-place? of what country is he a native?' Tell me, did he put all these questions to you?"

"I confess he asked me none."

"No; he merely came and freed me from the hands of Signor Vampa, where I can assure you, spite of all my outward appearance of ease and unconcern, I did not very particularly care to remain.)Now, then, Franz, when, in return for services so promptly and unhesitatingly rendered, he but asks me in return to do for him what is done daily for any Russian prince or Italian noble who may pass through Paris, merely to introduce him into society,—would you have me refuse? My good fellow, you must have lost your senses to think it possible I could act with such cold-blooded policy."

And this time it must be confessed, that in direct opposition to the ordinary discussions between the young men, all the good and powerful reasons were on Albert's side.

"Well!" said Franz, with a sigh, "do as you please, my dear viscount, for your arguments are beyond my powers of refutation. Still, in spite of all, you must admit that this Count of Monte-Cristo is a most singular personage."

"He is a philanthropist," answered the other; "and, no doubt, his motive in visiting Paris is to compete for the Monthyon prize, given, as you are aware, to whoever shall be proved to have most materially advanced the interests of virtue and humanity. If my vote and interest can obtain it for him, I will readily give him the one and promise the other. And now, my dear Franz, let us talk of something else. Come, shall we take our luncheon, and then pay a last visit to Saint Peter's?"

Franz silently assented, and the following afternoon, at half-past five o'clock, the young men parted, Albert de Morcerf to return to Paris, and Franz d'Epinay to pass a fortnight at Venice. But ere he entered his travelling carriage, Albert, in the fear of his expected guest forgetting the engagement he had entered into, placed in the care of the waiter of the hotel a card to be delivered to the Count of Monte-Cristo, on which, beneath the name of Albert de Morcerf, he had written in pencil,

"27 Rue du Helder, on the 21st May, half-past 10 A.M."

CHAPTER XXXIX

THE GUESTS

In the house in the Rue du Helder, where Albert had invited the Count of Monte-Cristo, every thing was being prepared on the morning of the 21st of May to fulfil the engagement.

Albert de Morcerf inhabited a pavilion situated at the corner of a large court, and directly opposite another building, in which were the servants' apartments. Two windows only of the pavilion faced the street; three other windows looked into the court, and two at the back into the garden. Between the court and the garden, built in the heavy style of the imperial architecture, was the large and fashionable dwelling of the Count and Countess de Morcerf. A high wall surrounded the whole of the mansion, surmounted at intervals by vases filled with flowers, and broken in the centre by a large gate of gilt iron, which served as the carriage entrance. A small door, close to the lodge of the concierge, gave ingress and egress to the servants and masters when they were on foot.

It was easy to discover that the delicate care of a mother, unwilling to part from her son, and yet aware he required the full exercise of his liberty, had chosen this habitation for Albert. On the other hand was visible the intelligent independence of youth, enchanted with the free and idle life of a young man. By means of these two windows, looking into the street, Albert could see all that passed; the sight of what is going on is so necessary to young men, who wish always to see the world traverse their horizon, be that horizon but the street only. Then, should any thing appear to merit a more minute examination, Albert de Morcerf could follow up his researches by means of a small gate, similar to that close to the concierge's door, and which merits a particular description. It was a little entrance that seemed never to have been opened since the house was built, so entirely was it covered with dust and dirt; but the well-oiled hinges and lock announced a frequent and mysterious employment. This door laughed at the concierge, from whose vigilance and jurisdiction it escaped, opening, like the door in the "Arabian Nights;" the "*open Sesame*" of Ali Baba, by a cabalistic word or a concerted tap without from the sweetest voices or whitest fingers in the world. At the end of a long corridor, with which the door communicated, and which formed the ante-chamber, was, on the right, Albert's breakfast-room, looking into the court, and on the left the saloon, looking into the garden. Shrubs and creeping plants covered the windows, and hid from the garden an l court these two apartments, the only rooms into which, as they were on the ground-floor, the prying eyes of the curious could penetrate. On the first floor were the same rooms with the addition of a third, formed out of the ante-chamber; these three rooms were a salon, a boudoir, and a bed-room. The salon down-stairs was only an Algerian divan, for the use of smokers. The boudoir up-stairs communicated with the bed-chamber by an invisible door on the staircase;— it is evident every precaution had been taken. Above this floor was a large studio, which had been increased in size by pulling down the partitions: a pandemonium, in which the artist and the dandy strove for pre-eminence. There were collected and piled up all Albert's successive caprices, hunting-horns, bass-viols, flutes,—a whole orchestra, for Albert had had not a taste but a fancy for music; easels, palettes, brushes, pencils, for music had been succeeded by painting; foils, boxing-gloves, broadswords, and single-sticks, for, following the example of the fashionable young men of the time, Albert de Morcerf cultivated, with far more perseverance than music and drawing, the three arts that complete a dandy's education, *i.e.* fencing, boxing, and single-stick; and it was in this apartment that he received Grisier, Cook, and Charles Lecour. The rest of the furniture of this privileged apartment consisted of old cabinets of the time of Francis I, filled with china and Japanese vases, earthenware from Lucca or Robbia, plates of Bernard de Palissy; of old arm-chairs, in which had perhaps reposed themselves Henri IV or Sully, Louis XIII or Richelieu, for two of these arm-chairs, adorned with a carved shield on which were engraved the fleur-de-lis of France on an azure field, evidently came from the Louvre, or, at least, some royal residence. On these dark and sombre chairs were thrown splendid stuffs, dyed beneath Persia's sun, or woven by the fingers of the women of Calcutta or of Chandernagor. What these stuffs did there, it was impossible to say; they awaited, whilst gratifying the eyes, a destination unknown to their owner himself; in the meantime they filled the room with their golden and silky reflexions. In the centre of the room was a rosewood piano of Roller and Blanchet, of small dimensions, but containing an orchestra in its narrow and sonorous cavity, and groaning beneath the weight of the chefs-d'œuvre of Beethoven, Weber, Mozart, Haydn, Grétry, and Porpora.

On the walls, over the doors, on the ceiling, were swords, daggers, Malay creeses, maces, battleaxes, suits of armour,

C.M.—N

gilded, damasked, and inlaid, dried plants, minerals, and stuffed birds, opening their flame-coloured wings as if for flight, and their beaks that never close. This was the favourite sitting-room of Albert.

However, the morning of the appointment, the young man had established himself in the small salon down-stairs. There, on a table, surrounded at some distance by a large and luxurious divan, every species of tobacco known, from the yellow tobacco of Petersburg to the black tobacco of Sinai, the Maryland, the Porto-Rico, and the Latakia, was exposed in those pots of crackled earthenware of which the Dutch are so fond; beside them, in boxes of fragrant wood, were ranged, according to their size and quality, pueros, regalias, havannas, and manillas; and in an open cabinet a collection of German pipes, of chibouques, with their amber mouth-pieces ornamented with coral, and of nargilas, with their long tubes of morocco, awaited the caprice or the sympathy of the smokers. Albert had himself presided at the arrangement, or, rather, the symmetrical derangement which, after coffee, the guests at a breakfast of modern days love to contemplate through the vapour that escapes from their mouth, and ascends in long and fanciful wreaths to the ceiling.

At a quarter to ten a valet entered; he composed, with a little groom named John, and who spoke only English, all Albert's establishment, although the cook of the hotel was always at his service, and on great occasions the count's chasseur also. This valet, whose name was Germain, and who enjoyed the entire confidence of his young master, held in one hand a number of papers, and in the other a packet of letters, which he gave to Albert. Albert glanced carelessly at the different missives, selected two written in a small and delicate hand, and inclosed in scented envelopes, opened them, and perused their contents with some attention.

"How did these letters come?" said he.

"One by the post, Madame Danglars' footman left the other."

"Let Madame Danglars know that I accept the place she offers me in her box. Wait: then, during the day, tell Rosa that when I leave the Opera I will sup with her, as she wishes. Take her six bottles of different wine, Cyprus, sherry, and Malaga, and a barrel of Ostend oysters; get them at Borel's, and be sure to say they are for me."

"At what o'clock, sir, do you breakfast?"

"What time is it now?"

"A quarter to ten."

"Very well, at half-past ten. Debray will, perhaps, be obliged to go to the minister,—and besides (Albert looked at his tablets), it is the hour I told the count, 21st May, at half-past ten, and though I do not much rely upon his promise, I wish to be punctual. Is Madame la Comtesse up yet?"

"If M. le Vicomte wishes I will inquire?"

"Yes, ask her for one of her liqueur cellarets, mine is incomplete; and tell her I shall have the honour of seeing her about three o'clock, and that I request permission to introduce some one to her."

The valet left the room. Albert threw himself on the divan, tore off the cover of two or three of the papers, looked at the playbills, made a face at perceiving they played an opera, and not a ballet; hunted vainly amongst the advertisements for a new tooth-powder of which he had heard, and threw down, one after the other, the three leading papers of Paris, muttering,—

"These papers become more and more stupid every day."

A moment after a carriage stopped before the door, and the servant announced M. Lucien Debray. A tall young man, with light hair, clear grey eyes, and thin and compressed lips, dressed in a blue coat with buttons of gold, beautifully carved, a white neckcloth, and a tortoiseshell eye-glass suspended by a silken thread, and which, by an effort of the superciliary and zygomatic nerves, he fixed in his eye, entered, with an half-official air, without smiling or speaking.

"Good morning, Lucien! good morning!" said Albert; "your punctuality really alarms me. What do I say? punctuality! You whom I expected last, you arrive at five minutes to ten, when the time fixed was half-past! Have ministers resigned?"

"No, my dear fellow," returned the young man, seating himself on the divan; "reassure yourself: we are tottering always, but we never fall; and I begin to believe that we shall pass into a state of immobility, and then the affairs of the Peninsula will completely consolidate us."

"Ah, true! you drive Don Carlos out of Spain."

"No, no, my dear fellow, do not confound our plans. We take him to the other side of the French frontier, and offer him hospitality at Bourges."

"At Bourges?"

"Yes, he has not much to complain of; Bourges is the capital of Charles VII. Do you not know that all Paris knew it yesterday, and the day before it had already transpired on the Bourse, and M. Danglars (I do not know by what means that man contrives to obtain intelligence as soon as we do) made a million?"

"And you another order, for I see you have a blue riband at your button-hole."

"Yes, they sent me the order of Charles III.," returned Debray carelessly.

"Come, do not affect indifference, but confess you were pleased to have it."

"Oh, it is very well as a finish to the toilette.   It looks very neat on a black coat buttoned up."

"And makes you resemble the Prince of Wales or the Duke de Reichstadt."

"It is for that reason you see me so early."

"Because you have the order of Charles III, and you wish to announce the good news to me?"

"No, because I passed the night writing letters,—five-and-twenty despatches.   I returned home at day-break and strove to sleep, but my head ached, and I got up to have a ride for an hour.   At the Bois de Boulogne ennui and hunger attacked me at once,—two enemies who rarely accompany each other, and who are yet leagued against me, a sort of Carlo-republican alliance.   I then recollected you gave a breakfast this morning, and here I am.   I am hungry, feed me; I am bored, amuse me."

"It is my duty as your host," returned Albert, ringing the bell, whilst Lucien turned over, with his gold-mounted cane, the papers that lay on the table.   "Germain, a glass of sherry and a biscuit.   In the meantime, my dear Lucien, here are cigars—contraband, of course; try them, and persuade the minister to sell us such instead of poisoning us with cabbage-leaves."

"*Peste!* I will do nothing of the kind; the moment they come from government you would find them execrable. Besides, that does not concern the home but the financial department.   Address yourself to M. Humann, section of the indirect contributions, Corridor A., No. 26."

"On my word," said Albert, "you astonish me by the extent of your acquaintance.   Take a cigar."

"Really, my dear count," replied Lucien, lighting a manilla at a rose-coloured taper that burnt in a stand beautifully enamelled—"how happy you are to have nothing to do; you do not know your own good fortune!"

"And what would you do, my dear diplomatist," replied Morcerf, with a slight degree of irony in his voice, "if you did nothing?   What! private secretary to a minister, plunged at once into European cabals and Parisian intrigues; having kings, and, better still, queens to protect, parties to unite, elections to direct; making more use of your cabinet with your pen and your telegraph than Napoleon did of his battle-fields with his sword and his victories; possessing five-and-twenty thousand francs a-year, besides your place; a horse for which Château Renaud offered you four hundred louis, and which you would not part with; a tailor who never disappoints you; with the Opera, the Jockey Club, and other varieties, can you not amuse yourself?   Well, I will amuse you."

"How?"

"By introducing to you a new acquaintance."

"A man or a woman?"

"A man."

"I know so many already."

"But you do not know this man."

"Where does he come from—the end of the world?"

"Farther still, perhaps."

"The devil! I hope he does not bring our breakfast with him."

"Oh, no; our breakfast comes from my father's kitchen. Are you hungry?"

"Humiliating as such a confession is, I am. But I dined at M. de Villefort's, and lawyers always give you very bad dinners. You would think they felt some remorse; did you ever remark that?"

"Ah! depreciate other persons' dinners; you ministers give such splendid ones."

"Yes! but we do not invite people of fashion. If we were not forced to entertain a parcel of country boobies because they think and vote with us, we should never dream of dining at home, I assure you."

"Well, take another glass of sherry and another biscuit."

"Willingly. Your Spanish wine is excellent. You see we were quite right to pacify that country."

"Yes; but Don Carlos?"

"Well, Don Carlos will drink Bordeaux, and in ten years we will marry his son to the little queen."

"You will then obtain the Golden Fleece, if you are still in the ministry."

"I think, Albert, you have adopted the system of feeding me on smoke this morning."

"Well, you must allow it is the best thing for the stomach: but I hear Beauchamp in the next room; you can dispute together, and that will pass away the time."

"About what?"

"About the papers."

"My dear friend," said Lucien, with an air of sovereign contempt, "do I ever read the papers?"

"Then you will dispute the more."

"M. Beauchamp," announced the servant.

"Enter, enter," said Albert, rising and advancing to meet the young man.

"Here is Debray, who detests you without reading you, so he says."

"He is quite right," returned Beauchamp, "for I criticise him without knowing what he does. Good-day, Commander!"

"Ah! you know that already," said the private secretary, smiling and shaking hands with him.

"*Pardieu!*"

"And what do they say of it in the world?"

"In which world? we have so many worlds in the year of grace 1838."

"In the entire political world, of which you are one of the leaders."

"They say that it is quite fair, and that you sow so much red, that you must reap a little blue."

"Come, come! that is not bad!" said Lucien. "Why do you not join our party, my dear Beauchamp? with your talents you would make your fortune in three or four years."

"I only await one thing before following your advice, that is, a minister who will hold office for six months. My dear Albert, one word, for I must get poor Lucien a respite. Do we breakfast or dine? I must go to the Chamber, for our life is not an idle one."

"You only breakfast: I await two persons, and the instant they arrive we shall sit down to table."

CHAPTER XL

THE BREAKFAST

"AND what sort of persons do you expect to breakfast?" said Beauchamp.

"A gentleman and a diplomatist."

"Then we shall have to wait two hours for the gentleman, and three for the diplomatist. I shall come back to dessert; keep me some strawberries, coffee, and cigars. I shall take a cutlet on my way to the Chamber."

"Do not do anything of the sort, for were the gentleman a Montmorency, and the diplomatist a Metternich, we will breakfast at eleven; in the meantime, follow Debray's example, and take a glass of sherry and a biscuit."

"Be it so, I will stay. I must do something to distract my thoughts."

"You are like Debray; and yet it seems to me that when the minister is out of spirits, the opposition ought to be joyous."

"Ah, you do not know with what I am threatened. I shall hear this morning M. Danglars make a speech at the Chamber of Deputies, and at his wife's this evening I shall hear the tragedy of a peer of France. The devil take the constitutional government! and since we had our choice, as they say at least, how could we choose that?"

"I understand; you must lay in a stock of hilarity."

"Do not run down M. Danglars' speeches," said Debray; "he votes for you, for he belongs to the opposition."

"*Pardieu!* that is exactly the worst of all; I am waiting until you send him to speak of the Luxembourg to laugh at my ease."

"My dear friend," said Albert to Beauchamp, "it is plain the affairs of Spain are settled, for you are most desperately out of humour this morning. Recollect that Parisian gossip has spoken of a marriage between myself and Mlle. Eugénie Danglars; I cannot, in conscience, therefore, let you run down the speeches of a man who will one day say to me, 'M. le Vicomte, you know I give my daughter eighty thousand pounds.'"

423

"Ah, this marriage will never take place," said Beauchamp. "The king has made him a baron and can make him a peer, but he cannot make him a gentleman; and the Count de Morcerf is too aristocratic to consent, for the paltry sum of eighty thousand pounds, to a *mésalliance*. The Viscount de Morcerf can only wed a marchioness."

"But eighty thousand pounds is a nice little sum," replied Morcerf.

"It is the social capital of a theatre on the boulevard, or a railroad from the Jardin des Plantes to la Râpée."

"Never mind what he says, Morcerf," said Debray, "do you marry her. You marry a ticket of a money bag, it is true; well, but what does that matter? it is better to have a blazon less and a figure more on it. You have seven martlets on your arms, give three to your wife, and you will still have four; that is one more than M. de Guise had who so nearly became King of France, and whose cousin was Emperor of Germany."

"On my word, I think you are right, Lucien," said Albert, absently.

"To be sure; besides, every millionaire is as noble as a bastard,—that is, he can be."

"Do not say that, Debray," returned Beauchamp, laughing, "for here is Château-Renaud, who, to cure you of your mania for paradoxes, will pass the sword of Renaud de Montauban, his ancestor, through your body."

"He will sully it then," returned Lucien, "for I am low,— very low."

"Oh, heavens!" cried Beauchamp, "the minister quotes Béranger, what shall we come to next?"

"M. de Château-Renaud! M. Maximilian Morrel!" said the servant, announcing two fresh guests.

"Now, then, to breakfast," said Beauchamp; "for if I remember, you told me you only expected two persons, Albert."

"Morrel!" muttered Albert, "Morrel! who is he?"

But before he had finished, M. de Château-Renaud, a handsome young man of thirty, gentleman all over, that is, with the figure of a Guiche and the wit of a Mortemart, took Albert's hand.

"My dear Albert," said he, "let me introduce to you M. Maximilian Morrel, captain of Spahis, my friend, and what is more—however the man speaks for himself—my preserver. Salute my hero, viscount."

And he stepped on one side, exhibiting the large and open brow, the piercing eyes and black moustache of the fine and noble young man, whom our readers have already seen at Marseilles under circumstances sufficiently dramatic not to be forgotten. A rich uniform, half French, half Oriental, set off his broad chest, decorated with the order of the Legion of Honour, and his graceful and stalwart figure.

The young officer bowed with easy and elegant politeness.

"Monsieur," said Albert, with affectionate courtesy, "M. le Comte de Château-Renaud knew how much pleasure this introduction would give me; you are his friend, be ours also."

"Well said!" interrupted Château-Renaud; "and pray that, if you should ever be in a similar predicament, he may do as much for you as he did for me."

"What has he done?" asked Albert.

"Oh! nothing worth speaking of," said Morrel; "M. de Château-Renaud exaggerates."

"Not worth speaking of!" cried Château-Renaud; "life is not worth speaking of!—that is rather too philosophical, on my word, Morrel. It is very well for you who risk your life every day, but for me, who only did so once——"

"What is evident in all this, baron, is that M. le Capitaine Morrel saved your life."

"Exactly so!"

"On what occasion?" asked Beauchamp.

"Beauchamp, my good fellow, you know I am starving," said Debray, "do not set him off on some long story."

"Well, I do not prevent your sitting down to table," replied Beauchamp; "Château-Renaud can tell us whilst we eat our breakfast."

"Gentlemen," said Morcerf, "it is only a quarter-past ten, and I expect some one else."

"Ah, true! a diplomatist!" observed Debray.

"I know not whether he be or not, I only know that I gave him a mission which he terminated so entirely to my satisfaction, that had I been king, I should have instantly created him knight of all my orders, even had I been able to offer him the Golden Fleece and the Garter."

"Well, since we are not to sit down to table," said Debray, "take a glass of sherry and tell us all about it."

"You all know that I had the fancy of going to Africa."

"It is a road your ancestors have traced for you," said Albert, gallantly.

"Yes, but I doubt that your object was like theirs—to rescue the Holy Sepulchre."

"You are quite right, Beauchamp," observed the young aristocrat. "It was only to fight as an amateur. I cannot bear duelling ever since two seconds, whom I had chosen to accommodate a quarrel, forced me to break the arm of one of my best friends, one whom you all know—poor Franz d'Epinay."

C.M.——N*

"Ah, true!" said Debray, "you did fight some time ago;—about what?"

"The devil take me, if I remember!" returned Château-Renaud. "But I recollect perfectly one thing: that, being unwilling to let such talents as mine sleep, I wished to try upon the Arabs the new pistols that had been given to me. In consequence, I embarked for Oran, and went from thence to Constantine, where I arrived just in time to witness the raising of the siege. I retreated with the rest, during eight-and-forty hours. I supported the rain during the day and the cold during the night tolerably well, but the third morning my horse died of cold. Poor brute! accustomed to be covered up and to have a stove in the stable, an Arabian finds himself unable to bear ten degrees of cold in Arabia."

"That's why you want to purchase my English horse," said Debray; "you think he will support the cold better."

"You are mistaken, for I have made a vow never to return to Africa."

"You were very much frightened then?" asked Beauchamp.

"I confess it, and I had good reason to be so," replied Château-Renaud. "I was retreating on foot, for my horse was dead. Six Arabs came up full gallop to cut off my head. I shot two with my double-barrelled gun, and two more with my pistols, but I was then disarmed, and two were left still, one seized me by the hair (that is why I now wear it so short, for no one knows what may happen), the other encircled my neck with the yataghan, when this gentleman, whom you see here, charged them, shot the one who held me by the hair with a pistol, and cleft the skull of the other with his sabre. He had assigned himself the task of saving the life of a man that day, chance caused that man to be myself; when I am rich I will order a statue of Chance from Klugmann or Marochetti."

"Yes," said Morrel, smiling, "it was the 5th of September, the anniversary of the day on which my father was miraculously preserved; therefore, as far as it lies in my power, I endeavour to celebrate it by some——"

"Heroic action," interrupted Château-Renaud. "I was chosen. But this is not all: after rescuing me from the sword, he rescued me from the cold, not by sharing his cloak with me, like St. Martin, but by giving me it all; then, from hunger, by sharing with me—guess what?"

"A Strasbourg pie?" asked Beauchamp.

"No, his horse; of which we each of us ate a slice with a hearty appetite: it was very hard."

"The horse?" said Morcerf, laughing.

"No, the sacrifice," returned Château-Renaud: "ask Debray if he would sacrifice his English steed for a stranger?"

"Not for a stranger," said Debray, "but for a friend, I might perhaps."

"I divined that you would become mine, M. le Comte," replied Morrel; "besides, as I had the honour to tell you, heroism or not, sacrifice or not, that day I owed an offering to bad fortune in recompense for the favours good fortune had on other days granted to us."

"The history to which M. Morrel alludes," continued Château-Renaud, "is an admirable one, which he will tell you some day when you are better acquainted with him; to-day let us fill our stomachs and not our memories. What time do you breakfast, Albert?"

"At half-past ten."

"Precisely?" asked Debray, taking out his watch.

"Oh! you will give me five minutes' grace," replied Morcerf, "for I also expect a preserver."

"Of whom?"

"Of myself," cried Morcerf; "*parbleu!* do you think I cannot be saved as well as any one else, and that there are only Arabs who cut off heads? Our breakfast is a philanthropic one; and we shall have at table—at least I hope so—two benefactors of humanity."

"What shall we do?" said Debray; "we have only one Monthyon prize."

"Well, but it will be given to some one who has done nothing to deserve it," said Beauchamp; "that is the way the Academy mostly escapes from the dilemma."

"And where does he come from?" asked Debray. "You have already answered the question once, but so vaguely, that I venture to put it a second time."

"Really," said Albert, "I do not know; when I invited him three months ago, he was then at Rome, but since that time who knows where he may have gone?"

"And you think him capable of being exact?" demanded Debray.

"I think him capable of every thing."

"Well, with the five minutes' grace we have only ten left."

"I will profit by them to tell you something about my guest."

"I beg pardon!" interrupted Beauchamp; "are there any materials for an article in what you are going to tell us?"

"Yes; and for a most curious one."

"Go on, then, for I see I shall not get to the Chamber this morning, and I must make up for it."

"I was at Rome the last Carnival."

"We know that," said Beauchamp.

"Yes, but what you do not know is that I was carried off by bandits."

"There are no bandits," cried Debray.

"Yes, there are, and most hideous, or rather most admirable, ones, for I found them ugly enough to frighten me."

"Come, my dear Albert," said Debray; "confess that your cook is behindhand, that the oysters have not arrived from Ostend or Marennes, and that, like Madame de Maintenon, you are going to replace the dish by a story. Say so at once, we are sufficiently well bred to excuse you, and to listen to your history, fabulous as it promises to be."

"And I say to you, fabulous as it may seem, I tell it as a true one from beginning to end. The brigands had carried me off, and conducted me to a most gloomy spot called the Catacombs of Saint Sebastian."

"I know it," said Château-Renaud; "I narrowly escaped catching a fever there."

"And I did more than that," replied Morcerf, "for I caught one. I was informed I was a prisoner until I paid the sum of 4,000 Roman crowns—about 24,000 francs (960l.). Unfortunately I had not above 1,500. I was at the end of my journey and of my credit. I wrote to Franz—and were he here he would confirm every word—I wrote then to Franz, that if he did not come with the four thousand crowns before six, at ten minutes past I should have gone to join the blessed saints and glorious martyrs, in whose company I had the honour of being; and Sig. Luigi Vampa, such was the name of the chief of these bandits, would have scrupulously kept his word."

"But Franz did come with the four thousand crowns," said Château-Renaud. "A man whose name is Franz d'Epinay or Albert de Morcerf has not much difficulty in procuring them."

"No! he arrived accompanied simply by the guest I am going to present to you."

"Ah! this gentleman is a Hercules killing Cacus, a Perseus freeing Andromeda!"

"No, he is a man about my own size!"

"Armed to the teeth?"

"He had not even a knitting-needle."

"But he paid your ransom?"

"He said two words to the chief, and I was free."

"And they apologised to him for having carried you off?" said Beauchamp.

"Just so."

"Why, he is a second Ariosto."

"No; his name is the Count of Monte-Cristo."

"There is not a Count of Monte-Cristo," said Debray.

"I do not think so," added Château-Renaud, with the air of a man who knows the whole of the European nobility perfectly.

"Does any one know any thing of a Count of Monte-Cristo?"

"He comes possibly from the Holy Land, and one of his ancestors possessed Calvary as the Mortemarts did the Dead Sea."

"I think I can assist your researches," said Maximilian. "Monte-Cristo is a little island I have often heard spoken of by the old sailors my father employed. A grain of sand in the centre of the Mediterranean, an atom in the infinite."

"Precisely!" cried Albert. "Well, he of whom I speak is the lord and master of this grain of sand, of this atom; he has purchased the title of count somewhere in Tuscany."

"He is rich, then?"

"I believe so."

"But that ought to be visible."

"That is what deceives you, Debray."

"I do not understand you."

"Have you read the 'Arabian Nights'?"

"What a question!"

"Well, do you know if the persons you see there are rich or poor, if their sacks of wheat are not rubies or diamonds? They seem like poor fishermen, and suddenly they open some mysterious cavern filled with the wealth of the Indies."

"Afterwards?"

"My Count of Monte-Cristo is one of those fishermen. He has even a name taken from the book, since he calls himself Sinbad the Sailor, and has a cave filled with gold."

"And you have seen this cavern, Morcerf?" asked Beauchamp.

"No! but Franz has: for Heaven's sake not a word of this before him. Franz went in with his eyes blindfolded, and was served by mutes and women, to whom Cleopatra was nothing. Only he is not quite sure about the women, for they did not come in until after he had taken some hashish so that what he took for women might have been simply a row of statues."

The two young men looked at Morcerf as if to say,—

"Are you mad, or are you laughing at us?"

"And I, also," said Morrel, thoughtfully, "have heard something like this from an old sailor named Penelon."

"Ah!" cried Albert, "it is very lucky that M. Morrel comes to aid me; you are vexed—are you not?—that he thus gives a clue to the labyrinth?"

"My dear Albert," said Debray, "what you tell us is so extraordinary."

"Ah! because your ambassadors and your consuls do not tell you of them—they have no time. They must not molest their countrymen who travel!"

"Now you get angry and attack our poor agents. How will you have them protect you? The Chamber cuts down their salaries every day, so that now they have scarcely any. Will you be ambassador, Albert? I will send you to Constantinople."

"No; lest on the first demonstration I make in favour of Mehemet Ali the Sultan send me the bowstring and make my secretaries strangle me."

"There, now!" said Debray.

"Yes, but this does not prevent the Count of Monte-Cristo from existing."

"*Pardieu!* every one exists."

"Doubtless, but not in the same way; every one has not black slaves, superb galleys, arms like those at La Casauba, Arabian horses, and Greek mistresses."

"Have you seen his Greek?"

"I have both seen and heard her. I saw her at the theatre, and heard her one morning when I breakfasted with the count."

"He eats, then?"

"Yes, but so little it can hardly be called eating."

"He must be a vampire."

"Laugh if you will; the Countess G——, who had known Lord Ruthven, declared the count was a vampire."

"Ah, capital!" said Beauchamp. "For a man not connected with newspapers here is the pendant to the famous sea serpent of the 'Constitutionnel.'"

"Wild eyes, the iris of which contracts or dilates at pleasure," said Debray, "facial angle strongly developed, magnificent forehead, livid complexion, black beard, sharp and white teeth, politeness unexceptionable."

"Just so, Lucien," returned Morcerf. "You have described him feature for feature. Yes, keen and cutting politeness. This man has often made me shudder; and one day that we were viewing an execution I thought I should faint, more from hearing the cold and calm manner in which he spoke of every description of torture than from the sight of the executioner and the culprit."

"Did he not conduct you to the ruins of the Colosseum and suck your blood?" asked Beauchamp.

"Or, after having delivered you, make you sign a blood-coloured parchment surrendering your soul to him?"

"Rail on,—rail on at your ease, gentlemen," said Morcerf, somewhat piqued. "When I look at you Parisians, idlers on the Boulevard de Gand or the Bois de Boulogne, and think of this man, it seems to me we are not of the same race."

"I am highly flattered," returned Beauchamp.

"At the same time," added Château-Renaud, "your Count of Monte-Cristo is a very fine fellow, always excepting his little arrangements with the Italian banditti."

"There are no Italian banditti!" said Debray.

"No vampire!" cried Beauchamp.

"No Count of Monte-Cristo!" added Debray. "There is half-past ten striking, Albert!"

"Confess you have dreamed this, and let us sit down to breakfast," continued Beauchamp.

But the sound of the clock had not died away when Germain announced,—

"His Excellency the Count of Monte-Cristo."

The involuntary start every one gave proved how much Morcerf's narrative had impressed them, and Albert himself could not prevent himself from feeling a sudden emotion. He had not heard a carriage stop in the street, or steps in the ante-chamber; the door had itself opened noiselessly.

The count appeared, dressed with the greatest simplicity, but the most fastidious dandy could have found nothing to cavil at in his toilette, every article of dress, hat, coat, gloves, and boots, were from the first makers. He seemed scarcely five-and-thirty; but what struck every body was his extreme resemblance with the portrait Debray had drawn.

The count advanced smiling into the centre of the room and approached Albert, who hastened towards him holding out his hand.

"Punctuality," said Monte-Cristo, "is the politeness of kings—according to one of your sovereigns, I think; but it is not the same with travellers. However, I hope you will excuse the two or three seconds I am behindhand; five hundred leagues are not to be accomplished without some trouble, and especially in France, where it seems it is forbidden to beat the postilions."

"M. le Comte," replied Albert, "I was announcing your visit to some of my friends, whom I had invited in consequence of the promise you did me the honour to make, and whom I now present to you. They are M. le Comte de Château-Renaud, whose nobility goes back to twelve peers, and whose ancestors had a place at the Round Table; M. Lucien Debray, private secretary to the Ministre de l'Intérieur; M. Beauchamp, an editor of a paper, and the terror of the French government, but of whom, in spite of his celebrity, you have not heard of in Italy, since his paper is prohibited there; and M. Maximilian Morrel, captain of Spahis."

At this name the count, who had hitherto saluted every one with courtesy, but at the same time with coldness and formality, stepped a pace forward, and a slight tinge of red coloured his pale cheeks.

"You wear the uniform of the new French conquerors, monsieur," said he. "It is a handsome uniform."

No one could have said what caused the count's voice to vibrate so deeply, and what made his eye flash, which was in general so clear, lustrous, and limpid when he pleased.

"You have never seen our Africans, M. le Comte?" said Albert.

"Never," replied the count, who was by this time perfectly master of himself again.

"Well, beneath this uniform beats one of the bravest and noblest hearts in the whole army."

"Oh, M. de Morcerf!" interrupted Morrel.

"Let me go on, captain! And we have just heard," continued Albert, "of a fresh action of monsieur, and so heroic a one, that, although I have seen him to-day for the first time, I request you to allow me to introduce him as my friend."

At these words it was still possible to remark in Monte-Cristo that fixed gaze, that passing colour, and that slight trembling of the eyelid, that shewed his emotion.

"Ah, you have a noble heart!" said the count; "so much the better."

This exclamation, which corresponded to the count's own thought rather than to what Albert was saying, surprised every body, and especially Morrel, who looked at Monte-Cristo with surprise. But, at the same time, the intonation was so soft, that, however strange the exclamation might seem, it was impossible to be offended at it.

"Why should he doubt it?" said Beauchamp to Château-Renaud.

"In reality," replied the latter, who, with his aristocratic glance and his knowledge of the world, had penetrated at once all that was penetrable in Monte-Cristo, "Albert has not deceived us, for the count is a most singular being. What say you, Morrel?"

"Ma foi! he has an open look about him, that pleases me, in spite of the singular remark he has made about me."

"Gentlemen," said Albert, "Germain informs me breakfast is ready. My dear count, allow me to shew you the way."

They passed silently into the breakfast-room; every one took his place.

"Gentlemen," said the count, seating himself, "permit me to make a confession which must form my excuse for any

inconvénences I may commit.   I am a stranger, and a stranger
to such a degree, that this is the first time I have ever been at
Paris.   The French way of living is utterly unknown to me,
and up to the present time I have followed the Eastern
customs, which are entirely in contrast to the Parisian.   I beg
you therefore to excuse if you find anything in me too Turkish,
too Italian, or too Arabian.   Now, then, let us breakfast."

"With what an air he says all this!" muttered Beauchamp;
"decidedly he is a great man."

"A great man in this country," added Debray.

"A great man in every country, M. Debray," said Château-
Renaud.

The count was, it may be remembered, a most temperate
guest.   Albert remarked this, expressing his fears lest, at the
outset, the Parisian mode of life should displease the traveller
in the most essential point.

"My dear count," said he, "I fear one thing, and that is,
that the fare of the Rue du Helder is not so much to your taste
as that of the Place d'Espagne.   I ought to have consulted
you on the point, and have had some dishes prepared
expressly."

"Did you know me better," returned the count, smiling,
"you would not give one thought of such a thing for a traveller
like myself, who has successively lived on macaroni at Naples,
polenta at Milan, olla podrida at Valencia, pilau at Constantinople, curry in India, and swallows' nests in China.
I eat every wnere, and of every thing, only I eat but little;
and to-day, that you reproach me with my want of appetite,
is my day of appetite, for I have not eaten since yesterday
morning."

"What!" cried all the guests, "you have not eaten for
four-and-twenty hours?"

"No," replied the count; "I was forced to go out of my
road to obtain some information near Nîmes, so that I was
somewhat late, and therefore I did not choose to stop."

"And you ate in your carriage?" asked Morcerf.

"No, I slept, as I generally do when I am weary without
having the courage to amuse myself, or when I am hungry
without feeling inclined to eat."

"But you can sleep when you please, monsieur?" said
Morrel.

"Yes."

"You have a receipt for it?"

"An infallible one."

"That would be invaluable to us in Africa, who have not
always any food to eat, and rarely any thing to drink."

"Yes," said Monte-Cristo, "but, unfortunately, a receipt

excellent for a man like myself would be very dangerous applied to an army, which might not awake when it was needed."

"May we inquire what is this receipt?" asked Debray.

"Oh, yes," returned Monte-Cristo, "I make no secret of it; it is a mixture of excellent opium, which I fetched myself from Canton in order to have it pure, and the best hashish which grows in the east, that is, between the Tigris and Euphrates. These two ingredients are mixed in equal proportions, and formed into pills. Ten minutes after one is taken the effect is produced. Ask M. le Baron Franz d'Epinay; I think he tasted them one day."

"Yes," replied Morcerf; "he said something about it to me."

"But," said Beauchamp, who, in his capacity of journalist, was very incredulous, "you always carry this drug about you?"

"Always."

"Would it be an indiscretion to ask to see those precious pills?" continued Beauchamp, hoping to take him at a disadvantage.

"No, monsieur," returned the count; and he drew from his pocket a marvellous *bonbonnière*, formed out of a single emerald, and closed by a golden lid, which unscrewed and gave passage to a small ball of a greenish colour, and about the size of a pea. This ball had an acrid and penetrating odour. There were four or five more in the emerald, which would contain about a dozen.

The *bonbonnière* passed round the table, but it was more to examine the admirable emerald than to see the pills that it passed from hand to hand.

"And is it your cook who prepares these pills?" asked Beauchamp.

"Oh, no, monsieur," replied Monte-Cristo; "I do not thus betray my enjoyments to the vulgar; I am a tolerable chemist, and prepare my pills myself."

"This is a magnificent emerald, and the largest I have ever seen," said Château-Renaud, "although my mother had some remarkable family jewels."

"I had three similar ones," returned Monte-Cristo; "I gave one to the Grand Signior, who mounted it in his sabre; another to our holy father the Pope, who had it set in his tiara, opposite to nearly as large, though not so fine a one, given by the Emperor Napoleon to his predecessor Pius VII. I kept the third for myself, and I had it hollowed out, which reduced its value, but rendered it more commodious for the purpose I intended it for."

Every one looked at Monte-Cristo with astonishment; he spoke with so much simplicity that it was evident he spoke the truth, or that he was mad. However, the sight of the emerald made them naturally incline to the former belief.

"And what did these two sovereigns give you in exchange for these magnificent presents?" asked Debray.

"The Grand Signior, the liberty of a woman," replied the count; "the Pope, the life of a man: so that once in my life I have been as powerful as if Heaven had made me come into the world on the steps of a throne."

"And it was Peppino you saved, was it not?" cried Morcerf—"it was for him that you obtained pardon?"

"Perhaps," returned the count, smiling.

"Monsieur le Comte, you have no idea what pleasure it gives me to hear you speak thus," said Morcerf. "I had announced you beforehand to my friends as an enchanter of the 'Arabian Nights,' a wizard of the middle ages; but the Parisians are people so subtle in paradoxes, that they mistake for caprices of the imagination the most incontestable truths, when these truths do not form a part of their daily existence. For example, here is Debray who reads, and Beauchamp who prints, every day,—'A member of the Jockey Club has been stopped and robbed on the Boulevard; that four persons have been assassinated in the Rue St. Denis or the Faubourg St. Germain; that ten, fifteen, or twenty thieves, have been arrested in a café on the Boulevard du Temple, or in the Thermes de Julien,' and who yet contest the existence of the bandits of the Maremna, of the Campagna di Romana, or the Pontine Marshes. Tell them yourself that I was taken by bandits, and that without your generous intercession I should now have been sleeping in the catacombs of St. Sebastian, instead of receiving them in my humble abode in the Rue du Helder."

"Ah," said Monte-Cristo, "you promised me never to mention the circumstance."

"It was not I who made that promise," cried Morcerf; "it must have been some one else whom you have rescued in the same manner, and whom you have forgotten. Pray speak of it, for I shall not only, I trust, relate the little I do know, but also a great deal I do not know."

"It seems to me," returned the count, smiling, "that you played a sufficiently important part to know as well as myself what happened."

"Well, you promise me if I tell all I know, to relate, in your turn, all that I do not know."

"That is but fair," replied Monte-Cristo.

"Well," said Morcerf, "for three days I believed myself the

object of the attentions of a mask, whom I took for a descendant of Tullia or Poppœa, whilst I was simply the object of the attentions of a *contadine*, and I say *contadine*, to avoid saying peasant.   What I know is, that, like a fool, a greater fool than he of whom I spoke just now, I mistook for this peasant a young bandit of fifteen or sixteen, with a beardless chin and slim waist, and who, just as I was about to imprint a chaste salute on his lips, placed a pistol to my head, and, aided by seven or eight others, led, or rather dragged, me to the Catacombs of St. Sebastian, where I found a highly educated chief of brigands perusing Cæsar's 'Commentaries,' and who deigned to leave off reading to inform me, that unless the next morning, before six o'clock, four thousand piastres were paid in to his account at his banker's, at a quarter past six I should have ceased to exist.   The letter is still to be seen, for it is in Franz d'Epinay's possession, signed by me, and with a postscript of M. Luigi Vampa.   This is all I know, but I know not, M. le Comte, how you contrived to inspire with such respect the bandits of Rome, who have so little respect for any thing; I assure you, Franz and I were lost in admiration."

"Nothing more simple," returned the count.   "I had known the famous Vampa for more than ten years.   When he was quite a child, and only a shepherd, I gave him, for having shewed me the way to a place, some pieces of gold; he, in order to repay me, gave me a poniard, the hilt of which he had carved with his own hand, and which you may have seen in my collection of arms.   In after years, whether he had forgotten this interchange of presents, which ought to have cemented our friendship, or whether he did not recollect me, he sought to take me, but, on the contrary, it was I who captured him, and a dozen of his band.   I might have handed him over to Roman justice, which is somewhat expeditious, and which would have been still more so with him; but I did nothing of the sort—I suffered him and his band to depart."

"With the condition that they should sin no more," said Beauchamp, laughing.   "I see they kept their promise."

"No, monsieur," returned Monte-Cristo; "upon the simple condition that they should respect myself and my friends. Perhaps what I am about to say may seem strange to you, who are socialists, and vaunt humanity and your duty to your neighbour, but I never seek to protect society who does not protect me, and whom I will even say, in general, occupies itself about me only to injure me; and thus giving them a low place in my esteem, and preserving a neutrality towards them, it is society and my neighbour who are indebted to me."

"Bravo!" cried Château-Renaud; "you are the first man I ever met sufficiently courageous to preach egotism. Bravo! M. le Comte, bravo!"

"It is frank, at least," said Morrel. "But I am sure that M. le Comte does not regret having once deviated from the principles he has so boldly avowed."

"How have I deviated from those principles, monsieur?" asked Monte-Cristo, who could not help looking at Morrel with so much intensity, that two or three times the young man had been unable to sustain the clear and piercing eye of the count.

"Why it seems to me," replied Morrel, "that, in delivering M. de Morcerf, whom you did not know, you did good to your neighbour and to society."

"Of which he is the brightest ornament," said Beauchamp, drinking off a glass of champagne.

"Monsieur le Comte," cried Morcerf, "you are at fault; you, one of the most formidable logicians I know—and you must see it clearly proved, that instead of being an egotist, you are a philanthropist. Ah! you call yourself Oriental, a Levantine, Maltese, Indian, Chinese; your family name is Monte-Cristo; Sinbad the Sailor is your baptismal appellation, and yet the first day you set foot in Paris, you instinctively possess the greatest virtue, or rather the chief defect, of us eccentric Parisians—that is, you assume the vices you have not, and conceal the virtues you possess."

"My dear vicomte," returned Monte-Cristo, "I do not see, in all I have done, any thing that merits, either from you or these gentlemen, the pretended eulogies I have received. You are no stranger to me, for I knew you since I had given up two rooms to you—since I had invited you to breakfast with me—since I had lent you one of my carriages—since we had witnessed the Carnival together, and since we had also seen from a window of the Place del Popolo the execution that affected you so much that you nearly fainted. I will appeal to any of these gentlemen, could I leave my guest in the hands of a hideous bandit, as you term him? Besides, you know, I had the idea that you could introduce me into some of the Paris salons when I came to France. You might, some time ago, have looked upon this resolution as a vague project, but to-day you see it was a reality, and you must submit to it under penalty of breaking your word."

"I will keep it," returned Morcerf; "but I fear that you will be much disappointed, accustomed as you are to picturesque events and to fantastic horizons. Amongst us you will not meet with any of those episodes with which your adventurous existence has so familiarised you; our Chimborazo is

Montmartre, our Himalaya is Mount Valerien, our Great Desert is the Plain of Grenelle, where they are now boring an Artesian well to water the caravans. We have plenty of thieves, though not so many as is said; but these thieves stand in far more dread of a policeman than a lord. France is so prosaic, and Paris so civilised a city, that you will not find in its eighty-five departments—I say eighty-five, because I do not include Corsica—you will not find, then, in these eighty-five departments a single hill on which there is not a telegraph, or a grotto in which the commissary of police has not put up a gas-lamp. There is but one service I can render you, and for that I place myself entirely at your orders; that is, to present, or make my friends present, you every where: besides, you have no need of any one to introduce you—with your name, and your fortune, and your talent" (Monte-Cristo bowed with a somewhat ironical smile), "you can present yourself every where, and be well received; I can be useful in one way only: —if knowledge of Parisian habits, of the means of rendering yourself comfortable, or of the bazaars, can assist, you may dispose of me to find you a fitting dwelling here. I dare offer to share my apartments with you, as I shared yours at Rome— I, who do not possess egotism, but am yet egotistical *par excellence;* for, except myself, these rooms would not contain a shadow, unless it were the shadow of a female."

"Ah," said the count, "that is a most conjugal reservation; I recollect that at Rome you said something of a projected marriage. May I congratulate you?"

"The affair is still in projection."

"And he who says 'in projection,' means already decided," said Debray.

"No," replied Morcerf, "my father is most anxious about it; and I hope, ere long, to introduce you, if not to my wife, at least to my intended—Mademoiselle Eugénie Danglars."

"Eugénie Danglars!" said Monte-Cristo; "tell me, is not her father M. le Baron Danglars?"

"Yes," returned Morcerf; "a baron of a new creation."

"What matter," said Monte-Cristo, "if he has rendered the state services which merit this distinction?"

"Enormous ones," answered Beauchamp. "Although in reality a liberal, he negotiated a loan of six millions (240,000*l.*) for Charles X, in 1829, who made him a baron and chevalier de la Légion d'Honneur; so that he wears the riband, not as you would think, in his waistcoat-pocket, but at his button-hole."

"Ah," interrupted Morcerf, laughing, "Beauchamp, Beauchamp, keep that for the 'Charivari,' but spare my future father-in-law before me." Then turning to Monte-Cristo, "You just now pronounced his name as if you knew the baron?"

"I do not know him," returned Monte-Cristo; "but I shall probably soon make his acquaintance, for I have a credit opened with him by the house of Richard and Blount of London, Arstein and Eskeles of Vienna, and Thomson and French of Rome."

As he pronounced the two last names, the count glanced at Maximilian Morrel.

If the stranger expected to produce an effect on Morrel, he was not mistaken—Maximilian started as if he had been electrified.

"Thomson and French!" said he; "do you know this house, monsieur?"

"They are my bankers in the capital of the Christian world," returned the count, quietly. "Can my influence with them be of any service to you?"

"Oh, M. le Comte, you could assist me, perhaps, in researches which have been, up to the present, fruitless. This house, in past years, did ours a great service, and has, I know not for what reason, always denied having rendered us this service."

"I shall be at your orders," said Monte-Cristo, inclining himself.

"But," continued Morcerf, "àpropos of Danglars,—we have strangely wandered from the subject. We were speaking of a suitable habitation for the Count of Monte-Cristo. Come, gentlemen, let us all propose some place; where shall we lodge this new guest in our great capital?"

"Faubourg Saint-Germain," said Château-Renaud. "The count will find there a charming mansion, with a court and garden."

"Bah! Château-Renaud," returned Debray, "you only know your dull and gloomy Faubourg Saint-Germain; do not pay any attention to him, M. le Comte—living in the Chaussée d'Antin, that's the real centre of Paris."

"Boulevard de l'Opéra," said Beauchamp; "on the first floor—a house with a balcony. M. le Comte will have his cushions of silver cloth brought there, and as he smokes his chibouque see all Paris pass before him."

"You have no idea, then, Morrel?" asked Château-Renaud: "you do not propose any thing?"

"Oh yes," returned the young man, smiling; "on the contrary, I have one; but I expected the count would be tempted by one of the brilliant proposals made him, yet as he has not replied to any of them, I will venture to offer him a suite of apartments in a charming mansion in the Pompadour style, that my sister has inhabited for a year, in the Rue Meslay."

"You have a sister?" asked the count.

"Yes, monsieur, a most excellent sister."

"Married?"

"Nearly nine years."

"Happy?" asked the count, again.

"As happy as it is permitted to a human creature to be," replied Maximilian. "She married the man she loved, who remained faithful to us in our fallen fortunes—Emmanuel Herbaut."

Monte-Cristo smiled imperceptibly.

"I live there during my leave of absence," continued Maximilian; "and I shall be, together with my brother-in-law, Emmanuel, at the disposition of M. le Comte, whenever he thinks fit to honour us."

"One minute!" cried Albert, without giving Monte-Cristo the time to reply. "Take care, you are going to immure a traveller, Sinbad the Sailor, a man who comes to see Paris; you are going to make a patriarch of him."

"Oh, no," said Morrel; "my sister is five-and-twenty, my brother-in-law is thirty; they are gay, young, and happy: besides, M. le Comte will be in his own house, and only see them when he thinks fit to do so."

"Thanks, monsieur," said Monte-Cristo, "I shall content myself with being presented to your sister and her husband, if you will do me the honour to introduce me; but I cannot accept the offer of any of these gentlemen, since my habitation is already prepared."

"What!" cried Morcerf, "you are, then, going to a hotel—that will be very dull for you."

"Was I so badly lodged at Rome?" said Monte-Cristo, smiling.

"*Parbleu!*—at Rome you spent fifty thousand piastres in furnishing your apartments, but I presume that you are not disposed to spend a similar sum every day."

"It is not that which deterred me," replied Monte-Cristo; "but as I determined to have a house to myself I sent on my valet-de-chambre, and he ought, by this time, to have bought the house and furnished it."

"But you have, then, a valet-de-chambre who knows Paris?" said Beauchamp.

"It is the first time he has ever been in Paris. He is black, and cannot speak," returned Monte-Cristo.

"It is Ali!" cried Albert, in the midst of the general surprise.

"Yes, Ali himself, my Nubian mute, whom you saw, I think, at Rome."

"Certainly," said Morcerf; "I recollect him perfectly. But how could you charge a Nubian to purchase a house, and a mute to furnish it? he will do every thing wrong."

"Undeceive yourself, monsieur," replied Monte-Cristo; "I am quite sure that, on the contrary, he will choose every thing as I wish. He knows my tastes, my caprices, my wants; he has been here a week, with the instinct of a hound, hunting by himself; he will organise every thing for me. He knew I should arrive to-day at ten o'clock; since nine he awaited me at the Barrière de Fontainbleau. He gave me this paper; it contains the number of my new abode; read it yourself," and Monte-Cristo passed a paper to Albert.

"Ah, that is really original," said Beauchamp.

"And very princely," added Château-Renaud.

"What! do you not know your house?" asked Debray.

"No," said Monte-Cristo; "I told you I did not wish to be behind my time; I dressed myself in the carriage, and descended at the vicomte's door."

The young men looked at each other; they did not know if it was a comedy Monte-Cristo was playing; but every word he uttered had such an air of simplicity, that it was impossible to suppose what he said was false: besides, why should he tell a falsehood?

"We must content ourselves, then," said Beauchamp, "with rendering M. le Comte all the little services in our power. I, in my quality of journalist, open all the theatres to him."

"Thanks, monsieur," returned Monte-Cristo; "my steward has orders to take a box at each theatre."

"Is your steward also a Nubian?" asked Debray.

"No, he is a countryman of yours, if a Corsican is a countryman of any one's. But you know him, M. de Morcerf."

"Is it that excellent M. Bertuccio, who understands hiring windows so well?"

"Yes, you saw him the day I had the honour of receiving you; he has been a soldier, a smuggler—in fact, every thing. I would not be quite sure that he has not been mixed up with the police for some trifle,—a stab with a knife, for instance."

"And you have chosen this honest citizen for your steward?" said Debray. "Of how much does he rob you every year?"

"On my word," replied the count, "not more than another. I am sure he answers my purpose, knows no impossibility, and so I keep him."

"Then," continued Château-Renaud, "since you have an establishment, a steward, and an hôtel in the Champs Elysées, you only want a mistress."

Albert smiled. He thought of the fair Greek he had seen in the count's box at the Argentina and Valle theatres.

"I have something better than that," said Monte-Cristo; "I have a slave. You procure your mistresses from the Opera, the Vaudeville, or the Variétés; I purchased mine at Constantinople; it cost me more, but I have nothing to fear."

"But you forget," replied Debray, laughing, "that we are Franks by name and frank by nature, as King Charles said; and that the moment she puts her foot in France your slave becomes free."

"Who will tell her?"

"The first person who sees her."

"She only speaks Romaic."

"That is different."

"But at least we shall see her," said Beauchamp; "or do you keep eunuchs as well as mutes?"

"Oh, no," replied Monte-Cristo; "I do not carry brutalism so far. Every one who surrounds me is free to quit me, and when they leave me will no longer have any need of me or any one else; it is for that reason, perhaps, that they do not quit me."

They had long since passed to dessert and cigars.

"My dear Albert," said Debray, rising; "it is half-past two. Your guest is charming; but you leave the best company to go into the worst sometimes. I must return to the minister's. I will tell him of the count, and we shall soon know who he is."

"Take care," returned Albert; "no one has been able to accomplish that."

"Oh, we have three millions for our police; it is true they are almost always spent beforehand; but no matter, we shall still have fifty thousand francs to spend for this purpose."

"And when you know, will you tell me?"

"I promise you. Au revoir, Albert. Gentlemen, good morning."

As he left the room, Debray called out loudly,—

"My carriage!"

"Bravo!" said Beauchamp to Albert; "I do not go to the Chamber, but I have something better to offer my readers than a speech of M. Danglars."

"For Heaven's sake, Beauchamp!" returned Morcerf, "do not deprive me of the merit of introducing him everywhere. Is he not peculiar?"

"He is more than that," replied Château-Renaud; "he is

one of the most extraordinary men I ever saw in my life. Are you coming, Morrel?"

"Directly I have given my card to M. le Comte, who has promised to pay us a visit at Rue Meslay, No. 14."

"Be sure I shall not fail to do so," returned the count, bowing.

And Maximilian Morrel left the room with the Baron de Château-Renaud, leaving Monte-Cristo alone with Morcerf.

CHAPTER XLI

WHEN Albert found himself alone with Monte-Cristo, "M. le Comte," said he, "allow me to commence my ciceroneship by shewing you a specimen of a bachelor's apartment. You, who are accustomed to the palaces of Italy, can amuse yourself by calculating in how many square feet a young man who is not the worst lodged in Paris can live. As we pass from one room to another I will open the windows to let you breathe."

Monte-Cristo had already seen the breakfast-room and the salon on the ground-floor. Albert led him first to his studio, which was, as we have said, his favourite apartment. Monte-Cristo was a worthy appreciator of all that Albert had collected here,—old cabinets, Japan porcelain, Oriental stuffs, Venice glass, arms from all parts of the world,—every thing was familiar to him; and at the first glance he recognised their date, their country, and their origin. Morcerf had expected he should be the guide; on the contrary, it was he who, under the count's guidance, followed a course of archæology, mineralogy, and natural history. They descended to the first floor; Albert led his guest into the salon. The salon was filled with the works of modern artists; there were landscapes of Dupré, with their long reeds and tall trees, their lowing oxen and marvellous skies; Delacroix' Arabian cavaliers, with their long white burnous, their shining belts, their damasked arms, their horses, who tore each other with their teeth whilst their riders contended fiercely with their maces; *aquarelles* of Boulanger, representing Nôtre Dame de Paris with that vigour that makes the artist the rival of the poet; there were paintings by Dias, who makes his flowers more beautiful than flowers, his suns more brilliant than the sun; designs of Decamp, as vividly coloured as those of Salvator Rosa, but more poetic; *pastels* of Giraud and Müller, representing children like angels, and women with the features of a virgin; sketches torn from the album of Dauzats' "Travels in the East," that had been made in a few seconds on the saddle of a camel or beneath the dome of a mosque: in a word, all that modern art can give in exchange and as recompense for the art lost and gone with ages long since past.

Albert expected to have something new this time to shew to the traveller, but, to his great surprise, the latter, without seeking for the signatures, many of which, indeed, were only initials, named instantly the author of every picture in such a manner that it was easy to see that each name was not only known to him, but that each of their styles had been appreciated and studied by him.

From the salon they passed into the bed-chamber; it was a model of taste and simple elegance. A single portrait, signed Leopold Robert, shone in its carved and gilded frame.

This portrait attracted the Count of Monte-Cristo's attention, for he made three rapid steps in the chamber, and stopped suddenly before it. It was the portrait of a young woman of five or six-and-twenty, with a dark complexion, and light and lustrous eyes veiled beneath their long lashes. She wore the picturesque costume of the Catalan fisherwomen, a red and black bodice and the golden pins in her hair. She was looking at the sea, and her shadow was defined on the blue ocean and sky.

The light was so faint in the room, that Albert did not perceive the paleness that spread itself over the count's visage, or the nervous heaving of his chest and shoulders. Silence prevailed for an instant, during which Monte-Cristo gazed intently on the picture.

"You have there a most charming mistress, viscount," said the count, in a perfectly calm tone; "and this costume—a ball-costume, doubtless, becomes her admirably."

"Ah, monsieur!" returned Albert, "I would never forgive you this mistake if you had seen another picture beside this. You do not know my mother; she it is whom you see here: she had her portrait painted thus six or eight years ago. This costume is a fancy one, it appears, and the resemblance is so great that I think I still see my mother the same as she was in 1830. The countess had this portrait painted during the count's absence. She doubtless intended giving him an agreeable surprise, but, strange to say, this portrait seemed to displease my father, and the value of the picture, which is, as you see, one of the best works of Leopold Robert, could not overcome his dislike to it. It is true, between ourselves, that M. de Morcerf is one of the most assiduous peers at the Luxembourg, a general renowned for theory, but a most mediocre amateur of art. It is different with my mother, who paints exceedingly well, and who, unwilling to part with so valuable a picture, gave it to me to put here where it would be less likely to displease M. de Morcerf, whose portrait by Gros I will also shew you. Excuse my talking of family matters; but as I shall have the honour of introducing you to the count, I tell you this to prevent you making any allusions to this picture. The picture seems to have a malign influence, for my mother rarely comes here without looking at it, and still more rarely does she look at it without weeping. This disagreement is the only one that has ever taken place between the count and countess, who are still as much united, although married more than twenty years, as the first day of their wedding."

Monte-Cristo glanced rapidly at Albert, as if to seek a hidden meaning in his words, but it was evident the young man uttered them in the simplicity of his heart.

"Now," said Albert, "that you have seen all my treasures, allow me to offer them to you, unworthy as they are. Consider yourself as in your own house; and to put yourself still more at your ease, pray accompany me to the apartments of M. de Morcerf, to whom I wrote from Rome an account of the services you rendered me, and to whom I announced your promised visit, and I may say that both the count and countess anxiously desire to thank you in person. You are somewhat *blasé* I know, and family scenes have not much effect on Sinbad the Sailor who has seen so many others. However, accept what I propose to you as an initiation into Parisian life—a life of politeness, visiting, and introductions."

Monte-Cristo bowed without making any answer; he accepted the offer without enthusiasm and without regret, as one of those conventions of society which every gentleman looks upon as a duty. Albert summoned his servant, and ordered him to acquaint M. and Madame de Morcerf of the arrival of the Count of Monte-Cristo.

Albert followed him with the count. When they arrived at the ante-chamber, above the door was visible a shield, which, by its rich ornaments and its harmony with the rest of the furniture, indicated the importance the owner attached to this blazon: Monte-Cristo stopped and examined it attentively.

"Azure seven merlets, or, placed bender," said he. "These are, doubtless, your family arms? Except the knowledge of blazons that enables me to decipher them, I am very ignorant of heraldry,—I, a count of a fresh creation, fabricated in Tuscany by the aid of a commandery of St. Stephen; and who would not have taken the trouble had I not been told that when you travel much it is necessary. Besides, you must have something on the panels of your carriage to escape being searched by the custom-house officers. Excuse my putting such a question to you."

"It is not indiscreet," returned Morcerf, with the simplicity of conviction. "You have guessed rightly. These are our arms; that is, those of my father: but they are, as you see, joined to another shield, which has gules, a silver tower, which are my mother's. By her side I am Spanish, but the family of Morcerf is French, and, I have heard, one of the oldest of the south of France."

"Yes," replied Monte-Cristo, "these blazons prove that almost all the armed pilgrims that went to the Holy Land took for their arms either a cross, in honour of their mission, or birds of passage, in sign of the long voyage they are about to undertake, and which they hoped to accomplish on the wings of faith. One of your ancestors had joined the Crusades; and supposing it to be only that of St. Louis, that makes you mount to the thirteenth century, which is tolerably ancient."

"It is possible," said Morcerf, "my father has in his study a genealogical tree which will tell you all that, and on which I made commentaries that would have greatly edified Hozier and Jaucourt. At present I no longer think of it; and yet I must tell you that we are beginning to occupy ourselves greatly with these things under our popular government."

"Well, then, your government would do well to choose from the past something better than the things that I have noticed on your monuments, and which have no heraldic meaning whatever. As for you, viscount," continued Monte-Cristo to Morcerf, "you are more fortunate than the government, for your arms are really beautiful and speak to the imagination. Yes, you are at once from Provence and Spain; that explains, if the portrait you shewed me be like, the dark hue I so much admired on the visage of the noble Catalan."

It would have required the penetration of Œdipus or the Sphinx to have divined the irony the count concealed beneath these words, apparently uttered with the greatest politeness. Morcerf thanked him with a smile, and pushed open the door above which were his arms, and which, as we have said, opened into the salon.

In the most conspicuous part of the salon was another portrait. It was that of a man from five to eight-and-thirty, in the uniform of a general officer, wearing the double epaulette *en torsade*, that indicates superior rank; the riband of the Legion of Honour round his neck, which shewed he was a commander; and on the breast, on the right, the star of a grand officer of the order of the Saviour, and on the left that of the grand cross of Charles III, which proved that the person represented by the picture had served in the wars of Greece and Spain, or, what was just the same thing as regarded decorations, had fulfilled some diplomatic mission in the two countries.

Monte-Cristo was engaged in examining this portrait with no less care than he had bestowed upon the other, when another door opened, and he found himself opposite to the Count de

Morcerf himself. He was a man of forty to forty-five years, but he seemed at least fifty, and his black moustache and eyebrows contrasted strangely with his almost white hair, which was cut short in the military fashion. He was dressed in plain clothes, and wore at his button-hole the ribands of the different orders to which he belonged. This man entered with a tolerably dignified step and with a species of haste. Monte-Cristo saw him advance towards him without making a single step. It seemed as if his feet were rooted to the ground and his eyes on the Count de Morcerf.

"Father," said the young man, "I have the honour of presenting to you M. le Comte de Monte-Cristo, the generous friend whom I had the good fortune to meet in the critical juncture of which I have told you."

"You are most welcome, monsieur," said the Count de Morcerf, saluting Monte-Cristo with a smile. "And monsieur has rendered our house, in preserving its only heir, a service which ensures him our eternal gratitude."

As he said these words, the Count de Morcerf pointed to a chair, whilst he seated himself in another opposite the window.

Monte-Cristo, whilst he took the seat Morcerf offered him, placed himself in such a manner as to remain concealed in the shadow of the large velvet curtains, and read on the care-worn and livid features of the count a whole history of secret griefs written in each wrinkle time had planted there."

"Madame la Vicomtesse," said Morcerf, "was at her toilette when she was informed of the visit she was about to receive. She would, however, be in the salon in ten minutes."

"It is a great honour for me," returned Monte-Cristo, "to be thus on the first day of my arrival in Paris brought in contact with a man whose merit equals his reputation, and to whom Fortune has for once been equitable; but has she not still on the plains of Mitidja or in the mountains of Atlas a marshal's staff to offer you?"

"Oh," replied Morcerf, reddening slightly, "I have left the service, monsieur. Made a peer at the Restoration, I served through the first campaign under the orders of Marshal Bourmont. I could, therefore, expect a higher rank, and who knows what might have happened had the elder branch remained on the throne? but the Revolution of July was, it seems, sufficiently glorious to allow itself to be ungrateful: and she was so for all services that did not date from the imperial period. I tendered my resignation, for when you have gained your epaulettes on the battle-field, you do not know how to manoeuvre on the slippery ground of the salons. I have hung up my sword and cast myself into politics. I have devoted myself to industry; I study the useful arts. During the twenty years I served, I often wished to do so, but I had not the time."

"These are the ideas that render your nation superior to any other," returned Monte-Cristo. "A gentleman of high birth, possessor of an ample fortune, you have consented to gain your promotion as an obscure soldier, step by step—this is uncommon; then become general, peer of France, commander of the Legion of Honour, you consent to again commence a second apprenticeship, without any other hope or any other desire than that of one day becoming useful to your fellow-creatures; this indeed, is praiseworthy,—nay, more, it is sublime."

Albert looked on and listened with astonishment, he was not used to see Monte-Cristo give vent to such bursts of enthusiasm.

"Alas!" continued the stranger, doubtless to dispel the slight cloud that covered Morcerf's brow, "we do not act thus in Italy; we grow according to our race and our species, and we pursue the same lines and often the same uselessness all our lives."

"But, monsieur," said the Count de Morcerf, "for a man of your merit, Italy is not a country, and France opens her arms to receive you: respond to her call. France will not, perhaps, be always ungrateful! She treats her children ill, but she always welcomes strangers."

"Ah, father!" said Albert with a smile, "it is evident you do not know M. le Comte de Monte-Cristo; he despises all honours, and contents himself with those that are written on his passport."

"That is the most just remark," replied the stranger, " I ever heard made concerning myself!"

"You have been free to choose your career," observed the Count de Morcerf, with a sigh, "and you have chosen the path strewed with flowers."

"Precisely, monsieur," replied Monte-Cristo, with one of those smiles that a painter could never represent or a physiologist analyse.

"If I did not fear to fatigue you," said the general, evidently charmed with the count's manners, "I would have taken you to the Chamber; there is a debate very curious to those who are strangers to our modern senators."

"I shall be most grateful, monsieur, if you will at some future time renew your offer; but I have been flattered with the hope of being introduced to the countess, and I will therefore wait."

"Ah! here is my mother!" cried the viscount.

Monte-Cristo turned round hastily, and saw Madame de

Morcerf at the entrance of the salon, at the door opposite to that by which her husband had entered, pale and motionless; when Monte-Cristo turned round, she let fall her arm, which for some unknown reason had been resting on the gilded door-post. She had been there some moments, and had overheard the last words of the visitor.

The latter rose and bowed to the countess, who inclined herself without speaking.

"Ah! good heavens, madame!" said the count, "are you unwell, or is it the heat of the room that affects you?"

"Are you ill, mother?" cried the viscount, springing towards her.

She thanked them both with a smile.

"No," returned she, "but I feel some emotion on seeing, for the first time, the man, without whose intervention we should have been in tears and desolation. Monsieur," continued the countess, advancing with the majesty of a queen, "I owe to you the life of my son, and for this I bless you. Now I thank you for the pleasure you give me in thus affording me the opportunity of thanking you as I have blessed you, from the bottom of my heart."

The count bowed again, but lower than before; he was even paler than Mercédès.

"Madame," said he, "M. le Comte and yourself recompense too generously a simple action. To save a man, to spare a father's feelings or a mother's sensibility, is not to do a good action, but a simple deed of humanity."

At these words, uttered with the most exquisite sweetness and politeness, Madame de Morcerf replied,—

"It is very fortunate for my son, monsieur, that he found such a friend, and I thank God that things are thus."

And Mercédès raised her fine eyes to heaven, with so fervent an expression of gratitude that the count fancied he saw tears in them.

M. de Morcerf approached her.

"Madame," said he, "I have already made my excuses to M. le Comte for quitting him, and I pray you to do so also. The sitting commences at two, it is now three, and I am to speak."

"Go, then, and monsieur and I will strive our best to forget your absence!" replied the countess, with the same tone of deep feeling. "M. le Comte," continued she, turning to Monte-Cristo, "will you do us the honour of passing the rest of the day with us?"

"Believe me, madame, I feel most grateful for your kindness, but I got out of my travelling carriage at your door this morning, and I am ignorant how I am installed in Paris, which

I scarcely know; this is but a trifling inquietude, I know, but one that may be appreciated."

"We shall have this pleasure another time!" said the countess; "you promise that?"

Monte-Cristo inclined himself, without answering, but the gesture might pass for assent.

"I will not detain you, monsieur," continued the countess, "I would not have our gratitude become indiscreet or importunate."

"My dear count," said Albert, "I will endeavour to return your politeness at Rome, and place my coupé at your disposal until your own be ready."

"A thousand thanks for your kindness, viscount," returned the Count of Monte-Cristo, "but I suppose that M. Bertuccio has suitably employed the four hours and a half I have given him, and that I shall find a carriage of some sort ready at the door."

Albert was used to the count's manner of proceeding; he knew that, like Nero, he was in search of the impossible, and nothing astonished him; only wishing to judge with his own eyes how far the count's orders had been executed, he accompanied him to the door of the hôtel.

Monte-Cristo was not deceived; as soon as he appeared in the Count de Morcerf's ante-chamber, a footman, the same who at Rome had brought the count's card to the two young men, and announced his visit, sprang into the vestibule, and when he arrived at the door the illustrious traveller found his carriage awaiting him.

It was a coupé of Koller's building, and with horses and harness, for which Drake had, to the knowledge of all the lions of Paris, refused on the previous day seven hundred guineas.

"Monsieur," said the count to Albert, "I do not ask you to accompany me to my house, as I can only shew you a habitation fitted up in a hurry, and I have, as you know, a reputation to keep up as regards not being taken by surprise. Give me, therefore, one more day before I invite you, I shall then be certain not to fail in my hospitality."

"If you ask me for a day, count, I know what to anticipate; it will not be a house I shall see, but a palace. You have, decidedly, some *génie* at your control."

"*Ma foi!* spread that idea," replied the Count of Monte-Cristo, putting his foot on the velvet-lined steps of his splendid carriage; "and that will be worth something to me among the ladies."

As he spoke, he sprang into the vehicle, the door was closed, but not so rapidly, that Monte-Cristo perceived the almost imperceptible movement which stirred the curtains of the apartment in which he had left Madame de Morcerf.

When Albert returned to his mother, he found her in the boudoir, reclining in a large velvet arm-chair; the whole room so obscure that only the shining spangle, fastened here and there to the drapery, and the angles of the gilded frames of the pictures, gave a kind of light to the room. Albert could not see the countenance of the countess, which was lost in a thin veil she had put on her head and which descended around her features like a cloud of vapour, but it seemed to him as though her voice had altered. He could distinguish amidst the perfumes of the roses and heliotropes in the flower-stands the sharp and fragrant odour of volatile salts, and he remarked in one of the chased cups on the mantel-piece the countess's smelling-bottle, taken from its shagreen case, and exclaimed in a tone of uneasiness, as he entered—

"My dear mother, have you been unwell during my absence?"

"No, no, Albert! but you know these roses, tuberoses, and orange flowers, exhale at first, before one is used to them, such violent perfumes."

"Then, my dear mother," said Albert, putting his hand to the bell, "they must be taken into the ante-chamber. You are really unwell, and just now were so pale as you came into the room——"

"Was I pale, Albert?"

"Yes; a paleness that suits you admirably, mother; but which did not the less alarm my father and myself!"

"Did your father speak of it?" inquired Mercédès, eagerly.

"No, madame; but do you remember that he remarked the fact to you?"

"Yes, I do remember!" replied the countess.

A servant entered, summoned by Albert's ring of the bell.

"Take these flowers into the anteroom or dressing-room," said the viscount; "they make the countess unwell."

The footman obeyed his orders.

A long pause ensued, which lasted until all the flowers were removed.

"What is this name of Monte-Cristo?" inquired the countess, when the servant had taken away the last vase of flowers; "is it a family name, or the name of the estate, or a simple title?"

"I believe, mother, it is merely a simple title. The count purchased an island in the Tuscan Archipelago, and, as he told you to-day, has founded a commandery. You know the same thing was done for Saint Stephen of Florence, Saint George, Constantinian of Parma, and even for the Order of Malta.

Except this, he has no pretension to nobility, and calls himself a chance count, although the general opinion at Rome is, that the count is a man of very high distinction."

"His manners are admirable!" said the countess; "at least, as far as I could judge in the few moments he remained here."

"They are perfect, mother—so perfect that they surpass by far all I have known in the leading aristocracy of the three proudest *noblesses* of Europe—the English aristocracy, Spanish aristocracy, and German aristocracy."

The countess paused a moment; then, after a slight hesitation, she resumed,—

"You have seen, my dear Albert—I ask the question as a mother—you have seen M. de Monte-Cristo in his house; you are quick-sighted, have much knowledge of the world, more tact than is usual at your age;—do you think the count is really what he appears to be?"

"What does he appear to be?"

"Why, you have just said,—a man of high distinction."

"I told you, my dear mother, he was esteemed such."

"But what is your own opinion, Albert?"

"I must tell you that I have not come to any decided opinion respecting him, but I think him a Maltese."

"I do not ask you of his origin, but what he is."

"Ah! what he is; that is quite another thing. I have seen so many remarkable things of him that if you would have me really say what I think, I shall reply that I really do look upon him as one of Byron's heroes, whom Misery has marked with a fatal brand;—some Manfred, some Lara, some Werner, one of those wrecks, as it were, of some ancient family, who, disinherited of their patrimony, have achieved one by the force of their adventurous genius which has placed them above the laws of society."

"You say——"

"I say that Monte-Cristo is an island in the midst of the Mediterranean, without inhabitants or garrison, the resort of smugglers of all nations, and pirates of every flag. Who knows whether or not these industrious worthies do not pay to their feudal lord some dues for his protection?"

"That is possible," said the countess, reflecting.

"Never mind," continued the young man, "smuggler or not, you must agree, mother dear, as you have seen him, that the Count of Monte-Cristo is a remarkable man, who will have the greatest success in the salons of Paris. Why, this very morning, at my abode, he made his *entrée* amongst us by striking every man of us with amazement, not even excepting Château-Renaud."

"And what do you suppose is the count's age?" inquired

Mercédès, evidently attaching great importance to this question.

"Thirty-five or thirty-six, mother."

"So young! it is impossible," said Mercédès, replying at the same time to what Albert said as well as to her own private reflection.

"It is the truth, however. Three or four times he has said to me, and certainly without the slightest premeditation, at such a period 1 was five years old, at another ten years old, at another twelve, and I, induced by curiosity, which kept me alive to these details, have compared the dates, and never found him inaccurate. The age of this singular man, who is of no age, is then, I am certain, thirty-five. Besides, mother, remark how vivid his eye, how raven-black his hair, and his brow, though so pale, is free from wrinkles,—he is not only vigorous, but also young."

The countess bent her head as if beneath a heavy wave of bitter thoughts.

"And has this man displayed a friendship for you, Albert?" she asked with a nervous shudder.

"I am inclined to think so."

"And—do—you—like—him?"

"Why, he pleases me in spite of Franz d'Epinay, who tries to convince me that he is a being returned from the other world."

The countess shuddered.

"Albert," she said, in a voice which was altered by emotion, "I have always put you on your guard against new acquaintances. Now you are a man, and are able to give me advice; yet, I repeat to you, Albert, be prudent."

"Why, my dear mother, it is necessary, in order to make your advice turn to account, that I should know beforehand what I have to distrust. The count never plays, he only drinks pure water tinged with a little sherry, and is so rich that he cannot, without intending to laugh at me, try to borrow money. What, then, have I to fear from him?"

"You are right," said the countess, "and my fears are weakness, especially when directed against a man who has saved your life. How did your father receive him, Albert? It is necessary that we should be more than complaisant to the count. M. de Morcerf is sometimes occupied; his business makes him reflective; and he might, without intending it——"

"Nothing could be in better taste than my father's demeanour, madame," said Albert; "nay, more, he seemed greatly flattered at two or three compliments which the count very skilfully and agreeably paid him with as much ease as if he had known him these thirty years. Each of these little tickling arrows must have pleased my father," added Albert, with a laugh. "And thus they parted the best possible friends; and M. de Morcerf even wished to take him to the Chamber to hear the speakers."

The countess made no reply. She fell into so deep a reverie that her eyes gradually closed. The young man, standing up before her, gazed upon her with that filial affection which is more tender and endearing with children whose mothers are still young and handsome. Then, after seeing her eyes closed, and hearing her breathe gently, he believed she had dropped asleep. and left the apartment on tiptoe, closing the door after him with the utmost precaution.

"This devil of a fellow!" he muttered, shaking his head. "I said at the time he would create a sensation here, and I measure his effect by an infallible thermometer. My mother has noticed him, and he must therefore, perforce be remarkable."

He went down to the stables, not without some slight annoyance, when he remembered that the Count of Monte-Cristo had laid his hands on a "turn-out," which sent his bays down to second place in the opinion of connoisseurs.

"Most decidedly," said he, "men are not equal, and I must beg my father to develop this theorem in the Chamber of Peers."

CHAPTER XLII

MONSIEUR BERTUCCIO

DURING this time the count had arrived at his house; it had taken him six minutes to perform the distance; but these six minutes were sufficient to induce twenty young men who knew the price of the equipage they had been unable to purchase themselves, to put their horses into a gallop in order to see the rich foreigner who could afford to give 20,000 francs a-piece for his horses.

The house Ali had chosen, and which was to serve as a town residence to Monte-Cristo, was situated on the right hand as you ascended the Champs Elysées. A thick clump of trees and shrubs rose in the centre, and masked a portion of the front; around this shrubbery two alleys, like two arms, extended right and left, and formed a carriage-drive from the iron gates to a double portico on every step of which stood a porcelain vase, filled with flowers. This house, isolated from the rest, had, besides the main entrance, another in the Rue Ponthieu. Even before the coachman had hailed the concierge the massy gates rolled on their hinges;—they had seen the count coming, and at Paris, as everywhere else, he was served with the rapidity of lightning. The coachman entered, and descending the half-circle without slackening his speed. The gates were closed ere the wheels had ceased to sound on the gravel. The carriage stopped at the left side of the portico, two men presented themselves at the carriage-window, the one was Ali, who, smiling with an expression of the most sincere joy, seemed amply repaid by a mere look from Monte-Cristo. The other bowed respectfully, and offered his arm to assist the count in descending.

"Thanks, Monsieur Bertuccio," said the count, springing lightly up the three steps of the portico; "and the notary?"

"He is in the small salon, excellency," returned Bertuccio.

"And the cards I ordered to have engraved as soon as you knew the number of the house?"

"M. le Comte, it is done already. I have been myself to the best engraver of the Palais Royal, who did the plate in my presence. The first card struck off was taken, according to

456

your orders, to M. le Baron Danglars, Rue de la Chaussée d'Antin, No. 7; the others are on the mantelpiece of your excellency's bedroom."

"Good; what time is it?"

"Four o'clock."

Monte-Cristo gave his hat, cane, and gloves to the same French footman, who had called his carriage at the Count de Morcerf's, and then he passed into the small salon, preceded by Bertuccio, who shewed him the way.

"These are but indifferent marbles in this antechamber," said Monte-Cristo. "I trust all this will soon be taken away."

Bertuccio bowed. As the steward had said, the notary awaited him in the small salon. He was a simple-looking lawyer's clerk, elevated to the extraordinary dignity of a provincial scrivener.

"You are the notary empowered to sell the country-house that I wish to purchase, monsieur?" asked Monte-Cristo.

"Yes, M. le Comte," returned the notary.

"Is the deed of sale ready?"

"Yes, M. le Comte."

"Have you brought it?"

"Here it is."

"Very well; and where is this house that I purchase?" asked the count carelessly, addressing himself half to Bertuccio, half to the notary.

The steward made a gesture that signified, "I do not know."

The notary looked at the count with astonishment.

"What!" said he, "does not M. le Comte know where the house he purchases is situated?"

"No," returned the count.

"M. le Comte does not know it?"

"How should I know it? I have arrived from Cadiz this morning. I had never before been at Paris; and it is the first time I have ever set my foot in France."

"Ah! that is different; the house you purchase is situated at Auteuil."

At these words Bertuccio turned pale.

"And where is Auteuil?" asked the count.

"Close here, monsieur," replied the notary, "a little beyond Passy; a charming situation in the heart of the Bois de Boulogne."

"So near as that?" said the count; "but that is not in the country. What made you choose a house at the gates of Paris, Monsieur Bertuccio?"

"I!" cried the steward, with a strange expression. "M. le

C.M.—O*

Comte did not charge me to purchase this house. If M. le Comte will recollect—if he will think——"

"Ah, true," observed Monte-Cristo; "I recollect now. I read the advertisement in one of the papers, and was tempted by a false title, 'a country-house.'"

"It is not yet too late," cried Bertuccio, eagerly; "and if your excellency will intrust me with the commission, I will find you a better at Enghien, at Fontenay-aux-Roses, or at Bellevue."

"Oh no," returned Monte-Cristo, negligently; "since I have this, I will keep it."

"And you are quite right," said the notary, who feared to lose his fee. "It is a charming place, well supplied with spring water, and fine trees; a comfortable habitation, although abandoned for a long time; without reckoning the furniture, which, although old, is yet valuable, now that old things are so much sought after. I suppose M. le Comte has the tastes of the day?"

"To be sure," returned Monte-Cristo, "it is very convenient, then?"

"It is more—it is magnificent."

"*Peste!* let us not lose such an opportunity," returned Monte-Cristo. "The deed, if you please, M. le Notaire." And he signed it rapidly, after having first ran his eye over that part of the deed in which were specified the situation of the house and the names of the proprietors.

"Bertuccio," said he, "give 55,000 francs to monsieur."

The steward left the room with a faltering step, and returned with a bundle of bank-notes, which the notary counted like a man who never gives a receipt for money until after legal examination.

"And now," demanded the count, "are all the forms complied with?"

"All, M. le Comte."

"Have you the keys?"

"They are in the hands of the concierge, who takes care of the house; but here is the order I have given him to instal Monsieur le Comte in his new possession."

"Very well;" and Monte-Cristo made a sign with his hand to the notary, which said, "I have no further need of you, you may go."

"But," observed the honest notary, "you are mistaken, I think, M. le Comte; it is only 50,000 francs, every thing included."

"And your fee?"

"Is included in this sum."

"But have you not come from Auteuil here?"

"Yes, certainly."

"Well, then, it is but fair that you should be paid for your loss of time and trouble," said the count, and he made a gesture of polite dismissal.

The notary left the room backwards, and bowing down to the ground; it was the first time he had ever met a similar client.

"See this gentleman out," said the count to Bertuccio.

And the steward followed the notary out of the room.

Scarcely was the count alone when he drew from his pocket a book closed with a lock, and opened it with a key which he wore round his neck, and which never left him. After having sought for a few minutes, he stopped at a leaf which had several notes, and compared them with the deed of sale that lay on the table, and recalling his *souvenirs:*—

"'Auteuil, Rue de la Fontaine, No. 28;' it is, indeed, the same," said he; "and now, am I to rely upon an avowal extorted by religious or physical terror? However, in an hour I shall know all."

"Bertuccio!" cried he, striking a light hammer with a pliant handle on a small gong. "Bertuccio!"

The steward appeared at the door.

"Monsieur Bertuccio," said the count, "did you never tell me that you had travelled in France?"

"In some parts of France,—yes, excellency."

"You know the environs of Paris, then?"

"No, excellency, no," returned the steward, with a sort of nervous trembling, which Monte-Cristo, a connoisseur in all emotions, rightly attributed to great disquietude.

"It is unfortunate," returned he, "that you have never visited the environs, for I wish to see my new property this evening, and had you gone with me you could have given me some useful information."

"To Auteuil!" cried Bertuccio, whose copper complexion became livid. "I go to Auteuil!"

"Well, what is there surprising in that? When I live at Auteuil, you must come there, as you belong to my service."

Bertuccio hung down his head before the imperious look of his master, and remained motionless, without making any answer.

"Why, what has happened to you?—are you going to make me ring a second time for the carriage?" asked Monte-Cristo, in the same tone that Louis XIV pronounced the famous "I have been almost obliged to wait."

Bertuccio made but one bound to the antechamber, and cried, in a hoarse voice,—

"His excellency's horses!"

Monte-Cristo wrote two or three notes, and as he sealed the last, the steward appeared.

"Your excellency's carriage is at the door," said he.

"Well, take your hat and gloves," returned Monte-Cristo.

"Am I to accompany you, M. le Comte?" cried Bertuccio.

"Certainly, you must give your orders, for I intend residing at the house."

It was unexampled for a servant of the count's to dare to dispute an order of his, so the steward, without saying a word, followed his master, who got into the carriage, and signed him to follow, which he did seating himself respectfully on the front seat.

CHAPTER XLIII

THE HOUSE AT AUTEUIL

MONTE-CRISTO had remarked, that as they descended the staircase, Bertuccio signed himself in the Corsican manner, that is, had formed the sign of the cross in the air with his thumb, and as he seated himself in the carriage, muttered a short prayer.

Any one but a curious man would have had pity on seeing the steward's extraordinary repugnance for the count's projected drive *extra muros;* but it seemed the count was too curious to excuse Bertuccio this little journey. In twenty minutes they were at Auteuil; the steward's emotion had continued to augment as they entered the village. Bertuccio, crouched in a corner of the carriage, began to examine with a feverish anxiety every house they passed.

"Tell them to stop at Rue de la Fontaine, No. 28," said the count, fixing his eyes on the steward, to whom he gave this order.

Bertuccio's forehead was covered with perspiration, but, however, he obeyed, and, leaning out of the window, he cried to the coachman,—

"Rue de la Fontaine, No. 28."

No. 28 was situated at the extremity of the village; during the drive night had set in, or rather a black cloud, charged with electricity, gave to these vapours the appearance and solemnity of a dramatic episode. The carriage stopped, the footman sprang off the box, and opened the door.

"Well," said the count, "you do not get out, M. Bertuccio —you are going to stay in the carriage, then?—What are you thinking of this evening?"

Bertuccio sprang out and offered his shoulder to the count, who, this time, leaned upon it as he descended the three steps of the carriage.

"Knock," said the count, "and announce me."

Bertuccio knocked, the door opened, and the concierge appeared.

"What is it?" asked he.

"It is your new master, my good fellow," said the footman. And he held out to the concierge the notary's order.

"The house is sold then?" demanded the concierge; "and this gentleman is coming to live here?"

"Yes, my friend," returned the count; "and I will endeavour to give you no cause to regret your old master."

"Oh, monsieur," said the concierge, "I shall not have much cause to regret him, for he came here but seldom; it is five years since he was here last, and he did well to sell the house, for it did not bring him in any thing at all."

"What was the name of your old master?" said Monte-Cristo.

"M. le Marquis de Saint-Méran. Ah, I am sure he has not sold the house for what he gave for it."

"The Marquis de Saint-Méran!" returned the count. "The name is not unknown to me; the Marquis de Saint-Méran!" And he appeared to meditate.

"An old gentleman," continued the concierge, "a staunch follower of the Bourbons; he had an only daughter, who married M. de Villefort, who had been the procureur du roi at Nîmes, and afterwards at Versailles."

Monte-Cristo glanced at Bertuccio, who became whiter than the wall against which he leaned to prevent himself from falling.

"And is not this daughter dead?" demanded Monte-Cristo; "I fancy I have heard so."

"Yes, monsieur, one-and-twenty years ago; and since then we have not seen the poor marquis three times."

"Thanks, thanks," said Monte-Cristo, judging from the steward's utter prostration that he could not stretch the cord further without danger of breaking it. "Give me a light."

"Shall I accompany you, monsieur?"

"No, it is unnecessary; Bertuccio will shew me a light." And Monte-Cristo accompanied these words by the gift of two pieces of gold, which produced a torrent of thanks and blessings from the concierge.

"Ah, monsieur," said he, after having vainly searched on the mantelpiece and the shelves, "I have not got any candles."

"Take one of the carriage-lamps, Bertuccio," said the count, "and shew me the apartments."

The steward obeyed in silence; but it was easy to see, from the manner in which the hand that held the light trembled, how much it cost him to obey.

They went over a tolerably large ground-floor, a first floor consisting of a salon, a bath-room, and two bedrooms; by one of these beds they arrived at a winding-staircase that opened on to the garden.

"Ah! here is a private staircase," said the count; "that is convenient. Light me, M. Bertuccio, and go first; we will see where it leads to."

"Monsieur," replied Bertuccio, "it leads to the garden."

"And, pray, how do you know that?"

"It ought to do so, at least."

"Well, let us be sure of that."

Bertuccio sighed, and went on first; the stairs led, in reality, to the garden. At the outer door the steward paused.

"Go on, Monsieur Bertuccio," said the count.

But he to whom he spoke was stupefied, bewildered, stunned; his haggard eyes glanced around, as if in search of the traces of some terrible event, and with his clenched hands he seemed striving to shut out some horrible recollections.

"Well!" insisted the count.

"No, no," cried Bertuccio, setting down the lantern at the angle of the interior wall. "No, monsieur, it is impossible; I can go no further."

"What does this mean?" demanded the irresistible voice of Monte-Cristo.

"Why you must see, M. le Comte," cried the steward, "that this is not natural; that having a house to purchase, you purchase it exactly at Auteuil; and that, purchasing it at Auteuil, this house should be No. 28 Rue de la Fontaine. Oh! why did I not tell you all? I am sure you would not have forced me to come. I hoped your house would have been some other one than this; as if there was not another house at Auteuil than that of the assassination!"

"Ah! ah!" cried Monte-Cristo, stopping suddenly, "what words did you utter? Devil of a man, Corsican that you are—always mysterious or superstitious. Come, take the lantern, and let us visit the garden; you are not afraid of ghosts with me, I hope?"

Bertuccio raised the lantern, and obeyed. The door, as it opened, disclosed a gloomy sky, in which the moon strove vainly to struggle through a sea of clouds that covered her with their sombre wave that she illumined for an instant, and was then lost in the darkness. The steward wished to turn to the left.

"No, no, monsieur," said Monte-Cristo. "What is the use of following the alleys? Here is a beautiful lawn, let us go on straight forwards."

Bertuccio wiped the perspiration from his brow, but obeyed; however, he continued to take the left hand. Monte-Cristo, on the contrary, took the right hand; arrived near a clump of trees, he stopped. The steward could not restrain himself.

"Move, monsieur,—move away, I entreat you; you are exactly in the spot!"

"What spot?"

"Where he fell."

"My dear monsieur Bertuccio," said Monte-Cristo, laughing, "recover yourself; we are no longer at Sartène or at Corte. This is not a *mâquis*, but an English garden; badly kept, I own, but still you must not calumniate it for that."

"Monsieur, I implore you do not stay there!"

"I think you are going mad, Bertuccio," said the count, coldly. "If that is the case, I warn you, I shall have you put in a lunatic asylum."

"Alas! excellency," returned Bertuccio, joining his hands, and shaking his head in a manner that would have excited the count's laughter, had not thoughts of a superior interest occupied him, and rendered him attentive to the least revelation of this timorous conscience. "Alas! excellency, the evil has arrived!"

"M. Bertuccio," said the count. "I am very glad to tell you, that while you gesticulate, you wring your hands and roll your eyes like a man possessed by a devil who will not leave him; and I have always remarked, that the devil most obstinate to be expelled is a secret. I knew you were a Corsican. I knew you were gloomy, and always brooding over some old history of the vendetta; and I overlooked that in Italy, because in Italy those things are thought nothing of. But in France they are considered in very bad taste; there are gendarmes who occupy themselves with such affairs, judges who condemn, and scaffolds which avenge."

Bertuccio clasped his hands, and as, in all these evolutions, he did not let fall the lantern, the light shewed his pale and altered countenance. Monte-Cristo examined him with the same look that, at Rome, had viewed the execution of Andrea, and then, in a tone that made a shudder pass through the veins of the poor steward,—

"The Abbé Busoni, then, told me an untruth," said he, "when, after his journey in France in 1829, he sent you to me, with a letter of recommendation, in which he enumerated all your valuable qualities. Well, I shall write to the abbé; I shall render him responsible for his protégé's misconduct, and I shall soon know all about this assassination. Only I warn you, that when I reside in a country, I conform to all its code, and I have no wish to put myself within the compass of the French laws for your sake."

"Oh, do not do that, excellency; I have always served you faithfully," cried Bertuccio in despair. "I have always been an honest man, and, as far as lay in my power, I have done good."

"I do not deny it," returned the count; "but why are you thus agitated? It is a bad sign; a quiet conscience does not occasion such paleness in the cheeks, and such fear in the hands of a man."

"But, M. le Comte," replied Bertuccio, hesitatingly, "did not M. l'Abbé Busoni, who heard my confession in the prison at Nîmes, tell you I had a heavy reproach to make against myself?"

"Yes; but as he said you would make an excellent steward, I concluded you had stolen,—that was all."

"Oh, Monsieur le Comte!" returned Bertuccio, contemptuously.

"Or, as you are a Corsican, that you had been unable to resist the desire of making a *peau*, as you call it."

"Yes, my good master," cried Bertuccio, casting himself at the count's feet, "it was simply a vengeance,—nothing else."

"I understand that; but I do not understand what it is that galvanises you in this manner."

"But, monsieur, it is very natural," returned Bertuccio, "since it was in this house that my vengeance was accomplished."

"What, my house!"

"Oh, M. le Comte, it was not yours then."

"Whose, then? M. le Marquis de Saint-Méran, I think the concierge said. What had you to revenge on the Marquis de Saint-Méran?"

"Oh, it was not on him, monsieur; it was on another."

"This is strange," returned Monte-Cristo, seeming to yield to his reflections, "that you should find yourself without any preparation in a house where the event happened that causes you so much remorse."

"Monsieur," said the steward, "it is fatality, I am sure. First, you purchase a house at Auteuil; this house is the one where I have committed an assassination; you descend to the garden by the same staircase by which he descended; you stop at the spot where he received the blow; and two paces further is the grave in which he had just buried his child. That is not chance; for chance, in this case, resembles Providence too much."

"Well, M. le Corse, let us suppose it is Providence. I always suppose any thing people please; and, besides, you must concede something to diseased minds. Come, collect yourself, and tell me all."

"I have never related it but once, and that was to the Abbé Busoni. Such things," continued Bertuccio, shaking his head, "are only related under the seal of confession."

"Then," said the count, "I refer you to your confessor: turn Chartreux or Trappist, and relate your secrets; but, as for me, I do not like any one who is alarmed by such phantasms, and I do not choose that my servants should be afraid to walk in the garden of an evening. I confess I am not very desirous of a visit from the commissaire de police; for, in Italy, justice is only paid when silent, in France she is paid only when she speaks. *Peste!* I thought you somewhat Corsican, a great deal smuggler, and an excellent steward; but I see you have other strings to your bow. You are no longer in my service, Monsieur Bertuccio."

"Oh, M. le Comte! M. le Comte!" cried the steward, struck with terror at this threat, "if that is the only reason I cannot remain in your service, I will tell all; for if I quit you, it will only be to go to the scaffold."

"This is different," replied Monte-Cristo; "but if you intend to tell an untruth, reflect it were better not to speak at all."

"No, monsieur, I swear to you, by my hopes of salvation, I will tell you all, for the Abbé Busoni himself only knew a part of my secret; but, I pray you, go away from that plane-tree, the moon is just bursting through the clouds, and there, standing where you do, and wrapped in that cloak that conceals your figure, you remind me of M. de Villefort."

"What!" cried Monte-Cristo, "it was M. de Villefort?"

"Your excellency knows him?"

"The former procureur de roi at Nîmes?"

"Yes."

"Who married the Count de Saint-Méran's daughter?"

"Yes."

"Who enjoyed the reputation of being the most severe, the most upright, the most rigid magistrate on the bench?"

"Well, monsieur," said Bertuccio, "this man with this spotless reputation —"

"Well?"

"Was a villain."

"Bah!" replied Monte-Cristo; "impossible!"

"It is as I tell you."

"Ah! really," said Monte-Cristo. "Have you the proof of this?"

"I had it."

"And you have lost it. How stupid!"

"Yes; but by careful search it might be recovered."

"Really," returned the count; "relate it to me, for it begins to interest me."

And the count, humming an air from *Lucia di Lammermoor*, went to sit down on a bench, whilst Bertuccio followed him, collecting his thoughts. Bertuccio remained standing before him.

CHAPTER XLIV

THE VENDETTA

"From what point shall I commence my story. M. le Comte?" asked Bertuccio.

"From where you please," returned Monte-Cristo, "since I know nothing at all of it."

"I thought M. l'Abbé Busoni had told your excellency."

"Some particulars, doubtless; but this is seven or eight years ago, and I have forgotten them."

"Then I can speak without fear of tiring your excellency."

"Go on, M. Bertuccio; you will supply the want of the evening papers."

"The story begins in 1815."

"Ah!" said Monte-Cristo, "1815 is not yesterday."

"No, monsieur; and yet I recollect all things as clearly as if they had happened but then. I had a brother, an elder brother, who was in the service of the emperor; he had become lieutenant in a regiment composed entirely of Corsicans. This brother was my only friend; we became orphans, I at five, he at eighteen. He brought me up as if I had been his son; and, in 1814. he married. When the emperor returned from the Island of Elba. my brother instantly joined the army, was slightly wounded at Waterloo, and retired with the army behind the Loire."

"But that is the history of the Hundred Days, M. Bertuccio," said the count; "unless I am mistaken, it has been already written."

"Excuse me, excellency, but these details are necessary, and you promised to be patient."

"Go on, I will keep my word."

"One day we received a letter. I should tell you that we lived in the little village of Rogliano, at the extremity of Cape Corse. This letter was from my brother. He told us that the army was disbanded, and that he should return by Châteauroux, Clermont-Ferrand, le Puy, and Nîmes; and, if I had any money, he prayed me to leave it for him at Nîmes, with an innkeeper with whom I had dealings."

"In the smuggling line?" said Monte-Cristo.

"Eh, M. le Comte, every one must live."

"Certainly; continue."

"I loved my brother tenderly, as I told your excellency, and I resolved not to send the money, but to take it to him myself. I possessed a thousand francs. I left five hundred with Assunta, my sister-in-law, and with the other five hundred I set off for Nîmes. It was easy to do so; and, as I had my boat and a lading to take in at sea, every thing favoured my project.

"But, after we had taken in our cargo, the wind became contrary, so that we were four or five days without being able to enter the Rhône. At last, however, we succeeded, and worked up to Arles. I left the boat between Bellegarde and Beaucaire, and took the road to Nîmes."

"We are getting to the story now?"

"Yes, your excellency; excuse me, but, as you will see, I only tell you what is absolutely necessary. Just at this time, the famous massacres of the South of France took place. Two or three brigands, called Trestaillon, Truphemy, and Graffan, publicly assassinated every body whom they suspected of Bonapartism. You have, doubtless, heard of these massacres, M. le Comte?"

"Vaguely, I was far from France at that period. Go on."

"As I entered Nîmes, I literally waded in blood; at every step you encountered dead bodies and bands of the murderers, who killed, plundered, and burned. At the sight of this slaughter and devastation I became terrified, not for myself,— for I, a simple Corsican fisherman, had nothing to fear; on the contrary, that time was most favourable for us smugglers,— but for my brother, a soldier of the empire, returning from the army of the Loire, with his uniform and his epaulettes, there was every thing to apprehend.

"I hastened to the innkeeper. My presages had been but too true; my brother had arrived the previous evening at Nîmes; and, at the very door of the house where he was about to demand hospitality, he had been assassinated.

"I did all in my power to discover the murderers, but no one durst tell me their names, so much were they dreaded. I then thought of that French justice of which I had heard so much, and which feared nothing, and I went to the procureur du roi."

"And this procureur du roi was named Villefort?" asked Monte-Cristo carelessly.

"Yes, your excellency; he came from Marseilles, where he had been deputy procureur. His zeal had procured him advancement, and he was said to be one of the first who had informed the government of the departure from the island of Elba.''

"Then,'' said Monte-Cristo, "you went to him?''

" 'Monsieur,' I said, 'my brother was assassinated yesterday in the streets of Nîmes, I know not by whom, but it is your duty to find out. You are the head of justice here; and it is for justice to avenge those she has been unable to protect.'

" 'Who was your brother?' asked he.

" 'A lieutenant in the Corsican battalion.'

" 'A soldier of the usurper army, then?'

" 'A soldier of the French army.'

" 'Well,' replied he, 'he has smitten with the sword, and has perished by the sword.'

" 'You are mistaken, monsieur,' I replied; 'he has perished by the poniard.'

" 'What do you want me to do?' asked the magistrate.

" 'I have already told you; avenge him.'

" 'On whom?'

" 'On his murderers.'

" 'How should I know who they are?'

" 'Order them to be sought for.'

" 'Why, your brother has been involved in a quarrel, and killed in a duel. All these old soldiers commit excesses which were tolerated in the time of the emperor, but which are not suffered now; for the people here do not like soldiers of such disorderly conduct.'

" 'Monsieur,' I replied, 'it is not for myself that I entreat your interference,—I should grieve for him or avenge him; but my poor brother had a wife, and, were any thing to happen to me, the poor creature would perish from want; for my brother's pay alone kept her. Pray, try and obtain a small government pension for her.'

" 'Every revolution has its catastrophes,' returned M. de Villefort. 'Your brother has been the victim of this; it is misfortune, and government owes nothing to his family. If we are to judge by the vengeance that the followers of the usurper exercised on the partisans of the king when, in their turn, they were in power, your brother would be here to-day, in all probability, condemned to death; what has happened is quite natural, and is only the law of reprisals.'

" 'What!' cried I, 'do you, a magistrate, speak thus to me?'

" 'All these Corsicans are mad, on my honour,' replied M. de Villefort; 'they fancy that their countryman is still emperor. You have mistaken the time; you should have told me this two months ago; it is too late now. Depart instantly, or I will compel you to do so.'

"I looked at him an instant to see if, by renewed entreaties, there was anything to hope.

"But this man was of stone. I approached him and said, in a low voice,—

"'Well, since you know the Corsicans so well, you know that they always keep their word. You think that it was a good deed to kill my brother who was a Bonapartist, because you are a royalist! Well! I who am a Bonapartist, also, declare one thing to you, which is, that I will kill you; from this moment I declare the vendetta against you; so protect yourself as well as you can, for the next time we meet your last hour has come.'

"And before he had recovered from his surprise, I opened the door and left the room."

"Ah! ah!" said Monte-Cristo. "With your innocent appearance you do those things, M. Bertuccio; and to a procureur du roi! Moreover, did he know what was meant by this terrible word 'vendetta'?"

"He knew so well, that from this moment he shut himself in his house, and never went out unattended, seeking me high and low. Fortunately, I was so well concealed that he could not find me.

"Then he became alarmed, and dared not reside any longer at Nîmes, so he solicited a change of residence, and as he was in reality very influential, he was nominated to Versailles; but as you know, a Corsican who has sworn to avenge himself, cares not for distance; so his carriage, fast as it went, was never above half a day's journey before me, who followed him on foot.

"The most important thing was, not to kill him only, for I had an opportunity of doing so a hundred times, but to kill him without being discovered—at least, without being arrested.

"I no longer belonged to myself, for I had my sister-in-law to protect and provide for. During three months I watched M. de Villefort; for three months he took not a step out of doors without my following him. At length I discovered that he went mysteriously to Auteuil, I followed him thither, and I saw him enter the house where we now are; only instead of entering by the great door that looks into the street, he came on horseback, or in his carriage, left the one or the other at the little inn, and entered by the gate you see there!"

Monte-Cristo made a sign with his hand that he could discern amid the darkness the door to which Bertuccio alluded.

"As I had nothing more to do at Versailles, I went to Auteuil, and gained all the information I could. If I wished to surprise him, it was evident this was the spot to lie in wait for him. The house belonged, as the concierge informed your excellency, to M. de Saint-Méran, Villefort's father-in-law; M. de Saint-Méran lived at Marseilles, so that this country-house was useless to him, and it was reported to be let to a young widow known only by the name of the baroness.

"One evening as I was looking over the wall, I saw a young and handsome woman, who was walking alone in that garden, which was not overlooked by any windows, and I guessed that she was awaiting M. de Villefort. When she was sufficiently near to distinguish her features, I saw she was from eighteen to nineteen, tall and very fair. As she had a loose muslin dress on, and as nothing concealed her figure, I saw she would ere long become a mother. A few moments after, the little door was opened and a man entered; the young woman hastened to meet him; they threw themselves into each other's arms, embraced tenderly, and returned together to the house. This man was M. de Villefort; I fully believed that when he went out in the night he would be forced to traverse the whole of the garden alone."

"And," asked the count; "did you ever know the name of this woman?"

"No, excellency," returned Bertuccio: "you will see I had not time to learn it."

"Go on."

"That evening," continued Bertuccio; "I could have killed the procureur du roi, but as I was not sufficiently master of the localities, I was fearful of not killing him on the spot, and that should his cries give the alarm, I could not escape; I put it off until the next occasion, and in order that nothing should escape me, I took a chamber looking into the street along which ran the wall of the garden.

"Three days after, about seven o'clock in the evening, I saw a servant on horseback leave the house at full gallop, and take the road that led to Sèvres. I conjectured he was going to Versailles, and I was not deceived. Three hours after, the man returned covered with dust, his errand was performed; and ten minutes after, another man on foot muffled in a mantle, opened the little door of the garden, which he closed after him. I descended rapidly; although I had not seen Villefort's face, I recognised him by the beating of my heart. I crossed the street, and stopped at a post placed at the angle of the wall, and by means of which I had once before looked into the garden. This time I did not content myself with looking, but I took my knife out of my pocket, felt that the point was sharp and sprang over the wall. My first care was to run to the door; he had left the key in it, taking the simple precaution of turning it twice in the lock. Nothing then, preventing my escape by this means, I examined the localities. The garden formed a long square, a terrace of smooth turf extended in the middle, and at the corners were tufts of trees with thick and massy foliage, that mingled with the shrubs and flowers.

"In order to go from the door to the house, or from the house to the door, M. de Villefort was compelled to pass by one of these clumps.

"It was the end of September; the wind blew violently. The faint glimpses of the pale moon, hidden at every instant by the masses of dark clouds that were sweeping across the sky, whitened the gravelled walks that led to the house, but were unable to pierce the obscurity of the thick shrubberies, in which a man could conceal himself without any fear of discovery. I hid myself in the one nearest to the path Villefort must take; and scarcely was I there than, amidst the gusts of wind, I fancied I heard groans; but you know, or rather you do not know, M. le Comte, that he who is about to commit an assassination fancies he hears low cries perpetually ringing in his ears. Two hours passed thus, during which I imagined I heard these moans repeated. Midnight struck. As the last stroke died away, I saw a faint light shine through the windows of the private staircase by which we have just descended. The door opened and the man in the mantle reappeared. The terrible moment had come! but I had so long been prepared for it that my heart did not fail in the least; I drew my knife from my pocket again, opened it, and prepared myself to strike. The man in the mantle advanced towards me, but as he drew near I saw he had a weapon in his hand. I was afraid, not of a struggle, but of a failure. When he was only a few paces from me, I saw that what I had taken for a weapon was only a spade. I was still unable to divine for what reason M. de Villefort had this spade in his hands, when he stopped close to the clump, glanced round and began to dig a hole in the earth. I then perceived that he hid something beneath his mantle, which he laid on the grass in order to dig more freely. Then, I confess, curiosity became mixed with my hatred; I wished to see what Villefort was going to do there, and I remained motionless and holding my breath. Then an idea crossed my mind, which was confirmed when I saw the procureur du roi lift from under his mantle a box two feet long, and six or eight inches deep. I let him place the box in the hole he had made, then, whilst he stamped with his feet to remove all traces of his occupation, I rushed on him and plunged my knife into his breast exclaiming—

"'I am Giovanni Bertuccio; thy death for my brother's; thy treasure for his widow; thou seest that my vengeance is more complete than I had hoped.'

"I know not if he heard these words. I think he did not,

for he fell without a cry; I felt his blood gush over my face, but I was intoxicated, I was delirious, and the blood refreshed, instead of burning me. In a second I had disinterred the box: then, that it might not be known I had done so, I filled up the hole, threw the spade over the wall, and rushed through the door, which I double-locked, carrying off the key."

"Ah!" said Monte-Cristo, "it seems to me that this was only a murder and robbery."

"No, your excellency," returned Bertuccio; "it was a vendetta followed by a restitution."

"And was the sum a large one?"

"It was not money!"

"Ah! I recollect," replied the count: "did you not say something of an infant?"

"Yes, excellency; I hastened to the river, sat down on the bank and with my knife forced open the lock of the box. In a fine linen cloth was wrapped a new-born child. Its purple visage, and its violet-coloured hands, shewed it had perished from suffocation; but as it was not yet cold, I hesitated to throw it into the water that ran at my feet; in reality, at the end of an instant I fancied I felt a slight pulsation of the heart; and as I had been assistant at the hospital at Bastia, I did what a doctor would have done—I inflated the lungs by blowing air into them, and at the expiration of a quarter of an hour I saw the breathing commence, and a feeble cry was heard. In my turn I uttered a cry, but a cry of joy. 'God has not cursed me, then,' I cried; 'since he permits me to save the life of a human creature, in exchange for the life I have taken away!'"

"And what did you do with the child?" asked Monte-Cristo; "it was an embarrassing load for a man seeking to escape."

"I had not, for a moment, the idea of keeping it, but I knew that at Paris there was an hospital where they receive these poor creatures. As I passed the barrier, I declared I had found this child on the road, and I inquired where the hospital was; the box confirmed my statement; the linen proved it belonged to wealthy parents; the blood with which I was covered might have proceeded from the child as well as from any one else. No objection was raised, but they pointed out to me the hospital, which was situated at the upper end of the Rue d'Enfer, and after having taken the precaution of cutting the linen in two pieces, so that one of the two letters which marked it was wrapped round the child, whilst the other remained in my possession, I rang the bell and fled with all speed. A fortnight after I was at Rogliano, and I said to Assunta,—

" 'Console thyself, sister, Israel is dead, but he is avenged.'

"She demanded what I meant, and when I had recounted all to her,—

" 'Giovanni,' said Assunta; 'you should have brought this child with you, we would have replaced the parents it has lost, have called it Benedetto, and then in consequence of this good action God would have blessed us.'

"In reply I gave her the half of the linen I had kept in order to reclaim him if we became rich."

"What letters were marked on the linen?" said Monte-Cristo.

"An H and an N, surmounted by a baron's coronet."

"By heaven, M. Bertuccio, you make use of heraldic terms! where did you study heraldry?"

"In your service, excellency; where every thing is learned."

"Go on; I am curious to know two things."

"What are they, monseigneur?"

"What became of this little boy, for I think you told me it was a boy, Monsieur Bertuccio."

"No, excellency, I do not recollect telling you that!"

"I thought you did; I must have been mistaken!"

"No, you were not, for it was in reality a little boy; but your excellency wished to know two things; what was the second?"

"The second was the crime of which you were accused when you asked for a confessor, and the Abbé Busoni came to visit you at your request in the prison at Nîmes."

"The story will be very long, excellency."

"What matter? you know I take but little sleep, and I do not suppose you are very much inclined for it, either."

Bertuccio bowed, and resumed his story.

"Partly to drown the recollections of the past that haunted me, partly to supply the wants of the poor widow, I eagerly returned to my trade of smuggler, which had become more easy since that relaxation of the laws which always follows a revolution. The southern districts were ill watched in particular, in consequence of the disturbances that were perpetually breaking out in Avignon, Nîmes, or Uzés. We profited by the kind of respite government gave us to make friends every where. Since my brother's assassination in the streets of Nîmes, I had never entered the town; the result was, the aubergiste, with whom we were connected, seeing we would no longer come to him, was forced to come to us, and had established a branch to his inn, on the road from Belle-garde to Beaucaire, at the sign of the Pont du Gard. We had thus, both on the side of Aigues-Mortes, Martigues, or at Bouc, a dozen places where we left our goods, and where, in case of necessity, we concealed ourselves from the gendarmes and custom-house officers. Smuggling is a profitable trade when a certain degree of vigour and intelligence is employed; as for myself, brought up in the mountains, I had a double motive for fearing the gendarmes and custom-house officers, as my appearance before the judges would cause an inquiry, and an inquiry always looks back into the past. And in my past life they might find something far more grave than the selling of smuggled cigars or barrels of brandy without a permit. So, preferring death to capture, I accomplished the most astonishing deeds, and which, more than once, shewed me that the too great care we take of our bodies is the only obstacle to the success of those projects which require a rapid decision and vigorous and determined execution. In reality, when you have once devoted your life, you are no longer the equal of other men, or, rather, other men are no longer your equals; and whosoever has taken this resolution feels his strength and resources doubled."

"Philosophy, Monsieur Bertuccio," interrupted the count; "you have done a little of every thing in your life."

"Oh, excellency."

"No, no, but philosophy at half-past ten at night is somewhat late; yet I have no other observation to make, for what you say is correct, which is more than can be said for all philosophy."

"My journeys became more and more extensive and more productive. Assunta took care of all, and our little fortune increased. One day that I was setting off on an expedition, 'Go,' said she; 'at your return I will give you a surprise.' I questioned her, but in vain; she would tell me nothing, and I departed.

"Our expedition lasted nearly six weeks; we had been to Lucca to take in oil, to Leghorn for English cottons, and we ran our cargo without opposition, and returned home full of joy.

"When I entered the house, the first thing I beheld in the centre of Assunta's chamber was a cradle, that might be called sumptuous compared with the rest of the furniture, and in it a baby of seven or eight months old; I uttered a cry of joy; the only moments of sadness I had known since the assassination of the procureur du roi were caused by the recollection that I had abandoned this child. For the assassination itself I had never felt any remorse.

"Poor Assunta had guessed all. She had profited by my absence, and furnished with the half of the linen, and having written down the day and hour at which I had deposited the child at the hospital, had set off for Paris, and had reclaimed it. No objection was raised, and the infant was given up to her. Ah, I confess, M. le Comte, when I saw this poor creature sleeping peacefully in its cradle, I felt my eyes fill with tears.

"'Ah, Assunta,' cried I, 'you are an excellent woman, and Heaven will bless you.'"

"This," said Monte-Cristo, "is less correct than your philosophy, it is only faith."

"Alas! your excellency is right," replied Bertuccio, "and God made this infant the instrument of our punishment. Never did a perverse nature declare itself more prematurely; and yet it was not owing to any fault in his bringing up. He was a most lovely child, with large blue eyes, of that deep colour that harmonises so well with the general fairness of the complexion; only his hair, which was too light, gave his face a most singular expression, which redoubled the vivacity of his look and the malice of his smile. Unfortunately, there is a proverb that says, that 'red is either altogether good or altogether bad.' The proverb was but too correct as regarded Benedetto, and even in his infancy he manifested the worst disposition. It is true that the indulgence of his mother encouraged him. This child, for whom my poor sister would go to the town, five or six leagues off, to purchase the earliest fruits and the most tempting sweetmeats, preferred to the grapes of Palma or the preserves of Genoa the chestnuts stolen from a neighbour's orchard, or the dried apples in his loft, when he could eat as well of the nuts and apples that grew in my garden.

"One day, when Benedetto was about five or six, our neighbour, Wasilio, who according to the custom of the country, never locked up his purse or his valuables,—for, as your excellency knows, there are no thieves in Corsica,—complained that he had lost a louis out of his purse; we thought he must have made a mistake in counting his money, but he persisted in the accuracy of his statement. One day, Benedetto, who had quitted the house since the morning, to our great anxiety, did not return until late in the evening, dragging a monkey after him, which he said he had found chained to the foot of a tree. For more than a month past, the mischievous child, who knew not what to wish for, had taken it into his head to have a monkey. A boatman who had passed by Rogliano, and who had several of these animals, whose tricks had greatly diverted him, had doubtless suggested this idea to him.

"'Monkeys are not found in our woods chained to trees,' said I; 'confess how you obtained this animal.'

"Benedetto maintained the truth of what he had said, and accompanied it with details that did more honour to his imagination than to his veracity. I became angry; he began to laugh; I threatened to strike him and he made two steps backwards.

"'You cannot beat me,' said he; 'you have no right, for you are not my father.'

"We never knew who had revealed this fatal secret, which we had so carefully concealed from him; however, it was this answer, in which the child's whole character revealed itself, that almost terrified me, and my arm fell without touching him. The boy triumphed, and this victory rendered him so audacious that all the money of Assunta, whose affection for him seemed to increase as he became more unworthy of it, was spent in caprices she knew not how to contend against, and follies she had not the courage to prevent. When I was at Rogliano every thing went on properly, but no sooner was my back turned than Benedetto became master and every thing went ill. When he was only eleven, he chose his companions from among the young men of eighteen or twenty, the worst characters in Bastia, or, indeed, in Corsica; and they had already, for some pieces of mischief, been several times threatened with a prosecution.

"I became alarmed, as any prosecution might be attended with serious consequences. I was compelled at this period to leave Corsica on an important expedition; I reflected for a long time, and with the hope of averting some impending misfortune, I resolved that Benedetto should accompany me. I hoped that the active and laborious life of a smuggler with the severe discipline on board would have a salutary effect on his character, well-nigh, if not quite, corrupted.

"I spoke to Benedetto alone, and proposed to him to accompany me, endeavouring to tempt him by all the promises most likely to dazzle the imagination of a child of twelve years old.

"He heard me, patiently, and when I had finished, burst out laughing.

"Are you mad, uncle? (he called me by this name when he was in a good-humour,) 'do you think I am going to change the life I lead for your mode of existence; my agreeable indolence for the hard and precarious toil you impose on yourself? exposed to the bitter frost at night, and the scorching heat by day, compelled to conceal yourself, and when you are perceived, receive a volley of balls, and all to earn a paltry sum? Why, I have as much money as I want; mother Assunta always furnishes me when I ask for it! You see that I should be a fool to accept your offer.'

"The arguments, and this audacity, perfectly stupefied me. Benedetto rejoined his associates, and I saw him from a distance point me out to them as a fool."

"Sweet child!" murmured Monte-Cristo.

"Oh! had he been my own son," replied Bertuccio, "or even my nephew, I would have brought him back to the right road, for the knowledge that you are doing your duty gives you strength; but the idea that I was striking a child whose father I had killed, made it impossible for me to punish him. I gave my sister, who constantly defended the unfortunate boy, good advice; and as she confessed that she had several times missed money to a considerable amount, I shewed her a safe place in which to conceal our little treasure for the future. My mind was already made up, Benedetto could read, write, and cipher perfectly, for when the fit seized him, he learned more in a day than others in a week; my intention was to enter him as clerk in some ship, and without letting him know anything of my plan, to convey him some morning on board: by this means his future treatment would depend upon his own conduct.

"I set off for France after having fixed upon this plan.

"All our cargo was to be landed in the Gulf of Lyons, and this was the more difficult, since we were in 1829. The most perfect tranquillity was restored, and the vigilance of the custom-house officers was redoubled, and this strictness was increased at this time in consequence of the fair of Beaucaire.

"Our expedition commenced favourably. We anchored our bark, which had a double hold, where our goods were concealed, amidst a number of other vessels that bordered the banks of the Rhône from Beaucaire to Arles. On our arrival there we began to discharge our cargo in the night, and to convey it into the town, by the help of the aubergistes with whom we were connected. Whether success rendered us imprudent, or whether we were betrayed, I knew not; but one evening, about five o'clock, our little cabin-boy hastened, breathless, to inform us that he had seen a detachment of custom-house officers advancing in our direction. It was not their vicinity that alarmed us, for detachments were constantly patrolling along the banks of the Rhône; but the care, according to the boy's account, they took to avoid being seen. In an instant we were on the alert, but it was too late; our vessel was surrounded, and amongst the custom-house officers I observed several gendarmes; and, as terrified at the sight of their uniform as I was brave at the sight of any other, I sprang into the hold, opened a port, and dropped into the river, dived, and only rose at intervals to breathe until I reached a cutting that led from the Rhône to the canal that runs from Beaucaire to Aiguesmortes. I was now safe, for I could swim along the cutting without being seen, and I reached the canal in safety. I had designedly taken this direction. I have already told your excellency of an innkeeper of Nîmes who had set up a little inn on the road from Bellegarde to Beaucaire."

"Yes," said Monte-Cristo, "I perfectly recollect him; I think he was your colleague."

"Precisely," answered Bertuccio; "but he had, seven or eight years before this period, sold his establishment to a tailor at Marseilles, who, having almost ruined himself in his old trade, wished to make his fortune in another. Of course, we made the same arrangements with the new landlord that we had with the old; and it was of this man that I intended to ask shelter."

"What was his name?" inquired the count, who seemed to become somewhat interested in Bertuccio's story.

"Gaspard Caderousse; he had married a woman from the village of Carconte, and whom we did not know by any other name than that of her village. She was suffering from the marsh-fever, and seemed dying by inches. As for her husband, he was a strapping fellow of forty, or five-and-forty, who had more than once, in time of danger, given ample proof of his presence of mind and courage."

"And you say," interrupted Monte-Cristo, "that this took place towards the year——"

"1829, M. le Comte."

"In what month?"

"June."

"The beginning or the end?"

"The evening of the 3d."

"Ah," said Monte-Cristo, "the evening of the 3d of June, 1829. Go on."

"It was from Caderousse that I intended demanding shelter; and, as we never entered by the door that opened on to the road, I resolved not to break through the rule, and, climbing over the garden-hedge, I crept amongst the olive and wild fig-trees; and, fearing that Caderousse might have some one there, I entered a kind of shed in which I had often passed the night, and which was only separated from the inn by a partition, in which holes had been made in order to enable us to watch an opportunity of announcing our presence. My intention was, if Caderousse was alone, to acquaint him with my presence, finish the meal the custom-house officers had interrupted, and profit by the threatened storm to return to the Rhône, and ascertain the state of our vessel and its crew.

I stepped into the shed, and it was fortunate I did so, for at that moment Caderousse entered with a stranger.

"I waited patiently, not to overhear what they said, but because I could do nothing else; besides, the same thing had occurred often before. The man who was with Caderousse was evidently a stranger to the south of France; he was one of those merchants who come to sell jewellery at the fair of Beaucaire, and who, during the month the fair lasts, and during which there is so great an influx of merchants and customers from all parts of Europe, often have dealings to the amount of 100 to 150,000 francs.

"Caderousse entered hastily.

"Then, seeing that the room was, as usual, empty, and only guarded by the dog, he called to his wife,—

"'Hilloa! Carconte!' said he, 'the worthy priest has not deceived us; the diamond is real.'

"An exclamation of joy was heard, and the staircase creaked beneath a feeble step.

"'What do you say?' asked his wife, pale as death.

"'I say that the diamond is real, and that this gentleman, one of the first jewellers of Paris, will give us 50,000 francs for it. Only in order to satisfy himself it really belongs to us, he wishes you to relate to him, as I have done already, the miraculous manner in which the diamond came into our possession: in the meantime, please to sit down, monsieur, and I will fetch you some refreshment.'

"The jeweller examined attentively the interior of the inn and visible poverty of the persons who were about to sell him a diamond that seemed to have come from the casket of a prince.

"'Relate your story, madame,' said he, wishing, no doubt, to profit by the absence of the husband, so that the latter could not influence the wife's story, to see if the two recitals tallied.

"'Oh!' returned she, 'it was a gift of Heaven! My husband was a great friend, in 1814 or 1815, of a sailor named Edmond Dantès. This poor fellow, whom Caderousse had forgotten, had not forgotten him; and at his death bequeathed this diamond to him.'

"'But how did he obtain it?' asked the jeweller; 'had he it before he was imprisoned?'

"'No, monsieur; but it appears that in prison he made the acquaintance of a rich Englishman; and as in prison he fell sick, and Dantès took the same care of him as if he had been his brother. The Englishman, when he was set free, gave this stone to Dantès, who, less fortunate, died, and, in his turn, left it us, and charged the excellent abbé who was here this morning to deliver it.'

C.M.—P

"'The same story!' muttered the jeweller; 'and, improbable as it seems at first, the history may be true: there's only the price we are not agreed about.'

"'How not agreed about?' said Caderousse; 'I thought we agreed for the price I asked.'

"'That is,' replied the jeweller, 'I offered 40,000 francs.'

"'Forty thousand!' cried La Carconte, 'we will not part with it for that sum; the abbé told us it was worth 50,000 without the setting.'

"'What was the abbé's name?' asked the indefatigable questioner.

"'The Abbé Busoni,' said La Carconte.

"'He was a foreigner?'

"'An Italian from the neighbourhood of Mantua, I believe.'

"'Let me see this diamond again,' replied the jeweller; 'the first time you are often mistaken as to the value of a stone.'

"Caderousse took from his pocket a small case of black shagreen, opened, and gave it to the jeweller. At the sight of the diamond, which was as large as a hazel-nut, La Carconte's eyes sparkled with cupidity."

"And what did you think of this fine story, eavesdropper?" said Monte-Cristo; "did you credit it?"

"Yes, your excellency. I did not look on Caderousse as a bad man, and I thought him incapable of committing a crime, or even a theft."

"That did more honour to your heart than to your experience, M. Bertuccio. Had you known this Edmond Dantès, of whom they spoke?"

"No, your excellency, I had never heard of him before, and never but once afterwards, and that was from the Abbé Busoni himself, when I saw him in the prison at Nîmes."

"Go on."

"The jeweller took the ring, and, drawing from his pocket a pair of steel pliers and a small set of copper scales, taking the stone out of its setting, he weighed it carefully.

"'I will give you 45,000,' said he, 'but not a halfpenny more; besides, as that is the exact value of the stone, I brought just that sum with me.'

"'Oh, that's no matter,' replied Caderousse, 'I will go back with you to fetch the other 5,000 francs.'

"'No,' returned the jeweller, giving back the diamond and the ring to Caderousse; 'no, it is worth no more, and I am sorry I offered so much, for the stone has a flaw in it, which I had not seen. However, I will not go from my word, and I will give 45,000.'

"'At least replace the diamond in the ring,' said Carconte, sharply.

"'Ah, true,' replied the jeweller, and he reset the stone.

"'No matter,' observed Caderousse, replacing the box in his pocket, 'some one else will purchase it.'

"'Yes,' continued the jeweller; 'but some one else will not be so easy as I am, or content himself with the same story. It is not natural that a man like you should possess such a diamond. He will inform against you; you would have to find the Abbé Busoni, and abbés who give diamonds worth two thousand louis are rare. Justice would seize it, and put you in prison; if at the end of three or four months you are set at liberty the ring will be lost, or a false stone worth three francs will be given you instead of a diamond worth 50 or perhaps 55,000 francs; but which you must allow one runs considerable risk in purchasing.'

"Caderousse and his wife looked eagerly at each other

"'No,' said Caderousse, 'we are not rich enough to lose 5,000 francs.'

"'As you please, my dear sir,' said the jeweller; 'I had, however, as you see, brought you the money in bright coin.'

"And he drew from his pocket a handful of gold, which he made to sparkle in the dazzled eyes of the innkeeper, and in the other hand he held a packet of bank-notes.

"There was evidently a severe struggle in the mind of Caderousse; it was evident that the small shagreen case, which he turned and re-turned in his hand, did not seem to him commensurate in value to the enormous sum which fascinated his gaze.

"He turned towards his wife.

"'What do you think of this?' he asked, in a low voice.

"'Let him have it,—let him have it,' she said: 'if he returns to Beaucaire without the diamond, he will inform against us; and, as he says, who knows if we shall ever again see the Abbé Busoni? in all probability we shall never see him.

"'Well, then, so I will!' said Caderousse: 'so you may have the diamond for 45,000 francs. But my wife wants a gold chain, and I want a pair of silver buckles.'

"The jeweller drew from his pocket a long flat box, which contained several samples of the articles demanded.

"'Here,' he said: 'I am very plain in my dealings,—take your choice.'

"The woman selected a gold chain worth about five louis, and the husband a pair of buckles, worth, perhaps, fifteen francs.

"'I hope you will not complain now?' said the jeweller

"'The abbé told me it was worth 50,000 francs,' muttered Caderousse.

"'Come, come,—give it to me! What a strange fellow you are!' said the jeweller, taking the diamond from his hand. 'I gave you 45,000 francs,—that is, 2,500 livres of income, —a fortune such as I wish I had myself, and you are not satisfied!'

"'And the five-and-thirty thousand francs,' inquired Caderousse, in a hoarse voice, 'where are they? Come,—let us see them!'

"'Here they are,' replied the jeweller; and he counted out upon the table 15,000 francs in gold, and 30,000 francs in bank-notes.

"'Wait whilst I light the lamp,' said La Carconte; 'it is growing dark, and there may be some mistake.'

"In fact the night had come on during this conversation, and with the night the storm which had been threatening for the last half hour. The thunder was heard growling in the distance; but neither the jeweller, nor Caderousse, nor La Carconte, seemed to heed it, absorbed as they were all three with the demon of gain. I myself felt a strange kind of fascination at the sight of all this gold and all these bank-notes. It seemed to me that I was in a dream; and, as it always happens in a dream, I felt myself riveted to the spot. Caderousse counted and again counted the gold and the notes; then handed them to his wife, who counted and counted them again in her turn. During this time, the jeweller made the diamond play and sparkle beneath the ray of the lamp, and the gem threw out jets of light which made him unmindful of those which—precursors of the storm—began to play in at the windows.

"'Well,' inquired the jeweller; 'is the cash all right?'

"'Yes,' said Caderousse. 'Give me the pocket-book, La Carconte, and find a bag somewhere.'

"La Carconte went to a cupboard, and returned with an old leathern pocket-book, from which she took some greasy letters, and put in their place the bank-notes and a bag, in which were, at the moment, two or three crowns of six livres each, and which, in all probability, formed the entire fortune of the miserable couple.

"'There,' said Caderousse; 'and now, although you have wronged us of perhaps 10,000 francs, will you have your supper with us? I invite you with good-will.'

"'Thank you,' replied the jeweller; 'it must be getting late, and I must return to Beaucaire,—my wife will be getting uneasy.' He drew out his watch, and exclaimed, '*Morbleu!* nearly nine o'clock!—why, I shall not get back to Beaucaire before midnight! Good night, my dears. If the Abbé Busoni should by any accident return, think of me.'

"'In another week you will have left Beaucaire,' remarked Caderousse, 'for the fair finishes in a few days.'

"'True; but that is no consequence. Write to me at Paris, to M. Joannes, in the Palais Royal, Stone Gallery, No. 45: I will make the journey on purpose to see him, if it is worth while.'

"At this moment there was a tremendous clap of thunder, accompanied by a flash of lightning so vivid that it quite eclipsed the light of the lamp.

"'Oh, dear!' exclaimed Caderousse. 'You cannot think of going out in such weather as this?'

"'Oh, I am not afraid of thunder!' said the jeweller.

"'And then there are robbers,' said La Carconte. 'The road is never very safe during fair-time.'

"'Oh! as to the robbers,' said Joannes, 'here is something for them;' and he drew from his pocket a pair of small pistols, loaded to the muzzle. 'Here,' said he, 'are dogs who bark and bite at the same time: they are for the two first who shall have a longing for your diamond, Daddy Caderousse.'

"Caderousse and his wife again interchanged a meaning look. It seemed as though they were both inspired at the same time with some horrible thought.

"'Well, then, a good journey to you!' said Caderousse.

"'Thank ye,' replied the jeweller. He then took his cane, which he had placed against an old cupboard, and went out. At the moment when he opened the door, such a gust of wind came in that the lamp was nearly extinguished. 'Oh!' said he, 'this is very nice weather; and two leagues to go in such a storm!'

"'Remain,' said Caderousse. 'You can sleep here.'

"'Yes,—do stay,' added La Carconte, in a tremulous voice; 'we will take every care of you.'

"'No; I must sleep at Beaucaire. So, once more, good night!'

"Caderousse followed him slowly to the threshold.

"'I can neither see heaven nor earth!' said the jeweller, who was outside the door. 'Do I turn to the right or left hand?'

"'To the right,' said Caderousse. 'You cannot go wrong, —the road is bordered by trees on both sides.'

"'Good,—all right!' said a voice, almost lost in the distance.

"'Close the door!' said La Carconte; 'I do not like open doors when it thunders!'

"'Particularly when there is money in the house, eh?' answered Caderousse, double-locking the door.

"He came into the room, went to the cupboard, took out the bag and pocket-book, and both began, for the third time, to count their gold and bank-notes. I never saw such an expression of cupidity as the flickering lamp revealed in the two countenances. The woman especially was hideous: the feverish tremulousness she usually had was redoubled: her countenance had become livid, and her eyes resembled burning coals.

"'Why,' she inquired, in a hoarse voice, 'did you invite him to sleep here to-night?'

"'Why?' said Caderousse with a shudder; 'why, that he might not have the trouble of returning to Beaucaire.'

"'Ah!' responded the woman, with an expression impossible to render; 'I thought it was for something else.'

"'Woman, woman,—why do you have such ideas?' cried Caderousse; 'or if you have them, why don't you keep them to yourself?'

"'Well!' said La Carconte, after a moment's pause; 'you are not a man!'

"'What do you mean?' added Caderousse.

"'If you had been a man, you would not have let him go from here.'

"'Woman!'

"'Or else he should not have reached Beaucaire.'

"'Woman!'

"'The road takes a turn,—he is obliged to follow it,—whilst alongside of the canal there is a shorter road.'

"'Woman!—you offend the *bon Dieu!* There!—listen!' And at this moment there was heard a tremendous peal of thunder, whilst the livid lightning illumined the room; and the thunder then rolling away to a distance, seemed as though it left the cursed abode lingeringly.

"'Mercy!' said Caderousse, crossing himself.

"At the same moment, and in the midst of the silence so full of terror which usually follows claps of thunder, they heard a knocking at the door. Caderousse and his wife started and looked aghast at each other!

"'Who's there?' cried Caderousse, rising, and drawing up in a heap the gold and notes scattered over the table, and which he covered with his two hands.

"'It is I!' shouted a voice.

"'And who are you?'

"'Eh, *pardieu!* Joannes, the jeweller!' .

"'Well, and you said I offended the *bon Dieu,*' said Carconte, with a horrid smile. 'Why, it is the *bon Dieu* who sends him back again.'

"Caderousse fell back, pale and breathless, in his chair.

"La Carconte, on the contrary, rose, and going with a firm step towards the door, opened it, saying, as she did so,—

"'Come in, dear M. Joannes.'

"'*Ma foi!*' said the jeweller, drenched with rain, 'it seems as if I was not to return to Beaucaire to-night. The shortest follies are best, my dear Caderousse. You offered me hospitality, and I accept it, and have returned to sleep beneath your friendly roof.'

"Caderousse stammered out some words, whilst he wiped away the damp that started to his brow. La Carconte double-locked the door behind the jeweller."

CHAPTER XLV

THE RAIN OF BLOOD

"As the jeweller returned to the apartment, he cast around him a scrutinising glance—but there was nothing to excite suspicion, if it existed not, or to confirm it, if already awakened. Caderousse's hands still grasped his gold and bank-notes, and La Carconte called up her sweetest smiles while welcoming the reappearance of their guest.

"'Heyday!' said the jeweller, 'you seem, my good friends, to have had some fears respecting the accuracy of your money, by counting it over so carefully directly I was gone.'

"'No, no,' answered Caderousse, 'that was not my reason, I can assure you; but the circumstances by which we have become possessed of this wealth are so unexpected, as to make us scarcely credit our good fortune, and it is only by placing the actual proof of our riches before our eyes that we can persuade ourselves the whole affair is not a dream.'

"The jeweller smiled.

"'Have you any other guests in your house?' inquired he.

"'Nobody but ourselves,' replied Caderousse; 'the fact is, we do not lodge travellers—indeed, our auberage is so near to the town, that nobody would think of stopping here.'

"'Then I am afraid I shall very much inconvenience you!'

"'Oh, dear me, no!—indeed, good sir, you will not,' said La Carconte, in her most gracious manner. 'I vow and protest your passing the night under shelter of our poor roof will not make the slightest difference in the world to us.'

"'But where will you manage to stow me?'

"'In the chamber overhead.'

"'Surely that is where you yourselves sleep?'

"'Never mind that, we have a second bed in the adjoining room.'

"Caderousse stared at his wife with much astonishment.

"The jeweller, meanwhile, was humming a song as he stood warming himself by the bright, cheering blaze of a large fagot kindled by the attentive Carconte, to dry the wet garments of her guest, and this done, she next occupied herself in arranging his supper, by spreading a napkin at the end of the table, and placing on it the slender remains of their dinner, to which she added three or four fresh-laid eggs.

"Caderousse had once more parted with his treasures—the bank-notes were replaced in the pocket-book, the gold put back into the bag, and the whole carefully locked in the *armoire*, which formed his stronghold; he then commenced pacing the room with a pensive and gloomy air, glancing from time to time at the jeweller, who stood reeking with the steam from his wet clothes, and merely changing his place on the warm hearth, to enable the whole of the garments to be in turns dried by the genial heat that issued from it.

"'Now then, my dear sir,' said La Carconte, as she placed a bottle of wine on the table, 'supper is ready whenever you are inclined to partake of it.'

"'But you are going to sit down with me, are you not?' asked Joannes.

"'I shall not take any supper to-night,' said Caderousse.

"'We dined so very late,' hastily interposed La Carconte.

"'Then it seems I am to eat alone,' remarked the jeweller.

"'Oh, we shall have the pleasure of waiting upon you,' answered La Carconte, with an eager attention she was not accustomed to manifest even to guests who paid for what they took.

"From one minute to another, Caderousse darted on his wife keen, searching glances, but rapid as the lightning-flash.

"'The storm still continued.

"'There! there!' said La Carconte, 'do you hear that? Upon my word, you did well to return hither.'

"'Nevertheless,' replied the jeweller, 'if by the time I have finished my supper, the tempest has at all abated, I shall make another attempt to complete my journey.'

"'Oh,' said Caderousse, shaking his head, 'there is not the slightest chance of its abating—it is the mistral, and that will be sure to last till to-morrow morning.' He then sighed heavily.

"'Well!' said the jeweller, as he placed himself at table, 'all I can say is, so much the worse for those who are abroad and cannot obtain a shelter.'

"'Ah!' chimed in La Carconte, 'they will have a wretched night of it, be they who they may.'

"The jeweller commenced eating his supper, and the woman who was ordinarily so querulous and indifferent to all who approached her, was suddenly transformed into the most smiling and attentive hostess. Had the unhappy man on whom she lavished her assiduities been previously acquainted with her, so sudden an alteration might well have excited suspicion in his mind, or at least have greatly astonished him.

C.M.—P*

"Caderousse, meanwhile, continued in gloomy silence to pace the room, sedulously avoiding the sight of his guest; but as soon as the stranger had completed his repast, the agitated aubergiste went eagerly to the door, and opened it.

"'The storm seems over,' said he.

"But as if to contradict his statement, at that instant a violent clap of thunder seemed to shake the house to its very foundation, while a sudden gust of wind, mingled with rain, extinguished the lamp he held in his hand. Trembling and awe-struck, Caderousse hastily shut the door and returned to his guest, while La Carconte lighted a candle by the smouldering ashes that glimmered on the hearth.

"'You must be tired,' said she to the jeweller; 'I have spread a pair of my finest and whitest sheets on your bed, so you have nothing to do but to sleep as soundly as I wish you may—you can easily find your room, it is exactly over this.'

"Joannes remained a short time listening whether the storm seemed to abate in its fury, but a brief space of time sufficed to assure him that, far from diminishing, the violence of the rain and thunder momentarily increased; resigning himself, therefore, to what seemed inevitable, he bade his host good night, and mounted to his sleeping apartment. As he passed over my head, the flooring seemed to creak beneath his tread, proving how slight must be the division between us. The quick, eager glance of La Carconte followed him as he ascended the staircase, while Caderousse, on the contrary, turned his back, and seemed most anxiously to avoid even glancing at him.

"All these particulars did not strike me as painfully at the time as they have since done; in fact, all that had happened (with the exception of the story of the diamond, which certainly did wear an air of improbability) appeared natural enough, and called for neither apprehension nor mistrust; but, worn out as I was with fatigue, and fully purposing to proceed onwards directly the tempest abated, I determined to take advantage of the comparative silence and tranquillity that prevailed to obtain the refreshment of a few hours' sleep. Overhead I could accurately distinguish every movement of the jeweller, who, after making the best arrangements in his power for passing a comfortable night, threw himself on his bed, and I could hear it creak and groan beneath his weight. Insensibly my eyelids grew heavy, deep sleep stole over me, and having no suspicion of any thing wrong, I sought not to shake it off. For the last time I looked in upon the room where Caderousse and his wife were sitting; the former was seated upon one of those low wooden stools which, in country places, are frequently used instead of chairs; his back being turned towards me, prevented me from seeing the expression of his countenance—neither should I have been able to do so had he been placed differently, as his head was buried between his two hands. La Carconte continued to gaze on him for some time in contemptuous silence, then, shrugging up her shoulders, she took her seat immediately opposite to him. At this moment the expiring embers threw up a fresh flame from the kindling of a piece of wood that lay near, and a bright gleam was thrown on the scene and the actors in it. La Carconte still kept her eyes fixed on her husband, but as he made no sign of changing his position, she extended her hard, bony hand, and touched him on the forehead.

"Caderousse shuddered!—the woman's lips seemed to move, as though she were talking!—but whether she merely spoke in an under tone, or that my senses were dulled by sleep, I did not catch a word she uttered. Confused sights and sounds seemed to float before me, and gradually I fell into a deep heavy sleep. How long I had been in this unconscious state, I know not; when I was suddenly aroused by the report of a pistol, followed by a fearful cry. Weak and tottering footsteps resounded across the chamber above me, and the next instant a dull, heavy weight seemed to fall powerless on the staircase! I had not yet fully recovered my recollection, when again I heard groans, mingled with half-stifled cries, as if from persons engaged in a deadly struggle. These evidences of the perpetration of some violent deed effectually roused me from my drowsy lethargy. Hastily raising myself on one arm, I looked around, but all was dark; and it seemed to me as if the rain must have penetrated through the flooring of the room above, for some kind of moisture appeared to fall, drop by drop, upon my forehead, and when I passed my hand across my brow I felt it wet and clammy.

"To the fearful noises that had awakened me had succeeded the most perfect silence,—unbroken, save by the footsteps of a man walking about in the chamber above. By the creaking of the staircase, I judged the individual, whoever he was, was proceeding to the lower apartment. In another minute I heard some person moving there; and, looking through, I saw a man stooping towards the fire to light a candle he held in his hand. As he turned round, I recognised the features of Caderousse,—pale, ghastly, and convulsed,—while the front and sleeves of his dress were covered with blood! Having obtained the light he had evidently descended to seek, he hurried up stairs again, and once more I heard his rapid and uneasy step in the chamber above. Ere long he came below, holding in his hand the small shagreen case, which he opened, to assure himself it contained the diamond,—seemed to hesitate as to which pocket he should put it in; then, as if dissatisfied with the security of either pocket, he deposited it in his red handkerchief, which he carefully rolled round his head. After this he took from his cupboard the bank-notes and gold he had put there, thrust the one in the pocket of his trousers, and the other into that of his waistcoat,—hastily tied up a small bundle of linen, and rushing towards the door, disappeared in the darkness of the night!

"Then all became clear and manifest to me; and I reproached myself with what had happened, as though I myself had done the guilty deed. I fancied that I still heard faint moans, and imagining that the unfortunate jeweller might not be quite dead, I determined to go to his relief, by way of atoning in some slight degree, not for the crime I had committed, but for that which I had not endeavoured to prevent; for this purpose I applied all the strength I possessed to force an entrance from the cramped spot in which I lay, to the adjoining room; the badly arranged planks which alone divided me from it yielded to my efforts and I found myself in the house; hastily snatching up the lighted candle, I hurried to the staircase, towards the middle of it I stumbled over a human body lying quite across the stairs. As I stooped to raise it, I discovered in the agonised features those of La Carconte.

"The pistol I had heard had doubtless been discharged at the unfortunate woman, whose throat it had frightfully lacerated, leaving a gaping wound from which, as well as the mouth, the blood was welling in sanguinary streams.

"Finding the miserable creature past all human aid, I strode past her and ascended to the sleeping chamber, which presented an appearance of the wildest disorder. The furniture had been knocked over in the deadly struggle that had taken place there, and the sheets, to which the unfortunate jeweller had doubtless clung, were dragged across the room; the murdered man lay on the ground, his head leaning against the wall, weltering in a gory stream poured forth from three large wounds in his breast; there was a fourth gash, but the blood was prevented escaping in consequence of the weapon (a large table-knife) still sticking in it.

"I stumbled over some object; I stooped to examine, it was the second pistol, which had not gone off, probably from the powder being wet. I approached the jeweller, who was not quite dead, and at the sound of my footsteps, causing as they did the creaking of the floor, he opened his eyes, fixed them on me with an anxious and inquiring gaze; moved his lips as though trying to speak, then overcome by the effort, fell back and expired.

"This appalling sight almost bereft me of my senses, and finding that I could no longer be of service to any one in the house, my only desire was to fly from such an accumulation of horrors as quickly as I could; almost distracted, I rushed towards the staircase, clasping my burning temples with both hands, and uttering cries of horror.

"Upon reaching the room below, I found five or six custom-house officers accompanied by an armed troop of soldiery, who immediately seized me, ere, indeed, I had sufficiently collected my ideas to offer any resistance; in truth, my senses seemed to have wholly forsaken me, and when I strove to speak a few inarticulate sounds alone escaped my lips.

"As I noticed the significant manner in which the whole party pointed to my blood-stained garments, I involuntarily surveyed myself, and then I discovered that the thick warm drops that had so bedewed me as I lay beneath the staircase, must have been the blood of La Carconte. Paralysed with horror, I could barely indicate by a movement of my hand the spot where I had concealed myself.

"'What does he mean?' asked a gendarme.

"One of the douaniers went to the place I directed—

"'He means,' replied the man upon his return, 'that he effected his entrance by means of this hole;' shewing the place where I had broken my way through the planks into the house.

"Then, and not before, the true nature of my situation flashed on me, and I saw that I was considered the guilty author of all that had occurred; with this frightful conviction of my danger, I recovered force and energy enough to free myself from the hands of those who held me, while I managed to stammer forth,—

"'I did not do it! indeed, indeed, I did not!'

"A couple of gendarmes held the muzzle of their carbines against my breast,—

"'Stir but a step,' said they, 'and you are a dead man!'

"'Why should you threaten me with death?' cried I; 'when I have already declared my innocence!'

"'Tush! tush!' cried the men; 'keep your innocent stories to tell to the judge at Nîmes. Meanwhile, come along with us, and the best advice we can give you is to do so unresistingly.'

"'Alas! resistance was far from my thoughts, I was utterly overpowered by surprise and terror; and without a word I suffered myself to be handcuffed and tied to a horse's tail, in which disgraceful plight I arrived at Nîmes.

"It seems I had been tracked by a douanier, who had lost sight of me near the auberge; feeling assured that I intended to pass the night there, he had returned to summon his comrades, who just arrived in time to hear the report of the pistol, and to take me in the midst of such circumstantial proofs of my guilt as rendered all hopes of proving my innocence utterly at an end.   One only chance was left me, that of beseeching the magistrate before whom I was taken to cause every inquiry to be made for an individual named the Abbé Busoni, who had stopped at the auberge of the Pont du Gard, on the morning previous to the murder.   If, indeed, Caderousse had not invented the story relative to the diamond, and that there existed no such person as the Abbé Busoni, then, indeed, I was lost past redemption, or, at least, my life hung upon the feeble chance of Caderousse himself being apprehended and confessing the whole truth.

"Two months passed away in hopeless expectation on my part, while I must do the magistrate justice by declaring he used every means to obtain information of the person I declared could exculpate me if he would.   Caderousse still evaded all pursuit, and I had resigned myself to what seemed my inevitable fate.   My trial was to come on at the approaching sessions; when on the 8th of September, that is to say, precisely three months and five days after the events which had perilled my life, the Abbé Busoni, whom I never ventured to believe I should see, presented himself at the prison doors, saying he understood one of the prisoners wished to speak to him; he added, that having learned the particulars of my imprisonment he hastened to comply with my desire.   You may easily imagine with what eagerness I welcomed him, and how minutely I related the whole of what I had seen and heard. I felt some degree of nervousness as I entered upon the history of the diamond; but to my inexpressible astonishment he confirmed it in every particular, and to my equal surprise, he seemed to place entire belief in all I stated.   And then it was, that won by his mild charity, perceiving him acquainted with all the habits and customs of my own country, and considering also that pardon for the only crime of which I was really guilty might come with a double power from lips so benevolent and kind, I besought him to receive my confession, under the seal of which I recounted the affair of Auteuil, in all its details, as well as every other transaction of my life.   That which I had done by the impulse of my best feelings produced the same effect as though it had been the result of calculation.   My voluntary confession of the assassination at Auteuil, proved to him that I had not committed that with which I stood accused. When he quitted me, he bade me be of good courage, and rely upon his doing all in his power to convince my judges of my innocence.

"I had speedy proofs that the excellent abbé was engaged

in my behalf, for the rigours of my imprisonment were alleviated by many trifling though acceptable indulgences; and I was told that my trial was to be postponed to the assizes following those now being held.

" In the interim it pleased Providence to cause the apprehension of Caderousse, who was discovered in some distant country, and brought back to France, where he made a full confession, refusing to make the fact of his wife's having suggested and arranged the murder any excuse for his own guilt. The wretched man was sentenced to the galleys for life, and I immediately set at liberty."

"And then it was, I presume," said Monte-Cristo, "that you came to me as the bearer of a letter from the Abbé Busoni?"

" It was, your excellency; the benevolent abbé took an evident interest in all that concerned me.

"' Your mode of life as a smuggler,' said he to me one day, ' will be the ruin of you if you persist in it; let me advise you when you get out of prison to choose something more safe as well as respectable.'

"' But how,' inquired I, 'am I to maintain myself and my poor sister?'

"' A person, whose confessor I am,' replied he, 'and who entertains a high regard for me, applied to me a short time since to procure him a confidential servant. Would you like such a post? If so, I will give you a letter of introduction to the friend I allude to.'

"' With thankfulness shall I profit by your permitting me to wait upon the gentleman you speak of.'

"' One thing you must do; swear solemnly that I shall never have reason to repent my recommendation.'

" I extended my hand, and was about to pledge myself by any promise he would dictate, but he stopped me.

"' It is unnecessary for you to bind yourself by any vow,' said he; ' I know and admire the Corsican nature too well to fear you! Here, take this,' continued he, after rapidly writing the few lines I brought to your excellency, and upon receipt of which you deigned to receive me into your service, and I venture most respectfully, and humbly, to ask whether your excellency has ever had cause to repent having done so?"

"On the contrary, Bertuccio, I have ever found you faithful, honest, and deserving. One fault I find with you, and that is, your not having placed sufficient confidence in me."

" Indeed, your excellency, I know not what you mean!"

"Simply this; how comes it, that having both a sister and an adopted son, you have never spoken to me of either?"

"Alas! I have still to recount the most distressing period of my life. Anxious as you may suppose I was to behold and comfort my dear sister, I lost no time in hastening to Corsica, but when I arrived at Rogliano I found a house of mourning and of desolation, the consequences of a scene so horrible that the neighbours remember and speak of it to this day. Acting by my advice, my poor sister had refused to comply with the unreasonable demands of Benedetto, who was continually tormenting her for money, as long as he believed there was a sous left in her possession. One morning that he had demanded money, threatening her with the severest consequences if she did not supply him with what he desired, he disappeared throughout the whole of the day, leaving the kind-hearted Assunta, who loved him as if he were her own child, to weep over his conduct and bewail his absence. Evening came, and still with all the patient solicitude of a mother she watched for his return.

"As the eleventh hour struck, he entered with a swaggering air, attended by two of the most dissolute and reckless of his ordinary companions. As poor Assunta rose to clasp her truant in her arms, forgetting all but the happiness of seeing him again, she was seized upon by the three ruffians, while the unnatural Benedetto exclaimed—

"'Come, if the old girl refuses to tell us where she keeps her money, let us just give her a taste of the torture; that will make her find her tongue, I'll engage.'

"It unfortunately happened that our neighbour, Wasilio, was at Bastia, leaving no person in his house but his wife; no human creature except her could hear or see anything that took place within our dwelling; two of the brutal companions of Benedetto held poor Assunta, who, unable to conceive that any harm was intended to her, smiled innocently and kindly in the face of those who were soon to become her executioners, while the third ruffian proceeded to barricade the doors and windows, then returning to his infamous accomplices, the three united in stifling the cries uttered by the poor victim at the sight of these alarming preparations; this effected, they dragged the unoffending object of their barbarity towards the fire, on which they forcibly held her feet, expecting by this diabolical expedient to wring from her where her supposed treasure was secreted; in the struggles made by my poor sister, her clothes caught fire, and her fiendish and cowardly tormentors were compelled to let go their hold in order to preserve themselves from sharing the same fate. Covered with flames, Assunta rushed wildly to the door, but it was fastened; tortured by the agony she endured, the unfortunate sufferer flew to the windows, but they were also strongly barricaded; then her cries and shrieks of anguish filled the place, to these succeeded convulsive sobs and deep groans, which, subsiding in faint moans, at length died away, and all was still as the grave.

"Next morning, as soon as the wife of Wasilio could muster up courage to venture abroad, she caused the door of our dwelling to be opened by the public authorities, when Assunta, although dreadfully burnt, was found still breathing: every drawer and closet in the house had been forced open and everything worth carrying off stolen from them.

"Benedetto never again appeared at Rogliano, neither have I since that day either seen or heard anything concerning him.

"It was subsequently to these dreadful events that I waited on your excellency, to whom it would have been folly to have mentioned Benedetto, since all trace of him seemed entirely lost, or of my sister, since she was dead."

"And in what light did you view the tragical occurrence?" inquired Monte-Cristo.

"As a punishment for the crime I had committed," answered Bertuccio. "Oh! those Villeforts are an accursed race!"

"Truly they are," murmured the count, with a most singular expression of countenance.

"And now," resumed Bertuccio, "your excellency may, perhaps, be able to comprehend that this place, which I revisit for the first time,—this garden, the positive scene of my crime, must have given rise to reflections of no very agreeable nature, and produced that gloom and depression of spirits which excited the notice of your excellency, who was pleased to express a desire to know the cause. At this instant, a shudder passes over me as I reflect that possibly I am now standing on the very grave in which lies M. de Villefort, by whose hand the ground was dug to receive the corpse of his child."

"It may be so," said Monte-Cristo, rising from the bench on which he had been sitting: "but," added, he, in a lower tone, "whether the procureur du roi be dead or not, the Abbé Busoni did right to send you to me, and you have also acted extremely properly in relating to me the whole of your history, as it will prevent my forming any erroneous opinions concerning you in future. As for that Benedetto, who so grossly belied his name, have you never made any effort to trace out whither he has gone, or what has become of him?"

"No! far from wishing to learn whither he had betaken himself, I should have shunned the possibility of meeting him, as I would a wild beast or a savage monster. Thank God, I have never heard his name mentioned by any person, and I hope and believe he is dead."

"Flatter not yourself that such is the case," replied the count; "an all-wise Providence permits not sinners to escape thus easily from the punishment they have merited on earth, but reserves them to aid his own designs, using them as instruments whereby to work his vengeance on the guilty."

"I am content to have him live," continued Bertuccio, "so that he spares me the misery of ever again beholding him. And now, M. le Comte," added the steward, bending humbly forward, "you know every secret of my life,—you are my judge on earth, as the Almighty is in heaven: have you no words of consolation to bestow on a repentant sinner?"

"My good friend, I know of none more calculated to calm your mind than the expressions employed by the Abbé Busoni when speaking of you to me; Villefort, the man you killed, merited the punishment he received at your hands, as a just reward for the wrongs he had done you, and it may be for other crimes likewise. Benedetto, if still living, will become the instrument of divine retribution in some way or other, and then be duly punished in his turn. As far as you, yourself, are concerned, I see but one point in which you are really guilty. Ask yourself wherefore, after rescuing the infant from its living grave, you did not restore it to its mother? There was the crime, Bertuccio! that was where you became really culpable."

"True, my lord! there, as you say, I acted wickedly, and moreover cowardly. My first duty directly I had succeeded in recalling the babe to life should have been to have restored it to its mother; but in order to do so I must have made close and careful inquiry, which would, in all probability, have led to my own apprehension; and I clung to life partly on my sister's account, and partly from that feeling of pride inborn in our hearts of desiring to come off untouched and victorious in the execution of our vengeance. Perhaps, too, the natural and instinctive love of life made me wish to avoid endangering my own. And then, again, I was not formed as brave and courageous as my poor brother."

Bertuccio hid his face in his hands as he uttered these words, while Monte-Cristo fixed on him a long and indescribable gaze.

After a brief silence, rendered still more solemn by the time and place, the count said, in a tone of melancholy wholly unlike his usual manner,—

"In order to bring this conversation to a befitting termination (as I promise you never again to revert to it), I will repeat to you some words I have heard from the lips of the Abbé Busoni himself, and which I recommend you to treasure up for your consolation—that all earthly ills yield to two all-potent remedies, time and silence. And now leave me, I would enjoy the cool solitude of this place; the very circumstances which inflict on you as a principal in the tragic scene enacted here such painful emotions, are to me, on the contrary, a source of extreme delight, and serve but to enhance the value of this dwelling in my estimation. The chief beauty of trees consists in the deep shadow of their umbrageous boughs, while fancy pictures a moving multitude of shapes and forms flitting and passing beneath that shade. Here, I am agreeably surprised by the sight of a garden laid out in such a way as to afford the fullest scope for the imagination, and furnished with thickly grown trees, beneath which leafy screen a visionary like myself may conjure up phantoms at will, and revel in the dreamy reveries of his own mind: this to me, who expected but to find a black enclosure surrounded by a straight wall, is, I assure you, a most agreeable surprise. I have no dread of supernatural things, and I have never heard it said that so much harm had been done by the dead during six thousand years, as is wrought by the living in one single day. Retire within, Bertuccio, and tranquillise your mind: should your confessor be less indulgent to you in your dying moments than you found the Abbé Busoni, send for me, if I am still on earth, and I will soothe your ear with words that shall effectually calm and soothe your parting soul ere it goes forth to that 'bourn from whence no traveller returns.'"

Bertuccio bowed lowly and respectfully, and turned away, sighing heavily as he quitted his patron.

When he had quite disappeared Monte-Cristo arose, and taking three or four steps onwards, he murmured,—

"Here beneath this plane-tree must have been where the infant's grave was dug. There is the little door opening into the garden. At this corner is the private staircase communicating with the sleeping apartment. There will be no necessity for me to make a note of these particulars, for there, before my eyes, beneath my feet, all around me, I have the plan sketched with all the living reality of truth."

After making the tour of the garden a second time, the count regained the house and re-entered his carriage; while Bertuccio, who perceived the thoughtful expression of his master's features, took his seat beside the driver without uttering a word. The carriage proceeded rapidly towards Paris.

That same evening, upon reaching his abode in the Champs Elysées, the Count of Monte-Cristo went over the whole building with the air of one long acquainted with each nook or corner. Nor, although preceding the party, did he once mistake one door for another, or commit the smallest error when choosing any particular corridor or staircase to conduct him to a place or suite of rooms he desired to visit. Ali was his principal attendant during the somewhat late hour of his survey. Having given various orders to Bertuccio relative to the improvements and alterations he desired to make in the house, the count, drawing out his watch, said to the attentive Nubian,—

"It is half-past eleven o'clock, Haydée will not be long ere she arrives. Have the French attendants been summoned to await her coming?"

Ali extended his hands towards the apartments destined for the fair Greek, which were at a distance from the habitable part of the dwelling, and so effectually concealed by means of a tapestried entrance, that it would have puzzled the most curious to have divined that beyond that spot lay hid a suite of rooms, fitted up with a rich magnificence worthy of the lovely being who was to tenant them.

Ali having pointed to the apartments, counted three on the fingers of his right hand, and then, placing it beneath his head, shut his eyes, and feigned to sleep.

"I understand," said Monte-Cristo, well acquainted with Ali's pantomime; "you mean to tell me that three female attendants await their new mistress in her sleeping chamber."

Ali with considerable animation made a sign in the affirmative.

"The young lady must needs be fatigued with her journey," continued Monte-Cristo, "and will no doubt wish to retire to rest immediately upon her arrival. Desire the French attendants not to weary her with questions, but merely pay their respectful duty and retire. You will also see that the Greek servant holds no communication with those of this country."

Ali bowed obediently and reverentially.

Just at that moment voices were heard hailing the concierge. The gate opened, a carriage rolled down the avenue and stopped at the flight of steps leading to the house. The count hastily descended, and presented himself at the already opened carriage-door to assist a young female, completely enveloped in a mantle of green and gold, to alight.

The female raised the hand extended towards her to her lips and kissed it with a mixture of love and respect. Some few words passed between them in that sonorous language in which Homer makes his gods converse. The female spoke with an expression of deep tenderness, while the count replied with an air of gentle gravity.

Preceded by Ali, who carried a rose-coloured flambeau in his hand, the female, who was no other than the lovely Greek who had been Monte-Cristo's companion in Italy, was conducted to her apartments, while the count retired to the pavilion reserved for himself.

In another hour every light in the house was extinguished, and it might have been thought that all its inmates slept.

CHAPTER XLVI

UNLIMITED CREDIT

ABOUT two o'clock the following day a calèche, drawn by a pair of magnificent English horses, stopped at the door of Monte-Cristo, and a person dressed in a blue coat, with buttons of a similar colour, a white waistcoat, over which was displayed a massive gold chain, brown trousers, and a quantity of black hair, descending so low over his eyebrows as to leave it doubtful whether it were not artificial, so little did its jetty glossiness assimilate with the deep wrinkles stamped on his features; a person, in a word, who, although evidently past fifty, desired to be taken for not more than forty, bent forwards from the carriage-door, on the panels of which were emblazoned the armorial bearings of a baron, and directed his groom to inquire at the porter's lodge whether the Count of Monte-Cristo resided there, and if he were within.

While waiting, the occupant of the carriage surveyed the house, the garden, so far as he could distinguish it, and the livery of the servants who passed to and fro, with an attention so close as to be somewhat impertinent. The glance of this individual was keen, but evincing rather cunning than intelligence; his lips were straight, and so thin that, as they closed, they were compressed within the mouth; his cheek-bones were broad and projecting—a never-failing proof of audacity and craftiness, while the flatness of his forehead, and the enlargement of the back of his skull, which rose much higher than his large and vulgarly shaped ears, combined to form a physiognomy anything but prepossessing, save in the eyes of such as considered that the owner of so splendid an equipage must needs be all that was admirable and enviable, more especially when they gazed on the enormous diamond that glittered in his shirt, and the red riband that depended from his button-hole.

The groom, in obedience to his orders, tapped at the windows of the porter's lodge, saying,—

"Pray, does not the Count of Monte-Cristo live here?"

"His excellency does reside here," replied the concierge, "but——" added he, glancing an inquiring look at Ali.

Ali returned a sign in the negative.

"But what?" asked the groom.

"His excellency does not receive visitors to-day."

"Then take my master's card. You'll see who master is —M. le Baron Danglars! Be sure to give the card to the count, and say that, although in haste to attend the Chamber, my master came out of his way to have the honour of calling upon him."

"I never speak to his excellency," replied the concierge; "the valet-de-chambre will carry your message."

The groom returned to the carriage.

"Well?" asked Danglars.

The man, somewhat crestfallen by the rebuke he had received, detailed to his master all that had passed between himself and the concierge.

"Bless me!" murmured M. le Baron Danglars; "this must surely be a prince instead of a count by their styling him 'excellency,' and only venturing to address him by the medium of his valet-de-chambre. However, it does not signify; he has a letter of credit on me, so I must see him when he requires his money."

Then, throwing himself back in his carriage, Danglars called out to his coachman, in a voice that might be heard across the road,—

"To the Chambre des Députés."

Apprised in time of the visit paid him, Monte-Cristo had, from behind the blinds of his pavilion, as minutely observed the baron by means of an excellent lorgnette as Danglars himself had scrutinised the house, garden, and servants.

"That fellow has a decidedly bad countenance," said the count, in a tone of disgust, as he shut up his glass into its ivory case. "How comes it that all do not retreat in aversion at sight of that flat, receding, serpent-like forehead, round, vulture-shaped head, and sharp-hooked nose, like the beak of a buzzard? Ali!" cried he, striking at the same time on the brazen gong.

Ali appeared.

"Summon Bertuccio!" said the count.

Almost immediately Bertuccio entered the apartment.

"Did your excellency desire to see me?" inquired he.

"I did," replied the count. "You no doubt observed the horses standing a few minutes since at the door?"

"Certainly, your excellency; I noticed them for their remarkable beauty."

"Then how comes it," said Monte-Cristo, with a frown, "that when I desired you to purchase for me the finest pair of horses to be found in Paris, you permitted so splendid a couple as those I allude to to be in the possession of any one but myself?"

At the look of displeasure, added to the angry tone in which the count spoke, Ali turned pale and held down his head.

"It is not your fault, my good Ali," said the count, in the Arabic language, and in a tone of such gentleness as none would have given him credit for being capable of feeling, "it is not your fault. You do not profess to understand the choice of English horses."

The countenance of poor Ali recovered its serenity.

"Permit me to assure your excellency," said Bertuccio, "that the horses you speak of were not to be sold when I purchased yours."

Monte-Cristo shrugged up his shoulders.

"It seems, M. l'Intendant," said he, "that you have yet to learn that all things are to be sold to such as care to pay the price."

"M. le Comte is not, perhaps, aware that M. Danglars gave 16,000 francs for his horses?"

"Very well! then offer him double that sum; a banker never loses an opportunity of doubling his capital."

"Is your excellency really in earnest?" inquired the steward.

Monte-Cristo regarded the person who durst presume to doubt his words with the look of one equally surprised and displeased.

"I have to pay a visit this evening," replied he. "I desire that these horses, with completely new harness, may be at the door with my carriage."

Bertuccio bowed, and was about to retire; but when he reached the door, he paused, and then said,—

"At what o'clock does your excellency wish the carriage and horses ready?"

"At five o'clock," replied the count.

"I beg your excellency's pardon," interposed the steward, in a deprecating manner, "for venturing to observe that it is already two o'clock."

"I am perfectly aware of that fact," answered Monte-Cristo, calmly. Then, turning towards Ali, he said, "Let all the horses in my stables be led before the windows of your young lady, that she may select those she prefers for her carriage. Request her, also, to oblige me by saying whether it is her pleasure to dine with me; if so let dinner be served in her apartments. Now leave me, and desire my valet-de-chambre to come hither."

Scarcely had Ali disappeared than the valet entered the chamber.

"M. Baptistin," said the count, "you have been in my service one year, the time I generally give myself to judge of the merits or demerits of those about me. You suit me very well."

Baptistin bowed low.

"It only remains for me to know whether I also suit you?"

"Oh, M. le Comte!" exclaimed Baptistin, eagerly.

"Listen, if you please, till I have finished speaking," replied Monte-Cristo. "You receive 1,500 francs per annum for your services here, more than many a brave subaltern who continually risks his life for his country obtains. You live in a manner far superior to many clerks and placemen who work ten times harder than you do for their money, and certainly are quite as faithful in the discharge of their duties as you may be. Then, though yourself a servant, you have other servants to wait upon you, take care of your clothes, and see that your linen is duly prepared for you. Again, you make a profit upon each article you purchase for my toilette, amounting in the course of a year to a sum equalling your wages."

"Nay, indeed, your excellency!"

"Do not interrupt me, M. Baptistin, I am not entering into these particulars with a view to complain or reproach you; on the contrary, I see nothing unfair or unreasonable in all I have enumerated: but let your notions of gain end with the advantages you have hitherto possessed. You know as well as myself, that were I to dismiss you it would be long indeed ere you would find so lucrative a post as that you have now the good fortune to fill. I neither ill-use nor ill-treat my servants by word or action. An error I readily forgive, but a wilful negligence or forgetfulness of my orders I never look over, and for that purpose I always endeavour, when issuing commands, to make them as short as they are clear and precise; and I would rather be obliged to repeat my words twice, or even three times, than they should be misunderstood. I am rich enough to become acquainted with whatever I desire to know, and I can promise you I am not wanting in curiosity. If, then, I should learn that you had taken upon yourself to speak of me to any one favourably or unfavourably, to comment on my actions, or watch my conduct, that very instant you would quit my service. You may now retire. I never caution my servants a second time,—remember that. You have been duly admonished, and if the warning is given in vain you will have nobody to blame but yourself."

Again Baptistin bowed reverentially, and was proceeding towards the door when the count bade him stay.

"I forgot to mention to you," said he, "I lay yearly aside a certain sum for each servant in my establishment: those whom I am compelled to dismiss lose (as a matter of course) all participation in this money, while their portion goes to the fund accumulating for those domestics who remain with me, and among whom it will be divided at my death. You have been in my service a year, your fortune has commenced, do not prevent its full accomplishment by your own folly."

This address, delivered in the presence of Ali, who, not understanding one word of the language in which it was spoken, stood wholly unmoved, produced an effect on M. Baptistin only to be conceived by such as have occasion to study the character and disposition of French domestics.

"I assure your excellency," said he, "at least it shall be my study to merit your approbation in all things, and I will take M. Ali as my model."

"Pray do no such thing," replied the count, in the most frigid tone; "Ali has many faults mixed with most excellent qualities; he cannot possibly serve you as a pattern for your conduct, not being as you are a paid servant, but a mere slave —a dog! who, should he fail in his duty towards me, I should not discharge from my service but kill!"

Baptistin opened his eyes with strong and unfeigned astonishment.

"You seem incredulous," said Monte-Cristo, who repeated to Ali in the Arabic language what he had just been saying to Baptistin in French.

The Nubian smiled assentingly to his master's words, then, kneeling on one knee, respectfully kissed the hand of the count.

This corroboration of the lesson he had just received put the finishing stroke to the wonder and stupefaction of M. Baptistin.

The count then motioned the valet-de-chambre to retire, and to Ali to follow himself into his study, where they conversed long and earnestly together.

As the hand of the pendule pointed to five o'clock the count struck thrice upon his gong. When Ali was wanted one stroke was given, two summoned Baptistin, and three Bertuccio.

The steward entered.

"My horses!" said Monte-Cristo.

"They are at the door harnessed to the carriage as your excellency desired. Does M. le Comte wish me to accompany him?"

"No, the coachman, Ali, and Baptistin, will be sufficient without you."

The count descended to the door of his mansion, and beheld

his carriage drawn by the very pair of horses he had so much admired in the morning as the property of Danglars. As he passed them he said,—

"They are extremely handsome certainly, and you have done well to purchase them, although you were somewhat remiss not to have procured them sooner."

"Indeed, your excellency, I had very considerable difficulty in obtaining them, and, as it is, they have cost an enormous price."

"Does the sum you gave for them make the animals less beautiful?" inquired the count, shrugging his shoulders.

"Nay, if your excellency is satisfied, all is as I could wish it. Whither does M. le Comte desire to be driven?"

"To the residence of M. le Baron Danglars, Rue de la Chaussée d'Antin."

This conversation had passed as they stood upon the terrace from which a flight of stone steps led to the carriage drive. As Bertuccio, with a respectful bow, was moving away the count called him back.

"I have another commission for you, M. Bertuccio," said he; "I am desirous of having an estate by the sea-side in Normandy, for instance, between Havre and Boulogne. You see I give you a wide range. It will be absolutely necessary that the place you may select have a small harbour, creek, or bay, into which my vessel can enter and remain at anchor. She merely draws fifteen feet water. She must be kept in constant readiness to sail immediately I think proper to give the signal. Make the requisite inquiries for a place of this description, and when you have met with an eligible spot, visit it, and if it possess the advantages desired, purchase it at once in your own name. The corvette must now, I think, be on her way to Fécamp, must she not?"

"Certainly, your excellency; I saw her put to sea the same evening we quitted Marseilles."

"And the yacht?"

"Was ordered to remain at Martigues."

"'Tis well! I wish you to write from time to time to the captains in charge of the two vessels, so as to keep them on the alert."

"And the steam-boat? Has your excellency any orders to give respecting her?"

"She is at Chalons, is she not?"

"She is, my lord."

"The directions I gave you for the other two vessels may suffice for the steam-boat also."

"I understand, my lord, and will punctually fulfil your commands."

"When you have purchased the estate I desire, I mean to establish constant relays of horses at ten leagues' distance one from the other along the northern and southern road."

"Your excellency may fully depend upon my zeal and fidelity in all things."

The count gave an approving smile, descended the terrace steps, and sprang into his carriage, which, drawn by the beautiful animals so expensively purchased, was whirled along with incredible swiftness, and stopped only before the hôtel of the banker.

Danglars was engaged at that moment presiding over a railroad committee. But the meeting was nearly concluded when the name of his visitor was announced. As the count's title sounded on his ear he rose, and addressing his colleagues, many of whom were members of either Chamber, he said,—

"Gentlemen, I must pray you to excuse my quitting you thus; but a most ridiculous circumstance has occurred, which is this,—Thomson and French, the bankers at Rome, have sent to me a certain individual calling himself the Count of Monte-Cristo, who is desirous of opening an account with me to any amount he pleases. I confess this is the drollest thing I have ever met with in the course of my extensive foreign transactions, and you may readily suppose it has greatly roused my curiosity; indeed so much did I long to see the bearer of so unprecedented an order for an unlimited credit, that I took the trouble this morning to call on the pretended count, for his title is a mere fiction—of that I am persuaded. We all know counts nowadays are not famous for their riches. But would you believe, upon arriving at the residence of the *soi-disant* Count of Monte-Cristo, I was very coolly informed, 'He did not receive visitors that day!' Upon my word such airs are ridiculous, and befitting only some great millionaire or a capricious beauty. I made enquiries and found that the house where the said count resides in the Champs Elysées is his own property, and certainly it was very decently kept up and arranged as far as I could judge from the gardens and exterior of the hôtel. But," pursued Danglars, with one of his sinister smiles, "an order for unlimited credit calls for something like caution on the part of the banker on whom that order is given. These facts stated, I will freely confess I am very anxious to see the individual just now announced. I suspect a hoax is intended, but the good folks who thought fit to play it off on me knew but little whom they had to deal with. Well! well! we shall see. 'They laugh best who laugh last!'"

Having delivered himself of this pompous address, uttered

with a degree of energy that left the baron almost out of breath, he bowed to the assembled party and withdrew to his drawing-room, whose sumptuous fittings-up of white and gold had caused a great and admiring sensation in the Chaussée d'Antin.

It was to this apartment he had desired his guest to be shewn, fully reckoning upon the overwhelming effect so dazzling a *coup-d'œil* would produce.

He found the count standing before some copies of Albano and Fattore that had been passed off to the banker as originals; but which, copies of the paintings of those great masters as they were, seemed to feel their degradation in being brought into juxtaposition with the gaudy gilding that covered the ceiling.

The count turned round as he heard the entrance of Danglars into the room.

With a slight inclination of the head, Danglars signed to the count to be seated, pointing significantly to a gilded arm-chair, covered with white satin embroidered with gold.

The count obeyed.

" I have the honour, I presume, of addressing M. de Monte-Cristo?"

The count bowed.

"And I of speaking to Baron Danglars, Chevalier de la Légion d'Honneur, and Member of the Chamber of Deputies?"

With an air of extreme gravity Monte-Cristo slowly enumerated the various titles engraved on the card left at his hôtel by the baron.

Danglars felt all the irony contained in the address of his visitor. For a minute or two he compressed his lips as though seeking to conquer his rage ere he trusted himself to speak. Then turning to his visitor he said,—

"You will, I trust, excuse my not having called you by your title when I first addressed you, but you are aware we are living under a popular form of government, and that I am, myself, a representative of the liberties of the people."

"So much so," replied Monte-Cristo, "that while preserving the habit of styling yourself baron, you have deemed it advisable to lay aside that of calling others by their titles."

"Upon my word," said Danglars, with affected carelessness, " I attach no sort of value to such empty distinctions, but the fact is, I was made Baron, and also Chevalier de la Légion d'Honneur, in consequence of some services I had rendered government, but——"

"You have abdicated your titles after the example set you by Messrs. de Montmorency and Lafayette? Well; you cannot possibly choose more noble models for your conduct!"

"Why," replied Danglars, "I do not mean to say I have altogether laid aside my titles; with the servants, for instance —there I think it right to preserve my rank with all its outward forms."

"I see, by your domestics you are, 'My lord!' 'M. le Baron!' the journalists of the day style you 'Monsieur!' while your constituents term you 'Citizen.'"

Again Danglars bit his lips with baffled spite, he saw well enough that he was no match for Monte-Cristo in an argument of this sort, and he therefore hastened to turn to subjects more familiar to him, and calculated on having all the advantages on his side.

"Permit me to inform you, M. le Comte," said he, bowing, "that I have received a letter of advice from Thomson and French of Rome."

"I am glad to hear it, M. le Baron, for I must claim the privilege of so addressing you as well as your servants; I have acquired the bad habit of calling persons by their style and title from living in a country where barons are still met with, simply because persons are never suddenly elevated to a rank which is possessed only in right of ancestry. But as regards the letter of advice, I am charmed to find it has reached you; that will spare me the troublesome and disagreeable task of coming to you for money myself. You have received a regular letter of advice, therefore my cheques will be duly honoured, and we shall neither of us have to go out of our way in the transaction."

"There is one slight difficulty," said Danglars; "and that consists in my not precisely comprehending the letter itself!"

"Indeed?"

"And for that reason I did myself the honour of calling upon you in order to beg you would explain some part of it to me."

"With much pleasure! Pray, now I am here, let me know what it was that baffled your powers of comprehension?"

"Why," said Danglars, "in the letter—I believe I have it about me—(here he felt in his breast-pocket)—yes, here it is! Well, this letter gives M. le Comte de Monte-Cristo unlimited credit on our house."

"And what is there that requires explaining in that simple fact, may I ask, M. le Baron?"

"Merely the term *unlimited*, nothing else, certainly."

"Is not that word known in France? Perhaps, indeed, it does not belong to the language; for the persons from whom you received your letter of advice are a species of Anglo-Germans, and very probably do not write very choice or accurate French."

"Oh, as for the composition of the letter, there is not the smallest error in it, but as regards the competency of the document, I certainly have doubts."

"Is it possible?" asked the count, assuming an air and tone of the utmost simplicity and candour. "Is it possible that Thomson and French are not looked upon as safe and solvent bankers? Pray tell me what you think, M. le Baron, for I feel uneasy, I can assure you, having some considerable property in their hands."

"Thomson and French are bankers of the highest repute," replied Danglars, with an almost mocking smile; "and it was not of their solvency or capability I spoke, but of the word *unlimited*, which in financial affairs is so extremely vague a term,—that—that——"

"In fact,—said Monte-Cristo, "that its sense is also without limitation."

"Precisely what I was about to say," cried Danglars. "Now what is vague is doubtful; and, says the wise man, 'where there is doubt there is danger!'"

"Meaning to say," rejoined Monte-Cristo, "that however Thomson and French may be inclined to commit acts of imprudence and folly, M. le Baron Danglars is not disposed to follow their example."

"How so, M. le Comte?"

"Simply thus; the banking-house of Thomson and Co. set no bounds to their engagements, while that of M. Danglars has its limits; truly he is wise as the sage whose prudent apophthegm he quoted but just now."

"Monsieur!" replied the banker, drawing himself up with a haughty air, "the amount of my capital, or the extent and solvency of my engagements, have never been questioned."

"It seems, then, reserved for me," said Monte-Cristo, coldly, "to be the first to do so."

"And by what right, sir?"

"By right of the objections you have raised, and the explanations you have demanded, which certainly imply considerable distrust on your part, either of yourself or me,—the former, most probably."

Again did Danglars, by a forcible effort, restrain himself from betraying the vindictive passions which possessed his mind at this second defeat by an adversary who calmly fought him with his own weapons: his forced politeness sat awkwardly upon him, while his splenetic rage, although essaying to veil itself under a playful, jesting manner, approached at times almost to impertinence. Monte-Cristo, on the contrary, preserved a graceful suavity of demeanour, aided by a certain degree of simplicity he could assume at pleasure, and thus, calm and wholly at his ease, possessed an infinite advantage over his irascible companion.

"Well, sir," resumed Danglars, after a brief silence, "I will endeavour to make myself understood, by requesting you to inform me for what sum you propose to draw upon me?"

"Why, truly," replied Monte-Cristo, determined not to lose an inch of the ground he had gained, "my reason for desiring an 'unlimited' credit was precisely because I did not know what money I might expend."

The banker now thought it his turn to shew off, and make a display of wealth and consequence; flinging himself back therefore in his arm-chair, he said, with an arrogant and purse-proud air,—

"Let me beg of you not to hesitate in naming your wishes; you will then be convinced that the resources of the house of Danglars, however limited, are still equal to meeting the largest demands; and were you even to require a million——"

"I beg your pardon!" interposed Monte-Cristo.

"I observed," replied Danglars, with a patronising and pompous air, "that should you be hard pressed, the concern of which I am the head would not scruple to accommodate you to the amount of a million."

"A million?" retorted the count; "and what use can you possibly suppose so pitiful a sum would be to me? My dear sir, if a trifle like that could suffice me, I should never have given myself the trouble of opening an account for so contemptible an amount. A million! Excuse my smiling when you speak of a sum I am in the habit of carrying in my pocket book or dressing-case."

And with these words Monte-Cristo took from his pockets a small case containing his visiting cards, and drew forth two orders on the treasury for 500,000 francs each, payable at sight to the bearer.

A man like Danglars was wholly inaccessible to any gentler method of correction; his upstart arrogance, his ostentatious vulgarity, were only assailable by blows dealt with the force and vigour of the present *coup ;* its effect on the banker was perfectly stunning; and as though scarcely venturing to credit his senses, he continued gazing from the paper to the count with a confused and mystified air.

"Come, come," said Monte-Cristo, "confess honestly, that you have not perfect confidence in the responsibility of the house of Thomson and French: there is nothing very strange in your exercising what seems to you a necessary caution;

However, foreseeing that such might be the case, I determined, spite of my ignorance in such matters, to be provided with the means of banishing all scruples from your mind, and at the same time leaving you quite at liberty to act as you pleased in the affair. See, here are two similar letters to that you have yourself received; the one from the house of Arstein and Eskeles of Vienna to Baron de Rothschild, the other drawn from Baring of London to M. Laffitte. Now, sir, you have but to say the word, and I will spare you all uneasiness and alarm on the subject, by presenting my letter of credit at one or other of the establishments I have named."

The blow had struck home, and Danglars was entirely vanquished; with a trembling hand he took the two letters from Vienna and London from the count, who held them carelessly between his finger and thumb, as though to him they were mere every-day matters to which he attached but very little interest. Having carefully perused the documents in question, the banker proceeded to ascertain the genuineness of the signatures, and this he did with a scrutiny so severe as might have appeared insulting to the count, had it not suited his present purpose to mislead the banker in every respect.

"Well, sir," said Danglars, rising, after he had well convinced himself of the authenticity of the documents he held, and bowing, as though in adoration of a man, the thrice happy possessor of as many orders for unlimited credit on the three principal banks of Paris, "you have there signatures worth untold wealth; although your conversation and vouchers put an end to all mistrust in the affair, you must pardon me, M. le Comte, for confessing the most extreme astonishment."

"Nay, nay," answered Monte-Cristo, with the easiest and most gentlemanly air imaginable, "'tis not for such trifling sums as these to startle or astonish the banking-house of M. le Baron Danglars. Then, as all is settled as to forms between us, I will thank you to send a supply of money to me to-morrow."

"By all means, M. le Comte! What sum do you want?"

"Why," replied Monte-Cristo, "since we mutually understand each other,—for such I presume is the case?"

Danglars bowed assentingly.

"You are quite sure that not a lurking doubt or suspicion lingers in your mind?"

"Oh, M. le Comte!" exclaimed Danglars; "I never for an instant entertained such a feeling towards you."

"No, no! you merely wished to be convinced you ran no risk, nothing more; but now that we have come to so clear an understanding, and that all distrust and suspicion are laid at

C.M.—Q

rest, we may as well fix a sum as the probable expenditure of the first year:—suppose we say six millions to——"

"Six millions!" gasped out Danglars,—"certainly, whatever you please."

"Then, if I should require more," continued Monte-Cristo, in a careless and indifferent manner, "why, of course, I should draw upon you; but my present intention is not to remain in France more than a year, and during that period I scarcely think I shall exceed the sum I mentioned. However, we shall see."

"The money you desire shall be at your house by ten o'clock to-morrow morning, M. le Comte," replied Danglars. "How would you like to have it? in gold, silver, or notes?"

"Half in gold, and the other half in bank-notes, if you please," said the count, rising from his seat.

"I must confess to you, M. le Comte," said Danglars, "that I have hitherto imagined myself acquainted with the degree of fortune possessed by all the rich individuals of Europe, and still wealth such as yours has been wholly unknown to me. May I presume to ask whether you have long possessed it?"

"It has been in the family a very long while," returned Monte-Cristo, "a sort of treasure expressly forbidden to be touched for a certain period of years, during which the accumulated interest has doubled the capital. The period appointed by the testator for the disposal of these riches occurred only a short time ago; and they have only been employed by me within the last few years. Your ignorance on the subject, therefore, is easily accounted for. However, you will be better informed as to me and my possessions ere long."

And the count, while pronouncing these latter words, accompanied them with one of those ghastly smiles that used to strike terror into poor Franz d'Epinay.

"With your tastes and means of gratifying them," continued Danglars, "you will exhibit a splendour that must effectually put us poor miserable millionaires quite in the background. If I mistake not you are an admirer of paintings, at least I judged so from the attention you appeared to be bestowing on mine when I entered the room. If you will permit me I shall be happy to shew you my picture-gallery, composed entirely of works by the ancient masters—warranted as such. Not a modern picture among them. I cannot endure the modern school of painting."

"You are perfectly right in objecting to them, for this one great fault—that they have not yet had time to become old."

"Or will you allow me to shew you several fine statues by Thorwaldsen, Bartoloni, and Canova—all foreign artists? for, as you may perceive, I think but very indifferently of our French sculptors."

"You have a right to be unjust to your own countrymen, if such is your pleasure."

"But perhaps you will prefer putting off your inspection of my poor pictures, &c., until another opportunity, when we shall be better known to each other. For the present I will confine myself (if perfectly agreeable to you) to introducing you to Madame la Baronne Danglars,—excuse my impatience, M. le Comte, but a person of your wealth and influence cannot receive too much attention."

Monte-Cristo bowed in sign that he accepted the proffered honour, and the financier immediately rang a small bell which was answered by a servant in a showy livery.

"Is Madame la Baronne at home?" inquired Danglars.

"Yes, M. le Baron," answered the man.

"And alone?"

"No, M. le Baron, madame has visitors."

"Have you any objection to meet any persons who may be with madame, or do you desire to preserve a strict incognito?"

"No, indeed," replied Monte-Cristo, with a smile, "I do not arrogate to myself the right of so doing."

"And who is with madame? M. Debray?" inquired Danglars, with an air of indulgence and good nature that made Monte-Cristo smile, acquainted as he was with the secrets of the banker's domestic life.

"Yes, M. le Baron," replied the servant, "M. Debray is with madame."

Danglars nodded his head, then turning to Monte-Cristo said, "M. Lucien Debray is an old friend of ours, and private secretary to the Ministre de l'Intérieur. As for my wife, I must tell you, she lowered herself by marrying me, for she belongs to one of the most ancient families in France. Her maiden name was De Servières, and her first husband was M. le Colonel Marquis de Nargonne."

"I have not the honour of knowing Madame Danglars, but I have already met M. Lucien Debray."

"Ah! indeed!" said Danglars, "and where was that?"

"At the house of M. de Morcerf."

"Oh! what! you are acquainted with the young viscount, are you?"

"We were together a good deal during the Carnival at Rome."

"True, true!" cried Danglars; "let me see—have I not heard talk of some strange adventure with bandits or thieves hid in ruins, and of his having had a miraculous escape?—

I forget how, but I know he used to amuse my wife and daughter by telling them about it after his return from Italy."

"Madame la Baronne is waiting to receive you, gentlemen," said the servant, who had gone to inquire the pleasure of his mistress.

"With your permission," said Danglars, bowing, "I will precede you to shew you the way."

"By all means," replied Monte-Cristo; "I follow you."

CHAPTER XLVII

THE DAPPLED GREYS

THE baron, followed by the count, traversed a long suite of apartments, in which the prevailing characteristics were heavy magnificence and the gaudiness of ostentatious wealth, until he reached the boudoir of Madame Danglars, a small octagonal-shaped room, hung with pink satin, covered with white Indian muslin; the chairs were of ancient workmanship and materials; over the doors were painted sketches of shepherds and shepherdesses after the style and manner of Boucher; and at each side pretty medallions in crayons, harmonising well with the fittings-up of this charming apartment, the only one throughout the vast hôtel in which any distinctive taste prevailed: the truth was, it had been entirely overlooked in the plan arranged and followed out by M. Danglars and his architect, who had been selected to aid the baron in the great work of improvement he meditated, solely because he was the most fashionable and celebrated decorator of the day. The ornamental part of the fittings-up of Madame Danglars' boudoir had then been left entirely to herself and Lucien Debray. M. Danglars, however, while possessing a great admiration for the antique as it was understood during the time of the Directory, entertained the most sovereign contempt for the simple elegance of his wife's favourite sitting-room—where, by the way, he was never permitted to intrude, unless, indeed, he excused his own appearance by ushering in some more agreeable visitor than himself; and even then he had rather the air and manner of a person who was himself introduced than as being the presenter of another, his reception being either cordial or frigid in proportion as the individual who accompanied him chanced to please or displease his lady wife.

As Danglars now entered he found Madame la Baronne (who, although past the first bloom of youth, was still strikingly handsome) seated at the piano, a most elaborate piece of cabinet and inlaid work, while Lucien Debray, standing before a small work-table, was turning over the pages of an album. Lucien had found time, preparatory to the count's arrival, to relate many particulars respecting him to Madame Danglars. It will be remembered that Monte-Cristo had made a lively impression on the minds of all the party assembled at the breakfast given by Albert de Morcerf; and although Debray was not in the habit of yielding to such feelings, he had never been able to shake off the powerful influence excited in his mind by the impressive look and manner of the count, consequently the description given by Lucien to the baroness bore the highly coloured tinge of his own heated imagination. Already excited by the wonderful stories related of the count by De Morcerf, it is no wonder that Madame Danglers eagerly listened to, and fully credited, all the additional circumstances detailed by Debray. The sound of approaching footsteps compelled the animated pair to assume an appearance of calm indifference and worldly ease; the lady flew to her piano, and her companion snatched up an album which fortunately lay near, and seemed as though really interested in its contents. A most gracious welcome and unusual smile were bestowed on M. Danglars, the count, in return for his gentlemanly bow, received a formal though graceful curtsy, while Lucien exchanged with the count a sort of distant recognition and with Danglars a free and easy nod.

"Baroness," said Danglars, "give me leave to present to you the Count of Monte-Cristo, who has been most warmly recommended to me by my correspondents at Rome. I need but mention one fact to make all the ladies in Paris court his notice, and that is, that the noble individual before you has come to take up his abode in our fine capital for one year, during which brief period he proposes to spend six millions of money,—think of that! It sounds very much like an announcement of balls, fêtes, dinners, and picnic parties, in all of which I trust M. le Comte will remember us, as he may depend upon it we shall him, in all the entertainments we may give, be they great or small."

Spite of the gross flattery and coarseness of this address, Madame Danglars could not forbear gazing with considerable interest on a man capable of expending six millions in twelve months, and who had selected Paris for the scene of his princely extravagance.

"And when did you arrive here?" inquired she.

"Yesterday morning, madame."

"Coming as usual, I presume, from the extreme end of the globe? Pardon me—at least, such I have heard is your custom."

"Nay, madame! this time I have merely proceeded from Cadiz hither."

"You have selected a most unfavourable moment for your first visit to our city. Paris is a horrible place in summer! Balls, parties, and fêtes, are over; the Italian opera is in London, the French opera every where except at Paris. As for the Théâtre Français, you know, of course, that it is nowhere; the only amusements left us are the indifferent races held in the Champ de Mars and Satory. Do you propose entering any horses at either of these races, M. le Comte?"

"I assure you, madame," replied Monte-Cristo, "my present intentions are, to do whatever will tend to render my sojourn in Paris most agreeable to myself and others. I only pray I may find some kind, pitying friend who will commiserate my lamentable ignorance of such matters, and instruct me rightly to understand the habits and etiquette of this polished city."

"Are you fond of horses, Monsieur le Comte?"

"I have passed a considerable part of my life in the East, madame; and you are, doubtless, aware that the inhabitants of those climes value only two things—the fine breeding of their horses and the beauty of their women."

"Nay, M. le Comte!" said the baroness, "it would have been somewhat more gallant to have placed the ladies before the animals."

"You see, madame, how rightly I spoke when I said I required a preceptor to guide me in all my sayings and doings here."

At this instant the favourite attendant of Madame Danglars entered the boudoir; approaching her mistress, she spoke some words in an under tone. Madame Danglars turned very pale, then exclaimed,—

"I cannot believe it; the thing is impossible!"

"I assure you, madame," replied the woman, "it is even as I have said."

Turning impatiently towards her husband, Madame Danglars demanded,—

"Is this true?"

"Is what true, madam?" inquired Danglars, visibly agitated.

"What my maid tells me."

"But what does she tell you?"

"That when my coachman was about to prepare my carriage, he discovered that the horses had been removed from the stables without his knowledge. I desire to know what is the meaning of this?"

"Be kind enough, madam, to listen to me," said Danglars.

"Fear not my listening,—ay, and attentively, too; for, in truth, I am most curious to hear what explanation you purpose offering for conduct so unparalleled. These two gentlemen shall decide between us; but, first, I will state the case to them. Gentlemen," continued the baroness, "among the ten horses in the stables of M. le Baron Danglars, are two that belong exclusively to me; a pair of the handsomest and most spirited creatures to be found in Paris. But to you, at least, M. Debray, I need not give a further description; because to you my beautiful pair of dappled greys were well known. Well! I had promised Madame de Villefort the loan of my carriage to drive to-morrow to the Bois de Boulogne; but when my coachman goes to fetch the greys from the stables, they are gone,—positively gone. No doubt, M. Danglars has sacrificed them to the selfish consideration of gaining some thousands of paltry francs. Oh! how I hate and detest that money-grasping nature! Heaven defend me from all the race of mercenary speculators!"

"Madame," replied Danglars, "the horses were not sufficiently quiet for you; they were scarcely four years old, and they made me extremely uneasy on your account."

"Nonsense!" retorted the baroness; "you could not have entertained any alarm on the subject, because you are perfectly well aware that I have recently engaged a coachman who is said to be the best in Paris. But, perhaps, you have disposed of the coachman as well as the horses?"

"My dear love! pray do not say any more about them, and I promise you another pair exactly like them in appearance, only more quiet and steady."

The baroness shrugged up her shoulders with an air of ineffable contempt, while her husband, affecting not to observe it, turned towards Monte-Cristo, and said,—

"Upon my word, M. le Comte, I am quite sorry I was not sooner aware of your establishing yourself in Paris."

"And wherefore?" asked the count.

"Because I should have liked to have made you the offer of these horses. I have almost given them away, as it is; but, as I before said, I was anxious to get rid of them upon any terms. They were only fit for a young man; not at all calculated for a person at my time of life."

"I am much obliged by your kind intentions towards me," said Monte-Cristo; "but this morning I purchased a very excellent pair of carriage-horses, and I do not think they were dear. There they are! Come, M. Debray, you are a connoisseur, I believe, let me have your opinion upon them."

As Debray walked towards the window, Danglars approached his wife.

"I could not tell you before others," said he, in a low tone, "the reason of my parting with the horses; but a most enormous price was offered me this morning for them. Some madman or fool, bent upon ruining himself as fast as he can, actually sent his steward to me to purchase them at any cost; and the fact is, I have gained 16,000 francs by the sale of them. Come, don't look so angry, and you shall have 4,000 francs of the money to do what you like with, and Eugénie shall have 2,000. There! what do you think now of the affair? Wasn't I right to part with the horses?"

Madame Danglars surveyed her husband with a look of withering contempt.

"What do I see?" suddenly exclaimed Debray.

"Where?" asked the baroness.

"I cannot be mistaken; there are your horses! The very animals we were speaking of harnessed to the count's carriage!"

"My dear, beautiful dappled greys?" demanded the baroness, springing to the window. "'Tis indeed they!" said she.

Danglars looked absolutely stupefied.

"How very singular!" cried Monte-Cristo, with well-feigned astonishment.

Madame Danglars whispered a few words in the ear of Debray, who approached Monte-Cristo, saying, "The baroness wishes to know what you paid her husband for the horses."

"I scarcely know," replied the count; "it was a little surprise prepared for me by my steward; he knew how desirous I was of meeting with precisely such a pair of horses,— and—so he bought them. I think, if I remember rightly, he hinted that he had given somewhere about 30,000 francs."

Debray conveyed the count's reply to the baroness.

Poor Danglars looked so crest-fallen and discomfited that Monte-Cristo assumed a pitying air towards him.

"See," said the count, "how very ungrateful women are! Your kind attention, in providing for the safety of the baroness by disposing of the horses, does not seem to have made the least impression on her. But so it is; a woman will often, from mere wilfulness, prefer that which is dangerous to that which is safe. Therefore, in my opinion, my dear baron, the best and easiest way is to leave them to their fancies, and allow them to act as they please; and then, if any mischief follows, why, at least, they have no one to blame but themselves."

Danglars made no reply; he was occupied in anticipations of the coming scene between himself and the baroness, whose threatening looks and frowning brow, like that of Olympic Jove, predicted a fearful storm.

Debray, who perceived the gathering clouds, and felt no desire to witness the explosion of Madame Danglars' rage, suddenly recollected an appointment, which compelled him to take his leave; while Monte-Cristo, unwilling to destroy the advantages he hoped to obtain by prolonging his stay, made a farewell bow and departed, leaving Danglars to endure the angry reproaches of his wife.

"Excellent!" murmured Monte-Cristo to himself, as he retraced the way to his carriage. "All has gone according to my wishes. The domestic peace of this family is henceforth in my hands. Now, then, to play another master-stroke, by which I shall gain the heart of both husband and wife— delightful! Still," added he, "amid all this, I have not yet been presented to Mademoiselle Eugénie Danglars, whose acquaintance I should have been glad to make. But never mind," pursued he, with that peculiar smile that at times lighted up his countenance, "it matters not for the present. I am on the spot, and have plenty of time before me—by and bye will do for that part of my scheme."

The count's further meditations were interrupted by his arrival at his own abode.

Two hours afterwards, Madame Danglars received a most flattering epistle from the count, in which he entreated her to receive back her favourite "dappled greys;" protesting that he could not endure the idea of making his *début* in the Parisian world of fashion with the knowledge that his splendid equipage had been obtained at the price of a lovely woman's regrets. The horses were sent back, wearing the same harness they had done in the morning: the only difference consisted in the rosettes worn on the heads of the animals being adorned with a large diamond placed in the centre of each, by order of the count.

To Danglars Monte-Cristo also wrote, requesting him to excuse the whimsical gift of a capricious millionaire, and to beg of Madame la Baronne to pardon the Eastern fashion adopted in the return of the horses.

During the evening Monte-Cristo quitted Paris for Auteuil, accompanied by Ali.

The following day, about three o'clock. a single blow

struck on the gong, summoned Ali to the presence of the count.

"Ali," observed his master, as the Nubian entered the chamber, "you have frequently explained to me how more than commonly skilful you are in throwing the lasso, have you not?"

Ali drew himself up proudly, and then returned a sign in the affirmative.

"I thought I did not mistake. With your lasso you could stop an ox?"

Again Ali repeated his affirmative gesture.

"Or a tiger?"

Ali bowed his head in token of assent.

"A lion, even?"

Ali sprung forwards, imitating the action of one throwing the lasso; then of a strangled lion.

"I understand," said Monte-Cristo; "you wish to tell me you have hunted the lion?"

Ali smiled, with triumphant pride, as he signified that he had indeed both chased and captured many lions.

"But do you believe you could arrest the progress of two horses rushing forwards with ungovernable fury?"

The Nubian smiled.

"It is well," said Monte-Cristo; "then listen to me. Ere long a carriage will dash past here, drawn by the pair of dappled grey horses you saw me with yesterday; now, at the risk of your own life, you must manage to stop those horses before my door."

Ali descended to the street, and marked a straight line on the pavement immediately at the entrance of the house, and then pointed out the line he had traced to the count, who was watching him. The count patted him gently on the back—his usual mode of praising Ali—who, pleased and gratified with the commission assigned him, walked calmly towards a projecting stone forming the angle of the street and house, and, seating himself thereon, began to smoke his chibouque, while Monte-Cristo re-entered his dwelling, perfectly assured of the success of his plan. Still, as five o'clock approached, and the carriage was momentarily expected by the count, the indication of more than common impatience and uneasiness might be observed in his manner. He stationed himself in a room commanding a view of the street, pacing the chamber with restless steps, stopping merely to listen from time to time for the sound of approaching wheels, then to cast an anxious glance on Ali; but the regularity with which the Nubian puffed forth the smoke of his chibouque proved that he at least was wholly absorbed in the enjoyment

of his favourite occupation. Suddenly a distant sound of
rapidly advancing wheels was heard, and almost immediately
a carriage appeared, drawn by a pair of wild, ungovernable
horses, who rushed forward as though urged by the fiend
himself, while the terrified coachman strove in vain to restrain
their furious speed.

In the vehicle was a girl, apparently young, and a child
of about seven or eight years of age. Terror seemed to have
deprived them even of the power of uttering a cry, and both
were clasped in each other's arms, as though determined not
to be parted by death itself. The carriage creaked and
rattled as it flew over the rough stones; and had it encountered
the slightest impediment to its progress, it must inevitably
have upset; but it still flew on, and the cries of the affrighted
spectators testified the universal sense of the imminent peril
its occupants were threatened with.

Then Ali knew the right moment was come; and, throwing
down his chibouque, he drew the lasso from his pocket—
threw it so skilfully as to catch the forelegs of the near horse
in its triple fold—suffered himself to be dragged on for a few
steps, by which time the tightening of the well-cast lasso
had so completely hampered the furious animal as to bring
it to the ground, and falling on the pole, it snapped, and
therefore prevented the other animal from pursuing its
headlong way. Gladly availing himself of this opportunity,
the coachman leaped from his box; but Ali had promptly
seized the nostrils of the second horse, and held them in his
iron grasp, till the maddened beast, snorting with pain,
sunk beside his companion. All this was achieved in much
less time than is occupied in the recital. The brief space
had, however, been sufficient for an individual, followed by
a number of servants, to rush from the house before which
the accident had occurred, and. as the coachman opened the
door of the carriage, to take from it a lady who was convulsively
grasping the cushions with one hand, while with the other
she pressed to her bosom her young companion, who had lost
all consciousness of what was passing.

Monte-Cristo carried them both to the salon, and deposited
them on a sofa.

"Compose yourself, madam," said he; "all danger is
over."

The girl looked up at these words, and, with a glance
far more expressive than any entreaties could have been,
pointed to her child, who still continued insensible.

"I understand the nature of your alarms, madam," said
the count, carefully examining the child, "but I assure you
there is not the slightest occasion for uneasiness; your little

charge has not received the least injury,—his insensibility is merely the effects of terror, and will soon cease."

"Are you quite sure you do not say so to tranquillise my fears? See how deadly pale he is! My child! my darling Edward! speak to your mother; open your dear eyes and look on me once again!—Oh, sir, in pity send for help! my whole fortune shall not be thought too much for the recovery of my blessed boy."

With a calm smile and gentle wave of the hand, Monte-Cristo signed to the distracted mother to lay aside her apprehensions; then opening a casket that stood near, he drew forth a phial composed of Bohemian glass, containing a liquid of the colour of blood, of which he let fall a single drop on the child's lips. Scarcely had it reached them, ere the boy, though still pale as marble, opened his eyes, and eagerly gazed around him.

At this unhoped-for sight, the wild delight of the mother equalled her former despair.

"Where am I?" exclaimed she, when her first raptures at her son's recovery were past, "and to whom am I indebted for so happy a termination to my late dreadful alarm?"

"Madam," answered the count, "you are under the roof of one who esteems himself most fortunate in having been able to save you from a further continuance of your sufferings."

"My wretched curiosity has brought all this about," pursued the lady. "All Paris rung with the praises of Madame Danglars' beautiful horses, and I had the folly to desire to know whether they really merited the high character given of them."

"Is it possible," exclaimed the count, with well-feigned astonishment, "that these horses belong to Madame la Baronne?"

"They do, indeed. May I inquire if you are acquainted with Madame Danglars?"

"I have that honour; and my happiness at your escape from the danger that threatened you is redoubled by the consciousness that I have been the unwilling and unintentional cause of all the peril you have incurred. I yesterday purchased these horses of the baron; but as the baroness evidently regretted parting with them, I ventured to send them back to her, with a request that she would gratify me by accepting them from my hands."

"You are then, doubtless, the Count of Monte-Cristo of whom Hermine has talked to me so much?"

"You have rightly guessed, madam," replied the count.

"And I am Madame Héloïse de Villefort."

The count bowed with the air of a person who hears a name for the first time.

"How grateful will M. de Villefort be for all your goodness! how thankfully will he acknowledge that to you alone it is owing that his wife and child exist! Most certainly but for the prompt assistance of your intrepid servant, this dear child and myself must both have perished."

"Indeed, I still shudder at the recollection of the fearful danger you were placed in, as well as your interesting child."

"I trust you will not object to my offering a recompense to your noble-hearted servant, proportionate to the service he has rendered me and mine."

"I beseech you, madam," replied Monte-Cristo, "not to spoil Ali, either by too great praise or rewards. I cannot allow him to acquire the habit of expecting to be recompensed for every trifling service he may render. Ali is my slave, and in saving your life he was but discharging his duty to me."

"Nay," interposed Madame de Villefort, on whom the authoritative style adopted by the count made a deep impression,—"nay, but consider that to preserve my life he has risked his own."

"His life, madam, belongs not to him; it is mine, in return for my having myself saved him from death."

Madame de Villefort made no further reply; her mind was utterly absorbed in the contemplation of the singular individual, who, from the first instant of her beholding him, had made so powerful an impression on her.

During the evident preoccupation of Madame de Villefort, Monte-Cristo scrutinised the features and appearance of the boy she kept folded in her arms, lavishing on him the most tender endearments. The child was small for his age, and unnaturally pale. A mass of straight black hair, defying all attempts to train or curl it, fell over his projecting forehead, and hung down to his shoulders, giving increased vivacity to eyes already sparkling with a youthful love of mischief and fondness for every forbidden enjoyment. His mouth was large, and the lips, which had not yet regained their colour, were particularly thin; in fact, the deep and crafty look, forming the principal character of the child's face, belonged rather to a boy of twelve or fourteen years of age than to one so young. His first movement was to free himself by a violent push from the encircling arms of his mother, and to rush forwards to the casket from whence the count had taken the phial of elixir, then, without asking permission of any one, he proceeded, in all the wilfulness of a spoiled child unaccustomed to restrain either whims or caprices, to pull the corks out of all the bottles in the casket.

"Touch nothing, my little friend," cried the count, eagerly; "some of those liquids are not only dangerous to taste, but even to smell."

Madame de Villefort became very pale, and, seizing her son's arm, drew him anxiously towards her; but once satisfied of his safety, she also cast a brief but expressive glance on the casket, which was not lost upon the count. At this moment Ali entered. At sight of him, Madame de Villefort uttered an expression of pleasure, and holding the child still closer towards her, she said,—

"Edward, dearest! do you see that good man? He has shewn very great courage and resolution, for he exposed his own life to stop the horses that were running away with us, and would certainly have dashed the carriage to pieces ere long. Thank him, then, my child, in your very best manner, for had he not come to our aid, neither you nor I would have been alive to speak our thanks."

This address, however, excited no similar feeling of gratitude on the part of the child, who, instead of obeying his mother's directions, stuck out his lips and turned away his head in a disdainful and contemptuous manner, saying,—

"I don't like him—he's too ugly for me!"

The count witnessed all this with internal satisfaction, and a smile stole over his features as he thought that such a child bade fair to realise one part of his hopes; while Madame de Villefort reprimanded her son with a gentleness and moderation very far from conveying the least idea of a fault having been committed.

"This lady," said the count, speaking to Ali in the Arabic language, "is desirous that her son should thank you for saving both their lives, but the boy refuses, saying, 'You are too ugly!'"

Ali turned his intelligent countenance towards the boy, on whom he gazed without any apparent emotion, but the sort of spasmodic working of the nostrils shewed to the practised eye of Monte-Cristo how deeply the Arab was wounded by the unfeeling remark.

"Will you permit me to inquire," said Madame de Villefort, as she rose to take her leave, "whether you usually reside here?"

"No, I do not," replied Monte-Cristo; "it is a small place I have purchased quite lately. My place of abode is No. 30 Avenue des Champs Elysées; but I am delighted to see your countenance seems expressive of a perfect return to tranquillity. You have quite recovered from your fright, and are no doubt desirous of returning home. Anticipating your wishes, I have desired the same horses you came with to be put to one of my carriages, and Ali, he whom you think so very ugly," continued he, addressing the boy with a smiling air, "will have the honour of driving you home, while your coachman remains here to attend to the necessary repairs of your calèche. Directly that important business is concluded, I will have a couple of my own horses harnessed to convey it direct to Madame Danglars."

"I dare not return with those dreadful horses," said Madame de Villefort.

"You will see," replied Monte-Cristo, "that they will be as different as possible in the hands of Ali. With him they will be gentle and docile as lambs."

Ali had, indeed, given proof of this; for, approaching the animals, who had been got upon their legs with considerable difficulty, he rubbed their foreheads and nostrils with a sponge soaked in aromatic vinegar, and wiped off the sweat and foam that covered their mouths. Then, commencing a loud whistling noise, he rubbed them well all over their bodies for several minutes; and, undisturbed by the noisy crowd collected round the broken carriage, Ali quietly harnessed the pacified animals to the count's chariot, took the reins in his hands, and mounted the box, when, lo! to the utter astonishment of those who had witnessed the ungovernable spirit and maddened velocity of the same horses, he was actually compelled to apply his whip in no very gentle manner ere he could induce them to start, and even then all that could be obtained from the celebrated "dappled greys," now changed into a couple of as dull, sluggish, stupid brutes as "the most timid driver" would desire to meet with, was a slow, pottering pace, kept up with so much difficulty that Madame de Villefort was more than a couple of hours returning to her residence in the Faubourg St. Honoré.

Scarcely had the first congratulations upon her miraculous escape been gone through than she retired to her room, ostensibly for the purpose of seeking a little repose, but in reality to write the following letter to Madame Danglars,—

"Dear Hermine,—I have just had a wonderful escape from the most imminent danger, and I owe my safety to the very Count of Monte-Cristo we were talking about yesterday, but whom I little expected to see to-day. I remember how unmercifully I laughed at what I considered your eulogistic and exaggerated praises of him, but I have now ample cause to admit that your enthusiastic description of this wonderful man fell far short of his merits. But I must endeavour to render the account of my adventures somewhat more intelligible. You must know, then, my dear friend, that when I had proceeded with your horses as far as Ranelagh, they darted forwards like mad things, and galloped away at so fearful a rate that there seemed no other prospect for myself and my poor Edward but that of being dashed to pieces against the first object that impeded their progress, when a strange-looking man, an Arab or a Nubian, at least a black of some nation or other, at a signal from the count, whose domestic he is, suddenly seized and stopped the infuriated animals, even at the risk of being trampled to death himself, and certainly he must have had a most wonderful escape. The count then hastened to us, and carried myself and son into his house, where, by some skilful application, he speedily recalled my poor Edward (who was quite insensible from terror) to life. When we were sufficiently recovered, he sent us home in his own carriage. Yours will be returned to you to-morrow. I am fearful you will not be able to use your horses for some days; they seem thoroughly stupefied, as if sulky and vexed at having allowed this black servant to conquer them after all. The count, however, has commissioned me to assure you that two or three days' rest, with plenty of barley for their sole food during that time, will bring them back to their former fine condition, which means, I suppose, that they will be ready to run off with the carriage again, and play their wild pranks with as much headstrong fury as they evinced yesterday: do not let them endanger your life, dear Hermine, as they did mine; for Providence may not send a Monte-Cristo, or his Nubian servant, to preserve you from destruction, as it did me. Adieu! I cannot return you many thanks for the drive of yesterday; but after all, I ought not to blame you for the misconduct of your horses, more especially as it procured me the pleasure of an introduction to the Count of Monte-Cristo,—and certainly that illustrious individual, apart from the millions he is said to be so very anxious to dispose of, seemed to me one of those curiously interesting problems I, for one, delight in solving at any risk or danger. Nay, so bent am I on following up my acquaintance with this remarkable personage, that if all other means fail, I really believe I shall have to borrow your horses again and make another excursion to the Bois de Boulogne. My sweet Edward supported the accident with admirable courage —he did not utter a single cry, but fell lifeless into my arms, nor did a tear fall from his eyes after it was over. I doubt not you will consider these praises the result of blind maternal affection; but the delicate, fragile form of my beloved child contains a mind of no ordinary strength with the heroic firmness of a Spartan boy. Valentine sends many affectionate remembrances to your dear Eugénie—and with best love to her and yourself, I remain,

"Ever yours, truly,
"Héloïse de Villefort."

"P.S.—Do pray contrive some means for my meeting the Count of Monte-Cristo at your house. I must and will see him again. I have just made M. de Villefort promise to call on him, in order to acknowledge the signal service he has rendered our family in preserving our child, if my unworthy self goes for nothing, and I flatter myself my husband's visit will be returned by the count."

Nothing was talked of throughout the evening but the adventure at Auteuil. Albert related it to his mother, Château-Renaud recounted it at the Jockey Club, and Debray detailed it at length in the salons of the minister, even Beauchamp accorded twenty lines in his journal to the relation of the count's courage and gallantry, thereby placing him as the greatest hero of the day before the eyes of all the fair members of the aristocracy of France. Vast was the crowd of visitors and inquiring friends, who left their names at the hotel of Madame de Villefort, with the design of renewing their visit at the right moment of hearing from her lips all the interesting circumstances of this most romantic adventure. As Héloïse had stated, M. de Villefort donned his best black suit, drew on a pair of new white kid gloves, ordered the servants to attend the carriage dressed in their full livery, and forthwith drove to the hotel of the count, situated, as the reader is already informed, in the Avenue des Champs Elyseés.

CHAPTER XLVIII

IDEOLOGY

IF the Count of Monte-Cristo had lived for a very long time in Parisian society, he would have fully appreciated the value of the step which M. de Villefort had taken. Standing well at court, whether the king regnant was of the elder or younger branch, whether the government was doctrinaire, liberal, or conservative: esteemed clever by all, just as we generally esteem those clever who have never experienced a political check; hated by many, but warmly protected by others, without being really liked by anybody, M. de Villefort held a high position in the magistracy, and maintained his eminence like a Harlay or a Molé. His drawing-room, regenerated by a young wife and a daughter by his first marriage scarcely eighteen, was still one of those well-regulated Paris salons where the worship of traditional customs, and the observance of rigid etiquette, were carefully maintained. A freezing politeness, a strict fidelity to government principles, a profound contempt for theories and theorists, a deep-seated hatred of ideality,—these were the elements of private and public life displayed by M. de Villefort.

M. de Villefort was not only a magistrate, he was almost a diplomatist. His relations with the ancient court, of which he always spake with dignity and respect, made him respected by the new one, and he knew so many things, that not only was he always carefully considered, but sometimes consulted. Perhaps this would not have been so had it been possible to get rid of M. de Villefort; but, like the feudal barons who rebelled against their sovereign, he dwelt in an impregnable fortress. This fortress was his post as procureur du roi, all the advantages of which he worked out marvellously, and which he would not have resigned, but to be made deputy, and thus have converted neutrality into opposition.

Ordinarily M. de Villefort made and returned very few visits. His wife visited for him, and this was the received thing in the world where they assigned to the heavy and multifarious occupations of the magistrate what was really only a calculation of pride, an off-shoot of aristocracy, in fact the application of the axiom, *"Pretend to think well of yourself, and the world will think well of you,"* an axiom a hundred times more useful in our society than that of the Greeks, *"Know thyself,"* a knowledge, for which, in our days, we have substituted the less difficult and more advantageous science of *knowing others.*

For his friends M. de Villefort was a powerful protector; for his enemies he was a silent, but bitter enemy; for those who were neither the one nor the other, he was a statue of the law made man. Haughty air, immovable countenance, look steady and impenetrable, or else insultingly piercing and inquiring, such was the man for whom four revolutions skilfully piled one on the other had first constructed and afterwards cemented the pedestal on which his fortune was elevated.

M. de Villefort had the reputation of being the least curious and least wearisome man in France. He gave a ball every year, at which he appeared for a quarter of an hour only,—that is to say, five-and-forty minutes less than the king is visible at his balls. He was never seen at the theatres, at concerts, or in any place of public resort. Occasionally, but seldom, he played at whist, and then care was taken to select partners worthy of him—sometimes they were ambassadors, sometimes archbishops, or sometimes a prince, or a president, or some dowager duchess. Such was the man whose carriage had just now stopped before the Count of Monte-Cristo's door.

The valet-de-chambre announced M. de Villefort at the moment when the count, leaning over a large table, was tracing on a map the route from St. Petersburg to China.

The procureur du roi entered with the same grave and measured step he would have employed in entering the court of justice. He was the same man, or rather the completion of the same man, whom we have heretofore seen as *substitut* at Marseilles. Nature, following up its principles, had changed nothing for him in the course he had chalked out for himself. From slender he had become meagre; from pale, yellow; his deep-set eyes were now hollow, and gold spectacles, as they shielded his eyes seemed to make a portion of his face. All his costume was black, with the exception of his white cravat, and this funereal appearance was only broken in upon by the slight line of red riband which passed almost imperceptibly through his button-hole, and which appeared like a streak of blood traced with a pencil.

Although master of himself, Monte-Cristo scrutinised with irrepressible curiosity the magistrate, whose salute he returned, and who, distrustful by habit, and especially incredulous as to social marvels, was much more disposed to see in the noble stranger, as Monte-Cristo was already called, a *chevalier d'industrie*, who had come to try new ground, or some malefactor who had broken his prescribed limits, than a prince of the Holy See, or a sultan of the Arabian Nights.

"Sir," said Villefort, in the tone assumed by magistrates in their oratorical periods, and of which they cannot, or will not, divest themselves in society,—"sir, the signal service which you yesterday rendered to my wife and son has made it a duty in me to offer you my thanks. Allow me, therefore, to discharge this duty, and express to you all my gratitude."

And as he said this, the "eye severe" of the magistrate had lost nothing of its habitual arrogance. These words he articulated in the voice of a procureur-général, with the rigid inflexibility of neck and shoulders, which caused his flatterers to say (as we have said before) that he was the living statue of the law.

"Monsieur," replied the count, with a chilling air, "I am very happy to have been the means of preserving a son to his mother, for they say that the sentiment of maternity is the most holy of all; and the good fortune which occurred to me, monsieur, might have enabled you to dispense with a duty which, in its discharge, confers an undoubtedly great honour; for, I am aware that M. de Villefort is not lavish of the favour he bestows on me, but which, however estimable, is unequal to the satisfaction which I internally experience."

Villefort, astonished at this reply, which he by no means expected, started like a soldier who feels the blow levelled at him over the armour he wears, and a curl of his disdainful lip indicated that from that moment he noted in the tablets of his brain that the Count of Monte-Cristo was by no means a highly bred gentleman. He glanced around, in order to seize on something on which the conversation might turn, and seem to fall easily. He saw the map which Monte-Cristo had been examining when he entered, and said,—

"You seem geographically engaged, sir? It is a rich study for you who, as I learn, have seen as many lands as are delineated on this map."

"Yes, sir," replied the count, "I have sought to make on the human race, taken as a mass, what you practise every day on individuals—a physiological study. I have believed it was much easier to descend from the whole to a part than to ascend from a part to the whole. It is an algebraic axiom, which makes us proceed from a known to an unknown quantity, and not from an unknown to a known; but sit down, sir, I beg of you.

Monte-Cristo pointed to a chair, which the procureur du roi was obliged to take the trouble to move forwards himself, whilst the count merely fell back into his own, on which he had been kneeling when M. Villefort entered. Thus the count was half-way turned towards his visitor, having his back towards the window, his elbow resting on the geographical chart which afforded the conversation for the moment,—a conversation which assumed, as had done those with Danglars and Morcerf, a turn analogous to the persons, if not to the situation.

"Ah, you philosophise," replied Villefort, after a moment's silence, during which, like a wrestler who encounters a powerful opponent, he took breath; "well, sir, really, if, like you, I had nothing else to do, I should seek a more amusing occupation."

"Why, in truth, sir," was Monte-Cristo's reply, "man is but an ugly caterpillar for him who studies him through a solar microscope; but you said, I think, that I had nothing else to do. Now, really, let me ask, sir, have you?—do you believe you have anything to do? or, to speak in plain terms, do you really think that what you do deserves being called any thing?"

Villefort's astonishment redoubled at this second thrust so forcibly made by his strange adversary. It was a long time since the magistrate had heard a paradox so strong, or rather, to say the truth more exactly, it was the first time he had ever heard it. The procureur du roi exerted himself to reply.

"Sir," he responded, "you are a stranger, and I believe you say yourself that a portion of your life has been spent in Oriental countries: thus, then, you are not aware how human justice, so expeditious in barbarous countries, takes with us a prudent and well-studied course."

"Oh, yes,—yes, I do, sir; it is the *pede claudo* of the ancients. I know all that, for it is with the justice of all countries especially that I have occupied myself—it is with the criminal procedure of all nations that I have compared natural justice, and I must say, sir, that it is the law of primitive nations; that is, the law of retaliation that I have most frequently found to be according to the law of God."

"If this law were adopted, sir," said the procureur du roi, "it would greatly simplify our legal codes, and in that case the magistrates would not (as you have just observed) have much to do."

"It may, perhaps, come to this in time," observed Monte-Cristo; "you know that human inventions march from the complex to the simple, and simplicity is always perfection."

"In the meanwhile," continued the magistrate, "our codes are in full force with all their contradictory enactments derived from Gallic customs, Roman laws, and Frank usages; the knowledge of all which, you will agree, is not to be acquired without lengthened labour, and it requires a tedious study to acquire this knowledge, and when that is acquired, a strong power of brain is necessary in order to retain it."

"I agree with you entirely, sir: but all that even you know with respect to the French code, I know, not only in reference to that code, but as regards the codes of all nations—the English, Turkish, Japanese, Hindoo laws, are as familiar to me as the French laws, and thus I was right when I said to you that relatively (you know every thing is relative, Sir)—that relatively to what I have done, you have very little to do; but that relatively to all I have learned, you have yet a great deal to learn."

"But with what motive have you learned all this?" inquired Villefort, astonished.

Monte-Cristo smiled.

"Really, sir," he observed, "I see that in spite of the reputation which you have acquired as a superior man, you contemplate every thing in the material and vulgar view of society, beginning with man, and ending with man—that is to say, in the most restricted, most narrow view which it is possible for human understanding to embrace."

"Pray sir, explain yourself," said Villefort, more and more astonished, "I really do—not—understand you—perfectly."

"I say, sir, that with the eyes fixed on the social organisation of nations, you see only the springs of the machine, and lose sight of the sublime workman who makes them act: I say that you do not recognise before you and around you any but those placemen whose brevets have been signed by the minister or the king; and that the men whom God has put above those titulars, ministers, and kings, by giving them a mission to follow out, instead of a post to fill—I say that they escape your narrow, limited ken. It is thus that human weakness fails from its debilitated and imperfect organs. Tobias took the angel who restored him to light for an ordinary young man. The nations took Attila, who was doomed to destroy them, for a conqueror merely similar to other conquerors, and it was necessary for both to reveal their missions, that they might be known and acknowledged; one was compelled to say, 'I am the angel of the Lord;' and the other,

'I am the hammer of God,' in order that the Divine essence in both might be revealed."

"Then," said Villefort, more and more amazed, and really supposing he was speaking to a mystic or a mad man, "you consider yourself as one of those extraordinary beings whom you have mentioned?"

"And why not?" said Monte-Cristo, coldly.

"Your pardon, sir," replied Villefort, quite astounded, "but you will excuse me, if, when I presented myself to you, I was unaware that I should meet with a person whose knowledge and understanding so far surpass the usual knowledge and understanding of men. It is not usual with us corrupted wretches of civilisation to find gentlemen like yourself, possessors, as you are, of immense fortune—at least so it is said —and I beg you to observe that I do not inquire, I merely repeat;—it is not usual, I say, for such privileged and wealthy beings to waste their time in speculations on the state of society, in philosophical reveries, intended at best to console those whom fate has disinherited from the goods of this world."

"Really, sir," retorted the count, "have you attained the eminent situation in which you are without having admitted or even without having met with exceptions? and do you never use your eyes, which must have acquired so much finesse and certainty, to divine, at a glance, the kind of man who has come before you? Should not a magistrate be not merely the best administrator of the law, but the most crafty expounder of the chicanery of his profession, a steel probe to search hearts, a touchstone to try the gold which in each soul is mingled with more or less of alloy?"

"Sir," said Villefort, "upon my word, you overcome me. I really never heard a person speak as you do."

"Because you remain eternally encircled in a round of general conditions, and have never dared to raise your wing into those upper spheres which God has peopled with invisible or marked beings."

"And you allow then, sir, that spheres exist, and that these marked and invisible beings mingle amongst us?"

"Why should they not? Can you see the air you breathe, and yet without which you could not for a moment exist?"

"Then we do not see those beings to whom you allude?"

"Yes, we do;—you see them whenever God pleases to allow them to assume a material form: you touch them, come in contact with them, speak to them, and they reply to you."

"Ah!" said Villefort, smiling, "I confess I should like to be warned when one of these beings is in contact with me."

"You have been served as you desire, monsieur, for you have been warned just now, and I now again warn you."

"Then you yourself are one of these marked beings?"

"Yes, monsieur, I believe so; for until now, no man has found himself in a position similar to mine. The dominions of kings are limited, either by mountains or rivers, or a change of manners, or an alteration of language. My kingdom is bounded only by the world, for I am neither an Italian, nor a Frenchman, nor a Hindoo, nor an American, nor a Spaniard —I am a cosmopolite. No country can say it saw my birth. God alone knows what country will see me die. I adopt all customs, speak all languages. You believe me to be a Frenchman, for I speak French with the same facility and purity as yourself. Well, Ali, my Nubian, believes me to be an Arab; Bertuccio, my steward, takes me for a Roman; Haydée, my slave, thinks me a Greek. You may, therefore, comprehend, that being of no country, asking no protection from any government, acknowledging no man as my brother, not one of the scruples that arrest the powerful, or the obstacles which paralyse the weak, paralyse or arrest me. I have only two adversaries—I will not say two conquerors, for with perseverance I subdue even them, though they are time and distance. There is a third, and the most terrible—that is my condition as a mortal being. This alone can stop me in my onward career, and before I have attained the goal at which I aim, for all the rest I have calculated. What men call the chances of fate, namely, ruin, change, circumstances —I have anticipated them all, and if any of these should overtake me, yet they will not overwhelm me. Unless I die, I shall always be what I am, and therefore it is that I utter the things you have never heard, even from the mouths of kings—for kings have need, and other persons have fear, of you. For who is there who does not say to himself, in society as incongruously organised as ours, 'Perhaps some day I shall have to do with the procureur du roi?'"

"But can you not say that, sir? for the moment you become an inhabitant of France you are naturally subjected to the French laws."

"I know it, sir," replied Monte-Cristo; "but when I visit a country I begin to study, by all the means which are available, the men from whom I may have any thing to hope or to fear, until I know them as well, perhaps better, than they know themselves. It follows from this, that the procureur du roi, be he who he may, with whom I should have to deal, would assuredly be more embarrassed than I should."

"That is to say," replied Villefort, with hesitation, "that

human nature being weak, every man, according to your creed, has committed faults."

"Faults or crimes," responded Monte-Cristo, with a negligent air.

"And that you alone, amongst the men whom you do not recognise as your brothers—for you have said so," observed Villefort, in a tone that faltered somewhat, "you alone are perfect?"

"No, not perfect," was the count's reply; "only impenetrable, that's all. But let us leave off this strain, sir, if the tone of it is displeasing to you: I am no more disturbed by your justice than are you by my second sight."

"No! no—by no means," said Villefort, who was afraid of seeming to abandon his ground. "No; by your brilliant and almost sublime conversation you have elevated me above ordinary level; we no longer talk—we rise to dissertation. But you know how the theologians in their collegiate chairs, and philosophers in their controversies, occasionally say cruel truths; let us suppose, for the moment, that we are theologising in a social way, or even philosophically, and I will say to you, rude as it may seem, 'My brother, you sacrifice greatly to pride; you may be above others, but above you there is God.'"

"Above us all, sir," was Monte-Cristo's response, in a tone and with an emphasis so deep that Villefort involuntarily shuddered. "I have my pride for men—serpents always ready to erect themselves against every one who may pass without crushing them. But I lay aside that pride before God, Who has taken me from nothing to make me what I am."

"Then, M. le Comte, I admire you," said Villefort, who, for the first time in this strange conversation, used the aristocratical form to the unknown personage whom, until now, he had only called *monsieur*. "Yes, and I say to you, if you are really strong, really superior, really pious, or impenetrable, which you were right in saying amounts to the same thing—yet be proud, sir, that is the characteristic of predominance—yet you have unquestionably some ambition."

"I have, sir."

"And what may it be?"

"I, too, as happens to every man once in his life, have been taken by Satan into the highest mountain in the earth, and when there he shewed me all the kingdoms of the earth, and as he said before, so said he to me, 'Child of earth, what wouldst thou have to make thee adore me?' I reflected long, for a gnawing ambition had long preyed upon me, and then I replied, 'Listen,—I have always heard tell of Providence, and yet I have never seen Him, nor any thing that resembles Him, or which can make me believe that He exists. I wish to be

Providence myself, for I feel that the most beautiful, noblest, most sublime thing in the world, is to recompense and punish.' Satan bowed his head and groaned. 'You mistake,' he said; 'Providence does exist, only you have never seen him, because the child of God is as invisible as the parent. You have seen nothing that resembles Him, because He works by secret springs and moves by hidden ways. All I can do for you is to make you one of the agents of that Providence.' The bargain was concluded. I may sacrifice my soul, but what matters it?" added Monte-Cristo. "If the thing were to do again, I would again do it."

Villefort looked at Monte-Cristo with extreme amazement. "Monsieur le Comte," he inquired, "have you any relations?"

"No, sir, I am alone in the world."

"So much the worse."

"Why?" asked Monte-Cristo.

"Because then you might witness a spectacle calculated to break down your pride. You say you fear nothing but death?"

"I did not say that I feared it; I only said that that alone could check me?"

"And old age?"

"My end will be achieved before I grow old."

"And madness?"

"I have been nearly mad; and you know the axiom—*non bis in idem*. It is an axiom of criminal law, and, consequently, you understand its full application."

"Sir," continued Villefort, "there is something to fear besides death, old age, and madness. For instance, there is apoplexy—that lightning-stroke which strikes but does not destroy you, and yet after which all is ended. You are still yourself as now, and yet you are yourself no longer; you who, like Ariel, touch on the angelic, are but an inert mass, which, like Caliban, touches on the brutal; and this is called in human tongue, as I tell you, neither more nor less than apoplexy. Come, if so you will, M. le Comte, and continue this conversation at my house, any day you may be willing to see an adversary capable of understanding and anxious to refute you, and I will shew you my father, M. Noirtier de Villefort, one of the most fiery Jacobins of the French Revolution; that is to say, the most remarkable audacity, seconded by a most powerful organisation,—a man who, perhaps, has not, like yourself, seen all the kingdoms of the earth, but who has helped to overturn one of the most powerful; in fact, a man who, like you, believed himself one of the envoys—not of God, but of a Supreme Being; not of Providence, but of Fate. Well, sir, the rupture of a blood-vessel on a lobe of the brain has destroyed all this—not in a day, not in an hour—but in a second. M. Noirtier, who on the previous night was the old Jacobin, the old senator, the old Carbonaro, laughing at the guillotine, laughing at the cannon, laughing at the dagger,—M. Noirtier, playing with revolutions,—M. Noirtier, for whom France was a vast chess-board, from which pawns, rooks, knights, and queens, were to disappear, so that the king was checkmated,—M. Noirtier, so redoubted, was the next morning *poor M. Noirtier*, the helpless old man, at the tender mercies of the weakest creature in the household, that is, his grandchild, Valentine; a dumb and frozen carcase, in fact, who only lives without suffering, that time may be given to his frame to decompose without his consciousness of his decay."

"Alas, sir!" said Monte-Cristo, "this spectacle is neither strange to my eye nor my thought. I am something of a physician, and have, like my fellows, sought more than once for the soul in living and in dead matter; yet, like Providence, it has remained invisible to my eyes, although present to my heart. A hundred writers since Socrates, Seneca, St. Augustin, and Gall, have made, in verse and prose, the comparison you have made, and yet I can well understand that a father's sufferings may effect great changes in the mind of a son. I will call on you, sir, since you bid me contemplate, for the advantage of my pride, this terrible spectacle, which must spread so much sorrow throughout your house."

" It would have done so unquestionably, had not God given me so large a compensation. In presence of the old man, who is dragging his way to the tomb, are two children just entering into life—Valentine, the daughter by my first wife Mademoiselle Renée de Saint-Méran, and Edward, the boy whose life you have this day saved."

"And what is your deduction from this compensation, sir?" inquired Monte-Cristo.

"My deduction is," replied Villefort, "that my father, led away by his passions, has committed some fault unknown to human justice, but marked by the justice of God! That God, desirous in his mercy to punish but one person, has visited this justice on him alone."

Monte-Cristo, with a smile on his lips, had yet a groan at his heart, which would have made Villefort fly had he but heard it.

"Adieu, sir," said the magistrate, who had risen from his seat; "I leave you, bearing a remembrance of you—a remembrance of esteem, which I hope will not be disagreeable to you when you know me better; for I am not a man to bore my friends, as you will learn. Besides, you have made an eternal friend of Madame de Villefort."

The count bowed, and contented himself with seeing Ville-fort to the door of his cabinet, the procureur being escorted to his carriage by two footmen, who, on a signal from their master, followed him with every mark of attention. When he had gone, Monte-Cristo drew a hard breath from his oppressed bosom, and said,—

"Enough of this poison, let me now seek the antidote." Then sounding his bell, he said to Ali, who entered, "I am going to madam's chamber—have the carriage ready at one o'clock."

CHAPTER XLIX

HAYDÉE

IT will be recollected that the new, or rather old acquaintances of the Count of Monte-Cristo, residing in the Rue Meslay, were no other than Maximilian, Julie, and Emmanuel.

The very anticipations of delight to be enjoyed in his forth-coming visits—the bright, pure gleam of heavenly happiness it diffused over the almost deadly warfare in which he had voluntarily engaged, illumined his whole countenance with a look of ineffable joy and calmness, as, immediately after the departure of Villefort, his thoughts flew back to the cheering prospect before him, of tasting, at least, a brief respite from the fierce and stormy passions of his mind. Even Ali, who had hastened to obey the count's summons, went forth from his master's presence in charmed amazement at the unusual animation and pleasure depicted on features ordinarily so stern and cold; while, as though dreading to put to flight the agreeable ideas hovering over his patron's meditations, what-ever they were, the faithful Nubian walked on tiptoe towards the door, holding his breath, lest its faintest sound should dissipate his master's happy reverie.

It was the hour of noon, and Monte-Cristo had set apart one hour to be passed in the apartments of Haydée; as though his so-long-crushed spirit could not all at once admit the feeling of pure and unmixed joy, but required a gradual succession of calm and gentle emotions to prepare his mind to receive full and perfect happiness, in the same manner as ordinary natures demand to be inured by degrees to the reception of strong or violent sensations.

The young Greek, as we have already stated, occupied apartments wholly unconnected with those of the count. The rooms had been fitted up in strict accordance with the Eastern style, that is to say, the floors were covered with the richest carpets Turkey could produce; the walls hung with brocaded silk of the most magnificent designs and texture; while, around each chamber, luxurious divans were placed, with piles of soft and yielding cushions, that needed only to be arranged at the pleasure or convenience of such as sought repose.

Haydée's female establishment consisted of three French attendants, and a fourth who was, like herself, a native of the climes of Greece. The three first remained constantly in a small waiting-room, ready to obey the first sound of a small golden bell, or to receive the orders of the Romaic slave, who just knew sufficient French to be enabled to transmit her mistress's orders to the three other waiting-women, who had received most peremptory instructions from Monte-Cristo to treat Haydée with all the respect and deference they would observe to a queen.

The fair Greek herself generally passed her time in the apartment forming the extremity of the suite of rooms assigned to her. It was a species of boudoir, circular, and lighted only from the top, which consisted of pale pink glass. Haydée was reclining upon soft downy cushions, covered with blue satin spotted with silver; her head, supported by one of her exquisitely moulded arms, rested on the divan immediately behind her, while the other was employed in adjusting to her lips the coral tube of a rich nargileh, whose flexible pipe, placed amid the coolest and most fragrant essences, permitted not the perfumed vapour to ascend until fully impregnated with the rich odours of the most delicious flowers. Her attitude, though perfectly natural for an Eastern female, would have been deemed too full of coquettish straining after effect in an European. Her dress, which was that of the women of Epirus, consisted of a pair of white satin trousers, embroidered with pink roses, displaying feet so exquisitely formed and so delicately fair, that they might well have been taken for Parian marble, had not the eye been undeceived by their constantly shifting in and out of the fairy-like slippers in which they were encased; these tiny coverings were beautifully ornamented with gold and pearls, and turned up at the point; a blue and white striped vest, with long open sleeves, trimmed with silver loops and buttons of pearls. She also wore a species of bodice, which, closing only from the centre to the waist, exhibited the whole of the ivory throat and upper part of the bosom; three magnificent diamond clasps fastened it where requisite. The junction of the bodice and drawers was entirely concealed by one of those many-coloured scarfs, whose brilliant hues and rich silken fringe have rendered them so precious in the eyes of Parisian belles. A small cap of gold, embroidered with pearls, was placed with tasteful elegance on one side of the fair Greek's head; while, on the other, a natural rose, of that dark crimson almost inclining to purple, mingled its glowing colours with the luxuriant masses of her hair, which, for jetty lustre, out-rivalled the raven's wing.

The extreme beauty of the countenance, that shone forth in loveliness that mocked the vain attempts of dress to augment it, was peculiarly and purely Grecian—there were the large dark melting eyes, the finely formed nose, the coral lips, and pearly teeth, that belonged to her race and country. And to complete the whole, Haydée was in the very springtide and fulness of youthful charms—she had not yet numbered more than eighteen summers.

Upon Monte-Cristo entering the apartments of the fair girl, he summoned her Greek attendant and bade her inquire whether it would be agreeable to her mistress to receive his visit?

Haydée's only reply was to direct her servant, by a sign, to withdraw the tapestried curtain that hung before the door of her boudoir, the frame-work of the opening thus made serving as a sort of border to the graceful tableau presented by the picturesque attitude and appearance of Haydée.

As Monte-Cristo approached, she leaned upon the elbow of the arm that held the nargileh, and, extending to him her other hand, said with a smile of captivating sweetness, in the sonorous language spoken by the females of Athens and Sparta, "Why demand permission ere you enter? Are you no longer my master; or have I ceased to be your slave?"

Monte-Cristo returned her smile. "Haydée," said he, "you well know."

"Why do you address me so coldly—so distantly?" asked the fair Greek. "Have I by any means displeased you? Oh, if so, punish me as you will; but do not—do not speak to me in tones and manner so formal and constrained!"

"Listen to me, Haydée," replied the count. "I was about to remind you of a circumstance you are perfectly acquainted with; namely, that we are now in France, and that you are consequently free!"

"Free!" repeated the fair girl. "Of what use would freedom be to me?"

"It would enable you to quit me!"

"Quit you! Wherefore should I do so?"

"That is not for me to say; but we are now about to mix in society—to visit and be visited."

"I desire to see no one but yourself."

"Nay, but hear me, Haydée. You cannot remain in seclusion in the midst of this gay capital; and should you see one whom you could prefer, think not I would be so selfish or unjust as to——"

"No, no!" answered Haydée, with energetic warmth,

"that can never be. No man could appear charming in my eyes but yourself None save yourself and my father have ever possessed my affection; nor will it be bestowed upon any other."

"My poor child!" replied Monte-Cristo, "that is merely because your father and myself are the only men with whom you have ever conversed."

"And what care I for all others in the world? My father called me *his joy*—you style me your *love*,—and both of you bestowed on me the endearing appellation of *your child!*"

"Do you remember your father, Haydée?"

The young Greek smiled. "He is here, and here," said she, touching her eyes and her heart.

"And where am I?" inquired Monte-Cristo, laughingly.

"You?" cried she, with tones of thrilling tenderness, "you are every where."

Monte-Cristo took the delicate hand of the young girl in his, and was about to raise it to his lips, when the simple child of nature hastily withdrew it, and presented her fair cheek instead.

"You now understand, Haydée," said the count, "that from this moment you are absolutely free; that here you exercise unlimited sway, and are at liberty to lay aside or continue the costume of your country, as it may suit your inclination. Within this mansion you are absolute mistress of your actions, and may go abroad or remain in your apartments, as may seem most agreeable to you. A carriage waits your orders, and Ali and Myrta will accompany you whithersoever you desire to go. There is but one favour I would entreat of you."

"Oh, speak!"

"Preserve most carefully the secret of your birth. Make no allusion to the past; nor upon any occasion be induced to pronounce the names of your illustrious father or ill-fated mother!"

"I have already told my lord, it is not my intention to hold converse with any one save himself."

"It is possible, Haydée, that so perfect a seclusion, though conformable with the habits and customs of the East, may not be practicable in Paris. Endeavour, then, to accustom yourself to our manner of living in these northern climes, as you did to those of Rome, Florence, Milan, and Madrid: it may be useful to you one of these days, whether you remain here or return to the East."

The fair girl raised her tearful eyes towards Monte-Cristo, as she said, with touching earnestness, "My lord would mean

C.M.—R

whether *we* return to the East or continue here, would he not?"

"My child," returned Monte-Cristo, "you know full well, that whenever we part, it will be by no fault or wish of mine: the tree forsakes not the blossom that embellishes it—it is the flower that falls from the tree on which it grew."

"My lord," replied Haydée, "never will I quit you, for sure I am I could not exist if banished your presence; alas! what would life be worth then?"

"My poor girl, you forget that ten years will effect an essentially different change in both of us; to you that space of time will bring but the perfection of womanly graces, while it will wrinkle my brows and change my hair to grey."

"My father had numbered sixty years, and the snows of age were on his head, but I admired and loved him far better than all the gay, handsome youths I saw about his court."

"Then tell me, Haydée, do you believe you shall be able to accustom yourself to our present mode of life?"

"Shall I see you?"

"Every day."

"Then what does my lord apprehend for me?"

"I fear your growing weary."

"Nay, my lord! that cannot be. In the morning I shall rejoice in the prospect of your coming, and in the evening dwell with delight on the happiness I have enjoyed in your presence; then, too, when alone, I can call forth mighty pictures of the past, see vast horizons bounded only by the towering mountains of Pindus and Olympus. Oh, believe me, that when three great passions, such as sorrow, love, and gratitude, fill the heart, *ennui* can find no place."

"You are a worthy daughter of Epirus, Haydée, and your charming and poetical ideas prove well your descent from that race of goddesses who claim your country as their birth-place; depend on my care, to see that your youth is not blighted, or suffered to pass away in ungenial solitude; and of this be well assured, that if you love me as a father, I, in my turn, feel for you all the affection of the fondest parent."

"Let not my lord be deceived, the love I bear you resembles in no degree my feelings towards my father; I survived *his* death; but were any evil to befall you, the moment in which I learned the fatal tidings would be the last of my life."

The count, with a look of indescribable tenderness, extended his hand to the animated speaker, who carried it reverentially and affectionately to her lips. Monte-Cristo, thus soothed and calmed into a befitting state of mind to pay his visit to the Morrels, departed, murmuring as he went these lines of Pindar, "Youth is a flower, of which love is the fruit; happy is he, who after having watched its silent growth, is permitted to gather and call it his own."

The carriage was prepared according to orders, and stepping lightly into it, the count drove off at his usual rapid pace.

CHAPTER L

THE MORREL FAMILY

In a very few minutes the count reached No. 7 in the Rue Meslay. The house was of white stone, and in a small court before it, were two small beds full of beautiful flowers. In the concierge that opened the gate the count recognised Coclès; but as he had but one eye, and that eye had considerably weakened in the course of nine years, Coclès did not so readily recognise the count.

The carriages that drove up to the door were compelled to turn, to avoid a fountain that played in a basin of rockwork, in which sported a quantity of gold and silver fishes, an ornament that had excited the jealousy of the whole quarter, and had gained for the house the appellation of "*le Petit Versailles.*"

The house, raised above the kitchens and cellars, had, besides the ground-floor, two stories and attics. The whole of the property, consisting of an immense workshop, two pavilions at the bottom of the garden, and the garden itself, had been purchased by Emmanuel, who had seen at a glance that he could make a profitable speculation of it. He had reserved the house and half the garden, and building a wall between the garden and the workshops, had let them upon lease with the pavilions at the bottom of the garden. So that for a trifling sum he was as well lodged, and as perfectly shut out from observation, as the inhabitant of the finest hotel in the Faubourg St. Germain.

The breakfast-room was of oak; the salon of mahogany and blue velvet; the bed-room of citron-wood and green damask; there was a study for Emmanuel who never studied, and a music-room for Julie who never played. The whole of the second story was set apart for Maximilian; it was precisely the same as his sister's apartments, except that the breakfast-parlour was changed into a billiard-room, where he received his friends. He was superintending the dressing of his horse and smoking his cigar at the entrance to the garden when the count's carriage stopped at the door.

Coclès opened the gate, and Baptistin, springing from the box, inquired whether Monsieur and Madame Herbault and

Monsieur Maximilian Morrel would see M. le Comte de Monte-Cristo.

"M. le Comte de Monte-Cristo?" cried Morrel, throwing away his cigar and hastening to the carriage, "I should think we would see him. Ah, a thousand thanks, M. le Comte, for not having forgotten your promise."

And the young officer shook the count's hand so warmly that the latter could not be mistaken as to the sincerity of his joy, and he saw that he had been expected with impatience, and was received with pleasure.

"Come, come!" said Maximilian; "I will serve as your guide; such a man as you are ought not to be introduced by a servant. My sister is in the garden, plucking the dead roses; my brother reading his two papers, *la Presse* and *les Débats*, within five steps of her, for wherever you see Madame Herbault, you have only to look within a circle of four yards and you will find M. Emmanuel, and 'reciprocally,' as they say at the École Polytechnique."

At the sound of their steps, a young woman of twenty to five and twenty, dressed in a silk robe de chambre, and busily engaged plucking the dead leaves off a splendid rose-tree, raised her head.

This female was Julie, who had become, as the clerk of the house of Thomson and French had predicted, Madame Emmanuel Herbault.

She uttered a cry of surprise at the sight of a stranger, and Maximilian began to laugh.

"Don't disturb yourself, Julie," said he.

"M. le Comte has only been two or three days in Paris, but he already knows what a woman of fashion of the Marais is, and if he does not, you will shew him."

"Ah, monsieur!" returned Julie; "it is treason in my brother to bring you thus, but he never has any regard for his poor sister. Penelon! Penelon!"

An old man who was digging busily at one of the beds of roses stuck his spade in the earth and approached cap in hand, and striving to conceal a quid of tobacco he had just thrust into his cheek. A few locks of grey, mingled with his hair which was still thick and matted, whilst his bronzed features and determined glance announced the old sailor who had braved the heat of the equator and the storms of the tropics.

"I think you hailed me, Mademoiselle Julie?" said he.

Penelon had still preserved the habit of calling his master's daughter "Mademoiselle Julie," and had never been able to change the name to Madame Herbault.

"Penelon," replied Julie, "go and inform M. Emmanuel

of this gentleman's visit, and Maximilian will conduct him to the salon."

Then turning to Monte-Cristo,—

"I hope you will permit me to leave you for a few minutes," continued she, and without awaiting any reply, disappeared behind a clump of trees, and entered the house by a lateral alley.

"I am sorry to see," observed Monte-Cristo to Morrel, "that I cause no small disturbance in your house."

"Look there," said Maximilian, laughing; "there is her husband changing his jacket for a coat. I assure you you are well known in the Rue Meslay."

"Your family appears to me a very happy one!" said the count, as if speaking to himself.

"Oh, yes, I assure you, M. le Comte, they want nothing that can render them happy; they are young and cheerful, they are tenderly attached to each other, and with twenty-five thousand francs a-year, they fancy themselves as rich as Rothschild."

"Five and twenty thousand francs is not a large sum, however," replied Monte-Cristo, with a tone so sweet and gentle that it went to Maximilian's heart like the voice of a father; "but they will not be content with that: your brother-in-law is a barrister? a doctor?"

"He was a merchant, M. le Comte, and had succeeded to the business of my poor father. M. Morrel, at his death left 500,000 francs (20,000*l*.), which were divided between my sister and myself, for we were his only children. Her husband, who, when he married her, had no other patrimony than his noble probity, his first-rate ability, and his spotless reputation, wished to possess as much as his wife. He laboured and toiled until he had amassed 250,000 francs; six years sufficed to achieve this object. Oh, I assure you, M. le Comte, it was a touching spectacle to see these young creatures destined by their talents for higher stations toiling together, and who unwilling to change any of the customs of their paternal house, took six years to accomplish that which innovators would have effected in two or three. Marseilles resounded with their well-earned praises. At last, one day Emmanuel came to his wife, who had just finished making up the accounts.

"'Julie,' said he to her, 'Coclès has just given me the last rouleau of a hundred francs; that completes the 250,000 francs we had fixed as the limits of our gains. Can you content yourself with the small fortune which we shall possess for the future? Listen to me. Our house transacts business to the amount of a million a-year, from which we derive an income of 40,000 francs. We can dispose of the business, if we please, in an hour, for I have received a letter from M. Delaunay, in which he offers to purchase the good-will of the house, to unite with his own, for 300,000 francs. Advise me what I had better do.'

" 'Emmanuel,' returned my sister, 'the house of Morrel can only be carried on by a Morrel. Is it not worth 300,000 francs to save our father's name from the chances of evil fortune and failure?'

" 'I thought so,' replied Emmanuel; 'but I wished to have your advice.'

" 'This is my counsel:—Our accounts are made up and our bills paid; all we have to do is to stop the issue of any more, and close our office.'

"This was done instantly. It was three o'clock; at a quarter past, a merchant presented himself to insure two ships; it was a clear profit of 15,000 francs.

" 'Monsieur,' said Emmanuel, 'have the goodness to address yourself to M. Delaunay. We have quitted business.'

" 'How long?' inquired the astonished merchant.

" 'A quarter of an hour,' was the reply.

"And this is the reason, monsieur," continued Maximilian, "of my sister and brother-in-law having only 25,000 francs a-year."

Maximilian had scarcely finished his story, during which the count's heart had seemed ready to burst, when Emmanuel entered, clad in a hat and coat. He saluted the count with the air of a man who is aware of the rank of his guest; then, after having led Monte-Cristo round the little garden, he returned to the house.

A large vase of Japan porcelain filled with flowers, that impregnated the air with their perfume, stood in the salon. Julie, suitably dressed and her hair arranged (she had accomplished this feat in less than ten minutes), received the count on his entrance.

The songs of the birds were heard in an aviary hard by:— the branches of false ebony-trees and rose acacias forming the border of the blue velvet curtains. Everything in this charming retreat, from the warble of the birds to the smile of the mistress, breathed tranquillity and repose.

The count had felt, from the moment he entered the house, the influence of this happiness, and he remained silent and pensive, forgetting that he was expected to recommence the conversation, which had ceased after the first salutations had been exchanged. He perceived the pause, and, by a violent effort, tearing himself from his pleasing reverie,—

"Madame," said he at length, " I pray you to excuse my emotion, which must astonish you who are only accustomed to the happiness I meet here; but satisfaction is so new a sight to me, that I could never be weary of looking at yourself and your husband."

"We are very happy, monsieur," replied Julie; "but we have also known unhappiness, and few have ever undergone more bitter sufferings than ourselves."

The count's features displayed an expression of the most intense curiosity.

"Oh, all this is a family history, as Château-Renaud told you the other day," observed Maximilian. "This humble picture would have but little interest for you, accustomed as you are to behold the pleasures and the misfortunes of the wealthy and illustrious; but such as we are, we have experienced bitter sorrows."

"And God has poured balm into your wounds as He does to all those who are in affliction?" said Monte-Cristo, inquiringly.

"Yes, M. le Comte," returned Julie, "we may indeed say He has for He has done for us what He grants only to His chosen; He sent us one of His angels."

The count's cheeks became scarlet, and he coughed, in order to have an excuse for putting his handkerchief to his mouth.

"Those born to wealth, and who have the means of gratifying every wish," said Emmanuel, "know not what is the real happiness of life; just as those who have been tossed on the stormy waters of the ocean on a few frail planks can alone estimate the value of a clear and serene sky."

Monte-Cristo rose, and, without making any answer (for the tremulousness of his voice would have betrayed his emotion), walked up and down the apartment with a slow step.

"Our magnificence makes you smile, M. le Comte?" said Maximilian, who had followed him with his eyes.

"No, no," returned Monte-Cristo, pale as death, pressing one hand on his heart to still its throbbings, whilst with the other he pointed to a crystal cover, beneath which a silken purse lay on a black velvet cushion, "I was wondering what could be the use of this purse, which contains a paper at one end and at the other a large diamond."

"M. le Comte," replied Maximilian, with an air of gravity, "those are our most precious family treasures."

"The stone seems very brilliant," answered the count.

"Oh, my brother does not allude to its value, although it has been estimated at 100,000 francs (4,000*l.*); he means, that the articles contained in this purse are the relics of the angel I spoke of just now."

"This I do not comprehend; and yet I may not ask for an explanation, madam," replied Monte-Cristo, bowing. "Pardon me, I had no intention of committing an indiscretion."

"Indiscretion!—oh, you make us happy by giving us an occasion of expatiating on this subject. Did we intend to conceal the noble action this purse commemorates, we should not expose it thus. Oh! would we could relate it every where, and to every one; so that the emotion of our unknown benefactor might reveal his presence."

"Ah! really," said Monte-Cristo, in a half-stifled voice.

"Monsieur," returned Maximilian, raising the glass cover and respectfully kissing the silken purse, "this has touched the hand of a man who saved my father from suicide. us from ruin, and our name from shame and disgrace,—a man by whose matchless benevolence we, poor children, doomed to want and wretchedness, can at present hear every one envying our happy lot. This letter,"—(as he spoke. Maximilian drew a letter from the purse and gave it to the count)—"this letter was written by him the day that my father had taken a desperate resolution; and this diamond was given by the generous unknown to my sister as her dowry."

Monte-Cristo opened the letter, and read it with an indescribable feeling of delight. It was the letter written (as our readers know) to Julie, and signed "Sinbad the Sailor."

"Unknown, you say, is the man who rendered you this service—unknown to you?"

"Yes, we have never had the happiness of pressing his hand," continued Maximilian. "We have supplicated Heaven in vain to grant us this favour, but all the affair has had a mysterious direction we cannot comprehend; all has been guided by a hand invisible, but powerful as that of an enchanter."

"Oh," cried Julie, "I have not lost all hope of some day kissing that hand, as I now kiss the purse which he has touched. Four years ago, Penelon was at Trieste,—Penelon, M. le Comte. is the old sailor you saw in the garden, and who from quartermaster has become gardener,—Penelon, when he was at Trieste, saw on the quay an Englishman, who was on the point of embarking on board a yacht; and he recognised him as the person who called on my father the 5th of June, 1829, and who wrote me this letter the 5th of September. He felt quite convinced of his identity, but he did not venture to address him."

"An Englishman!" said Monte-Cristo, who grew uneasy at the attention with which Julie looked at him "An Englishman, you say?"

C.M.—R*

"Yes," replied Maximilian, "an Englishman, who represented himself as the confidential clerk of the house of Thomson and French at Rome. It was this that made me start when you said the other day, at M. de Morcerf's, that Messrs. Thomson and French were your bankers. That happened, as I told you, in 1829. For God's sake, tell me, did you know this Englishman?"

"But you tell me also, that the house of Thomson and French have constantly denied having rendered you this service?"

"Yes."

"Then is it not probable that this Englishman may be some one who, grateful for a kindness your father had shewn him, and which he himself had forgotten, has taken this method of requiting the obligation?"

"Every thing is possible on such an occasion, even a miracle."

"What was his name?" asked Monte-Cristo.

"He gave no other name," answered Julie, looking earnestly at the count, "than that at the end of his letter—'Sinbad the Sailor.'"

"Which is evidently not his real name, but a fictitious one."

Then, noticing that Julie was struck with the sound of his voice,—

"Tell me," continued he, "was he not about my height, perhaps a little taller; his chin imprisoned, to use the word, in a high cravat; his coat closely buttoned up, and constantly taking out his pencil?"

"Oh, do you then know him?" cried Julie, whose eyes sparkled with joy.

"No," returned Monte-Cristo, "I only guessed. I knew a Lord Wilmore, who was constantly doing actions of this kind."

"Without revealing himself?"

"He was an eccentric being, and did not believe in the existence of gratitude."

"Oh Heaven!" exclaimed Julie, clasping her hands. "In what did he believe, then?"

"He did not credit it at the period when I knew him," said Monte-Cristo, touched to the heart by the accent of Julie's voice: "but, perhaps, since then he has had proofs that gratitude does exist."

"And do you know this gentleman, monsieur?" inquired Emmanuel.

"Oh, if you do know him," cried Julie, "can you tell us where he is—where we can find him? Maximilian—Emmanuel —if we do but discover him, he must believe in the gratitude of the heart!"

Monte-Cristo felt tears start into his eyes, and he again walked hastily up and down the room.

"In the name of Heaven!" said Maximilian, "if you know any thing of him, tell us what it is."

"Alas!" replied Monte-Cristo, striving to repress his emotion, "if Lord Wilmore was your unknown benefactor, I fear you will never again see him. I parted from him, two years ago, at Palermo, and he was then on the point of setting out for the most remote regions; so that I fear he will never return."

"Oh, monsieur, this is cruel of you," said Julie, much affected; and the young lady's eyes swam with tears.

"Madame," replied Monte-Cristo, gravely, and gazing earnestly on the two liquid pearls that trickled down Julie's cheeks, "had Lord Wilmore seen what I now see, he would become attached to life, for the tears you shed would reconcile him to mankind;" and he held out his hand to Julie, who gave him hers, carried away by the look and accent of the count.

"But," continued she, "Lord Wilmore had a family or friends, he must have known some one, can we not——"

"Oh, it is useless to inquire," returned the count; "he was not the man you seek for, he was my friend; he had no secrets from me, and he would have confided this also to me."

"And he told you nothing?"

"Not a word."

"And yet you instantly named him."

"Ah, in such a case one supposes——"

"Sister, sister," said Maximilian, coming to the count's aid, "monsieur is quite right. Recollect what our excellent father so often told us, 'It was no Englishman that thus saved us.'"

Monte-Cristo started.

"What did your father tell you, M. Morrel?" said he eagerly.

"My father thought that this action had been miraculously performed,—he believed that a benefactor had arisen from the grave to serve us. Oh, it was a touching superstition, monsieur, and although I did not myself believe it, I would not for the world have destroyed my father's faith in it. How often did he muse over it and pronounce the name of a dear friend,—a friend lost to him for ever; and on his death-bed, when the near approach of eternity seemed to have illumined his mind with supernatural light, this thought which had until then been but a doubt became a conviction, and his last words were, 'Maximilian, it was Edmond Dantès!'"

At these words the count's paleness which had for some time been increasing, became alarming; he could not speak, he looked at his watch like a man who has forgotten the time; said a few hurried words to Madame Herbault, and pressing the hands of Emmanuel and Maximilian,——

"Madame," said he, "I trust you will allow me to visit you from time to time; I value your friendship, and feel grateful to you for your welcome, for this is the first time for many years that I have thus yielded to my feelings;" and he hastily quitted the apartment.

"This Count de Monte-Cristo is a singular man," said Emmanuel.

"Yes," answered Maximilian; "but I feel sure he has an excellent heart, and that he likes us."

"His voice went to my heart," observed Julie; "and two or three times I fancied I had heard it before."

CHAPTER LI

ABOUT the centre of the Faubourg Saint-Honoré, and at the back of one of the most distinguished-looking mansions in this rich neighbourhood, where the various hotels vie with each other for elegance of design and magnificence of construction, extended a large garden whose widely-spreading chestnut-trees raised their heads above the walls high and solid as those of a rampart, scattering, each spring, a shower of delicate pink and white blossoms into the large stone vases placed at equal distances upon the two square pilasters, supporting an iron gate, curiously wrought, after the style and manner of the reign of Louis XIV. This noble entrance, however, spite of its striking appearance and the graceful effect of the geraniums planted in the two vases, as they waved their variegated leaves in the wind, and charmed the eye with their scarlet bloom, had fallen into utter disuse, from the period when the proprietors of the hotel (and many years had elapsed since then) had confined themselves to the possession of the hotel with its thickly-planted court-yard, opening into the Faubourg Saint-Honoré, and the garden shut in by this gate which formerly communicated with a fine kitchen-garden of about an acre in extent. But the demon of speculation having drawn a line, or in other words projected a street, at the extremity of this kitchen-garden, and even before the foundations of the said street were dug, its name being duly affixed upon an iron plate at the corner of the situation chosen, it occurred to the then possessor of the hotel we are describing, that a handsome sum might be obtained for the ground now devoted to fruits and vegetables, for the purpose of adding it to the projected street intended to form a great branch of communication with the Faubourg Saint-Honoré itself, one of the most important thoroughfares in the city of Paris.

In matters of speculation, however, though "*man* proposes," yet *money* "disposes." From some such difficulty the newly-named street died almost in birth, and the purchaser of the "kitchen-garden," having paid a high price for it, and being quite unable to find any one willing to take his bargain off his hands without a considerable loss, yet still clinging to the belief that at some future day he should obtain a sum for it that would repay him, not only for his past outlay, but also the interest upon the capital locked up in his new acquisition, contented himself with letting the ground temporarily to some market-gardeners at a yearly rent of 500 francs.

Thus, then, as already stated, the iron gate leading into the kitchen-garden had been closed up and left to the rust, which bade fair to destroy its hinges ere long, while, to prevent the ignoble glances of the diggers and delvers of the ground from presuming to sully the aristocratical enclosure belonging to the hotel, the gate in question had been boarded up to a height of six feet. True, the planks were not so closely adjusted but that a hasty peep might be obtained between their interstices; but the strict decorum and rigid propriety of the inhabitants of the hotel left no grounds for apprehending that advantage would be taken of that circumstance.

Horticulture seemed, however, to have been abandoned in the deserted kitchen-garden, and where the most choice and delicate of fruits and vegetables once reared their heads, a scanty crop of lucerne alone bore evidence of its being deemed worthy of cultivation. A small, low door gave egress from the walled space we have been describing into the projected street, the ground having been abandoned as unproductive by its various renters, and had now fallen so completely in general estimation as to return not even a fraction of the poor ten shillings per cent. it had originally paid.

Towards the hotel the chestnut-trees we have before mentioned rose high above the wall, without in any way affecting the growth of other luxuriant shrubs and flowers that eagerly pressed forward to fill up the vacant spaces, as though asserting their right to enjoy the boon of light, and air also. At one corner where the foliage became so thick as almost to shut out day, a large stone bench and sundry rustic seats indicated that this sheltered spot was either in general favour or particular use by some inhabitant of the hotel, which was faintly discernible through the dense mass of verdure that partially concealed it, though situated but a hundred paces off.

Whoever had selected this retired portion of the grounds as the boundary of their walks or scene of their meditative musings, was abundantly justified in their choice by the absence of all glare, the cool, refreshing shade, the screen it

afforded from the scorching rays of the sun that found no
entrance there even during the burning days of hottest
summer, the incessant and melodious warbling of birds and the
entire removal from either the noise of the street or the bustle
of the hotel.

On the evening of one of the warmest days spring had yet
bestowed on the inhabitants of Paris might be seen, negligently
thrown upon the stone bench, a book, a parasol, and a work-
basket, from which hung a partly-embroidered cambric handkerchief, while, at a little distance from these articles, was a
young girl, standing close to the iron gate, endeavouring to
discern something on the other side by means of the openings
in the planks, whilst the earnestness of her attitude and the
fixed gaze with which she seemed to seek the object of her
wishes, proved how much her feelings were interested in the
matter.

At that instant the little side-door leading from the
waste ground to the street was noiselessly opened, and a
tall, powerful, young man, dressed in a common grey blouse
and velvet cap, but whose carefully-arranged hair, beard,
and moustaches, all of the richest and glossiest black, but
ill accorded with his plebeian attire, and after casting a
rapid glance around him, in order to assure himself he was
unobserved, entered by this door, and carefully closing and
securing it after him, proceeded with a hurried step towards
the iron gate.

At the sight of him she expected, though probably not
under such a costume, the girl we have before mentioned
started in terror, and was about to make a hasty retreat.
But the eye of love had already seen, even through the narrow
chinks of the wooden palisades, the movement of the white
robe, and observed the fluttering of the blue sash fastened
around the slender waist of his fair neighbour. Pressing
his lips close to the envious planks that prevented his
further progress, he exclaimed, "Fear nothing, Valentine—
it is I!"

Again the timid girl found courage to return to the gate,
saying as she did so, "And wherefore come you so late to-day?
It is almost the dinner hour, and I have been compelled to
exercise my utmost skill to get rid of the incessant watchfulness
of my mother-in-law, as well as the espionage of my maid, who,
no doubt, is employed to report all I do and say. Nor has it
cost me a little trouble to free myself from the troublesome
society of my brother, under pretence of coming hither to
work undisturbed at my embroidery, which, by the way, I
am in no hurry to finish. So pray excuse yourself as well
as you can for having made me wait, and, after that, tell me

why I see you in so singular a dress, that at first I did not recognise you."

"Dearest Valentine!" said the young man, "the difference between our respective stations makes me fear to offend you by speaking of my love, but yet I cannot find myself in your presence without longing to pour forth my soul and to tell you how fondly I adore you. If it be but to carry away with me the recollection of such sweet moments, I could even bless—thank you for chiding me, for it leaves me a gleam of hope, that if not expecting me (and that indeed would be worse than vanity of me to suppose), at least I was in your thoughts. You asked me the cause of my being late, as also why I come thus disguised. I will candidly explain the reason of both, and I trust to your goodness to pardon me. But first, let me tell you I have chosen a trade."

"A trade? Oh, Maximilian, how can you jest at a time when we have such deep cause for uneasiness?"

"Heaven keep me from jesting with that which is far dearer to me than life itself! But listen to me, Valentine, and I will tell you all about it. Tired out with ranging fields and scaling walls, and seriously alarmed at the idea suggested by yourself, that if caught hovering about here your father would very likely have me sent to prison as a thief, a sort of thing not very desirable for an officer in the French army, whose continual presence in a place where no warlike projects could be supposed to account for it might well create surprise; so from a captain of Spahis I have become a gardener, and, consequently, adopted the costume of my calling."

"What excessive nonsense you talk, Maximilian!"

"Nonsense! Pray do not call what I consider the wisest action of my life by such a name. Consider, by becoming a gardener I effectually screen our meetings from all suspicion or danger."

"I beseech of you, Maximilian, to cease trifling, and tell me what you really mean."

"Simply, that having ascertained that the piece of ground on which I stand was to let, I made application for it, was readily accepted by the proprietor, and am now master of this fine crop of lucerne! Think of that, Valentine! There is nothing now to prevent my building myself a little hut on my plantation, and residing not twenty yards from you. Only imagine what happiness that would afford me. I can scarcely contain myself at the bare idea. Such felicity seems above all price—as a thing impossible and unattainable. But would you believe that I purchase all this delight, joy, and happiness, for which I would cheerfully have surrendered ten years of my life, at the small cost of 500 francs per annum, paid quarterly! Henceforth we have nothing to fear. I am on my own ground, and have an undoubted right to place a ladder against the wall, and to look over when I please, without having any apprehensions of being taken off by the police as a suspicious character. I may also enjoy the precious privilege of assuring you of my fond, faithful, and unalterable affection, whenever you visit your favourite bower; unless, indeed, it offends your pride to listen to professions of love from the lips of a poor working man, clad in a blouse and cap."

A faint cry of mingled pleasure and surprise escaped from the lips of Valentine, who almost instantly said, in a saddened tone, as though some envious cloud darkened the joy which illumined her heart,——

"Alas! No, Maximilian, this must not be for many reasons! We should presume too much on our own strength, and like others, perhaps, be led astray by our blind confidence in each other's prudence."

"How can you for an instant entertain so unworthy a thought, dear Valentine? Have I not, from the first blessed hour of our acquaintance, schooled all my words and actions to your sentiments and ideas? And you have, I am sure, the fullest confidence in my honour. When you spoke to me of your experiencing a vague and indefinite sense of coming danger, I placed myself blindly and devotedly at your service, asking no other reward than the pleasure of being useful to you; and have I ever since, by word or look, given you cause of regret for having selected me from the numbers that would willingly have sacrificed their lives for you? You told me, my dear Valentine, that you were engaged to M. d'Epinay, and that your father was resolved upon completing the match, and that from his will there was no appeal, as M. de Villefort was never known to change a determination once formed. I kept in the background as you wished; waiting not the decision of your heart or my own, but hoping Providence would graciously interpose in our behalf and order events in our favour. But what cared I for delays or difficulties so long as my sweet Valentine confessed she loved me, and accepted my fervent vows of unfailing constancy? Blessed avowal! the very recollection of which can at all times raise me even from despair itself. To hear you repeat those enrapturing words from time to time is all I ask, and to obtain that privilege I would cheerfully endure even double my present disquietudes."

"Ah, Maximilian! that is the very thing that makes you so bold, and which renders me at once so happy and unhappy, that I frequently ask myself whether it is better for me to endure the harshness of my mother-in-law, and her blind preference for her own child, or to be, as I now am, insensible to any pleasure save such as I find in these our meetings, so fraught with danger to both."

"I will not admit that word," returned the young man; "it is at once cruel and unjust; is it possible to find a more submissive slave than myself? You have permitted me to converse with you from time to time, Valentine, but forbidden my ever following you in your walks or elsewhere—have I not obeyed? And since I found means to enter this enclosure to exchange a few words with you through this door—to be close to you without being enabled to obtain a view of your dear features, I have even solicited to touch the tip of your glove through the small openings of the palisades, think you that at my age, and with my strength, this wall that now parts us would keep me from your side one instant were it not that my respect for your wishes presents an impassable barrier? Never has a complaint or a murmur of your rigour escaped me. I have been bound by my promises as rigidly as any knight of olden times. Come, come, dearest Valentine, confess that what I say is true, lest I be tempted to call you unjust."

"It is, indeed, most true!" said Valentine, as she passed the end of her slender fingers through a small opening in the planks, thus permitting her lover to press his lips to the taper finger that almost instantly disappeared; "and you are a true and faithful friend, but still you acted from motives of self-interest, my dear Maximilian, for you well knew that from the moment in which you had manifested an opposite spirit all would have ended between us. You promised to bestow on me the friendly affection of a brother. I who have no friend but yourself upon earth, who am neglected and forgotten by my father, harassed and persecuted by my mother-in-law, and left to the sole companionship of a paralysed and speechless old man, whose withered hand can no longer press mine, and whose eye alone converses with me, while doubtless, however fixed, chilled his frame, there still lingers in his heart the warmest tenderness for his poor grandchild. Oh, how bitter a fate is mine to serve either as a victim or an enemy to all who are stronger than myself, while my only friend and supporter is but a living corpse! Indeed, indeed, Maximilian, I am very miserable, and you are right to love me for myself alone."

"Dear Valentine!" replied the young man, deeply affected, "I will not say you are all I love in the world, for I dearly prize my sister and brother-in-law, but my affection for them is calm and tranquil, in no manner resembling that I feel for you. At the mere thoughts of you my heart beats more quickly, my blood flows with increased rapidity through my veins, and my breast heaves with tumultuous emotions; but I solemnly promise you to restrain all this ardour, this fervour and intensity of feeling, until you yourself shall require me to render them available in serving or assisting you.   M. Franz is not expected to return home for a year to come, I am told; in that time many favourable and unforeseen chances may befriend us.   Let us then hope for the best,—hope is so sweet a comforter!   Meanwhile, Valentine, while reproaching me with selfishness, think a little what you have been to me—the beautiful but cold resemblance of a marble Venus.   What promise of future reward have you made me for all the submission and obedience I have evinced?—none whatever! What granted me?—scarcely more!   You tell me of M. Franz d'Epinay, your betrothed lover, and you shrink from the idea of being his wife; but tell me, Valentine, is there no other sorrow in your heart?   You see me devoted to you body and soul, my life and each warm drop that circles round my heart are consecrated to your service; you know full well that my existence is bound up in yours, that were I to lose you I would not outlive the hour of such crushing misery; yet you speak with calmness of the prospect of your being the wife of another!   Oh, Valentine! were I in your place, and did I feel conscious, as you do, of being worshipped, adored, with such a love as mine, a hundred times at least should I have passed my hand between these iron bars, and said to poor Maximilian, 'Take this hand, dearest Maximilian, and believe that, living or dead, I am yours,—yours only, and for ever!'"

The poor girl made no reply, but her lover could plainly hear her sobs and tears.

A rapid change took place in the young man's feelings—

"Dearest, dearest Valentine!" exclaimed he; "forgive me if I have offended you, and forget the words I spoke if they have unwittingly caused you pain."

"No, Maximilian, I am not offended," answered she; "but do you not see what a poor, helpless being I am, almost a stranger and an outcast in my father's house, where even he is seldom seen; whose will has been thwarted, and spirits broken, from the age of ten years beneath the iron rod so sternly exercised over me; oppressed, mortified, and persecuted, day by day, hour by hour, minute by minute; no person has cared for, or even observed my sufferings, nor have I ever breathed one word on the subject, save to yourself. Outwardly, and in the eyes of the world, I am surrounded by kindness and affection, but the reverse is the case. The general remark is, 'Oh, it cannot be expected that one of so stern a character as M. Villefort could lavish the tenderness some fathers do on their daughters! What, though she has lost her own mother at a tender age, she has had the happiness to find a second mother in Madame de Villefort.' The world, however, is mistaken; my father abandons me from utter indifference, while my mother-in-law detests me with a hatred so much the more terrible as it is veiled beneath a continual smile."

"Hate you, sweet Valentine!" exclaimed the young man; "how is it possible for any one to do that?"

"Alas!" replied the weeping girl; "I am obliged to own that my mother-in-law's aversion to me arises from a very natural source—her overweening love for her own child, my brother Edward."

"But why should it?"

"Nay! I know not; but though unwilling to introduce money matters into our present conversation, I will just say thus much, that her extreme dislike to me has its origin in mercenary motives; and I much fear she envies me the fortune I already enjoy in right of my mother, and which will be more than doubled at the death of M. and Madame Méran, whose sole heiress I am. Madame de Villefort has nothing of her own, and hates me for being so richly endowed. Alas! how gladly would I exchange the half of this wealth for the happiness of at least sharing my father's love! God knows, I would prefer sacrificing the whole, so that it would obtain me a happy and affectionate home."

"Poor Valentine!"

"I seem to myself as though living a life of bondage, yet at the same time am so conscious of my own weakness, that I fear to break the restraint in which I am held lest I fall utterly powerless and helpless. Then, too, my father is not a person whose orders may be infringed with impunity: protected as he is by his high position, and firmly established reputation for talent and unswerving integrity, no one could oppose him; he is all powerful with even his king; you he would crush at a word, and myself he would cause to expire of terror at his feet. Dear Maximilian, believe me when I assure you that I attempt not to resist my father's commands, more on your account than my own, for, though I could willingly sacrifice myself, I would not peril your safety."

"But wherefore, my sweet Valentine, do you persist in

anticipating the worst, and in viewing every thing through so gloomy a medium, why picture the future so fraught with evil?"

"Because I judge it from the past."

"Still consider that although I may not be, strictly speaking, what is termed an illustrious match for you, I am for many reasons not altogether so much beneath your alliance. The days when such distinctions were so nicely weighed and considered no longer exist in France, and the first families of the monarchy have intermarried with those of the empire. The aristocracy of the lance has allied itself with the nobility of the cannon. Now I belong to this last-named class; and certainly my prospects of military preferment are most encouraging as well as certain. My fortune, though small, is free and unfettered, and the memory of my late father respected in our country, Valentine, as that of the most upright and honourable merchant of the city;—I say our country, because you were born not far from Marseilles."

"Name not Marseilles, I beseech you, Maximilian, that one word brings back my mother to my recollection,—my angel mother, who died too soon for myself, and all who knew her; but who, after watching over her child, during the brief period allotted to her in this world, now I fondly hope, and fully believe, contemplates her with pitying tenderness from those realms of bliss to which her pure spirit has flown. Ah, were she still living, we need fear nothing, Maximilian, for I would confide our love to her, and she would aid and protect us."

"I fear, Valentine," replied the lover, "that were she living I should never have had the happiness of knowing you; you would then have been too happy to have stooped from your grandeur to bestow a thought on an humble, obscure individual like myself."

"It is you who are unkind, ay, and unjust too, now, Maximilian," cried Valentine; "but there is one thing I wish to know?"

"And what is that?" inquired the young man, perceiving that Valentine hesitated and seemed at a loss how to proceed.

"Tell me, truly, Maximilian, whether in former days, when our fathers dwelt at Marseilles, there ever existed any misunderstanding between them?"

"Not that I am at all aware of," replied the young man, "unless, indeed, any ill-feeling might have arisen from their being of opposite parties; your father being, as you know, a zealous partisan of the Bourbons, while mine was wholly devoted to the emperor—there could not possibly be any other difference between them; but now, that I have answered your question to the best of my power and knowledge, tell me, dearest, why you ask?"

"I will," replied his fair companion, "for it is but right you should know all. Then, I must begin by referring to the day when your being made an officer of the Legion of Honour was publicly announced in the papers. We were all sitting in the apartments of my grandfather, M. Noirtier; M. Danglars was there also,—you recollect M. Danglars, do you not, Maximilian, the banker, whose horses ran away with my mother-in-law and little brother, and very nearly killed them?—while the rest of the company were discussing the approaching marriage of Mademoiselle Danglars, I was occupied in reading the paper aloud to my grandfather; but when I came to the paragraph concerning you, although I had done nothing else but read it over to myself all the morning (you know you had told me all about it the previous evening), I felt so happy, and yet so nervous, at the idea of pronouncing your beloved name aloud, and before so many people, that I really think I should have passed it over, but for the fear that my so doing might create suspicions as to the cause of my silence, so I summoned up all my courage, and read it as firmly and steadily as I could."

"Dear Valentine!"

"Well, would you believe it, directly my father caught the sound of your name, he turned round quite hastily, and, like a poor silly thing, I was so persuaded that every one must be as much affected as myself, by the utterance of your name, that I was not surprised to see my father start, and almost tremble; but I even thought (though that surely must have been a mistake) that M. Danglars underwent a similar emotion.

"'Morrel! Morrel!' cried my father, 'stop a bit;' then knitting his brows into a deep frown, he added, 'Surely this cannot be one of the Morrel family who lived at Marseilles, and gave us so much trouble from their being such violent Buonapartists—I mean about the year 1815.'

"'I fancy,' replied M. Danglars, 'that the individual alluded to in the journal mademoiselle is reading is the son of the large ship-owner there.'"

"Indeed!" answered Maximilian; "and what said your father then, Valentine?"

"Oh, such a dreadful thing, I dare not repeat it."

"Nay, dearest!" said the young man, "be not afraid to tell *me*—say, what was it?"

"'Ah,' continued my father, still frowning severely, 'their

idolised emperor treated these madmen as they deserved, he called them "*food for cannon*," which was precisely all they were good for; and I am delighted to see that the present government have adopted this salutary principle with all its pristine vigour; if Algiers were good for nothing but to furnish out the means of carrying so admirable an idea into practice, it would be an acquisition well worthy of struggling to obtain. Though it certainly does cost France somewhat dear to assert its rights in that uncivilised country.'"

"The sentiments expressed were somewhat unfeeling I must confess," said Maximilian; "but do not let that tinge your fair cheek with the blush of shame, my gentle Valentine; for I can assure you, that although in a different way, my father was not a jot or tittle behind yours in the heat of his political expressions: 'Why,' said he, 'does not the emperor, who has devised so many clever and efficient modes of improving the art of war, not form a regiment of lawyers, judges, and legal practitioners, sending them in the hottest fire the enemy could maintain, and using them to save better men?' You see, my sweet Valentine, that for mildness of expression and imaginative benefits, there is not much to choose between the language of either Royalist or Buonapartist. But what said M. Danglars to this burst of party spirit on the part of the procureur du roi?"

"Oh, he laughed, and in that singular manner so peculiar to himself—half-malicious, half-ferocious; his smile, even, has always made me shudder, it has so very unnatural a look—he almost immediately rose and took his leave; then, for the first time, I observed the agitation of my grandfather, and I must tell you, Maximilian, that I am the only person capable of discerning emotion in the paralysed frame of my poor afflicted relative. And I suspected that the conversation that had been carried on in his presence (for no one ever cares to refrain from saying and doing what they like before the dear old man, without the smallest regard to his feelings) had made a strong impression on his mind; for, naturally enough, it must have pained him to hear the emperor he so devotedly loved and served spoken of in that depreciating manner."

"The name of M. Noirtier," interposed Maximilian, "is celebrated throughout Europe, he was a statesman of high standing; and I know not whether you are aware, Valentine, that he took a leading part in every Buonapartean conspiracy set on foot during the restoration of the Bourbons."

"Oh, I have often heard whispers of things that seem to me most strange—the father a Buonapartist, the son a

Royalist; what can have been the reason of so singular a difference in parties and politics? But to resume my story: I turned towards my grandfather, as though to question him as to the cause of his emotion; he looked expressively at the newspaper I had been reading.

"'What is the matter, dear grandfather?' said I, 'are you pleased?'

"He gave me a sign in the affirmative.

"'With what my father said just now?'

"He returned a sign in the negative.

"'Perhaps you liked what M. Danglars remarked?'

"Another sign in the negative.

"'Oh, then, you were glad to hear that M. Morrel (I durst not pronounce the dear name of Maximilian) had been made an officer of the Legion of Honour, was that it, dear grandpapa?'

"He signified assent in a way that convinced me he was more than glad—that he was delighted; only think of the poor old man's being so pleased to think that you, who were a perfect stranger to him, had been made an officer of the Legion of Honour! Perhaps, though, it was a mere whim on his part, for he is almost falling into a second childhood; but for all that I love him dearly, and pray that he may long be spared to me."

"How singular," murmured Maximilian, "that your father should apparently hate the very mention of my name, while your grandfather, on the contrary—— Well, well, it is no use to endeavour to find a reason for these things; strange, indeed, are the feelings brought into play by the action of party likes or dislikes."

"Hush!" cried Valentine, suddenly, "conceal yourself!— Go, go! Some one comes!" Maximilian leaped at one bound into his crop of lucerne, which he commenced pulling up in the most pitiless manner, under the pretext of being occupied in weeding it.

"Mademoiselle! mademoiselle!" exclaimed a voice from behind the trees. "Madame is searching for you every where; there are visitors in the drawing-room."

"Who is it?" inquired Valentine, much agitated, "are they ladies?"

"Oh no, mademoiselle! I believe it is some grand prince, or a duke, or a king, perhaps; stay, now I remember, they said he was the Count of Monte-Cristo, and that he wished particularly to see you."

"I will come directly," said Valentine aloud.

The name caused an electric shock to the individual on the other side of the iron gate, on whose ear the "*I will come!*" of

Valentine, sounded the usual parting knell of all their interviews.

"Now then," said Maximilian, as, tired with his unusual employment, he stopped to rest himself, by leaning on the handle of a spade he had taken care to furnish himself with, "would I give much to know how it comes about that the Count of Monte-Cristo is acquainted with M. de Villefort."

CHAPTER LII

TOXICOLOGY

IT was really the Count of Monte-Cristo who had just arrived at Madame de Villefort's, for the purpose of returning the visit of the procureur du roi, and at this name, as may be easily imagined, the whole house was in confusion.

Madame de Villefort, who was alone in her drawing-room when the count was announced, desired that her son might be brought thither instantly to renew his thanks to the count; and Edward, who heard nothing and nobody talked of for two whole days but this great personage, made all possible haste to come to him, not from obedience to his mother, not from any feeling of gratitude to the count, but from sheer curiosity, and that he might make some remark, by help of which he might find an opportunity for saying one of those small pertnesses which made his mother say,—

"Oh that sad child! but pray excuse him, he is really *so* clever."

After the first and usual civilities, the count inquired after M. de Villefort.

"My husband dines with the chancellor," replied the young lady, "he has just gone, and I'm sure, he'll be exceedingly sorry not to have had the pleasure of seeing you before he went."

Two visitors who were there when the count arrived, having gazed at him with all their eyes, retired after that reasonable delay which politeness admits and curiosity requires.

"Ah! what is your sister Valentine doing?" inquired Madame de Villefort of Edward; "tell some one to bid her come here, that I may have the honour of introducing her to the count."

"You have a daughter, then, madame?" inquired the count; "very young, I presume?"

"The daughter of M. de Villefort," replied the young wife, "by his first marriage, a fine well-grown girl."

"But melancholy," interrupted Master Edward, snatching the feathers out of the tail of a splendid parroquet, that was screaming on its gilded perch, in order to make a plume for his hat.

Madame de Villefort merely cried,—

"Silence, Edward!"

She then added,—

"This young madcap is, however, very nearly right, and merely re-echoes what he has heard me say with pain a hundred times; for Mademoiselle de Villefort is, in spite of all we can do to rouse her, of a melancholy disposition and taciturn habit, which frequently injure the effect of her beauty. But what detains her? Go, Edward, and see."

"Because they are looking for her where she is not to be found."

"And where are they looking for her?"

"With grandpapa Noirtier."

"And do you think she is not there?"

"No, no, no, no, no, she is not there," replied Edward, singing his words.

"And where is she, then? If you know, why don't you tell?"

"She is under the great chestnut-tree," replied the spoiled brat, as he gave, in spite of his mother's cries, live flies to the parrot, who appeared to relish such 'small deer' excessively.

Madame de Villefort stretched out her hand to ring, intending to direct her waiting-maid to the spot where she would find Valentine, when the young lady herself entered the apartment. She appeared much dejected; and any person who considered her attentively might have observed the traces of recent tears in her eyes.

Valentine, whom we have in the rapid march of our narrative presented to our readers, without formally introducing her, was a tall and graceful girl of nineteen years of age, with bright chestnut hair, deep blue eyes, and that languishing air so full of distinction which characterised her mother. Her white and slender fingers, her pearly neck, her cheeks tinted with varying hues, gave her at the first view the aspect of one of these lovely Englishwomen who have been so poetically compared in their manner to a swan admiring itself. She entered the apartment, and seeing near her step-mother the stranger of whom she had already heard so much, saluted him without any girlish awkwardness or even lowering her eyes, and with an elegance that redoubled the count's attention. He rose to return the salutation.

"Mademoiselle de Villefort, my daughter-in-law," said Madame de Villefort to Monte-Cristo, leaning back on her sofa and motioning towards Valentine with her hand.

"And M. de Monte-Cristo, king of China, emperor of Cochin-China," said the young imp, looking slyly towards his sister.

Madame de Villefort at this really did turn pale, and was very nearly angry with this household plague, who answered to the name of Edward; but the count, on the contrary, smiled and appeared to look at the boy complacently, which caused the maternal heart to bound again with joy and enthusiasm.

"But, madame," replied the count, continuing the conversation and looking by turns at Madame de Villefort and Valentine, "have I not already had the honour of meeting yourself and mademoiselle before? I could not help thinking so just now; the idea came over my mind, and as mademoiselle entered, the sight of her was an additional ray of light thrown on a confused remembrance; excuse me the remark."

"I do not think it likely, sir; Mademoiselle de Villefort is not very fond of society, and we very seldom go out," said the young lady.

"Then it was not in society that I met with mademoiselle or yourself, madame, or this charming little merry boy. Besides the Parisian world is entirely unknown to me, for, as I believe I told you, I have been in Paris but very few days. No—but, perhaps, you will permit me to call to mind—stay!"

The count placed his hand on his brow as if to collect his thoughts.

"No—it was somewhere—away from here—it was—I do not know—but it appears that this recollection is connected with a lovely sky and some religious fête; mademoiselle was holding flowers in her hand, the interesting boy was chasing a beautiful peacock in a garden, and you, madam, were under the trellis of some arbour. Pray come to my aid, madame, do not these circumstances bring to your mind, some reminiscences?"

"No, indeed," replied Madame de Villefort, "and yet it appears to me, sir, that if I had met you any where, the recollection of you must have been imprinted on my memory."

"Perhaps M. le Comte saw us in Italy," said Valentine, timidly.

"Yes, in Italy; it was in Italy most probably," replied Monte-Cristo, "you have travelled then in Italy, mademoiselle?"

"Yes, madame and I were there two years ago. The doctors were afraid of my lungs, and prescribed the air of Naples. We went by Bologna, Perusa, and Rome."

"Ah, yes—true, mademoiselle," exclaimed Monte-Cristo, as if this simple indication was sufficient to determine his recollections. "It was at Perusa, on the day of the Fête-Dieu in the garden of the Hôtel des Postes, when chance brought us together; you, Madame de Villefort, and your son, I now remember having had the honour of meeting you."

"I perfectly well remember Perusa, sir, and the Hôtel des Postes, and the fête to which you allude," said Madame de Villefort, "but in vain do I tax my memory, of whose treachery I am ashamed, for I really do not recall to mind that I ever had the pleasure of seeing you before."

"It is strange, but neither do I recollect meeting with you," observed Valentine, raising her beautiful eyes to the count.

"But I remember it perfectly," interposed the darling Edward.

"I will assist your memory, madam," continued the count; "the day had been burning hot: you were waiting for horses, which were delayed in consequence of the festival. Mademoiselle was walking in the shade of the garden, and your son disappeared in pursuit of the bird."

"And I caught it, mamma, don't you remember?" interposed Edward, "and I pulled three such beautiful feathers out of his tail."

"You, madam, remained under the arbour formed by the vine; do you not remember, that whilst you were seated on a stone bench, and whilst, as I told you, Mademoiselle de Villefort and your young son were absent, you conversed for a considerable time with somebody?"

"Yes, in truth, yes," answered the young lady, turning very red, "I do remember conversing with an individual wrapped in a long woollen mantle; he was a medical man, I think."

"Precisely so, madam, this man was myself; for a fortnight I had been at that hotel, during which period I had cured my valet-de-chambre of a fever, and my landlord of the jaundice, so that I really acquired a reputation as a skilful physician. We discoursed a long time, madam, on different subjects; of Perugino, of Raffaelle, of manners, customs, of the famous *aqua-tofana* of which they had told you, I think you said, that certain individuals in Perusa had preserved the secret."

"Yes, true," replied Madame de Villefort, with a kind of uneasiness; "I remember now."

"I do not recollect now all the various subjects of which we discoursed, madam," continued the count, with perfect calmness; "but I perfectly remember that, falling into the error which others had entertained respecting me, you consulted me as to the health of Mademoiselle de Villefort."

"Yes, really, sir, you were in fact a medical man," said Madame de Villefort, "since you had cured the sick."

"Molière or Beaumarchais would reply to you, madam, that it was precisely because I was not, that I had cured my patients; for myself, I am content to say to you that I have studied chemistry and the natural sciences somewhat deeply, but still only as an amateur, you understand."

At this moment the clock struck six.

"It is six o'clock," said Madame de Villefort, evidently agitated. "Valentine, will you not go and see if your grandpapa will have his dinner?"

Valentine rose, and saluting the count, left the apartment without replying a single word.

"Oh, madam!" said the count, when Valentine had left the room, "was it on my account that you sent Mademoiselle de Villefort away?"

"By no means," replied the young lady, quickly; "but this is the hour when we give to M. Noirtier the sad repast which supports his sad existence. You are aware, sir, of the deplorable condition of my husband's father?"

"Yes, madam, M. de Villefort spoke of it to me—a paralysis, I think."

"Alas, yes! there is an entire want of movement in the frame of the poor old gentleman; the mind alone is still active in this human machine, and that is faint and flickering, like the light of a lamp about to expire. But excuse me, sir, for talking of our domestic misfortunes; I interrupted you at the moment when you were telling me that you were a skilful chemist."

"No, madam, I did not say so much as that," replied the count, with a smile; "quite the contrary. I have studied chemistry, because, having determined to live in Eastern climates, I have been desirous of following the example of King Mithridates."

"*Mithridates, rex Ponticus,*" said the young scamp, as he tore some beautiful portraits out of a splendid album, "the individual who breakfasted every morning with a cup of poison à la crême."

"Edward, you naughty boy!" exclaimed Madame de Villefort, snatching the mutilated book from the urchin's grasp; "you are positively past bearing; you really disturb the conversation: go, leave us, and join your sister Valentine in dear grandpapa Noirtier's room."

"The album," said Edward, sulkily.

"What do you mean?—the album!"

"I want the album."

"How dare you tear out the drawings?"

"Oh, it amuses me."

"Go—go directly."

"I won't go unless you give me the album," said the boy, seating himself doggedly in an arm-chair, according to his habit of never giving way.

"Take it, then, and pray disturb us no longer," said Madame de Villefort, giving the album to Edward, who then went towards the door, led by his mother.

The count followed her with his eyes.

"Let us see if she shuts the door after him," he muttered.

Madame de Villefort closed the door carefully after the child, the count appearing not to notice her; then casting a scrutinising glance around the chamber, the young wife returned to her chair, in which she seated herself.

"Allow me to observe, madam," said the count, with that kind tone he could assume so well, "you are really very severe with that dear clever child."

"Oh, sometimes severity is quite necessary," replied Madame de Villefort, with all a mother's real firmness.

"It was his Cornelius Nepos that Master Edward was repeating when he referred to King Mithridates," continued the count, "and you interrupted him in a quotation, which proves that his tutor has by no means neglected him, for your son is really advanced for his years."

"The fact is, M. le Comte," answered the mother, agreeably flattered, "he has great aptitude, and learns all that is set before him. He has but one fault, he is somewhat wilful: but really, on referring for the moment to what he said, do you truly believe that Mithridates used these precautions, and that these precautions were efficacious?"

"I think so, madam, because I—I who now address you have made use of them, that I might not be poisoned at Naples, at Palermo, and at Smyrna—that is to say, in three several occasions of my life, when, but for these precautions, I must have lost my life."

"And your precautions were successful?"

"Completely so."

"Yes, I remember now your mentioning to me at Perusa something of this sort."

"Indeed! did I?" said the count, with an air of surprise, remarkably well counterfeited; "I really did not remember it."

"I inquired of you if poisons acted equally, and with the

same effect, on men of the north as on men of the south, and you answered me that the cold and sluggish habits of the north did not present the same aptitude as the rich and energetic temperaments of the natives of the south."

"And that is the case," observed Monte-Cristo. "I have seen Russians devour, without being visibly inconvenienced, vegetable substances which would infallibly have killed a Neapolitan or an Arab."

"And you really believe the result would be still more sure with us than in the East, and in the midst of our fogs and rains a man would habituate himself more easily than in a warm latitude to this progressive absorption of poison."

"Certainly; it being at the same time perfectly understood that he should have been duly fortified against the poison to which he had not been accustomed."

"Yes, I understand that; and how would you habituate yourself, for instance, or rather how did you habituate yourself to it?"

"Oh, very easily. Suppose you knew beforehand the poison that would be made use of against you; suppose the poison was, for instance, brucine——"

"Brucine is extracted from the *Brucæa ferruginea*, is it not?" inquired Madame de Villefort.

"Precisely, madam," replied Monte-Christo; "but I perceive I have not much to teach you. Allow me to compliment you on your knowledge, such learning is very rare amongst ladies."

"Oh, I am aware of that," said Madame de Villefort; "but I have a passion for the occult sciences, which speak to the imagination like poetry, and are reducible to figures, like an algebraic equation; but go on, I pray of you; what you say interests me to the greatest degree."

"Well," replied Monte-Cristo, "suppose, then, that this poison was brucine, and you were to take a milligramme the first day, two milligrammes the second day, and so on. Well! at the end of ten days, you would have taken a centigramme; at the end of twenty days increasing another milligramme, you would have taken three hundred centigrammes; that is to say, a dose which you would support without inconvenience, and which would be very dangerous for any other person who had not taken the same precautions as yourself. Well, then, at the end of a month, when drinking water from the same *carafe*, you would kill the person who had drank this water as well as yourself, without you perceiving, otherwise than from slight inconvenience, that there was any poisonous substance mingled with this water."

"Do you know any other counter-poison?"

"I do not."

"I have often read and read again the history of Mithridates," said Madame de Villefort, in a tone of reflection, "and had always considered it as a fable?"

"No, madam, contrary to most history, it is a truth; but what you tell me, madam, what you inquire of me is not the result of a chance question, for two years since you asked me the same questions, and said, too, that for a very long time this history of Mithridates occupied your mind."

"True, sir. The two favourite studies of my youth were botany and mineralogy; and subsequently, when I learned that the use of simples frequently explained the whole history of a people, and the entire life of individuals in the East, as flowers betoken and symbolise a love-affair, I have regretted I was not a man, that I might have been a Flamel, a Fontana, or a Cabanis."

"And the more, madam," said Monte-Cristo, "as the Orientals do not confine themselves, as did Mithridates, to make a cuirass of his poisons, but they also make them a dagger. Science becomes, in their hands, not only a defensive weapon, but still more frequently an offensive one; the one serves against all their physical sufferings, the other against all their enemies; with opium, with belladonna, with brucæa, snake-wood, the cherry-laurel, they put to sleep all those who would arouse them. There is not one of those women, Egyptian, Turk, or Greek, whom here you call 'good women,' who do not know how, by means of chemistry, to stupefy a doctor, and in psychology to amaze a confessor."

"Really!" said Madame de Villefort, whose eyes sparkled with strange fire at this conversation.

"Eh, indeed! Yes, madame," continued Monte-Cristo, "the secret dramas of the East begin and end thus, from the plant which can create love to the plant that can cause death; from the draught which opens heaven before your eyes to that which plunges a man in hell! There are as many shades of every kind as there are caprices and peculiarities in human, physical, and moral nature; and I will say further, the art of these chemists knows excellently well how to accommodate and proportion the remedy and the ill to its yearnings of love or its desire for vengeance."

"But, sir," remarked the lady, "these eastern societies, in the midst of which you have passed a portion of your existence, are as wild and visionary as the tales that come from their strange land—a man can easily be put out of the way there then: it is, indeed, the Bagdad and Bassora of M. Galland. The sultans and viziers, who rule over such society, and who constitute what in France we call the government, are, in fact, really these Haroun-al-Raschids and Giaffars, who not only pardon a poisoner, but even make him a prime minister if his crime has been an ingenious one, and who, under such circumstances, have the whole story written in letters of gold to divert their hours of idleness and ennui."

"By no means, madam; the fanciful exists no longer in the East. There are there now, disguised under other names, and concealed under other costumes, agents of police, magistrates, attorney-generals, and bailiffs. They hang, behead, and impale their criminals in the most agreeable possible manner; but some of these, like clever rogues, have contrived to escape human justice, and succeed in their fraudulent enterprises by cunning stratagems. Amongst us a simpleton, possessed by the demon of hate or cupidity, who has an enemy to destroy, or some near relation to dispose of, goes straight to the grocer's or druggist's, gives a false name, which leads more easily to his detection than his real one, and purchases, under a pretext that the rats prevent him from sleeping, five or sixpennyworth of arsenic—if he is really a cunning fellow he goes to five or six different druggists or grocers, and thereby becomes only five or six times more easily traced—then, when he has acquired his specific, he administers duly to his enemy, or near kinsman, a dose of arsenic which would make a mammoth or mastodon burst, and which, without rhyme or reason, makes his victim utter groans which alarm the entire neighbourhood. Then arrive a crowd of policemen and constables. They fetch a doctor, who opens the dead body, and collects from the entrails and stomach a quantity of arsenic in a spoon. Next day a hundred newspapers relate the fact, with the names of the victim and the murderer. The same evening, the grocer or grocers, druggist or druggists, come and say, ' It was I who sold the arsenic to the gentleman accused;' and rather than not recognise the guilty purchaser, they will recognise twenty. Then, the foolish criminal is taken, imprisoned, interrogated, confronted, confounded, condemned, and cut off by hemp or steel; or, if she be a woman of any consideration, they lock her up for life. This is the way in which you Northerns understand chemistry, madam. Desrues was, however, I must confess, more skilful."

"What would you have, sir?" said the lady, laughing; "we do what we can. All, the world has not the secret of the Medicis or the Borgias."

"Now," replied the count, shrugging his shoulders, "shall I tell you the cause of all these stupidities? It is because, at your theatres, by what at least I could judge by reading the pieces they play, they see persons swallow the contents of a phial, or suck the button of a ring, and fall dead instantly. Five minutes afterwards, the curtain falls and the spectators depart. They are ignorant of the consequences of the murder; they see neither the commissary of police with his badge of office, nor the corporal with his four men; and that is an authority for weak brains to believe that this is the way that things pass. But go a little way from France—go either to Aleppo or Cairo, or only to Naples or Rome, and you will see people passing by you in the streets,—people erect, smiling, and fresh-coloured, of whom Asmodeus, if you were holding on by the skirt of his mantle, would say, 'That man was poisoned three weeks ago; he will be a dead man in a month.'"

"Then," remarked Madame de Villefort, "they have again discovered the secret of the famous *aqua-tofana* that they said was lost at Perusa."

"Eh, indeed, does mankind ever lose anything? The arts are removed, and make a tour of the world! things change their names, and the vulgar do not follow them—that is all; but there is always the same result. Poison acts particularly on one organ or the other; one on the stomach, another on the brain, another on the intestines. Well, the poison brings on a cough, the cough an inflammation of the lungs, or some other complaint catalogued in the book of science, which, however, by no means precludes it from being decidedly mortal; and if it were not, would be sure to become so, thanks to the remedies applied by foolish doctors, who are generally bad chemists, and which will act in favour of or against the malady as you please; and then there is a human being killed according to all the rules of art and skill, and of whom justice learns nothing, as was said by a terrible chemist of my acquaintance, the worthy Abbé Adelmonte de Taormine, in Sicily, who had studied these national phenomena very profoundly."

"It is quite frightful, but deeply interesting," said the young lady, motionless with attention. "I thought, I must confess, that these tales were inventions of the middle ages."

"Yes, no doubt, but improved upon by ours. What is the use of time, encouragements, medals, crosses, Monthyon prizes, &c. &c., if they do not lead society towards more complete perfection? Yet man will never be perfect until he learns to create and destroy—he does know how to destroy, and that is half way on the road."

"So," added Madame de Villefort, constantly returning to her object, "the poisons of the Borgias, the Medicis, the Renés, the Ruggieris, and later, probably, that of Baron de Trenck, whose story has been so misused by modern drama and romance——"

"Were objects of art, madam, and nothing more," replied the count. "Do you suppose that the real *savant* addresses himself stupidly to the mere individual? By no means. Science loves eccentricities, leaps and bounds, trials of strength, fancies, if I may be allowed so to term them. Thus, for instance, the excellent Abbé Adelmonte, of whom I spake to you just now, made in this way some marvellous experiments."

"Really!"

"Yes; I will mention one to you. He had a remarkably fine garden, full of vegetables, flowers, and fruit. From amongst these vegetables he selected the most simple—a cabbage, for instance. For three days he watered this cabbage with a distillation of arsenic; on the third, the cabbage began to droop and turn yellow. At that moment he cut it. In the eyes of every body it seemed fit for table, and preserved its wholesome appearance. It was only poisoned to the Abbé Adelmonte. He then took the cabbage to the room where he had rabbits, for the Abbé Adelmonte had a collection of rabbits, cats, and guinea-pigs, equally fine as his collection of vegetables, flowers, and fruit. Well, the Abbé Adelmonte took a rabbit, and made it eat a leaf of the cabbage. The rabbit died. What magistrate would find, or even venture to ins'nuate anything against this? What procureur du roi has ever ventured to draw up an accusation against M. Magendie or M. Flourens, in consequence of the rabbits, cats, and guinea-pigs they have killed?—not one. So, then, the rabbit dies, and justice takes no notice. This rabbit dead, the Abbé Adelmonte has its entrails taken out by his cook and thrown on the dunghill; on this dunghill was a hen, who, pecking these intestines, was, in her turn, taken ill, and dies next day. At the moment when she was struggling in the convulsions of death, a vulture was flying by (there are a good many vultures in Adelmonte's country); this bird darts on the dead bird and carries it away to a rock, where he dines off his prey. Three days afterwards, this poor vulture, who has been very much indisposed since that dinner, feels very giddy, suddenly, whilst flying aloft in the clouds, and falls heavily into a fish-pond. The pike, eels, and carp eat greedily always, as every body knows—well, they feast on the vulture. Well, suppose, the next day, one of these eels, or pike, or carp, is served at your table, poisoned as they are to the third generation. Well, then, your guest will be poisoned in the fifth generation, and die, at the end of eight or ten days, of pains in the intestines, sickness, or abscess of the pylorus.

The doctors open the body and say, with an air of profound learning, 'The subject has died of a tumour on the liver, or typhoid fever!'"

"But," remarked Madame de Villefort, "all these circumstances which you link thus one to another may be broken by the least accident: the vulture may not pass at the precise moment, or may fall a hundred yards from the fish-pond."

"Ah, this it is which is art. To be a great chemist in the East, we must direct chance; and this is to be achieved."

Madame de Villefort was deep in thought, yet listened attentively.

"But," she exclaimed suddenly, "arsenic is indelible, indestructible; in what way soever it is absorbed, it will be found again in the body of the creature from the moment when it has been taken in sufficient quantity to cause death."

"Precisely so," cried Monte-Cristo—"precisely so; and this is what I said to my worthy Adelmonte. He reflected, smiled, and replied to me by a Sicilian proverb, which I believe is also a French proverb. 'My son, the world was not made in a day —but in seven. Return on Sunday.' On the Sunday following I did return to him. Instead of having watered his cabbage with arsenic, he had watered it this time with a solution of salts, having their bases in strychnine, *strychnos colubrina*, as the learned term it. Now, the cabbage had not the slightest appearance of disease in the world, and the rabbit had not the smallest distrust; yet, five minutes afterwards, the rabbit was dead. The fowl pecked at the rabbit and next day was a dead hen. This time we were the vultures, so we opened the bird, and this time all particular symptoms had disappeared, there were only general symptoms. There was no peculiar indication in any organ—an excitement of the nervous system—that was it;—a case of cerebral congestion— nothing more. The fowl had not been poisoned—she had died of apoplexy. Apoplexy is a rare disease amongst fowls, I believe, but very common amongst men."

Madame de Villefort appeared more and more reflective.

"It is very fortunate," she observed, "that such substances could only be prepared by chemists; for else, really, all the world would be poisoning each other."

"By chemists and persons who have a taste for chemistry," said Monte-Cristo, carelessly.

"And then," said Madame de Villefort, endeavouring by a struggle, and with effort, to get away from her thoughts, "however skilfully it is prepared, crime is always crime; and if it avoid human scrutiny, it does not escape the eye of God. The Orientals are stronger than we are in cases of conscience, and very prudently have no hell—that is the point."

"Really, madame, this is a scruple which naturally must occur to a pure mind like yours, but which would easily yield before sound reasoning. The bad side of human thought will always be defined by the paradox of Jean Jacques Rousseau, you know, the mandarin, who is killed at 500 leagues distance by raising the tip of the finger. Man's whole life passes in doing these things, and his intellect is exhausted by reflecting on them. You will find very few persons who will go and brutally thrust a knife in the heart of a fellow-creature, or will administer to him, in order to remove him from that surface of the globe on which we move with life and animation, that quantity of arsenic of which we just now talked. Such a thing is really out of rule—eccentric or stupid. To attain such a point, the blood must be warmed to thirty-six degrees, the pulse be, at least, at ninety, and the feelings excited beyond the ordinary limit. But if passing, as we do in philology, from the word itself to its softened synonym, you make an elimination—a simple change of words; instead of committing an ignoble assassination, if you merely and simply remove from your path the individual who is in your way, and that without shock or violence, without the display of those sufferings which, becoming a punishment, make a martyr of the victim, and of him who inflicts them a butcher, in every sense of the word; if there be no blood, no groans, no convulsions, and, above all, that horrid and compromising moment of accomplishing the act, then one escapes the clutch of the human law, which says to you, 'Do not disturb society!' This is the mode in which they manage these things, and succeed, in Eastern climes, where there are grave and phlegmatic persons who care very little for the questions of time in conjunctures of importance."

"Yet conscience remains!" remarked Madame de Villefort, in an agitated voice and with a stifled sigh.

"Yes," answered Monte-Cristo,—"happily, yes! conscience does remain, and if it did not, how wretched we should be! After every action requiring exertion it is conscience that saves us, for it supplies us with a thousand good excuses, of which we alone are judges; and these reasons, how excellent so ever in producing sleep, would avail us but very little before a tribunal when we were tried for our lives. Thus Richard III, for instance, was marvellously served by his conscience after the putting away of the two children of Edward IV; in fact, he could say, 'These two children of a cruel and persecuting king, who have inherited the vices of their father, which I alone could perceive in their juvenile propensities,—these two children are impediments in my way of promoting the happiness of the English people, whose unhappiness they (the children) would infallibly have caused.' Thus was Lady Macbeth served by her conscience, when she sought to give her son and not her husband (whatever Shakespeare may say) a throne! Ah! maternal love is a great virtue, a powerful motive, so powerful that it excuses a multitude of things, even if after Duncan's death, Lady Macbeth had been at all pricked by her conscience."

Madame de Villefort listened with avidity to these appalling maxims and horrible paradoxes delivered by the count with that ironical simplicity which was peculiar to him.

After a moment's silence, the lady inquired,—

"Do you know," she said, "M. le Comte, that you are a very terrible reasoner, and that you look at the world through a somewhat distempered medium? Have you really measured the world by scrutinies, or through alembics and crucibles? For, truth to say, you are a great chemist, and the elixir you administered to my son which recalled him to life almost instantaneously——"

"Oh, do not place any reliance on that, madame; *one* drop of that elixir sufficed to recall life to a dying child, but three drops would have impelled the blood into his lungs in such a way as to have produced most violent palpitations; six would have suspended his respiration and caused syncope more serious than that in which he was; ten would have destroyed him. You know, madame, how suddenly I snatched him from those phials which he so imprudently touched?"

"Is it, then, so terrible a poison?"

"Oh, no! In the first place, let us agree that the word poison does not exist, because in medicine use is made of the most violent poisons, which become, according as they are made use of, most salutary remedies."

"What, then, is it?"

"A skilful preparation of my friend's, the worthy Abbé Adelmonte, who taught me the use of it."

"Oh!" observed Madame de Villefort; "it must be an admirable antispasmodic."

"Perfect, madam, as you have seen," replied the count; "and I frequently make use of it, with all possible prudence though, be it observed," he added with a smile of intelligence.

"Most assuredly," responded Madame de Villefort, in the same tone; "as for me, so nervous, and so subject to fainting fits, I should require a Doctor Adelmonte to invent for me some means of breathing freely and tranquillising my mind in the fear I have of dying some fine day of suffocation. In the meanwhile, as the thing is difficult to find in France, and your abbé is not probably disposed to make a journey to Paris on my account, I must continue to use the antispasmodics of M. Pianché; and mint and Hoffmann's drops are amongst my favourite remedies. Here are some lozenges which I have made up on purpose, they are compounded doubly strong."

Monte-Cristo opened the tortoise-shell box, which the lady presented to him, and imbibed the odour of the pastilles with the air of an amateur who thoroughly appreciated their composition.

"They are, indeed, exquisite," he said; "but as they are necessarily submitted to the process of deglutition,—a function which it is frequently impossible for a fainting person to accomplish, I prefer my own specific."

"Undoubtedly, and so should I prefer it, after the effects I have seen procured; but of course it is a secret, and I am not so indiscreet as to ask it of you?"

"But I," said Monte-Cristo, rising as he spoke,—"I am gallant enough to offer it you."

"Oh, sir!"

"Only remember one thing, a small dose is a remedy, a large one is poison. One drop will restore life as you have witnessed; five or six will inevitably kill, and in a way the more terrible, inasmuch as, poured into a glass of wine, it would not in the slightest degree affect its flavour. But I say no more, madam, it is really as if I were advising you."

The clock struck half-past six, and a lady was announced, a friend of Madame de Villefort, who came to dine with her.

"If I had had the honour of seeing you for the third or fourth time, M. le Comte, instead of only for the second," said Madame de Villefort, — "if I had had the honour of being your friend, instead of only having the happiness of lying under an obligation to you, I should insist on detaining you to dinner, and not allow myself to be daunted by a first refusal."

"A thousand thanks, madam," replied Monte-Cristo, "but I have an engagement which I cannot break; I have promised to escort to the Académie, a Greek princess of my acquaintance who has never seen your grand Opera, and who relies on me to conduct her thither."

"Adieu, then, sir! and do not forget my recipe."

"Ah, in truth, madam, to do that, I must forget the hour's conversation I have had with you, which is indeed impossible."

Monte-Cristo bowed and left the house.

Madame de Villefort remained immersed in thought.

"He is a very strange man," she said; "and in my opinion is himself the Adelmonte he talks about."

As to Monte Cristo the result had surpassed his utmost expectations.

"Good!" said he, as he went away; "this is a fruitful soil, and I feel certain that the seed sown will not be cast on barren ground."

Next morning, faithful to his promise, he sent the prescription requested.

CHAPTER LIII

THE pretext of an Opera engagement was so much the more feasible as there chanced to be on that very night a more than ordinary attraction at the Académie Royale. Levasseur, who had been suffering under severe illness, made his reappearance in the character of Bertram, and, as usual, the announcement of the most admired production of the favourite composer of the day had attracted an audience consisting of the very *élite* of Parisian fashion. Morcerf, like most other young men of rank and fortune, had his orchestral stall, with the certainty of always finding a seat in at least a dozen of the principal boxes occupied by persons of his acquaintance; he had moreover his right of entry into the omnibus box. Château-Renaud rented a stall beside his own, while Beauchamp, in his editorial capacity, had unlimited range all over the theatre.

It happened that on that particular night the minister's box was placed at the disposal of Lucien Debray, who offered it to the Count de Morcerf, who again, upon his mother's rejection of it, sent it to Danglars with an intimation that he should probably do himself the honour of joining the baroness and her daughter during the evening in the event of their accepting the box in question. The ladies received the offer with too much pleasure to dream of a refusal. To no class of persons is the presentation of a gratuitous opera-box more acceptable than to the wealthy millionaire, who still hugs economy while boasting of carrying a king's ransom in his waistcoat-pocket.

Danglars had, however, protested against shewing himself in a ministerial box, declaring that his political principles, as well as being a member of the opposition party, would not permit him so to commit himself; the baroness had, therefore, despatched a note to Lucien Debray, bidding him call for them, it being wholly impossible for her to go alone with her daughter to the Opera. There is no gainsaying the plain fact, that a very unfavourable construction would have been put upon the circumstance of two ladies going together to a public place, while the addition of a third, in the person of her mother's admitted lover, enabled Mademoiselle Danglars to defy malice and ill-nature while visiting so celebrated a place of amusement. Thus, then, we perceive that for a mother, however innocent and pure-minded, to conduct her child alone to operas or spectacles, would be deemed a breach of decorum; but to go thither under the guidance of one who, if not actually her seducer, might in time become so, made all right, and set the world at defiance: let others reconcile these strange inconsistencies if they will, we confess it above our powers!

The curtain rose as usual to an almost empty house, it being one of the absurdities of Parisian fashion never to appear at the Opera until after the commencement of the performances, so that the first act is generally played without the slightest attention being paid to it, that part of the audience already assembled being too much occupied in observing the fresh arrivals and noting each batch of *élégantes* as they take possession of their boxes, to have eyes or ears for the business of the stage, while the noise of opening and shutting doors, with the mingled buzz of many conversations, effectually prevents even those few who would listen to the orchestra from being able to do so.

"Surely!" said Albert, as the door of a box on the first circle opened, and a lady entered, resplendent with beauty and jewels, "that must be the Countess G——."

"And who may she be, pray?" inquired Château-Renaud, carelessly.

"What a question! Now do you know, baron, I have a great mind to pick a quarrel with you for asking it, as if all the world did not know who the Countess G—— was."

"Ah, to be sure!" replied Château-Renaud, "I remember now—your lovely Venetian, is it not?"

"Herself!"

At this moment the countess perceived Albert, and returned his salutation with a graceful smile.

"You are acquainted with her, it seems?" said Château-Renaud.

"Franz introduced me to her at Rome," replied Albert.

"Well, then, will you do as much for me in Paris as he did for you in the 'Queen of Cities?'"

"With much pleasure!"

"Silence!" exclaimed the audience.

This manifestation on the part of the spectators of their wish to be allowed to enjoy the rich music then issuing from the stage and orchestra produced not the slightest effect on the two young men, who continued talking as though they had not even heard it.

"The countess was present at the races in the Champ de Mars," said Château-Renaud.

"To-day?"

"Yes."

"Bless me! I quite forgot the races—did you bet?"

"Oh, merely a paltry fifty louis."

"And who was the winner?"

"Nautilus. I staked on him."

"But there were three races, were there not?"

"Yes; there was the prize given by the Jockey Club—a gold cup, you know—and a very singular circumstance occurred about that race."

"What was it?"

"Silence!" again vociferated the music-loving part of the audience.

"Why, that it was gained by a horse and rider utterly unknown on the course."

"Is that possible?"

"True as day; the fact was, nobody had observed a horse entered by the name of Vampa, or that of a jockey styled Job; when at the last moment a splendid roan, mounted by a jockey about as big as your fist, presented themselves at the starting-post, they were obliged to stuff at least twenty pounds weight of shot in the small rider's pockets to make him weight; but with all that he outstripped Ariel and Barbaro, against whom he ran, by at least three whole lengths."

"And was it not found out at last to whom the horse and jockey belonged?"

"No!"

"You say that the horse was entered under the name of Vampa?"

"Exactly; that was the title."

"Then," answered Albert, "I am better informed than you are, and know who the owner of that horse was!"

"Silence there!" cried the whole collective force of the pit. And this time the tone and manner in which the command was given betokened such growing hostility, that the two young men perceived, for the first time, that the mandate was addressed to them; leisurely turning round, they calmly scrutinised the various countenances around them, as though demanding some one person who would take upon himself the responsibility of what they deemed excessive impertinence; but as no one responded to the challenge, the friends turned again to the front of the theatre, and affected to busy themselves with the stage.

At this moment the door of the minister's box opened, and Madame Danglars, accompanied by her daughter, entered, escorted by Lucien Debray, who assiduously conducted them to their seats.

"Ha, ha!" said Château-Renaud, "here comes some friends of yours, viscount!—What are you looking at there? don't you see they are trying to catch your eye?"

Albert turned round just in time to receive a gracious wave of the fan from Madame le Baronne; as for Mademoiselle Eugénie, she scarcely vouchsafed to waste the glances of her large black eyes even upon the business of the stage.

"I tell you what, my dear fellow," said Château-Renaud, "I cannot imagine what objection you can possibly have to Mademoiselle Danglars—that is, setting aside her want of ancestry and somewhat inferior rank, which, by the way, I don't think you care very much about; now, barring all that, I mean to say she is a deuced fine girl!"

"Handsome, certainly," replied Albert, "but not to my taste, which, I confess, inclines to a softer, gentler, and more feminine style than that possessed by the young lady in question."

"Bless my heart!" exclaimed Château-Renaud, who, because he had seen his thirtieth summer, fancied himself duly warranted in assuming a sort of paternal air with his more youthful friend, "you young people are never satisfied; why, what would you have more? your parents have chosen you a bride who might serve as the living model of the 'Hunting Diana,' and yet you are not content."

"No, for that very resemblance affrights me; I should have liked something more in the manner of the Venus of Milo or Capua; but this chase-loving Diana, continually surrounded by her nymphs, gives me a sort of alarm, lest she should some day entail on me the fate of Actæon."

And, indeed, it required but one glance of Mademoiselle Danglars to comprehend the nature, as well as justness, of Morcerf's remark: "she was certainly handsome," but her beauty was of too marked and decided a character to please a fastidious taste; her hair was raven black, but amid its natural waves might be seen a species of rebellion to the hand that sought to band and braid it; her eyes, of the same colour as her hair, were richly fringed and surmounted by well-arched brows, whose great defect, however, consisted in an almost habitual frown; while her whole physiognomy wore that expression of firmness and decision so little in accordance with the gentler attributes of her sex—her nose was precisely what a statuary would have chosen for a chiselled Juno. Her mouth, which might have been found fault with as too large, displayed teeth of pearly whiteness, rendered still more conspicuous by the over-redness of her lips, beside which her naturally pale complexion seemed even more colourless. But that which completed the almost masculine look Morcerf found so little to his taste, was a dark mole, of much larger dimensions than these freaks of nature generally are, placed just at the corner of her mouth; and the effect tended to increase the expression of unbending resolution and self-dependence that formed the characteristics of her countenance. The rest of Mademoiselle Eugénie's person was in perfect keeping with the head just described; she, indeed, reminded you of the Hunting Diana, as Château-Renaud observed, but with a more haughty and resolute air than statuaries have bestowed on the "Chaste Goddess of the silver bow." As regarded her attainments, the only fault to be found with them was the same a fastidious connoisseur might have found with her beauty, that they were somewhat too erudite and masculine for so young a person: she was a perfect linguist; a first-rate artist; wrote poetry, and composed music; to the study of the latter, she professed to be entirely devoted, studying it with indefatigable perseverance, assisted by a schoolfellow who, having been educated with the view of turning her talents to account, was now busily engaged in improving her vocal powers, in order to take (what she was assured by her friends she would infallibly attain) a leading position at the Academy of Music. It was rumoured that she was an object of almost paternal interest to one of the principal composers of the day, who excited her to spare no pains in the cultivation of her voice, which might hereafter prove a source of wealth and independence. But this counsel effectually decided Mademoiselle Danglars never to commit herself by being seen in public with one destined for a theatrical life; and acting upon this principle, the banker's daughter, though perfectly willing to allow Mademoiselle Louise d'Armilly (for so was the future *débutante* named) to practise with her through the day, took especial care not to compromise herself by being seen in her company. Still, though not actually received at the Hôtel Danglars in the light of an acknowledged friend, Louise was treated with far more kindness and consideration than is usually bestowed on that most unfortunate class of deserving females styled governesses.

The curtain fell almost immediately after the entrance of Madame Danglars into her box, the band quitted the orchestra for the accustomed half-hour's interval allowed between the acts, and the audience were left at liberty to promenade the salon or lobbies, or to pay and receive visits in their respective boxes. Morcerf and Château-Renaud were amongst the first to avail themselves of this permission. For an instant the idea struck Madame Danglars that this eagerness on the part of the young viscount arose from his impatience to join her party, and she whispered her expectations to her daughter that Albert was hurrying to pay his respects to them. Mademoiselle Eugénie, however, merely returned a dissenting movement of the head, while, with a cold smile, she directed the attention of her mother to an opposite *loge* situated on the first circle, in which sat the Countess G——, and where Morcerf had just made his appearance.

"So we meet again, my travelling friend, do we?" cried the countess, extending her hand to him with all the warmth and cordiality of an old acquaintance; "it was really very good of you to recognise me so quickly, and still more so to bestow your first visit on me."

"Be assured," replied Albert, "that if I had been aware of your arrival in Paris, and had known your address, I should have paid my respects to you long ere this. Allow me to introduce my friend, Baron de Château-Renaud, one of the rare specimens of real gentlemen now to be found in France, and from whom I have just learned that you were a spectator of the races in the Champ-de-Mars yesterday."

Château-Renaud bowed to the countess.

"Were you at the races, then, M. le Baron?" inquired the countess, eagerly.

"I was."

"Well, then," pursued Madame G——, with considerable animation, "you can, probably, tell me to whom belonged the winner of the Jockey Club stakes?"

"I am sorry to say I cannot," replied the baron; "and I was just asking the same question of my friend Albert."

"Are you very anxious to know, Madame la Comtesse?" asked Albert.

"To know what?"

"The name of the owner of the winning horse?"

"Excessively; only imagine—but do tell me, M. le Vicomte, whether you really are acquainted with it or no?"

"I beg your pardon, madam, but you were about to relate some story, were you not? You said, 'Only imagine,'—and then paused. Pray, continue."

"Well, then, listen! You must know I felt so interested for the splendid roan horse, with his elegant little rider so tastefully dressed in a pink satin jacket and cap, that I could not help praying for their success with as much earnestness as though the half of my fortune were at stake; and when I saw them outstrip all the others, and come to the winning-post in such gallant style, I actually clapped my hands with joy. Imagine my surprise when, upon returning home, the first object I met on the staircase was the identical jockey in the pink jacket! I concluded that, by some singular chance, the owner of the winning horse must live in the same hotel as myself; but lo! as I entered my apartments I beheld the very gold cup awarded as a prize to the unknown horse and rider. Inside the cup was a small piece of paper, on which were written these words, 'From Lord Ruthven to Countess G——.''

"Precisely; I was sure of it," said Morcerf.

"Sure of what?"

"That the owner of the horse was Lord Ruthven himself."

"What Lord Ruthven do you mean?"

"Why, our Lord Ruthven—the Vampire of the Salle Argentino!"

"Mercy upon me!" exclaimed the countess; "is he here too?"

"To be sure,—why not?"

"And you visit him?—meet him at your own house and elsewhere?"

"I assure you he is my most intimate friend, and M. le Château-Renaud has also the honour of his acquaintance."

"But what makes you so convinced of his being the winner of the Jockey Club prize?"

"Was not the winning horse entered by the name of Vampa?"

"What of that?"

"Why, do you not recollect it was the appellation of the celebrated bandit by whom I was made prisoner?"

"True."

"And from whose hands the count extricated me in so wonderful a manner?"

"To be sure, I remember it all now."

"Now I argue from the circumstance of the horse and bandit bearing the same singular name, that the count was the person to whom the unknown horse belonged."

"But what could have been his motive for sending the cup to me?"

"In the first place, because I had spoken much of you to him, as you may believe; and in the second, because he delighted to see a countrywoman take so lively an interest in his success."

"I trust and hope you never repeated to the count all the foolish remarks we used to make about him?"

"I should not like to affirm upon oath that I have not.

Besides, his presenting to you the cup under the name of Lord Ruthven proves his knowledge of the comparison made between himself and that individual."

"Oh, but that is dreadful! Why, the man must owe me a fearful grudge for so doing."

"Does his offering you the fruits of his victory seem like the conduct of one who felt ill-will towards you?"

"No! certainly not!"

"Well then——"

"And so this singular being is in Paris?"

"He is."

"And what effect does he produce?"

"Why," said Albert, "certainly, during the first week of his arrival here, he was the great lion of the day; nothing else was thought of or talked about but the wonderful Count of Monte-Cristo and his extraordinary actions; then the coronation of the Queen of England took place, followed almost immediately afterwards by the robbery of Mademoiselle Mars' diamonds; and two such interesting events turned public attention into other channels."

"My good fellow," said Château-Renaud, "the count happens to be so great a favourite of yours, that you treat him as carefully and delicately as though he were your best and most intimate friend. Do not believe what Albert is telling you, Madame la Comtesse; so far from the sensation excited in the Parisian circles by the appearance of the Count of Monte-Cristo having abated, I take upon myself to declare that it is as strong as ever. His first astounding act upon coming amongst us was to present a pair of horses worth 32,000 francs to Madame Danglars; his second, the almost miraculous preservation of Madame de Villefort's life, now it seems that he has carried off the prize awarded by the Jockey Club! I, therefore, assert and maintain, in despite of whatever Morcerf may advance, that not only is the count the object of universal remark, interest, and curiosity, at this present moment, but also that he will continue to be so while he pleases to exhibit an eccentricty of conduct and action which, after all, may be his ordinary mode of amusing himself as well as the world."

"Perhaps you are right," said Morcerf; "but just cast your eyes towards the box formerly belonging to the Russian ambassador, and tell me, if you can, who is the present occupant of it?"

"Which box do you mean?"

"The one between the pillars on the first tier—it seems to have been fitted up entirely afresh."

"Did you observe any one during the first act?"

"Where?"

"In that box."

"No!" replied the countess, "it was certainly empty during the first act;" then, resuming the subject of their previous conversation, she said, "And so you really believe it was your mysterious Count of Monte-Cristo that gained the prize?"

"I am sure of it."

"And who afterwards sent the golden cup to me?"

"Undoubtedly!"

"Then do you know," said the countess, "I have a strong inclination to return it? I cannot understand receiving such presents from a person wholly unknown to you."

"Do no such thing, I beg of you; it would only produce a second goblet, formed of a magnificent sapphire, or hollowed out of a gigantic ruby. It is his manner of acting, and you must take him as you find him."

At this moment the bell rang to announce the drawing up of the curtain for the second act. Albert rose to return to his place.

"Shall I see you again?" asked the countess.

"If you will permit me to make a second visit during the next interval, I will do myself the honour of coming to inquire whether there is any thing in which I can be useful to you in Paris?"

"Pray take notice," said the countess, "that my present residence is 22 Rue de Rivoli, and that I am at home to my friends every Saturday evening. So now, you gentlemen cannot plead ignorance both of when and where you may see me if so inclined."

The young men bowed, and quitted the box. Upon reaching their stalls they found the whole of the audience in the parterre standing up and directing their gaze towards the box formerly possessed by the ambassador of Russia. Following the universal example, the friends perceived that an individual of from thirty-five to forty years of age, dressed in deep black, had just entered, accompanied by a female dressed after the Eastern style; the lady was young and surpassingly beautiful, while the rich magnificence of her attire drew all eyes upon her.

"By heavens!" said Albert, "it is Monte-Cristo himself with his fair Greek!"

The strangers were, indeed, no other than the count and Haydée. The sensation excited by the beauty and dazzling appearance of the latter soon communicated itself to every part of the theatre, and even ladies leaned forwards from the boxes to admire the many-coloured coruscations that darted their sparkling beams whenever the superb diamonds worn by the young Greek played and glittered among the cut-glass lustres with their waxen lights.

The second act passed away during one continued buzz of voices, one deep whisper, intimating that some great and universally interesting event had occurred; all eyes, all thoughts were occupied with the young and beautiful female, whose gorgeous apparel and splendid jewels threw an air of insignificance upon all the fair visitants of the theatre; the business of the stage was utterly neglected—all seemed to consider the contemplation of so much loveliness far more deserving attention.

Upon this occasion an unmistakeable sign from Madame Danglars intimated her desire to see Albert in her box directly the curtain fell on the second act, and neither the politeness nor good taste of Morcerf would permit his neglecting an invitation so unequivocally given. At the close of the act he therefore proceeded to the baroness's *loge*. Having bowed to the two ladies, he extended his hand to Debray. By the baroness he was most graciously welcomed, while Eugénie received him with her accustomed coldness.

"My dear fellow!" said Debray, "you have just come in the very nick of time to help a fellow-creature regularly beaten and at a stand-still. There is madam overwhelming me with questions respecting the count; she insists upon it that I can tell her his birth, education, and parentage, where he came from and whither he is going. Being no disciple of Cagliostro, I was wholly unable to do this; so, by way of getting out of the scrape, I said, 'Ask Morcerf, he has got the whole history of his beloved Monte-Cristo at his fingers' ends;' whereupon the baroness made you a sign to come hither, and now I leave the solution of her questions in your hands."

" Is it not almost incredible," said Madame Danglars, "that a person having the command of at least half a million of secret service money at his command, should possess so little information upon so every-day a matter as the present?"

"Let me assure you, madam," said Lucien, "that had I really the sum you mention at my disposal, I would employ it more profitably than in troubling myself to obtain particulars respecting the Count of Monte-Cristo, whose only merit in my eyes consists in his being twice as rich as a nabob. However, I have turned the business over to Morcerf, so pray settle it with him as may be most agreeable to you. for my own part, I care nothing about the count or his mysterious doings."

" I am very sure no nabob of our time would have sent me

a pair of horses worth 32,000 francs, wearing on their heads four diamonds valued at 5,000 francs each."

"He seems to have a mania for diamonds," said Mercerf, smiling; "and I verily believe that, like Potemkin, he keeps his pockets filled for the sake of strewing them along the road, as little Thumb did his flint-stones."

"Perhaps he has discovered some mine," said Madame Danglars. "I suppose you know he has an order for unlimited credit on the baron's banking establishment?"

"I was not aware of it," replied Albert, "but I can readily believe it."

"And, further, that he stated to M. Danglars his intention of only staying a year in Paris, during which time he proposed to spend six millions. He must be the Shah of Persia travelling incog."

"Have you remarked the extreme beauty of that young girl by whom he is accompanied. M. Lucien?" inquired Eugénie.

"I really never met with one woman so ready to do justice to the charms of another as yourself;—let us see how far she merits your praises," continued Lucien, raising his lorgnette to his eye. "A most lovely creature, upon my soul!" cried he, after a long and searching scrutiny.

"Who is this young person, M. Morcerf," inquired Eugénie; "does any body know?"

"Allow me to state," said Albert, replying to this direct appeal, "that I can give you very tolerable information on that subject, as well as on most points relative to the singular person of whom we are now conversing—the young girl is a Greek."

"So I should presume by her dress; if, therefore, you know no more than one self-evident fact, the whole of the spectators in the theatre are as well informed as yourself."

"I am extremely sorry you find me so ignorant a cicerone," replied Morcerf, "but I am reluctantly obliged to confess, I have nothing further to communicate—yes, stay, I do know one thing more, namely, that she is a musician, for one day that I chanced to be breakfasting with the count, I heard the sound of a guzla—it is impossible it could have been touched by any finger than her own."

"Then your count entertains visitors, does he?" asked Madame Danglars.

"Indeed he does, and in a most noble manner, I can assure you."

"I must try and persuade M. Danglars to invite him to a ball or dinner, or something of the sort, that he may be compelled to ask us in return."

"What!" said Debray, laughing; "do you really mean you would go to his house?"

"Why not? my husband could accompany me."

"But do you know this mysterious count is a bachelor?"

"You have ample proof to the contrary if you look opposite," said the baroness, as she laughingly pointed to the beautiful Greek.

"No, no!" exclaimed Debray; "that lady is not his wife, he told us himself she was his slave; do you not recollect, Morcerf, his telling us so at your breakfast?"

"Well, then," said the baroness, "if slave she be, she has all the air and manner of a princess."

"Of the Arabian Nights?"

"If you like; but tell me, my good Lucien, what is it that constitutes a princess? gold, silver, and jewels, and our Greek beauty there is one blaze of diamonds; I doubt if any queen's could equal them."

"To me she seems overloaded," observed Eugénie; "she would look far better if she wore fewer, and we should then be able to see her finely formed throat and wrists."

"See, how the artist peeps out!" exclaimed Madame Danglars; "my poor Eugénie, you must conceal your passion for the fine arts."

"I admire all that is beautiful in art or nature," returned the young lady.

"What do you think of the count?" inquired Debray; "he is not much amiss, according to my ideas of good looks."

"The count?" repeated Eugénie, as though it had not occurred to her to observe him sooner "the count? oh,—he is so dreadfully pale."

"I quite agree with you," said Morcerf; "and it is in that very paleness that consists the secret we want to find out. The Countess G—— insists upon it he is a vampire."

"Then the Countess G—— has returned to Paris, has she?" inquired the baroness.

"Is that she, mamma?" asked Eugénie; "almost opposite to us, with that profusion of beautiful light hair?"

"Yes, yes, there she is!" cried Madame Danglars; "shall I tell you what you ought to do, Morcerf?"

"Command me, madam, I am all attention."

"Well, then, you should go and bring your Count of Monte-Cristo to us."

"What for?" asked Eugénie.

"What for? why to converse with him, of course; if you have no curiosity to hear whether he expresses himself like other people, I can assure you I have. Have you really no desire to be introduced to this singular being?"

"None whatever," replied Eugénie.

"Strange girl!" murmured the baroness.

"He will very probably come of his own accord," said Morcerf: "There! do you see, madam, he recognises you, and bows."

The baroness returned the salute in the most smiling and graceful manner.

"Well," said Morcerf, " I may as well be magnanimous and tear myself away to forward your wishes; adieu; I will go and try if there are any means of speaking to him."

"Go straight to his box, that will be the simplest plan."

"But I have never been presented."

"Presented to whom?"

"To the beautiful Greek."

"You say she is only a slave?"

"While you assert that she is a queen, or at least a princess —No, no! I cannot venture to enter his box; but I hope, that when he observes me leave you, he will come and take my place."

"We shall see, it is just probable, therefore go at once."

"Adieu! I sacrifice myself, remember that," said Albert, as he made his parting bow.

As he had predicted, just as he was passing the count's box the door opened, and Monte-Cristo came forth. After giving some directions to Ali, who stood in the lobby, the count observed Albert, and, taking his arm, walked onwards with him. Carefully closing the box-door, Ali placed himself before it, while a crowd of wondering spectators assembled round the unconscious Nubian.

"Upon my word," said Monte-Cristo, "Paris is a strange city, and the Parisians a very singular people; do pray observe that cluster of persons collected round poor Ali, who is as much astonished as themselves, really one might suppose he was the only Nubian they had ever beheld; now I will pledge myself, that a Frenchman might shew himself in public, either in Tunis, Constantinople, Bagdad, or Cairo, without drawing a circle of gazers around him."

"That shews that the Eastern nations have too much good sense to waste their time and attention on objects undeserving of either. However, as far as Ali is concerned, I can assure you, the interest he excites is merely from the circumstance of his being your attendant; you who are at this moment the most celebrated and fashionable person in Paris."

"Really? and what has procured me so flattering a distinction?"

"What? why, yourself to be sure! You give away horses worth a thousand guineas; you save the lives of ladies of high rank and beauty; you send thoroughbred racers to contest the prize of the Jockey Club, the horses being rode by tiny urchins not larger than marmots; then, when you have carried off the golden trophy of victory, instead of setting any value on it, you give it to the first handsome woman you think of!"

"And who has filled your head with all this nonsense?"

"Why, in the first place, I heard it from Madame Danglars, who, by the by, is dying to see you in her box, or to have you seen there by others; secondly, I learned it from Beauchamp's journal; and thirdly, from my own imagination. Why, if you sought concealment, did you call your horse Vampa?"

"That was an oversight, certainly," replied the count, "but tell me, does the Count de Morcerf never visit the Opera? I have been looking for him, but without success."

"He will be here to-night."

"In what part of the house?"

"In the baroness's *loge*, I believe."

"Is the charming young female with her—her daughter?"

"Yes."

"Indeed! then, I congratulate you."

Morcerf smiled. "We will discuss that subject at length some future time," said he. "But what think you of the music?"

"What music?"

"That which you have just heard."

"Oh, it is admirable as the production of a human composer, sung by a party of bipeds without feathers, as Diogenes styled mankind."

"Why, my dear count, would you have me understand that you undervalue our terrestrial harmony, because you can at pleasure enjoy the seraphic strains that proceed from the seven choirs of paradise?"

"You are right in some degree; but when I wish to listen to sounds so exquisitely attuned to melody as mortal ear never yet listened to, I go to sleep."

"Then, why not indulge yourself at once? Sleep, by all means, if such be your means of procuring the concord of celestial sounds. Pray, do not hesitate; you will find every incentive to slumber, and for what else but to send people asleep was the opera invented?"

"No, thank you. Your orchestra is rather too noisy to admit the soft wooing of the drowsy god. The sleep, **after** the manner I have mentioned, and to produce the desired effects, absolute calm and silence are necessary, a certain preparation must also be called in aid."

"I know, the famous hashish!"

"Precisely. Now you know my secret, let me recommend you, my dear viscount, to come and sup with me whenever you wish to be regaled with music really worth listening to."

"I have already enjoyed that treat when breakfasting with you," said Morcerf.

"Do you mean at Rome?"

"I do."

"Ah, then I suppose you heard Haydée's guzla; the poor exile frequently beguiles a weary hour in playing to me the airs of her native land."

Morcerf did not pursue the subject, and Monte-Cristo himself fell into a silent reverie.

The bell rang at this moment for the rising of the curtain.

"You will excuse my leaving you," said the count, turning in the direction of his *loge*."

"What! Are you going?"

"Pray, say every thing that is kind to Countess G—— on the part of her friend the Vampire."

"And what message shall I convey to the baroness?"

"That, with her permission, I propose doing myself the honour of paying my respects in the course of the evening."

The third act had now commenced; and during its progress the Count de Morcerf, according to promise, made his appearance in the box of Madame Danglars.

The Count de Morcerf was not one of those persons whose aspect would create either interest or curiosity in a place of public amusement; his presence, therefore, was wholly unnoticed, save by the occupants of the box in which he had just seated himself.

The quick eye of Monte-Cristo, however, marked his coming; and a slight though meaning smile passed over his lips as he did so.

Haydée, whose soul seemed centred in the business of the stage, like all unsophisticated natures, she delighted in whatever addressed itself to the eye or ear.

The third act passed off as usual. Mesdemoiselles Noblet, Julie, and Lerous, executed the customary number of pirouettes; Robert duly challenged the Prince of Grenada; and the royal parent of the Princess Isabella, taking his daughter by the hand, swept round the stage with majestic strides, the better to display the rich folds of his velvet robe and mantle. After which the curtain again fell, and the spectators poured forth from the theatre into the lobbies and salon. The count also, quitting his box, proceeded at once to that of Madame Danglars, who could scarcely restrain a cry of mingled pleasure and surprise.

"Welcome, M. le Comte!" exclaimed she, as he entered. "I have been most anxious to see you that I might repeat verbally those thanks writing can so ill express."

"Surely so trifling a circumstance cannot deserve a place in your remembrance! Believe me, madame, I had entirely forgotten it!"

"But it is not so easy to forget, M. le Comte, that the very day following the one in which you kindly prevented my disappointment respecting the horses, you saved the life of my dear friend Madame de Villefort, which I had placed in danger by lending her the very animals your generosity restored to me."

"This time, at least, I cannot accept of your flattering acknowledgments. In the latter affair you owe me nothing. Ali, my Nubian slave, was the fortunate individual who enjoyed the privilege of rendering to your friend the trifling assistance you allude to."

"Was it Ali," asked the Count de Morcerf, "who rescued my son from the hands of bandits?"

"No, M. le Comte," replied Monte-Cristo, pressing with friendly warmth the hand held out to him by the general; "in this instance I may fairly and freely accept your thanks; but you have already tendered them, and fully discharged your debt—if, indeed, there existed one—and I feel almost mortified to find you still revert to the trifling aid I was able to render your son."

"May I beg of you, Madame la Baronne, to honour me with an introduction to your charming daughter?"

"Oh! you are no stranger—at least not by name," replied Madame Danglars, "and the last two or three days we have really talked of nothing else but yourself. Eugénie," continued the baroness, turning towards her daughter, "M. the Comte de Monte-Cristo."

The count bowed, while Mademoiselle Danglars returned a slight inclination of the head.

"You have a charming young person with you to-night, M. le Comte," said Eugénie. "Your daughter, I presume?"

"No, indeed," said Monte-Cristo, astonished at the coolness and freedom of the question. "The girl you allude to is a poor unfortunate Greek left under my care."

"And what is her name?"

"Haydée," replied Monte-Cristo.

"A Greek?" murmured the Count de Morcerf.

"Yes, indeed, count," said Madame Danglars; "and tell me, did you ever see at the court of Ali Tebelin, whom you so gloriously and valiantly served, a more exquisite beauty or richer costume than is displayed in the fair Greek before us?"

"Did I hear rightly, M. le Comte," said Monte-Cristo, "that you served at Janina?"

"I was inspector-general of the pasha's troops," replied Morcerf; "and I seek not to conceal that I owe my fortune, such as it is, to the liberality of the illustrious Albanese chief."

"But look! pray look," exclaimed Madame Danglars.

"Where?" stammered out Morcerf.

"There, there!" said Monte-Cristo, as wrapping his arms around the count he leaned with him over the front of the box, just as Haydée, whose eyes were occupied in examining the theatre in search of the count, perceived his pale marble features close to the countenance of Morcerf, whom he was holding in his arms.

This sight produced on the astonished girl an effect similar to that of the fabulous head of Medusa. She bent forwards as though to assure herself of the reality of what she beheld, then uttering a faint cry, threw herself back in her seat. The sound that burst from the agitated Greek reached the ear of the watchful Ali, who instantly opened the box-door to ascertain the cause.

"Bless me!" exclaimed Eugénie, "what has happened to your ward, M. le Comte? she seems taken suddenly ill?"

"Very probably!" answered the count. "But do not be alarmed on her account! Haydée's nervous system is delicately organised, and she is peculiarly susceptible of the odours even of flowers—nay, there are some which cause her to faint if brought into her presence. However," continued Monte-Cristo, drawing a small phial from his pocket, "I have an infallible remedy for such attacks."

So saying, he bowed to the baroness and her daughter, exchanged a parting shake of the hand with Debray and the count, and quitted the box.

Upon his return to Haydée, he found her extremely pale and much agitated. Directly she saw him she seized his hand, while the icy coldness of her own made Monte-Cristo start.

"With whom was my lord conversing a few minutes since?" asked she, in a trembling voice.

"With the Count de Morcerf," answered Monte-Cristo. "He tells me he served your illustrious father, and that he owes his fortune to him!"

"Base, cowardly traitor that he is!" exclaimed Haydée, her eyes flashing with rage; "he it was who sold my beloved parent to the Turks, and the fortune he boasts of was the price of his treachery! Knowest thou not that, my dear lord?"

"Something of this I heard in Epirus," said Monte-Cristo; "but the particulars are still unknown to me. You shall relate them to me, my child. They are, no doubt, both curious and interesting."

"Yes, yes! but let us go hence, I beseech you. I feel as though it would kill me to remain longer near that dreadful man."

So saying, Haydée arose, and wrapping herself in her burnouse of white cashmire embroidered with pearls and coral, she hastily quitted the box at the moment when the curtain was rising upon the fourth act.

"Do you observe," said the Countess G—— to Albert, who had returned to her side, "that man does nothing like other people; he listens most devoutly to the third act of *Robert le Diable* and when the fourth begins makes a precipitate retreat."

END OF THE FIRST VOLUME